Thirteen

Make yourself uncomfortable...

Thirteen
Volume One

Edited by Andrew Hannon

Cloontubrid Press

Easkey Castle Books

Published by Cloontubrid Press
A division of Easkey Castle Books
Copyright © 2010 Edited by Andrew Hannon

All rights reserved

The right of Andrew Hannon to be identified as the editor of this work has been asserted by him in accordance with the Copyright, Designs and Patents Act 1988 With the exception of having their stories published under Thirteen, the economic rights to the short stories in this anthology are those of the individual respective authors, including the right to authorize the reproduction of the work in any form (Article 9, Berne Convention). Furthermore, the perpetual moral right to be identified as the author of the work and the right to object to any distortion or mutilation of the work which would be prejudicial to his or her honour or reputation remains with the individual respective authors.

First published in the United States in 2010

This edition published 2011

ISBN 9781453867501

It is a criminal offence to distribute this work in Italy unless the first short story has been physically removed.

CONTENTS

The 113 Stories

The Magic, *Darran York*	Page 13
Joshua's Room, *Lee Betteridge*	Page 15
One Night In the Graveyard, *Hector Summers*	Page 17
Shift, *Matthew Batham*	Page 19
Day Trip, *Christopher Staples*	Page 22
The Stranger the Lie, *David Christopher*	Page 23
Sick Puppy, *Lee Betteridge*	Page 26
Checking, *Craig Dutton*	Page 31
The Undertaker, *Andrew Hannon*	Page 32
The Cluster, *Todd Langley*	Page 36
Ghost Writer, *Lee Betteridge*	Page 39
Express Delivery, *Robert Bell*	Page 43
Pigeon Morning, *Matthew Batham*	Page 46
The Storm, *Leisa Parker*	Page 50
Jokerman, *Hilda Stringer*	Page 52
Random, *Thomas Gilbert*	Page 53
Hell, *Andrew Hannon*	Page 54
Bete Noir, *Pádraig Ó Méalóid*	Page 58

Thirteen

That First Cup of Joe, *Leisa Parker* — Page 61

All Aboard The Love Train, *James Cooper* — Page 63

Last Meal, *Ibrahim Amin* — Page 70

Weight, *David Christopher* — Page 72

Powers, *James Doggett* — Page 74

The Assassin, *Lavie Tidhar* — Page 77

Bobby Moon, *Lee Betteridge* — Page 79

The Cemetery, *Susan Conway* — Page 84

The Tokoloshe, *Paul Crilley* — Page 86

Friends Of The Earth, *James Cooper* — Page 93

Big Mice, *Robert Neilson* — Page 98

Looking Back, *Mark Patrick Lynch* — Page 103

The Perfect Spot, *Matthew Batham* — Page 107

The Show, *Thomas Gilbert* — Page 113

Thanks For Watching, *Claire Shevlin* — Page 117

See How They Dance, *Tyler Keevil* — Page 119

Mr Thirteen, *Robert Nielson* — Page 124

Boxing Clever, *Mark Patrick Lynch* — Page 132

The Toll Of Finnegan's Bridge, *Brian Showers* — Page 134

Thirteen

Samuel, *Rebecca Billings*	Page 140
Doggy, *Roger Freedman*	Page 143
When She Grew Old, *Mark Patrick Lynch*	Page 145
Frozen On Film, *Kevin Roach*	Page 150
Cobbled Connely, *Matthew Ward*	Page 152
Warts And All, *Colin Mulhern*	Page 153
Fucking Vampires, *Erik Tomblin*	Page 155
Steve, *John Lee*	Page 157
Drop Dead Gorgeous, *James Bernthal*	Page 159
The Tomb, *Leila Eadie*	Page 161
Pandora's Box, *Stephen Owen*	Page 164
Bon Appetit, *Ernest DeVore*	Page 169
The A.C.I., *Julian Urquhart*	Page 173
Brief Future, *John Lee*	Page 176
The Steps Where I Sinned, *J. G. Craig*	Page 180
All Sales Final, *Philip Tinkler*	Page 182
A New Life, *Stephen Tyson*	Page 188
One Night Stand, *Michael O'Connor*	Page 190
Alone in the Cataloochee Valley, *Lee Clark Zumpe*	Page 192

Thirteen

Faux Paw, *Nancy Jackson*	Page 196
Gordy Starts On Days, *Lee Betteridge*	Page 198
Perhaps I'm Not Dark Enough, *Stephanie Simpson-Woods*	Page 204
Sorry, Charlie, *Greg Vest*	Page 206
Last Season's Ghost, *Mike Beeman*	Page 212
How To Know A Body, *Stephen Francis Decky*	Page 217
By The Shore, *Matthew Brolly*	Page 222
Death Of The Apostrophe, *Pamela K. Kinney*	Page 228
The Lidenbrock Duty, *Martyn Prince*	Page 231
The Bed, *Kelli Lowry*	Page 234
Family Ties, *Lavie Tidhar*	Page 235
The Makeshift, *Gary McMahon*	Page 237
Deadline, *Joseph Paul Haines*	Page 240
A Mother's Love, *Andrew Hand*	Page 243
Calendar Girl, *Robert Bell*	Page 245
Freeing The Prisoner, *Darryl Slater*	Page 253
Just In Case, *Edward Rodosek*	Page 258
Falling In Love Again, *Dawn Wingfield*	Page 261
The Accident, *Leisa Parker*	Page 264

Thirteen

Grallabelle, *Philip Tinkler*	Page 268
In Your Grocer's Freezer, *Roger Dale Trexler*	Page 275
Appendix, *Sara Joan Berniker*	Page 278
451208: A Man Like Any Other, *Lee Betteridge*	Page 281
Death to the Switchblade Queen, *James Bennett*	Page 287
The Healthy Man, *Jane Mackenzie*	Page 293
Her Little Secret. *William I Lengeman III*	Page 295
Possession, *Steven Southworth*	Page 296
Hell Inside, *Nate Southard*	Page 297
Shelby's Witch, *Kenneth Ryan*	Page 304
Presence of Mind, *James Lane*	Page 309
The Magician, *Gareth Fry*	Page 314
Night Tiger, *Donia Carey*	Page 316
The Tower, *Matthew Batham*	Page 318
The Snow Came Softly Down, *Brian Showers*	Page 330
The Art Of Eula Mae, *Bonnie J. Glover*	Page 341
Vigilante Man, *Nigel Atkinson*	Page 348
Balance of the Devils, *Christopher Cathrine*	Page 354
Playtime, *Aliya Whiteley*	Page 368

Thirteen

Klaus, *Matthew King*	Page 372
Swept Away, *Richard Hipson*	Page 374
The Cockroach Collector, *Ben Repton*	Page 375
Catalyst, *Brian Dowell*	Page 378
Lester, *Steven Southworth*	Page 382
Me, Marc and It, *Matthew Batham*	Page 384
In Her Place, *M.S. Hart*	Page 388
Whitecaps, *Thea Atkinson*	Page 389
The Eulogy Pills, *Ken Goldman*	Page 392
Laughter in the Dark, *Joseph Wakeling*	Page 397
The True Master of the Desert, *Sean M. Foster*	Page 399
Chicken List, *Zoe Lea*	Page 402
The Asylum & The Sundowner Captain, *James Field*	Page 405
The Urge, *Bryan Woolf*	Page 407
Thoughtform, *Dee Weaver*	Page 413
Appetite for Destruction, *John Glass*	Page 415
Sidewalks, *Joshua Scribner*	Page 419
Darkness, *Bill West*	Page 424
Two Faced, *Paul McAvoy*	Page 425

Thirteen

The Thirteen Editorials

January	Page 432
February	Page 434
March	Page 435
April	Page 436
May	Page 437
June	Page 438
July	Page 439
August	Page 440
September	Page 441
October	Page 442
Hallowe'en	Page 443
November	Page 444
December	Page 445

thirteen

the one-hundred & thirteen stories

Thirteen

THE MAGIC
DARRAN YORK

Have you ever read something and enjoyed it so much you wished you'd never read it, just so you could read it again for the first time? The first time is magical, right? It doesn't matter how many times you read it again, it's never quite as good.

This is your chance to read something truly amazing for the first time. You'll only get this chance once, so don't blow it. I want you to get the most out of this, so you're going to have to trust me. Do exactly as you're told.

If you're not alone right now then put this away immediately. Magic - real magic - is shy of company. It's not going to happen if you're reading this in a crowded coffee shop or sat on a packed train.

Only read from here if you're alone.

Good. We've started.

Now I need you to do a few more things for me - just a few small things. Think of this as an instruction manual, a process you have to follow if you want a thing to work. I'm not trying to be pushy or boss you around just for the sake of it. I just want this to work for you.

Go somewhere you can close the door behind you and read this without being disturbed. It doesn't matter where - your bedroom will do, or a toilet. Anywhere you can go without someone walking in on you. And like I said, close the door after you.

Maybe some of you are reading this and haven't done as you've been instructed. Do you wish you'd played along? I guarantee you, it's better to be a part of this than to simply eavesdrop on the magic. It mightn't be too late though. I can't promise anything but if you go to a quiet place now and close the door... I'll see what I can do.

So, here we are. Or rather, there you are. I really hope you're enjoying this so far. I know nothing has actually happened yet, but aren't you excited? Is your curiosity growing larger and larger? Enjoy this. This is the only time you can feel what you are feeling now. The wonder of what's going to happen, the half-formed conclusions some of you may already have made - all of this can only happen once, can only happen now, can only happen the first time.

Some of the magic has begun already. You are alone in a room, true, but you are also unified with all the people who have ever done this before you, and all of those who will do it after you. Can you feel each other? Perhaps you feel silly about this whole thing, or maybe you feel privileged. You are each a part of an invisible crowd, gathered together outside of time, reading the same words.

Don't worry, that's not the punch of it, and this certainly isn't a joke. I'm not here to waste your time with talk of the metaphysical. And to prove it, we'll move on.

I take it there's light in your chosen room or you wouldn't be able to read this, right?

Come on, you can answer me if I ask you a question! In fact you have to answer me if you want this to work. I'll ask you again. Answer this time. Loud and clear, don't be afraid. Just say, "Right".

Now, now, everybody, let's all play along. All I want is one little spoken word in exchange for all the words I've given you so far. Remember, I'm doing this for you - this is the only chance you'll get and I want it to work.

Answer my question.

Well done! You might have felt silly saying it aloud but there's nobody here to hear you and what harm has been done? Now you can continue to enjoy this, knowing that you've followed the instructions perfectly. And when you follow instructions perfectly, things tend to work.

Do whatever it takes to get your room as dark as possible so that there's just enough light for you to still make out these words. Draw the curtains closed, turn off the main light and put on a side-light. Better still, light a candle or read with the flame from a cigarette lighter. I hate to keep reminding you, but it really will be worth it if you do as I say. It would be such a shame for you to miss out having already come as far as you have.

Allow me to describe your scene. That's kind of strange, isn't it? Shall we take a moment to consider that? Usually when you read something the scene is described for you so that you can picture it in your mind, but here you are reading your very own scene, in which you are sat in a dark room, all alone, reading from wherever you chanced upon this magic. What mighty implications! When you were younger, did you ever pretend to yourself that you were a character in a book or a film and that millions of people read about you and watched what you did? Perhaps the pretence was real?

Don't worry, though, that's not the magic I spoke of earlier.

Enjoy this moment. Here it comes. Here comes the magic.

Very quickly, get up off your bed or chair or place against the wall. Get up and walk over to the door you closed behind you a few minutes ago. Put your ear against the door and listen. Hold your breath.

I wonder if you can hear me.

Let me expand on the scene I described a moment ago. You remember, the one with you in the dark room, reading. Yes, well, outside of that room, on the other side of that closed door, someone you can't see is standing. It's me. I wonder if you can guess my name. The slightly autistic among you may have already registered the first letters of the last five paragraphs and what they spell. It's the closest I have to a name.

Can you hear me breathe? No? Perhaps I'm holding my breath too, with an ear pressed up against the door, trying to hear you.

Or perhaps there is one last step, one last instruction you must follow in order to make this magic work.

Invite me in.

Come now, don't be bashful! You already spoke to me earlier when you answered my question about the light. All you have to do is ask me to come in. You see. I know you're alone in there, all by yourself in the dark. And I want to prove to you that the magic works.

Thirteen

JOSHUA'S ROOM
LEE BETTERIDGE

Daniel grabbed the TV remote control off the settee beside him and stabbed at the mute button. The newsreader fell silent and continued to mouth the evening's headlines wordlessly. Daniel glared at the BabySafe intercom that sat on the sideboard. He was sure he'd heard the baby stir. He strained his ears, listening. He heard the rain against the conservatory roof. He heard the wind whistling over the chimney. He heard the constant hum of the heater in the bathroom where Caroline was having a bath. A bead of sweat ran from his temple, down his face. He could hear the baby softly gurgling to itself.

Daniel gave the newsreader his voice back and turned the volume up slightly. He felt sweat run down his side under his dressing gown, and a chill passed through him. He took a swig of the lager bottle he cradled in his hand and it slid down his throat like ice. He shivered again.

The baby let out a cry; a troubled yelp that had a slightly static quality to it as it came from the intercom. Daniel thought of unplugging it, but then thought better of it. He'd done that once before and Caroline had yelled at him. She'd really lost her temper, sobbing and crying and screaming. He left the intercom on, but turned the fire up an extra bar. Despite the sweat that leaked out of his skin, Daniel felt chilled to the bone.

He sat back in his place on the settee and heard a high-pitched squeak. Standing backup, he lifted the cushion he'd just sat on and pulled out the toy that had made the noise. It was a rubber giraffe that squeaked when you squeezed it. He tossed it into Joshua's toy box and sat down again.

The baby let out another cry. Daniel glared at the intercom. There was another cry, then a sob. Daniel drank some Carlsberg. The baby started to cry. Daniel felt sick. The crying coming from the intercom was shrill and piercing and he turned the volume up even further on the TV. The weatherman was smiling like an idiot now while he told of the gales of rain, sleet and snow that were heading for the area. Daniel finished his beer. The baby's cries started to sound more desperate, more anxious.

Daniel went into the kitchen, and after dropping the empty beer bottle into the bin, he took another from the fridge. He stood in the kitchen for a while after closing the fridge door. Sweat ran from under his arms and down his face, yet he felt cold. He walked back into the living room.

Joshua was still crying, screaming almost. Daniel knew he should go to the baby's room but he couldn't. He couldn't bring himself to go into the hallway, up the stairs, open the door with the little 'Joshua's Room' sign. He couldn't do it.

He sat down with his beer and watched the sports news. He could hardly hear what the reporter was saying. Joshua's screaming was too loud now. He wailed and screamed, wave after wave of piercing noise coming from the intercom. Sweat ran from Daniel's body. Shivers wracked him as he tried to ignore the baby and listen to the football results. Joshua screamed and cried. Daniel sweated and shivered. He couldn't take it anymore. He had to turn the intercom off.

Caroline walked into the room just before Daniel had time to stand up. She wore her dressing gown and one of the bathroom towels tied up in a bundle on top of her head. She glared at Daniel fiercely.

"Can't you hear that?" snapped Caroline, pointing at the intercom. "Are you deaf? He's screaming for God sake."

Daniel just looked at her. Tears welled up in his eyes.

"You could have gone up to him Daniel. You are his father, you know. It shouldn't all be up to me." The baby's screaming continued.

15

Thirteen

Tears started to roll down Daniel's cheek and he whimpered, "... I can't."

Caroline gave him another severe glance and then she was out in the hall. Daniel jumped to his feet.

"Wait!" he gasped as he followed her out of the living room. She stomped up the stairs, and as Daniel started up them he experienced a strange sensation. Joshua's screaming came from upstairs and from the intercom on the sideboard in the living room at the same time. It was strange - real-life stereo - and he went dizzy. He tried to catch up with Caroline.

At the top of the stairs she walked straight through the door marked 'Joshua's Room' without any hesitation, and he heard her softly cooing. The screams halted slightly, then proceeded, but quieter than before.

Daniel reached the top of the stairs and stood in the doorway, watching his wife sat in the rocking chair. She was softly saying, "Its OK honey-bunny. Mummy's here, I'm here. You're all right now...

The icy cold of the room chilled Daniel straight to the bone and made the hair on his arms bristle up, but Caroline didn't seem to notice. Daniel looked at the empty cot and started to sob. Caroline continued to talk softly to her empty arms, held as if cradling an infant, her breath making a mist in front of her. The sobbing of the baby that surrounded them, the sobbing that came from everywhere in the room but from nowhere in particular, became quieter and sleepier.

Daniel sobbed into his hands, then slumped down to his knees and cried in despair. As Caroline talked to the baby that was no longer there, he remembered little Josh's beautiful hands, his tiny feet and beautiful ears. And he remembered the doctor saying that cot death was just one of those horrible but unavoidable things that happened. There was nothing that could be done, and it was so, so sad. Daniel sobbed into his hands as Caroline talked into the empty room and her empty arms. The baby's cries softened to just a gurgle again.

ONE NIGHT IN THE GRAVEYARD
HECTOR SUMMERS

The two ghosts smiled at each other in the moonlit graveyard. One of them was dressed in a naval uniform, a cheeky but likeable shine emanating from his face as he leaned against his gravestone.

"Hello, mate!" he chirped at the other ghost, who had been wandering rather aimlessly among the tombs and faded headstones.

"Hi," he answered softly.

"Didn't expect to see anyone else out on a night like this, but pleased to meet you. I ain't seen you before - new boy, are ya?"

"Erm... yeah. Yeah, I... I think so."

"Well, that proves it! All new 'uns have the bad memories to begin with. Bet you can't remember how you got here, either."

The other ghost looked down at his feet. He looked like an embarrassed schoolboy forced to stand in front of a new class and introduce himself.

"No. I can't."

"Don't worry 'bout that, mate. It'll come to ya. It might take a while, but it always comes to ya in the end."

A sudden flash of lightning lit up the sky over to the east, followed shortly by a slow rumble of thunder.

"It's funny," started the naval ghost, "how quiet this place gets when it rains. When I was a kid I thought ghosts would love the rain."

"So... so we are ghosts then?"

The naval ghost laughed, but not maliciously.

"Of course we are, mate! Of course we are!"

"Oh."

A look of pity crossed the naval ghost's face.

"Look, why don't ya take a seat? I remember how confused I was when I arrived here. Thought I was off me bleedin' head, I tell ya."

The other ghost accepted the invitation and sat down on the damp grass.

"How long have you been here?"

The ghost smiled sadly.

"A long time."

Lightning flashed again, and the thunder came quicker this time. "And you remember... you can recall..."

"How I died? Yeah. I can remember."

"What happened?"

"Died at sea, but not in the heroic way. Blimey, no, not like a hero."

"Was it during the war?"

"War?"

"The First World War? The Second?"

"Oh, those! No, I missed them, thank God. Only heard about them through me brother."

"Your brother? Is he here too?"

"No, no, he used to come and visit me. He was a sailor too. Always looked after me when we was kids and always came to me grave on me birthday. I'm sure he's long dead now. Said he was moving to America after the second one of them wars. Must be over there now."

"But, if we're all dead, isn't there somewhere you can meet?"

"How'd ya mean?"

"Well, I don't know. Like Heaven or something?"

"Nope, at least not as far as I know. Haven't got my invite yet, anyway!"

The naval ghost laughed at this, a loud, good-natured laugh that made his

Thirteen

new companion smile, despite the confusion and fear he'd been feeling since he found himself in this graveyard. How long had that been? A week? A month? It was hard to tell.

"So what happened?" he asked the naval ghost after his laughter had faded back into that cheeky grin.

"It was me twenty-third birthday and I was out at sea in the middle of the Pacific bleedin' Ocean. Homesick, I was, and the lads knew it, so they decided to get me drunk. Only problem was, I was s'posed to be on duty early in the morning. Fell off the bloody ship just before dawn. A couple of people saw me fall in, but by the time I was pulled in it was too late."

The cheeky look left his face. The other ghost felt slightly uncomfortable, as though maybe he'd pushed him too far.

"Look," he said, pushing himself up off the ground. "I'm going to head back to my place. Try and think how I got here."

"All right, mate. See you again."

"Yeah. See you."

The other ghost turned and walked back the way he'd come, a lonely figure with a lot to think about. The sailor shook his head sadly as he watched him round a tomb, the noose tied around his neck dragging along the floor after him like a snake.

Thirteen

SHIFT
MATTHEW BATHAM

Harris hated trendy bars, particularly expensive trendy bars. He'd pleaded with Annette to meet him somewhere else but she'd insisted on this particular venue. He'd also begged her not to be late, leaving him on his own feeling utterly conspicuous and spending a fortune on gin and tonics to hide his nerves.

Annette was late, and sitting at the ridiculously small table for two, surrounded by obviously wealthy twenty and thirty-somethings. Harris did fell utterly conspicuous. One thing he didn't feel was drunk. Despite having tried every technique he knew to attract the waitress's attention, he was still dry. He was toying with a cocktail stirrer left by the table's previous occupant and eyeing the waitress, who was chatting happily to a glamorous young couple on a nearby table. Harris wondered if the couple were famous. He didn't watch enough TV or go to see enough popular films to know, but they looked like they belonged in Hollywood.

The woman was blond, hair shoulder length and cut with absolute precision. The man was as dark as she was fair, his jaw-line like that of a comic book hero.

The waitress giggled and flicked her fringe self-consciously. Harris began to feel irritated. Maybe he just wasn't beautiful enough to get served.

He coughed loudly, fist pressed to his lips, and waited for the waitress to notice him. She continued to chat to the beautiful couple.

He recalled a story a friend had told him about her time in New York. The friend, Jennifer, had been sitting in a less salubrious bar than this, trying to get the attention of a member of staff. A group of lads on the next table called across 'Hey gorgeous, you want a drink?'

Jennifer had answered in the affirmative. One of the lads had picked up an empty cigarette packet and thrown it at the waitress's head. 'The lady here would like a drink!' the lad had called when the waitress turned. 'Be right there!' she'd answered.

Harris didn't think the same approach would work here.

He glanced at his watch. Annette was twenty minutes late. She was always late. He coughed again and, miracle of miracles, the waitress glanced in his direction, before continuing her conversation with the couple. 'Whenever you're ready,' Harris called.

He'd gone through the 'I'm too ugly for this bar' phase now and was squarely in the 'I'm sick of waiting to get served' phase. Soon he would be in the 'I really need a drink' phase and that's when things could get nasty.

The waitress moved on to another table and began taking orders from two stunning females. Harris snapped the cocktail stirrer and stood. He was entering phase three earlier than expected.

He pushed his way between tables and beautiful people and tapped the waitress on the shoulder. She looked round, seemingly stunned at someone making physical contact.

'When you've finished auditioning for Hollywood directors and mixing with models, perhaps you could come and serve the ugly guy in the corner. I've been waiting half an hour,' he said.

The waitress didn't smile. 'I'll be over as soon as I can,' she said, turning back to the models.

Young people have no appreciation of irony, thought Harris, who was 35 going on seventy. Sardonic wit was a dying skill. Who would be the great raconteurs of the future? Robbie Williams? Kylie Minogue? Madonna? They were about the only three figures of pop culture he knew. He didn't care much for popular culture.

Thirteen

He sidled back to his table. He didn't even have the cocktail stick to fiddle with now. He glanced towards the entrance, hoping to see Annette tottering through in a pair of dangerously high heels and a little black dress. No sign, and now the waitress was wandering off towards the bar.

He sent dagger stares into her back and continued to stare almost as aggressively when she turned and headed back to the models' table, handing them their drinks with a big, white grin.

He waved and signalled her over. Harris couldn't swear to it, but he thought he saw her consider ignoring him and than decide she'd made him suffer enough.

'Hi,' she said, standing by his table, face sour.

'Hi,' replied Harris with sardonic sweetness - not that she'd understand he was being sardonic, of course.

'Gin and tonic please,' he said, adding 'Better make it a treble, in case I have to wait as long for my second drink.' He smiled, thinking, why not? She's here, she's taken the order, I'll be getting my drink soon. Why bear grudges?

'Treble G & T,' said the waitress. 'That'll be twenty three pounds.'

It wasn't a request, it was a warning.

'I was joking,' said Harris. 'A single will be fine.'

'So that's a single G&T,' said the waitress, face still not cracking.

'Please. And could you make sure I get a cocktail stirrer with that. Gives me something to fiddle with between drinks.'

'Sure,' said the waitress, walking away.

'No sense of irony,' muttered Harris. 'Not the faintest recognition of sarcasm.'

Ten minutes passed. Still no Annette. And still no drink.

The waitress reappeared and began taking another order from the 'Hollywood' couple.

Where's my fucking drink?

He banged his fist on the metal table in frustration. The waitress and several customers looked his way, most of them frowning pompously.

He fished his mobile from his jacket pocket and looked at it grudgingly. He hardly ever used the thing. Didn't like it. Didn't like the idea of being contactable wherever he went. He managed to negotiate the address book and highlight Annette's number. It rang several times before clicking onto the answer service. He considered asking her to meet somewhere else, so that he could make an exit in protest at the appalling service, but hung up without speaking.

'Waitress!' he called, and she glanced at him, plucked eyebrows raised.

'Just wondered what had happened to my drink?'

'Oh sorry,' she called. 'I forgot to put in the order. You'll have to ask the next waitress I'm afraid. I'm finishing my shift.'

'I hope she's as efficient as you,' he called.

'She will be,' said the waitress.

'I was being sarcastic,' said Harris, deciding to spell it out this time. 'Do you know what sarcasm is? Have you ever heard of irony?'

'Why don't you explain it to the next waitress?' she replied, walking off. He watched her hovering round the bar, chatting with two impossibly good-looking barmen.

Bitch, bitch, bitch!

And then he snapped, stood and shoved through the crammed tables to the bar.

'I have never been subjected to such dreadful service,' he said.

At first she kept her back to him, continuing her conversation with the barmen, who were eying him nervously.

'Any chance you could actually look at me while I'm complaining?'

She turned.

Thirteen

'What's the problem exactly?'

'The problem is, I've been here about forty minutes and I still don't have a drink. This is a bar isn't it? I haven't inadvertently walked into a fashion shoot, or Madame fucking Tussaud's?'

'Don't swear at me please,' she said, barely ruffled.

'I haven't even started!'

'Harris?'

Now Annette decided to show up.

'Is everything okay?'

She was wearing a little black number and a pair of dangerously high heels. She'd made a real effort and now Harris felt bad for spoiling things.

'I'm sorry,' he said, taking her arm. 'I think we'd better leave.'

'I need the loo,' said Annette, looking from Harris to the impassive waitress.

'I'll show you to it,' said the waitress, which shocked Harris.

'Thanks.'

Annette followed the suddenly amicable hostess through the bar and disappeared behind a partition wall.

Harris sat on the edge of a stool and waited, avoiding eye contact with the bar staff.

Annette returned ten minutes later without the waitress.

Harris glanced at his watch. 'Is there still time to get a drink somewhere else?' he asked.

'Yes, it's only nine o'clock,' said Annette. Now even she was missing the acid in his wit.

'Let's just get out of here,' he said, pulling her gently towards the exit.

'I know a good place,' she said. 'Just round the corner. It's a bit off the beaten track, but great atmosphere.'

'Doesn't sound like your kind of place. Have you got a cold? Your voice is kind of husky.'

'No,' said Annette, now leading Harris by the arm down a succession of small side streets.

'Where is this place?' he asked, as she tugged him towards a narrow alleyway.

'Just up here,' she said.

'There's nothing down here.'

Harris surveyed the stacks of crates and piles of old blankets. Water was dripping somewhere like in a public toilet.

'That's how I like it,' said Annette, turning to face him. Except she wasn't Annette anymore; she was the waitress from the bar, wearing Annette's clothes.

'How...?' Harris took a step backwards toward the meagre light of the street.

'I'm thirsty,' said the waitress, and she opened her mouth to reveal teeth a sharp as pins. Her face began to bubble like molten plastic. It ran across her bones, reforming into something hideous. The eyes that glared from the mess of flesh were feral.

Harris just stared.

And then she was on him, teeth ripping into his throat. He felt the throbbing of warm blood. Saw it pumping into his white shirt. Heard her guzzling. She'd got her drink.

Now that was ironic.

Thirteen

DAY TRIP
CHRISTOPHER STAPLES

The coach driver tapped impatient fingers on the steering wheel as, one by one, the elderly people from the Royal Oak Residential Home were helped onto the coach. He'd given up saying good morning to them after the first four or five had slowly passed him. Most were obviously senile so the driver decided to keep quiet lest he be mistaken for one of their sons, or whatever roles their warped minds attributed to him.

The stench of urine and faeces was already overpowering, and the coach was only half full.

"Come on, Mary, you have to get onto the coach if you want to go to the gallery."

"No. The driver is a horrible man."

Upon hearing this, the driver turned his head. The exchange had been between one of the carers and an old lady. The old lady stood staring at him, her eyes squinted in hate while the carer offered an apologetic 'She doesn't mean it' kind of look. The driver turned away.

As Mary was eventually coaxed onto the coach, the driver found himself wondering who had planned this day excursion. He was pretty confident that most of his passengers didn't know their own second names, so he couldn't see any point in taking them to the National Gallery, spreading their god-awful stink, making everyone feel awkward just being near them. They wouldn't appreciate any of the art; they wouldn't even remember it by dinnertime.

"I said we're all set," said a voice by his side.

The driver returned from his thoughts.

"Oh, okay. Off we go."

The carer noticed the way the driver's hands were gripped to the steering wheel, as though he were trying to strangle it. She almost asked him if everything was all right - it wasn't like Mary to take a disliking to someone either - and when the driver drove headfirst right into a speeding lorry, she wished she had.

THE STRANGER THE LIE
DAVID CHRISTOPHER

It was Christmas morning and my nose was bleeding again. I was numb from the cold and stood in the dark by the fireplace eating the mince pie my wife had left out, inhaling sugar dusting and coughing into the brandy. The coals were still warm; she'd waited up for me, must have just gone to bed.

Someone switched the hall light on and I shrank back behind the tree. The living room door opened to a sliver of light and my daughter Lilly came in wearing her vest and pink pants. Spruce needles bent against my face as I watched her sit crossed legged, her hands like humming birds among the presents. She picked one with white paper and red metallic snowflakes and turned it in her little hands until her fingers found a fold.

"Lilly-Anne!" I said.

She snatched her hands away, "Who's there?"

"I hope you're not going to open that."

She looked up to the top of the tree and the angel whose eyes were dots of glitter. "No," She said, "It's for morning."

"Good girl," I stepped out into the light, she took a strangled breath, horrified by my face.

"What's wrong?" I wiped my nose with the back of my hand, there was plenty of blood, "It's nothing honey, just a bloody nose," I said. "Come give daddy a hug." She began to scream.

I bent down to scoop her up, "It's daddy," I said, "It's me, daddy," but she tumbled back and screamed harder. Because of the blood on my face or my torn clothes she didn't recognise me and kept on screaming. I held out my palms and hushed her.

"It's daddy,"

"No," she whispered, "Daddy's upstairs."

My suitcase was stolen on Christmas Eve at a cash point in Kings Cross. It was the kind you keep your whole life in, wallet, train ticket, presents, everything.

There was a man my age with curly brown hair and yellowing teeth. He smiled and asked for change.

"I don't have any," I said, putting my card in the slot.

"You're lying," he replied.

"Excuse me?"

"You're lying to me."

As I remember it he was sitting on the floor with his back to the wall, fixing me with eyes grey like London stone.

"I know liars," he said, *"I see liars."*

I ignored him, pretended I hadn't heard and tapped in my pin, "There's change in your pocket," he said. "Liar."

He stood up. He had a powerful, square set jaw and thick fingers with long dirty nails. I reached into my pocket and handed him a coin. "There," I said, "It's all I have."

"You've got more," his teeth were sharp, "I want everything."

"I'm sorry, but I need it."

He spat on the pavement by my feet, "You're a liar!"

I handed him a few more coins saying, "Look, I don't want any trouble," then turned back to the cash machine while he counted them out. It beeped and swallowed my card. I mashed my fist into the keypad and swore at the screen. When I leant down to pick up my suitcase it was gone and so was he.

A flush of nerves boiled me under my coat. I rushed through the crowded

Thirteen

station looking for him. A suitcase caught my eye, my suitcase, thrown onto the train on platform seven, my train. The man's ratty green parka followed it into the carriage.

I ran to catch it but an old guard with round glasses and bloodshot eyes stopped me as it pulled away.

"Tickets please."

"That's my train."

"Can't let you through without a ticket."

I dropped my shoulder, knocked him to the ground and ran alongside first class hammering on the windows. A young woman with braided hair and a neatly pressed red uniform opened the nearest carriage door.

"Hurry, sir," she said holding out her hand.

I had one foot in the carriage by the time the old guard regained his feet. He limped up the platform swearing, calling me dangerous, crooked. The girl heard, her smile dropped and she let go of my hand. I lost my balance, reached out for a hold on her uniform but grabbed her tightly packed breasts. She lashed out with a fist as quick as a bee sting that knocked me back out the carriage. I rolled along the platform and lay winded on the concrete.

Blood tricked down my cheek. The guard stood over me adjusting his glasses, one eye squinting through a cracked lens.

"You crazy bastard," he said, "You could have broken my hip."

I can still taste spiced fruit.

"Who are you?" Lilly asked.

I tried to smile. "I travelled hundreds of miles to be here when you woke up." I wanted to hold her, rest her head on my shoulder so she couldn't see my broken face, but she wouldn't let me near.

There were heavy footsteps on the stairs.

"I just need to get cleaned up, then you'll see."

The living room door opened. A man stood naked in the doorway, silhouetted by the light from the hall. He was tall with long sinuous muscles and hairy legs, his eyes hidden in the shadow covering his face.

"Go to bed Lilly," he said, "Go on, quickly now."

He spoke firmly to her like a father, and I wanted to smash his brains out with the poker, but not until Lilly was safe in bed. She did as she was told and disappeared upstairs.

"Who are you?" asked the man.

She was always such a good girl.

"Well? What are you doing in my house?"

The poker was the type with a nasty barbed hook on the shaft. I took a casual step towards the fireplace.

"This is *my* house." I wrapped my fingers round the handle, the metal was warm. "Get out!"

"You're crazy," he said, "You're filthy, there's blood all over you. Who are you?"

"I'm Lilly's father."

The man brought his face into the light and I recognised him instantly, the decaying mouth and grey godless eyes like London stone. "You're a liar," he said.

I lunged at him. I wanted to stick the metal in his soft belly, to skewer him like a pig, but he was too quick, my joints were brittle from the cold. He stepped aside and ploughed a fist like a cannonball into my neck.

I woke in the snow; face down in a mask of frozen blood. My cheek stung. I explored it with my tongue and found a hole where I'd bitten through. There were

Thirteen

teeth missing too.

The sun hung low and pale as a new moon. There was a thin film of mist in the air. I tried the back door but it was locked so I wiped some frost from the living room window with my coat sleeve and looked inside. The Christmas lights were on and the fire was lit. Lilly sat in her mother's lap, nesting in her thighs and the silk of her white negligee.

I brought my face closer to the glass and held my breath.

He sat warming himself by the fire in my pyjamas and traded the gifts from my suitcase for kisses.

He kissed Lilly on the forehead then wrapped his thick fingers round my wife's head and kissed her with an open mouth, his long dirty nails working through her hair.

I banged my fists against the glass. Banged and screamed, grim and frozen and the whole family looked at me, just looked at me in silence like I'd lost my mind, some crazy stranger trying to ruin Christmas.

I stopped screaming and stood dumbly looking at them looking at me. Then I sat back in the snow. All I could think to do was shiver.

Thirteen

SICK PUPPY
LEE BETTERIDGE

...No, Inspector. I don't need no frigging solicitor. I know what I'm gonna tell ya and I don't need no gimp in a suit to help me. I'll tell you the whole truth and nothing but the truth; all that shite; because I might be a lot of things, but I ain't no liar. Listen up, Inspector, and you, darling, because I'm only gonna tell you this once.

I hadn't seen Skeet for about just over three years when, out of the blue yesterday, I got a letter from him. He'd never really been much of a clever guy, like you'd guess, but the writing in this letter was bad. I mean real bad. It looked like he'd writ it with the pen up his arse. It said that I had to go round to his place, and it told me the address, because I had to do him a big favour. It was hard to read, but that was the ring of it. It said I owed him one, big time, and he was right.

I sold Skeet some stuff a few years back and he got caught 'in possession'. Your guys said they'd drop the charges if he told them who his dealer was. He didn't grass on me though, so he was right when he said I owe him one. He got fourteen months cos of me. His scraggy letter said he was different now, as well. It said he was off the stuff and he had changed. He reckoned I'd hardly know him.

Shit, how right was he?

So I set off round there at about dinnertime. I was clean all yesterday so I could tell it was a nice day. Sun shining, birds singing, all that shite.

Aye.

Course I bloody walked. What, did you think I went in my own private chopper or something? When you have as much money as I do, you walk everywhere. Then it costs a bloody fortune in shoes, though. It's a shite life, mate, but someone's gotta live it.

So, it takes me about an hour to find his spot and I'm sweating like a rapist in church by the time I get there. The lift's knackered so I go up the stairs to the third floor. I knock on Skeet's door, or I think it's Skeet's anyway, but no one answers. I knock again and still the same. So this time I bray the door with my fist and a half-arsed voice shouts, "Who's there?" I shouts back. "Skeet, it's me," even though I'm not sure it was Skeet who asked. Then the voice shouts, "Who the fuck's me?" and I recognise Skeet's voice.

"It's Harker," I shouts. "I got your letter."

"Aye. Come in, Mike. The door's not locked." And so I went in.

'This was about one o'clock. I just said I set off at dinnertime and it took me about an hour. Give him a nudge, will ya love, wake him up.

So I goes in and it's pitch black and stinks. I've smelt worse like, but Skeet had always been one of the cleanest guys I knew. But, like I said before, I hadn't seen him since ages.

"Where are ya, Skeet?" I asks. "I can't see a fucking thing."

"Shut the door and I'll turn the light on," says Skeet, so I do.

It took a bit for my eyes to get used to the light, and when they had, I wished they fucking hadn't. What a fucking mess!

"What the hell happened, Skeet?" I ask, and he tells me.

Poor guy. He'd always been a bit screwed up, in the head like, but I never really knew how bad. Shit, he was one sick puppy. His parents were to blame, I suppose. When we was kids his ma' used to keep him off school to keep her company. She'd get lonely and try to slit her wrists or take an overdose. All that shite. So Skeet would stay at home and then his da' would kick seven shades of shit out of him for bunking school. He'd come to school sometimes with a black eye or a bust lip, all that shite.

His da' made him lose his finger as well. He shut the car door on his hand

Thirteen

and sliced his ring finger, that one there. Clean off. There was blood everywhere but he made Skeet walk to the hospital cos he didn't want blood all over his leather car seats. They couldn't fix it so poor Skeet had a finger missing from dead young.

When Skeet was seven, his da' and him were walking down the street as a bus passed. His da' tripped and fell under the wheels and he died when his head popped under a tyre. People say Skeet pushed him. I don't know what to think. I asked 'im about it once but he didn't like to talk about it.

About a month after his da' died his ma' got a boyfriend. She was right ugly, face like a rat catcher's dog, but she got another bloke anyway. He was a real big guy called Gerry, and Skeet was shit-feared of him. Years later he told me Gerry used to feel him up, grope him and that. He'd creep into Skeet's room for an hour or so every other night. Don't tell your ma. It's our little secret; all that shite. Skeet's ma' thought he was the dog's dongers, like, but Skeet hated him.

Big Gerry went with Skeet's ma' for about a year before he died. He was fishing with Skeet when he fell off the riverbank and drowned. He'd been out drinking the night before and was still pissed. Skeet tried to save him but Gerry was too heavy. That's what the story was anyway. Skeet told me what really happened, that Gerry got touchy-feely 'cos there was no one about so Skeet booted him in the bollocks and pushed him in the river. Then he ran in after him and shoved Gerry's head under. He said Gerry kept trying to straighten up so he kept having to give his knackers a good fist. We were both nine then. Poor Skeet. He never really had a chance.

I'm getting to it. I just want you to know what Skeet was like when I knew him. And why he was such a sicko.

After Gerry died his ma' couldn't get another bloke. I suppose she'd have a bit of a...thing ...a reputation. She killed herself on Skeet's eleventh birthday by slicing her wrists with the same knife she'd sliced his birthday cake with. Skeet was real upset 'cos his ma was the only person he loved, I think. 'part from Samantha Fox, of course.

So then he had to go live up Scotland somewhere, with his auntie and uncle. He hardly knew them so he didn't really want to go. But it wasn't up to him. He was there from just after he was eleven, till he was seventeen. That was nearly six years I hadn't seen him. When he came back I thought he was a bit weird, but it was the stuff. He got me into it and then I started to make some dough from it. He told me his auntie and uncle had been all right. They were both sound, but he'd come back cos they'd nagged on at him about finding work.

He lived with me for a bit in my bed-sit, then he got his own spot through the council. They gave it to someone else when he got banged up.

Aye, cheers darling. Milk, three sugars, ta. And a chocolate biscuit if you've got one. Heh heh.

So that's pretty much Skeet's life story. From then he was like me and loads others. Get money where you can, buy the stuff that you can't do without, use it up and get some more. Every now and then, when you remember, you buy food and some liquor, or clothes if you're desperate. You forget to wash and end up smelling like a witch's knickers. At least Skeet was always clean, which was a bit weird for a guy like him. He showered every day and changed his clothes every other. That's how come I was surprised when his digs stunk yesterday. It was piss and shit and sweat, worse than my place.

When I saw him sat there though, looking like something from a cheap horror film, it was obvious why the place stunk. He was over by the doorway into the kitchen, sat in a wheel chair. He'd put on some meat, around the face and that, and his belly looked like it had been drinkin'. It had a hang over! Heh heh. I guess he probably weighed just the same as he used to with all them bits missing and...

Thirteen

Oh. Cheers, love. Where's the biscuit though? Heh.

Right, yeah. So he's there, looking at me, and sitting in his wheel chair but he had no frigging legs, see. That's why he had his wheel chair. His legs were gone. His... wait a minute... his right leg stopped about the centre of his thigh. It had a pointed stump that was covered by the leg of his jeans. His other leg finished about an inch above where his knee used to be and the leg of his jeans covered that one too. No wonder he's put weight on, I thought, he can't go any-frigging-where.

You might think he could do some weights or something. To lose weight I mean. He couldn't though, and do you know why? One of his fucking arms was missing as well, that's why. I couldn't believe it. His right arm. It was gone from here, just a shoulder with no fucking arm hanging off it. He was wearing a T-shirt with a picture of a dog on it, but he also had an old tea towel or something over the stump. The tea towel looked mouldy and fucking horrible. I felt like throwing up. Jesus H Christ. He looked like an extra from that Saving Private Ryan film, for God sake.

Skeet's left arm was fine, apart from the finger he'd lost in his da's car door, and he was running his hand through his greasy hair.

So I asks him, "What the hell happened, Skeet?" and he says. "It's a long story, Mike."

I tell him I got all day so he tells me to sit down. His sofa was covered in crap; pizza boxes, cock mags, liquor cans, all that shite. I just sat on the chair arm and watched as the freak that used to be Skeet tried to wheel his chair nearer me. When he'd moved about a foot he gave up, panting like a fat dog. I told him he was a fucking mess and he agreed. He said that was why he'd writ to me.

Skeet said I had no idea what it was like in prison. He didn't blame me for landing him there, but he said that he couldn't hack it. He said every day he either had his head kicked in or his arse ...well ...you know... He didn't know why but a couple of guys seemed to target him as easy game. He said he started going a bit crazy and without any stuff to help, he just kept on going.

He said he'd remembered when he was a kid, when he'd lost his finger. All the kids had been different to him. They'd all thought he was dead good. The teachers had beer different too. They'd helped him out and cheered him on when they used to always dump on him. See. that's what had been going through his head when he'd put his right leg in the door of the industrial washing machine in the basement of the prison. He thought someone would take pity on him. The door was electric, Skeet said, and it just cut his leg right off.

Yeah. I know. Crazy bastard!

Anyway, he'd been near the end of his stretch so after the hospital they let him out. His leg had been ripped off more than cut off, according to the quacks, so they couldn't put it back on. He got a flat and started trying to get back to the old life. He started on the stuff again, from some other dealer, but it was bad and it gave him the downies. He got depressed, he said, and started hallucinating.

Skeet reckons he was like that for about three months, until one day he had an idea. He must have thought back to other times in his life when he'd felt shitty. And what did he do to cheer himself up? The sick fucker hacked his own leg off with a fire-axe. It would have hurt like hell. So I think he must have been on something. He said he wasn't though. He told the quacks that he'd been hallucinating and there was a giant scorpion on his leg or something. He'd lied though, he told me, he'd known exactly what he was frigging doing, he just didn't want to get chucked into the nut house.

They sent him to rehab instead. For six months. And he said that when he came out he was clean and felt great. I don't know if that's true, his two legs were both fucking missing for Christ sake; but that's what he said.

Thirteen

Skeet said he'd been clean ever since. He got about not too bad in his wheel chair, although he'd have given anything for an electric one. Heh, he'd have given his right arm! Only kidding.

Yeah, it was his right arm that was missing. He did it for a buzz. He thought it would cheer him up one day when there was nowt on telly, so he got the tire axe from down the hall and lobbed his bloody arm off. He said he made a right cock up of it cos he had to hold the axe with his left hand. He said it looked like a blind man's dog had done it. This is where it gets a bit shitty. You don't have any fags on ya, do ya?

Cheers.

Well he couldn't go to the quacks cos they'd lock him up for sure, the sick bastard. Chopping his own leg off and then his arm. So he tried to clean himself up. He said he soaked his stump in boiling water and TCP. I bet he screamed the friggin' spot down. Then he sewed it up using the same needle and cotton that he sews his socks and the arse of his pants with. He had to peel the tea towel off to show me it and by his lace I knew it was hurting. It looked disgusting, like something gone off in a butcher's shop. There were tatty bits of skin dangling and dripping blood and pus. Bits of the stump looked black and scabbed over, and other bits looked fucking mouldy-green and putty and all that shite. One bit was just dripping strings of blood like a leaky tap. And the skin around it, the bit that didn't look like a shark's breakfast, was all yellow and purple with bruises.

He told me that it hurt like shit and half the time he couldn't feel the right-hand side of his body. He couldn't sleep cos of the pain. He had trouble keeping food down and if anything touched the stub he said it felt like red-hot nails being hammered in.

Skeet said he was sure that he was dying, that he was sure his arm had gone septic and he didn't have much time. When I looked at his face I realised how ill he looked. His face was pale and flabby and his eyes looked like piss-holes in snow. His hair was all matted and greasy and I asked how often he had a bath. Although I didn't want to, I would have helped him have a bath if he'd wanted. He said he had an all-over wash and changed his clothes once a fortnight. He'd have done it more often, he said, but it took him a whole fucking day to do it and he was knackered afterwards.

He took me in to the bedroom of his flat. Well, I took him really; I pushed his wheel chair - where there was a huge thing covered in a piss-stained sheet. It stood taller than me by about a foot. There was a rope coming from high up under the sheet, and it was tied to the door handle of his wardrobe. Skeet said all I had to do was pull the rope tree when he told me to. It was tied like cowboys tied up their horses and one sharp pull would undo it, he said. He asked if I'd be able to do that and I said course I frigging would. He said that was my one favour I owed him. I didn't realise how big a favour it was till he pulled the dirty sheet away. That was when I almost shit myself.

It was one of those multi-gym things with all the weights on. Some have a bench as well: you know what I mean.

Well, the rope that was tied to the door handle was holding up about six of the black weights. They were right up the top of the frame and how the hell he got them up there I'll never friggin' know. Fastened to the weights was a big, fuck-off axe blade. It hung below the weights about ten inches. It looked like a kind of home-made guillotine and it wasn't till I saw Skeet lean forward in his wheel chair and put his fat head on the wooden base that I realised that was exactly what the bloody thing was. If I pulled that rope, the weights and the big-bastard blade would drop and the blade would chop Skeet's head clean off. He looked at me with sad eyes and told me to do it. He said that he needed me to do it: that this was the only way he could go. Fucking do it Mike.

Thirteen

I couldn't. I've known him all my life and even though he was living in shite and in fuck-knows how much pain, I couldn't do it.

I suddenly felt I had to get out of there. I was choking on the smell of shit and piss and I was trying damn hard not to puke up.

I ran. I headed straight for the door to the corridor, tripping over the shit on the floor.

The door from the flat wouldn't bloody open. Skeet was coming up behind me like he should be in the fucking Olympics and the door wouldn't open. He was shouting stuff like. "You owe me one, Mike" and "I need you, Mike" - all that shite.

I fumbled with the key in the door as though my hands were someone else's. Skeet grabbed my jacket. He was still shouting at me to help him but I shoved him back, turned the key and got the door open.

I charged down the corridor and, looking over my shoulder, saw Skeet tearing after me with a look on his face that made my hair bristle up. Big, fat, round moon-face with eyes all wild and scary. He must have been pissing about when he had been struggling with his chair. Now he was like greased fucking lightning. I knew I'd be free of him if I got to the top of the stairs, and when I did, I sighed and looked back. Skeet was about three-foot away. And he wasn't stopping. He wasn't even slowing down.

Shite. I thought. He's gonna ram me down the fucking stairs.

I ran down kinda sideways, looking up the stairs. When Skeet hit the top, the front of his chair dropped and his stumpy body shot into the air, straight towards me. His face... Jesus. I'll never forget it as long as I live. His mouth was wide and looked like a big black rip in his pale moon-face, and his hand was stretched out like a claw trying to grab me.

I was at the bottom of the first flight and I just stood and watched as Skeet bounced off two or three steps like a fucking Guy Fawkes dummy. Then he landed at my feet. His head was a funny shape now, looked like a fucking punctured football. He looked at me and mumbled something. I think it was "You owe me one, Mike."

Then the bloody wheelchair clattered down the stairs and landed on him. I heard something crack. Not like a stick or a twig, but a wet crack. You know, like when you drop a coconut. I knew it was Skeet's skull.

I sat there and cried for a bit. I haven't cried for ages and I forgot what it was like. It was weird. Like flushing the chain after taking a dump and letting all the shite out. Then you guys showed up and shoved me in a van like I was Jack the fucking Ripper or something.

So any way, there you go, that's what happened. I told you he was a crazy bastard, didn't I? He was one sick puppy all right. I blame his parents.

So what happens to me now?

What? That's it? I can just walk outa here.

No problem. I'm not doing anything else tomorrow. I could just go for a good ol' statement signing. I tell you what though, I couldn't have another coffee could I, before I go? Aw, go on. I won't even need a chocolate biscuit. Heh heh. Aw. You're a cheating bastard, Inspector, you know that? How about another fag then?

Aw, fucking great. That's the last time I help you out. Fucker! I come all the way down here, help you out, and you won't even give me another coffee. I didn't have to co-operate, you know...

Thirteen

CHECKING
CRAIG DUTTON

The lake was as cold as ice and I was up to my knees in it before I'd reached the small boat. I threw my underwater spotlight and my paddle into it and then pulled myself out of the black water, plant life clinging to my feet.

The sun had set just over an hour ago and I was sure I was alone on the lake. I'd been fortunate to find the boat.

I lifted the anchor out of the water and in the moonlight I could see that I'd brought up some algae with it. Then I reached for my paddle and began to beat at the water, propelling my vessel towards the middle of the lake, breaking the reflection of the moon on the still water into a thousand shimmering pieces.

Eventually I reached the middle of the lake, lining my craft up with the two promontories on either side of me, which pointed to my secret, glowing in the moonlight like the fingers of ghosts. This was the place. Right here.

I dropped anchor and turned on the underwater spotlight. Next, I jumped into the water.

I sank towards the bottom in an orb of light, which gave me approximately three feet of visibility in each direction. I could see the anchor rope on my left.

I sank lower and lower. The water was freezing and my lungs desperately wanted to take in a breath.

And then I saw her, still with her foot tied around the large rock, still in her wedding dress, still with her long black hair.

Still dead.

Satisfied, I swam back up to the boat and clambered in. I paddled back to shore.

THE UNDERTAKER
ANDREW HANNON

When I first read it, my initial reaction was that it must be a joke. My wife, seeing the look on my face as I read the hand-written letter at the breakfast table, asked what it was about.

"It's from a student at Finchley High," I told her. "Apparently the whole of the fourth year need to find two weeks of work experience over the beginning of summer. This young fellow wants to know if I can offer him a placement."

"And why should that cause you to look so worried?"

"Well, come on. How many fourteen year olds do you know who'd want to spend two weeks working at an undertaker's?"

"I don't know any fourteen year olds," my wife smiled. "Pass the sugar."

I passed her the sugar.

"All I'm saying is, when I was fourteen I didn't want to be an undertaker."

"And what did you want to be? A spaceman? A cowboy? Maybe this boy - what's his name? - "

I checked the name at the bottom of the page.

"Geoff Capper."

"- Geoff Capper. Maybe Geoff Capper *does* want to be an undertaker when he's older. You're always complaining about the prejudice you get from people when you tell them what it is you do. I'd have thought you would have been pleased by this lad showing some interest."

My wife sipped some tea, giving me the chance to think about what she'd just said. She had a point; she always did. That's why I loved her. Thirty years of marriage and not another living soul had ever come between us. Maybe this Geoff Capper was a lot more mature than I'd been at fourteen. Also, it was kind of flattering for someone to show an interest in what I did for a living, rather than to associate me with death and want nothing more to do with me than a quick 'Good morning' whenever it couldn't be avoided.

"I think I'll offer him a placement," I told my wife. She winked at me as she bit into her toast.

Geoff showed up at my place of work a couple of weeks later. I'd already formed an image of him in my head - a tall, pale, gangly boy dressed all in black, with hollow eyes and a deep, monotone voice. My wife had told me not to be so silly and said I was a fine one to talk about prejudice, accusing me of being as bad as some of the locals I so often moaned about.

"I'm sure he'll look like any normal fourteen year old boy," she said.

However, when he arrived that dismal, grey morning, I realised that for the first time in as long as I cared to remember my wife had been wrong.

"You must be Geoff," I ventured to the long string of misery stood on the doorstep, nervously chewing on a fingernail. "Come on in. My name's Mr. Granby."

He stepped into the reception area and I offered him my hand to shake. I realised my mistake immediately when he took his right hand away from his mouth and shook my own with it. I preferred to think that the dampness I felt was just a bit of sweat rather than saliva. As I looked at his hand I could just about see that his fingernails had been bitten down as far as possible. Four angry red fingertips and a raw thumb all conspired to produce the weakest handshake I'd ever felt.

I knew it was going to be a long two weeks.

"So? How'd it go?" my wife called when she heard me arrive home that evening. I found her in the kitchen, putting the finishing touches on my dinner. I gave her a kiss on the cheek before I sat down at the table.

"I don't suppose I can withdraw the offer of a placement at this stage, can I?"

"Oh, George! Bad day at the office?"

"You have no idea. I tried to make him feel at ease as I could but I couldn't get anything out of him. I asked him questions about school, why he'd applied for work experience with me, about football, music..."

"And?"

"Nothing. Hardly a squeak."

"Maybe he was just nervous."

My wife put my dinner plate in front of me and gave my shoulders a rub. She always did that, and to be perfectly honest it often hurt, but I never said anything to stop her.

"Maybe. I don't know. He's just... weird. I told him to take a two hour lunch because he was really bothering me, but he came back after forty minutes and said it was too cold for him. In the end I just gave him a brochure on coffins and he sat in a corner flicking through that until five o'clock, biting his fingernails non-stop."

My wife laughed at that.

"Poor George! Maybe tomorrow will be better."

"I don't think it could be much worse."

The next few days were pretty much the same. Geoff barely spoke and always took short lunches. It was driving me mad, so I took a bit of action. I had the idea of unplugging the phone when he wasn't looking and taking my lunch at a different time to him so he couldn't do any damage if anyone tried to call.

"Just take a message if anyone calls," I'd say to him.

"Okay," he'd mumble, finger in his mouth and head down, reading whatever literature I'd given him to go through that day.

On the Friday, however, things changed. I came back from my lunch at about half past two and found him pacing around the office, a grin on his face. It was hard to believe he could look so animated.

"We had a call!" he practically yelled at me as I came through the door. "The phone line must have fallen out but I put it back in and a few minutes later it rang. Here! I've got all the details."

He thrust a piece of paper at me and I sat down behind my desk to read what was on it. I recognised his handwriting from the letter he'd sent me a few weeks ago: *Susan Coventry, 25 years old, death c/b -*

"What does 'c/b' mean?" I asked.

"Caused by."

"Oh."

"*... death c/b mountaineering accident. Extensive damage to face but family desire open-coffin if poss.*"

"Coventry?" I thought out loud.

"Do you know the family?"

I looked at Geoff and was going to ask if he realised he'd said more to me in the past twenty seconds than in the past four and a half days.

"I think so," I said. "Yes, I'm pretty sure I do. I think her father used to own the bakery a few years ago. Anyway, I'd better call the hospital and arrange all the necessaries."

Geoff sat opposite me, smiling and frantically chewing his fingernails as I spoke to the hospital and sorted out the delivery of Susan Coventry's remains.

I was surprised to find Geoff standing outside my office the next day. He waved at me with his free hand (the other was raised to his mouth, being chewed

Thirteen

upon) as I made my way down the hill towards him.

"Good morning, Mr Granby," he said.

"Geoff. What are you doing here? You do realise you get Saturdays and Sundays off, don't you? I thought I'd told you that already."

"Yes, you did Mr Granby, but that lady is coming today and I thought you could use a hand."

"Lady? Do you mean the remains of the Coventry girl?"

"Yes. I wanted to help you if I could, or just watch what you do."

I unlocked the door to my reception area. What advice would my wife give me if she were here right now? I'd told her about Geoff's sudden change in personality, but whereas I thought it was him getting excited about the possibility of seeing a dead body, she thought it was just him coming out of his shell at last.

I turned to look at Geoff

"Listen, Geoff, I don't think this is a good idea. Just come by on Monday and I'll give you a few more brochures to look through."

"Mr Granby, I don't mean to be rude, but surely you realised I was here on work experience to help me make up my mind as to what career path I wanted to take. I can't really do that if I'm not exposed to as many elements of the job as possible." It was like talking with my wife. I knew I couldn't win.

"Come in," I said.

Geoff seemed pretty calm when the remains of Susan Coventry arrived from the hospital later on that morning. She had been a very large woman and when I weighed her I discovered her to be just over eighteen stone. Quite what a woman of that size had been doing climbing mountains, I couldn't understand. All I was sure of was that she must have left quite a crater where she landed. Sorry - undertaker's humour.

Her face was pretty messed up. Her forehead had been completely shattered and had caved in badly on the left hand side. It would take a lot of work to put right if the family were to insist on an open coffin at the funeral service, but I knew it wasn't an impossible task.

Geoff watched everything I did and listened intently to everything I said. He asked question after question - what was this for? what was I doing next? how did this work? I must admit, it was quite an ego boost for me to see someone so enraptured with my work.

Now and again I would have to leave Geoff alone with the body while I made some calls. I had to call Susan Coventry's brother to tell him that the burial could take place the following Sunday. Usually it wouldn't have taken so long, but the facial reconstruction would add at least two days. He thanked me, and made plans to come in on Tuesday to look at coffins for his sister. Meanwhile, Geoff would carry out simple tasks for me, like mixing certain chemicals or testing various shades of make-up on Susan's skin. He worked hard, and it was nice to have some company now that he'd suddenly seemed to learn how to talk.

The facial reconstruction of Susan Coventry turned out to be one of the hardest jobs I'd ever had to carry out. Geoff and I had two photographs given to us by her brother when he came by on Tuesday, and they helped us to an extent. By Saturday afternoon, it was safe to say we'd finished and Susan Coventry, though still a far cry from a Sleeping Beauty comparison, at least looked like she was sleeping.

"Well, Geoff, that's the end of that," I said to him as he was preparing to leave my office for the last time. "Did you enjoy your placement?"

"Yes, Mr Granby. I'd like to thank you for giving me the chance to work with you. I've enjoyed it so much and it's helped me to make up my mind about what I want to do when I leave school."

I laughed. "I'm glad for you, Geoff. Who knows, maybe I'll have a job here

Thirteen

for you if you feel the same way in a few years. Thanks for all your hard work. Here's a little something."

I took an envelope from my back pocket and handed it to him.

"Oh, no, Mr Granby, honestly, it's okay," he protested.

"Nonsense! You worked very hard while you were here and you've earned every penny. Just don't spend it all at once."

"Thanks, Mr Granby."

"You're welcome. Now, run along. Have a great summer."

He extended his hand and I shook it. I was reminded of our first handshake a couple of weeks ago and I involuntarily looked down at his hand.

"I see you've let your nails grow," I said.

The smile on his face faltered for a second.

"Yes. Anyway, I'd better be off. Thanks again."

And off he went.

I closed the door behind him and locked it, turning the sign on the door from 'OPEN' to 'CLOSED'.

Something didn't seem right. The fact that his nails had grown bothered me a bit, and I wasn't sure why. I had an inkling but...

I went through the reception area and out into the preparation room. Susan Coventry lay there in her coffin, gloved hands folded across her ample chest. I removed the gloves one after the other and had my suspicions confirmed.

Her fingernails had been bitten down as far as they could be.

I stared down at her for a few moments, then my lips formed a secret smile. "I suppose we've all got our little fetishes," I said, unbuckling my belt.

Thirteen

THE CLUSTER
TODD LANGLEY
_____

I managed to pick the phone up on its third ring and mumbled something that sounded nothing like hello but would have to make do.

"I'm sorry to wake you, Mr. O'Leary, but I really think you should see this."

"That you, Liddle?"

"Yes."

"What time is it?"

I could have found out the answer to my question by looking at my bedside clock, but that would have involved opening my eyes.

"It's nearly four am," Liddle said. "Sir, I don't quite..."

He trailed off.

"You don't quite what, Liddle?"

He stayed silent for a few moments and I was just beginning to doze off when I heard a sob.

"Liddle?" I said, sitting up and opening one eye. "Are you crying?"

"Sir, please..."

A couple more sobs sounded at the other end of the phone. I'd never particularly liked Liddle – he's fat, has a limp handshake and never talks about girls, but I didn't like hearing him cry. For one thing, I didn't want him getting his tears into the computers at the observatory.

"Liddle? Liddle? I'm about to open my left eye. My right one is already open. That means I'm going to get out of bed, get dressed, get into my car and drive to the observatory. If this is about one of your cats dying or anything equally uninteresting, there'll be trouble."

"Hurry," he blubbered.

Mercifully, Liddle had stopped crying at some point between me hanging up the phone on him and reaching the observatory. His eyes were still a little red when he greeted me at the entrance and I felt embarrassed just looking at him.

"Thanks for coming," he said, his voice wavering a little. I can often be quite sarcastic but decided to avoid descents to the lowest form of wit in case I set him off.

"That's okay," I lied. "What were you crying... what's the problem?"

Liddle's answer was to point one of his fat fingers towards his computer screen. His desk, as always, was immaculate, a far cry from the chaos of my own, which was situated just behind his.

"Take a look," he urged.

I moved past him to get a better look at the image. For a full ten seconds I looked at the screen. I could hear Liddle shifting about behind me. I turned to face him and looked him in his bloodshot eyes. He looked at me as though I ought to say speak first, unconsciously nodding his head as though he was trying to get me to agree with him about something.

"It's a new cluster of stars," I finally said. "Mate, hundreds of new clusters are discovered each month now that we're using the new telescopes. Is this all you've brought me here for?"

"_Read_ them."

"Read them? Read what?" I turned to the screen again. "Liddle, what is there to read? They're just a cluster of..."

Someone with very cold feet walked very slowly over my grave.

"Fucking hell, Liddle."

Thinking back, they probably weren't the best words I could have used after I'd seen what I'd just seen.

Thirteen

Liddle made us both coffees and we sat hunched in front of his screen. How had I not seen it straight away? Of the hundreds of stars in the cluster, several were much brighter than the majority. These clearly formed letters, blatantly obvious to me now after my initial lack of realisation. And when I say they formed letters I don't mean in some kind of Greek-mythological-oh-look-there's-a-winged-horse way; I mean letters, real, bona fide, alphabet letters.

And the letters formed words.

Written in the cluster, from left to right across the computer screen, was the following:

I made ths

Not 'I made this' (although Liddle and I both misread it as this until I noticed there was no second 'i'), but 'I made ths'.

"What do you think it means?" Liddle asked me.

"Nuh uh. You first."

Liddle took quite a melodramatic swig of his coffee before he spoke. I still hadn't touched mine.

"The odds... the odds of it being a coincidence... perfectly formed letters... there has to be some intelligence... a higher power governing..."

"Liddle, promise me you'll never pack in all this science stuff to become a public speaker, okay?"

We both managed smiles.

"What do you make of it then?"

"I'm not so quick to rule out coincidence."

"But they're letters. They spell words."

"Yes, but one of them is spelt wrong."

"But the meaning is obvious."

"So you think, what, God has graffitied the universe? Signed it at the bottom so that people could tell it was His work? Come on."

"Why not? If you'd created something like – "

"My own universe."

" – your own universe, wouldn't you want people to know about it? Wouldn't you leave a message?"

"If I did, I'd write more than three words."

We sat in silence for a bit, both thinking.

"Horoscopes," Liddle finally said.

"I was waiting for you to say that."

"But you get my point, right? People have been reading the stars for thousands of years."

"True. Maybe next week you'll discover a new cluster which advises you to change jobs and to expect a surprise through the post."

"Be serious."

"I am. Look, Liddle, I admit I was shocked at first, but the more I think about it, the less surprising this is. Surely you've heard that thing about the hundred monkeys and the hundred typewriters?"

"Monkeys? Typewriters?"

"Yeah, you know. Put a hundred monkeys in a room with a hundred typewriters and one of them will eventually come up with the complete works of Shakespeare."

"I'm not sure I – "

"Chance! Randomness! They're not letters we're seeing on the screen, they're just stars which happen to form letters. For all we know, there's an alien civilisation looking at the Milky Way and, in their language, it reads 'Who's your daddy?'"

"No, Mr. O'Leary. I'm not convinced. The chances of those stars shining brighter than the others, forming words which they predate by billions and billions of years... it's too much."

I pushed myself away from the screen and got up from my chair.

"What about the misspelling?" I asked.

"It must mean something."

"It means I'm probably right. What we've got in front of us doesn't change a thing. Don't let it bother you. If you do, you'll make it mean what you want it to mean."

"Like you're doing by denying it means anything?"

I groaned. This was getting too confusing for me.

"Like I said, it doesn't change a thing. You think it's the handwriting of God, I think it's a few stars that just happen to be where they are. We balance each other out, Liddle. Goodnight."

"Where are you going?"

"Home. Bed. Sleep."

"But..."

"But nothing. I'm tired. If you want to stay here and stare at it for a few more hours then be my guest."

Liddle stood up and approached me as I walked to the door.

"How can you be so blasé about something as monumental as this?"

"Be careful how much credence you put into this. If this convinces you of the existence of a higher power, what will happen to your faith?"

Liddle stopped. He dropped his gaze to the floor and I left him to it.

GHOST WRITER
LEE BETTERIDGE

"Aw, Christ on a crutch!" said Alfie as he stepped off the curb into a puddle that came up to the cuffs of his jeans. His shoe quickly allowed the water to drench the sock within. The rain was pouring as heavily now as it had been all day, making the evening look grey and miserable. Alfie, in turn, felt grey and miserable as he shook his foot and proceeded across the rain-drenched street to his house. A yellow transit van was parked outside his house and he wondered if the creepy guy with the earrings next door was having some work done.

Alfie juggled the stack of magazines he held from one hand to the other and finally managed to find his door key. He went into his house and let out a sigh of relief as he shut out the horrible night. He flicked on the hall light and noticed a brown envelope on the floor. Setting the magazines on the hall table he picked up the envelope and started to rip it open while he used his feet to kick off his wet shoes.

The envelope contained a magazine that he'd ordered over the Internet entitled Ghost Writer and it boasted itself to be 'the home of the best short horror stories in the world'. Alfie shrugged out of his dripping coat, picked up the other magazines and made his way to the kitchen, his right foot making squelch noises with every step.

After getting showered and changed into some warmer clothes, Alfie slammed a frozen turkey dinner in the microwave and left it buzzing away as he considered his pile of magazines. Three of them were of the bedroom variety - the kind that his dad used to say should come with a free pack of Kleenex - so he put them to one side for later. Then he had a Loaded, an FHM, an Official Playstation 2 magazine, a Fangora and an Empire. Plus the Ghost Writer that had been waiting for him when he came home. His newsagent's bill was ridiculous every month, what with most magazines being over £3 a pop these days, but what the hell. It was his money, and at least he didn't just piss it away on drink like most people.

The microwave made a BING! and Alfie brought the steaming pile of solids masquerading as food over to the table. He opened Ghost Writer and started to read the Editorial inside the front cover. Here again, like on the website, it claimed to have the most spine chilling tales and scrotum shrivelling stories to be found this side of Hell's front door. Alfie laughed to himself as he chewed. After all, that was what all these type of publications said, but most of them contained plot-less drivel containing corny monsters and sex-crazed maniacs. He turned to the first story and grinned at the title.

"The Box," he said, then sarcastically to the empty house: "Whooo!"
He started to read.
Bang! Bang! Bang!
Alfie lurched back in his seat and his heart seemed to lurch in his chest too. The knock at the door had surprised him, totally goosed him in fact, and he didn't really know why. The story he was reading, although quite well written and atmospheric, was still very basic and unoriginal. To sum it up, a bloke who lived on his own had received a parcel which, when he opened it, had released some kind of ghost/demon/poltergeist thing that had wrecked his house before battering the bloke (yeah, right!) and ultimately possessing him.

However, somehow this lame-arse tale must have got to him, subconsciously perhaps, because the knock at the door had most definitely caused him to almost shit his pants. Or maybe it was because the story, The Box, started with a knock at the door.

Alfie pushed the plate aside that still held most of the turkey dinner, now cold

Thirteen

and unbelievably looking less like food than it had done, and went to the front door. Opening it let in a breath of icy wind and a sprinkling of rain that made Alfie shiver. He also shivered when he saw that there was nobody there waiting for him. Instead, there was a square box sitting ominously on the step. Alfie glared through the rain up and down the dark street. There was no movement except for a black cat with white feet running under a parked car. He could see no one who might have left the package. Alfie sighed, picked up the box and brought it inside. After shutting the door he carried it through to the kitchen and set it on the table.

The package was a cube about as long as a school ruler in all directions. It was wrapped in brown paper and then tied with tatty brown string. It had a ripped corner and a cardboard tag that was blank. It was identical to the one described in the story.

Alfie looked at it. He picked it up and shook it. No rattle, no nothing, and then he remembered that that was exactly what Graham, the character in 'The Box', had done.

"For Christsake," Alfie growled to himself. "That's just a story and that's just a box. Nothing more." And before he lost the nerve he pulled off the string and started ripping at the brown paper. It came off easily and Alfie was suddenly holding a battered-looking wooden box with a brass-hinged top and a latch.

"This must be a wind-up," he said, his voice sounding slightly shrill as it broke the silence. "Wooden boxes don't fall out of stories, especially run-of-the-mill pulp fiction like that." The box was also identical to the one Graham had opened in the story.

Yeah, story.

Fiction, right.

This was obviously just a strange coincidence. Alfie touched the hinges with a finger that shook almost imperceptibly, then the latch, but the latch flipped open with his touch.

Alfie said, "Oh Fuck!" while the lid of the wooden box sprang open as if pushed from inside. Foul-smelling air blew into Alfie's face from within the box, making his hair flap and his eyes squint. The smell made his stomach clench into a knot and he dropped the box. It landed with a clack that cracked one of the ceramic tiles on the floor. Alfie didn't notice. He spun round on the spot and followed a wave of destruction that swept round the room.

A mug and two plates jumped off the draining board and smashed on the floor. Something unseen landed in the sink, splashing water everywhere. The curtains billowed and then the framed picture of Bela Lugosi as Dracula leaped from the wall and shattered. The microwave door flew open, sparks shot from the toaster, a mug exploded as it sat on the worktop. A cupboard door sprang open so hard that it pulled loose of one of its hinges. Two glass jars, one full of wine gums and one full of aniseed balls, fell from the cupboard and smashed on the floor. A stack of papers, shopping lists and old lottery tickets blew up into the air and scattered about the room. Then all was silent and still.

Alfie stared in amazement, shocked and in awe of what he had just witnessed. Then he felt the chill. His breath plumed in front of him as the room's temperature dropped considerably. All this had happened in the story, all this had happened and the character had recalled reading something once about ghosts and hauntings and dramatic drops in temperature and now Alfie recalled them too. He struggled to control his thoughts. What had happened next in the story? And then it came to him. The ghost/demon/poltergeist had written 'you are mine' on the mist on the window. Alfie spun on his heels to face the window. There was writing there but he had to step closer to see what it said. It read 'you are min', and as Alfie watched the final 'e' appeared on its own. His breath suddenly

Thirteen

seemed difficult to gather, and a sickening feeling roiled in his guts. He supposed it was shock or fear or insanity or all three. This couldn't be happening.

As he gazed at the writing on the window his vision blurred for a second and he became aware of his mouth being dry and the sound of his blood pumping round his skull.

Then he decided to leave. Alfie ran to the front door, totally ready to leave the house in his stocking feet and without a coat. But the door wouldn't open. He twisted the latch and pulled but the door wouldn't move and it didn't make sense because there was no sliding bolt and nothing else that could be holding the door shut. Then he felt a cold gust against the side of his neck and heard a faint whisper saying something he couldn't make out. He let out an uncontrollable wail and ran into the living room. The TV set switched itself on and started randomly flicking through channels, some of which Alfie knew for sure he didn't get with his Sky subscription. And then he noticed that the channel changes weren't random at all.

"You are..." said Michael J. Fox.

"...Mine. I will have..." a rock band screamed.

"You..." Rita off Coronation Street.

"You are mine..." Some American sitcom woman.

"...For ever and ever." A cute puppet dog.

Alfie gaped at the TV and listened to the sound clips as they played over and over.

"You are..."

"...Mine. I will have..."

"You..."

"You are mine..."

"...For ever and ever."

He recalled this exact scene from the story and realised that he had to get out of here. He knew what was coming next and he had to leave. Alfie left the living room at high speed and caught his shoulder painfully on the doorframe. He didn't slow down though, but sprinted down the hall, the TV channel hopping of its own accord behind him. Back in the kitchen he looked at the writing on the window. You are mine. Then he looked at the back door.

Without thinking he raced through the messy kitchen - and his foot landed on the aniseed balls that had smashed onto the floor. His foot skidded under him as he painfully performed the splits, then his momentum carried him over side ways. Alfie fell with his full body weight against the table, the solid edge hitting him square in the throat. He slumped to the floor and blood started to form a puddle on the floor just below his gaping mouth. There was no sound in the room except the ticking of the wall clock and the thick dripping of blood onto tiles. The whole house was blanketed with stillness. Several lottery tickets found resting places now that the turbulent air had become calm. Nothing moved.

Then there was the sound of the front door opening, quick footsteps down the hall and a large man strode over to Alfie. The man's latex-gloved hand touched Alfie's cold neck.

"Shite! We killed the poor bugger," he said into his hands-free microphone.

"Oh great," said the voice in his ear. "Just fucking great. You sure he's dead?"

"Of course I'm sure. He's got no pulse, he's not breathing and his neck looks like someone hit it with a cricket bat. The poor bugger's dead all right."

Static and then a sigh in his ear.

"Well, there's nothing we can do for him now. Better clear our stuff out."

The man strode around the kitchen clutching a canvass holdall and started to collect the pieces of machinery he had planted there earlier in the day. The little

Thirteen

fan to blow the curtains, the pressure pads that had knocked the picture off the wall and the crockery from the draining board. And the two that had been responsible for throwing the sweets on the floor and scattering the bits of paper everywhere. He took the gizmo off the microwave door and the one from the toaster. Then he dunked his hand in the sink and took out the little water jet.

"I don't know," said the voice in his ear. "We spend hours setting this shit up to give the guy a good scare. It's like a well rehearsed orchestra in here, pressing all these buttons at the right time to make it look like there's something spinning round the room. Then he has to go and fuck it up royally. Still, he did look scared, didn't he?"

The man said nothing and proceeded to collect the cameras. Three in the kitchen, two in the hall. Then back to the kitchen and into the holdall he threw in the wooden box that they had compressed thirty pounds of air into, and its wrapping and string. Then he picked up the Ghost Writer magazine and its envelope. He read the slogan on it. 'The home of the best short horror stories in the world.' He sighed and dropped them into his bag. Confident he was finished, he glanced round the room for a final check. Then he noticed the writing on the window. Where it had said 'you are mine' it now read 'you forgot this, you numpty'. Hearing the laughing in his ear he peeled the clear membrane from the window and reminded himself to wrap the cord from the touch-pad that it was linked to round the other guy's neck when he got back.

Giving the room a final glance, his gaze rested on Alfie's lifeless body.

"Poor bugger," he said under his breath, then turned and headed down the hall.

He opened the front door, the door he'd held shut with all his strength not ten minutes ago, and was about to leave. Then he remembered something. He grabbed the miniature fan clipped to the mirror that had blown in the poor bugger's ear when he'd tried to exit the house. Then the man shut the door and dashed through the rain to the yellow van that already had the engine running.

Thirteen

EXPRESS DELIVERY
ROBERT BELL

Everything happened so fast - he opened the door, pulled me inside, closed the door, and thrust a gun in my face. Then he pushed up against me, one hand gripping the collar of my grey uniform, the other forcing the gun to my temple.

"You do anything I don't say, I shoot. Understand?"

I nodded, the pizza box still in my hand.

"Good."

A drop of sweat ran down his brow and over his greasy face. He had deep acne scars. He took the gun away from my head and let go of my collar. Before he spoke again, he licked his right index and middle finger and rubbed them against his thumb, as if trying to feel the texture of his saliva.

He moved down a darkened hallway.

"Come on," he said. We entered a kitchen. The blinds were closed and the backdoor had two metal bars running horizontally across, bolted into the wall and the door. There were tiny pieces of concrete and plaster lying on the floor, and a drill and hammer rested on the edge of the sink. Dusty footsteps dotted the floor.

Again he licked his two fingers.

"Sit down, put the pizza on the table." He pointed with the gun to the two chairs and table. When I didn't move, he shouted, "Sit down now!"

I heard a whimper from the opposite corner, alongside the fridge. Three men sat on the floor - pizza delivery boys - their arms and legs tied, their mouths taped shut. Two of them watched me. The third had dark patches of blood on his chest. He was slumped forward, his head tilted to the right.

I sat down.

"Good, great," he said, taking the other chair. He opened the pizza box - Hawaiian, no tomato, extra cheese - and picked up three slices. While he pointed the gun at me, he forced the food into his mouth until his cheeks bloated like a hamster's.

"It's good," he said. It sounded like 'hith hood'.

Halfway through, he went to the cupboard and returned with peanut butter and syrup. He dipped the pizza in both jars, and stuffed it down his throat. He licked his fingers.

"Yeah, that's good - you know why?"

I shook my head.

"'Cause I can mix my pizza with syrup and peanut butter - ain't that right, boys?" He leaned to the side; the two guys nodded.

"You're thinking, I'm mad, I've lost it, I've gone off - well you're wrong. I'm as sane as it gets, and I'll stay that way. Come tomorrow, I'll be alive and healthy and normal."

Looking at the clock on the wall, he exhaled a deep breath. The time was twenty minutes to midnight.

"Twenty minutes, boys."

Chunks of peanut butter were stuck in the stubble around his mouth.

"Right, let's get you the same as the boys." He bent down and picked up a rope. "You know," he said as he walked over to me, "them three cried like you've never seen. One of them tried to hit me with his pizza box. Pity I had to shoot him."

I raised my hands and he tied them.

"That too tight?"

I shook my head.

After he taped my mouth, he closed the door leading to the hallway. Then he drilled and bolted two more rods into the door, same as the other.

Thirteen

We were now locked in.

He sat down, sweat rolling over his reddened cheeks. "Let's see him get in here now - ain't that right, boys?" He leaned back, his eyebrows raised; the two men nodded again.

He looked at me and grinned.

"I don't know when he's coming. I know he's coming this week, but it could be any day."

I watched him look around the kitchen, appraising it.

"Nice house, this. I really like this one - I've got five, you know."

I raised my eyebrows.

"It's true. It's a pity I can't show you around. I've got a Ferrari in the garage - I like my Ferrari. I've got seven cars, but I like the Ferrari best. He can have the others. Just leave me with my Ferrari and this house."

He picked up a packet of fags off the table. Even though I had tape over my mouth, he offered me one. I shook my head.

"Good, only got three left." He glanced at the clock. "Doesn't matter, this'll be over in ten minutes, then I'll pop to the shops and get ten cartons."

He lit the cigarette after three attempts; his shaking hands dropping first the fag, then the lighter.

"I've had a good two years. Good two years." He put the lighter on the table and twirled it around. Then he placed the fag in the ashtray, and lifted his shirt. There were three large scars across his stomach. "See here? Should've been dead two years ago. Should've been on the other side already."

He licked and rubbed his fingers.

"Back then I was a driver for a company called Safeguard, we used to transport the money for the banks in armoured vehicles. Used to have more ammunition on us than the second fucking battalion. Ain't that right, boys?"

He leaned back; they nodded.

"They blocked the highway, formed a circle, and shot us to bits. They didn't even give us a chance to give them the money. They wanted to kill us." Again he lifted his shirt. "They thought I was dead -- hell, I thought I was dead. They took all the money, then fucked off, leaving me in the middle of nowhere, bleeding to death."

He smiled and shook his head, and picked up his cigarette. Half had turned to ash, resting in the ashtray like a fossil.

"You know what happened then?"

I shook my head.

"He appeared out of nowhere. I didn't hear no cars stop, didn't see anyone coming. I remember he was dressed in a white suit and had slicked-back hair that he kept smoothing back while he spoke." He mimicked the action, running his hand over his hair.

"So he kneels next to me and puts his hand on my shoulder - fuck. His touch burned like a thousand fires. It was as if fire ran through my veins."

He turned, showing me his left ear. The skin looked burned.

"See that?"

I nodded.

"That's what his breath did to my ear. Burned like hell. Everything burned like hell."

He inhaled three longs puffs, and glanced at the clock.

Five minutes till midnight.

A tear trickled down his cheek.

"The bullets, they were hurting, everything was goddamn hurting. I just wanted it to end. He said I had a choice: I could die, or I could sign a contract with him and he'd let me live two more years, with all the money I wanted."

Thirteen

He looked at me and laughed; his eyes flooded with tears. "Shit, someone tells you if you sign a contract, you can not only be safe from the pain, but also have all the money you want and an extra two years - you telling me you're not going to sign it?"

He put his index and middle finger together and signed the air. "Signed it right there. I didn't believe in it, but it was worth a shot. He took a paper out of his pocket, then dipped a pen in my own blood - there was enough of it lying around to fill a thousand Parkers."

He glanced up at the clock. Two minutes.

"After I signed it, I passed out, and woke up in hospital. And for the last two years I've been living the good life."

He flicked the fag against the edge of the ashtray. "I like living like this - hell, I like *living*. He can have everything - 'cept the Ferrari and the house. I like the house. But he can have everything else."

He looked at me. "That's why I've got you boys. I figure if I offer you to him, he might let me live. It's the only chance I've got."

One minute to midnight.

"Hell, each day this week has been the best of my life." He wiped tears from his eyes. "I'll give him you three, he'll let me live - he has to, ain't that right, boys?"

This time the two guys cried.

Something clanked outside the backdoor. It was midnight.

He jumped up, knocking the chair back. "Get up, get up, get up, go over there!"

He waved the gun in my face. I stood and jumped over to the fridge.

Something scratched on the door.

The first bolt started to unscrew itself.

He whimpered, holding the gun out in front of him. "He's going to take you, you hear me? He'll take you, not me."

He must have thought we didn't believe him. Perhaps he didn't believe himself. He walked back to us.

"You hear me? I said he will take you, not me, now nod!"

He slammed the butt of the gun into the face of the second man. Blood splattered against the side of the fridge.

He moved to me. Behind him, the screws were nearly out, and the scratching on the door was growing louder. "You hear me? He will take you, not me!"

Smiling, I raised my hand and slicked back my hair.

Thirteen

PIGEON MORNING
MATTHHEW BATHAM

I emerge from my quilt like a moth, soggy from its rebirth. It's too early to spread my wings and show their not so glorious colours. First I need caffeine and three cigarettes. These will be consumed while feeding on the mental nectar of breakfast television, staring bleary-eyed, blank-faced at the inane antics of the presenters.

Perhaps an hour from now I will tentatively unfold, uncurl, lick off the remnants of sleep and fly into the day.

Breakfast TV is as stupid as ever. The presenter, who is highly rated, I understand, talks like a school yob while his co-host giggles in a helium-high voice at everything he says. I could turn over to one of the less infantile offerings, but they irritate me even more because they try to be serious but give even the most horrendous news a morning make-over. I feel angry at myself because I find the ludicrously upbeat female presenter attractive.

The pigeons are courting outside the living-room window. It is a black, sickening sound. The worst sound to wake up to. Before I open my eyes I see the male's bloated, dirty body, head held up so proud. I have bought rat poison to kill them. I'm intending to mix it with some bread and other tasty tit-bits and leave it on the ledge outside my bedroom window. I hope they won't die there. I don't fancy finding stiff, maggot invested pigeons when I open the window to a new day.

The pompous male reminds me of businessmen, swollen beneath their grey plumage, full of self-admiration for their commercial achievements.

Soon I will be crushed against such pigeon-men on the sweating tube, my head glued to someone's stale armpit, or cocked unnaturally against a shoulder dusted with dandruff.

I swig the cold remains of coffee and surrender to the pull of work.

The tube is as packed as ever. Morning breath hangs like smog. Someone is prodding my back. I'm not sure if it's deliberate, but I still want to lash out. I can feel their breath on my neck, their thigh pressed to my leg. This is the closest I get to intimacy.

They prod me again and I try to edge away, but the slightest movement brings me uncomfortably close to molesting someone. I strain to see the culprit, but they are just out of range.

The doors open at Oxford Circus and the carriage breathes out, spraying commuters onto the grey platform. I feel the prodder back up a little, but not as much as they could. I slide into a new space, leaning against the glass partition. I'm aware that my back is sweating and that I will leave a large smear behind me. I glance towards the prodder.

She is short and a little stout. She is carrying a rolled up magazine under her arm. Her linear shoulders are at the level of the tender area of my back. She looks fierce, like a small dog trained to kill. Her mouth is puckered like the bottom of the same animal. I resent that screwed up face. I imagine her prodding me again, deliberately, painfully, urging me off the train.

"Quickly," she barks, "I'm late for a meeting."

I grab her by the ears and spit into her face: "Fuck off you stupid little bitch. Poke me again and I'll fucking kill you!"

I pull a black curtain across the scene before it turns grisly. Sometimes I disturb myself with the images of revenge I conjure up. Self-censorship has become instinctive. Once I shoved a young lad through the tube window. Posted him like a fat, fleshy letter, stuffed with bubble-wrap. His crime had been to fire a

Thirteen

ball of spit and paper at my head from the gutted body of a pen. His head had caught in the narrow gap, the flesh pealing back, the skull scraping on metal.

I had drawn the black curtain before the screech of brakes or the crack of bone.

By my stop the train is almost empty. The prodder is long gone to her executive job, unaware of my dark intentions towards her.

Air quells my mood a little. The sun is out and London is bright and warm. I walk through a small park to the office block where I work. There are more fat pigeons strutting around the benches, eating scraps even as they prepare to mount their chosen partners. I feel queasy again and a cloud covers the sun. Black mood returns.

I'm employed by a company that sells financial packages to individuals and commercial enterprises. It's a high-powered environment. I'm responsible for taking calls and directing them to the correct person.

I've been working here for six years.

I can't smoke in the offices so by mid-morning I'm desperate for a cigarette. Sometimes Edith covers for me while I slip outside. Edith is about sixty. Too old to be working. The company keeps her on because she's related to the managing director. If she wasn't here, maybe I would have been promoted by now.

I imagine slipping arsenic into Edith's tea. Her face blows up like a blue football, her neck swells like a snake that has eaten an antelope. She drops dead and everyone turns to me, her successor, their faces a mixture of horror and relief.

I draw aggressively on my cigarette. There are pigeons on the pavement in front of the office block, pecking at the ash as I flick it.

Ashley Hayes, one of the company's most successful young reps, strides towards me from the park. He is swinging his black briefcase like a school child on his way home for summer holidays would a satchel.

"Just clinched a major deal!" he chirps.

I smile, go to respond, then hear the deep reply of another rep who has been smoking in the doorway just behind me. I shrink, feel ugly, puff even more violently on my cigarette.

The reps give each other a high five and jog up the stairs to the office, grey plumage fluffed up with arrogant air.

I follow them a few seconds later. Edith is laughing with a female colleague as I approach my desk. I assume they are talking about me and give the second woman a cold stare as I relieve Edith of her temporary duties.

"Thank you," says Edith crisply as she returns to her own position, still gossiping with her friend.

My desk is next to a window, tarnished brown by pollution. I can just about make out the small park and the grey dots, the pigeons. Around me grey-suited reps strut and peck between the desks.

The rep who has just scored the great deal approaches, barely looking at me, and asks if I can call Interflora and order his wife some flowers.

"It's her birthday he says," dropping a slip of paper in front of me, on which he has scrawled her name and address, and walking off before I can reply.

It is not my job to order flowers for the wives of young, superior reps. But I do it anyway, making sure her name is miss-spelt.

I think I am becoming paranoid. The reps seem to be looking at me more than usual. Not staring, but glancing from behind their computer screens and looking quickly away when I turn.

A pigeon has landed on the ledge outside my window. It is the fattest, ugliest bird I have ever seen. It has a tumour-like growth on one leg, which looks blue and bloody, like the knuckle of a joint of meat.

Thirteen

Some people eat pigeon meat. That makes me feel sick.

David Blakely is the boss of the company. He is only thirty-seven, but looks older, probably because of the stress. He has his own office not far from my desk. It is made from partitions which are half glass, but he has blinds on every wall so that he can shut out the work force.

He rarely speaks to me so I am surprised when he pops his head round the door of his office and beckons me over. At first I look to see if anyone is standing nearby, but he points at me and beckons again.

I push my chair back, still hesitant even though there is no doubt now as to whom he is beckoning. I glance around the office and forty heads duck back behind their computer screens. Edith is in the midst of making tea so she ducks behind the kettle, pretending to hunt for a dropped sugar sachet.

My legs are starting to feel weightless. I hope that the reps will stay behind their screens while I make my way to the office. If I feel them watching I will think too much about how I am walking and then walking will seem like an alien activity.

I stand and begin the journey. I focus on a spot just to the left of the boss's head, desperately trying not to think about what my legs are doing. I reach the office without stumbling and fall into a chair facing Blakely, who has already sat down.

"Thanks for coming," he says, as if I had received a formal invitation. I nod.

"I'm afraid I have some rather bad news."

For a brief moment I think that someone I know has died, but it is far worse than that.

"I need to make some cutbacks," he continues. "And there really isn't anyone else I can let go, except you. Please don't take it personally..."

I have stopped hearing him. I am leaping across the desk, and gripping his long white neck in my hands. We both fall, me forwards, him backwards, me still fastened to his throat. His Adams apple is cracking under my grip.

"...I really am sorry," he concludes, and insults me with a patronising smile of sympathy.

I know I should say something. "Why not Edith," seems like a good start, but my tongue is too big and my throat too dry, so I stand and wander back into the main office, eyes fixed to the grey carpet.

I know that forty-one pairs of eyes are staring at me from behind forty-one computer screens; Edith will have returned to hers by now.

The first thing I notice when I reach my desk is a trail of pigeon shit dripping down the window. It looks like anaemic snot.

I fumble my jacket from the back of the chair and push my shaking hands into the sleeves. At least I manage that manoeuvre without too much difficulty. I should be asking about redundancy pay, my pension, references, but I feel stunned. If I try to speak I will either fly into a rage or cry. I don't want to do either until I am somewhere private.

I head for the stairs without looking back at the office. Once through the exit door I light a cigarette. My hands are shaking so violently I have to clasp one in the other to steady it enough to hold the lighter.

Each stair seems like a drop of three feet. I reach the outside and react to the sun like a vampire, covering my eyes with my right arm.

Squinting, I head for the park. I chance one glance up at the office and forty-one heads duck from view - or so I imagine.

In the park the pigeons are swarming, tumbling over each other. Some are fighting over pieces of bread or potential mates. I want to kick one, send its bloated body rocketing into the trees, feel the weight of it against my shoe.

"It's pigeons that have put me here," I think angrily.

I sit on a bench, not yet overcome with the rat-birds. Usually when I sit here I

Thirteen

eat a sandwich bought from the cafe just round the corner. I won't be doing that any more. I feel hot tears in my eyes, but fight them. I start to think about sales reps and pigeons, and soon the two have become one. I glance at the sandwich and have an idea.

I'm greeted with wary looks when I appear in the office a couple of hours later, brandishing the large white box of cakes.

"Thought I should have some sort of leaving-do," I say. "Who's for a cake?"

I see their expressions flicker between uncertainty and sympathy. It's super-rep Ashley that makes the first move.

"Thanks mate, that's really good of you. How about we take you for a beer later?"

"Great!" I say, grinning, watching him bite into the doughnut, hoping the extra jam I have shoved into the middle will disguise the taste of the other added ingredients – a little rat poison, and some arsenic I bought over the Internet months ago when the pigeons were really getting me down. I'm glad now I didn't waste it on them.

The rest of the office comes forward, following the example of their champion. I stay long enough to see the first of them drop, blood spurting from their mouths, eyes bloated with shock.

I don't enjoy their rattling screams and wet, bubbling cries as much as I'd imagined, and this time it's not just a matter of closing my eyes for a few seconds and thinking of something else. This time it's real.

Thirteen

THE STORM
LEISA PARKER

Hedar sat on the porch, admiring his two great loves - the woods and his garden. He lovingly toiled in his garden, day in and day out, pulling milkweeds and dandelions, killing mites and aphids and slugs. He harvested carrots and cukes, squash and rhubarb, and an assortment of herbs (basil being his favourite) for his active vegetarian diet.

Meat, he shuddered. He hadn't eaten meat for 11 years and didn't miss it at all. No sir'ree bob. He felt healthier, stronger, younger, and even more energized for his late evening jaunts into the deep green woods. He never missed a day. Ever. He found the woods relaxing, soothing, even magical; the massive oaks, the wildflowers, the thistle, even the storms he enjoyed. The dazzling crazy power of them was awe-inspiring. Majestic. Of course you could lose your way in the tangle of trees and wild-grass. Five hikers this year and counting....

The storm had come out of nowhere.

Hedar ran for shelter, for cover, as the trees thrashed against a swirling black sky, their branches cracking and splintering and crashing throughout the air, about the swaying ground - the winds screaming and howling. Finding nothing, nary a rock nor cave nor hole, Hedar crouched by a shrub and marvelled, mouth gaping at the sky. The raging power and unbridled strength, the crack of ear-shattering light that lit up the skies like a display of fireworks.

And that's when he saw them.

Lightly swaying, almost floating amidst the chaos of the shrieking winds and the whipping branches and the swirls of debris - they fell; tenderly as if guided by a soft hand - little green leaves with stick legs and stem arms. Falling and falling.

Then darkness.

Hedar smiled at his silliness.

His spooked imagination.

His little grey cells working overtime.

How quaint.

Then again and again and again. The blackness shook and flashed alive with an electric booming radiance. And there, clearly visible in vivid light. Them.

From the highest treetop, inside a cracked branch, its jagged hollowness, they spilled out - little stick legs and stem arms falling, toppling head over feet and feet over heads. Tumbling and tossing, tumbling and tossing...

Again, darkness.

Hedar's brow deepened, the lines flexing as his mind raced and scattered, attempting to make sense. To make order. What with the swirling winds, the flashes of light, the adrenaline, who knows what strangeness the mind can conjure...?

BOOM!

Hedar jumped as the sky broke again.

He stared intently.

Concentrating.

They were still there.

Just a trickle now, out of the splintered branch. But they were there, definitely there. For his eyes didn't lie, they never had. And he rubbed at them then, at his drooping eyes, his heavy lids falling. No, it was most definitely not silliness or insanity. Not a trick or confusion of the mind, of the storm, of the light, or the winds or anything else. They were there. For he was not a silly-goose of a man or losing his marbles, and he was most definitely not one short of a six-pack. He was a solid, clear-thinking, level minded individual, the most sane of all men, of all

Thirteen

six-packs. And as he began to ball up on the ground, he pictured them in his mind. The little leaves, the little legs, the little grins.

He awoke in the woods, to the sun's warmth and the birds' chirping, and he remembered. Remembered everything and remembered well. He knew it had happened. He was sure of that. Positive. And although he had always felt at peace in these woods, always safe, he now felt unsure, he felt strange, he felt...

Watched.

And not alone. He slowly got up, brushing the twigs and leaves and dirt off of his shirt and his pants, and then, despite his misgivings, his uneasy feelings, he moved deeper into the woods. For it was something that could not be ignored. A situation that longed for more. A compulsion, a beckoning perhaps, something that persuaded him to go on, to...

Go... go... go...

Beyond the bushes and thickets. Beyond the thorns and the spikes, to a clearing. Unknown to him before. Something new. And that's where he saw them. A few hundred perhaps, maybe more, little leaves dancing and chanting, their little stick legs bouncing up and down, up and down. Some slammed little pebbles together with their tiny stem hands while the wildflowers clapped their petals, swaying and giggling, twirling and spinning.

And then they stopped.

Sudden and quick.

Dead silence.

Nothing.

And they all looked up, their little flat green faces facing the sky.

Hedar stiffened.

A horrid rigidness shot through him from head to toe as he slowly looked up. Up and up, higher and higher, until he too saw it, and his mouth contorted into a twisted mixture of awe and terror as a giant oak bent forward. Its branches and leaves smacking him in the face, the twigs poking at his eyes, the rough bark scraping his neck and arms and legs. The rawness, the bleeding, the endless cuts, and then its mighty branches grasped him; up...up...up... into the air, his arms and legs thrashing and kicking, thrashing and kicking.

Fruitlessly.

And as wonderful as it here in the woods, the peace, the beauty, the tranquillity, my green friends, big and small, there have been some problems. A period of adjustment, if you will. My former garden occupants have visited and they are not happy. Not happy at all. The cucumbers, the peppers, the squash, the carrots, even the basil, attempting to attack me with their little name spikes for the generations of slaughter they have endured. And mealtimes here, well, they are grand spectacles and there is plenty, don't get me wrong.

It's just that the main course, the middle course, the side course, the dessert, and every other course in-between, well, it's meat. And since I can no longer eat my greens, for they are now my friends, they are of the soil, of the seed, of the ground, and forbidden; what can I do? And so they heap great mountains of flesh upon me and they are savages I tell you, pure savages. For their little mouths hold rows upon rows of tiny little fangs that pull and yank and drool and growl and smile as the blood drips down their little green faces and drenches their little wood legs. Bird and deer, squirrel and possum, rabbit and horse, and once, just once, a woman. Quite plump, her elastic pushed to its limits, her ruby-lined mouth stuffed with a crushed tin can. And I tried desperately to avoid her eyes, her blazing stare. To read the battered can, the brand of beer, as her blues bulged and bulged, disbelieving and pleading...as my little green friends began to growl and feed.

JOKERMAN
HILDA STRINGER

Deep holes where the eyes are gouged
blood and mucus blend in its ugly mouth,
its face a mask, cruel and obscene
inside my head a piercing scream

Garish clothes hang in tatters
stained with fetid matter,
pitilessly it pursues its quest
gratified at my distress.

Hideous mouth moving in mime
unseeing eyes search mine,
transfixed by its ghastly leer
I'm held in a web spun from fear.

Gasping for breath I claw the air
seeking escape from my nightmare,
alone amongst the crowd I stand
it offers me its oversized hand.

It's dancing and twirling
the leaflets it thrusts unfurling
telling the circus is in town,
I look at the face of a clown.

Thirteen

RANDOM
THOMAS GILBERT

Ah, decisions, decisions!

I love this part of it, it really heightens the senses. Yes, stood here in the park, feeling the wind and rain, listening to the sounds of... well, everything. The traffic, the birds, the chimes of the bells over at Saint Stephen's, the people.

The people.

I like to choose one at random – honestly, I do. But it's more difficult than you might imagine. I'm getting better at it. In fact, I'm finding ways to be more and more random. Last week, for example, I made myself find someone wearing red. It took a while – I was in the city, you see, among all the workers, and they all seem to wear black. Anyway, I eventually noticed a gentleman wearing a red tie.

But I didn't kill him.

I killed the first person I saw him speak to. A newspaper vendor. I waited all day in a coffee shop opposite his stand. I had four chocolate muffins and fifteen coffees. Then, when the vendor finally closed up, I left the coffee shop, crossed the road, broke his fat neck, giggled a bit, then ran away.

Today, I chose the first lethal weapon I saw, which happened to be a kitchen knife. I'm going to stick with that 'first person they talk to' thing, once I find someone...

Now...

Oh, goody! There's a young man! I'll follow him! I can't let him out of my sight. He looks rather sprightly so if he strays too far I'll not know who to kill.

I'll jog towards him a bit. There are lots of joggers in the park, I'll look perfectly natural.

Woo! I'm so excited! I'll pass him and get a quick look at him.

Oh! Oh, I saw him well! Young, in his late teens. I hope he talks to a young lady first! Oh!

"Bloody hell!"

What?

I stop and turn.

The young man is holding up my knife. He examines it. He examines me.

"Did you drop this?" he asks.

"Yes," I say. "Yes, I must have done."

I approach him and snatch the knife from his hand.

I'm not looking forward to this.

HELL
ANDREW HANNON

"Hell."

Mrs Fenn sits behind the Customer Enquiry desk is Groundwater Library and looks up at the boy standing in front of her. Moments earlier, she had taken off her glasses in order to massage the bridge of her nose. For this reason, the boy's face is just a blur to her. She can make out blonde hair and big blue eyes, but that is all.

"Hell," the boy repeats. There is a sense of frustration in his voice, along with something else that Mrs Fenn doesn't feel comfortable with.

Mrs Fenn picks her glasses up from the desk and puts them on. The world, after a couple of seconds, comes into focus. Standing in front of her is a

retard? is that the right word or are you not allowed to call them that anymore?

Mrs Fenn composes herself.

"Hello," she says.

"Hell."

The boy must only be ten or eleven years old. His voice, however, is quite deep. He is dressed in faded white jeans and a white t-shirt and Mrs Fenn can't decide if he looks more like an angel or an asylum inmate. She takes a moment to look beyond him, beyond his too-large eyes and wet mouth, hoping to see an accompanying mother or father somewhere nearby who might come and end this embarrassing situation. Seeing no-one, she returns her gaze to the boy.

"I think you mean 'hello', don't you?"

Mrs Fenn tries a smile but it feels so false she abandons it.

"No, my mummy says I can't say hello to peepull who I don't know."

"So you say 'Hell' instead, do you?"

"No, I want to know baud Hell."

Mrs Fenn is slightly confused and again looks for an accompanying adult.

"Where is your mummy?" she asks.

"My mummy is at home but I am in da libree because dat is where you go if you want to know fings."

This time Mrs Fenn smiles for real.

Poor little bastard, she thinks. *I wonder why he wants to know about Hell. Maybe he means helicopters but can't remember the rest of the word.*

"Do you mean helicopters?" she asks.

The boy stares at her for a few moments. He hasn't the foresight or capacity to attempt to hide his emotions and, in much the same way as Mrs Fenn looked around for a parent, the boy seems to look around for someone else who might be able to help him instead of this old lady who is talking about helicopters.

"Or Hell, the place?" she ventures.

The boy's attention is immediately and entirely focused on Mrs Fenn once more.

"Hafoohbeendare?" he blurts out, his already wide eyes widening further.

"I'm sorry?"

"Haff you *been* dare, haff you *been* dare?"

"Have I...been there? To Hell? My lord, no. Nor do I intend to."

"Do you know where it is?"

"No, not exactly. Although I do know how people get there."

"Howhowhow, I wanna go to Hell!"

The boy has raised his voice to a level which causes a few heads to turn. Mrs Fenn doesn't realise, however, as she is suddenly completely and utterly fascinated by the boy and what's going on inside his head.

Thirteen

"You definitely don't want to go to Hell."

The boy looks at her. His big blue eyes seem to shimmer and his breathing quickens rapidly before he starts to cry. It is a pathetic yet unashamed cry, raw and somehow naked. The boy doesn't care who hears him, doesn't even give a thought to it. He had thought he was close to his goal but now this old lady has snatched it away from him.

"Sssh, sssh, sssh, sssh, sssh," pleads Mrs Fenn. A dozen or so patrons are staring over and she gets up from the desk she is sat behind. She walks around it and crouches down beside the

blubbering retard. Pauline, don't be so cruel. He can't help himself.

Crouched down, Mrs Fenn's face is about level with the boy's. She puts a tentative hand on one of his shuddering shoulders.

"Why don't you tell me your name? I'll tell you mine and we can be friends. Then I'll take you into the staff-room, give you a nice drink of lemonade, and I'll answer all your questions about Hell. How's that?"

The boy is confused for a moment but, after he realises that the old lady is now going to help him (and give him lemonade), he stops crying and smiles.

"My name is Thomas and I am ten."

"My name is Pauline and I am... I am very pleased to meet you."

Thomas has a sip of lemonade. It tastes good. He sits in a comfortable chair and his eyes never leave his new friend

Poor lyn, dat's what she is called

as she removes a pile of books from the chair opposite him, places them on a coffee table, and sits down.

"Okay then, Thomas, we've got to be quick because I've got work to do."

Thomas smiles.

Poor lyn's voice is nice. The words are clear and sound good, not like mummy's. Mummy's voice is slurred most of da time. Mummy drinks a lot, but it isn't melonlaid dat is in her glass.

"So you want to know about Hell? Is it for a school project or something? Do you need a paper and pen?"

"No, it is just for me, not for the schools. I want to go there. How do I go there?"

Careful not to start him crying, Mrs Fenn decides against telling him he doesn't want to go there.

"Hell is where people go if they've been really, really bad."

"Really bad like if maybe dey have hitted someone?"

Mrs Fenn ponders this.

"It's unlikely."

"If I hitted someone, den would I go to Hell?"

"No, no, not if you just hit someone – you should say 'hit', by the way, not 'hitted'. You have to do something really, really bad to go to Hell. Most people are more concerned with getting to Heaven though. Don't you want to go to Heaven?"

"No, Hell. Fank you for da melonlaid."

Thomas puts his glass down on the coffee table and stands up, his hand outstretched to Mrs Fenn. She smiles, takes his hand, and leads him out of the staff-room.

The three boys see Thomas before he sees them. They watch him from the top of the park as he stands by the edge of the lake, hurling badly aimed stones at the ducks.

As they move closer, one of the boys realises that Thomas is

Thirteen

"A fucking spastic!"
"Are you sure?"
"Yeah, I saw his face when he turned just then."
Thomas is too busy throwing stones to hear their clumsy approach. The boys get near enough to establish that Thomas is alone before one of them pounces, grabbing Thomas's mop of blonde hair and yanking him back, causing him to drop to the grass.
The three boys stand around him, expecting him to attempt to get up and make a run for it. But Thomas is too shocked to do anything except look up at his three assailants. He looks pathetic just lying there. The boy who pulled his hair feels instantly ashamed but doesn't want to lose face in front of his friends.
"Why are you throwing stones at my ducks?" he asks.
The other two boys snigger, although they too secretly feel sorry for the boy on the ground.
"I didn't know dey were your ducks. I was trying to kill all of dem."
The three boys exchange looks, trying to take in what Thomas has just said.
"Why do you want to kill ducks? That's fucking stupid."
"I want to be really, really bad."

It is Jason's last day working at the shop, and thank fuck for that. The only thing he will miss about it will be the occasional fivers or tenners he could help himself to when he was sure the owner wouldn't miss them.
Does he feel guilty about that? Does he fuck. As far as he is concerned he is collecting money owed to him. He didn't get paid enough to stand around all day, putting up with all kinds of shit. No, the sooner he left this dump and started at the telesales firm, the better.
The shop door opens and Jason looks up from the porno he was studying, one of which he always keeps on a shelf below the counter.
"Oh, great," he mutters.
The little retard walks right up to him.
"Paul oh mag."
Jason screws his eyes up at the kid, perplexed.
"What did you say?"
"Paul oh mag. Where are the paul oh mag?"
The kid's meaning gets through to Jason, his first crazy thought is that he is the victim of some hidden camera show. He can almost hear a voice in his head saying 'Take a look at our next prank. This shop assistant likes to look at porn all day, not to mention help himself to an odd tenner. How will he react to this kid coming in –'
Jason shakes his head.
"Porno mags are over there," he says, pointing to the far wall of the shop. He leans over the counter and whispers to Thomas. "But you ain't fucking getting any. I doubt you could reach for starters."
Thomas walks towards the magazines before Jason has even finished his sentence. He doesn't have time to listen to him – it's getting late and he wants to go to Hell and back before his mummy realises he is not in the house.
Thomas doesn't know what a porno magazine is, but the man pointed in this direction so he must be close. He picks up the first brightly coloured magazine he sees and, like the three boys instructed, sticks it up under his white t-shirt before running out of the shop.
Jason watches all of this. Does he leap over the counter, catch the child-thief and take the magazine back?
Does he fuck.

*

Thirteen

The sun is almost setting and Thomas wanders around the edge of the lake, near the bushes where the boys said they'd wait for him.

He listens intently.

"There he is, look. Thomas! Thomas!"

Thomas walks hurriedly towards the sound of the voice calling his name. A pair of hands shoot out from the bushes and pull him in.

Thomas finds himself in a small clearing, most of the space of which is taken up by himself and the three boys.

"Did you do it?" one of them asks him.

Thomas smiles as he pulls the magazine out from under his t-shirt. Three pairs of hands all grab for it at once but it doesn't take long until it is thrust back at him.

"You stupid fucking shit, what's this? We said a porno mag, not a fucking kiddies' arts and crafts mag."

Thomas looks down at the magazine. He cannot understand why the boys don't seem to like it. It is bright and colourful and even has a pair of blue scissors attached to it. His mummy doesn't let him play with scissors.

"Go back and steal a porno, you prick. I thought you said you wanted to be bad?"

The boys watch him fumble with the magazine and then, in a scene two of them will play over and over in their minds for many years, watch as he plunges the scissors into their friend's left eye. The scissors, designed with safety in mind to assist children of four years and upwards in cutting out dinosaur shapes from the magazine, prove to be equally useful for puncturing the eye and embedding in the brain of a boy who moments earlier had been anticipating seeing his first naked women.

Twenty minutes later, Thomas sits in the bushes with the dead boy. He can't wait to see his daddy who, so his mother told him last night, is burning in Hell.

The two other boys have run away, but that's all right. Thomas can hear the sirens in the distance getting closer by the second. He smiles. He always wondered what the *please cars* were for, and now he knows.

They are coming to take him to Hell.

Thirteen

BETE NOIR
PÁDRAIG Ó MÉALÓID

Professor Gerry Whyte strode purposefully into Trinity College's room 4026 at three o'clock exactly, as he always did. Taking his seat at the desk, he carefully placed a box of Camel Light cigarettes, his ancient, battered Zippo lighter, and an old saucer he had borrowed from the staff canteen on the desk in front of him. Only after this ritual did he finally look up.

Professor Whyte's students were well used to his punctual ways, and were all in their seats before him.

The Professor lit his first cigarette.

"As this is our final folklore tutorial of the college year," he began, after blowing out a long plume of grey-white smoke, "I thought I'd finish with a more recent tale than those we have been discussing up until now. All the folktales we have dealt with over the last three terms have been rooted several hundred years in the past, at least. This afternoon's story, however, is so recent that it could be said that the ink is still wet on it."

Professor Whyte paused to allow his students to laugh at his - admittedly weak - witticism, which, after a momentary pause, they dutifully did.

"This is the legend of the Black Beast of Dublin Castle.

"Ms. Margaret Keating was hurrying along Dame Street late one October evening. The freezing rain showed absolutely no sign of abating any time soon, despite Margaret's impassioned prayers to God, Saint Jude, and - in hopeful desperation - the met office. If she had known who the patron saint of taxi drivers was, she would have sent a few prayers that direction as well. 'Why is it,' she wondered, 'that the more you need a taxi, particularly in the pouring rain, the less likely you are to find one? Yet another sub-clause of Murphy's Law, perhaps?'

"Margaret Keating's idle thoughts were suddenly cut short as she passed by the Viking bar.

"Despite her stray musings, Margaret had been continuously scanning the street, still vainly hoping to spot a taxi. As she drew level with the Viking, she found herself looking directly up Palace Street at the main tourist entrance to Dublin Castle."

At this point Professor Whyte paused to light another cigarette. After snapping his Zippo lighter shut with a sound like a gunshot, he resumed his narrative.

"Margaret Keating had walked along Dame Street many times over the last number of years, both day and night, and was very familiar with the various gates leading off it into Dublin Castle. This time, however, she saw something she had never seen before."

Professor Whyte paused again.

"At this point I'm going to quote directly from Ms. Keating's oral testimony.

"She says, 'I saw what seemed to be an enormous pair of glowing blood-red eyes, high over the Castle gates. Although the night was very dark, and the rain was still pelting down, I'm willing to swear that I saw a huge black dog-like body attached to those hideous eyes. I also got a very strong feeling that, whatever it was that I had seen, it's main purpose was to protect the Castle gates.' End of quote.

"Funnily enough," said the Professor, "Margaret's 'strong feeling' proved to be dead right, as you will see later.

"So, onto the next sighting.

"Ms. Anne Leonard was walking home towards Rathmines after finishing her night's work behind the bar in The Porter House on Parliament Street. On this occasion it was a crystal-clear, cloudless, rainless night. Anne was taking her

Thirteen

usual short cut through The Liberties, which involved turning right at the top of Parliament Street, walking up Lord Edward Street, cutting onto Werburgh Street, and then along Little Ship Street before finally arriving into Aungier Street.

"It was as Anne was passing the Little Ship Street gate of Dublin Castle that she saw, and again I quote 'An enormous shaggy black dog, with eyes like balls of liquid fire, crouched on the wall over the gate, staring right down at me.' Again, end of quote.

"There were a number of other sightings of the beast of Dublin Castle, always at night, and always describing a pair of fiery eyes seen on the walls high over the various gates into the Castle.

"Sadly," said Professor Whyte, "none of the other witnesses were anywhere near as articulate -or lyrical - as Margaret and Anne were.

"OK. So far, so good. Would anyone like to comment on what I've told you so far?"

The first hand in the air was, as usual, that of Frank Toner.

Frank Toner was probably the most enthusiastic of Professor Whyte's tutorial students, and seemed to have read nearly as widely in his subject as the Professor himself had.

"Right Frank," said the Professor, "the floor, for the moment, is yours."

"This sounds like a classic example of the folkloric phenomenon known as 'Black Dog'. Black dogs are one of the five major groups of anomalous creatures generally recognised by folklorists. The other four groups are..."

At this point Professor Whyte stopped Frank, because he knew that if he let him, Frank would still be talking when the tutorial was over.

"Just this once, Frank, why don't we let someone else tell us about the other groups of creatures?"

Frank Toner sat down, disgruntled, as Anne-Marie O'Meara shot her hand into the air.

Professor Whyte smiled. His favourite student.

Anne-Marie began.

"The other four types are, firstly, Giant Lake Monsters, of which the Loch Ness Monster is the most famous, although there are numerous other examples, including several here in Ireland. Secondly, Big Hairy Men - or BHMs - in this case the most obvious example is the Himalayan Yeti, or Abominable Snowman. Thirdly, Alien Big Cats – ABCs - such as the Surrey Puma, and many others.

"The last - and probably most obscure - category, Giant Birdmen - on which I'm writing my dissertation, by the way - includes such wonderful examples as the 'Jersey Devil', a malevolent flying creature with a long thin tail seen over New Jersey in the early 1900s, and the red-eyed 'Mothman' which haunted West Virginia in the 1960s."

"Thank you, Anne-Marie," said the Professor. "It's good to see Frank isn't the only one reading the course literature. I look forward to seeing your dissertation, by the way.

"After all that, let's get back to the subject in hand. Black Dogs.

"The lore of Black Dogs stretches back into the distant past. Tales of these creatures have always been particularly prevalent amongst the Celtic races, and they were often described as being about the size of a pony, with blazing red eyes, and jet-black coats. It was commonly believed that they were the hounds of the Devil himself, roaming the countryside in search of the souls of the newly dead. Others thought that those who had the misfortune of seeing one would die within the coming year. Black Dogs were also somehow connected with running water - I don't know if you are all aware that the River Poddle flows underground directly beneath Dublin Castle before it joins the Liffey at Wellington Quay - and churchyards. One of them, the Yorkshire 'Padfoot,' even seems to have had a sense of humour. It would creep up unheard behind an unsuspecting traveller, then suddenly rattle a chain, which, as I'm sure you can imagine, was a trifle unsettling."

Once again Professor Whyte's students tittered obligingly.

"Black Dogs go under numerous different names. In Scotland it is known as the 'Wangye.' In Wales it is 'Gwyllgi.' English versions include the 'Skriker' from Lancashire, 'Black Shuck' from East Anglia, and 'Guytrash' from Cheshire.

"One of my own personal favourites is the 'Moddey Dhoo,' which is said to haunt the corridors of Peel Castle in the Isle of Man. Those of you studying Celtic languages should recognise the similarity between 'Moddey Dhoo' and the Irish 'Madra Dubh,' which translates into English as, would you believe, black dog."

Professor Whyte's students laughed one more time.

"There are a number of specifically Dublin-based Black Dogs. The Black Dog of Cabra haunts the ruins of Beggsboro House, which was once the home of John Toler, first Earl of Norbury. Lord Norbury, known as 'The Hanging Judge' is chiefly remembered as the judge who tried and convicted Robert Emmet after the 1798 rebellion.

"Inevitably, the Hellfire Club in the Dublin mountains has it's own Black Dog legend. On one occasion a priest visiting the area found himself confronted by an enormous black hound with horns. As the priest began to say the rite of exorcism, the dog changed into a hellish demon, let forth a great howl, and vanished before the priest's very eyes."

Professor Whyte lit his third, and last, cigarette of the day.

"All this leads us fairly neatly back to Dublin Castle, where we began.

"What was it that Margaret Keating and Anne Leonard had seen on those October nights on the walls over the Castle gates?

"Certainly the Castle is steeped in history, and has a rich store of ghostly sightings and mysterious occurrences. The - still unexplained - disappearance of the Irish Crown Jewels early this century is just one example still remembered by local historians. But, sadly, the Black Beast was not destined to join this illustrious company. In the end, it had a very prosaic explanation.

"After the story had been circulating for a few months it finally came to the attention of Detective Inspector John Moran.

"D.I. Moran was head of security in Dublin Castle, and took a certain malicious glee in pointing to the new night-time security cameras that had recently been attached to the Castle wall over the gates. He particularly enjoyed drawing people's attention to the pair of large infrared lights attached to the top of each camera. At night, he said, these lights glowed a dull, fiery red... You see, the lights were what people were seeing all along. The rest of it was supplied by their own imaginations.

"I see our time is up," said the Professor. "Go gently, children, and don't believe all you read, or half of what you hear."

Cigarettes and lighter in hand, and smiling broadly, Professor Gerry Whyte left the room.

Author's Note.

With one obvious exception, all the folk tales quoted here come from already existing documentary sources. Anyone interested in reading further should check their local library. The cameras, however, are there for all to see.

Thirteen

THAT FIRST CUP OF JOE
LEISA PARKER

Myers slumped into the shop, the door banging behind him. He was worn already and he'd just gotten up. Just thinking of all his flights, here and there and there and back. It was exhausting, it was. The meetings and squabbles, the jerks and morons. Oh well, he thought, such was his life. A cup of joe would probably help; it usually did.

And as he rubbed at his eyes, he stepped towards the glass. The lad at the counter, Zye (who, by the way, was always at the counter), nodded at him, and filled a deep blue cup with the usual. His usual. His ever-the-trusty picker upper. And the waves of heat, the warm thick currents; they swarmed out of the spicket and into the air, across the counter, and into his nostrils. And he breathed in deep, feeling better already: more alive, more vibrant. For just the smell alone, so rich and so deep, so calming and smooth, was of a pure heaven - an absolute gift.

But then he panicked, his heart breaking stride, as he caught sight of the machine, its small silver spicket. For it was dripping just barely. Just a bit of a trickle. And then it sputtered loudly, coarsely and sharp, a blast of thin liquid spraying all over. And he bit at his lip, bit at it hard. For what would he do? Without his first cup? Be a basket of nerves is what he would be. Unruly, unpleasant, rude and quite evil. And he would cause quite a ruckus, quite a horrible scene. Yelling and screaming, shouting and cursing, at the top of his lungs, his arms all about. For how could it be? How could they run out?

But then he relaxed, and breathed in quite deep, for Zye spun around, facing his way. And the cup was well full, filled to the brim. And he laughed just a little, quite shrill and quite soft, at his almost display, his almost outburst. And then Zye turned again, and sprinkled a bit, just the way that he liked. Of dry, and of brown, of sweet cinnamon.

"Luck's with you today Mr. Myer." he laughed. "You got the last cup of joe."

And Writ smiled, his hand dropping metals across the counter.

"Yes indeed, thank the heavens for that."

And he grasped the wide cup and strode to his favourite table, his orange painted chair.

And then he shuddered, he did, from the tips of his shoes to the top of his hat, as he swirled the hot liquid, the sweet cinnamon. To think that he might've had to sample another flavour, another taste. Something different. For he was a creature of habit - he didn't like change. No, not at all. Not in the least. It gave him the willies, it gave him the shakes. And he looked upwards then, above the dispensers, the silver machines. At the slanted wide rafters, his ultimate dread. For that's where they were.

The alternate flavours.

The alternate tastes.

The tracy and sue, the steve and the mark. The todd and the brian, the ruth and the phil. All suspended by thick steel wires and thick steel bolts. Their bodies wound tight, around and around, with twine and with copper, with metal and cord. And their heads jutted back, their chins to the sky, their necks all exposed, so thin and so taut. With long thin tubes, plunged into the jugular, seeping out of their necks. For that was the freshest of spots, the purest of drain. And their eyes they bulged wide, though their mouths remained closed. For sewn they were, the lips tightly shut. With thick black thread, round and about, again and again. And Writ laughed softly, as he remembered back, the very first days. When the shop had first settled, had opened its doors. And the mouths were not bound, not in the least. And oh what a noise, the gawd awful racket. The chatter and screams, the

Thirteen

wails and the sighs. It had proved bad for business. Quite bad indeed. And now the workers, with their wings flapping wide, were removing his favourite full-flavour, his limp-bodied joe. The tubing plucked out, the hooks and wires, the bolts and the screws. Yanked out of the toes and the back, the sides and spine; the unwinding of twine. The splash on the floor, of pinks and of clear, of reds and of bile, yellows and greens.

And as he brought the cup up, to his quivering lips, the scarlet red crimson, it splashed all about. Warming his tongue and his mind, his cheeks and his throat. And as they dragged joe by, the body it did, it gave one last jerk. Its mouth spitting up, its blue eyes so wide. And Myers smiled softly, and raised his cup high, in salute to his favourite - his full flavoured joe.

ALL ABOARD THE LOVE TRAIN
JAMES COOPER

> *'Ha, ha, ha; ho, ho, ho*
> *and a couple of tra la las.'*
> *- The Wizard of Oz*

It is dark; of course it is. And the moon is full in the sky. The train rattles along, making perfect time, weaving its way through the hills, carrying twenty-four newly-weds to a night of secluded bliss. It could have taken place in any part of the country, on any night of the year, it wouldn't matter; the mystery would remain the same. You may even have heard it, whistling through the English countryside, trying to outrun the night. The Love Train. Caught in an endless loop between cities. Travelling tirelessly between the living and the dead.

The train slows down as it passes through a minor station, and that's when they clamber aboard. No one to this day knows how many of them there were, but they must have numbered at least twenty because some of them were later found in pieces scattered around the various compartments of the train.

One of them isn't agile enough to join its brothers and spills beneath the wheels of the main carriage, its ravaged head silently exploding, having fallen foul of the Love Train's crazy impulse for speed. It will later be discovered wandering aimlessly through the countryside, its headless body pivoting without direction in the dark.

Once aboard, though, the zombies are relentless in their pursuit of fresh meat. They smash easily through the glass of the carriage and clamber over each other in a frenzy of hunger, desperate to be the first to tear the flesh of the beautiful people safely assembled within.

The couples look on in horror and disbelief as the zombies tumble inside. There is a moment of mock comedy, completely lost on all but the most remote onlooker, when the beautifully presented newly-weds, still in their morning suits and frocks, stand opposite ranks of decomposing, reanimated bodies that are bracing themselves, ready to pounce. It is an exquisite moment of true horror that only the zombies fail to sense. The kind of horror that needs the absurd and the obscene to co-exist on the same stage, before the tragedy and the terror can intrude.

The zombies have no time for such meandering philosophy though. They want to feed. They launch themselves at the party of young people and begin to smash and maim and rip and maul. They have done it before and they will do it again. They are experts in the art of bad death. They have blood in their hair, in their eyes, and in their mouth; they have clumps of flesh and brain between their teeth. This is what it's like when they feast. They are quick and destructive and strong. Not a single one of the newly-weds, in that moment of initial onslaught, can quite believe their eyes. They have been betrayed by the very force that has brought them here. It is love that has let them down.

Also on board is Keith Carrick, best man to one of the grooms. He is trying to catch some sleep before they arrive at the hotel where his next duty is to sabotage the bridal suite, a tradition he has little time for but is willing to carry out courtesy of the money gratefully received from the doting father of the bride. Fine, he thinks; I'll trash the room. But then it's straight back home to Bess and his own bed; he wants to be there when his children awake.

A noise in the adjacent carriage rouses him from his slumber and he unsteadily gets to his feet. He is mildly surprised to discover that he is alone, before remembering that the first two carriages have been reserved solely for those invited by Tag's family to take their place aboard the Love Train. A perfectly

Thirteen

tacky way to bring the day's festivities to a close.

Carrick hears the noise again and this time he feels a pulse of alarm. That sure sounds like one hell of a party, he thinks. In fact, unless he's much mistaken, he is hearing the sound of his dream all over again: the metallic squeal of a room being thoroughly and efficiently trashed.

He steps through the connecting carriage doors and feels a slab of cold meat smack him squarely in the face. The leering countenance that follows it up is like a Halloween ghoul out scaring up candy for a feast. He has no time to dwell on the bloodstained teeth or the dead eyes because the zombie's arm is raised again ready to strike, and Carrick does the only thing he can to protect himself: he launches his own attack.

He grabs the creature's arm and surprises the strength from it, twisting it along the metal filaments of the door. Realising he has only a short time in which to capitalise on his advantage, he smashes the connecting door on the thing's arm and listens to the zombie's howls of outrage through the glass.

Then, nothing.

As quickly as the creature attacked, it is gone, leaving the jettisoned arm still writhing in the rim of the door. It tears itself free and scuttles about for a moment before it realises the hopelessness of its task. Not one to stand on ceremony, Carrick opens the carriage door and kicks the arm out into the night, where it cartwheels across the landscape and disappears, to be found and partly devoured early the next morning by a dog. A fitting end, perhaps, for a severed limb that has executed its fair share of horrors in the dark.

Carrick, however, has already forgotten it. He peers through the glass of the carriage door and feels numb. The celebrations have been transformed into a gala of homicide and destruction. The surviving couples, all three of them, are trapped in a corner of the carriage being toyed with by half a dozen creatures from hell. The rest of the wedding fraternity are gone, gorily scattered around every possible surface of the room, their life force irrevocably spent. The carriage is a red nightmare of blood and offal and utter mayhem. He can see heads that have had the pulp pounded out of them, bones that have been ground down to dust. In one corner of the carriage a zombie with a face like stretched rubber is gnawing on a human leg. When any of its mates get too close, it bares foul teeth matted with hair and prepares to defend its prize to the death, twitching with the kind of fury usually reserved only for politicians and the criminally insane.

Carrick is almost blinded by the monstrous intensity of it; he can barely believe his eyes. Tag is in there, or at least, he was, anticipating his first night of marriage with Lou. Where are they now, he wonders? How could they have been so quickly consumed?

He idly checks the surviving couples, who are being penned in like cattle, as though the zombies are rationing themselves, and none of the faces staring back at him is Tag's. One of them, however, looks familiar, and as he stares closer, peering through the muck on the glass, he realises that Lou is still very much alive. No longer looking radiant, it's true, but she is definitely still alive. Her face is smeared with the blood of her fellow brides, but he is certain it's her; even through the blood, it's her. The petrified face, he realises, now belongs to the widow of his best friend, and he can feel the rage bubbling up inside.

He tries to get Lou's attention, but she is mesmerised by her captors, the zombies feeding and prodding them with the gnawed bones of the other guests, grunting in amusement when they flinch.

He is considering how he can best reach her when the glass in the door is once again filled with the mottled face of a zombie he has already seen. The thing smiles and raises its arm, which has been severed at the elbow and now hangs in ugly tatters to the floor. The zombie waves the stump at Carrick, and then

Thirteen

smashes it through the glass into his face, the force of it slamming him to the floor of the train. The creature's stump is still waving stupidly in the air, but the zombie is trying to push its way through the widening hole in the door. Within seconds it will be on him and those ridiculous teeth will no doubt be tearing out his throat.

Carrick looks around and seizes hold of the first thing his hand alights upon: a fire extinguisher, perfect for crushing a dead assassin's skull.

He hefts it in his hands, rises to his full height, and brings the extinguisher crashing down onto the bobbing head of the corpse. The zombie emits no sound, but it doesn't have to. Where its head used to be there is now just a hole, slowly oozing a grey glutinous muck. Its head, what's left of it, is a crushed scallop unevenly spread across the floor.

Carrick treads on it and gives it the same treatment as the creature's arm, sending it high and wide into the night. The carriage, he thinks, now has one zombie less than it did before. The odds of him surviving the night are looking up. All he has to do now is rescue the girl, save the planet, and reach for the man in the moon.

He collapses to the floor and clutches his stomach but it doesn't prevent him from being violently sick. He has no idea what to do next. He has already run out of ideas.

Carrick leans out of the carriage window and takes in enormous lungfuls of air. Were the zombies not otherwise engaged with their alternative food source, he has no doubt that he would already have been crudely parted from his head and the soup inside poured down the gullets of the damned.

So far, he has been lucky. Louisa, on the other hand, has not. In fact, he can see through the connecting door that her time is about to run out. One of the zombies has decided it's time to open a fresh can of worms. He is corralling the dazed survivors into a bloody corner of the room where a dozen zombies are already sharpening their claws.

Carrick will have to think fast, but his mind is not functioning properly, has decided to betray him at the most inopportune moment imaginable. He can see Louisa and the others slipping in the blood, moving closer to the massed ranks of their antagonists, having almost given up the fight. Not, Carrick thinks, that it was ever much of a contest.

He has to think; has to come up with something, even if it only offers the most fragile source of hope.

And then he has it. Like a slap in the face, it comes to him, as simply and as tellingly as great ideas have a tendency to, the sharpness of it taking him by surprise.

What he has to do is obvious. He must derail the train.

While Carrick is arriving at his rather extreme solution to the problem, Louisa is discovering something new about herself with every passing minute. She had imagined herself, before this evening, a rather prim, cautious, unadventurous type, but she has come to realise that she possesses reserves of strength that she has never had to call upon before. It strikes her that, were she within reach of any sort of weapon at all, she would have no hesitation in using it. In fact, she thinks she would take enormous pleasure in laying waste to every single zombie in the room. Had her hands not been manicured for the wedding, she thinks sombrely, she would even have considered using her bare hands.

She looks down at her wedding dress and feels like weeping, but she senses that she must remain strong. Isn't it enough, she thinks, that she has been forced to witness the terrible mutilation of her husband? Must she be reminded of it every time she glances at the dress? She tries not to focus on it, but it's impossible not to; she is drenched in Tag's blood, and trying to pretend that it isn't

Thirteen

so is simply not enough to alleviate the dull ache of the horror she's endured. It is there, in all its vivid glory, and it is all she can do not to collapse to the floor in tears.

She turns to look out of the window, but there are thick clots of intestine on it, and she is unable to penetrate the mess. A glance at her fellow survivors doesn't help matters either; in fact, it makes her feel sick, for they look as deranged as she feels, and it suddenly dawns on her that she will not be leaving this carriage alive.

The zombies no longer appear interested in them, however; not for the moment. They are tearing at the meat they have already procured, fighting senselessly over morsels and scraps when there is clearly more than enough to sustain them for days.

The two zombies appointed to watch over Louisa and the others, though, look less than thrilled about being left out of the food loop, and she wonders how long it will be before their appetite finally overwhelms them.

She doesn't have to ponder the matter for long; the nearest zombie, with a face left in tatters by its emergence from the grave, can contain itself no more. It turns to Louisa's nearest neighbour, a young man who has already watched his wife ripped apart at the seams, extends a purple, distended hand, and almost playfully squeezes the eyes from his head. It looks, she thinks, a horribly simple process, but the creature's phenomenal strength appals her. Not that the zombie has noticed; it is clearly unaffected by anything else around it and awkwardly stoops to collect the ejected eyes, which it pops into its mouth like gum.

The young man, who is understandably screaming in agony, has not, however, felt the worst of it. Once the zombie has devoured its ghoulish appetiser, it bends with a clumsy inevitability and plunges its hand into the man's stomach, twisting it like a knife so that belly and body fat are beyond repair. There is no resistance; the stomach yields with a ludicrous farting sound and the zombie uncoils the man's innards before Louisa has even processed what has been done. Neither is there any time to. Without any regard for the reaction of its terrorised audience, the zombie begins to feed. The intestines unspool like steaming lengths of rubber and are slipped effortlessly into the zombie's gaping, yellow mouth.

It grins at Louisa and wipes blood from its lips, as though suddenly self-conscious of its eating habits. The man, his stomach now completely emptied, no longer cares. If his body is fodder for zombies, then so be it. At least he has been spared any more pain.

Louisa thinks she can just discern a faint smile on his face as his gutted carcass cools on the Love Train's floor.

Carrick opens the carriage door and climbs up onto the roof of the train. He has seen this done a thousand times in films and knows it has become a genre staple, but the cliché has suddenly taken on a daunting new perspective, and he idly wonders whether he should reconsider his options before the opportunity is irretrievably lost.

Too late. He clambers onto the roof and feels the wind trying every trick in the book to dislodge him. The train, too, is not making it easy, shaking with a ferocity that he hadn't anticipated down below. Still, it's no use whining about difficult circumstances. The zombies sort of trump all that anyway. If he wants to help the few people still alive, including Louisa, his best chance is to guide the train from the tracks. There is no other way that he can think of that might sufficiently unsettle the zombies so that some of the passengers may be able to escape. Yes, it will be dangerous, he's aware of that, and a huge risk, but what other choice does he have? Should he simply step aside and allow those fucking

Thirteen

monstrosities a free run at the entire train? There are others on board besides the wedding guests and he has no doubt whatsoever that the zombies will not be satisfied until every warm body has been destroyed.

Carrick crawls along the top of the carriage, his throat licked raw from the wind. His thinking is clear and logical, though not without holes, for he is aware that if he does manage to derail the train there is a strong likelihood that many on board will die in the ensuing disaster. Hopefully, though, it will be quick and painless and those that do die will at least be spared the horror of being devoured. He is equally aware that, should his plan result in the kind of mayhem he is anticipating, his own life is in jeopardy too.

Fuck it, he thinks. If it destroys some of those creatures and forces them to disband it'll be worth it. More pertinently, if a single passenger is saved in the process, all the better.

If he was to stay on board and do nothing, he reflects, his life would be forfeit anyway, along with countless others. The bottom line is a simple equation that takes very little figuring out. He is convinced that every single passenger on board this ill-fated train would, given the choice, prefer to die in a train wreck rather than be split from navel to neck by a zombie. Simple, really; and it is with this assertion in mind that Carrick moves with painful slowness towards the front of the speeding train.

The zombies stop feeding and listen for a sound in the night. At first, Louisa is uncertain what it is that they're attuned to, but then she hears a crumpled vibration in the roof. Is somebody out there? Her heart leaps and she vaguely marvels at how the human mind can trick itself into manufacturing any excuse for hope.

Still, the zombies seem concerned by it. They have been forced to postpone their feeding and Louisa can see in their blank, lifeless eyes that they are not best pleased about it. There is some garbled form of undead communication, and one of the zombies is instructed to venture out into the night.

The large window, which still has the drying viscera smeared across it, is punched into a million fragments and the creature leans out, bits of flesh flying from its face as the wind flays it, reminding Louisa of a bad clown whose make-up has been twisted out of true. It grunts and propels itself onto the rim of the window and then flings itself onto the roof. There is a thunderous bang followed by silence; and then nothing.

The next thing Louisa sees is a large body tumbling through the darkness onto the tracks.

Carrick has heard the noise in the carriage below and is waiting for the zombie to appear. When it finally declares itself, Carrick has positioned himself between the window and the access point, where he wastes no time in kicking the zombie as hard as he can in the face.

Fortunately, it's enough. The creature, unaware of what has happened to it, spins into the dark and falls onto the line, where the train itself makes light work of finishing it off.

Another one of the fuckers erased; how many does that leave, Carrick wonders? He has no idea, but he is in no doubt that where there is one there will soon be another. They are clearly onto him, and if he wants to execute his plan he really has to get his arse across this roof.

Without pausing to consider the consequences, he begins to slide towards the lead train. He is making enough noise now to wake the dead (had they been safely tucked up in their graves where they belong) but he no longer cares. There is no discretion to protect; the quicker he gets to the controls, the sooner these

Thirteen

bastards will be destroyed.

He makes the leap between the carriages, dreading a last-minute fall, and slides down the ladder to the engine room. There is a small night light illuminating the area and a large man with a cap peering out at the endless dark.

'We have a problem,' Carrick begins, but before the sentence is complete, the zombie steering the train has turned around and has swung its enormous fist into Carrick's unprotected face.

'Not for much longer,' it says, its gravelly voice resonating with its own delight. 'I've been expecting you.'

Another hammer blow to the head sends Carrick reeling, and it is all he can do to prevent himself from being flung from the train.

So close, he thinks stupidly. So agonisingly close.

The zombie moves towards him, arms extended in what would have been a glorious moment of Hollywood pastiche had it not been so real, and Carrick realises that he has no time at all for self-pity. If he is to survive this, he must act now. He must do something instantly that will disable this thing before it can do any more harm.

He glances around but sees nothing that he might be able to utilise in his defence. Unless . . .

The zombie advances, closing in, its arms cheesily outstretched to claim him, and Carrick leans forward and flips the peak of the cap over the creature's unsuspecting, baleful eyes. Not much, perhaps, but in the grander scheme of things, it just might be enough.

Carrick eases past his disorientated assailant and takes a firm hold of the train's controls. He has a moment of doubt, but it is quickly overcome. There is nothing else he could realistically have done.

He yanks the lever to the right and prays. There is a grinding of metal, a derelict hiss of air, and then the Love Train is spun from its tracks.

The train remains upright for longer than any engineer would have believed, but eventually the lead carriage capitulates and is tilted by the unevenness of the land onto its side where it slides through the countryside destroying crops and hedgerows and trees. The rest of its family is not far behind, of course, and within seconds the only sound to be heard for miles around is the bellow of the Love Train as it concertinas into a deformed and twisted jalopy.

When it finally grinds to a halt, over half a mile from where it originally left the track, there is a moment of decompression before the first tiny sounds of survival break out.

Then, an accompanying wrench of metal, and the first zombie eases itself out of the carnage, its sunken eyes dead to the world.

Carrick stirs and realises that his life has not been forfeit after all. He is bruised and battered and his head feels ground to a pulp, but he is still, by the grace of God, alive. The same, however, can't be said of his companion, whose head has been rammed into the Love Train's controls. The peaked cap is smoking slightly in the middle of the console where two live wires are competing to set it alight. The zombie's head, on which the cap had jauntily perched, is mercifully nowhere in sight.

The smoking cap, however, is warning enough; Carrick should immediately exit the train. Gingerly, he gets to his feet and grimly wonders what he'll see if he succeeds in clambering out.

He pulls himself to the door of the toppled train, climbs onto the damaged console, and hauls himself out of the wreckage.

The night is cold and dark, and the remainder of the train is steaming in the midnight air. There are screams resounding around the scene of the tragedy, though Carrick is almost relieved to hear them, for it indicates that some of the

Thirteen

passengers have been fortunate enough to get out alive.

A few people are moving slowly across the pitch-black field, walking with some trepidation, almost crippled by panic and shock. Some, he notices, are supporting their fellow passengers, hobbling alongside them, refusing to forego their obligation, even giving piggy-back rides to those too injured or too distressed to walk alone.

Carrick peers into the dark, looking hard, and listens to the timbre of the screams.

Shit, he thinks. Those people aren't being given piggy-back rides; they're mobilising an attack. Even in the shaky light from the train wreck he can see a handful of zombies relentlessly pursuing three women across a landscape destined to lead them to the grave; two more are making a meal of yet another unfortunate survivor by tearing out his throat as he gainfully hobbles closer and closer to his death, probably yearning for it, Carrick thinks, as the zombies efficiently exploit their advantage in the dark.

The piggy-back riders, of course, are not survivors of the train wreck, clinging to their saviours for dear life; they are zombies, couriers of death and destruction, riding their victims to hell.

Carrick feels his bowels loosen and something vital in his spirit gives way. He experiences such a sudden sense of dread and nausea that he barely even realises when he is dead, the arm of the zombie who killed him still protruding from his belly like a deformity he can never correct.

He had done his best, but in the final reckoning it simply wasn't enough. The dead have their own agenda and they will never stop until their hunger is satisfied, their terrible work complete.

Postscript

Louisa's fate was rather more prosaic than Carrick's, though it's doubtful she would have been grateful for that. She certainly fared the better of the two because she died instantly, her heart rendered defunct by a cable shot through it in the crash, her hopes of escaping, in the end, as futile as she'd always feared.

The zombies, of course, went on. They always do, don't they? They headed towards the lights in the distance where they would eventually discover a town. There weren't that many of them left, but that was of little consequence. All that mattered was the yearning to feed. A pattern of existence repeated endlessly in all manner of creature dotted around the globe.

They traipsed over the fields and through the woodland and across a landscape they had yet to explore. Two of them had a banner of some sort draped unwittingly around their neck. It was from the Love Train. In gold lettering it read 'Just Married', though, in life, the two zombies had never met and the declaration was utterly untrue.

LAST MEAL
IBRAHIM AMIN

He looked down at the knife in his hand, and tentatively, almost unconsciously, let go of the handle. His eyes then flicked to the knife in his gut, and his hand came to rest on its handle instead. He glanced up, saw a wide-eyed expression on her face, then staggered back and slumped into a sitting position against the wall. Her movements mirrored his, making the whole scene seem surreal, and she collapsed against the adjoining wall. The two of them sat there for a moment, gasping in pain, each not quite knowing what to say or how to react.

"Well, this is awkward," she said, breaking the uncomfortable silence, her voice managing to sound more amused than pained.

"Yeah." He stifled a cry, and shifted his position slightly, causing the pain in his gut to become dull rather than screaming. "Sorry," he said, knowing that the word seemed absurd under these circumstances.

"No problem," she gasped. "As much my fault as yours. So, why?"

"Why?"

"I know why I stabbed you," she explained rather patiently, "but I'd like to know why you stabbed me. Is this how you treat all the girls you pick up in bars?"

He opened his mouth to answer, an illogical trickle of blood escaping from the corner of his lip as he did so (I was stabbed in the abdomen, so why the hell am I bleeding from the mouth?), then hesitated. "Promise you won't laugh?"

She pointedly indicated the knife protruding from her body, and raised an eyebrow in a universal gesture of cynicism. "I think I can manage."

"I was going to eat you." He waited for a reaction, either ridicule or disgust.

"Really?" Despite her previous comment, she did give a small laugh (though by her sudden grimace she clearly regretted it, the vibrations no doubt causing her wound to open and close in harmony with her mouth). "Me too."

Again an uncomfortable quiet fell, as the two would-be cannibals sat and bled in surprise, their gazes meeting with comical shyness.

"What gave you the taste?" she asked at last.

For some reason a million lies flew to his lips, but he dismissed them with a sigh. What better time for a confession... "Last month my neighbours' house caught fire. The fire brigade wasn't there yet, so I broke down the door and tried to help them. I managed to grab one of their children, and got her outside. I didn't notice it inside – too much smoke and adrenaline, I guess – but she was burned all over. When I laid her on the grass outside, I sat there staring at her like a retard, wondering why she looked like that. By the time I snapped out of it the paramedics had arrived, but there was nothing they could do.

"When I was a kid, I used to suck my thumb all the time, even when my bitch grandmother rubbed chillies on it to stop me. Looking at that kid, it was like my brain just forgot the last two decades. I was sucking my thumb like a baby. And I tasted her. I didn't know what the hell it was at first, but eventually I realised that it was her juices on my thumb, and it tasted..." He frowned, clearly trying to grope for the right word.

"I know," she said. "You can't compare it to anything else."

"Yeah," he said with a wistful smile. "So, how about you? What got you started?"

"Nothing quite so dramatic. I used to date this guy who was into biting. I got a little tired of it, and decided to show him what a proper bite was. Never saw him again after that. I suppose the joke was on me, since it got me hooked. I tried to find a substitute. Dog, cat, zebra... I tried all sorts of stuff. But nothing was quite right."

"Dog's pretty good, though. Just not what you were looking for."

Thirteen

"I thought it tasted lousy."
They both smiled, and drifted into silence once more.
"You know..." he began.
"Yeah?"
"Since we're dying anyway..."
"And my mum always said it was a sin to waste food..."
They each tentatively inched along their respective walls, wincing as even these slow and careful movements caused explosions to rip through their nerves, until they were close enough to share a bizarre embrace, each making sure not to touch the handle protruding from the other's abdomen. Then, they fed.

Thirteen

WEIGHT
DAVID CHRISTOPHER

Kate's puking in the toilet because she drank too much. She's been in there a while, but she's a big girl so I figure she's got a lot to bring up.

Leo's in my room with her pretty friend, I want him to get lucky so I leave them to it and get comfortable on the sofa-bed in the lounge. I'm just drifting off when Kate stumbles through the door.

"Is anyone in here?" she asks.

"Yeah me, Hal."

"I was sick but I cleaned it up."

"Forget about it."

She lets the door close behind her. "Everyone's gone to bed," I say. "You should go home." The bolt slides closed.

"Is that a double?" she asks.

I hear the rustle of fabric, the unzipping of jeans. "No," I lie.

Her breath whistles through clogged nostrils. I can't see her, but I hear that whistle as she stumbles out of her pants towards me.

"It's cold in here."

I tuck the duvet under my body, make an airtight cocoon. The wooden supports creak as she sits on the bed next to me.

"I'll turn the heating on." I say.

She rests a hand on my calf, a clumsy, heavy hand that squeezes its way up to my thigh.

"No need."

I knock it away.

"Kate," I say. "You're drunk, go home."

The hand comes back, but more determined, ferrets its way under the duvet. It's cold, painfully cold and clammy.

"I've got a girlfriend," I say.

Her hand slips down my stomach like it's greased. "I don't care."

I push her away, but she's strong, too strong, freakishly strong. "I don't want to."

"Of course you do," her hand's on my dick, she's rubbing it, her fingers wrapped right round, "You're already hard."

And she's right, I am. Somehow I am.

She slips under the covers and presses her big naked body to mine, then hooks her leg round my hip and grinds against me. Her coarse pubic hair burns my thigh. "Fuck me," she says, her breath smells of stomach. She rolls on top of me, squeezing the air from my body.

"Get the fuck off me!"

I grab her wrists but she presses my arms back into the pillow and kisses me, encasing my mouth, poking at my teeth with her fat tongue. She bites my lip and pushes me inside her. The bed moans.

"Fuck me!" she shudders, rocking backwards.

I grab her head in both hands and flip her over with all my strength. Flip her right off the bed and onto the floor.

Except she doesn't hit the floor, she hits the glass coffee table next to the bed, hits it hard. Head first, then the rest, and it shatters, breaks into shards and slivers that stick in her fat body like a pin cushion.

She doesn't move. The breath whistles through her nose once and then stops. Leo bangs on the door.

"Hal? What's going on?" He tries the handle but it's locked. "We heard a noise."

Thirteen

Then another voice, the girl.

"Kate? Are you in there?"

I get off the bed. Leo's rattling the handle.

"Unlock the door Hal, let me in."

I pull back the bolt and they're standing next to me in the dark. One of them asks if I'm all right.

"I think so," I say.

Then Leo turns on the light.

There's glass everywhere, glass and blood and by the bed, a dead girl, naked. She doesn't seem so big now.

"What have you done?"

Blood wells from inside her, her virginity trickles down between her legs.

"What did you do to her?"

I look down. My dick's still hard and stained a slimy, clotted red.

Thirteen

POWERS
JAMES DOGGETT

The Christmas lights alternated every two seconds between white and blue. Here and there bulbs had blown along the cold plastic wire, but it was only a temporary thing. Bob would change any broken ones in the morning; he always did. Even the blown ones above the large bay window at the top of the house would be put right. Bob would get a ladder and make the effort. It knew this, because it had watched the house for some time... it had seen him do it before. It also knew that Bob would meticulously grit the whole path the next morning, in a gesture of protection towards his family, after the icy weather was through this evening. It even knew that Bob would dress as Santa Claus on Christmas Eve and act out an elaborate charade to please his two youngest children. It knew *many* things... and they did nothing to help its pain; they merely incensed it.

It existed now, as a faint shimmering light beside the rose bushes in the front garden. As it contemplated its pitiful situation, it would occasionally flair up an iridescent yellow, much like the street lights above it. But most of the time it was just pale, barely noticeable amongst all the festive lights on Brewer Street. It had hazy mental images of its old physical form, but its strongest moments of clarity were reserved for recalling the faces of loved ones. Loved ones who had shared Christmas after Christmas with it in this house. One time when all the hurt had faded for a time. One time where it was momentarily aware of the worth and potential it possessed. One time where all the agony of its alcoholism and drug abuse had been momentarily segregated from its life by the ones who cared. Put to one side, no doubt to return shortly after New Years Eve, but for one moment at least, put blissfully away.

To a degree it had control of those demons now. Indeed, it could not yearn for drugs that would have an impact on a physical body, yet it still sought some sort of piece to fill the lonely hole that remained in its soul. As an apparition it now existed more in a series of jagged dream like sequences than a steady continued existence, but it still knew it was here for a reason; it was desperately unhappy. Not in an overtly emotional sense. It knew a lot of the despairing, depressing and forlorn feelings had departed with its toxin ridden body. All human beings were cursed with bad chemical responses that made situations seem worse than they were, unbearable and soul destroying. This was simpler than that it decided... yes... it was simply missing 'a piece'. It had the right to feel unfulfilled; it had had far too little of what was good, far too much of what was self destructive and far too much pent up and unrefined talent. It had moved on quicker than intended and there was an absolute somewhere that could help with that moving on. Somewhere in that house...

A child laughed from inside the house and a huge roar of laughter followed shortly. There was some minor clattering of cutlery and then a wine glass was being tapped. Bob was trying to make a speech. A passer-by would not have heard or been aware of these things, regardless of the acuteness of their senses. But it always existed inside the house, at least in part. Even though its epicentre was now situated next to the rose bushes, its radius easily covered the house, its awareness reaching into every room like feelers...

As was fitting with the inconsistent and dreamlike state of its existence, there were days when its presence in the house dimmed, but there were also times like today, where its spectral eyes burned like a sentinel into every corner. It watched as the youngest children played with Pokemon and Spiderman dolls; it watched as the family bulldog brushed past the Christmas tree, causing it to sway dangerously for a moment; it watched as a drunk Grandfather idly watched James Bond with glazed eyes; it watched as the majority of the family played

Thirteen

Monopoly at the large dining table that had been dragged into the center of the room for Christmas Day. It pondered the sight of a 21st century family enjoying the festive season, before switching its eye inwards.

The tree was real, like Bob's, and was decorated with a multitude of goodies, ranging from snowflakes through to edible mini Yule-logs. Two bands of silver tinsel intertwined their way around the tree. Her Father sat at the head of the table drinking brandy, as was his tipple during the later stages of Christmas Day, smiling as his family played Rummy and bantered. Various family members laughed and joked about each other. Mother was grinning at her older sister and narrowing her eye; none of the family could bluff and it quickly became a particularly funny game. Her Grandfather snored in the small armchair in the corner. He would wake up shortly and attempt to make the family gamble real money, as opposed to the piles of one and two pence pieces that lay in front of the players already. The cat was treating this day no differently to any other, lying in front of the fire and stretching hard. The children played with Early Learning Centre animals and fairy tale castles. She felt warmth inside, more vivid than she had, felt in as long as she could remember. These people loved her, encouraged her, and carried her through. She became aware that this was a memory... suddenly she is clawing to retain it this clearly, God please, it was almost like she was back there all those years (how many?) ago. But it is too late, the image is already being replaced with another; she shudders with horror as the portable heater slides towards the bath, unable to stop it, unable to do anything but watch this deadly slow motion replay. It was so cold... she knew it was foolish to perch it there, but it had been cold in the old bathroom... and of course she was hopelessly drunk. That was her prevailing memory now... the violent shaking, the brief pain... then the all consuming cold and blackness.

It burst out of its frightening reverie with an outraged cry. Not an audible one, but a single physical shockwave that caused the windows on Bob's house to shake and Christmas lights to rattle against brick. The sudden recall of emotion had caused it to flare up into an incandescent ball; it had lost itself for a minute, but it was back now, aware that Bob was gazing out the window in its direction. Surely he didn't see it? It concentrated on its withdrawal and slowly but surely, Bob looked up and pulled the curtains shut. Just as it tried to shrink back and pull some presence from the living room, it heard a single voice:

"Nothing love, just all the lights in this street have left me a bit dazed. Seeing stars!"

He had seen it. Whereas normally it was a barely detectable speck of light whilst outside, Bob had stared directly at it. Could it be that its most vivid recollection yet of its previous life had something to do with it? But it was more than that wasn't it? It looked down at the thorn bushes and couldn't comprehend what it beheld; a pair of poorly defined spectral hands now shimmered just above the spindly plants.

Helen.

She remembered her name and suddenly she was aware again. Not complete, but aware of where she was and what she was, free of the floaty paralysis that had been her existence. She moved closer to a patch of ice that had begun to form on the driveway and recoiled at the sight of a humanoid reflection. Helen Cole stared back at her. Not quite the self loathing flesh and bone person she had known, but a glowing effigy of herself with faint features. She became aware that she appeared to be naked... but she thought little of it; she was a thing of beauty and she felt simultaneously proud and powerful. Memories came to her again but did not dissipate; the dream like state had disappeared in favour of a savagely aware and focused one. She had somehow

Thirteen

gained a power that she would not even have comprehended before. From a barely aware cloud of energy that did little more than observe, she had suddenly become substantial, motivated... *real*... and she did not intend to waste it. As if to confirm her suspicions, she passed a hand through the wing mirror of Bob's Ford; it moved an inch before flicking back to its original position. She had felt something solid! Her ghostly digits may have passed through it, but she had something resembling touch!

Something else too. She was humanoid now, in *senses* as well as shape. Her cloud like form, her radius, her awareness of the house; it had all gone. In a way she felt even more alone now without the constant presence of the family in her 'grasp', but who cared if she could physically touch them now? And wasn't that the other thing, the most prevailing thing? She was *emotional;* anger, resentment, individualism, pride, relief, sorrow, *love*. Sensations that seemed age old, yet new and exciting simultaneously. But she had to hurry... this incredible transition might be a temporary one and there was one ever present sensation under all these rekindled ones; she was missing something, some deep unfulfilled desire went unsated. Her *talent*. She had written things. Songs, stories, poems... all, she realized now, works of art. Under the floor... she had put them *under the floor in her room*. If she could just...

The family had been semi-aware of her presence before, be it manifested in a brief chill or a feeling that someone else was in a room with them, yet they had never had any feelings of dread from either experience. Helen was going to dispel any doubts about her existence. She had one more Christmas to get through, hell she deserved it and she had something very important to take care of. Wait 'till they got a load of her. They would love her or they would be terrified; she realised she was not giving either a preference. She looked up at the clear night sky and marvelled at how crisp the stars were tonight. She began to walk across the front lawn.

Across the road, Mrs Chapple's hand shakes wildly as she holds the curtain. Her wine glass lies on the floor, its red contents seeping irreparably into the cream carpet. Her bottom lip quivers and her eyes grow lachrymose, but it matters not. Through her tears she can still see the nude ghost of her ex-neighbours' dead daughter walking up her old driveway.

THE ASSASSIN
LAVIE TIDHAR

"Hi Dad." The girl smiled and walked into the living room, her uniform rumpled after a day of school. Her father looked up distractedly from the paper he was working on and smiled back. "Hi pumpkin," he said. "There's lunch ready for you in the kitchen. How was school?"

The girl shrugged. "It was OK."

She went to the kitchen and took out the plate left for her in the oven. "I'm gonna eat in my room," she called over her shoulder. "Dad?"

"No problem pumpkin!" he was miles away again, choosing and discarding sentences, occasionally grunting as he used a red marker to cross out a particularly annoying specimen. "Give you a shout when your mum gets here..." His voice ebbed away and disappeared behind her. She walked up the stairs carefully, balancing a tray with her lunch and a glass of water, and the sweet that will remain untouched that mum always left for her.

The girl closed the door behind her with a sigh of relief, putting the tray down on the small worktable before falling back on her bed. The quiet was good.

After eating, she turned on the computer, waiting patiently as it went through the motions of counting the amount of memory it had before finally bringing up the little icons on the screen. She clicked on an icon the shape of a white bunny, and was greeted by a dark screen and the sound of a modem dialling. Then lines of text appeared.

Peter Rabbit BBS. It said. And:
Login:
The cursor blinked, on and off, waiting after the colon.
The girl typed in a string of characters.
Password:
Another string.
There was a pause, then a message appeared, like a slow wave of characters rolling over the screen.
1 contact online. It said. The cursor blinked once, then continued its
sluggish movement: Chat Y/N?
She pressed Y on the keyboard.
Aura. The name appeared on the screen hesitantly, as if typed by a person inexperienced with such an activity. It is good of you to show up. The cursor hesitated, as if the person on the other side of the phone line was weighing their words very carefully. Then
I have another job for you.

Dad dropped her at school the next morning, pecking her on the cheek before driving off. "Your mother and I have an important meeting today!" he shouted out of the car window, waving at her distractedly.

She dusted imaginary lint off her immaculately pressed uniform and walked through the gate of the school, into the main building, ignoring the other children around her. She walked to the end of the long hall, pushed open the fire doors, and was out in the street again.

The whole thing had taken only three minutes. Nobody noticed her.

She hefted her school bag onto her shoulder and began walking away, her movements casual. Nobody paid her any attention.

She got on a bus, paid, sat at the back and watched the streets go by, and got off on a street corner, where several tall buildings cluttered the skyline.

She walked through the glass doors of a large office block, entering a plush waiting room. A security guard stopped her. "Can I help you, Miss?" He smiled as

Thirteen

he said it.

"I hope so," she said earnestly. She beckoned him closer, so that he had to stoop to listen to her. "I'm visiting my uncle – he's on the fifth floor – it's his birthday and I wanted to surprise him." She ended on a questioning note, her large blue eyes imploring the guard.

He smiled. "No problem. Come on." He took her to the elevator and waited while she got in. "Won't say a word," he promised, and smiled again at the young schoolgirl as the doors silently closed.

The fifth floor was a bustle of activity, men and women in power suits marching along corridors of metal and glass, piles of papers in their hands. In the hubbub she was all but ignored.

She walked, quickly but unhurriedly, to the office she needed. She didn't knock.

"Yes?" the man's face looked annoyed. "What are you doing here kid?" he demanded. "Get the hell out of my office."

She smiled and came closer to the desk.

"What is this?" the man complained theatrically to the sky. "First the coffee machine breaks, now kids come wandering in – I mean, what next? Dogs and cats?" He waved his hand at her, as if getting rid of a fly. "Shoo. Shoo."

The girl smiled and moved closer. Her uniform was immaculate.

She plunged the knife into the man's neck, watching with detached satisfaction as the beating vein burst, spraying a fine mist of dark blood on the floor.

She extracted the knife, ran its edge smoothly along the circumference of the man's neck. Her moves were precise. Confident. The assassin they called Aura began cleaning the blade on the man's Saville Row jacket.

"Mr. Bergerstorm?" Loud voices and footsteps and the door to the office opening, two faces staring at her in utter shock.

The girl felt her heart slowing, time halting to a stand still as she recognised them. Behind her, the severed head of a man looked up at the ceiling, a look of mild surprise on his plump face.

"Mum? Dad?" she said.

She absent-mindedly weighed the knife in her hand.

"I can explain everything..."

Thirteen

BOBBY MOON
LEE BETTERIDGE

The night was dark and icy, and a biting wind pulled at my hair and clothes. I crept alongside a leafy hedge as quietly as I could and kept my eyes peeled. The grass underfoot made wet, crunching noises with each step. There was hardly any light in the park as the nearest streetlamp was…well, at the street, which was about three hundred yards from where I was. Long shadows from the surrounding trees enclosed me like a cloak and everywhere seemed to be a possible hiding place.

The hedge I was following, running one leather-gloved hand lightly across it, abruptly stopped and the grass beneath my feet gave way to concrete. I stepped back, crouching behind the bush, and surveyed the area. My eyes are good in the dark (I eat my carrots!) and I could tell that the long grey snake of concrete was a path that ran up the hill of the park. If I went right it would lead me to the tennis courts, then the children's play area, then back through the green metal gate (or over, at this time of night), to the quiet street again. If I followed the path left, up the hill, I would pass the bowling green before entering the picnic area with its lovely collection of overgrown trees and bramble bushes.

Eanie meanie minie mo!

I went left.

I ran up the path slightly stooped, probably looking like an SAS man from a movie, wearing all black as I was. I was fast and silent, and I entered the picnic area not by the opening in the foliage, but by an unintended gap between a tangle of nettles and a low hanging tree of some kind.

The picnic area of the park was a collection of five or six tables with benches, surrounded by a U-shaped collection of trees, and as I slowly made my way through the throng of plant life and undergrowth, I heard a noise.

It was coming from the picnic area: a kind of low moaning noise. I slowly inched forward, trying not to make any noise. Then, without warning, I had my head out of the bushes and was looking into the picnic area.

There were a few picnic tables and benches, plus I could see a number of litter bins. The moaning sound was still going on and I could see what looked like a couple of people sprawled on a bench. I put my hand in the small leather pouch that hangs from my belt and grabbed a handful of the tiny metal pieces I keep there, being careful not to prick my fingers. Then I slowly stepped out of the covering of the bush.

As I crept up on the two people, I ascertained that it was a women doing the groaning. I couldn't see much of them, the only light in here was the moonlight, and I couldn't make out which limb belonged to who. There seemed to be a lot of them. Something was stuck up in the air, and it was only when I got about twelve feet away that I noticed it was a leg. A bare leg, a very long and slim one, dappled with a milky sheen of moonlight. With that as a point of reference, all the other body parts dropped into place. The moaning seemed to be very fitting.

The woman was stretched out on her back on the picnic table, totally starkers. She looked mighty fine in the moonlight. Her legs were held up in the air, spread open slightly. This is where the other person enters, if you pardon the crude pun. The man, who was dressed in a white shirt and black pants, had his head between her legs and was making slobbery noises with his mouth. The woman was moaning and groaning and writhing on the table. You work it out!

Anyway, I didn't know what to do. I was certain of my gut-feeling, I knew one of them was nearby. But neither of the two people in front of me seemed to be what I was looking for. But my stomach still churned painfully, my balls had that dull ache and a sickly taste came to the back of my throat. I knew there was one

Thirteen

here. I crept closer to the two on the picnic table, my hand holding the metal pieces loosely. I kept low and concentrated on making my footsteps silent, ready for action, ready for anything.

Except the lump of dog shit that my foot landed in!

My foot shot straight out from under me and I landed on my backside awkwardly. The woman screamed in alarm and stared at me. The man's head popped up from between her legs like a jack-in-the-box and glared at me. His white shirt was partly unbuttoned and his flies were open, Humpty Dumpty poking his old bald head out.

"You dirty goddam perv," he snarled, zipping up his fly, and then I was on my feet and running. Neither the man nor the woman had been what I was looking for, so I decided the best bet was to get the hell out of there. I crashed through the trees and bushes that made up the boundaries of the picnic area, not looking back. I'd seen the man's uniform before, millions of times, in every town and village. They meant trouble at the best of times, and I'd just interrupted one of them having his supper, as it were. I was in the deepest kind of shit ever, if he caught me.

As I broke out the other side of the bushes, my feet slammed the concrete and I charged down the path towards the gate of the park. I could see the ghostly silhouettes of a set of swings, a climbing frame, a seesaw and other apparatus. They looked like strange giant insects, back lit by the moon as they were.

And then I saw it. The reason for my sickly, aching guts. It was sat on the crossbeam of the swings, perched there like an evil monstrous ape on a branch, watching me. I stopped in my tracks, and glared at the shape sat on the swing frame, one leg dangling down. I put the small metal pieces that were still in my hand back in the pouch, then started walking towards the play area. I'd totally forgotten my pursuer, that is how dedicated I am with my work.

He hadn't forgotten me though, and he rushed at me like a frigging prop-forward on steroids. If my attention hadn't been on the shape that sat on the crossbeam of the swings I would have easily dodged him. But as it was, I remembered the bobby too late, and his truncheon caught me just above the ear.

I went down like a sack of ropes, and as my vision blurred I heard, "You deserve that, you perving prick! What's your name?"

"*Goddamn...Bobby!*" I said drowsily. In the sky the pale blue moon looked down at us with its constant expression of shock.

"Bobby what?" snapped the bobby.

"*Moon...*" I whispered.

"Well, Bobby Moon, you're under arrest for perving on a man and his wife trying to get some goddamn privacy."

I heard him say that, and I saw the dark figure leap from the swing frame, land on the ground smoothly, and lope off on all fours like a disfigured primate. Then there was nothing.

I wasn't out of it for long. I woke up in the back of a police car looking at the back of a copper's head. It was the big guy who I'd interrupted in the park whose truncheon I'd assaulted with my head. Thirty minutes later, after being bossed and pushed around I found myself in the small police station's only holding cell. I was booked under the name of Bobby Moon, which I found quite amusing, and I had a headache and a bump above my ear like a goose egg, which wasn't amusing in the slightest. Apparently, someone was going to look at my bump for me, but I wasn't going to hold my breath until they came. For some reason I didn't expect Naylor (I heard someone call the big bobby that as I'd stumbled through the station) to go out of his way to make my stay more comfortable, whether I had a bump on my head, Alzheimer's or an axe in my skull. Mr. 'Lucky Licky' Naylor

Thirteen

just didn't seem the type.

I shared the cell with a bunk, a chair, a table and a chrome toilet and was debating whether to use it and risk catching some unsavoury disease when I heard a harsh scream. It came from outside my barred window, I was sure, but it was cut off before I could be positive.

I strained my ears.

I needn't have bothered.

Suddenly, it seemed that everyone within the police station was either screaming, yelling, shouting or generally adding to the onslaught of my ears. My hair prickled up on my arms and the back of my neck. It was awful. Every shriek seemed to stem from sheer terror and panic, and each one was more painful than the last.

I felt terrible, listening to all that fear and not being able to help. Then the violence started. The shouts were punctuated with horrid cracking and ripping noises, wet crunches and the odd animal-like groan.

It didn't last long. Five minutes at the most. The screams got less and less, many ending in mid-wail. There were a few bangs, like furniture clattering about, and I was sure I heard a gunshot. The last voice I heard was that of a woman close by screaming, "Don't! Oh for Godsake *DON'T...!*" And then it was gone with a sickening wet thud that sounded very close to my cell door. Then there was silence.

I stood stock still and waited and listened. My ears rang. I knew what was going on. It was the thing from the playground. I knew what was going on, I just wondered what would happen next.

SNICK! That's what happened next. It was the lock of my huge cell door with the closed peephole and the *'who gives a fuck'* scribbled in magic marker. The door swung inwards slightly and I took a step back, getting ready for something to rush in.

Nothing did. Instead I heard the padding of several feet walking away and I remembered the thing loping off into the dark on all fours. Then there was such a foul animal laugh that made my heart stop for a second, I'm sure, and then it kick-started itself again causing a pain to run across my chest and down my left arm.

I let out a sigh, rubbed a clammy hand down my sweaty face, then poked my head out the open door. In the corridor just next to me was a woman slumped on the floor with a squashed head. Above her was a lumpy bloody streak stretching down the wall. She was the only person in the short corridor, except myself of course. I walked past her, light on my toes, quiet as a cat, stealthy as a ninja, shitting bricks like a professional. There were two doors in addition to the one I'd just walked through and I knew the end one led to the main cop shop bust-em-and-bruise-em area so I tried the mystery door.

And what's behind mystery door number one?

Nothing to worry about in here, but not a lot to get excited about either. It was a store cupboard. I went in, switched on the light and closed the door. It was so small, if I'd stood in the centre of the closet I could have touched all four walls with my outstretched hands. I had better and more urgent things to do with my time though. I looked around for a weapon or anything I could use as one. There wasn't much. Bottles of disinfectant and toilet cleaner, mop and bucket, set of stepladders, sweeping brushes and one of those dust pans with an upright handle. Then I spied something and grabbed it quickly. It was a pole about four feet long with a metal S shaped hook on the end. I remembered the windows in the police station's main room being high up, the tops touching the ceiling in fact, and this was the tool used for opening them. I recall them having one similar at school.

I took it out to the corridor and leaned it against the wall at an angle and

Thirteen

stomped on the middle of the pole with my boot. It snapped with a splintery crack and a clatter. I picked up both pieces - the piece with the hook in my right hand, the simple two-feet stake in my left - and shouldered the door open into the police station proper.

Now, I've seen a few blood baths in my time, but this one was more of a Jacuzzi with a blood mist sauna to follow. Furniture lay everywhere, some shattered to pieces, some hurled against walls, and amongst the ruined desks and chairs were ruined people. Corpses littered the room like discarded mannequins covered in red paint. Blood was sprayed up the walls and splattered in congealing puddles on the floor. I only had a few seconds to take in the carnage before I heard the voice but a few seconds was more than I needed.

"*So you've come,*" said a whispery voice. I turned and looked upwards. The thing from the play area was up in a shadowed top corner of the room, its head twisted sideways against the ceiling, its feet on the two connecting narrow window sills. "*The butcher I've heard tell of is here. The one that kills but can't be killed.*"

I said nothing. My stomach and balls were aching and I was scared. I didn't realise these creatures knew of me, or that they passed information from one to the other.

The thing let out that laugh again, that carnal whispered laugh and dropped from its perch, landing delicately on all fours. Now I could see it properly and I tried not to show my fear. I had expected the creature's face to be more manly, or *hu*manly, given it's ape-like posture but this was one of the most altered creatures I'd seen. Tiny yellow eyes and an almost reptilian two-slit nose made up it's elongated face along with a wide mouth so full of teeth that it brought to mind TV footage I've seen of great white sharks. The heavily muscled body, still in clothing surprisingly, hunched behind that horrific head with the shark's grin like a coiled spring. Now it was on the ground, there were only about ten metres between us. I could smell the raw meat on his breath.

The yellow eyes narrowed even more.

"*The one that kills but can't be killed is about to be just that.*"

"Er...killed, do you mean?" I asked. Sometimes sarcasm can't be held back.

"*Precisely,*" the thing said. "*Your blood is my wine,*" and with a roar it launched itself at me. As those big hands with the big claws got closer, my hands tightened on the two bits of the window opener.

Five minutes later I stepped out of the police station onto the street, nursing my right hand because two of the fingers were gone. The two nearest the thumb were now nothing more than squirting stumps. I also had a limp due to the fact that the bone below my knee seemed to be badly sprained. Still, you should see the other guy. Now that I'd killed him he had returned to his normal state - that of a man in his early twenties with sandy hair and pimples. Only a kid really. His shark's grin had been replace by a soft-lipped line.

I'd left him laying on the floor amongst the other already decomposing bodies with the wooden stake sticking out of his chest and one of his eyes missing. The eye, at first yellow but now a hazel colour, still clung to the window hook that lay next to him. The one that kills but can't be killed strikes again.

Outside, the chill wind started to grab at my clothes and hair again. The street was empty, the only occupants being a few cars and a van parked along the kerb. I recognised the van and the two men who got out of it.

"How's things?" asked the short one, the man I know as Fouse. "You look in bad shape. What happened?"

"He was strong," I said. "The strongest yet. Where's Tina and Molly?"

Fouse laughed. I felt like ripping his head off. "There's been a change of

Thirteen

plan."

"You said this was to be my last one," I said, trying to control my rage. "You promised you'd let them go."

"And we will," said Hall, the other man. He rubbed his beard. "We just need this one more job from you. We are struggling to get a replacement of your calibre."

I said, "That's *your* problem."

Fouse laughed again. "Not if you want your wife and kid back."

"Shut up!" growled Hall, but Fouse seemed not to notice.

"Its your problem if you don't want them pegged out in the sun and turned to crispy critter fritters. Its your problem...*oof!*"

Hall dug an elbow into his stomach. "I said shut up," then he turned to me. "I realise how you must feel, but you must trust us. Your family is safe and will remain unharmed. We ask of you just one more job, to kill one more of those monsters, and then our contract will be finished. What do you say?"

What could I say?

"OK. But this I promise. If I don't get Tina and Molly back after this next one, the two I kill next will be you two."

Fouse started to shiver over-dramatically with his fingers in his mouth. "Ooooh!" he said, until Hall glared at him and he stopped.

"Very well," said Hall. "That's a deal. Now how badly are you hurt?"

"Not too bad," I said. My shin bone had already mended itself and my two fingers were slowly and painfully growing back. Hall looked at his wristwatch.

"Well you've got about an hour until sun up. We have some supper for you." While he said this Fouse slid the van door open. "It's all we could find. I'm sure it will do."

Fouse dropped a large mongrel onto the road and it gave out a low whine. Drugged, no doubt.

"We'll be in touch," said Hall already climbing into the van. Fouse winked at me then climbed into the back. He laughed, then shouted, "See you soon." The van rumbled away.

"Not if I see you first," I muttered under my breath. I strode across the tarmac, wiggling my new-grown fingers to chase out the pins and needles. I picked up the dog by its scruff and dragged it into a back street. When I was well hidden in the shadows I squatted and rubbed at the matted fur on the dog's neck. Then I sunk my teeth into the exposed skin. Thin blood exploded into my mouth and I drank heavily. As I drank I thought of Tina and Molly and tears filled my eyes, so I changed my train of thought to those bastards Hall and Fouse. And I imagined how they would scream in agony when I got hold of them.

Several of my friends are working together to help me track them down. We are nearly there. Then I will have my beautiful wife and daughter back and the bearded Hall and the short-arsed Fouse will learn what a true monster is.

I gulped down the sweet liquid quickly. It would be sunrise soon.

Thirteen

THE CEMETERY
SUSAN CONWAY

For years, the cemetery was just a normal cemetery. By day, graves were dug, the dearly departed were buried, headstones were set, friends and family would pay their respects to friends and family no longer with us.

By night, although a little creepy to look at (but which cemetery isn't?), it was nothing out of the ordinary. Owls would dutifully twit-twoo, the moon would obligingly shine through the branches of the trees, and once in a while the odd couple, in an attempt to do something daring and different, would fornicate in the dense bushes.

It was just a normal cemetery. But then, all of a sudden, it became incredibly haunted.

The first recorded incident was reported by an elderly couple that had been taking a stroll in the forty acres the cemetery had to offer. After hearing screaming and sobbing coming from beneath their feet, they flagged down a contracted landscape gardener who was driving along, observing the 5mph speed limit and using his hazard lights. The common contention among the three was that someone had been buried alive. Grabbing a shovel from the back of his truck, the young, lithe, bare-chested gardener ran among the gravestones, searching for a tell-tale patch of newly dug earth under which he was already dreaming of finding and rescuing a prematurely buried beauty, who he would settle down with and start a family.

He couldn't find one.

A mobile phone call later, two police officers arrived. Their response time was just six minutes and ten seconds, but by the time they arrived the whole cemetery was resounding with screaming and moaning and shouting and sobbing from underground. Voices of old and young, male and female, different accents – all could be heard.

The police, quickly assessing the situation, decided that the issue was a council matter and promptly sped away in search of less supernatural activities. One of the officers, P.C. Robert Hendry, spotted the transparent figure of a woman in a white dress stamping her feet and pulling at her hair at the east gate of the cemetery in his rear-view mirror.

Yes, he thought decidedly. They hadn't covered this eventuality at Hendon. It was definitely a council matter.

The ghostly howling got louder and louder and eventually caught the attention of local residents who, for one reason or another, were not at work that afternoon. They left their homes, with some justifiable trepidation at first, until the old 'safety in numbers' mentality kicked in as the inhabitants from different streets converged and marched together in one inquisitive mass.

By the time the local residents (there were about sixty or so) got in sight of the cemetery, more transparent figures were decking the landscape. Two minutes later, the residents still in attendance (there were now only thirty or so – the rest had fled in terror) were frantically punching 999 into their phones. The police policy quickly filtered through – haunted graveyards were simply not a police matter. It was a council issue.

Thirty scared and confused taxpayers desperately tried to get through to the appropriate council department. Automated voices droned out lists of options. For a burst water main, you had to dial 'one'. To report offensive graffiti, you had to dial 'two', and so on. For a full five minutes the only sounds were the pathetic, spine chilling lamentations of the apparitions and the high-pitched beeps of keypads being pressed.

George Morgan (who claimed welfare but was regularly spotted up a ladder

Thirteen

cleaning windows) grew so infuriated at the robotic voice at the end of the line that, in sheer desperation, he pressed seven and got through to the Department for Controlled Parking Zones.

"Good afternoon, this is Amanda speaking, how can I help you?"

George, who suddenly realised he hadn't a clue what to say, finally screamed down the phone.

"It's the fucking devil!"

A recording of that call is now used for training purposes.

Someone finally got through to someone else who put them through to someone who took their details and passed them onto someone else who was in a position to contact someone who would be able to help. Two days later, a perimeter was put up around the cemetery. In fact, it was put up a good eighty feet around the cemetery because the workmen were too scared to get any nearer.

The fence didn't last long. As local news covered the story, national news quickly picked up on it. People wanted to come and see the ghosts – they were still audible from beyond the perimeter fence, but that wasn't good enough. The first person to knock down a section of the fencing was the producer of a live TV show. They had put together the motley crew of a vicar, a psychic investigator and a busty brunette presenter, and they weren't going to leave without a story.

The section came down, the crew moved forward, an entranced audience watched. But it was a non-event. Despite the vicar's best attempts to speak to the ghosts, they weren't having any of it. The only moment of note that got people talking (they'd already seen the ghosts on the news and weren't that impressed with seeing them again) was the psychic investigator's look of pure fright and his words "You mean they're *real*?" before he fainted. A career built up over years of apparently communicating with his spirit guide in all manner of so-called haunted locations was destroyed in an instant.

Bit by bit, the fence was dismantled and taken away. You can buy sections of it on Ebay, but there's no guarantee that it's genuine.

Property prices in the area within earshot of the morose ghostly wailing left estate agents scratching their heads. People desperate to leave the area sold their houses for a tenth of their value. Others, more shrewd and willing to invest in soundproofing materials, sold their homes for ten times their value to scientific research teams and bizarre cults from across the globe. The backlash was that those who had sold early and cheap formed a collective and began legal action against the estate agents and solicitors who had previously represented them. The judge dismissed the case, which became known as the 'Haunted Homes Affair', despite none of the homes being haunted.

And, in time, the spectacle of the sobbing spirits became just one of those things. It has never become normal as such, but the trappings of commercial venture has made it somehow acceptable – the homes which caused headlines in the 'Haunted Homes Affair' are now mainly gift shops, with names like 'Cemetery Souvenirs' and 'The Genuine Graveyard Shop'.

Although a few scientists remain and continue to study the activities, it is unlikely that they will ever uncover any kind of explanation. Perhaps the only way to find out why the ghosts are so upset is to be buried there yourself after you die. So far, there have been no volunteers.

Thirteen

THE TOKOLOSHE
PAUL CRILLEY

The witchdoctor – the umthakathi - owned a special silver spoon that he used to stir sugar into his tea. His grandfather had stolen it from a British colonist, way back when they first appeared on their shores. The umthakathi believed the spoon, with its intricate carvings and minute swirls, added something special to the taste.

Right now, he was using it to gouge the eyes out of a week old corpse. The eyes themselves were easy enough. They just popped out. But the stalks gave him a bit of trouble. They had become leathery over the days, and eventually he was forced to use the scissors on them.

The warm night wind caressed his face, and for a moment seemed to smooth his deep wrinkles, wiping the weariness and sickness from his small frame. He closed his eyes and turned his face into the strengthening breeze. He'd watched the liver-colored clouds build up all afternoon, towering higher and higher into the sky, and he prayed to the ancestors that the summer storm would hold off long enough for him to complete his task.

It pleased him that they granted his boon. It boded well for what lay ahead.

A whispering sound flicked his eyes open. The wind had picked up even more, was soughing through the long veldt grass. He frowned. He had become distracted again. He found that happening more and more lately. He shook his head in an attempt to clear it. There was still much to do before the storm hit.

He inserted his middle finger and thumb into the mouth and pulled out the shriveled tongue. It barely reached past the crooked teeth, so he worked the scissors into the mouth and snipped it from behind. The scissors kept losing their grip, but he succeeded eventually, although it was not as neat as he would have liked it. He examined the tongue by the light of the fire. The edge was ragged, as if a child had taken a butter knife to a piece of steak. He shook his head in irritation and dropped the tongue into the small fire he had built.

Now came the hard part. He wrapped his hands in ox skin and took the poker from the flames. It hissed at him as a stray drop of rain fell onto the tip, causing a small circle of black to appear on the glowing metal. He looked to the sky, saw the clouds outlined in a flicker of lightning. A rumble of thunder sounded soon after, discontented.

The umthakathi parted the brittle hair and prodded around until he found the centre. Then he positioned the tip of the poker against the skull. He ignored the smell of burning hair and pushed. The poker parted the skin, but stopped when it hit the skull. He pushed harder, but only succeeded in sliding the body over the grass. He solved the problem by kneeling lightly on the chest and pushing the poker towards him. He felt the skull give and the poker slid easily down, through the neck, the chest, the stomach.

The body twitched. He stood up and watched, eyes glittering, as the body slowly shriveled and shrank until it was barely knee high, a wizened gnome of a creature, an almost child-like expression on its face.

Conversely, the creature's penis increased in size until it was out of all proportion to the rest of it. It lay on the grass like a sickened snake.

The umthakathi opened a pouch on his belt and took a pinch of powder from within. He dropped it into the wrinkled creature's mouth. He stood back as it shuddered and spasmed as if in pain.

The umthakathi smiled. His tokoloshe was born.

A sound from her childhood woke Thandi from sleep, the tick-ticka-tick from above as the sun heated the metal sheeting that acted as roofing material for

Thirteen

most of the shacks in the township. It reminded her of summer mornings and holidays, of sleeping decadently late and not having to get up for school. She smiled at the memories.

She missed her home; the city depressed her. She would never <u>know</u> it, not like she knew her township, Nyuswa. The grey blocks and glass buildings of Durban pushed her away, the symmetry alienating and frightening her until she was forced to visit the police psychiatrist once a week. And she'd only lived there for a year.

She wondered why she was here, sleeping in the bed that had become her sister's after Thandi moved away to join the police force.

Then she remembered.

And she heard the quiet sounds of her mother weeping in the doorway.

The morning sun hit Thandi in the face as she walked out of the hut. It was a summer's day, close to Christmas, and the rain from the day before rose from the grass and mud as steam. The humidity was increased as the residents took advantage of the sun to hang out their washing, multicolored rainbows that hung between shacks and oozed dampness into the air.

She was at a loss. Her little sister had gone missing two days ago, and her mother had called her in after the local police failed to even turn up and take a report. Thandi didn't even know where to start. She wasn't a detective. She'd spent the last year following up burglary reports, filling in forms and trying to counsel those scarred by the sexual abuse that seemed to be on the increase. But she could not tell her mother that. Her mother assumed that if you were a member of the police then you solved crimes. Departments meant nothing to her.

All Thandi had to go on was that her sister had been washing clothes by the river when she disappeared. She headed that way now, acknowledging the greetings of those she knew from growing up here. It was mostly women. The men were all out working or looking for work. She noticed quite a few new families she didn't recognize, people forced to live here as the backlog for government housing grew longer and longer, the free housing promised in '94 still having mostly failed to materialize unless you were family or friend of a government minister.

She walked the familiar trail and arrived at the river, the same place where she used to wash the family's clothes as a child. The water was dirtier now, a muddy green color that partially obscured the riverbed and did not look healthy. She wandered aimlessly up and down the bank, feeling stupid as she surveyed the ground. What did she expect to find? A trail of torn clothing leading her to Virtue's hiding place? This was hopeless! She could better serve by going to the local station and demanding they take some action. But what could they do? Nobody had any clues.

She sat down on the bank and put her head in her hands. One thing she did know was that the first 24 hours were crucial. If no leads were found then, chances were nothing would turn up.

Virtue had been missing for 36 hours already.

"Are you the lady from the police?"

Thandi looked up and saw a young boy crouching on the ground before her. He looked about eight years old and held a thin metal rod in his hand that connected to a wire man on a bicycle. He pushed it around in circles, leaving a grooved circle in the dust. Thandi watched the knees of the man rise and fall, rise and fall.

The boy stopped pushing it, skidding the toy so that it appeared the man crashed his bike into the dust.

"Are you the police-woman?" he asked again.

Thirteen

"Yes."

"Gogo says Virtue is probably dead. That she was taken by a bad man and raped."

Thandi felt goose bumps rise over her skin. "That's not true!" she snapped. "You tell your grandmother not to say such evil things!"

"I did already."

Thandi squinted at the boy. "Did you know Virtue?"

Did you know Virtue? What was she saying? Did she also believe it was too late?

She corrected herself. "*Do* you know Virtue?"

The boy nodded. "She's my girlfriend."

It was such a simple sentence. Thandi stared at the boy blankly for a moment, and then started to cry. She lowered her head, saw her tears fall and form little dark craters in the dust.

A hand touched her shoulder. The boy patted her awkwardly, then took his hand away.

"Anyway, it wasn't a man that took her."

"What?" Thandi's head snapped up. "What do you mean? Do you know who took her?"

The boy nodded.

"Who!" Thandi was on her feet now, towering over the boy.

He looked up at her. Then he reached into his pocket and pulled out a stick wrapped with colored beads. He gave it to Thandi.

"What's this?"

"A charm. Gogo had the sangoma make it for me, but I think you will need it more."

Thandi shook her head. "I don't understand."

"It fights evil. You can use it against the thing that took Virtue. I don't need it, but you will. You're too old."

"Too old? What do you mean? And what thing?"

"The tokoloshe," he said simply.

Thandi watched the sun set over the freeway bordering the township. It lowered itself through the smog-filled air, causing the sky to glow a dirty red in color. She had spent the day searching through the hills to the south of the township. She had found nothing. Tomorrow she would turn to the north.

She sipped a glass of iced water and remembered when the view was cleaner than this. Or maybe it was her who had changed. She shook her head. A tokoloshe! What kind of nonsense was that? The tokoloshe was a myth, an evil little monster used to scare children with.

Not just children, she reminded herself. Adults raised their beds on bricks so the short creature could not attack and rape them in their sleep. The mere mention of the tokoloshe was enough to have most women crying out in fear. She couldn't believe that in this day and age people still believed in goblins and monsters. It was holding her people back, this primitive belief. And yet the charm the boy gave her was wrapped through her hair. She told herself it was simply to hold it in place, but she was fooling no one.

The man came to her again in her dreams. She sat huddled in a darkened room. She sensed a vast space all around her. She waved a hand behind her and felt cold, clammy air. The skin on the back of her neck prickled. She sensed someone else in the room, watching her through the darkness. She scrabbled backwards in the dirt until she hit up against a rough wall. She ran a hand over it, felt jagged bricks hard against her sweat-slicked skin.

Thirteen

And then his face was right in front of hers. She didn't know how she knew this, but it was the truth. She tried to move, but was frozen in place. The terror held her immobile. She wanted to raise a hand, to hide her face away from the scrutiny, for she knew he could see her in the dark.

For long minutes, nothing happened. Every second stretched into an hour, and her nerves screamed out in anticipation of the touch she knew would come. It always did. The only factor to be decided was how long she had to wait and where it would touch first.

It was her stomach this time. Ice cold and jarring, the finger stroked her stomach, back and forth, back and forth. Her skin became numb wherever the finger touched, so always she could trace its passage like a pathway on her skin.

Then the finger drifted slowly downwards, over her pelvis, cold, oh God, it was so cold—

She opened her mouth in a silent scream. It took a moment for Thandi to realize she could see vague shapes in the darkness, that she wasn't dreaming anymore.

She closed her mouth, tried to calm her breathing. Every night. She'd had that dream every single night for the past twelve years. Ever since the man tried to hurt her, tried to take from her what was not his to take.

He had not succeeded. Neither had anyone since. It was impossible for her to be intimate with anyone without thinking about that night, without remembering his breath, reeking of yeasty beer.

Thandi forced her mind away from these thoughts. She knew from past experience that once they got hold, it was hard to shake them off. They would haunt her for days. She turned over onto her side and closed her eyes. She needed sleep if she was to be alert tomorrow.

She was just drifting off when she realized there was another presence in the room.

Her pulse thudded in her throat, making too much noise as she tried to listen for sounds of movement. Her eyes searched the small room, flicking back and forth between shapes that were innocent before but which now took on sinister menace. Was that a pile of clothes on the chair, or was somebody sitting there watching her? Had she hung her jacket on the door? She couldn't remember. Was someone standing there?

God, what should she do? Her gun was sitting on the dresser beside her head. Could she grab it, flick the safety off, and point it before whoever was in the room was on her? She doubted it.

Then another thought struck her. Whoever? Or should it be whatever?

As her eyes slowly adjusted she could make out more of the room around her. The window was slightly ajar, even though she <u>knew</u> she had latched it. The night sky was visible, fast moving clouds outlined in silver as they passed before the moon.

She watched these clouds, waiting. And then the moment presented itself. The clouds parted. Moonlight shone through the window, directly onto a hideous dwarf-like creature that stood at the bottom of her bed, one hand carefully reaching beneath the bedclothes.

Thandi instinctively kicked out. The creature hissed in pain and snatched its hand back. It looked at her for a full second, black eyes glinting, then it whirled around and leapt through the window. Thandi jumped out of bed and pulled her shoes on. Out the window, careful not to land on any uneven stones. She looked around. There, weaving its way between the shacks. Thandi sprinted after it. It was heading out the township, up towards the hills where she had intended to start searching in the morning.

The tokoloshe led her on a chase for the next half hour, always managing to

Thirteen

just stay ahead while at the same time never disappearing from sight. Thandi had been on enough chases to know she was being led somewhere, but at the moment she had no choice in the matter. The creature was her only link to Virtue.

She paused to regain her breath. They were entering a more wooded area now. The wind was picking up, throwing branches around like arms waving in the sky. Lightning flickered behind the clouds, casting a brief light by which she could see the tokoloshe, waiting patiently for her atop the hill.

She straightened up. The tokoloshe was looking at her. She could not see so far, but she sensed their eyes meeting across the darkness. She set off again, but this time she walked. The tokoloshe kept its pace steady in front.

It led her like this for another three or four kilometers. Then, as she drew to the crest of another hill and started downwards, she realized two things. One, the tokoloshe had disappeared, and two, there was a small hut not twenty feet from her, surrounded by trees and bushes. The hut startled her. Her people lived together. They gathered in towns and villages. No one would live on their own like this. It was not safe.

The door to the hut opened. Orange light and smoke drifted out, followed by a small man wearing dirty trousers and smoking a home-made cigarette. Thandi sniffed the air, noting the unmistakably sweet smell of marijuana.

The man squinted at her. Thandi stared back, unsure as to what was going on. Then she looked again at the hut, saw the animal skulls hanging around the eaves, the different kinds of herbs growing in the garden.

She had just enough time to realize the man was an umthakathi – what her people called a wizard – before something leapt onto her back and forced her down onto the grass with a strength that was impossible to fight.

Thandi's cheek was pushed hard into the ground. She watched as the umthakathi ambled towards her. His bloodshot eyes regarded her with sleepy interest. He knelt down beside Thandi. He lowered and turned his head so that he was looking directly into her eyes. Then he sniffed. Like an animal he inhaled her scent, moving all over her body, down over her back, lingering over her buttocks. She tried to wriggle away from the grasp that held her prisoner, but the clawed hand holding her head into the grass tensed in warning, and she felt the creature's talons digging into her scalp.

The umthakathi's face appeared again in front of her. He seemed pleased with something. Dirty yellow teeth bared in a smile.

"You are a virgin, yes?" And he nodded without waiting for an answer. He waved a hand in front of her nose, rubbing his fingers together. The smell of vinegar wafted into her nostrils.

No! she screamed. Or at least tried to. Her mouth would not work. Lethargy overwhelmed her. All she wanted was sleep. *No!* she told herself. If she passed out she was as good as dead. She had a feeling she knew what the umthakathi wanted of her, wanted of her young sister.

Oh God, no, she sobbed. *Please, not Virtue.*

And then the vinegary smell lodged in the back of her throat and she found it difficult to breathe anymore.

Thandi awoke to find herself tied to a musty bed. She looked around in confusion. The room was wreathed in marijuana smoke. She tasted it in her mouth, smelt it everywhere about her person. How long had she been breathing it? Her head was spinning. Everything felt surreal. She blinked, then opened her heavy eyes and watched the umthakathi dancing around the little hut. He was naked, and he seemed to be dancing with a partner that was not there, one hand around an invisible waist, the other holding a hand. She tried to move her head, but it felt too heavy. She settled on moving her eyes around the hut. The tokoloshe was sitting

Thirteen

on a shelf just beneath the roof. His hand was moving rhythmically, and she realized he was masturbating a penis that was almost as tall as he was. She found this quite comical, and almost laughed until she suddenly saw that it was watching her with fierce concentration as it moved its hands up and down.

Thandi gagged, and felt the bile rise up in her throat. She tested the ropes that tied her arms. The left one was loose, but she could not pull it over her thumb. She still had her tracksuit pants on, so she had not been violated. Yet. She had no doubt about what was going to happen now. She'd spent enough time counseling victims of the crime to figure it out. Mostly young children and their parents. And all thanks to the commonly held belief that having sex with a virgin was the only way to cure Aids.

A thought suddenly occurred to Thandi, one that filled her with hope. If the umthakathi had her, and intended to use her as a "cure", where was Virtue? He would have no need of Thandi if he had already raped her sister. Had she escaped?

The thought went someway towards clearing her head. She looked towards the umthakathi. He was still busy dancing. She had to move now. There wouldn't be another chance. Thandi wriggled her left wrist back and forwards, pulling down on the rope. After a minute or so she had rubbed her skin raw and soaked the rope with blood. She gritted her teeth and pulled down with all her strength. The pain was excruciating but the blood-slick rope finally slid past her thumb. She breathed a sigh of relief and kept her hand where it was. The next moment had to be judged just right. She would not have much time.

She waited until the umthakathi turned his back to her as he danced with his invisible partner. Then she moved her hand and attempted to untie the knot that held her other wrist to the bedpost. This one was tighter. She yanked at the knot, bending her nail back as she tried to find something to grip. She was not getting it. Shit. No, wait. She felt a movement.

And then everything seemed to happen at once. The tokoloshe saw her and let out a screeching wail that startled her so much she actually stopped pulling at the knot and looked up. The umthakathi was running at her, his teeth bared in a snarl. Thandi sobbed in fear, yanked hard at the knot. It came apart slowly, oh God, it was too slow. The umthakathi was at the bottom of the bed, grasping for her feet. The tokoloshe was dropping from his shelf.

The knot parted. Thandi screamed and threw her body off the bed. She landed heavily on the floor, her ankles still tied to the bedposts. The umthakathi laughed and crawled over her legs. She pulled her arm out from underneath her ribs and lashed out in a backwards arc with all her strength. Her fist connected with the side of the umthakathi's head, snapping it back against the wood of the bed. The weight on her legs suddenly shifted as he collapsed onto the floor. She looked up. The tokoloshe stood right before her. It bent forward, teeth bared. Thandi did the only thing she could think of. She yanked the stick from her hair and stabbed it into the tokoloshe's chest. The creature screeched in pain. Greasy smoke poured from the wound. The tokoloshe pulled out the stick and dropped it to the floor. Then, mewling in pain, it turned from her and loped slowly towards the door.

Thandi pulled herself back onto the bed and untied her legs. She had fallen awkwardly and strained one of her ankles. She rubbed it briefly, then leapt up, intending to chase after the tokoloshe.

She froze. The tokoloshe was still standing in the doorway. Its wound was leaking a steady flow of black liquid onto the dirt. Its breath was coming in ragged gasps. But it was its eyes that held her attention. They bore into Thandi with such hurt and betrayal that she felt as though she had stabbed a child. It turned from her and walked away, looking back once and waiting for her to follow.

Thirteen

She did just that for a long time, up and over hills, amazed as she went that so much of the fluid could leak from the creature and yet still it lived and managed to stay far enough away from her that she could not catch it. Finally, however, she crested another hill. At the bottom a lake shone darkly in the moonlight. The tokoloshe had vanished.

Then she heard something crying. The tokoloshe? No, this was human. She strained her ears as a breeze flicked the sound in and out of hearing. It was the sound of a little girl.

Virtue.

Thandi ran down the hill, all thoughts of the tokoloshe driven from her mind. Her momentum carried her into the water. She splashed to a stop and looked around.

What she saw amazed her.

The tokoloshe was lying on the ground outside a small hole dug into the side of the hill. But this was not what had stunned her. It was the fact that Virtue was sitting on the ground cradling the dying creature in her lap, cooing over it and crying.

Thandi's heart leapt in fear. "Virtue!" she yelled, splashing out of the water, stumbling as she went. She righted herself, carried on running towards her sister.

"Virtue, get away from it! Don't let it touch you."

Virtue looked up as Thandi staggered to a stop, holding out her hand. "Come on, baby. Come away from the monster."

Virtue shook her head, looking puzzled through her tears. "He's not a monster. He helped me get away from the old man. He said he wanted to hurt me."

Thandi shook her head. "What? Who said? "

"The tokoloshe! He said he wouldn't let the old man hurt me like he wanted to. He hid me here."

Thandi sank to her knees. Fragments of childhood stories drifted through her mind. The tokoloshe, raping women, beating men to death with sticks. But then she thought of the boy giving her the charm, saying he did not need it, but that she would as she was old. And with that thought came other stories, not gruesome enough to make it into everyday fears: the tokoloshe making friends with children, playing with them in total innocence, protecting them like a faithful pet.

God, what had she done?

She realized the creature was staring at her. It bared its teeth and hissed. Then it rolled its tongue over its lips and grinned at her, a grin so full of malice and lasciviousness that a shudder ran through Thandi.

Then it closed its eyes and died in the arms of Virtue.

Thirteen

FRIENDS OF THE EARTH
JAMES COOPER

Everything needs a burial, because everything must return to the earth. There is no other certainty greater than this and yet it still leaves a chill in the bones, it still makes the blood sluice slower in the veins; it still fills us with an unquantifiable dread. When the realisation finally dawns that things must come to an end, it is as though our lives have been forfeit all along. How could we not have been better prepared? Every day should have been cherished and protected, not idly wasted away.

Everything needs a burial, you see, because everything must return to the earth. There is no certainty greater than this.

Hal still felt groggy from the night's events, and couldn't quite fathom why it seemed so important to walk endlessly through the January snow. It was midnight and neither he nor Frank were adequately dressed for the occasion. At some point, they had both taken leave of their senses, it seemed, though no matter how hard Hal tried, he could no longer remember what had triggered the midnight walk, nor why they had set out without their coats.

Maybe it had been a blessing in disguise, Hal thought, for the cold had quickly sobered him up, and he trudged through the falling snow with a faint headache and a distant yearning for home.

"Why are we doing this again?" Frank said, pulling up alongside him. His face was beaten red by the wind and the playful expression that he usually pulled off so effortlessly now just seemed tired and old. The snow had settled in his hair like shards of bone, as though the accumulated mass of it was trying to push him to the ground, where he would quickly become another unidentified oddity deftly concealed by the snow.

Hal felt himself shiver and pressed on, bracing himself against the unrelenting cold.

"There's something I want you to see," he told Frank, still not certain what he had in mind. "It's not too far now, I promise."

He heard Frank sigh and the wind carried it down the street like a Chinese whisper, the cadence of it changing as it was swept along.

"Can't it wait?" Frank asked.

"No," Hal said. "I want you to see it tonight. Like this. In the snow."

Frank grunted. "There'd better be either pussy or beer at the end of this, Hal, or I swear to God . . ."

Hal stopped and fresh snow bunched up at his feet. "There," he said, seeing for the first time the place that had called to him from afar. "There's something I want to show you inside."

Frank stared in irritation towards the end of the street, where the corpses of old cars stood in improbable towers, exquisitely illuminated by the snow.

"The scrap yard?" Frank said, unable to contain his frustration, though he had to admit that, in the unnatural light, the dead wrecks piled before him had an oddly fascinating quality, like something imported from a reality far removed from his own.

"It's beautiful," Hal said, stepping back to take it all in. And Frank realised that, in a peculiar way, it was. Whether it was the snow, or the added romance of midnight, or probably a combination of the two, the scrap yard had achieved a degree of symmetry and perfection it would never have been able to assume during the day. Indeed, even as Frank assessed it, he could barely credit that he was so enamoured with the place, yet he felt *privileged*, as though he was being granted access to a perspective others had been cruelly denied.

Thirteen

"It does look unusual," he said quietly, reluctant to disturb the mood.

Hal moved towards the scrap yard and Frank followed, aware that the bodies of countless jalopies were ominously poised above them. They stopped at the main gates and Hal read the sign nailed to the door: "Delaney's Salvage and Reclamation Yard". He took a quick look around, assessed the silence and began to lever himself over the gate.

Frank grabbed at his coat. "What the hell are you doing?" he said. "I don't want to actually *go in*."

Hal pulled himself free. "This isn't what I want to show you," he said. "We *have* to go in. Just stay close."

Hal nimbly pulled himself up and within seconds Frank heard a muffled thump as he launched himself into the snow.

"Jesus..." Frank muttered, clambering over the gate. "This had better be good, Hal. Seriously. I'm really not in the mood for any parlour tricks."

He landed next to Hal and the pair of them dusted themselves down, their bodies now numb to the cold, their faces pummelled and raw.

"What are we looking for exactly?" Frank said, feeling nervous and exposed.

"You'll know it when you see it," Hal said, hoping to God that he would too.

They waited a few minutes to ensure that the place wasn't guarded by dogs, and then began moving between the lines of cars, each row typically showing the same thing, vehicles mangled and torn beyond repair, their ageless ruin a testament to how everything grinds to a halt.

The strange glamour of the place that Frank had sensed outside had given way to an alarming reality, and Frank suddenly felt the oppressive violence and the urgent heat of destruction that had delivered each of the cars to this grim place long before their allotted time, where their death throes were insignificant and where they would stay buried until every asset was stripped to the bone. So it seemed to Frank now, as he looked at the dead bodies ranged before him, repulsed by how easily his irritation had been replaced by fear. There was something else, too, that troubled him, and no matter how hard he tried not to consider it, it remained with him, haunting his every step, the ghostly presences that still lingered around every car, as though each vehicle had made a sacrifice of its driver, taking something of humanity with it to compensate for its own distress.

Frank shuddered and felt a fresh gust of wind playfully meander through the yard. It echoed through the empty vessels and some of the cars rocked gleefully in their endless towers of pain. Were they singing to him, Frank thought wildly? He shook his head and hurried to catch up with Hal.

"Look, man, can we get out of here? I don't feel so good. I think maybe we made a mistake."

Hal indicated for him to be silent and pointed at a gap between the cars. "Did you see that?" he asked sharply.

Frank peered into the snow, angling for a clearer perspective between the body parts, and shook his head.

"What was it?"

"I think it was a woman," Hal said. "She was wearing a white dress. She may have been lost."

Frank resisted the urge to strangle his friend, feeling lost and disoriented himself. "It can't have been a woman," he said decisively. "It must have been a flurry of snow."

Hal shook his head, stepping down the line of cars. "No," he said. "It was definitely a woman. I think she must be looking for something too."

He set off deeper into the scrap yard and Frank felt a brief temptation to abandon him here, to whatever ghouls and monstrosities fate had assigned to

Thirteen

him as a result of his reckless behaviour. The very last thing he felt like doing right now was pursuing one of Hal's frivolous and demented amusements. He was tired and afraid, and wasn't ashamed to admit to either; all he wanted to do was lie down.

"Hal!" he shouted, chasing him down the avenue of wrecked cars. "Stop this horseshit right now. I've had enough, man. I mean it; this is ridiculous."

He drew to a halt, painfully gasping for breath, and watched a woman in a torn white dress run past him close enough to touch.

"Jesus Christ! Hal, I saw her! She's here, she's here!"

He could no longer see Hal but he heard him shout, and it seemed to Frank that his friend had drifted even further away: "Don't lose her, Frank," Hal instructed. "She needs our help. Follow her!"

Frank hesitated, not sure whether it was in his best interests to follow Hal's advice or not, but he realised that if he didn't act soon the woman would be quickly consumed by the snow. He gave chase, vaguely wondering whether he would have cause to regret it later, and spotted the woman weaving dangerously between the lines of cars.

"Wait!" he called, knowing it was futile but still driven by cliché, as everybody is when circumstances lurch beyond their grasp. "We want to talk to you!"

The woman kept running and then cast her head to one side, as though listening intently to a voice beyond Frank's perception. She drew alongside a small mountain of cars and then stopped, her white dress billowing in the snow.

Hal came coursing around the corner of the yard and saw the woman no more than five yards from where Frank was standing. He edged slowly towards them and patted Frank on the back.

"You managed to stop her," he said, unable to take his eyes from the woman.

"No," Frank said. "She just stopped. I think there's something here she wants us to see."

Frank watched the woman carefully and realised that she was wearing a ball gown, the beaded sequins busily reflecting the light. Her face was beautiful but undercut with some terrible tragedy, lost in the memory of what it was like to have a purpose and to be driven by it to the exclusion of everything else.

"Can we help you?" Hal asked tentatively.

The woman turned her eyes on him and smiled. She looked elegant and refined, untouched by the cold, and yet seemingly frozen in time.

"I think so," she said. "I've lost my car. Somebody told me it was here."

Frank cut in: "Are you aware what time it is, lady?" he said, but Hal gestured for him to remain silent.

"None of those things matter any more," the woman said, turning her attention to Frank. "Time only has meaning when you have a finite amount of it left."

Frank looked puzzled and on the verge of expressing it, and Hal quickly intervened before he got the chance.

"What car are you looking for?" he asked.

"My husband's," the woman said. "He let me borrow it. Do you think he'll be terribly upset?"

Hal shook his head, feigning a light hearted tone that he hoped wouldn't betray his fear.

"Of course not," he said. "It's just a car."

The woman looked unconvinced. "But I've killed it," she said. "Look. I think it's that one up there. They must have brought it here after the crash."

She pointed towards the top of the pile and Hal and Frank could just make out a silver Lexus, wedged into the pyramid of cars around it.

"Jesus," Frank said, and turned away appalled.

Thirteen

The front end of the Lexus had been completely destroyed, the engine block welded to the driver's seat as though the vehicle was preparing to drive itself out of the yard. It would have been difficult even to strip the front end down for parts, Frank mused, so atomised had that part of the vehicle become. Whatever it had hit, the Lexus had surrendered meekly to a superior force, and Frank began to wonder at the extent of the craziness of the woman standing before him in the snow. There was no doubt in his mind, as he looked at the demolished remains of the Lexus, that nothing had walked out of that accident alive.

"When did you say you crashed your car?" Hal asked, obviously having tuned in to the same frequency as Frank.

"Last night," the woman said, looking wistful. "I'd had a little too much to drink. I guess I must have misread the road."

Frank listened with astonishment as the woman tried to blind them with her lies. *Misread the road*? Shit, if this woman had been behind the wheel of the Lexus when it hit, she'd have been lucky to even *see* the road, let alone have time to read it.

"Lady," Frank said, growing tired of the woman's game, "take a look at that car. I guarantee that whoever *did* crash it certainly isn't walking around any scrap yard looking to be reunited with it any time soon. Do you understand?"

The woman appraised Frank with the provocative air of a woman in complete control of her fate.

"I understand your rejection of it," she said, "but I urge you to remember why you're here."

Frank looked at Hal, more confused than ever, and Hal too looked slightly bewildered now that this strange woman had called him to account.

"There's no reason for us being here at all," Frank explained, feeling a sudden rush of exasperation. "We belong somewhere else. It's just that some of us haven't realised it yet."

The woman shook her head and the flakes of snow in her hair looked like radioactive dust. "Come now, boys. That isn't true, is it Hal? We all know why we're here."

She pointed to another car in a darkened corner of the yard, presumably one that had only recently been brought in, and drew their attention to how flawlessly it deformed its space.

"Look familiar?" the woman asked, standing aside.

Hal and Frank pierced the gloom and the snow and tried to make out the features of this latest wreck. It was impossible. The car had been utterly demolished in whatever scandalous tragedy had consumed it.

"Take a closer look," the woman said. "I'm in no rush. I have all the time in the world."

Disconcerted now, Hal and Frank moved cautiously towards the car, each of them feeling a burgeoning recognition with every step they took. The midnight snow had begun to descend in waves, and they had to look hard to see what they were being shown, but finally Hal pulled back and grasped his friend by the arm.

"My God," he said softly, "it's my dad's."

Frank took a step closer and realised that Hal was correct; the wreck occupying the pool of darkness did look exactly like Hal's father's.

"It can't be his though," Frank said, laughing foolishly. "We drove to the party in it tonight. We left it on the Edgware Road."

The woman had followed them and was clearly taking no pleasure in her role as broker for the damned, despite being perfectly cast in the part.

"Look in the back," she said, unable to keep a trace of regret from her voice.

Frank and Hal obliged, craning amongst the mangled metal, to focus on the two items the woman had brought to light. They were the coats each of them had

Thirteen

brought to the party in case the night took an unexpected turn for the worse.

Frank screamed and looked at himself in the twisted mirror that was still hanging by a thread to the door. His face was fleshless and red, as was Hal's, and, in the cracked reflection, their bodies were no more functional than the car's, hideously grafted together and sustained only by a ludicrous desire to survive.

"I'm sorry," the woman whispered, already retreating towards the dark. "Truly I am."

Hal and Frank stood in the middle of the yard, no longer touched by the snow, the wind keening through the wreckage of a hundred metal coffins; the same sound the dying make, Frank thought, when they realise the grave is only a heartbeat away.

He glanced around and was unsurprised to find himself alone in Delaney's yard. He vaguely wondered why Hal had deserted him, but accepted that the moral certainty of their friendship no longer applied. He reflected briefly on what else was buried here, and why it would never be unearthed, and then, in an instant, he too was gone, too weak to offer any resistance. Blinded by what he'd suddenly become.

Thirteen

BIG MICE
ROBERT NEILSON

I never liked the house in Cavan Street. Most likely it was because we moved there after my dad left. But all the same, it was gloomy looking; sort of dispirited. As though it would like nothing better than to be knocked down.

The house itself was one of a terrace of three story red brick buildings. A flight of four granite steps led up to every front door and the small front gardens were enclosed by iron railings topped with spikes. All the paint on the doors and windows was peeling. The railings were rusty.

Inside number seventeen, where we had the top floor flat, the halls were decorated with dark brown wallpaper. The floors mouldered under worn lino which might have been blue once. Now it was a sort of scuffed grey.

Our flat comprised of three huge rooms with high ceilings. There was a monster fireplace in the sitting room but no matter how much my mother built up the fire, you'd freeze once you got more than five feet from it.

Of course we didn't always have enough money for a big fire. On the days we were short of cash, it meant going to bed early to stay warm. There was only one bedroom which mother had split into three with free-standing partitions: the type the girl used to get changed behind in old black and white films. On those early nights, she would drag in the television and rearrange the partitions so that we could both watch it from our beds.

We moved in on a bright June evening, so we had five months before we began to realise how cold it could get. It was November before the noises started.

In the beginning it wasn't so bad. All you could hear was a skittering, scratching noise under the floor. And only if you were awake late. It was worst in the kitchen. By the middle of December we stopped eating there and moved the dining table into the sitting room. It was not really a hardship. You'd hardly notice the table tucked away in the back corner.

At first, other people didn't seem to notice the skitterings, or if the did they never mentioned it. But gradually the noises got worse until you couldn't help but hear them. In the sitting room and the bedroom as well as the kitchen. And all the time. Even if we turned the telly up loud you couldn't ignore it. If you listened carefully there was squeaking and squealing also. By January it was beginning to drive my mother a bit crazy. I wouldn't go home after school until I was sure she would be back from work; nothing would persuade me to stay in that flat by myself.

The landlord was no help. It was shortly before Christmas when mother first complained to him about the noises. But it wasn't for another month, after a pile of phonecalls and after mother had already begun looking for another flat, that we got a response. He called around at half past six one evening, when we were in the middle of dinner. He was a big man with rounded shoulders and a thick neck. Hair spouted out from under his shirt collar, as thick and wiry as that on his head. He had piggy little eyes which were jammed tightly against the sides of his meaty nose. When he spoke you could see that his teeth were yellowed and broken. I didn't like him being in our home.

He frightened me. I could imagine someone like him as a murderer, despite the fact that I never saw him dressed in anything but a business suit with a white shirt underneath. It was unfortunate that the dirt which perpetually ringed the shirt's collar and cuffs spoilt the image he attempted to cultivate.

But even worse, he had a pair of Staffordshire Bull Terriers which went everywhere with him. Even if they were just sitting quietly at his feet, the dogs gave off an air of threatening malice. One of them kept on staring at me and licking his chops. I wished their leads were made of chain, even though the

Thirteen

leather looked thick and strong..

I was used to looking after myself. I had come across some right thugs playing soccer at under 15 level. For some reason they always picked on me because I was the tallest on the team; probably reckoning if they sorted me out the rest of the lads would be intimidated. But the landlord and his dogs were something else. They looked as though their whole aim in life was to scare people. And they were succeeding.

"What can I do for you, Mrs Shaw," the landlord asked, in a booming voice which made him sound as if he was shouting.

"We've got rats," Mother said.

"Rats?" He was even louder. "Rats, Mrs Shaw? We've never had rats before."

"Well you've got them now, Mr Ryan."

"Have you any evidence?"

"Listen," Mother said, holding her hands up for quiet.

For half a minute we stood in silence. One of the dogs began to strain at his leash and whimper. Ryan jerked on it viciously. "Shut up, Sykes."

The rats refused to perform. Not a sound would they make. Not a skitter or a squeak.

"Come with me," Mother said, leading the way to the kitchen. She opened a press and took out a bag of porridge. A big hole had been chewed in its side and most of the contents had spilled out. "I suppose you're going to tell me David did this?"

Ryan threw me a glance and laughed. "No, Mam," he said, holding out his hand for the offending bag. Mother passed it to him and he examined the hole carefully, grunting and nodding his head. "Mice," he said, handing it back.

"Mice?" Mother said, the word dripping disbelief.

"*Big* mice," I said.

The dogs swung their ugly heads in my direction when I spoke. I got the impression they would be glad of the opportunity to rip me limb from limb. All they required was the merest suggestion of a command from their master. Sykes's eyes narrowed. The other dog growled deep in his throat. Ryan snapped the lead. "Quiet, Bill."

Ryan retreated from the kitchen, hauling his terriers behind him. "Get yourself a dose of rat poison, Mrs Shaw," he said. "That'll take care of them."

"I put down enough rat poison to kill an elephant," Mother said.

"They didn't eat it?"

"They ate it all right. Lapped it up like mother's milk." She went to another press; the one that held the washing powder and bleach and the like. The box she took out was red and featured a picture of a rat on the front. This box also had a hole chewed in its side. "I didn't even have to disguise it. They couldn't get enough."

Ryan stood there staring at the box. Nobody spoke. Above our heads something with four feet and claws raced along the space between our ceiling and the attic floor. Ryan's head jerked upwards and a curse escaped his lips. "Excuse me, Mam," he said. The hair on the necks of both dogs stood on end. Their teeth bared and a terrifying, low-pitched growl purred out of them. I was glad they were staring at the ceiling, not at me.

"I'll get you something to put down for them," Ryan said. "Something the chemist doesn't stock."

The next day he returned with a brown paper bag containing a white powder with azure speckles through it. Mother dutifully poured powder onto half a dozen saucers and crumbled a Hobnob onto each as bait. As she had done on previous occasions, Mother laid the poison down at bed time. In the morning we eagerly

Thirteen

checked the saucers. They remained exactly as they had been the previous night: the poison and the biscuits were untouched. For another week we watched for a change. Eventually the Hobnob crumbs disappeared. The mice were not only big, they were intelligent.

Mother left it for a couple of weeks before contacting Mr Ryan again. Jokingly she wondered which was worse, the vermin or the landlord. In my opinion it was a close run thing, the vermin winning by a short head. But only because the noises were getting louder. It sounded as if there were armies of them in the spaces between the walls, above the ceilings and beneath the floors.

Mother had begun storing all our food in biscuit tins, collected from other members of the family. Granny was putting pressure on her to move back into the family home. But that was something she would never do. That would mean that my dad had beaten her. In some ways I think she would have preferred to move back in with him and put up with the drunken rows again.

For a month my mother telephoned Ryan on a daily basis. At first he tried to brush off the seriousness of the situation, later he began to promise action but failed to follow through. It was not until she threatened to stop paying the rent that he actually called.

He turned up with his attendant Staffordshire Bull Terriers on a Saturday, at lunch time. It was as though he wanted to cause us as much inconvenience as possible. When I answered the door to his knock the dogs growled at me and one of them, Sykes, barked. Ryan merely flashed a broken tooth grin and pushed his way into the flat without an invitation.

"Mrs Shaw," he said in his loud voice. "Are you there, Mrs Shaw? I haven't got all day to waste on your petty complaints."

Mother bustled out from the kitchen drying her hands on a dish cloth. I could see that she was annoyed. "I don't consider rats living in my home to be a petty matter," she said. "I doubt Dublin Corporation would either."

Mr Ryan's mouth set in a tight line. He spoke between clenched teeth. "Are you threatening me, Mrs Shaw?"

"Just stating facts, Mr Ryan," she replied. "David, would you get that shoe, please?"

I headed for the bedroom and returned carrying a pair of Doc's. The toe of the right shoe had had been gnawed off.

"Mice?" she said.

Ryan kept quiet.

"Big mice," I said.

The dogs stared at me, straining on their chains. Bill's top lip curled away from his teeth in a silent snarl. I looked from the dog to its master. They looked incredibly alike.

There was a gap of five paces between Mother and Mr Ryan. He halved it and held out his hand towards her. Both of us stared without understanding. The dogs shuffled forward, whining. My eyes followed a line from Ryan's outstretched hand to the dog's throats. The line was filled in by the links of steel chains. My mother took a step back, widening the gap again. She looked really jumpy, as though calculating her chances of making the bedroom before the dogs got her.

"I'm going to leave Bill and Sykes with you tonight. They'll take care of the problem. They've seen off a lot bigger than a few rats in their time." He grinned down at the dogs. Their barrel chests seemed to swell with pride. Sykes gave me a cocky glance which seemed to say, 'You're lunch'.

"I'm sorry, Mr Ryan, that's just not suitable."

"What?" he snapped. "Now you see here..."

"There's no way those dogs are coming into this flat while we're still here," she said. "I'll have to make arrangements for us to stay with my mother."

Thirteen

"I'm not leaving them on their own."

It was the first time I had seen Ryan show any concern for a living thing. Perhaps he had a good side that we hadn't seen.

"Then you can make arrangements to stay with them, Mr Ryan," Mother said.

Our landlord's mouth opened and closed but no sound sounds came out. I bit back on a smile as I thought how much like a goldfish he looked.

"You're not nervous of staying here by yourself, are you, Mr Ryan?" Mother asked.

His lips and his tongue were unable to form proper words. All he could get out were grunts.

"Afraid of the mice?" I said, daring the malevolent stare of the dogs.

"I can't just drop everything to spend the night in your flat," Ryan said.

"Of course not," Mother said. "You'll need time to make arrangements. What'll we say, tomorrow? The next day?"

"Well, I don't know. I'll have to check."

I realised he wasn't scared. Just lazy. He didn't want to give up whatever it was he did with his nights in order to solve our problem. It was too much like work.

"I don't think I can wait more than a day or two," Mother said. "But I'm sure the corporation will be able to help me."

"Now see here, Mrs Shaw," he blustered.

"No, Mr Ryan, you're the one who needs to see. I'm not prepared to put up with the rats any longer and that's that. Either you fix the problem or I get the Corporation to do it. I doubt they'll be able to do it at once and I doubt they'll leave us or your other tenants here in the meantime."

I was proud. My mother was taking on this bully-boy, head to head, and she was winning. Even the dogs were backing off.

"And I doubt any of your tenants will be paying rent if they're moved out," she said. "What do you think?"

"Wouldn't it be terrible if the Corporation wouldn't let us back in," I said, doing my best to sound as if I meant it.

Mother looked at me, following my lead. "You don't think they'd condemn the house because of the rats, do you, David?"

"Who knows what damage they've done, chewing away at stuff under the floors."

Ryan interrupted. "Can you make arrangements to spend tonight with your mother, Mrs Shaw?"

Mother shrugged. "Probably."

"Then do it." He turned and went to the door. "I'll be back by five o'clock." He opened the door, then added, "If that's all right with you."

Mother nodded and rewarded his attempt at politeness with a smile. She was enjoying herself. It was nice for her to win for a change.

Granny made a big fuss over us coming to stay and insisted on cooking a big Sunday lunch the next day, with a roast, three types of vegetable and mountains of mashed potato. Granddad carved the meat at the table as though it was a big family occasion like Christmas or something. Everything anybody said seemed to be funny and we laughed a lot. I knew it was from relief. The rats had caused Mother more worry than I had imagined, that was obvious. Now that there was a good chance the problem would be solved she could afford to admit, to herself as much as anybody, just how concerned she had been.

Going home on the bus was almost like the start of a holiday. Mother was actually keen to get there. She was annoyed that Ryan had left his dinner plate unwashed and dirty coffee cups in the sitting room. But no matter how hard we listened there were no rat noises. Mother wrapped her arms around me and gave

Thirteen

me a huge hug, something she hadn't done since I outgrew her during the summer.

We walked around looking for signs of our landlord's activities while we had been away. But at least, in that, he had been tidy. We checked the bins but there was nothing. No evidence of a single rodent. Then it struck me: the dogs would have eaten them. I decided to say nothing to Mother.

That night we went to bed in silence for the first time in months. Lying in bed, I strained to hear any unusual sounds. There were the usual creaks you would expect from an old house, creaks I had not been able to hear over the sound of the rats. And for the first time I noticed, very faintly, the sound of rock music from our downstairs neighbours. They had asked once or twice if the music disturbed us; they liked to play it loud. But we had never been able to hear it. I drifted off to sleep with the faint sound of Pearl Jam as a lullaby.

The golden silence lasted five days. By the following weekend I was sure I heard skittering under the floorboards. For a while I couldn't be certain. The noises were infrequent and not very loud. But on Sunday night they returned to full volume. Mother telephoned Mr Ryan at once. As usual she was unable to catch him and the messages she left on his answering machine got no response.

She was so angry that on Tuesday she went around to his house but got no reply when she knocked at the door. She called on his neighbours but they were of no help. It appeared that no-one had seen him for over a week. Not since the Saturday he spent in our flat, to be exact.

The next day Mother came home and announced that she had found us a new flat. We could move in on the next weekend. Although there were only three more nights to spend in Cavan Street, it felt like an eternity. The rats grew louder than ever, snuffling in the walls as though chasing an elusive scent. I felt like a little kid again, wrapping myself tightly in my bedclothes so that the boogey man won't get me.

But I had reason to be frightened. I didn't tell Mother; I didn't want to make things any worse for her than they already were. I found something while I was packing. Piled up in the corner beside my wardrobe. For a long time I couldn't work out what exactly I had discovered. There were a dozen small, brass rings - well, yellowy metal anyway. Tiny things. Smooth on top but ragged on the reverse side. Piled with them was a collection of small change amounting to eighty nine pence.

I think, I'm almost certain, the circular brass pieces are the eyelets from a pair of boots. I tried to think if there should be any other part of a human that would be indigestible. Like the zipper off a pair of trousers. If my thinking was correct, that should be somewhere around.

On Saturday morning we did one last clean up before leaving. I found a round metal disc in the space between the cooker and the press beside it. The metal was reasonably soft and there was a series of indentations on it. Teeth marks, I was certain. Etched into the disc was the word *Sykes* and Mr Ryan's telephone number.

Mother carried the last box of our belongings into the hall and waited for the van to arrive. From the corner of my eye I caught an impression of motion. The fridge moved as something pushed along behind it. Something large. Large enough to eat a bull terrier. At least. The big mice were coming out into the open. I dropped Sykes' identity disc and ran to the door. They could have the flat. We didn't need it any more. Neither, I suspected, did Mr Ryan.

LOOKING BACK
MARK PATRICK LYNCH

John Croswell awoke from a night of interrupted sleep to the soft sound of a zip being undone and the scented suggestion of pencil lead teasing the limits of his senses' range.

He blinked his glued together eyes a couple of times, trying to clear the gummy stickiness his sight fought to escape each morning, and, with stinging redness swarming in his vision, he forced the world into focus. John had been having trouble with dry eyes for as long as he could remember, since adulthood really. (John considered adulthood bequeathed to anyone who had made it past forty-five without either a case of drug dependency or a criminal record to their name.) But it was only in the last few months that he'd felt the pain enough for him to approach his physician about them. The optician had given him the all clear already; in every other respect John's eyes were as sharp as they had ever been. And his doctor, a softly spoken Scotsman who smelled of drink first thing of a Monday surgery, assured him that replacement tears were all that John required to keep his eyes good and fit.

The viscous tears were greasy and came in a short pale tube John squeezed a thin white worm from every morning and administered to his inside lower eyelids. The tears were cool and easing after the initial stinging sensation left, and John's eyes felt the moisture with all the relief of a parched lawn come summer rain.

Today, though, as his eyes swam into focus, John found the stinging ache in his eyes no longer there. And his memory of the scent of pencils and the unzipping sound now clashed with the chink of soft wooden sticks being bundled one upon the other, as if shuffled by a magician about the task of conjuring prophecy. *Dream,* he thought. *Must have been a dream.* But the memory lingered like a tongue come back to worry a loose tooth.

He sat up in bed and turned his head to the bedroom door. The doctor had said his eyes would probably start producing tears naturally after a few doses of the liquid grease, and it looked like this had happened. There was no dryness beneath his lids. The weight he normally found in his eyes was gone. And that sucking sensation he experienced when he blinked slowly was no longer there.

Fantastic! What a great start to the morning. Although John had never voiced the fear, he had often worried about his sight, and the dry eyes and constant ache on a morning had bothered him silly these last months. Even the assurances of the whisky doctor had done little to assuage his secret fears.

"It happens sometimes. No one really knows why. There're all sorts of things can lead to it. Suffering from a lot of stress lately? It's most often the case. Tires you out, and your eyes want to go back to stress-free times."

Oddly enough, or not, John hadn't been stressed at all. Everything he could possibly want to go right was doing so. He had a nice home, a wife he loved and didn't cheat on (and who, in return, he was sure, returned that love and didn't cheat on him either). His daughter was at Edinburgh University studying English, and she had a nice boyfriend from a good family. John's mortgage payments were at an end, he didn't have a bad pension deal, and he was now head of his sales division in the plastics firm. Another five years and he could take early retirement without his accountant breaking into a sweat and still treat himself to a new car every three years.

"John! Jo-ohn! Better be awake. It's nearly time."

His mother was calling him from downstairs. For a moment John almost forgot she'd been dead for close to a decade, felled by a heart attack that had seemed like a blessing back when he was in his late thirties.

Thirteen

"John. Come on. Move yourself. Andy'll be here soon."

When he heard his mother calling him the second time, he froze. The first time he heard her shout he could have put down to hearing things. How often since she had died had he heard her say his name when there was no one about, or thought he glimpsed her gliding through a busy throng in the shopping arcades? They were all misperceived visions or echoes, his brain wanting something it couldn't have. He'd mentally chided his parents often enough for giving him a single syllable name, one that could be misheard in a thousand daily activities. "John," said the washing machine on its final churn. "John," went the trucks barrelling along the York road by the house he shared with Jackie. "John," said his mother, dead all these years, from downstairs.

The realisation slowly dawned that he wasn't in his bed: except on one level he knew perfectly well that he was. The bed was different than the one he'd fallen asleep in; it was narrower for a start, and shorter. He must have slept with his legs curled up into his chest. How long had it been since he'd slept in such a position? Long before he'd married and started sharing a bed regularly, that was for sure.

This was the bed of his childhood home. And the wallpaper, now he came to scrutinise it, was the painted woodchip of his youth, his carpet the nondescript brown he'd always remembered it as. The curtains were thick and dull. The light shade was a paper construct, built from a kit they'd bought at Woolworths in the city centre. His wife Jackie was gone; he was alone in his single child's bed of yesteryear. And his mother was calling him down to breakfast.

John slid from the covers (sheets, not a duvet, he noticed) and was astonished to find his pyjamas, heavy flannel with a knotted cord tie holding them together at the waist, a run of large buttons to the top of his chest, were the same as his boyhood too. They fit him snugly as well, although he was sure his legs should have split the fabric, his breathing heavy chest sprayed the buttons everywhere. He moved to the creaking old wardrobe, a brown device of nightmare conjuring proportions that always seemed to sway open in his mind's eye at night, releasing a fear to take hold of him and plunge him into its terrible darkness.

A mirror hung on the inside of the door, and in its reverse John saw himself the way he had been aged nine. The silver glint had swung the room around, almost a mirror to his own dizziness, and there he stood, young and fresh-faced, smooth of skin, thick of hair, and clear-eyed as a crystal stream. Gone was the greying sight he'd forced his eyes to endure each morning for the last few years; no more developing gut, hairs sprouting from his ears and nose. Here he was vital and new, a whole life still ahead of him. And yet . . . And yet he couldn't remember a thing about how it was to be a nine-year-old.

Am I dreaming, he wondered? Is this all an illusion? At the core of him fluttered a panicked feeling that threatened to overwhelm him, confine him to madness.

His mother called again, this time more insistent, demanding he get himself ready because she didn't want another letter complaining at his poor time keeping. John remembered his school days with little clarity, but the mention of school letters reminded him of the times he had come home holding a sealed envelope for his parents. And the inevitable arguments about being late for school that would follow.

In a strange motion that was too real to be called floating, John sorted school clothes from his wardrobe, tugging on a sweater and fastening trousers that seemed so clumsy and unwieldy, yet which also brought a flood of familiarity back . . . if not actual memories. In the bathroom he cleaned his face, washing with soap and water in a way he never would have done as a child (the youthful John

Thirteen

would have wiped a damp flannel across his face and called the matter of washing for the day at an end, and proud of the fact he'd be too), and he marvelled at the face free of stubble and slow-to-respond flesh. He was blemish free in the mirror. There were no wrinkles; his eyes did not look tired, his skin was smooth as cream. The large pores he'd develop across his nose and forehead as he grew older were not yet in evidence. All that smudged the delicacy of his youth was a spray of gentle freckles, arching across his soft nose. And even then they seemed to fit his well-made face like the speckles on a bird's egg.

In this mirror, in this bathroom, he had drawn a disposable razor across his father's cheeks countless times, scraping away soap and bristles in long easy swipes. The smell of that soap and his father's heady aroma filled his head for a moment and John wondered if this wasn't a dream at all, but something very real which was *actually happening*. Perhaps he really was experiencing this.

His heart pounded at the thought. What if he were trapped here forever, caught in a loop of his youth? No, that couldn't happen. This was a dream, albeit an incredibly vivid one. But wait a second. This wasn't all bad. It would be over soon, he knew, surely. It must be a dream: logic dictated it be so. It would end before too long, and probably sooner rather than later. But mightn't he have a chance to see his mother again? His father would already have been up and away to work, but he could still experience the joy of seeing his mum again, years before she became frail and unsure. He could eradicate the memories of senility and that slow loss of expression she had slipped beneath in the old people's home.

John went to the top of the landing, and with only a little trepidation made his way down the stairs, wondering at how narrow they seemed in comparison with his memory of them being high and wide. Descending, John took note of all the colours he had forgotten had ever adorned these walls. The wallpaper's looping, flower-dazed, patterns were astonishingly garish, and the lightweight trim phone on the shelf at the bottom of the stairs brought back the little choice of phone the company would allow you to have.

His mother awaited him.

He walked into the kitchen and smiled at her, busy at the cooker warming milk for his cereal. "I don't know why I bother, I should just let you drink this cold."

John sat quietly, just watching his mum pouring the milk into a bowl already filled with cornflakes. He put a spoon to the cereal and lifted it to his lips, taking a mouthful to find himself in the echoing hallway of the church school. How had that happened? Streams of pupils were rushing by him; he was jostled as he came to a sudden halt. He must have been walking too, but why had his adult consciousness skipped the journey from home to school? He felt like a mind dropped in a body from a great height. Disorientation spun his thoughts around as he tried to get a grip on his senses. He wanted the experience of having a mother again, young and vibrant and fit to attend to his fears and needs.

One minute he had been in the kitchen of his old house, now he was in the middle of a school hall, the luminous shouts and echoes of children making his head hurt; his mind felt compressed by the child's skull he wore. People he recognised but couldn't put names to were talking to him, calling him on as they rode the rapids of the crowded corridor. They didn't know he was different, couldn't see he wasn't the person they thought they knew. Where was he going? What was next on his timetable? He felt the panic of a thousand anxiety dreams rush through his veins, skipping his heart along on a string.

John's eyes no longer hurt, as he saw all that surrounded him with pristine clarity and yet also with a dreamily detached panic. He followed his classmates through familiar unfamiliarity, along corridors and through doors, anxious not to lose sight of them and become lost in these strange halls. What lessons might he

Thirteen

have to endure today? What questions might he be called upon to answer? Would the leering giants who were adults punish and humiliate him? With a sinking feeling of being lost forever, John felt his inadequacy at who he was, at who he had always been, shrink his mind until it no longer seemed too large for the skull it was trapped in, and found himself contained within an echoing trap of bony darkness that seemed too huge to ever fill.

THE PERFECT SPOT
MATTHEW BATHAM

They chose the spot because it attracted the sun. It was not the most accessible place; hidden behind newly converted warehouses, it could be reached only via a narrow alleyway between two apartment buildings and a flight of treacherous steps worn smooth and more lethal, by centuries-worth of local explorers, workers and perhaps one or two murderers come to row their victim to the middle of the Thames and drop them unceremoniously into its depths.

Michael found it. He was always walking ten paces ahead of everyone else. He scampered onto the road, grinning.

"Here, here!" he squawked, jabbing his finger at the passage between the buildings.

"What's here?" asked Tom.

"The perfect spot!" Michael's wide face already red from the heat, glowed. "Quick," he called, darting back down the alleyway, as if the perfect spot was going somewhere.

Carol laughed, squeezed Tom's arm and followed Michael.

Michael held the most interest for her. She had pondered Tom's broody, sometimes stern personality, wondered about its compatibility with her own. She had pondered it at length, because Tom was by far the most attractive of the two men, but his earnest eyes always seemed to be accusing someone of something.

Tom did not quicken his pace. He waited for the fourth member of the work excursion, Wendy, to catch up. She had been left to buy sandwiches and cans of cola from the staff shop. Tom relieved her of the small burden and nodded towards the backs of Carol and Michael. "The perfect spot apparently."

Wendy glanced at her watch. "I need to be back at two. I've got a meeting with a new writer."

Tom nodded and led the way down the passage to the top of the stairs, which he viewed with disapproval.

"Come on," Michael shouted, already on the bank, throwing pebbles into the dark water.

"I'm coming," called Tom, taking a nervous step downwards. "Will you be okay?" he asked Wendy, but she had already overtaken him, jumping from step to step.

"Would you like me to take the bag?" she asked, turning back.

"No, it's fine." Tom tried to look confident.

By the time he reached the bank, the others had set up base, sitting on jackets, skirts and trousers hitched up to bare white legs.

"At last!" laughed Michael, holding out his hand for the bag.

Tom spread his own jacket on the small rocks and sat near to Wendy who was squinting into the sun, her pale, freckled face bound to burn.

"Perfect spot," repeated Michael, proud of his find.

"Why haven't we found it before?" asked Carol, who had stripped to a bikini.

"You came prepared." Michael surveyed her slim body. "Prepared for anything," said Carol with a grin and a wink.

Tom frowned in Carol's direction, then stared across the water. His view of the south bank was partly blocked by a passing pleasure cruise, the megaphone enhanced voice blaring out muffled information about Canary Wharf and Dickens novels.

"What kind of people go on those boats?" asked Carol, rubbing sun lotion into her legs.

"Tourists, I would imagine," replied Tom.

"Sad bastards, more like," laughed Michael. "American sad bastards mainly."

Thirteen

They were silent for a while, basking contentedly.

"Has anyone read any Dickens?" asked Tom suddenly. "What?" Michael, who had been lying with his head on Carol's thigh, lifted it slightly to stare at Tom.

"The man on the boat said something about Dickens as it went past," Tom explained.

"Oh." Michael raised his eyebrows, and rested his head again. "No, I haven't."

"I have," said Wendy, who was still sitting upright, looking into the sun, eyes closed. "Great writer. Better than any of the shit I have to deal with."

"I always found him a bit boring," said Carol. "Apart from that one with the songs - Oliver!"

Wendy's mouth dropped open.

"Not in the same league as Jackie Collins, aye Carol?" mocked Michael.

"Sod off," Carol responded. "Unless you want to deal with that mail-out yourself this afternoon."

Michael gave her calf a brief caress with the back of his hand. "It wasn't a good time to be living and working in London," said Tom. "Homelessness, real poverty, lots of desperate people."

"Bit like now then," said Michael, almost serious.

"Much worse," said Tom.

"It's hard to imagine it being any worse," said Wendy. "If I had money the first thing I'd do was give some of it towards helping the homeless."

"What do you mean 'if you had money?" asked Carol with a smirk. "I typed up your contract, don't forget, you're a lot better off than me."

"Hardly a millionaire, though," returned Wendy. She was concerned Carol would use the picnic to try and break down the barriers that existed in the office between publishing executives and their secretaries.

"It's all relative," said Tom. "To someone who sleeps in a doorway every night you'd seem incredibly wealthy."

"And how much do you give to the homeless, Tom?" asked Michael, without stirring.

"Not enough," said Tom.

Carol suddenly tutted loudly.

"What?" Michael opened his eyes.

"Someone else is on our beach."

Carol was glaring down the bank beyond the steps to the alleyway. The others looked too.

The intruder was sitting with his knees pulled to his chest, like a child sitting in a school assembly, but he was not young - perhaps forty, and dressed in a dark suit. A black brief case sat beside him like a faithful dog.

Carol tutted again. "Your perfect spot's been invaded, Michael."

"Where did he come from?" asked Wendy. "I didn't see him come down the steps."

"You've had your eyes closed," said Tom.

"Been watching me have you?" asked Wendy with a faint smile.

Tom blushed and looked back towards the man in the suit.

"He must be hot," said Carol. "Why doesn't he take off his jacket?"

"He's probably not stopping," said Michael, with a sly grin. "He's just dropping off the briefcase."

"What do you mean?" asked Carol.

"Bomb," whispered Michael in a menacing tone.

"Don't be stupid." Carol tutted again and closed her eyes.

"He might be right," said Wendy, "He doesn't look like the sort of person that would sit on a river bank for his lunch break."

"He doesn't look like a terrorist either," said Carol.
"Doesn't he?" asked Michael.
"He looks like he belongs in the city," said Wendy.
"He looks like every other businessman in a suit," said Tom. "Anyway forget about him, what were we talking about?"
"Desperate people," said Carol, faking a yawn.
"I'm desperate," said Michael jumping up, "Desperate for a piss."
Carol scowled. "Make sure you do it a long way from me. I don't want it running down into my hair or something."
"Why don't you come with me and give your approval," suggested Michael, already unzipping his fly.
"Sod off," said Carol, but she was smiling.
"I wonder how much the new government is planning to invest in the homeless?" said Tom, trying to resurrect the conversation.
"Only as much as they have to," said Wendy. "The National Health and Education are the big vote winners."
"They've already won the votes."
Wendy shrugged.
"Homeless people can't vote. Why bother with them when you can please the electorate by pumping money into their kids' education?"
Tom nodded. His gaze followed two canoes lined with muscular rowers as they sped past.
"Maybe we should do something," said Wendy.
"Like what?"
"Start a charity."
"There're already charities."
"We could get one of our writers to donate the profits from a book to Shelter, or something."
"Why would they do that? How many of our writers are likely to feel that generous?"
Wendy thought about the writers she represented. Most of them too full of their own importance to have room for a charitable thought.
"Michael's taking a long time," said Carol, rolling on her side and staring at the rotting wooden pillar behind which he had disappeared.
"I'm sure he's okay," said Wendy. She glanced again at the stranger.
"He hasn't moved."
Tom followed her gaze.
"He's just relaxing."
"He doesn't look very relaxed. I wonder what is in the briefcase."
"Files, reading glasses, sandwiches wrapped in tinfoil," suggested Tom.
"Maybe Michael's right. Maybe he is planning to plant a bomb under one of the office buildings."
"I doubt it."
"So do I," admitted Wendy, rubbing her left leg, which was already feeling sore, despite the lotion. She turned to ask Carol if she could use some more, but Carol had gone in search of Michael.
"Looks like the love birds are finally getting it together," she said, nodding at Carol's crushed red jacket.
Tom gave the row of wooden support columns behind which Michael and Carol had now both disappeared a disapproving look.
"It's like quicksand behind there," he said. "Did you see it as we passed? They've probably both sunk into it and suffocated."
"Charming," said Wendy. "Nothing like giving young love your blessing."
"What's love got to do with it?" asked Tom.

109

Thirteen

"As Tina Turner once said," laughed Wendy.

Tom nearly smiled.

"Careful," said Wendy, "You're face might crack."

"Don't," sighed Tom. "I know I'm too serious sometimes. I just don't find much to smile about these days."

"Oh dear."

Wendy was trying to lighten the atmosphere she had inadvertently created.

"Don't you ever wonder why you're so lucky?" asked Tom.

"How do you mean?"

"I don't know." Tom paused for a moment. "Don't you ever wonder when the really bad thing is going to happen to you?"

"The what?"

"Sometimes I lie awake wondering when the horrible thing is going to happen to me - the thing that's going to shatter my life."

"Oh God, Tom, don't think so much."

"I can't help it. You must think like that too. I get so panicky sometimes. I lie there hugging a pillow praying - not sure who to, but really praying - that nothing bad will happen to any of the people I care about. That's the worse fear, something happening to my sister or one of her kids."

"It just means you care. Most people don't. They're quite happy for everyone else to suffer as long as they're okay. You're not like that, which is nice."

"I'm not so sure. If there was a pill I could take to stop me feeling any pain if something awful did happen to someone close to me, I wonder if I'd be so bothered."

Wendy went to continue her tribute to Tom's better qualities, but her attention was caught suddenly by the stranger.

"What's he doing?" she asked, mouth wide.

Tom looked along the bank, shielding his eyes against the sun with his hand.

The man was dancing, twirling round like a ballerina, leaping and prancing - ludicrous in his pinstripe suit. But more disturbing was the sound he was making - a desperate wailing, like a fox on heat.

"He's mad," whispered Wendy, as if the man was more likely to hear this remark than any other that had been made about him by the group. "Or just a chronic attention seeker."

"Maybe we should make a move," said Tom, looking nervously at the stranger who was now punching the air as he skipped once more around his briefcase then fell to the ground, sobbing.

Carol and Michael ran giggling back down the bank.

"Crack open the cola!" yelled Michael. "We're celebrating!"

"What exactly?" asked Wendy, pulling two cans from the carrier back and holding them out for the panting couple to take.

"Our love," cackled Carol.

Michael joined in with the laughter, slapping her on the back as if she was a colleague who had just clinched a deal. Tom took a can of cola and tugged at the ring pull. It snapped in his fingers, cola fizzing through the insufficient crack he had created.

"Here," said Wendy, taking the can from him and prizing the broken seal open with a long, strong nail.

"So what have you two been talking about?" asked Carol jovially, moving her jacket so that it was not in the shadow of the warehouse behind.

"Oh nothing much," said Wendy. "Putting the world to rights I think they call it. I've been telling Tom he cares too much about other people. Oh, and that freak's been doing some kind of war dance," she nodded towards the spot where the stranger had fallen.

Thirteen

"He's gone," said Tom.

"His case is still there," said Carol, pressing a hand to her chest.

"Shit, look, he's left the case."

"Told you," said Michael, humourlessly.

"What should we do?" asked Wendy. "Maybe he's just taking a pee."

"Where?" asked Michael. "The only cover is that way." He jabbed a thumb over his shoulder. "And he wasn't there just now."

"Calm down," said Tom. "I'll go and take a look."

"Don't," squealed Carol grabbing his arm. "It might blow up in your face."

"It's just a brief case," said Tom, striding towards it.

For a moment the others remained huddled together, watching him go like frightened children whose father is checking the wardrobe for monsters. Then Wendy broke away and followed him. "Careful," she called.

But Tom was already kneeling by the briefcase, glancing around for a sign of its owner.

"Tell me when he's opened it," said Carol screwing her eyes closed, and digging her nails into Michael's arm.

She heard the disproportionately loud sound of the clasps being released and the click as the briefcase lid flipped open. Confident that there was no bomb, they approached the spot where Tom was crouched. He plucked something from the case, a note, and read it. He put a hand to his face and handed the paper to Wendy.

"What is it?" asked Michael, glancing over her shoulder. "I think we should get away from here," said Wendy. Michael snatched the note from Wendy and scanned it.

"I thought he was weird," he said. "Look at this."

Carol read the note aloud: "*I have never heard such a bunch of bleeding heart liberals talk so much bullshit in my life. How loud does a cry for help have to be before you take notice?*"

Carol frowned. "What's he talking about?"

A gunshot punctuated the question. Carol screamed, grabbing Michael's arm and turning to face the approaching man.

"No more bullshit today," he said and fired the gun again, obliterating the top of Carol's head. They all screamed this time, staring from Carol's twitching corpse to the suited man, as he fired again. This time Wendy fell, clutching her chest, blood spouting through her fingers.

"Wait....!" Tom held up his hands as if they could offer any resistance to the weapon.

"For what?" asked the man, shooting Michael in the back as he ran for the steps back to the road. "For you to stop bleating on about how much you want to help people and actually start doing something?

"How could you hear that?" Tom staggered backwards.

"Just so you know," said the man, slipping the gun into the inside pocket of his jacket, as if it were a wallet. "If you had actually come over to ask me what was wrong, I wouldn't have killed anyone. You can blame yourself for this," he nodded at each of Tom's dead colleagues. "That'll give you something to think about next time you wake up in the night. Now you've really got a reason to pray. I'd pray hard if I were you. Blately isn't a common name. It won't be hard to trace your family."

"How...?" Tom glanced down at his security pass, pinned, as always, to the front of his jacket.

"See you later, maybe," said the man, and he strode past Tom, grabbing the briefcase as he went. Tom watched him stroll casually along the bank. Watched until he was a dark speck. He didn't notice that residents from the luxury flats

Thirteen

overlooking the river had surrounded him and the corpses.

"Who did this?" someone asked him - a man, a woman, he couldn't see, didn't care.

"I did," he whispered.

Thirteen

THE SHOW
THOMAS GILBERT

It was my first time on TV in just over twenty-eight years, but seeing as I was only two days old when I was on the evening news in a report on hospital hygiene, I was pretty nervous about it.

This time would be different though. For a start, I'd actually be awake, and secondly I stood a good chance of winning a considerable amount of money if I could display the same amount of general knowledge in front of the cameras and studio audience as I did in front of the TV and my girlfriend when we were at home. It was actually Laura who was responsible for all of this. She was the one who suggested I use my intellect for a purpose other than annoying her, and she dialled the contestant application number herself before thrusting the cordless phone into my reluctant hand. My mild protests abated as soon as the recorded, accent-less female voice on the other end had invited me to answer three multiple-choice questions with my touch-tone buttons. I did so, then left my personal details, pretty confident that I'd done well.

The next couple of days I spent in a mildly paranoid frame of mind, convinced that the game-show producers wouldn't accept applicants who got all of the three phone questions right. However, I eventually received a call on my mobile from a withheld number. I answered it (I usually never answer it unless I know who's calling – I have a crazy ex-girlfriend who makes sporadic attempts to get back in touch, and I'm always frightened it might be her) and spoke to a lady called Jane.

"I'd like to invite you to a screening session," she explained. "It'll take a couple of hours but it's usually a good laugh and there's free coffee."

"Free coffee? Sold!"

She laughed at this, even though it wasn't particularly funny, and it was a pleasant sound, which made me smile.

"Good. There is a screening on Tuesday at noon in The Rehearsal Rooms, Brixton High Street, third studio. Will you be able to attend that?"

"Yeah, no problem. I'm a school teacher and it's half-term then, so I'm free all week."

I don't know why I'd volunteered that information. It hadn't been necessary and the mildly paranoid frame of mind I mentioned earlier made me think I was sounding like I wanted a date with her. Her silent pause added weight to my theory and I gently hit my forehead with my free left hand in a comical gesture of self-reprimand which attracted a couple of smiles from some of the people on the high Street who noticed me.

"Okay," Jane said, mercifully ending the awkward silence. "I'll see you then."

The screening session had been quite fun. I'd been slightly nervous about meeting Jane and had lain awake some nights, Laura snoring softly beside me, wondering what she looked like. I imagined her as blonde with bright blue eyes and the fashion sense of a GAP model, and when I first saw her I congratulated myself on a pretty accurate guess. She strolled into the studio and announced who she was to me and the thirty or so other applicants, who ranged from students to those in final preparation for the grave (one or two had already started to rot). The nervous conversation which strangers usually have with each other ground to a halt.

"Good afternoon, everybody! I'm Jane, the assistant producer of *Who's In Charge?* I'd like to thank you for making it down here today; I know some of you have made quite an effort.

"Okay, so, basically, everyone will be interviewed by either myself or Dan" –

Thirteen

everyone turned to face Dan, who Jane had indicated with a sweep of her arm, before looking at Jane again – "but it will be very informal, so that we get an idea of what you're like. So just relax – be yourself! You'll all be asked to do a quick quiz, similar in format to *Who's In Charge?* But that will be supervised by our colleague, Joseph Murdoch, who will join us in about an hour."

Unfortunately, I was interviewed by Dan, a balding Scottish man in his early forties. Even still, he made me feel incredibly nervous. All I could think was 'This man has the power – the *power* – to put people on television. Okay, it's just a stupid quiz show hosted by one of those overly buoyant hosts who look as though they spend every minute they're not on TV in a sun bed, but still... TV!'.

Despite my nerves, I think I came across okay, and I did well on the quiz afterwards too. I didn't get to talk to Jane (although I did have some of the free coffee she'd promised).

One week later I received a letter informing me I'd been successful. Filming would take place in exactly one month at the LWT studios in central London, and I had to leave a message on Jane's answer phone to confirm I'd be there.

Laura was proud of me and before long all of our mutual friends knew about my forthcoming TV appearance. To begin with, Laura was even more excited about me being on TV than I was, and she'd force me to watch every episode of *Who's In Charge?* while she calculated how much I was likely to win. I think that in her mind she had the money spent before I'd even come close to winning it. Poor Laura. If only she'd known what was going to happen.

Laura and I took the overhead from Welwyn Garden City to the LWT studios. I'd tried on four or five shirts before eventually deciding on the first one I'd tried, and Laura spent as long getting ready as she would do before a night out, even though the audience were always sat in almost total darkness.

"Are you nervous?" Laura asked me as we stepped off the train.

"A bit," I lied. I was more than a bit nervous – in fact, I felt like getting the next train back to Welwyn Garden City. Only Laura's proud smile made me continue to the studios.

Laura and I presented ourselves at reception. I was whisked away for a pre-filming briefing and Laura was rather rudely told to wait outside behind a security gate until they were letting members of the audience in.

Dan gave me and the four other contestants our briefing and we were quickly introduced to the host so that we wouldn't be star-struck once the cameras started to roll. I noticed one of the other contestants attempt to shake his hand. The host looked at the outstretched hand with disgust before turning away, leaving a very upset looking old lady in his wake.

"Oh," I heard her say. A pathetic little sound which summed up what had happened. They say you should never meet your heroes because you'll only be disillusioned. I'd just seen the proof of that.

The way *Who's In Charge?* works is quite simple once you've see it a few times, but I suppose I'll make a hash of it when I try to explain. Five people line up behind booths and are first asked individual questions. Whoever win the most money is 'in charge', but it's up to the other contestants to get in charge by forging alliances with other contestants, and by playing their Star Cards. Effectively, it's your typical, bog standard quiz, tarted up to look different to the other stuff on TV.

The audience were already seated when my fellow contestants and I took our places behind our answer-booths. The warm-up man sounded about as funny as a broken collarbone but the audience sounded as though they were enjoying it. I looked for Laura but I couldn't see her, partly due to the poor lighting

Thirteen

and partly due to the fact that there were close to seven hundred people sat in front of me. I knew she'd be looking at me though, so I mouthed "Hello Laura" anyway.

Suddenly, the game show music started and a happy, loud voice announced "Ladies and gentlemen, please welcome your host, the one, the only, Michael Benson!"

A huge round of applause erupted among the audience and a happy, smiling, jubilant Michael Benson came rushing out of the back-stage shadows to greet his fans. He was a far cry from the miserable and rude Michael Benson we'd briefly been treated to earlier, although I noticed even the old lady he had ignored was now smiling and clapping madly along with the audience. In a way, Michael Benson reminded me of that crazy ex-girlfriend I mentioned earlier – miserable and rude, but able to turn on the charm at the flick of a switch.

"Hello and welcome to *Who's In Charge?*" Benson sang at the camera directly opposite him. "This is the game show where you don't get charged –"

"Sorry, Michael, cut!"

This second voice came from the shadows. I presume it belonged to the director.

"What?" asked Benson. He was still smiling but I think I could see the annoyance in his eyes.

"Nothing too major. Got a bit of camera shadow on the lower half of your face."

I heard Benson mutter how it should have been tested beforehand as he retreated back to the shadows. His entrance was done again but this time he stood further away from the camera.

"Hello and welcome to *Who's In Charge?*, the game show where you don't get charged for being in charge, or barged for being in charge, even if you're large and live in a garage."

"Cut!" came the director's authoritive (yet audibly confused) voice.

Benson remained absolutely still, staring into the camera and smiling. He looked insane.

"Michael, what are you doing? You're not reading what's on the auto-cue."

"I wanted to change it."

The director, who had emerged from the shadows and taken the still-smiling Benson gently by the arm, looked very confused. I saw him cover Benson's clip-on microphone so that the audience wouldn't hear their conversation.

I could though.

"Michael, what you just said didn't make sense. Why are you grinning like that? Are you okay?"

"She left me, Charles. She just packed her fucking things and..."

"Look, let's talk about this after the show, okay? We'll have a drink."

"Okay, Charles."

For the third time, Benson made his entrance, and this time it went okay (although the audience could be forgiven for not being quite so animated). We were all introduced to the cameras and had to say where we were from and what we did for a living. My voice faltered a little when I spoke and I could imagine the stick I'd get for that from people later.

Pretty soon, we were under way. I answered all five of my opening questions correctly, as did one of the younger contestants, so we had a tie-break and I won, even though he attempted to play one of his Star Cards.

"So, at the end of round one, Paul is in charge. Who's in charge, audience?" Michael Benson yelled.

"Paul's in charge!" they roared back in unison.

I smiled, feeling slightly embarrassed.

115

Thirteen

"Oh, is he now?" shouted Benson. "Is he really?"

Benson reached into his jacket pocket and slowly produced a handgun. I distinctly remember hearing people laugh, which reminded me of the people laughing when Tommy Cooper had a heart-attack in front of a TV audience. They thought he was joking around, and he died.

Benson fired the gun three times, randomly pointing it towards the audience. The smell which followed reminded me of fireworks and the ringing in my ears sounded like a million Catherine wheels.

"I think you'll find that *I'm* in fucking charge!"

It seemed to take an eternity for anyone to react, myself included. All I could do was stare in horror at Benson's grinning face. It was only when the first scream came that I realised he was looking directly at me with the eyes of a lunatic.

"So you're in charge, are you, Paul?" he asked.

"No," I mumbled. I wanted to look away and hope that he'd leave me, but as scared as I was looking at those eyes, I couldn't shift my gaze from them.

"But these people - " *bang bang*, two more shots fired randomly at the audience " – seem to think you are. Look at you, with your fucking Star Cards, you lanky prick."

If I hadn't heard the conversation he'd had with the director less than ten minutes earlier, I know I would have been executed. Words escaped me before I even knew what I was saying and I know they saved my life.

"She's behind you!" I said.

Benson fell for it, in his craziness expecting to see whichever woman had recently had the good sense to leave him. In the time it took him to turn around I leaped over my booth.

"You lying - "

My punch knocked him down and sent the gun soaring.

Bodies around me. Benson shouting, roaring like an animal. The audience screaming, trampling over each other to escape, even though the threat was now being pinned to the floor. Then, surreally, the game show music starting – someone must have hit a button in the panic – and the screams got worse and worse, as though competing with the catchy tune.

One member of the audience sat still, enjoying the show. Laura. Laura watching the spectacle. Dressed to the nines. Head lolled to one side. A small red dot between her eyes.

Thirteen

THANKS FOR WATCHING
C.M. SHEVLIN

Hi there! My name is Sarah. I know the usual way to start one of these is to say I've never done this type of thing before, and that I'm really nervous... Well, I am nervous but that's because this is my second try at meeting someone through video dating and the first didn't really go so well. To make a very long story short, I ate him. Don't switch off the tape just yet. Really, don't. There were totally mitigating circumstances which I suppose I'd better explain to you so you can decide whether or not we'd be compatible.

To start with, since this is "Paranormal Partners Dating Agency", you've probably guessed that I'm not exactly what I seem. I'm not really one for labels but I guess you'd call me a 'werewolf', if you were going to call me anything. I have been working on a more PC term - maybe lupo-human or trans-human but nothing really fits yet. So, anyway, werewolf. Yeah, that's me. But just for three days out of every month. The rest of the time I'm just your average model-slash-actress-slash-fitness instructor from South London.

It's been two years since the first change and it wasn't something I asked for, believe me. I had just moved to London from Milton Keynes when I saw this guy at a flatmate's boyfriend's party. We were making some serious eye contact across the room, you know, and as he was leaving, he shot me this burning "follow me" stare and so I did. I don't want to give you the idea I hook up with just anyone but there must have been something about him - some kind of hypnotic power or whatever - because I like to get to know a person first before, you know. But even though he'd definitely been giving me the come-on in the party he went totally schizo when I caught up with him, ranting, raving, telling me to get away from him and so on. Then he falls to his knees and clutches his stomach like he was about to puke. I went over to see if he was all right, mug that I am. My mum always said to me, "Sarah, your soft heart is gonna get you in trouble someday," and it turns out she was right. Although I think she meant I was gonna get myself knocked up. He lifts his head up and let's just say it was not pretty. I really don't want to go into details but with all the oozing from the mouth and eyes and the melting skin, I started to back away thinking Ebola maybe or that flesh-eating bug. That's when he grabbed my wrist and squeezed it until I heard my bones crack. So I'm screaming with the pain as he's slashing away at my stomach with what could have been knives. I don't remember passing out but when I came to, I was in an ambulance covered in blood and I didn't know it yet, but I was a werewolf. Needless to say, my dress was completely ruined. Although on the upside there was no need for cosmetic surgery or anything because the scars healed completely and very fast.

Because of the scratches, the police put it down as a freak animal attack, probably by a puma that escaped from a private zoo last month. I nodded along, even did an appearance on "When Animals Attack" on cable - maybe you saw it? But really, I knew something was definitely up, I just wasn't feeling like myself. I went back to Milton Keynes shortly afterwards to recuperate and moved back in with my parents for a while which turned out to be a mistake because obviously, the next full moon produced a rather unexpected change. Unfortunately my mum chose that moment to call up the stairs to let me know 'Emmerdale' had started. It's weird, even now when I think about that first time, I can't remember the exact expression on her face or just what she said when she saw wolf-me. All I have are these vague impressions of sweet-smelling fear and sweaty meaty juicy flesh that's the best thing you ever tasted in your life... Now, Dad was fattier and a lot harder to digest. Mum was always on at him about cholesterol and reducing salt and so on. It's sad when people let themselves go, isn't it? The police put it down

Thirteen

as yes, you guessed it, a freak animal attack. Makes you wonder how many of those they see. So just like that, I found out I was a werewolf and lost my parents on the same night. My life has been touched by tragedy but I like to think of myself as a positive person. The way to look at it, I suppose, is that they'll always be with me, you know, in spirit or whatever. Plus after that I noticed a definite improvement in my complexion - far fewer open pores and fine lines - way more effective than that pricey moisturiser they pushed on me at Boots. And even though that was a very big meal, I didn't gain a pound! I'm not saying that I should eat people to stay thin and look good or anything, just that you've got to look on the bright side of things, right?

Anyway, on to Alan. Alan was the first guy I met through "Paranormal Partners". His father had been a leprechaun but he could still pass for normal, he was a little on the short side and a little tight with money but I really liked him. He was sweet and romantic and gave amazing foot rubs. He was perfect really except for being a smoker and having this one tiny sexual kink. He wanted to do it with me during a full moon, you know, when I was in my other form. I have to say I really wasn't into the idea, but sometimes guys want weird stuff even when you're not a werewolf. And you have to compromise in a relationship. But I guess we should have used chains because the nylon rope he bought at Budget DIY turned out to be quite easily broken. I think he died pretty happy, which is some consolation even if my Marks and Spencer's 'Floral Fantasy' duvet was completely ruined. I can't help feeling like it's a little my fault. If I wasn't a vegetarian maybe the urge for fresh meat wouldn't be so strong at that time of the month. But I know what you're thinking; you gotta have principles and respect your beliefs, right? Even if they cause you pain. And it makes me feel a little bit better that I really didn't enjoy him all that much. I mean, I've tasted better. He smoked like a chimney, and all that tobacco smoke, it doesn't just cling to your clothes, it permeates right through your tissues to your organs. They should put that on the packet.

So let's see, other things you should know about me regarding the whole werewolf thing: I'm hairy once a month, that's all. The rest of the time I am just so careful about personal hygiene and excess hair removal, I promise. I'm a part-time fitness instructor so I'm also extra picky about what I eat - as I said, I'm actually a vegetarian excepting when, well you know. I like candle lit dinners, long walks, and romantic comedies at the cinema. I'm flexible though, I'll give anything a go once but anything with gore and guts in it is not a good idea too near my time of the month. I'm looking for a very special guy. Someone warm, with a sense of humour, who cares about his body and his health. I'm a very non-judgmental person so I don't care if you're a shapeshifter, shaman, vampire, or whatever. I'm looking for someone who wants to make a genuine long-term connection. On the subject of sex, it's probably better if you're a paranorm yourself. Even when it's not full moon I'm still a lot stronger than an ordinary, there have been unfortunate incidents recently and staff at the local A&E have started to give me funny looks. On the other hand, I don't want to discriminate, I mean, I know how much I'd hate it if someone ruled me out just because of what I am. So I guess if you're a human watching this and you think we might be good together, we could give it a go - at your own risk of course. My view is if you're up for it and have private health insurance, why not?

I guess this is goodbye. I hope to be seeing you very soon. I'd like to finish with my favourite movie quote of all time "After all... I'm just a girl, standing in front of a boy, asking him to love her" - don't you just adore Julia Roberts? Oh, before I forget - no smokers please. So.... Bye! Thanks for watching!

Thirteen

SEE HOW THEY DANCE
TYLER KEEVIL

"She's a genius – nobody's ever matched the choreography of *La Vie en Noir*."

"Maybe, but she's also a hopeless egomaniac."

"I heard she'd been living in a desert compound for the last twenty years."

Amanda rolled her eyes. She knew all the rumours, too. Every dancer did. After practically rewriting the modern dance bible, Annie-José had gone into seclusion with a handful of trusted assistants, proclaiming all dancers to be 'inadequate' for her purposes. That had been when Amanda was first starting out.

"I think the injury did it – turned her into such a perfectionist, I mean."

Amanda tuned out the gossip, craning her neck to see if the queue was moving. It wasn't. The auditions were being held at a nondescript warehouse by the waterfront. The summer heat imbued the sea-breeze with the stench of fish and salt and oil, but that hadn't kept any dancers away. There were at least a hundred of them, both male and female, stretched out in a line two blocks long.

As she waited, Amanda considered her chances. They were slim. Annie-José's name had attracted the big fish as well as the minnows. Amanda knew she fell somewhere between those categories. She was a good dancer, but she wasn't great. Some people might have written this off to bad luck. Amanda knew better. Greatness makes it own luck, and she didn't have greatness in her. For this reason, at twenty-seven, she found herself scraping by on the independent circuit. She had almost resolved herself to this fate, but not quite. The dream was fading, like a star at dawn, but it continued to glimmer on her inward eye.

"Amanda Kinlock?"

It had been six hours since they'd been admitted into the warehouse, and in that time forty-eight names had been called. Those yet to be called waited in a single room which smelled of sweat and nerves and fishmeal. The man with the megaphone scanned the sea of hopeful faces, then called again, "Amanda Kinlock."

"That's me."

She had to fight her way to the front of the throng. The man glanced at her then gestured for her to follow him. He led her up a metal staircase to the second floor of the warehouse, which had been turned into a studio that was stifling hot. At the centre of the studio was a single, high-legged chair. On the chair was a petite woman with ivory-white hair. She had a cane across her knees and a smouldering cigarillo between her lips. A cloud of smoke, which smelled faintly of garlic, enshrouded the woman like gauze.

Despite her nerves, Amanda couldn't conceal her curiosity.

The woman smiled, displaying stained teeth. "You are surprised by me, no?"

"I just didn't expect you to be auditioning us all yourself."

"It is tedious, yes." Her words were precise, even through her heavy accent. "But there is a maxim, *qu'est que ce*? If you want something done right, do it yourself. As Annie-José, I have learned to do everything myself."

Amanda smiled politely.

"This is how it goes, *ma fille*. You dance. I watch." Annie-José checked her wristwatch. "You have seven minutes to impress me. After that – pffft."

"I brought my own music-"

"No music. Dance."

"But-"

"Six minutes, fifty seconds."

Amanda danced.

119

Thirteen

She flung herself about the space, fighting through the oppressive heat like a bushman through jungle. Annie-José watched and smoked. After one minute Amanda was soaked in sweat. After five, her breathing had become ragged and her movements sloppy.

"Stop," Annie-José said. "That is good."

But it wasn't, and Amanda knew it. She had shown herself to be just what she was – a desperate amateur. She stood and panted and tried not to look disappointed.

"You can go now."

"That's it? You don't want to interview me?"

Annie-José flicked her hand impatiently. "I know all I need from your dancing."

The same man who'd brought her into the studio led Amanda out. Like the others, she was asked to wait until the final decisions had been made. She didn't really see the point. After dancing like that, she didn't have a hope in hell. Yet Amanda waited. She waited because she couldn't shake an irritating grain of hope. It was stuck in her heart like sand in an oyster, and she couldn't walk out, not until she knew for certain.

She knew for certain by seven o'clock that night. Her name was one of the first to be announced. She'd obviously been an easy cut. She began gathering her things, stuffing her clothes into her bag. She should have known better. She was and always would be a talented amateur. These people were out of her league.

She heard, "The rest of you are free to go."

She froze. Groans and sighs rippled throughout the warehouse. People began to move, en masse, towards the exit. Amanda wasn't sure she'd heard right. Then the names were repeated. Hers was among them.

Somehow, she'd made it.

The remaining dancers were ordered into a cramped office on the main floor of the warehouse. Amanda didn't think the others looked any more confident, or less incredulous, than she did. Apparently, none of them had expected to be chosen, either. Standing in front of them, brandishing her cane to like a witch waving a wand, Annie-José snapped out her sentences in a manner that did not encourage discussion.

"I am not a nice person," she began. "But I am honest. This is the, how do you say, situation?" She emphasised the last syllable, so the word was almost unrecognisable. "You are not here because you were the best. For me, the best is still the worst. Nobody is good enough, you see?"

She looked around the room, letting that sink in. Amanda wasn't surprised. It had been too good to be true, but that didn't mean she hadn't landed on her feet.

"I pick you because I can use you. You are ambitious. You are skilled. But you do not have that." She snapped her fingers for effect. "Without that, you will never be great. You want to be great, I can make you great. I will give you that." She snapped again. "But you must pay. You give up everything, and I make you dance like never before. That is the choice for you."

A pause. Somebody asked, "What do you mean by everything?"

"*Quel idiot!* I mean everything."

More silence. Amanda knew how the other dancers felt, because she felt the same. The situation was completely bizarre, well beyond anything she'd expected, even from somebody as notoriously eccentric as Annie-José.

"You have tonight to decide. There are twenty dancers here, yes? I need only twelve. *Six hommes, et six filles.* Tomorrow morning, at six, there is a bus.

Thirteen

The first twelve *personnes* will be my twelve. I leave it, as they say, in your hands."

Before anybody could ask another question, she rapped her cane twice on the floor and marched out the door, which was opened by one of her assistants. The dancers sat in silence, glancing furtively at each other. They were all thinking the same thing. Annie-José had used the term 'ambitious,' but it was obvious she had meant 'desperate.'

A few dancers began to talk, voicing their concerns. Amanda didn't stick around to allay their fears. They could make their own choice.

For Amanda, it wasn't much of a choice at all.

She played it safe by turning up half an hour early. To her surprise, the bus wasn't just already waiting – it was nearly full. She was the tenth person to board, and the sixth female. A girl arrived two minutes later and was told to go home.

Amanda sat near the back. Most of the dancers in front of her had their heads down. Amanda knew how they felt. Annie-José had chosen her quarry well. She'd known who would swallow the bait. Like the others, Amanda was willing to give up everything because she'd almost done so already – she'd abandoned her friends, her family, and any chance at a normal life. She'd given it all up to become a dancer. If Annie-José could make her great, then whatever the sacrifice, it would be worth it.

When the twelfth person arrived, the bus lurched into motion.

The man sitting beside Amanda muttered, "I wonder how far we have to go."

It was just the kind of nervous comment that would have irritated Amanda under normal circumstances. At the moment, she sympathised. She was scared, too.

"Probably not far," she assured him.

In a sense, she was right. After four blocks, Amanda noticed a bitter scent emanating from the heating vent at her elbow. She turned to the man beside her. He was asleep. Amanda barely had time to register this before she blacked out.

She woke up in a bare room with white walls. She was lying on a bed, dressed in a beige gown, and as her senses returned she realised she had a serious problem.

She couldn't move.

She could crane her neck from side to side, work her mouth, even lift her head. But she couldn't move her limbs. At first, she thought she might be strapped down. The only problem was, she couldn't feel the straps. She couldn't feel anything below her neck.

She looked at her body by tilting her head. It looked perfectly normal. She focused on her arm and tried to lift it. She couldn't. Could drugs do that to you? She didn't know, but her head felt thick and bloated. She tried to remember what had happened. The bus. They'd got on the bus. Maybe there'd been an accident. That was possible. She looked around. The room looked almost like a hospital, but something – maybe the lack of activity – told her it wasn't.

She lay like that, helpless and bewildered, for what seemed like hours. Then the door opened, oily-smooth on its hinges, and Annie-José limped in, her cane cracking on the tiled floor. Later, Amanda would remember the relief she felt at seeing the old woman and cringe. She assumed her presence meant everything was all right.

"Ah, *ma fille*." Annie smiled at her as if she were a child. "You are awake."

"Why can't I feel my arms and legs?"

"I will be truthful, yes?" Annie-José took her time lighting a cigarillo. She

Thirteen

waved away the smoke before answering. "I am hoping you can be reasonable, not like some of the others."

Amanda tried to quell a rising wave of panic. "What do you mean?"

"*Ma fille*, you are paralysed. You are what they call quadriplegic."

Amanda didn't have the composure to frame a response. She just stared.

"You made your bargain, and I collected. It's bad, yes, but also *necessaire*. If it wasn't, I wouldn't have needed the likes of you."

"I don't understand," Amanda managed to say. Out of habit, she tried to sit up, forgetting that she couldn't. This was a joke. It had to be. Paralysed? That didn't make any sense. "How did this happen?"

Annie made a cutting motion across her neck. "Your spinal cord is, pffft."

"Don't lie to me!" Amanda shrieked. "You're lying!"

Annie sighed. "Just as the others. You are all so *incroyable*. You made your choice." She threw up her hands in exasperation. "Did I not give you a choice, no?"

Amanda began to weep. She was still half-drugged and the sheer insanity of the situation was overwhelming her. "You didn't tell us," she sobbed. "You lied."

"*C'est merde!*" Annie snapped. "I never lie. I said *toute*, everything. I have been more than fair – I left you your head. That's something, at least." The old woman checked her watch. "There are five others to see. *Quels imbeciles!* You are the ones who got on the bus. Remember that, why don't you!"

The cane rapped across the floor. She was leaving. Amanda couldn't let her go. As Annie neared the door, Amanda choked out, "But how can I dance if I can't move?"

The cane stopped. Annie-José flashed a brown-toothed smile.

"Oh, you will dance," she said. "You will dance as an angel.

Annie-José gave her a week to grow accustomed to her situation. Amanda cycled through the stages of trauma: denial, rage, despair. In the end she settled into a mild state of shock. She spent hours at a time staring at her body as if it were an alien creature. In many ways it was. She was still attached to it, but it was no longer hers. Periodically, she was forced to watch other people taking care of it. Assistants came in to bathe her, change her clothes and tubes, and to feed her gruel. In the hours between these visits, her limbs were left connected to wires which stimulated them, imitating exercise. The implications of this, and why it might be needed, eluded her.

Occasionally, reality would slash across her benumbed mind. She knew there was no hope. She'd been selected, not just because she was desperate, but because she wouldn't be missed. The others would be no different. Whenever she thought of how they'd been duped, she'd throw a fit – screaming, biting, spitting, and thrashing her head from side to side. By the end of the week, these fits were fewer and further between.

On the seventh day, Amanda heard the crack of cane-on-tile that signalled the return of her captor. When she entered, Annie-José looked relaxed and content.

"You are behaving better than some," she said. "Soon, you will rehearse."

Amanda searched the old crone's face. There was no sign of mockery.

"I don't understand," she said.

The smile again, witch-like and hideous. "You will."

The next morning two orderlies picked Amanda up, placed her in a wheelchair, and brought her to the rehearsal space. It was a vast black-box room. The ceiling was high and covered with a patterned grid. Amanda didn't pay much attention to any of this. Her attention was ensnared by the two dancers cavorting

Thirteen

and reeling across the performance space. She recognised the man who'd sat beside her on the bus. Her heart hammered in her chest. They were moving. They weren't paralysed after all.

Then she noticed their expressions. The woman's face was blank and white as paper. The man was crying. She watched them, puzzled. Both the dancers had a strand of transparent wire running from the back of their neck to the ceiling. When they moved, the wire followed them, ghosting across the grid. Amanda didn't make the connection, even when she saw one of the assistants preparing a third wire.

Then, as they bent her forward and she felt the slight pressure on her neck, she finally realised what was happening, even if she didn't understand it. They were plugging her in. Annie-José's words sprang into her mind, taunting her.

I have learned to do everything myself.

Amanda watched, horrified, as her hands gripped the rests of her wheelchair and pushed her upright. Her legs took tentative steps, like a baby learning to walk. It felt as if her head was disembodied and floating above the ground. She was only aware of her limbs when she could see them. A leg kicked up. An arm lifted. She began to move – slowly at first, as Annie-José grew accustomed to the nuances of her latest puppet – and then with increasing speed. Soon Amanda was leaping and spinning and whirling alongside the other marionettes. Annie-José had kept her promise. Amanda's movements were filled with a grace and precision she hadn't thought possible.

She was dancing like never before.

MR THIRTEEN
ROBERT NIELSON

Billy was a good kid, really. He obeyed his parents, showed respect for his elders and kept his room tidy. Sometimes he even helped his mother around the house. But despite all these good qualities he managed to get himself into trouble. In fact it was his willingness to help that sort of led to his problem. One evening after dinner Billy was helping his mother clear the table. As he reached out to lift his father's plate his sleeve caught the side of the salt cellar and knocked it over. He carefully brushed the spilt salt into a little pile and swept it off the table into the palm of his hand. Then he walked to the kitchen, without dropping a grain on the dining room carpet, and marched to the sink to dispose of it.

"Billy," his mother said, "you should throw a pinch of the salt over your shoulder for luck."

"Sure, Mum", he replied absently, dumping the salt down the waste-disposal and wiping his hands on a dishcloth. "I should throw some over my left shoulder with my right hand or I'll turn into a frog, or something."

"Don't make fun of things you don't understand, Bill," his Dad shouted from the dining room where he sat, finishing a cup of coffee and reading the evening paper.

Billy put on a frown and deepened his voice. "If you make faces the wind will change and leave you like that." He giggled, realising how like his father that sounded. He continued in his normal voice. "This is the twenty-first century folks. They stopped believing in witches and magic and that soft of stuff years ago."

"Don't talk like that to your mum, Bill", his dad called. "You apologise right now," he ordered in that tone that says: or else.

"Okay. Okay! I'm sorry. But I still think that all this superstitious stuff is real garbage."

The boy retreated rapidly upstairs to his room. He had a geography project to finish for school the next morning and if it wasn't finished he'd get it from old Rhino - whom Billy was sure had taken up teaching because he hated children. As he worked best in silence the radio stayed firmly off even though he fancied some music. Even the faint noise of the TV from downstairs distracted him sometimes. Oh well, he promised himself, the folks are going out tonight, so if I get his finished early enough I'll be able to watch Monsters of Rock. He set to his work with a smile of anticipation.

"Billy, we're off now," his mother called from the bottom of the stairs. "Are you sure you'll be all right alone?"

"Yes, Mum. See you later." Why do they still treat me like a child? he asked himself. I'm a teenager. What are they going to do, get a girl a year or so older than me to babysit? He thought about that one. Not a bad idea after all. "Snap out of it Bill," he said aloud. "You've got a project to finish."

"Ahem." It sounded as though someone was clearing his throat right there in the room with him. "Good evening, Billy."

The boy twisted about in his chair. Sitting behind him, perched on the edge of the bed, was a small, pink faced, wrinkled man with a shiny, bald head and piercing red eyes. He was wearing purple flowing robes with a hood hanging down the back, which made him look for all the world like a trendy, but very short, monk.

"I said, good evening, Billy," the stranger repeated, calmly.

"What the ..." was all the youngster could manage to reply.

The short, pinkish man pulled a black leather diary from the breast pocket of his robe and scribbled a short note inside. "Lacks manners also," he mumbled as he wrote.

Thirteen

"Who, or what, in the world are you?" whispered Billy.

"You may call me Mister Thirteen," the intruder said, hopping down from the bed and holding out a tiny pink hand to the boy. "How do you do."

Too stunned to do otherwise, Billy took the little man's hand and shook it mechanically. "What do you want from me?"

"Well, Billy, it's like this," Mister Thirteen began, climbing onto the edge of the boy's desk and sitting cross-legged, nose to nose with his host. "Another boy called Bill, you'll know his stuff from school, once said - 'There are more things in heaven and earth than you ever dreamed of." That's not it exactly, but it'll do for now".

Just what I need right now, thought Billy. A Goblin misquoting Shakespeare at me.

"One of these things, or forces, is what you call superstition." "Hey! That only works if you believe in it". -"Wrong, Billy. I'm in charge of superstition around here and I can make it work any way I like. Most of the time people who ignore my superstitions pay in small ways. Ways you'd hardly notice. You know - bad luck."

"Oh! I see. You're in charge of bad luck, are you?"

"Don't be silly, boy," snapped Thirteen angrily. "I just said I've got the local superstition franchise. That's all. You don't ever want to meet the guy who looks after luck. Not like this, anyhow."

"And what exactly do you mean by 'like this'?"

"You, my dear Billy, have got me rightly pissed. Not only did you ignore the rituals laid down for salt spillage earlier on, but you made fun of them. Then you had the cheek to say that superstition, my superstition, is garbage. Now, you're going to have to pay for that."

"You don't seriously expect me to believe all this, do you?".

"Think about it, Billy. How many people do you know have had a visit from a three foot tall man with red eyes? Not that many, I'll bet. My very presence here is proof of what I say."

"It's got to be something I ate," said Billy.

"Okay, fine. Have it your own way," said Mr Thirteen sliding down off Billy's desktop. "Tomorrow morning," he continued, pointing a finger at the boy's chest, "you're going to have a piece of bad luck. And that stroke of bad luck is going to stay with you all day, at least. You just remember why it's happening and I'll see you tomorrow night." The little man stamped angrily across Billy's bedroom and pulled open the door. "We'll see if it was something you ate tomorrow, won't we," sneered Thirteen, storming out.

Billy jumped out of his seat and ran to the door. "Listen, I don't care..."

He was talking to thin air. He raced downstairs but there wasn't a sign of his visitor to be found. He slowly mounted the stairs, shaking his head. "Weird", he said, in a shaky voice. "Truly... awesomely weird."

The next morning Billy rolled his bicycle out of the garage only to find that he had a flat tyre. "We all know how this happened," he said picturing a short pink man holding a knife. "Real mystical piece of bad luck that is." He glanced at his wristwatch, realising as he did so that he'd have to run if he was to catch the school bus. As he raced out of the driveway he saw the rear of the bus disappearing into the distance and with it his chances of getting to school on time.

"Great," he muttered, as he scuffed his way along the sidewalk to the bus-stop, to wait with the other commuters for the regular service. He arrived into his first class, Geography, fifteen minutes after the bell. "Sorry, I'm late, Sir," he said, slipping behind his desk.

Mr Ryan, the Geography teacher, grunted a dismissal of his apology.

"Your project is due in this morning," he said, without lifting his eyes from the homework he was correcting for his next class.

Thirteen

"Yes, sir. I've got it right here," Billy replied, pulling a large folder out of his schoolbag.

"Is it going to grow legs and walk up here by itself?" asked Rhino mildly, drawing muffled giggles from Billy's classmates. "Bring it up here," he roared.

Billy scrambled out of his seat and walked as fast as he could, without breaking into a trot, to Mr Ryan's desk. He handed the bad tempered teacher his project folder.

"Is this some kind of joke?"

"Joke, sir?"

"Joke, sir," mimicked Rhino. "Joke, boy," the teacher continued angrily. "It's a thing designed to make people laugh." He stared hard at Billy who had no idea what was going on. Had Rhino finally flipped his trolley? wondered the boy.

"The problem is, William, that I don't have much of a sense of humour, as you well know."

"I'm sorry, sir. I just don't understand what you're taking about."

"This, boy," he said, holding out Billy's project folder. "This is what I'm talking about."

Billy stared helplessly at the pages of his folder. Every one was blank. What had happened to his project? Mr Thirteen. Of course. He must have crept back into the bedroom during the night and replaced the project with blank pages. Even as the thought crossed his mind his eyes came to rest on the top page. It had a faint peanut butter smear in one corner. He'd dropped a smudge of peanut butter from a sandwich onto the top page of his project. And in exactly the same spot. And he hadn't been able to clean off the mark completely just like the mark on the page in front of him. I don't like what you're thinking, he said to himself. There is no way that writing can disappear without trace off a page. Just like magic, he thought.

"Well?" demanded Ryan.

"I thought... "

"What? You thought I wouldn't check your work?" The teacher paused for a few seconds, staring at the boy. "See me after school. Two hours detention. Now sit down."

"But, sir, Mr Ryan, I've got basketball practice this afternoon."

"Tough luck."

"If I don't go to practice they won't pick me for the game on Saturday."

"Isn't life tragic," said Rhino, smiling for the first time since Billy had arrived into class.

And so Billy spent two hours in detention and lost his place in the basketball squad. He brooded his way through dinner that evening and splashed and clunked his way though the washing-up afterwards. His parents cast concerned glances at one another but said nothing. He was a good kid. Everyone had bad moods once in a while.

Billy finished the dishes and retired to his room in silence to await the disappearance of Mr. Thirteen. Unable to doubt that the little man would return, after the evidence of his day's luck, the boy sat down at his desk staring though unseeing eyes at his unopened school books.

"Ahem!"

Billy whirled. As he had expected Thirteen was sitting on the edge of his bed. "You let the air out of my tyre," Billy accused him angrily.

"Hold it, Billy boy. I admit that I caused you a little bad luck, but nothing as crude as letting your tyre down."

"You also said one piece of bad luck."

"That's right. And that's all I did. One little thing."

"Little? I was late for school, I got into detention and I've been left out of the

Thirteen

basketball team."

"A little luck goes a long way. Especially when it's bad."

"Yeah! But that's three things." "No, Billy. The flat tyre was carelessness. If you remember it was soft last night when you got home. You were going to fix it after you did your homework but you forgot."

"Oh! That's right," admitted the boy. "But it's your fault I forgot. If you hadn't come along last night I would've remembered."

"Sorry Billy. That one's down to you."

"My project? Now, you can't say that you had nothing to do with that. Projects don't just disappear."

"The project was my doing," agreed Thirteen.

"And the basketball?"

"I did say that one piece of bad luck would stay with you. Didn't I?"

"Well, it's still your fault."

"Only indirectly. Anyway, that's the way luck works."

"Now I've got to do that project again. What about that?"

"Check the folder. I think you'll find that everything is back to normal. And I cleaned off that peanut-butter stain."

"Gee, thanks."

"And superstition?" asked Thirteen. "Do you still think it's all trash?"

"No," said Billy. "I'll watch my step from now on."

"And I'll be everywhere at once. So to be really sure that you've learned well I'm going to set you a little task for the next week."

"Aw! Come on. Haven't you done enough already. It was only a little bit of salt I spilt."

Thirteen ignored his outburst, deep in thought. "Got it," he cried, grinning at the boy. "For the next week you must avoid stepping on the cracks in the sidewalk. If for any reason, and I mean any reason Billy, you step on a crack I'm going to turn you into a frog." The little man's grin grew wider and wider until it threatened to swallow his ears.

"A frog?" blurted Billy. "Gimme a break."

"I knew you weren't truly convinced. That's why I'm setting you this test. If you fail it, you'll deserve to be a frog. If you pass, you'll remember to honour my superstitions for the rest of your life." The goblin-like man reached out and placed his hand on Billy's. It was strangely cold and clammy on the touch. "Goodbye for now, Billy. I'll be seeing you."

With that Thirteen vanished, just like switching off a light. Billy looked at his hand, where the little man had touched it. There, on the back, right in the middle, stood a large wart with long black hairs growing out of it. "That's just a reminder," said Thirteen's voice, sounding as if it came from inside his head. "But, hey! Don't worry about it, Billy boy. You'll do this standing on your head. I'll be back in a week and everything will be normal again." Then the voice chuckled evilly, causing the boy to shudder. "Or else I'll be back to pick up my frog. We can't have magical frogs hopping about the countryside, can we? I mean, what would happen if a passing princess gave you a kiss." The voice broke up in peals of uproarious laughter and faded out, like a weak radio station on a cheap transistor. Billy sat at his desk, frightened, for several minutes. He hadn't an idea what to do now. There was a gentle tap on the door. It opened and his mother came in.

"Why, Billy. You look as it you've seen a ghost."

"Not a ghost, Mum. A goblin" It was out before he had time to think. He glanced up at his mother. She looked worried.

"A goblin? You think you saw a goblin?"

Billy had visions of men in white coats coming to take him to the funny farm. Would his mother understand what had happened? She'd probably just laugh.

Thirteen

But he had to talk about this to somebody, and at least if she thought he'd gone nuts she's keep it to herself.

"Sit down, Mum. I've got something to tell you," he said, seriously.

His mother sat on the edge of his bed, in almost the exact spot Thirteen had occupied only minutes earlier. Then he told here the entire tale and as proof showed her his project folder complete with restored project. "If I was making this up do you think I'd have gone to the trouble of actually doing the project. You can check with Rhino... Mr Ryan. It's the same folder. And the project's good. I've been working on it for a couple of weeks."

"I'm sorry, Billy. I'm sure there's a rational explanation for what's happened. Maybe you only think it was the same folder. You probably fell asleep and dreamed up this Mr Thirteen. I know you're disappointed about the basketball game, but you'll get over it." She stood up. "I think you should go to bed and get some sleep. If you're still not feeling well in the morning you don't have to go to school. Alright?"

"But, Mum. It's true. I swear."

"You get a good night's sleep and you'll see things differently in the morning. Goodnight," she said, closing his bedroom door softly behind her.

For the next few days Billy was unusually quiet. His father figured it was because of losing his place on the team for Saturday. His mother thought it better that his father kept this belief. On the day of the game Billy couldn't bring himself to go along even as a spectator, even though is parents did their best to persuade him and all his friends would be there. After lunch his mother made a last attempt to cheer him up. "Isn't that movie you wanted to see, Death something or other, on at the Plaza this weekend?"

"Yeah!" he replied listlessly. "Well I stopped by the movie house yesterday and picked up tickets for this afternoon's show. I thought you and me could go along and then maybe on to McDonald's afterwards."

"You booked for Death Weekend?"

"Correct." Billy threw his arms about his mother and hugged her. For the first time all week he looked happy. "Okay! Let's get going. We don't want to miss the opening. I read in Horror Monthly that they used two hundred gallons of fake blood shooting the first five minutes. And that's only while they roll the credits. Are you coming, Dad?"

"Not me. Only one of us is being sacrificed to Death Weekend," his father laughed, relieved to see his son coming back to his normal, bouncy self. Billy and his mother drove to the theatre in good spirits, both of them avoiding the subject of the goblin. They couldn't get parking right outside but found a car park only two streets away. As they walked towards the Plaza Movie Theatre Billy's mother could not ignore the fact that her son was bobbing about avoiding the cracks in the sidewalk. "Stop that, Billy. You're making a show of us."

He didn't answer. He kept concentrating on missing the cracks.

"Billy, I'm talking to you. Walk beside me properly."

The boy stopped. His mother stopped a few paces further on.

"Mum. Whatever you may think, I was deadly serious when I told you about the goblin. Have you seen this?" he asked, holding up his warty hand for her inspection. "The goblin did this to prove his power to me and to remind me about his threat."

"It's only a wart, Billy," his mother said gently. "Lots of people get warts. Come on, we'll be late."

She turned on her heels and set off once again at a brisk pace towards the theatre. Billy bobbed along a little quicker and drew alongside her.

"Look, Billy," she said, beginning to get annoyed with his antics, "I'll take responsibility for you stepping on the cracks."

And as she said it she reached out and pushed lightly against his shoulder, throwing him off balance. Billy stumbled and his right foot plonked down right across a crack. He teetered for a Mument and then his left fell right across yet another.

"There you are," his mother said triumphantly. "You've stepped on a crack, two cracks, and you're not a frog. Now, let's forget all about this foolishness and enjoy the rest of our day out."

Doubt about Mister Thirteen's threat seeped into his mind for the first time since the wart. It was true that he'd stepped on a crack. It was also true that he was still a boy - not a frog. He shrugged his shoulders. His mum was right. There was nothing to do now but forget about the goblin and enjoy the movie.

When they got home Billy was his normal happy self, describing to his dad in detail all the goriest scenes from Death Weekend and acting out several murders, complete with horrible screams and leaping about.

"Are you quite finished, Bill?" his father asked as the boy paused to catch his breath.

"Oh! No Dad. There's lots more," he said happily.

"I see. It's just that Dave from the basketball team phoned. The team won and there's a bit of a party going on over at his house. He said that they'd all like you to come over."

"When?"

"Right away. They've been celebrating since the game finished."

"Your bike still punctured?" asked his mother. He nodded. "Okay then! I'll give you a ride."

"It's all right, Dave's isn't far. I'll walk."

"Never look a gift horse in the mouth," said his mother, picking up the car keys and heading for the door.

As they drove to Dave's, Billy sat with his elbow out the window. He smiled over at his mother. "Isn't it a lovely evening," he said.

"It's not like you to notice mundane things like the weather."

"Well, it's kind a like a weight has been lifted off my shoulders, you know? What with the worry over my goblin and the team and everything. You tend to appreciate the ordinary things after that sort of experience. It's nice to be able to just think about long sunny evenings and stuff like that."

They pulled up outside Dave's house and Billy hopped out. He walked around to the drivers side of the car, stuck his head through the open window and kissed his mum on the cheek.

"What's come over you? It's ages since you kissed me. I thought you'd grown out of that sort of thing."

"I just wanted to say thanks for being a great mum."

His mother drove off, leaving Billy looking fondly after her. Suddenly his attention was caught by a movement in the rear window of the car. Standing on the back seat, grinning hugely and waving at Billy was Mister Thirteen. His mother's words earlier in the day rang in his ears.

"I'll take responsibility for you stepping on the cracks."

As if the goblin could read the youngster's thoughts, Thirteen began nodding his head. Ignoring Dave, who was walking out of the house to greet him, Billy sprinted after the departing vehicle.

"Mum!" he called. "Mum, stop."

But she was too far away to hear him. He waved his arms, willing her to glance in her rear view mirror. In vain. He ran back to Dave.

"Forget something?" enquired Dave.

"No time to talk, Dave," he panted. "Can you loan me your bike?"

Thirteen

"Sure. No problem. But what's going on?"

"The bike, Dave. Please."

Dave read worry and fear in his friend's face. Without another word he hurried around the side of his house and half-wheeled, half dragged his bicycle out. "There you go Billy. You can tell me about it later."

"Yeah! Maybe later," Billy called over his shoulder. "And thanks, Dave," he yelled, standing up on the pedals and pushing with all his strength. He knew that his mother wasn't the fastest of drivers. There was a short cut across a field that would save him half a mile but it was still unlikely that he could overhaul the car before home. How long before Thirteen made his move, wondered Billy. Pushing thoughts of a green warty mother out of his mind he pedalled as fast as his legs would go.

It's the final burst into Paris in the Tour De France, he said to himself.

Greg Lemond is only five seconds in front and tiring. Go, go, go. He hit the final turn about ten miles an hour too fast. Suddenly the tyres lost grip as he leant too far over and the bike skidded off the road into a hedge. He lay for a Mument his legs tangled up in the bike.

From where he lay he could see his own house. The car stood in the driveway. Maybe everything was all right. He pulled his feet from under the bike and stood up. As he did so he saw Mr Thirteen appear out of the driveway to his home. The little man was holding one end of a dog leash in his left hand Behibd him, on the other end of the leash, hopped a large, fat, bright green frog. The goblin and his charge ambled casually away in the opposite direction and vanished around a bend in the road.

Billy stood by the crashed bicycle, unaware of some nasty gashes he had picked up in the fall. His legs didn't seem to want to move from the spot on which he stood. He was too afraid of what he would find at home.

"Mum!" he called, almost in a whisper. "Mum!" he screamed, regaining control of his limbs and running full speed to his house. He charged to the front door and pulled out his key. In his haste it dropped to the ground. "Mum!" he panted as he regained the key and operated the lock. He pushed the door open silently. Did his dad know what was going on? What was he going to tell him? The truth? He heard voices coming from the kitchen.

"Now, drink that," his father was saying. "And from the top, tell me what happened. I couldn't make head nor tail of what you were saying when you came in."

"When I arrived home," he heard his mother's voice say, relief washing over him, "there was a goblin standing in the porch."

"A goblin," repeated his father, his voice colourless.

"Yes. And he was holding this huge, revolting frog in his arms."

"Frog," his father repeated, seemingly unable to function other than as an echo.

"And when I walked up to the door, this horrible little creature pushes the frog up towards my face."

"Face," said Billy's Dad.

"Will you stop repeating every word I say."

"Sorry, love. It's just that this is a bit hard to take."

"Do you want to hear it, or not?"

"Yes, of course. Go on."

"Anyway, the goblin holds up the frog and he leers at me. 'Lady,' he says, 'you came that close.' And he holds the thumb and forefinger of his free hand a fraction apart. Then he drops the frog, which he's got on a dog's leash by the way, and begins to back away from the house. 'Just don't walk under any ladders,' he says, and strolls off from the driveway."

Thirteen

"Do you seriously expect me to believe this?" asked Billy's father, reasonably.

"It's all true. You can ask Billy, he's seen the goblin. He'll tell you."

"Don't bet on it," said Billy softly to himself, watching a look of mingled disbelief and pity cloud his father's face. Without a word he let himself quietly back out through the front door.

BOXING CLEVER
MARK PATRICK LYNCH

You should see the other guy.

I mean, really, you should see him. A big old bruiser the company had brought in from somewhere out of Eastern Europe. He'd been around for ages, a stranger to electric light and streetcars even. A fighter, you'd think, to have survived this long, a battler and a warrior ... and only recently brought out from his stronghold. But I'm good. They can bring in whoever they like. They're all the same to me. They all fall when you take them just right.

This one looked big, looked tough, but he wasn't a fighter; not really – he'd never been up against his own. Not the way I had.

One thing you learn pretty quickly in this game, it's how to deal with your own. When I was first made, nobody knew that much about us, we were shadows and whispers, misinterpreted glimpses from out the corner of your eye. London was our playground, for the few of us there were. That was one of the rules: that there should only be so many at a time. If the predators outnumber the prey, well you're in real trouble. You can't continue to function, not without being noticed.

Then came the ginger Irishman, and his book, his penny dreadful. It didn't cause all that much trouble at first; it was if anything a minor nuisance ... and some even used it to their advantage, dressing in evening suits and capes, gliding through the East End as if they were the Lords of the Last Days. Fiction had portrayed our like before with varying degrees of accuracy, but never to the popularity of the masses. A stage play was made, and some few of us – there were only ever a few of us back then – even attended one of the performances.

Paranormalists began to hunt for us, still others began to worship us; we were portrayed on celluloid, and conjured in poetry by half-inebriated fools. We became a little more shadowy, a little more of a quieted whisper – they wouldn't find us. We were so sure they wouldn't find us.

But then came science. The manipulation of light through prisms, the glass eye that could see what no human ever could. Devices were constructed which could detect sounds that previously only bats could hear, machines created that could sense subtle shifts in air pressure, and we were found. The introduction of the Van Helsing Generator during the first decade of the twenty-first century put paid to any thoughts we might have had of concealment. Devised by the great-great-great grandnephew of Abraham Stoker, the contrivance could generate that intrinsic quality of light that is inimical to the sun. I do not know what manner of device it is, only that it is effective, and that I suffer as I do because of it. I have overheard mechanics of such creations talk of particle streams and photons, such things as I am unable to comprehend but which I believe are components of the machinery of the universe itself.

It seems that while we were slipping between shadows, our prey had found a way to brighten their dark lack of understanding. Our sureness in our superiority has been our downfall. We should have nipped this science in the bud, should have curtailed the ability of genius to flourish in the herd. But now it is too late, and here we stand, paraded before them as entertainment.

The Carpathian they had ushered in to the arena was fearsome to behold. He was grey through his years of night feeding, his hair was gone and only thick green veins roamed over his distorted skull. His arms were powerful and the nails at his fingers' ends were sharpened like the blades of shovels. His needle teeth were prominent, but they had only been used to piercing human flesh ... and whatever scurried through his lair's walls, no doubt.

He was unleashed onto the stage through the heavy trap of the gates by an armoured human. The human's armour looked like marble, veined as it was with

Thirteen

stitches of specially grown garlic. No predator could break through to the tender skin without inflicting serious injury to itself. The Carpathian was confused. His eyes, staring black bulbs accustomed only to darkness, would be almost useless beneath the halogen spots shining down on us. Already I was at an advantage.

But he fought well, scuttling around the arena like an oversized spider, and I spared him too much discomfort by finishing him relatively quickly. The crowd didn't like that, protected as they were behind their high-impact plastic windows from us, and so far above, like spectators at the coliseum. I sometimes wonder when I shall meet someone old enough to have seen those Roman arenas of death.

After I had emerged victorious the jets were switched on, and I raised my face and arms to the downpour of blood, opening my mouth wide and losing myself in the ecstasy of the blood lust. I wish I could resist, wish I could hold firm enough to be ready when they march into the arena and pull me out to my coffin. The chance is always there; they are never entirely vulnerable, but if I am ever to make my move it will be then, when they believe me sated and unable to function like the predator I am.

Until then, until that time I am able to control my base urges, I will fight in the ring, I will take my umbilical in my coffin and suck whatever dregs of artificial nutrients keep me alive and restore me. But for now they carry me away, my bruises already healing thanks to the downpour of red, and box me away from the light. And sleeping, recovering, I dream of escape.

Like the light behind my eyes, everything in my dream is blood red.

THE TOLL OF FINNEGAN'S BRIDGE
BRIAN SHOWERS

Harvey Rabbitt's elbow slipped off the bar, his slumping body jerked as he nearly slid from his stool; his left hand jostled an empty pint glass. Aside from a man asleep in the corner, Harvey and the publican were the only ones in the vacant pub.

"Ar mhaith leat cupán tae?"

"What?" replied Harvey Rabbitt.

"Would you like a cup of . . . coffee?" repeated the man behind the counter.

Harvey Rabbitt opened his drooping eyelids and then squinted at the publican through smoke arabesques and alcohol vapour. "I'm not down for the count yet, chief. How about another brewskie?" he replied in a slurred Midwestern accent.

The publican looked at him for a long while before drawing another pint of Guinness. "You're from the States?" he said as he topped off the pint while simultaneously hoping the American wouldn't pass out on his bar.

Harvey Rabbitt snapped to attention. "You bet'cher ass I am," he said jabbing his forefinger at the publican. "Best damn purchasing rep this side of the Mississippi. The company sent me out here to hit another homer." In one practiced motion he pulled a business card from the inside pocket of his suit coat.

The publican slid the card off the dark, varnished bar top into his palm and put on his reading glasses: "'Harvey Rabbitt, International Purchases, Eastern Division. Anderson & Anderson, Ltd.' That sounds fancy, sir, very impressive," he said with sincerity. "What does it mean?"

"What does it mean? It means I go to foreign countries and look for exotic products for our imports boutique."

The publican looked at him blankly.

"Ain't you ever heard of Anderson & Anderson?" The publican smiled at him and shook his head. "The big department store?" Blank smile, slight embarrassment. "New York, Los Angeles, Chicago? Jesus, where do you do all your shopping?"

The publican thought hard. "Well, we got Kennedy's Post Office up the road. They sell things like milk, cheese, bread, and jam, if you're looking for things like that. But if you want more exotic stuff like low fat milk or those new frozen spring rolls, you gotta go someplace big like Tralee. Have you ever tried a frozen spring roll?"

Harvey Rabbitt sighed, disregarding the publican's attempt at changing the subject. "Look, you watch tv? You ever seen *Seinfeld*?"

"I'm afraid not. We barely got the Kerry, West Meath match last week, being such a distance from everything." With a wink and a laugh he added, "As they say, approximately one Irish mile from the whole of civilisation."

"Well, there's this character, Elaine Benes. She travels around the world and looks for stuff to sell in her clothing catalog. That's sorta what I do. I look for foreign junk that we can sell in our stores. You know, knick-knacks, clothing. *Objects d'art*." He said the last bit with authoritative panache.

"Ahh, right," said the publican, still not fully understanding. "And did you find any foreign junk around here, Mr. Rabbitt?"

"You're damn straight I did! Wool socks dyed locally, pottery made from indigenous clays, and for the final *coup de grace*," he burst out, "handmade lampshades! This place is a goddamn goldmine. Folks'll eat this shit up." Harvey Rabbitt nearly slid off his chair with the thought of his bonus check.

The publican merely smiled and went about his business of drying pint glasses as Harvey Rabbitt sat on his stool lost in a pecuniary haze.

Thirteen

After Harvey had finished his final drink, he drew himself up and cleared his throat, "Say, bartender," the words dripped out of his mouth, "Be a pal. Call me a cab."

"I'm afraid there's only one taxi in the area. That'll be aul' Johnny Sheehan."

"Great. Call'em up for me, would ya?"

"Oh, there's no need for that, sir."

"What? Why not?"

"Because he's over there asleep in the corner." The publican gestured to the man who had had his chin resting on his chest since Harvey had walked in. "Once aul' Johnny's asleep you wouldn't wanna wake him up; not with his temper. Besides, he's been drinking the black stuff since noon today. He's in no shape to be drivin'."

Harvey Rabbitt stood, slack-jawed with disbelief. "Jesus. Unbelievable. One cabbie?" The publican nodded. "And that's him? Is he *ever* in any shape to give *anyone* a ride?"

"Oh, of course! Aul' Johnny gives Father Callahan a ride to the pub after church every Sunday. Always on time, Johnny is. It takes him approximately fourteen minutes to get from St. Anthony's Blessed Refuge of Sinners to St. Arthur's blessed cosy of the holy pint!"

"And that qualifies him as a taxi driver?" The bartender beamed. "Look, just forget it. I'll walk. What's the fastest way to this place?" Harvey held up a brochure with a picture of a quaint seaside cottage. "It's the bed 'n' breakfast where I'm staying--however it's pronounced."

"Oh! Tígh Na Trá. That'll be Mrs. Walshe's place. Nice woman that Mrs. Walshe"

"Yeah, whatever. What's the fastest way there this time of night?"

"Well, there's Slea Head Drive. It's the long way around Mount Eagle, but if the moon's out it makes for a pleasant view Blaskets, especially if the ocean's calm. And as long as you keep your eye open for cars coming around the corners, it should be the safest way home this time o' night; what with all the tourists gone home for the season. And I'd say Johnny'll be asleep for at least another two and a half hours and you should be safe in bed by then."

"Two and a half hours? Christ, I practically have to be up in three. I'm flying out of Shannon airport early. You said that's the long way. You got any short ways around here?"

"Well, I suppose you could go along the Ballyferriter Road." The publican paused for a long while to scratch his head. He thought as fast as he poured Guinness--always with a pause to let things settle. "That will take you down along the coast, through Ballyferriter and then down into Ventry."

"And that's faster?"

"Oh, it's a lovely walk this time of year. A bit dark being on the north side of the hill, but I'll give you the loan of my torch. You can give it to Mrs. Walshe when you get back and she'll return it to me when she's in here tomorrow night," and before Harvey could reply, the publican produced a large flashlight from behind the counter.

"Super. And how fast will that get me there?"

"Oh, I'd say it's about fourteen kilometres give or take."

"Kilometres? How far is that in miles? Look, just tell me how long it will take me to walk back to whatever that place is called where I'm staying."

"Oh, I'd reckon about three," decided the publican

"Three hours? But that's longer than the other way you told me," replied Harvey.

The publican paused to let the bubbles settle. "I suppose it is. I suppose it is."

Thirteen

"Look, just tell me the straightest way back. The fastest."

"Well," began the publican hesitantly, "there's a trail next to the Kehoe Lodge. That'll take you up along the side of the hill,"

"Great. And how long will that take," said Harvey, pronouncing every syllable with great aim.

"About an hour," replied the publican softly.

"An hour? That's it? Now we're getting somewhere. Why didn't you tell me that before?" asked Harvey.

"Because of Finnegan's Bridge, Mr. Rabbitt," said the publican

"The bridge? And you weren't gonna tell me 'cause of some stupid bridge?"

"Well, not many people use the bridge," replied the publican in a grave tone.

"You're telling me that everyone around here walks the long way?" asked Harvey with wonder.

"Aye. But it is a lovely walk most of the year round. If you haven't walked around Slea Head, you haven't visited Ire--"

Harvey cut the publican short, "And no one walks the short way because of the bridge?"

"Well, you see, Mr. Rabbitt, it's not the bridge so much as the toll."

"Hold on. There's a toll?" At least that's what Harvey thought he heard through his drunken ears. "On a bridge? At... " Harvey checked his imitation Rolex, "nearly one in the morning?" He chuckled, "I don't think I'll ever understand this country. I think I can afford a little toll. How much do I owe ya, chief?"

"Well, you may get lucky, sir. Finnegan may be asleep. It's his bridge so we tend to leave him with it."

"Well, if it's the shortest way, I'll take my chances with Finnegan."

The publican decided it was no use arguing with the American. He punched the prices of the drinks into an antique register that in turn spit out a small receipt. He handed the scrap to Harvey.

"Is this in dollars?" Rabbitt asked half-astounded.

"No sir, we stopped using dollars five years ago," replied the publican with a wry smile.

"Really? You used to use dollars here? Hell, I was only jokin'." Rabbitt removed some money from his wallet. "Keep the change," he said as he slapped it on the bar top.

The publican watched as Harvey Rabbitt slowly rose from the stool, both palms flat on the bar and feet spread further apart than usual. And then, like a snake, Rabbitt weaved his way, dodging absolutely nothing, to the door.

When he reached the door he leaned heavily on the frame, using the knob for support. Turning he said, "Nice place. Not like the local Irish tavern we got back home, 'Hank's Irish Sports Bar and Grill,' but at least the beer's cheap. Maybe you oughta think about serving burgers and buffalo wings, get a couple of widescreens in here for the football games. Might pack the place out more often." He gave the room another brief glance, "But at least you got the Ballykissnagel thing down pat. See ya."

"*Slán abhaile*," said the publican softly, "*Go n'éirí an t-ádh leat.*"

It wasn't until Harvey Rabbitt had staggered out into the night that the publican noticed he had left a twenty-dollar bill laying on the bar.

Harvey left the pub slightly less level headed than when he nearly slipped off his stool earlier. Next to the pub was a small cottage that had converted into a woollen goods shop for tourists. He had visited there earlier in the day and had already penned a deal with them to supply Anderson & Anderson with the rights to their sock patterns and recipes for their homemade dyes.

Not long after the wool shop Harvey came upon a white cottage that had long

Thirteen

ago succumbed to entropy and had a slight and lazy lean to it. A wooden plaque mounted near the front door proclaimed the cottage to be the 'Kehoe Lodge'. It had probably seen better days, thought Harvey, a unique fixer-upper. A small overgrown path ran along the side of the decrepit house to the equally decrepit field that lay behind it at the base of the hill. A low wall made of tightly piled rocks ran right along the side of the path and up the hill for as far as Harvey could see.

Harvey Rabbitt took the path as described to him, brushing away the dewy grass that grew over the wall and hung over the path. He followed it past the cottage and alongside the brambly field. When Harvey reached the base of the hill he stopped to urinate on the wall, gently swaying back and forth in the salty sea breeze that blew in off the ocean. As he relieved himself, his eyes wandered up the dark hill in front of him. Harvey squinted at what first looked to be a solitary light tumbling down the hillside. It bobbed up and down, staggered left and right, all the while coming straight towards Harvey.

When the light was almost upon him, Harvey identified what it was - a lantern, the old type that Harvey had only seen before in movies like *The Wolf-Man*. And an old man not unlike Lon Chaney Jr. held the lantern aloft. His face was illuminated partly by the lantern's light and partly by its shadow, casting his countenance in a mould of great desperation. The old man resembled the man pictured on the postcard Harvey sent his brother earlier that day. In fact, all the old men around the village seemed like they could have served as the model for the postcard.

He wore a cobalt blue and rust red sweater, over which was one of those traditional tweed jackets and hats with the snap in front (both of which Harvey was bringing samples to the boss on Monday). The man's hair was iron with white stubble poking out from his jaw. Harvey thought the old man looked like he wasted a great deal of time propping up the bar or sitting on the bench in front of the post office. What he needs is to visit the gym a few times a week, thought Harvey as he zipped up.

The old man came up to him, gasping for breath. "Yeh're not going up to Finnegan's Bridge, are yeh, sir? Have yeh not been warned about the toll?" He was clearly shaken and between his wavering voice and heavy brogue, Harvey had a difficult time understanding him.

"As a matter of fact, I am going that way," said Harvey smugly. "Is the price high?" he asked slightly amused. He jangled the change in his pocket.

"It's dear enough I'd say!" replied the old man flabbergasted. "I just come from that way," he said thumbing the path behind him, "I wouldn'ta done it meself, but I'm meeting the gombeen man at the pub in a few minutes. And I can't be late fer that."

Harvey didn't have a clue what a gombeen man was, but considering the way the old man talked, he imagined it was something involving money. Harvey could always sense when money was at stake.

"O' course if Finnegan's asleep yeh'll stand a good chance o' sneaking across the bridge like I done. But waking Finnegan's a bad idea. A real beast if ever there was one. If he wakes and finds yeh on his bridge--" the old man's face went white like his stubble. "Yeh'll have to excuse me, sir. *Go n'éirí an t-ádh leat*, God bless," and he hurried down the path towards the pub.

Harvey smirked to himself, "These people buckle under authority. Got no sense of pride." He belched a few times to ease the tension in his beer-swollen belly before continuing up the increasingly steep path.

For the next twenty minutes or so the path was a ghost. Sometimes it was there, clear as day, other times it vanished from view by either overgrown brush or Harvey's bleary eyes. It wasn't long after that that the trail wound around the side

Thirteen

of the hill, cutting off Harvey's view of the small collection of lights that was the pub and surrounding cottages. Harvey followed the trail up the hill's southern face, until it levelled out just shy of the peak.

"That's probably what they'd call a river. Looks like run-off to me," said Harvey when he came upon a stream that trickled down through the brush from somewhere higher up on the hill. The path led right up to the moon-bathed trickle and then turned to follow it as it ran down the gradual slope. And it wasn't long after that when Harvey Rabbit came upon Finnegan's Bridge.

Finnegan's Bridge turned out to be a small wooden bridge that looked in the moonlight, to be painted rusty red. Where the bridge spanned, the stream wasn't more than six or seven feet across; and even at night Harvey could see the water flowing over loose rocks and rubble. It could be walked across without so much as getting your ankle wet. The bridge was more of a luxury than a necessity.

Harvey Rabbit walked up to the bridge and stopped himself with a laugh. As far as he could see, there was no trace of a booth or even a basket to throw your change into like on the Illinois interstate just outside of Chicago. "Dumb Micks. Where do they expect me to put the money?"

Harvey assumed that Finnegan must be drunk, asleep, or both, and in any case probably somewhere warm. "Smartest of the lot of them." Even if Finnegan were around, Harvey probably would have laughed in his face and hopped from stone to stone across the stream. His shoes would get wet, but it would be worth is just to see the look on Finnegan's face.

"The road less travelled," repeated Harvey as he, for the first time ever, had his own interpretation of a poem he was taught in high school. "But seeing as there's no one here to stop me from going across Mister Finnegan's Bridge..." Harvey said raising his voice at the end of the sentence. He stepped onto the rust-coloured planks.

His imitation leather shoes trip-trapped stiffly as he walked drunkenly to the centre of the bridge. "Hey Finnegan!" he yelled as he unzipped his fly, "I'm on your bridge and I don't plan on giving you a dime!" Harvey stamped his feet a few times on the planks for emphasis and arced a stream of piss off the bridge and into the water. He whistled 'Sweet Home Alabama' as at least three pints left him. When he had finished what he called 'shaking hands with Nixon,' he leaned over the side of the bridge and gazed drunkenly into the stream.

What looked back however was not his reflection, but something much ghastlier. The mug that stared at him was neither entirely canine nor simian, but something of a hybrid. Its matted, orange-ochre hair was a collection of twigs, leaves, and heath grass.

Harvey Rabbit staggered backwards to the opposite side of the bridge, and leaned on the rail in disbelief. His numbed legs refused to carry him anywhere even when a pair of great, black claws rose up from beneath the bridge and the creature pulled its bulk onto the planks. The beast stood on short legs so that it more resembled an oversized gorilla that Harvey had seen on a nature show about Africa. Harvey had seen real gorilla at the zoo and had even been to Africa on business, but never could he remember something as vicious, or as large, as this.

When the beast smiled, which is what it looked like it was doing when it opened its glistening maw; it revealed a set of razor sharp canines stained the same rusty red colour as the bridge.

"Y-You must be Finnegan," was all Harvey could mutter before another three pints unexpectedly left his body.

Ring-ring. Ring-ring. The phone echoed down the hallway of the guesthouse.
"Hello?"

Thirteen

"Hello, is that Mrs. Walshe?" asked a meek voice, "This is Finton from down at the pub."

"Oh, Finton, how're things?"

"Not at all bad, not at all bad. You wouldn't happen to have a gentleman lodger staying with you at the moment, would you? An American fellow."

"Surely you know so yourself, Finton. I talked to aul' Johnny this morning when he dropped off my shopping. He said that Mr. Rabbitt was down at your place all night. Left the place on rubber legs I hear."

"Aye, that's so. Did he come back last night?"

"Which way did you sent him home, Finton?" enquired Mrs. Walshe in a stern, matronly tone.

"I tried to get him to take the scenic route, but he insisted on the bridge. He was keen on saving time. You know how they are."

"Now Finton Fingal O'Flahertie Wills O'Toole, you should know better than to be sending a stranger that way with the toll and all." The receiver buzzed like an angry bee in Finton's ear.

"I'm sorry Mrs. Walshe, but I... so he never came home last night?"

"Well he certainly wasn't at breakfast, Mr. O'Toole," scolded Mrs. Walshe

"Oh dear, he probably woke up Finnegan," lamented Finton. "Would you do me a favour? If you see aul' Johnny again, would you ask him to pick up another torch at Kennedy's for me?" and then added thoughtfully, "And another packet of those frozen spring rolls?"

Thirteen

SAMUEL
REBECCA BILLINGS

I hate the dark. Samuel tells me about the creatures lurking there, and Samuel knows everything. When he comes round we play 'hiding from the monster.' We huddle tight under the duvet, and tickle each other and wriggle like the worms I throw at my sister in the garden, and giggle until we feel sick while he describes the jagged shadows outside, waiting to bite us if we stick out so much as a toe. The best times are when we shout rude words like willy and bum to make the ghouls and demons disappear, because Samuel says they don't like it if you are disrespectful. When he comes to play it is a safe kind of scared, just like when I hit Chloe with a worm, she screams and shudders, but then she just throws it back and I scream, until we are both covered in worm juice. It's a different kind of fear at night.

The first visitor grows from a picture on the wall. In the daytime it is Tea Airy Hon Ree (Dad taught me how to say it. He plays for Arsenal. Thierry Henri I mean, not Dad) but at night I can't see his smile, just a smudgy shape which begins to move. Red eyes grow from the wall on stalks just like the eyes on a snail and he has broken grey teeth. I know he will suck my eyeballs out if I let him so I squeeze them shut and screw my lips into a tight little button because he would like to cut out my tongue. I feel breath on my face as he whispers my name and there is a scent of pipe smoke and old wet dogs. I try to breath through my nose but it's bunged up so I am snorting through snot, but can't open my mouth even though I'm suffocating because I need my tongue for loads of things so I shout for Mum.

Mum is here, warm and snuggly. She smells of cake and flowers and her silky hair tickles my face. The hall light is on so when I look up at Thierry he is normal again, with his red shirt bright against the green grass of the pitch, grinning for his fans. Mum is murmuring that it was just a nightmare and I want to tell her that I was awake all the time but I remember Samuel's warning. He said that there are special people like us who can see the creatures and people like Mum and Dad who don't believe in them. Whenever you tell somebody about a creature and they say it's not real, it gives it more power and makes it even more angry and dangerous next time. So I say nothing, just cling to Mum while she tells me that Samuel will be coming to play with me tomorrow, and in the afternoon it's Josh Webster's birthday party. I want to say that sometimes the games I play with Samuel scare me, and that nobody likes Josh Webster because he is useless at sport and weird because his parents don't let him watch television, and he constantly picks his nose and eats it. Then I decide that if Samuel comes over I'll have somebody to talk to about the monsters, and remember that Josh Webster's mum always makes huge party bags to take away with proper toys and everything. People liked Josh for about a week after his birthday last year. Mum kisses me and leaves again.

The next phantasm (it's a word Samuel uses, it sounds more special than ghost) grows from my dressing gown on the back of the door. The black folds shiver into a face with hollow spaces where the eyes should be and lips the colour of mud at the bottom of a pond. I turn to the wall and lie still as I can, and I count backwards from twenty to one in my head. This is a trick Samuel taught me, and sometimes we lie gripping each other under the duvet and counting to make the monsters go away, with our breath making us hot and damp. I never see the ghosts in the daytime, but that's because Samuel warns me when they're about to come and we hide. I turn my head and the counting spell has worked, the face has vanished, then I taste something salty and realise that I have bitten my lip too hard concentrating on the numbers, and I hope that ghosts can't smell blood. I

Thirteen

curl into a ball and bury my nose in the pillow, trying to think about what I will get in my party bag tomorrow.

Then there is a scratching at the window and a shape at the curtains. It's Murphy, our dog. I want to let him in as he's been in the garden so long, but I'm scared to open the window because I don't know what I might see. I asked Samuel what he might look like after being run over and then buried under the cherry tree and he said he wouldn't be a skeleton yet, but his fur would be gone and his skin would have become a bit red and oozy, like when you get to the end of a slush puppy, and there might be maggots. Maggots is a special word for me and Samuel. When we're under the duvet and one of us shouts "Maggots!" we both tickle each other. But maggots aren't funny at night when I'm by myself. The scratching gets faster and Murphy starts to whine and whimper, and even though I put the pillow over my head, it doesn't dim the sound and a terrible howling fills the whole room, and there's a smell of earth and Murphy's old basket. The pillow is wrenched away from over my head and I screw my eyes tight shut again, because I want to remember Murphy like he used to be, and not all bleeding and rotten.

Dad is holding me. I realise that it was him taking the pillow away and me making the howling noise. His beard scratches but I don't mind. The hall light is on and as I am lying against him I look up at Thierry, who smiles down. Dad sees me watching him.

"There have been a lot of nightmares tonight, haven't there, Ben? You'll grow out of them soon. I bet Thierry doesn't do this at night." I want to tell him that if he lay here in the dark and watched Thierry he would see him do stranger things than have nightmares, but I don't, and I don't mention Murphy either. That's because I know he won't believe me, and because I know that talking about Murphy would make him sad. When Murphy was buried we all went out to say goodbye, and Mum and Dad talked about what a good friend he was and how we should be happy that he had gone to heaven, but Dad's eyes went all glittery and Mum's did too. Perhaps it's because heaven is a bit like ghosts, and you have to be special to really believe in it. He kisses my head and I can smell toothpaste, and then he is gone.

The next day is sunny, which is good because we can bounce on the big trampoline in Josh Webster's garden. I think it's the only thing that stops him picking his nose. I'm up in my bedroom watching cartoons when I hear footsteps on the path outside, and I look out of the window. Samuel sees me and starts to skip and wave. Dad saw him doing this the other day and muttered that he thought he was a bit strange. Mum said that you were entitled to be a bit odd at that age, and it was nice that he came round to play with me, but Mum is nice about everybody.

"Good morning, Mrs Byrne."

"Hello, Samuel," and Mum starts telling him to go and find me upstairs, and that she is popping out to the shops, and Dad is playing his Saturday football match as usual. I hear the door close and Mum glides down the garden path in her silky dress, cornflower blue, she calls it.

Samuel pokes his head around the door, grinning. His teeth are false and I want to ask if he takes them out at night, and the sunlight gleams through the window onto his bald head. Normally I smile back and start laughing but I haven't quite felt like that the last couple of times. He hugs me and I can smell soap and cough sweets, then he reaches up and turns the TV off. The first few times he came we watched TV together and he told wonderful stories and we played hangman and battleships, and it was only towards the end he would see the ghosts, but now the creatures come sooner and sooner, and we have to go under

Thirteen

the duvet and do our special cuddling and touching. This time it happens almost at once.

"Time to hide, Ben", he says, looking around as if he can hear the creatures. This time, I don't know why, the thought of it frightens me more than the ghosts. I try to think of a way out.

"Samuel, perhaps they're friendly ghosts. Perhaps we should stay outside and try to talk to them". I've never seen Samuel snarl before, I've never seen anybody old snarl, but he does it now, and grabs me and pulls the duvet over us. He doesn't normally do this, he just protects me from the monsters, but suddenly I feel his fingers clawing at my clothes and he is wheezing more than normal, and telling me about the awful things outside, when I realise I don't believe him. I don't want to see the awful creatures with empty eye sockets but I don't want this either. I grab the corner of the duvet and throw it off. I look around the room. It is all normal as crisps. For the first time I shout at a grownup who isn't Mum or Dad.

"You're lying! There aren't any ghosts. Only I see ghosts! You're not special!" and suddenly he pins me down, holding my arms, telling me to damn well behave. Even Dad doesn't speak to me like that, not even the time I left the taps running in the bathroom sink when I was four because I wanted to make a home made waterfall. This isn't the normal, friendly Samuel and I start to scream. Suddenly Samuel stops and stares at the corner of the room. Between the TV and the Wallace and Grommit alarm clock there is a fuzzy, blurry shape. It reminds me of the little whirlwinds that you get in Autumn which pick up the dead leaves and throw them around the garden. I don't know what happens next but I hear growling and Samuel is dragged off the bed and onto the floor, his face goes purple and blue, and he stops moving. I think he might be asleep but his eyes are wide open. The shape fades, but in the shadows in the corner, I see a wagging tail.

Lots of people come to the house. A nice policeman asks questions, especially about dogs. Samuel has nasty dog bites, quite a savaging, he says. Savaging is a good word, I might use it in a story at school one day. They say he had a heart attack. Mum says it was just like Samuel, not wanting something like that preventing him from babysitting. They're worried I might have nightmares, but I don't think I'll have any now. I get even more cuddles, and they want to know if there's anything special I want. We're off to collect a new puppy this afternoon.

Thirteen

DOGGY
ROGER FREEDMAN

I slammed on my brakes but before I'd even heard the dull thud of car hitting dog, I knew it was too late.

The view from behind the windshield looked like a beautifully painted theatre backdrop. Streaks of red, pink and yellow dissected the grey that had been so dominant when I had started my drive over an hour ago, tearing it apart and ripping away its solemnity. The snow that covered the road and the lawns of the suburban dwellings to either side of me was like a blank canvas waiting to surrender itself to the victor of the war of colours above.

Beautiful, except for the screeching of my tyres as they desperately tried to grip to something. Awe-inspiring, except for the shape of the big black dog which rolled over my bonnet and up, over my roof, seeming to cast me a reproachful look in the split-second its tortured face was level with mine.

The car skidded from side to side. As I desperately turned at the wheel, I noticed the dog behind me in my rear-view mirror, crashing down onto the ground and sliding a few feet.

I pumped the brakes ferociously until finally the tyres managed to cause enough friction with the ice and black sludge that covered the road to bring the car to a halt.

"Fuck," I whispered. "Idiot."

One moment. One moment was all it had taken and I could have gotten myself killed, all because of a stupid lapse in concentration. And the poor dog... if that had been a small child...

"Idiot."

I looked once more in my rear-view mirror, averting my eyes from their own reflected guilty gaze and looking further back along the road to the shape of the dog.

I looked around. The streets were empty of everything other than parked cars. I waited for the dark windows of the houses to suddenly fill with light as the people awoken by the sound of the last few seconds forsook their warm beds to investigate. One of them would look out to see their dog dead. But for the moment, they remained dark.

Drive, a voice said. *There's nothing you can do; it was an accident.*

The voice had hardly finished when I found my right hand turning off the ignition, unbuckling my seatbelt and pulling at the door handle. It wasn't right to drive off. It would only mean trouble. Someone might be watching after all and would have enough wits about them to get my registration. Then there'd be trouble.

Sssshh, whispered the black sludge as my feet swung out of the car and onto the icy ground. The cold hit me immediately and I was reminded of the cause of my lapse in concentration – I'd been turning the heater down, concentrating too much on what should have been a simple twist of a dial and not enough on the road in front of me.

I closed the door gently behind me and sucked in a lungful of the freezing air as I took slow, careful steps towards the dog. I walked in a straight line through one of the two trenches caused by the wheels, like I was walking a tightrope. The dog lay a few meters beyond where the trenches began.

My senses were searching for anything – the slightest signal that things weren't as bad as I had first thought. My ears strained for a whimper while my eyes looked for a quick wagging of the tale. I was close enough now to see the wind ruffling its thick black hair and prayed for a different kind of movement, one that came from the dog itself, not caused by the harsh environment in which it found itself.

And then I heard it, so slight but unmistakable. The dog whimpering.

I hurried my steps, not caring now that I had left the comfort of the mini-trenches and entered the feint tracks left by the car before impact. I almost fell as my leg slid out from under me but recovered myself and stood over the dog. The one baleful eye I could see was fixed ahead, unblinking and unwilling to look at me, the cause of its suffering.

It whimpered again, louder this time, and I crouched beside it and placed a hand on its head. It was enough to gain the dog's forgiveness as it turned to look at me for the second time this early morning.

"You'll be okay," I said. "Just a bit of a bang, you'll pull through."

The dog blinked and then looked away, unconvinced by my diagnosis. And then, catching me by complete surprise, a cold, icy tear ran town my cheek and landed on the dog. I heard myself sob and shuddered with shame at the pain I had caused this innocent.

I covered my head with my hands and crouched there in the snow until a subtle change in the shadows that penetrated the extremes of my vision caused me to look up towards one of the houses on my right. I lifted the heavy dog as gently as I could and then made my way up the path that led to the house, inside which someone had just turned on a light. Slipping most of the way, I got to the front door and raised an elbow high enough to press the doorbell in quick succession.

"Who is it?" came a far away voice, old and irritated. I realised that the chances were the source of the voice hadn't heard the accident and they had probably been making a 4 a.m. trip to the toilet.

"Please," I urged. "I've had an accident. I've hit a dog with my car and it needs help."

"Hold on," came the reply, followed by the sound of feet descending stairs and the wary opening of his front door by a wizened old man. Seeing the dog in my arms and deciding I was genuine, he opened the door further and revealed his attire of dressing gown and slippers.

"He's hurt pretty bad," I said needlessly.

"You don't say." The old man came closer. "Wouldn't worry though. That's old Doggy. No one's going to be after you if he doesn't make it."

"What do you mean?" I was getting impatient. I wanted this old man to do something constructive, like let me use his phone or pull out a degree in veterinary science, not stand there chatting.

"Doggy. That's what they call him. He's a stray. A nuisance. Terrorises the other dogs but isn't seen for hide nor hair when the council come to look for him. If I were you, I'd lay him by the side of the road and drive on home."

"I'm not going home," I snapped.

"It's four in the morning," the old man pushed. "Fella, where are you going?" He took a step closer to me and looked closely. "That's an awful lot of blood you got splattered over you. All that blood come from Doggy?"

I was naïve to think the dog had a chance. It breathed its last breath ten minutes later on the old man's kitchen table. I stayed with if for a while, sobbing almost silently and stroking it, before I left quietly and drove off, putting the heating onto full. With the old man's head rolling around in the boot, along with the heads of my wife and her interfering mother, they made quite a racket.

WHEN SHE GREW OLD
MARK PATRICK LYNCH

When I awoke that morning, I found the gift she'd left for me beside my bedside – flowers, desiccated dead things, a parody of their vital beauty in a cracked vase filled to the brim with stagnant water. It was a wonder the smell hadn't woken me earlier. She'd been in the night, of course, entering my third-storey bedroom by the window. Brown autumnal leaves, brittle as only such remnants can be, lay beneath the opened sash window which should by rights have been latched and bolted (I am fastidious about such things, almost to the point of obsession). As if I needed any further hint. Autumn leaves in summertime, darling. How wonderfully melodramatic. She's the last of them by any count, by any reckoning that matters – was always going to be the last of them. The others had all come in their time; had come and been dispatched quickly enough. Some were dead even before they'd time to register the fact. Poor little lost boys, all grown up and gone to the grave. But not her. Oh no. Why, she'd waited till the last, tracking me all these years, following my every move from country to country, directing her top-hatted generals and comfort-blanket assassins from faraway lands. Until they'd all gone, all been used up, and there was her alone remaining.

Now she'd come herself, and there were just the two of us, as it should have been from the first. She blamed me, you understand. Blamed it all on the telling, on my telling. "You should have told the truth," she would say. And who could blame her for that? Certainly not I. But then we all have our burdens, our shadows, to consider... don't we?

I cleaned away the leaves beneath the window, threw the dead flowers in the dustbin, flushed the stagnant water, and washed my hands to be free of the touch of unseasonable death. I dressed and made my way down to the street, taking a late breakfast in a small corner restaurant where I am familiar but not known, and mused over the coming night's encounter. I found myself absurdly pleased that she was still alive. Had I ever doubted as much? I do not know. Perhaps because it had been so long since the last of them came anywhere near me I had thought her slipped away to the other side. (If truly there be such a place. I do not know, nor do I intend to find out.) But then again, perhaps not, perhaps I am lying once more, though to myself this time. No, I can say I never honestly believed her gone. Not until I could see the evidence with my own eyes could I have believed that. And even then I would be fearful of shadows, of children's laughter around the statue in the park. I must tell you this: she was always the better at telling stories, more adept at fashioning beginnings and middles and ends - although, I'd flatter myself, mine would be one story she would not live to bring about to a conclusion – and so I was wary of her and her abilities. After all, there was always the danger of a twist in the tale, and she was more than capable of tightening her grip till the screw was driven in. Putting my thoughts of her behind me, I went about my business for the day, making market checks on my various stocks and shares, bringing it all to a fair conclusion, and being able to spend some time enjoying myself in the city library. I returned to my Edwardian townhouse in early summer's evening, enjoying the perfumes of a fine day's end, and finding myself wishing the night's events might be so delicately settled.

I lived alone and had done for some time. My infrequent visitors had seen to that over the years. It was hard enough to retain friendships and acquaintances as it was, given my unique position, and night-time assassins could be a tedious distraction or a deadly business depending on the circumstances. So better I was a singular household, a castle built of strong fortifications, for the duration of my ... siege. Yet even so, for all my securities, she could have had me last night. As I slept, did she gaze down at me, her face softened by the moonlight that must surely have streamed through the open window? Did she look on my sleeping form with her night-dark eyes and tremble at the thought of my demise? I shuddered at such imaginings. Lying prone before her, how fortunate I was that her whimsical nature ensured this be concluded in the shape of Story. But somehow I was responsible for that too – at least in part. Tonight would be different, though, because I had advance warning of her presence, and we would meet as close to equals as was possible. On entering my home I locked and bolted the door, wanting to be secure in the knowledge that at least when she came she would enter only where and how I permitted. In the downstairs rooms I pulled the heavy drapes together against the evening traffic, and then did the same in the first-floor library and study; a crime on any other day as beautiful as this but permissible given the sobriety of the task now at hand. On leaving each room I was careful to lock the door behind me and to pocket the key. Certainty can best be served by heavy mortise locks. I did the same on up to the third-floor, where I knew our encounter would take place. After all, she knew how the story went...

I found myself wondering how it would go, our meeting. And wondered as well how she would look, what ravages the ticking crocodile of time might have scarred her with. The others had worn the lines on their faces with all the solemnity of the terminally condemned, and I was put in mind of those poor children one sees ravaged by cancers; the same look of hope and confusion shining from a face reduced to its skeletal basics. Age can in turn do such things to men and women. Having checked that she had not arrived early, making a surprise entry during the day while I was away, I made my way back downstairs to the kitchen, returning to the third-floor with a bottle of chilled champagne and two glasses – fine crystal flutes – in the unlikely event things should progress from a civil point. Oh, and I brought one other thing up too: my twist in the tale, you might say. There in the bedroom, I waited by the open window, watching the sun set in a flush across the horizon and the first of the stars that peppered the night twinkle to life. The cold gently embraced me as the day's heat faded and the moon rose. It wasn't until the afterglow of day had vanished that I saw her. At first I wasn't sure ... a shooting star perhaps, though one low in the sky? But then came certainty: it was she, coming as I had known she would. Passing through the shadowed copses of chimneys and sloping meadows of roofs, she was little more than a glow journeying below the lowest watching stars, an inversion of the lights and traffic of the city streets beneath her. I watched, hardly able to take a breath as the distant glow became sharper, more clearly defined. Though still at a distance, I could tell she had on a white gown, possibly her nightdress, and her arms were spread wide, her trailing feet kicking as though she were swimming and not flying through the night air.

And she was terrible. Oh my Lord, how I was scared of her. I wanted only to cower away from the window then, to hide in the closet until morning came and she might be gone. Wanted her simply to not be. But I was frozen senseless, unable to release my grip on the windowsill. And there I remained, helpless and vulnerable, as all the while she grew ever closer...

She kept coming, a huge moth outside the window, reaching towards me, her arms extended, her fingers spread wide, the dreadful nails at their ends curling monstrously with age; yellowed and browned and eager for my throat. I broke my grip on the sill, backed away almost stumbling across the room, not even thinking to close the window and slide home its bolts. With horror I wondered what thoughts kept her buoyant. Of my end at her hands, of her revenge? Then all too suddenly, before I'd time to regain my senses and dash to the window and slam it shut, she had glided from the cold night and into my room. Had she timed her appearance to coincide with the appearance of unhindered moonlight into the room? Possibly. Whatever, the effect was to transcend terror. Here she was revealed as a creature borne of the night: her old beauty was the cold that cloaked the moon blue-white, her terribleness that same aloofness of the night's curve. Her bare feet touched the floorboards as she settled from her flight, her ragged toenails scraped the lacquer. She was centre-stage in the play tonight, and I was backed away up against the wall, wishing to be overlooked. Her sparse hair was pure white, thin as cobwebs, and draped over her bony skull; her face lined and venous, thin still, yet sagging to one side. The nightgown she wore was patched and ragged, hanging on her as though a shroud on a mouldering skeleton. When she looked at me after briefly examining the room (remember, she had been here the previous night and had so had time to give it a more leisurely inspection) she smiled, revealing sparse yellowed teeth protruding at crooked angles from pale, receding gums. I couldn't help but imagine her floating above me last night as I slept. Did she rise and fall to the rhythm of my breathing, while I lay beneath her, a dreamer unaware?

I banished such thoughts from my head, they would do me no good here, and I forced my attention back to the creature in front of me. She had worn lipstick for me, or an approximation thereof, but it looked as though it had been clumsily applied. Perhaps because of her long, curling fingernails she was not able to perform so delicate a task as apply make-up. And then I really noticed the sagging to the left side of her face, the immobility there that was like a mask. Stroke, I thought. One of the ravages of age. The unsteadiness of her stance now she was no longer airborne confirmed this to me. She seemed set to collapse, was favouring her right leg over the left, the bulk of her weight, what little there was, being taken by it. She was breathing heavily, the journey here having evidently caused her a great deal of exertion. Seeing her weakness, I was a little less afraid of her then.

"You," she whispered when she had her breathing better regulated. Her old woman's voice seemed to travel slowly across the room. "You killed him," she said. "You killed them all."

So this would be no easy meeting. But in truth, I'd hardly thought it would be. Let the champagne go to waste, then.

I was surprised at the strength of my voice as I said, "I did what I had to. I had no choice."

"There are always other choices!"

"No. The story demanded it."

I nodded at her. "You above all should know that, I made you the storyteller."

She thought about this for a moment, and I could see her mind working behind the side of her face still capable of expression. As if wary of traps, she said, "You gave him a shadow..."

"Gave it him back. The dog tore it away: the nanny slammed the window and it snapped off. He already had a shadow."

"No! No, he shouldn't ever have had one. That's why he couldn't die."

"We can all die, including him. And he did."

"Because of you!"

"No." She watched me, wondering if it was the truth I spoke. Moonlight streamed past her, making a web of light I was careful to avoid around her dark shadow on the floor.

"He couldn't grow up," she said confused, "so how could he die?"

I shook my head sadly. "Because he couldn't grow up. How else could we not grow old, other than by dying young?"

"You are no older."

"And who said I was alive?"

She shook her head at that, "Oh no, you're alive." She sniffed theatrically. "I

Thirteen

can smell you. I could hear you breathing and farting as you slept last night, see your chest rise and fall beneath the sheets."

"Then why didn't you kill me last night? You could have, you know."

"Because..." Her voice faded in confusion and her eyes left mine. And for a moment I took pity on her.

"Because of the story," I said. But oh no, she didn't want to hear that – it would make her no better than me. Her eyes flared with anger, but then they just as quickly seemed to die and she hung her head and stared at the floor. She needed help in bringing this to an end.

"Michael came closest."

She looked up slowly.

"What?"

"Yes. Swung his sword and nicked my ear. Here. Can you see?" I levered my head to one side so she might see the tiny scar, long since healed, across the lobe. "He didn't last long after that, but he was still the closest."

Darkness began to gather behind her eyes, far darker and more profound than any I had imagined in my dreams of her, seeming to gleam like oil. "And John? You want to know how easily John went – crying on his knees and calling for his mother, his sister, his god? Little cry-baby John." Still she held her ground in the middle of the room, though I sensed she wouldn't remain there much longer. I edged slowly around her, staying out of the moonlight and what it might reveal, keeping my back to the wall, running my hand softly over the textured paper. I dodged carefully around the tallboy, sliding ever closer to the tray I'd brought up from the kitchen. The champagne, the cut crystal flutes, that one last thing...

"The twins were fun too. In the guts of one – out the guts of another." A little zigzag cut of the hand for illustration. She watched from the centre of her moonlit web, silent all the time, her anger overcoming her confusion as she gauged my cruelty. "And for what?" I demanded. "For your petty revenge, your imagined sleights. And what's it worth now? You're not even real, Wendy. You're a figment of my imagination. And Peter... Peter was just the same. But you were his mother, don't you know. It was you who stitched the shadow back to him, not me. He was your child then. You gave birth to him in any sense that mattered with that one act. And what can be born can die, can grow old. Tick-tock, tick-tock, Wendy."

"But he was the pan! He couldn't die!"

"He did, though." I turned my back on her, reached down to the table and behind the champagne glasses for the final item I'd brought up from the kitchen. And she came at me, as I knew she would, furiously and without restraint. I heard her start, but I was quicker. I spun around, and the hook sank into her belly easily and without resistance, stopping her instantly in her tracks. Up, the sharpened curve of the hook slid, slicing a path through her sternum, rising further and further to burst her heart. And she came to a halt against me.

I held her upright, what little weight of her there was, as she slowly realised what had happened: that her life was trickling away. Her papery skin was so close to me, the last of her breath, smelling wonderfully of wild berries, a gentle tickle on my cheek, her painted lips an **O** of surprise and resignation. "I'm told," I said, speaking as gently as I could, "that it's an awfully big adventure. Sleep well, wendie-bird, Wendy Darling." Her eyes closed and there was no more breath, no more wild berries against my skin.

I stayed with her till just before dawn.

I decided against removing her body from the room, cleaning her ink-black blood from the floor, pretending she hadn't been there. Instead I elected to let the

Thirteen

cleaners find her when next they came. There would be a police investigation, of course, newspaper headlines – possibly concerning the hook murderer, if the public could remember that far back … if the journalists could remember that far back. But it was at an end at last. There would be no more of them. Leaving my townhouse for the last time, what few possessions I deemed necessary swinging in a bag at my side, I turned second to the right and straight on till morning. And when the sun rose, I cast no shadow.

FROZEN ON FILM
KEVIN ROACH

'Ibuycameras' is my log-in. I buy them, clean them up a little and then resell them. Hopefully at a profit. I like Manual focus Nikons, Leicas of course, maybe an old Pentax if the price is right. But it's the 1970's rangefinders I specialize in, Canonets, Yashica Electros, Olympus RCs and RDs, and the Ricoh 500G. I dust them off, replace the light seals, remove the old leatherette and recover them in colourful lizard skins. They sell pretty well and I can make 30-40 bucks for a couple hours work.

I got lucky on a Canon Canonet QL17, model G-III. The camera was introduced in 1972 and sold more than 1.2 million units. It was half the size of an SLR with a fast sharp lens, a great little "poor man's Leica." The Ebayer I got it from said it was from an estate sale. He didn't know anything about old cameras, didn't have a battery, and didn't test it. Strictly as-is. Paypal preferred.

Usually I avoid these auctions but this one looked ok in the photos and included a Canonlite D flash, which was probably worth what I bid. It sat around on my workbench for a couple weeks before I got around to checking it out.

When I opened the back I saw there was still film in the camera. I snapped it shut immediately but knew the last few frames would be destroyed. I've bought cameras with film in them before and always just tossed it but this time I figured I'd have it developed. Might be fun to see what the previous owner was shooting.

I took the film down to Wal-Mart with a couple rolls of my own and had them one-hour it. Later, when I got out to the car I dug the photos out of the blue plastic Wal-Mart bag. With the engine idling I did a quick check of my pictures. The first was my cousin's birthday party. One or two good shots of my friends and relatives, mostly a boring waste of film. The second envelope was a roll of Kim and Stephs' baby, cute in his 'I got 2 mommies' t-shirt. Next was a twelve-exposure test roll from an old Argus, all overexposed, sticky shutter. Finally I came to the prints from the Canonet.

The first ten shots looked like a college campus. The colours were a little off with grey-green grass and a pinkish tint to the sky. Lousy composition. Boring. A building entrance symmetrically centred in the frame. Some longhaired, blue jean clad boys playing Frisbee in a grassy area amid post-modern campus buildings. An empty hallway, underexposed, oooh spooky. A shot across the rooftops of a little college town, the horizon tilted like some freshman photog's attempt at artsy. I was starting to think this was a waste of money.

Then there was the girl. A distant shot crossing the grey-grass Frisbee yard. Straight long brownish blonde hair under a leather headband, patched bell bottoms, granny glasses, keds on her feet. Obviously no bra holding those perky breasts under a plain, white, men's t-shirt.

Medium range. Full figure shot. A straight white smile, hand at chest level reaching for a wave, nipples straining against tight cotton. Recognition and anticipation.

Close up. Head and shoulders fill the frame. Lens flaring off the reflections in her glasses. A sprinkle of freckles across the nose. Dimples in her smile. Lips pursed, a kiss?

Next shot, out of focus. Inside the lenses' focusing range of 2.6 feet. Golden brown blur, white corner, fuzzy skin tones, a cheek? Grey-green grass filling three quarters of the frame.

Then a series of six shots, taken in an outdoor cafe? Uncomfortable metal chairs, tables, concrete. The girl, familiar. Not her face, I have never seen her before. But her type. This is one of the girls of my youth. Back in the 70's all the girls looked like this. Or tried to anyway. Fashionably patched jeans, granny

Thirteen

glasses, (probably plain glass lenses) and that springy, summer of love attitude. (Even though the summer of love went up in flames five years earlier.) Fresh smooth skin, sunlight sparkling in her hair, the disaffected slouch, the animated laugh.

I remember her and all those girls like her. They're older now, older and wiser? I don't know. Husbands, children, SUVs, planting flower gardens to bright their mundane suburban lives. All the hopes, dreams, and plans of those perky breasted girls lost to mortgage, jobs, bills, bake sales, and divorce. But not this one. This girl is frozen in my youth. Frozen in my memory. Frozen in a thirty-year-old photograph.

Final frames, A cornfield. Iowa? Illinois? Rows and rows of eight foot corn, linear perspective, atmospheric perspective, acres of corn stretching to infinity. Only corn and sky, horizon broken by blue hazed barns and silos, miles away.

And the girl, peeking between the stalks, laughing, tassels in her hair, dimples deep in the bright sunlight. Shadows painting corn stalks on her clothes. I played this game myself once, in the cornfields of my youth. Top and bottom of the frame fogged. Exposed to the light when I opened the camera.

And running, blue jean rump, long hair flying, the bottom of her left sneaker. Rushing through the rows, leaves slapping bare arms, stalks rustling, a gust of girl blowing through the field. Corn and girl and earth blurred by camera shake, should have opened the aperture. More fogging.

Next frame, fog spreads across the top and bottom reaching for the centre. Faded girl, hands on hips. Anger? Defiance? True emotion lost in the light.

And the next, only the centre of the frame readable. Point of view from above aiming at the subject on the ground. Long hair plastered to her face. Eyes wide, mouth open. Fear. And a shadow blurred and fogged rising into the frame.

Final shot, almost entirely white, a strip of faded image clinging to the side of the photograph. Just a hand, reaching for the edge of the frame. Frozen thirty years. Frozen in the corn.

COBBLED CONNELY
MATTHEW WARD

I was there that night at the dance.

You were there too. You danced to Contra with all the rest. But I danced the Cobbled Connely. All the time looking at you! And you gazed back into my eyes, pupils wide with wonder, and I knew you wanted to dance it too.

It wasn't difficult. But the timing takes work, and this was the wrong time.

I saw you with lady friends, beaming gaily over your fruit punch and sandwich quarters. You cast that longing glance once more my way, enticing, pitching your request. But it was the wrong time! I shook my head to tell you, but oh, how I yearned to dance with you then. You bubbled and your lips quivered, frothing punch from lip to tongue, but all I would hear were your yearning cries of anguish. How did you think you could dance the Cobbled Connely amongst friends? "Fuck them!", I thought. "Fuck them and come, come and dance with me. Come and dance the Cobbled Connely!" But you did not leave them. And I waited.

I saw you with him - saw your false smile and, in his eyes, that love-puppet glint as he bowed, and took your hand in his claw. Saw the lock in his embrace, the swirls of petticoat and black suede as you combined and spun. Your colours made brown, and you did not dance the Cobbled Connely. I waited.

I did well to wait. Two hours, and there could not have been a more perfect time.

You were so beautiful! You shone pale as powder snow against the dark night, delicate as paper. Like a ballerina. I felt so close to you, could almost feel your spine in my open palms. Your tight sequined frock glistening like a lake in the moonlight. Your pinned back locks with ribbons, little gingham flags, your slippers as glass, noiseless and traceless as you walked the beaten track home. I met you there my little Cinderella. I showed you the moves.

How we must have looked, together the two of us, as we danced alone on that bridleway. It was cold, and you shivered! But I went through it all. We danced like lovers there. Then I took you home and we danced the Cobbled Connely some more. I took you down to the hollow amidst the fuchsia and, together, we danced along the riverbed. How I adored you then, my little partner, cavorting to those moves. Hand in hand, embraced, leaping to the steps of my eternal waltz.

And you danced so well!

WARTS AND ALL
COLIN MULHERN

I can still remember the first time that I noticed it. It was on the bookshelves in my Grandfather's study. I used to go in there because there was an enormous oak table. I would sit there with a pad of paper for hours at a time; drawing and colouring until the whole table was littered with my work. But on this day I had grown bored with my doodles and my attention turned to the bookshelves. These contained hundreds of books which were broken up every now and again with spaces containing ornaments. There were all sorts of treasures up there, but the one that gripped my attention was a tiny shoe.

I climbed up on a chair to get a better look. It was the strangest ornament I had ever seen. It was brown and ugly and stood on a small wooden mount. I did not hear my Grandfather come into the room, and I nearly jumped out of my skin when he leaned over my shoulder and whispered in my ear:

"It's made from human skin."

I turned to see him smiling, but his smile was directed at the ornament, not at me. He picked it up and brought it down so I could have a closer look.

"And not any old skin either." he said. "Warts," he whispered. "Every lump and bump. Four thousand, three hundred and eleven of them; each one dried then stitched together."

Now that I could see it close up I could see what he meant. The leather of the shoe was not in sheets as you would expect. It was made up from thousands of tiny lumps. Each lump had been pierced and stitched to the next in line and one below, like rings on a chain mail vest.

"Why?" I asked.

My grandfather smiled again and sat down. He placed the shoe on the table.

"When I was a young man," he said, "I worked as a hospital porter. During my time there we had an outbreak of Elephant Feet. I don't recall the medical expression but it got the name Elephant Feet because anyone who caught this nasty little virus developed the most horrendous warts all over their feet and ankles. The thing was, the only cure was to let the virus run its course. In the meantime these warts would grow wild, developing under other warts, cutting off the circulation to the warts above, which would die and fall off. Each morning the nurses would brush the patients' feet, removing the dead warts. Then they would brush the warts from the sheets into a pan. The pan was emptied into a bucket and we had the job of taking this, along with other waste, to the incinerator.

"Well, like I said, I was a young man, and young men are often daft, often disgusting. We started having a bit of fun with these warts. We used to get a piece of elastic and stretch it between thumb and forefinger. This would work like a mini catapult and we could fire these lumps of dead flesh at each other. This became such a popular pastime that we used to bring the bucket of warts straight to our mess room. We even used them as chips for card games.

"And then one day, we started talking about other things we could do with these horrible little things. The suggestion to make a shoe came about as a joke. It was meant to be ironic; you know, what with the warts coming from feet in the first place. Well, a joke soon turned into a bet, and the next thing I knew, I was spending my dinner times and tea breaks for the next few months stitching these things together. Four thousand, three hundred and eleven of them."

"And you made them into a shoe?"

"A shoe? No. This is not a shoe, although that was the original plan. There were not enough for that. So no, not a shoe but a sandal. Which is why it has the inscription on the plate on the base."

And there on the base was a tiny brass plaque, inscribed with a serif script.

Thirteen

'Wart Sandal.'

Thirteen

FUCKING VAMPIRES
ERIK TOMBLIN

I have one. I keep him in a room with no doors or windows. He is my gift to you. Granted, I put him there for a few selfish reasons, but ultimately, he is for your enjoyment. Make no mistake about that.

I guess I should give him a name. Something sexy and cool like "Tristan de Tartar," maybe? "Trissy" for short. That fits well, I think. He is sexy and cool. I've kept him well supplied with absinthe and nubile young boys to feed upon. Trissy is pretty wasted right about now.

When I placed him there he was pretty pissed, flying around the room in a fury of fangs and black fingernails. My laughing just fuelled his anger. He tore at his silky pirate-shirt in a futile attempt at intimidation. It didn't last long once he realized there was no way out.

He calmed down a bit, trying a more classic approach at getting to me. I must admit, he is quite beautiful, even more so than Bret Michaels on Poison's first album cover - high cheekbones, pouting lips, flawless complexion. His hair is raven black, falling down upon his shoulders and back like a river of night.

Trissy's eyes pulse green and gold when he's working that vampire hoodoo. Sexy, yes, but I don't swing that way. He tried anyway, talking softly and staring up into the ceiling, trying to get a fix on me. I laughed some more until he got pissed again, pounding against the walls and threatening my whole family.

The absinthe seemed to soothe him. He definitely appeared to feel a whole lot better about the situation after I sent in the first shivering boy, naked and curled up into a corner of the room. Trissy approached him cautiously at first, then like a mother comforting her sick child, took the boy into his arms. He held the boy in his lap for a few minutes, stroking his curly brown hair. Finally, when the child felt comfortable enough to lay his head upon Trissy's shoulder, that vampire ripped into him like a coyote on a pork chop.

Now Trissy just sits there on the bed of red silk pillows I laid out for him, sipping at the last bottle of absinthe and singing under his breath. Some music, perhaps? He must hear my thoughts because he looks up to see what I've placed against one wall. Trissy grunts, stands and walks over to the radio. He rummages through the small box of CDs: Bauhaus, Nick Cave, Dead Can Dance. He puts in "Disintegration" by The Cure, of course.

I've switched them all, anyway. When Slayer's "Angel of Death" engulfs the room he practically hits the floor, weighted down by terror and covering his ears. It takes him a few seconds to collect himself before he tries to turn the CD player off, but I won't let him. Trissy roars up at the ceiling, kicking the radio across the room, but I allow it to keep playing - an audible tidal wave of distortion and pain. On his bed of pillows, Trissy curls up and weeps, keeping his arms wrapped around his head to help drown out the music. I guess I'll give him a break. It's time to move on.

The radio is gone and Trissy hears the tapping of the large wooden stake I've placed on the opposite side of the room. He looks up just in time to see it flying at him, lodging deep into his chest. His mouth opens in a silent scream.

I count one... two... three... then the stake is gone. Trissy looks down at his chest. He sees no blood, no wound. He chokes out a nervous laugh and shakes his finger toward the ceiling. He's convinced I'm up here somewhere. Maybe I am.

What's that around your neck, Trissy?

Feeling the weight, he looks down at the ring of garlic cloves with which I've graced him. At first, he jerks with surprise, apparently not sure what it could be. He seems to figure it out quickly - he's smart that way - and laughs aloud, mocking my attempt to hurt him. He says something about "ignorant myths". He has forgotten that he is mine.

A steamy, sizzling stench wafts to his nose, like garlic chicken on the grill. It is, of course, his fragrant necklace searing his smooth, ivory neckline. Trissy yelps and rips the garlic from his body, suffering blisters to his hands as well. He rolls off the pillows and reaches for the last of his drink, but I've taken it from him. Now, much like the young boy I fed him earlier, Trissy curls up into a corner of the room and weeps.

Fucking vampires. Where's your power now, Trissy? Where's all that sound and fury, signifying nothing? Your eyeliner is running and it's not very flattering. You smell of booze and blood. To sum it up: you've lost your cool. Of course, that's assuming you had it to begin with.

He's had enough. I've had enough. This game is too easy and the poor guy is ready to be put out of his misery. I apologize if you disagree; after all, he was my gift to you. However, it is late, Trissy is very tired and all things, good or bad, must come to an end.

So with two simple words I'll put poor Trissy to rest.

Thirteen

STEVE
JOHN LEE

It was a large jar with two glass rings at the side of the stubby neck; the sort of jar that is commonly used for home wine making. Tim had first seen it when he was six years old. Before that he had been too short to notice it, hidden away as it was, at the back of a shelf up near the ceiling of the laundry room where most of the household junk migrated.

The jar was made of clear glass and filled with a clear liquid. A pale, pink form hung suspended inside. At first Tim thought it was a huge lump of cod's roe, a delicacy his father enjoyed in season. Later, as he grew taller and could see it better, he decided it was a skinned rabbit. Tim had a stuffed rabbit which lay across the foot of his bed. It was a well-loved toy and most of the fur had worn away. He bent it experimentally at the middle, its feet nestling between its long, floppy ears. From certain angles, with a little imagination, it was the double of the sample in the wine making jar.

Tim's house was miles from anywhere. There were no children nearby for him to play with. Even if there were, he reckoned, his parents would not allow it. They were not fond of strangers. So Tim had been forced from an early age to amuse himself, which trained him in the use of a highly active and fertile imagination.

He was occasionally allowed to watch TV with his father. It was always sports programmes. Football was Tim's favourite. He played football for hours in the back garden. He took the parts of both teams, gave a running commentary to each match and invented elaborate competitions which often took weeks to complete as his team battled through round after round of the World Championships before winning the final. Naturally, Tim always scored the winning goal, though seldom more than one in the final. He felt it was important to maintain perspective with regard to his abilities.

Imagination and invention kept Tim entertained most of the time. But there were moments of introspection when he realised how empty his life was without a companion. What he really needed was a friend. Or, better still, a brother. Why, if his parents loved him, as they continually claimed to, had they denied him a sibling.

Or had they?

Tim's thoughts turned to the jar in the laundry room. If you bent a tiny child the way he bent his stuffed rabbit, they would look pretty similar. In fact, a human child would be the right colour and also hairless. He gave this a great deal of thought and, at the age of eight, came to the conclusion that his parents had indeed given birth to two children. Probably twins.

Now he realised why they were so secretive. It was obvious why they kept the world at arm's length. Tim knew their melancholy secret. He sympathised with his parents though, naturally, he would never discuss it with them. That would be far too painful for all concerned.

Now that he was at long last aware of his brother's existence, Tim welcomed him wholeheartedly into his fantasy worlds, even allowing his team to win the Championship on occasion. In the beginning Tim always thought about his brother as *Tim's Brother*, calling him that in his football commentaries and discussing him with third parties under that title. But eventually he felt the need for his brother to have a name. And so the curled pink figure in the wine making jar became Steve.

For a long time Tim was content merely knowing that Steve existed. It was nice to have company. At bedtime Tim would hold long, one-sided conversations with his brother, holding forth on subjects as diverse as the modern detective

Thirteen

novel (of which both Tim and his father were huge fans), social diseases, brotherhood (a subject close to his heart, and one which Tim was learning more about with every passing day) and the place of the professional foul in contact sports.

The trouble with Steve was that he didn't really have opinions of his own. Oh sure, Tim would often argue for Steve, but he felt it wasn't realistic, all he could do was take an opposing viewpoint and call it Steve's. He was sure that in many cases his brother would agree with him, if only he could speak for himself. But agreeing with himself seemed pointless so, necessarily, Tim and Steve fought a lot.

In the end there was only one thing for it. Tim knew that he would have to confront his brother. He was nine years old - being twins they were both nine - and the time for fantasy was over. Taking pains to ensure that he wasn't spotted by his parents, Tim went to the garage, another repository for junk, and dragged a step ladder from the bottom of a pile containing bicycles, fishing rods, a length of wooden fencing and a rusted lawnmower.

Getting the step ladder past his parents and into the laundry room was an operation that took planning, ingenuity and a liberal dose of luck. He set up the ladder below the spot on the shelving where Steve hung out. Looking upwards, Tim estimated the gap between the top step and his brother's jar. It was somewhere in the region of his own height. He grinned in anticipation, sure that the jar could be reached.

Tim mounted the step ladder with great deliberation. He wished to savour the experience so that he could remember every moment, every circumstance of his first meeting with Steve. On the top step Tim's forehead was level with the shelf which held his brother's jar. He reached over the lip of the shelf and placed a hand on either side of the jar. It was heavier than he had imagined but he was able to slide it to the edge where he could properly see the contents.

The curled figure within was wrinkled all over, like a walnut. Tim could see a fine line of downy hair running along a ridge that bisected it long ways. That had to be Steve's spine. He took careful hold of the jar and attempted to lift it. It tipped backwards slightly and he allowed it to plonk back onto the shelf.

The movement caused a ripple to course through the clear liquid that surrounded his brother's tiny body. Slowly the figure began to rotate, both vertically and horizontally. Tim held his breath. He was fairly sure his legs had ceased to function.

Slowly, then faster, like a cork righting itself, the figure made a one eighty degree turn in both planes. The head, which had always been hidden due to Steve's posture, was hideous. The tightly shut eyes bulged from their sockets, the mouth was huge and fleshy over a receding chin, the brow was deeply ridged. Tim was suddenly glad that his twin had failed to live past the very moment of his birth.

Or had he? Perhaps Tim's father, seeing his wife deliver such a monstrosity, had taken the child's fate in his own hands. Perhaps Steve could have lived had he been allowed. The thought caused Tim to shudder. He stared into the face of the brother he never knew, realising that even the faint existence he had given this unfortunate creature must cease.

A tiny bubble of air slipped from the wrinkled body's mouth. First one, then the second eye blinked open. Slowly, ever so slowly, Steve's mouth spread into a smile.

DROP DEAD GORGEOUS
DAVID BERTHNAL

She swept the last of the bones under the beautiful Chinese rug. That had to be husband number fifteen. No, no, of course, she'd forgotten Henry. How could she forget Henry? Yes, David was husband sixteen; the third David she'd married.

Some would blame the men for falling into her clutches, but she'd said in the Lonely Hearts columns that she was a real man-eater.

David didn't taste as good as he looked. He needed a lot of ketchup.

Bella-Donna Metzger wiped the gravy from her new blouse, slipped on an overcoat, and reapplied her rich red lipstick. She washed up the Wedgwood, and placed David's head in the second drawer down of the filing-cabinet in her bedroom, where she'd cleared a vacancy between Cuthbert and one of the other Davids. She'd pickle it later. Too many chores. Cuthbert had become a little pungent recently, she'd have to buy some more vinegar.

She closed the door and locked it; one can never be too careful, with all these nasty people about.

She slid into her latest late husband's Porsche and switched on the CD-player. The track was *Bright Eyes*. She liked this song, and tapped a highly-polished talon against the steering-wheel in rhythmic approval. By the time she'd arrived at the post-office, the mysterious lady was already prowling for fresh prey. Her eyes finally rested on a nervous-looking young man, with a twitch. He was holding a Royal Mail Overseas Postage Costs leaflet with shaking hands, and seemed absorbed in it.

He looked up when she approached him.

"Hello," she said, smiling. "When you've finished, can I look at that leaflet?"

"Of course," he replied, rather shyly. "I've finished with it now." He handed the document to the stunning lady.

"My name's Josie Murdoch," said Bella-Donna Metzger.

"I'm Victor," said the man. "Victor Morley."

"Oooh..." The widow's eyes lit up; there was a gap between Ulrick and Walter. She said slowly, "I hope I'm not being too presumptuous, but I've really taken to you, and I know you have to me."

"I have." He was watching Josie Murdoch, as she continued:

"There is a special place in my life that I feel was made for you."

Victor looked suddenly excited. "Where in your life?"

She murmured significantly "In my bedroom..."

A few weeks later (when David's remains had been safely disposed of), Josie Murdoch and Victor Morley were married in secret. The honeymoon was not remarkable. She'd had better.

"Wow, Victor," she had remarked coming home, "You're quite a lady-killer."

Husband number seventeen strolled into the lounge, and sat down on the settee.

"I thought we'd have something special for dinner tonight, darling," his wife called to him from the kitchen.

"Ah, that reminds me," Victor was rising, "I thought we might invite my parents round. They're looking forward to meeting you."

Bella-Donna hissed, "I thought we'd agreed not to tell anyone about us."

"Well, yes, but they are my *parents*." He noticed the almost inhuman fire in his new wife's eyes. It was a rage he had never known in her before.

"You-" She cut herself short, and recomposed herself. "Of course they can come," she said at last with a grimace, "I was just worried that there wasn't

Thirteen

enough cutlery to go around."

"Don't worry about that, I always carry a knife and fork around with me for emergencies."

Josie Morley's ambiguous reply was: "So do I. You never know when there might be somebody for dinner." She coughed. "When are they coming?"

"I haven't asked them yet," Victor explained. "I'll go and call them now. If that's alright, my sweet?"

"Of course."

Bella-Donna Metzger watched her new husband disappear into the study. She heard him pick up the phone, dial a number, and say:

"Hello, mum... I'd like you to come and meet Josie... That's right... The address is-"

It was at that moment that she picked up the somewhat battered, over-used frying-pan. She also entered the study.

Mrs. Morley savoured the last mouthful of the delicious dinner. She and her husband agreed that Josie could cook an exquisite gourmet meal.

"Where did you say she was again, Victor, dear?" she asked, sipping her wine.

"I really don't know," replied Victor Morley, slipping the blonde hair he had found in his soup under the table. He topped up his mother's glass. "But it feels like she's with us now," he continued through mouthfuls. "You can just feel her presence at the table. She has that effect. Was the meat a bit coarse, Dad?"

"No, of course not, son. By the way, what did you say this was?" He gesticulated with his stainless-steel fork to the food on the plate.

"It Jodie's special recipe."

"I thought you said she was called Josie."

"That's what I meant. Josie's unique meal."

When the parents had left, Victor went into the hall. The rug was getting a bit lumpy now. He picked up the spotless frying pan, and the bloodstained telephone, and dropped them both into an open manhole on the street outside. He gathered together Josie's remains. Poor woman. But she really was going to fill that void.

There was an empty space in his study between Ingrid and Katy.

Thirteen

THE TOMB
LEILA EADIE

"OK, gather round now. Settle down," Professor Hill told the excited group. "I think we're ready to open the tomb." He removed his wide brimmed panama hat and wiped the sweat from his pink forehead. The white-hot sun was blazing, despite having risen less than an hour ago. The bleached land surrounding the dig site reflected the heat like a mirror. Replacing the hat, he turned to face the steps leading down into the shadowed passageway. A quick stroke of his ever-growing belly did nothing to quell the fluttering therein. "Steve?"

The professor's quick gesture brought the research assistant forward, camera at the ready.

"Now rolling, Prof," Steve told him, watching the glowing screen, keeping everything in the frame.

"Let's go, then." Hill started down the stone steps, his heavy boots crunching on the perpetual layer of dust. Steve followed, with the small troupe of students not far behind.

It was dark as they reached the door, after the bright sunlight above, and Hill switched on the flashlight. He licked his lips, tasting dust. The workers had done the difficult part earlier, and now all that was needed was a gentle push to open the door.

He pushed the door open, and felt cool air caress his weathered skin as he stepped inside. A side-to-side sweep of the high lux light revealed only a bare corridor. There wasn't even any of the damned desert grit underfoot.

It could have been disappointing, but Hill still felt like a jittery teenager. This was what the job was all about! Discovery; just think, he was the first person to set foot in this corridor for nearly a thousand years. Maybe more.

After checking air quality, he walked onward, following the corridor round a ninety degree turn where he found another door, with a wheel protruding from it.

"Make sure you capture the interesting opening mechanism," Hill told Steve, pointing at the door. "It's almost an early version of the double twist system we use today."

"It's amazing how well preserved it is," Steve said, training the camera on the floodlit area.

"This corridor has been sealed – airtight - until we got here. It has stood undisturbed for up to a thousand years. Of course, we'll only be able to accurately date it when we see what's inside."

Making sure Steve was still filming, Hill grabbed the cool wheel and tried to turn it. His muscles strained, and he worried that he'd have to ask one of the students, with their younger, fresher bodies to help him. But it grated and slowly, so slowly, it began to turn.

Would the mechanism still work? Despite his confident words, it was terribly possible that the door might not unlock, delaying the dig until the workers could break through. The wheel continued to turn.

A hiss filled the air, overwhelming their surroundings, and everyone, even the professor, ducked, bending double and covering their heads. The susurrus of sound died away, and Hill opened his eyes. He brought the air monitor up, testing for poison gas, and relaxed as it blinked green, safe.

"It's okay. More CO_2 than we're used to, but it's breathable."

An audible sigh of relief echoed the escaping gas, and the crowd shifted, embarrassed at the scare. A girl giggled nervously, and was shushed.

"Ready, Steve?" Hill asked.

"Ready."

Hill pulled the door open. It was heavy, and the unseen hinges were stiff, but

Thirteen

it moved, revealing only darkness beyond.

"Onward," Hill said, his voice barely audible. He swung the flashlight around, trying to get a view of the room the geo-survey had revealed from the surface. He would have a better look later when he let the workers bring proper lighting in, but he always preferred to get the first experience of a tomb by the single steady beam of a flashlight.

The room was large and mainly empty. A lower ceiling than Hill was used to gave a feeling of oppression. He took a few more steps forward and Steve joined him.

"So, any more clues as to what this place was?" he said.

"I have a funny feeling..." Hill trailed off. He glanced at the walls and ceiling, at the places where the room would have been lit. "I think it might be a tomb like the one found in the Far Northern Quarter."

"Gardiner's Tomb?"

"That's the one." Hill trained the beam on an open door directly across the room from them. "Her discovery was controversial, but if this is the same, why, then it must be seen as compelling proof. Proof of the social behaviour and beliefs of the ancient inhabitants of the land."

"You agree with Gardiner's theories, then?"

"She drew the only sensible conclusions from the evidence."

Hill walked on, and Steve followed.

"You see the undecorated walls, the bare floor underfoot. This was merely an entrance room. Through here we should find more evidence of their culture."

Through the doorway, Steve saw that Hill was right. Pictures adorned the walls, showing strange-looking buildings, groups of people, even a map of the land as it was.

"Do you expect to find any..." Steve swallowed, took a deep breath, "remains?"

"I shouldn't think so. Not after all this time. They're probably dust by now. Preservation techniques were poor, when they bothered at all."

Steve nodded, thankful.

Textiles were heaped on the floor in small piles.

"It's very sad, really," Hill said as he walked over to one such heap of material. "They brought all this down here, perhaps to take with them to the afterlife."

"They were alive when they came down here?"

"Oh yes. The big question posed by Gardiner's findings, for me at least, is *why* they did so. They lived in chaotic times, rife with war and power struggles. Was this a form of escape, or punishment? Was it a prison they were locked in, to be tortured to death? Or was it a religious matter, purely voluntary?"

"Or religious torture?" Steve said, smiling.

Hill frowned at him, and the grin fell from his face. Steve studied the camera's screen to avoid the professor's glare.

"I'm talking about *beliefs*, Steve. There is one unconfirmed clue, though. Gardiner said she found some written communications. They apparently crumbled to dust before she could record them properly, but she said those buried here believed they could be saved by staying locked up in these rooms. They wanted immortality."

"Madness."

"Possibly. But who knows how many more of these tombs are out there? How widespread this belief was?" Hill shrugged and turned away. "Look out for any writing, but if you do find any, don't touch it." He raised his voice to make sure the whole group heard. "Nobody is to touch *anything*, do you understand?"

They moved on. The burial complex was extensive, with rooms disappearing

Thirteen

off in all directions. Most of the contents of the rooms had dissolved into dust thanks to the effects of time, though some funerary furniture and tubular food containers still remained. It was hard to make sense of.

In one room Hill found a heap of bones, extremely fragile, but essentially intact.

"Wonderful," he said, and called Steve over to document the find. "Gardiner never found anything like this!"

"There's at least six skulls there," Steve commented. "Is this a known burial practice?"

"No remains have ever been found before. Perhaps the conditions in this room were different, allowing preservation of the bodies for longer."

"Some form of refrigeration?"

"Maybe. We'll check over the rooms - all the rooms - much more closely in the next few weeks. But for now, I think we need to get lighting in here. I need to make notes and document the site in detail. The world needs to know about this. Wait till Gardiner hears!"

The two men walked back through the complex, herding the students out in front of them. Just as they were passing through the door with the wheel mechanism, Hill paused.

"Hold on a moment, Steve," he said. Bringing out a tiny compressed air device, he held it up to a section of wall and fired small jets of air. As the dust flew away, markings were revealed.

"I don't believe it. We've got an identification plate." Hill continued to clear the area of the centuries' dust. "Get that camera going again."

DOWNING STREET DEFENCE SHELTER: NUCLEAR BUNKER N° 3, it read.

"I'll translate it properly when we get back to the base, but this confirms it. We've got a Gardiner's Tomb all right. I can't wait to tell her!"

PANDORA'S BOX
STEPHEN OWEN

Hi, I'm 'niceguyalex' and guess what... I'm probably the most dangerous person in this chat room, but hell, with a name like mine, who's going to know, eh?

It's not normal I know but I like to use my real name, not like most of the jerks in here, hiding behind unimaginative four-letter word pseudonyms designed to attract like-minded pervs so they can spend their nights talking filth... a lousy and pointless existence isn't it?

But I'm better than them, chat rooms maybe crawling with vermin out for a cheap thrill, but my needs stretch beyond those of any ordinary person... my ambitions are on a completely different level if you get my meaning... there's something I've been craving to do for such a long time now and this place has given me the perfect opportunity to act out my fantasy...

It's not sex I'm after, Christ, that would be too simple wouldn't it? You can get that anywhere can't you, I mean, if you really want it all you've got to do is visit the local whorehouse and let's face it, there's enough of them in this shit-hole of a town. No, I want to find someone special... I guess it all looks a bit sad to you people that I spend my nights in these imaginary rooms talking to people I don't really know and trying to win their affections, but it's all I've got... for now...

Ultimately, I don't give a shit if she really likes me... I want her for myself, that's all...I want to meet her and take her somewhere real special for a meal, a classy joint, and we would talk and share a few soft words in the golden candlelight, and afterwards we would take a quiet walk along by the river, a warm gentle breeze blowing as the evening skies faded, and we would hold hands, talking and laughing, sharing and learning about each other... and then I would take her somewhere quiet... away from the real world... where we could be alone and nobody could see us...

And then, without a second thought, I would place my hands around that person's neck and squeeze the fucking life out of them... niceguyalex, huh? I have my off days.

Anyway, at least I use my real name, even if I'm not really a 'nice guy', unlike some of the goddam pervs stalking these chat rooms... I'm telling you, most of them don't even attempt to disguise their motives, they just come out and say it... like *'bi-guy-4sex'*, I could never do that, even if I thought like that which I don't, I couldn't just come out and say it, I'd be too embarrassed, I really would. But then it doesn't really matter where you go, there's always going to be mad people about, it's not just in chat rooms, they're everywhere aren't they?

You see them everyday, but they're invisible, you must walk past a hundred psychos each time you go into town, but they don't look crazy do they? They look like me and you, that's how clever they are, they operate incognito, otherwise we would all see them for what they were and that would just be too easy. This whole crumby world's a cesspit of diseased minds so don't dismiss the chat room as the centre of this perverted plague, it really isn't all that bad, the world was a sick place long before the internet, believe me.

There are good people in here too, just like in real life, it's finding them, that's the tricky bit... I have found myself a 'friend' in here you know and I'm starting to think that she might actually be the *one* I'm looking for...She's so nice, so vulnerable, she really shouldn't be talking to people like me, but hey, you get What you deserve in this life and this flirty little bitch is going to get what's coming to her... Tonight I'm going to ask her if she wants to meet up...Yeah, I know what you're thinking, about how would anybody in their right mind meet up with someone from a chat room or give out personal details like email addresses and stuff, but I got myself a live one here folks, she really is hooked, we swapped

Thirteen

email addresses last night and I sent her a picture of me...

I don't know who the hell it really was, I found the picture in a fucking holiday brochure, it was some cool looking guy lying on a beach, you know all bronze and muscles, not like the real niceguyalex at all, I'm a balding pasty faced sixteen stone slob, she won't even know who the hell I am, she won't see me coming...anyway, tonight it's her turn to send a pic...

So I'm sitting here staring at my screen watching the sickos flicker in and out of the chat room and then I see her... *pandora*, did I tell you she was called that? I don't know if it's her real name or not, I've never heard of a real life pandora, have you? She says 'Hi', sweet, huh? And she loves the picture, thinks I'm cute, *daft bitch*, says she's sending one of her right now. So I type back I want to meet her and the broad just says for me to hold on and see what she looks like first, says I might not fancy her... who gives a shit about looks, what's with this world, it's her life I want... her soul for Christ's sake...

Outlook Express tells me I'm receiving mail, but you know how long these things take - long enough for *bi-guy-4sex* to hijack the screen and start giving me the come on, look you sick bastard I'm not interested, okay? *So hornymonkey*, his mental accomplice puts on the pressure offering his oral services and his hairy ass for rent and I feel sick, I reckon it's time for niceguyalex to get the hell out of chat for now and sit quietly in my inbox and wait for my pic...Sure enough a box appears on the screen giving me a load of shit about how some files can harm my computer, so what do I know about it? I got all the latest anti-virus stuff installed on here, that's what I'm paying for isn't it, so how can anything get in that could damage the pc?

Mouse on open and CLICK, I've opened pandora's box...

Pupils shrivel to pinholes as the sunniest summer's day you could ever dream of floods golden rays into my dingy room, an azure sky meets an iron grey sea which glistens and twinkles in the magnificent sunlight... I can feel it's warmth... and to the right of the picture a young girl dances upon a glittering white sand, her dainty footprints spiralling into the distance into a yawning cave that looks like he's seen this dance a hundred times before, and the blurred figure twirls in her own carefree way, her pure white face turning away, almost as though she changed her mind about being photographed at the last minute, but not so much that I can't make out her soft enigmatic features, piercing black eyes, flashing ivory smile, and her eyes looking back over her shoulder and it's like she really knows me and my heart flips...

Yeh, you'll know me soon enough little girl, just got to persuade you to come and meet me first...

Bi-guy-4sex or hornymonkey... pandora would never even consider meeting shit like that, she told me so... said fuck-heads like that ruin it for everybody and I agree with her, those crazy people are scum, why don't they just crawl back into the sewer where they came from?

I'm thirsty, so I go to the fridge and grab a cold beer.

I stand in the kitchen and stare out at the cobalt sky... a new day is dawning, in the distance through the open window the sea gently ripples on the sandy shore and a girl laughs as her skipping feet *splish-splash splish-splash* through the clear warm water... and she sings...a beautiful voice... the kind you would imagine a mermaid to have... pure and irresistible...I jump... what happened there? Did I fall asleep standing up for a second?

What the hell was that all about? The sea? Girl singing?

Fuck... down the can and open another please...I want to look at that pandora bitch again, I grab can number two and sit myself back down in front of the pc and stare at the screen... a naked Jordan is giving me the come on... *fucking screensaver*... so I wiggle my mouse...

Thirteen

And then my leaden heart suddenly sinks into my stomach... something's changed here... she's moved... I'm sure of it... the lethargic yawning cave is now shouting to me to shut down and get the fuck out of here, because he was directly behind her just a moment ago, but now she is to the left and she is nearer to the camera and her face has turned so that she is almost looking straight at me...

That's not all... the perfect summer sky now has a few unwelcome blemishes upon its horizon...It seems the storm is coming whether we like it or not.

How in God's name did the bitch switch pics?

Time for niceguyalex to go back into chat and see if pandora is in... not very likely at five in the morning, I'm telling you, she is one weird broad, soon to be a dead one I think, don't you? Christ, she's in... at this time..? Is she nuts? So I click on pandora and... 'Hey you bitch, yeah, real clever, freaked me out real good - how d'you do it, huh?'

Pandora says, '???????????????'

So I explain tonight's shit, I still think she's fooling around here you know, and she tells me to close the box.

I'm thinking, *why's she saying that?* But I'll do it anyhow just for you my dearest pandora, so I close the box... just need another drink first before reopening... 'BRB pan.'

'OK' she says.

In my grotty kitchen I ping the ring from can number 3... sssssssssssssssss.... and tip and swallow... it's like freezing cold medicine... thick and strong and I'm feeling a little numb now as I look blearily to the east... the poppy-coloured sky now casting an unearthly hue across the run-down housing estate...

Red sky at morning - shepherds warning...

Outside the ocean gathers momentum, crashing in against jagged rocks, the girl laughs and sings now accompanied by an eerie harpsichord and the tune is hollow... soulless... and suddenly I don't feel like niceguyalex anymore, I feel like I'm made out of fucking glass and this pandora bitch can see right into me, for the first time since I met her I don't feel like I'm in control anymore and let me tell you, I don't like it, I don't like it all...

My clammy face is dripping with sweat, trembling hands wipe the damp from my brow as I walk back over to my computer... pandora has already left a message telling me to open the box back up again and I watch my shaking right hand do the honours even though my brain is screaming for it not to.

And *she's somehow done it again*... pandora the witch has magicked a new picture onto my screen... now isn't she the clever one?

She is so much closer than before, the black storm clouds are filling the sky fast and something else... she looks older now, her hair is greying, her perfect smile is more like a wolf's grin... only her eyes remain the same, but now they are looking *into* me, not at me...

'Hey pan, cut it out'

'Look to the top right niceguyalex and click on the attachment, it's a piece of music, you think changing pics is clever, wait til you see this...'

I see what looks like a paperclip and sure enough the word 'attachment' appears when I move the cursor over it... CLICK... my right hand is now out of my control...

The harpsichord swirls up its tuneless discord... a disharmony from hell... a twisted musical mess so painful to my ears... so much so that I immediately try to turn it off, but guess what..?

'I'll be up and out of your screen in no time... LOL... and God help you then...'

'Fuck you pan, you got a crazy sense of humour'

'No joke niceguyalex, I'm coming for you.'

Thirteen

Outside the shepherds' warning sky is darkening, a rumble of thunder, deep and hollow in the distance and the humidity is becoming unbearable... sweat drips from my forehead... and above all this, the sloshing of the waves and the incessant girlish giggling of the dancing pandora roll around in my head... as her dainty feet pitter patter onwards...

I click again and again, desperately trying to close pandora's box, but her once sweet smile seems so far away now... a snarling and malevolent sneer glares at me with pure contempt. I try to close down the computer...

Outside the rain is now falling... the wind howls through swaying trees... lightning zigzags a crazy path through the ever-darkening sky... and with a pure terror now surging through me I see that the picture on the screen has actually come to life...

Slowly but *oh so very* surely the scene is starting up...I try to stand... more alcohol... but my head is not right and a million black dots swirl rapidly before my bloodshot gaze... I'm switching off... I feel faint and I stumble to the floor...

And all the while the devilish harpsichord plays on and on whilst pandora's feet slap around in the wet sand as she skips towards me...

I manage to get to my feet running a filthy hand across my unshaven face before reaching for the half empty beer can and I turn back to the screen... fuck...

It's true enough, she *really* is moving, almost within touching distance now, her eyes now dark and evil, an old hag, no longer laughing but cackling, no longer dancing but bent and crippled squinting through the monitor with bony hands shielding the light from her side as if she's having difficulty looking in.

Another bolt of fluorescent blue branches its way across the grey sky outside the window illuminating my petrified glistening features for a split second, but it's enough for her wretched face to see who I am and she smiles...

The tinny tuneless music is fading as the ghastly old woman nears her exit... even the sea is quietening... and the yawning cave just screams a silent scream at the madness before him...

'Nearly there now niceguyalex...'

I grab the plug and yank it from its socket...

No way can this be really happening, I'm asleep, I've got to be... this must be some kind of nightmare... the computer is *really* still running...

I'm at a total loss... pandora's twig-like fingers are pressing against the glass , clawing and scratching, her breath is making it misty as she presses up to look out into *my* world...

I turn and run to escape but the door slams shut.

I *pull and push, push and pull*...fuck, I can't even remember which way the damn thing opens now and I look back over my shoulder to see the dreaded pandora gliding effortlessly out of the screen and into the room...

An evil stench fills my lungs as the phantom snakes around, she looks like a million tiny crystals tailing her evil ghastly face and eventually she rests in the darkest of dark places...

Underneath the table, the old woman slowly evolves, a hideous hunched figure, naked but for her straggling white hair that seems to cascade over her body like a silver waterfall across her sagging witch's teats, and there she sits, huddled up, knees against her chin and skinny arms wrapped around bony legs...

She stares into me with dark sunken eyes, a terrible evil that bores into my soul and I'm frozen, unable to move... the life seems to drain from me...

'I've been dead four hundred years or more,' she croaks, '... burnt at the stake I was, but you let me out, you brought me back niceguyalex, you're mine now...'

The ghastly apparition breaks out into mad cackles of insane laughter and with each ear-splitting shriek my back arches in pure agony, like my spine is

Thirteen

being ripped apart and my head drops, a demoralised niceguyalex with tears streaming down my face I look back at the screen and through my blurred vision I can just about make out the words that tell me what I already know...
    PANDORA HAS LEFT THE CHATROOM.

Thirteen

BON APPETIT
ERNEST DeVORE

In Les Catacombs below the teeming city of Paris, Franco Chenard changed the batteries in the handheld recorder he carried with him. His dirty and scratched hands shook slightly as he dropped one of the used batteries into the dirt. The dim light from his helmet lamp wavered once again, reminding him of his decision to split the batteries between the light source which might lead him to the surface and the recorder which chronicled his explorations below.

"I estimate roughly eight more hours of light before I am consigned to darkness." The recorder light had been turned off to save power and only the weak helmet lantern illuminated the rough hewn walls of the ancient labyrinth. "It has now been twenty-nine hours since I entered Les Catacombs, may God have mercy on my soul."

He continued his relentless journey, trying the branching passages to find the one which lead him back into familiar territory. Dead ends led to grim ossuary piles of bones, as old as the tunnels themselves. He cursed the builders, those malcontents who had dug beneath Denfert Rochereau to move the bodies from Cimetiere des Innocents.

"I have dedicated my life to exploration." He turned at a branch in the passage to find yet another tunnel leading downwards, ever downwards into the cold bowels of the Earth. "I did not leave my bones on Everest or in the Congo, but this man-made Hell has defeated me. The chalk marks I have left are nowhere to be found. They are gone."

More exhausting paths led him nowhere and he paused in a wider passage to fumble in his pocket for the last of his energy bars. His hands shook as he opened up the wrapper and let it drop to the ground. The red foil lay forgotten in the dust.

"The walls have changed again." He turned the recorder towards his face, hoping the terror he felt did not show. "I believe I have crossed over into an older Roman section, dug centuries before the 1786 excavations. How deep I am I can not tell."

He swallowed hard and blinked away tears.

"I pity the ego and folly which led me to make this trek alone. I would give up all of the glory now to simply hear another human voice." He lifted the camera and tilted it to its side, the blinking red battery light signalling the end of the chronicle.

"If this record is ever found, know that I failed. I never reached the bottom. The historians and anthropologists were wrong. It is far deeper than imagined."

He shifted the camera in his hands, struggling visibly.

"Tell Lilly that I love her."

He thumbed off the recorder and removed the batteries. The rest of their feeble power would be used in the helmet lamp. Perhaps it would buy him a few more hours.

Six more hours of wandering and he was forced to swap out the batteries in the lamp again. The stale, damp air choked him in some passageways and methane pockets had accumulated in others. As the helmet lamp grew dim he changed out the batteries yet again and held the final set in his hand for a long while, willing them to power and not leave him blind and stumbling in the cursed darkness.

Will alone was not enough and eventually he was left in the dark. His backup flashlight had failed him many hours before, using more power than the small head lamp and thus bigger batteries. That was not the worst of it, however. The food was gone and his water as well. He sloshed the tiny amount in the plastic

Thirteen

bottle and cursed himself.

Ten more hours passed and Franco wandered like a broken thing through the crypt. His hands groped at walls and his parched tongue licked at the acrid and bitter moss that he sometimes encountered. The dampness of the moss did nothing to ease the thirst but he fancied he had become an animal, a small subterranean creature doomed to a blind and meaningless existence below the soil.

For two more days he wandered half-mad, and ranted at the darkness which imprisoned him. Some vestige of sanity remained to him for he did not destroy the recorder he carried in his small pack, nor did he abandon his water containers in the hopes he might find another one of the countless puddles he had stepped over on his way downwards into the catacombs.

His hands and knees were raw from crawling through the tomb. His groping outstretched hand came into contact with something small and flimsy and he picked it up, completely blind in the absolute darkness. Unable to determine what this alien object could be, he held it to his nose and sniffed. As the faint smell of the strawberry energy bar wafted from the foil wrapper, he began to scream, throwing it from him in rage. He rolled on the ground and clawed at his hair, beating his fists ineffectually against the uncaring walls. When he finally calmed himself he searched with outstretched hands for the wrapper and then licked it hungrily for the flavour and crumbs which still clung to it.

It was then that he imagined a light moving through the corridor. A distant light, dimmed by distance and a corner, but he rubbed at his eyes and was amazed to see the faintest outline of his hand in front of him. How many times in the past two days had he imagined he had seen light?

His rasped out a call for help and the light grew stronger. Still on his hands and knees he crawled towards the corner junction to meet it. Like an answered prayer, the light revolved itself into the flickering flame of a candle, carried by hands that stopped before him. As his eyes slowly resolved to the presence of light again, he looked up into the gruesome face of his rescuer.

The man wore a threadbare brown robe, patched many times, like a monk. His torso was too small and his arms and legs too long and almost spider-like with their swollen joints. The warty hand which clutched at the tallow candle was steady and the hideously deformed face peered down at him with eyes full of compassion.

"Am I mad?" Franco spoke in French as he reached out to clutch at the figure's hem.

"I can not tell from here, monsieur." With his overlarge mouth and crooked teeth the man smiled down at him. "Perhaps you are the better judge of your sanity."

Franco began to laugh and when the figure motioned for him to follow he did so, if only to stay in the presence of the light.

A few winding twists and turns away they entered a small room, little more than a widening of the passageway where it became clear the man made his home. Books in English, French, and Spanish were piled in orderly stacks and a small fire was lit in a crude hearth. Old clothes of all sorts were spread in one corner, obviously as a bed for the strange fellow who dwelled here.

"Would you prefer wine or water?" The hideous man peered at Franco curiously but benignly.

"Wine. Merci, monsieur." Franco gasped as the bottle was handed to him and he drank greedily from it, slaking his thirst. His mysterious benefactor laughed and pronounced Franco a true Frenchman to take wine before water, even in this situation.

"You have my gratitude, monsieur, but I am amazed. Do you live down

Thirteen

here?"

"But of course." The man bustled with a small pan that hung from a hook over the hearth. "There are a number of us who live in Les Catacombs, each equally hideous as myself. We make occasional forays to the surface world for food, books, and fuel for our meagre fires."

"You are truly not so hideous," Franco began but the stranger cut him off with a wave and a laugh.

"I have seen my face before, mon ami. I am not vain."

"And to be truthful, it is not a bad life." He poured a small amount of the wine into the pan and placed it over the hearth fire to simmer. "I have my books and companionship when I desire it. And today I have you to entertain me."

"Truly!" Franco's hunger seemed to double as the stranger took a long piece of meat from where it hung drying and delicately seasoned it with herbs from a pouch. He watched slavering as the man placed it into the pan to sear.

"I have taken liberties to feed you." The stranger produced a fork and began to drift wine and seasoning over the browning meat. "I hope that you like rat."

At that point in time Franco would have eaten one raw, much less sautéed and he said so. The stranger beamed at him happily before bending back to his task.

"So there is a community down here! We never suspected."

"We value our privacy, as you can imagine. And it is true that visitors from above never come here. I believe you are the first in my lifetime."

"You've been down here your entire life?" Franco was stunned. He remembered his recorder and cursed the death of the batteries.

"All my life," the stranger answered. He turned the rat over and the smell of the cooking meat wafted over Franco, who licked his dry lips. His stomach, long since ceasing to growl, came alive all over again.

The stranger laughed. "Why even in the company of neighbours here, I am considered an unusual fellow."

"Oh? Do they not look like you?"

"Not so much for my appearance, for we are a rather tolerant lot." The stranger looked up and gave him a wink. The shadows of the hearth fire played over his twisted and alien face in gruesome fashion. "More so due to my habits. I am quite different from them in taste and culture."

"You appear to be well read and quite the gourmet."

"You are too kind." The man lifted the meat with his fork, testing its preparation. "They think me odd for the care I put into my food."

"How absurd! It is simply a choice of hobby, like chess or darts. I have known many men with far worse habits."

"Too true. I find pleasure not only in preparing my food, but also in the procuring of it. Why be cruel? It is just a meal, do you agree?"

"We all have our place in this world." Franco nodded, but his mind was on the sautéed rat simmering in the pan.

"Well put. And if I talk to my food, even keep company with it for awhile or feed it to bring flavour to the meat, then am I so wrong?"

"Not at all! Is the farmer cruel to his cows? His chickens?"

"Precisely." The stranger removed the pan from the fire and retrieved a small, cracked plate upon which he slid the filet of meat. The juices simmered and the smell of herbs was strong in the enclosed space. He sighed deeply. "But I must endure their barbs and jests. Many of your fellows above would find our diet here quite horrifying."

"I suppose that is true." Franco couldn't take his eyes off the meal being prepared for him. "But one can not overlook the necessity of having food close to hand. And a learned and well-mannered fellow such as yourself has many virtues which far outweigh the minor peculiarity of eating rats."

In the silence that fell and from the strange look the hideous man gave him, Franco suddenly realized that a monstrous misunderstanding had taken place. The stranger placed the fork on the plate and held it out to Franco.

"Oh, I never eat rats," the stranger said with a wry smile.

Thirteen

THE A.C.I.
JULIAN URQUHART

The room is dark – so dark that we cannot see how large it is beyond the glow of the light that hangs above the table. The table is mahogany – it looks sturdy and efficient, a no-nonsense table for the no-nonsense matters frequently discussed around it.

As we move around the table, we notice the group of a dozen people sat around it. Nine men, all of discernibly strong builds; three women, all coldly beautiful. To put an age on any of them, the men or the women, is difficult. They look like they are in their thirties, yet something about each and every one of them seems to put them beyond that. Nothing physical – no grey hairs, no spectacles, no deep wrinkles. It's something that is at once subtle and obvious – something manufactured.

In front of each of them are copies of the same report. They read it in silence, seemingly able to do so at great speed despite the poor lighting. The substantial document is finished by each of them in less than thirty minutes.

Man 7: Do we have a date of implementation?

Man 9: As soon as it is approved, it will be implemented.

Man 1: The first stages, at least. We have to appreciate that an initiative like this will take some time.

Man 7: Of course.

Man 1: We can also expect a significant reaction. And some strong resistance.

Woman 1: Possibly the largest yet.

Man 7: Why so? I know they have been troublesome in the past when our decisions have interfered with their emotions, but this...?

Woman 1: They react. They always do. But with this A.C.I. we are tampering with a side to them we cannot fully appreciate.

Man 7: Nor should we attempt to appreciate it. Their peculiarities need phasing out and this A.C.I. will be a large step towards our goal.

Woman 3: I agree. A hugely important step such as this must be taken. I feel the time is right. Any resistance we face must be dealt with.

A member of the group, Man 8, reaches out to take a sip of water from his glass while the conversation continues. As he attempts to put it down, the glass slips from his grip and hits the table. Although it doesn't break, it makes a loud noise. The eleven other heads turn to look at him, their expressions unreadable. He holds the gaze of one of them for a few moments.

Man 8: Shall we continue?

Woman 1: Yes. We were talking about the resistance we will face.

Thirteen

Man 8: What measures will be taken against any?

Man 10: If the reaction is as strong as it has been in the past, then the most extreme measures. It is all they know. But I feel we are troubling ourselves here unnecessarily. Our last eight initiatives have been accepted peacefully.

Woman 1: I reject your unconcern.

Man 8: So do I.

Man 10: Then please enlighten me.

Woman 1: Something like this is a lot more akin to the initiative implemented before the eight you mention.

Man 10: I fail to see how.

Man 9: So do I. I appreciate their peculiarity as much as anyone here but fail to see a similarity that might lead to another attempted uprising.

Man 8: Don't be so naïve. You cannot underestimate this. The challenge mounted ten or so years ago was because we acted rashly. We forgot to at least consider that our implementations, however necessary we knew they were, might not prove popular. How can you execute all prisoners – *all prisoners* – in jails across the country in one day and expect there not to be a reaction? How can you judge a fraudster against a paedophile, or a petty criminal against a mass-murderer? You thought the public would welcome it because it meant an undesirable section of society would be instantly wiped out? Those prisoners had mothers, fathers, sisters, brothers, friends! And this A.C.I. will be just as deplorable in their eyes.

Man 10: Don't you mean 'we'? You are sounding slightly emotional.

Man 8, beneath the table, clutches the sides of his chair and squeezes them hard. He tries to control the anger that is bubbling up inside of him and the quaver that is threatening to distort his voice.

Man 8: That's just an issue of semantics. I do not want to be sidetracked.

Man 10: My point is that I cannot see how the A.C.I. is in anyway comparable to our Penal Reform Initiative. In fact, I am surprised it has even reached this tier of government. Why isn't it being discussed as part of the Education Policies?

Man 4: It was. They passed it on to us. It seems someone down there realised it could be a sensitive subject.

Man 10: Well, I think it's a waste of time. I appreciate it is a large step on the way to achieving our goal but to me it is a natural progression and I cannot for-see any major resistance. Of course, there are always upstarts, but that's just the way they are. They won't pose a problem.

Man 9: Just explain… why the trepidation? What is the link? I can reel off the consequences of the Penal Reform Initiative word for word. Our best

Thirteen

sociologists wrote it. I don't fully understand it – obviously a family connection is something none of us can empathise with – but the A.C.I., in my opinion, does not threaten that tie in the slightest.

Man 8 gets up from his seat. His emotions take over and it takes him a moment to realise that attacking any of the people around the table will be futile. Their reflexes are too quick, their strength too much to overcome. He takes three long strides backwards, screaming abuse at the nonplussed eleven about evil and murder.

Reaching into his blazer pocket, he pulls out a device. It is small and metallic and, moments after he depresses its activator, it kills everyone in the room and obliterates half of the building in which the meeting was taking place.

But Man 8's sacrifice was in vain. And Man 8, or David Seward as he is normally known, was probably aware of this. His martyrdom, in the grand scheme of things, meant absolutely nothing. It meant nothing to the government of genetically engineered individuals he had almost impossibly managed to infiltrate, nor did it mean anything to those he might call his sympathisers, as they would never hear of it.

To infiltrate the government in the way he had, reaching a mid-to-low level tier group of Initiative Consultants, had taken all of his will and dedication. His peers were literally designed and created to be efficient, to tackle complexities and strategies with the power of a computer and the heart of man.

But it had gone wrong.

The result – madcap schemes and policies and initiatives and programmes and dictations and a whole host of other names for their aims.

The A.C.I. was the Accent Correlation Initiative. Its aim, to abolish regional accents and have one all encompassing way of speaking... unity.

Its practical purpose, none.

The means to which it would have been enforced, terrifying.

All teachers were to be replaced with Conforming Speech teachers; mothers and fathers would be forced to change their accents and take tests, which they would have to pass before they were allowed to bring up their children: massive, impenetrable walls were to be built around cities such as Liverpool, Newcastle and Birmingham, where accents were deemed too entrenched to be successfully changed. No food would be allowed in – the cities would be reclaimed in fifty years and made efficient.

All of this for a unifying accent. All of it for nothing.

Thirteen

BRIEF FUTURE
JOHN LEE

Another damn retro sixties CD clicked through the auto-changer. Their Satanic Majesties had requested the Rolling Stones. I wanted two paracetamol and a cold beer to wash them down. Saturday night parties are habit forming. That's the only reason I was there.

The barman had called time. Somebody ordered six-packs. I overheard a stranger shout the address of a flat across the top of the pub roar. "Thanks, Andy," the recipient of the information yelled. I nodded. "Yeah, thanks, Andy."

If I had stopped to think about what I was doing, I would have gone home. I had been on the piss since early afternoon. Our league match had kicked off at eleven AM. We won. We celebrated. By closing time I had been drunk twice, sobered once and hung over. I figured a naggin of Scotch would give me a good buzz and take care of the vice grip across my forehead. My confidence in my prescribing abilities should have come in suppository form.

Peter Green's Fleetwood Mac had been survived but the pounding of Charlie Watts' drums was an obstacle my weakened constitution failed to overcome. I wandered into the kitchen. At least the noise level was bearable. The crush of heaving bodies was its own drawback. The humid air was difficult to breathe, like hot treacle. I pushed my way across the room to its second door. Perhaps there was somewhere quiet and empty through it.

The door gave onto a tiny square space with doors on each side. One stood ajar revealing a bathroom. The next was a cupboard. The last room stood in a darkness surrounding a dense mound shaped like a giant anthill. I fumbled on the light. The mound consisted of coats lying on a bed. I extinguished the light and stumbled to the bed. The coats offered little resistance on their way to the floor. A patchwork quilt rose quickly to meet me. My inner ear informed me I was doing the moving. Thankfully, everything went black.

It was dark and it was quiet. Vague recollections of a gate-crashed party guttered at the back of my mind like a dying candle. I grasped the shredded memories and clutched them to me for comfort. After a while I realised I knew where the flat was and was fairly confident of finding my way home. Except for a lone parka, the pile of dislodged coats had disappeared from the floor. It was late.

My watch read two twelve, but then it always did. I rolled onto my back, swung my legs over the side of the bed and sat up. My head spun a bit, but I felt good. Except for my mouth, which tasted like a urinal for incontinent German Shepherds. The dogs, that is.

Back in the kitchen I discovered human dregs, most of who looked like they should have joined me face down on the bed. I peered though bloodshot eyes at my fellow revellers. Nobody I knew remained. The rest of the lads had split. I felt abandoned. A voice in my head laid a bet they hadn't even bothered looking for me before they went. It was a sucker bet I was having no part of.

I opened the fridge and discovered a litre carton of milk. Every receptacle in the room looked like a breeding ground for typhus. I knocked the milk back straight from the waxed cardboard. Afterwards my mouth tasted like a dog's urinal down which milk had been swilled. The raging thirst retreated. The coldness of the milk reminded me of my earlier headache. But all in all I felt good. Rested. Sobered. To a degree.

Muffled strains of music edged under the door from the main room. It was too low to identify. I succumbed to its siren call. The room, illuminated by a single lamp sitting on a low table, was like a layered confection, half dark chocolate and half milk. The casualties on the floor were thrown into soft relief. Anything much

Thirteen

above knee height was in shade. The chair beside the stereo was occupied; there was no way of taking control of the musical entertainment. I was going to have to put up with someone else's taste. Not always a bad thing. I would never have thought of playing the Beach Boys. The achingly sweet lead vocals of *God Only Knows* gave me a feeling of intense well-being. I sat on the floor, just inside the door. There was a spot available on the couch but the silhouette lolling in the next seat looked unsociably drunk. The risk of being vomited on was too great.

The Beach Boys finished their song and the figure by the stereo unit rejected the remainder of the CD and replaced it. The new music was something by Michael Nyman. Probably a film score. I recognised it vaguely.

I found myself staring intently at the figure by the stereo. Tall, slender, shoulder length hair that could have been blonde, an exquisite profile. She turned slightly. Great cheekbones. Was she looking at me? It was impossible to tell where her eyes were focused. She had an unfair advantage. Being on the floor, my face was lit by the weak glow of the lamp. She would know I was staring. But I couldn't help myself.

She was probably way out of my league. A full-length leather coat cascaded to the floor on either side of her low chair. She was wearing denims but I would have given good odds they had a designer label. Her shoes were simple leather slip-ons, but definitely Italian. A splash of white sock gave her the appearance of one of those boyish foreign students who seem to spend their days wandering the city looking mysterious and desirable and unattainable. I thought I had grown out of that phase.

She slumped in the chair, all angle and line like a Vogue model. Her legs seemed impossibly long. She had slipped a little lower in her seat. The light caught her throat. Her neck was slim and long and white like a swan's. No matter how remote the chance of success, I was going to have to go over and speak to her. I would never forgive myself for not trying.

Getting to my feet without swaying or stumbling was an achievement. Upright, the shadows surrounding the girl by the stereo unit appeared denser. Her head and shoulders were curves of darkness. The mystery of her face intensified. I was as nervous as I'd been on my first day of school. Every opening line I had ever heard or used sounded faintly ridiculous. She deserved something original. In the moment it took me to reach her chair my mind blanked, denying me access to even the most banal of 'lines'.

Waving my hand in the general direction of the floor beside her chair I said, "Do you mind if..."

"It's a free country."

The voice was a surprising husky contralto, which would have harmonised beautifully with the Beach Boys, octaves below their soaring falsettos. I briefly considered perching on the chair's arm. That would have been too familiar. The real choice was between squatting and kneeling alongside the chair. I choose kneeling. It was safer, though less dignified.

At this range, facial details were recognisable. Vivid, ultramarine eyes swept across me. A sensuous mouth allowed itself a half smile. A pink tip of tongue flicked over crimson painted lips.

The subtle make-up at eye and lip was not a statement. Few men look natural when using cosmetic enhancements. He was a natural. This close, there was no mistaking him for a woman any longer, though the total effect of his appearance was androgynous. He smiled as he observed my recognition. Our eyes met. Though I have never thought of myself as homophobic, I have always been resolutely hetero in my desires. But right then and right there his sex made no difference. There was an aura about him. If it were not such an overused word I would describe what he had as charisma. But they talk about politicians and

Thirteen

footballers as charismatic.

Within seconds of the electric charge of those eyes I knew I would be prepared to follow wherever he desired to go. For him, I would do anything, no matter how monstrous. And it would be monstrous. That was certain. There was an ageless satiation behind those ultramarine mirrors. I could feel him reading my entire history from the lines on my face, the way I held my head, my breathing, the words I was afraid to speak.

He ran one of his hands down my cheek. I shuddered from the sensuousness of his touch. No woman's skin had ever felt so soft, so inviting. I watched his lips as he spoke to me. The words slipped away into the darkness, like echoes on a storm. They didn't matter. I knew what he wished me to know. He was communicating directly with my soul.

His hand slid around to the back of my neck and he drew me close, lips brushing the tiny fine hairs coating my ear as he whispered the secrets of the ancients to me. Or perhaps it was the raging, psychotic outpourings of a sociopath. It didn't matter. Whatever he wanted to say, I would listen. So long as he allowed me to look upon his face, to smell the cinnamon sweetness of his breath, to flounder in the swell behind his eyes.

"What will I do with you?" He gazed at me in the puzzled, fond way a man will look at a dog that has surprised him by a flash of intelligence beyond the animal. I would not have been surprised had he stroked my head, scratched behind my ears. Nor would I have resisted. For a long time he stared at me in silence. I sat at his feet accepting his stare, drinking it in.

"You know what I will do, don't you?" He spoke the question rhetorically.

Yes. I knew what he would do with me. And I would accept it willingly. I would indulge him in any manner he could imagine merely to extend the period of his regard. Somehow, I knew he could imagine anything. Had done things I could not even conceive of.

The door opened, casting a brief wash of pale light across our still forms. He looked away. The wrench was almost physical, as though I had been slapped in the face. His eyes fell upon another. *No*, my mind screamed, *there is only me. Here. Look here*. But not so much as a whimper passed my lips.

He smiled. Breathing was impossible. I was not holding my breath, the function of oxygenation was suspended. My lungs paused, slowly deflating. In some dark corner of my psyche a voice of sanity cried out for attention. It replayed stills from movies. Violent, hideous movies. Abhorrent scenes of degradation and suffering. This is what he means for you, the voice cried. This is your brief future.

A hint of blackness pushed at the periphery of my vision. I felt myself begin to topple forward ever so slowly. A shuddering breath revived me. His glance flashed onto me for a fraction of time so short as to be immeasurable. The displeasure in it caused my eyes to fill with tears. Holding back a bitter sob required an act of heroism I am incapable of reproducing.

He sat forward in his chair, gaze never moving from the open door. He said nothing but I could hear him call to that other. I watched his face avidly for a sign, a flicker of disappointment in my rival. There was none. His concentration was total. Nothing existed apart from his prey. I wanted to cry out, break the spell he was creating. My tongue refused to respond. It was like a cold, dead fish in my mouth. My vocal chords flexed impotently.

At last he returned his attention to me. The relief was almost orgasmic in its intensity. I leant against the chair arm, too weak to support my immense weight. He spoke. One word. One titanic, final, damning word.

"Go," he said.

My body obeyed at once and without question. My mind screamed in silent protest. *No.* Over and over again. *Take me.*

I staggered back to where I had sat on first entering the room as though it were a refuge, a safe haven from this storm of cruelty. Now, my back propped against the cold wall, I was an outsider. An observer where formerly I had been a principal.

The newcomer was a skinny youth, little more than a boy. His hair was close cropped, almost shaven. His ears stuck out like trumpets. Arms lacking in all muscle definition hanging from a white tee shirt. Legs like pipe cleaners in jeans which must have been sprayed on. Ratty sneakers with open laces. I wanted to cry out, *Take me. Not him. Never him.*

The skinny youth replaced me at the slender man's feet. He stood where I had knelt. Did he know nothing? How did he dare stand?

Surely now it would be obvious that I was the one. I understood his needs. I knew every move he wished me to make, before the thought was fully formed.

The slender man stood. The youth turned and preceded him to the door. Without even a glance in my direction, they left. Suddenly it was as though I was sitting in the wilds of Patagonia, thousands of miles from the nearest human habitation. Despite the sleeping and unconscious bodies on the floor, I had never been so alone. My soul was as desolate as the wind-scoured wilderness of my imagination. I drew my knees up under my chin. Tears flowed freely down my cheeks, wetting the front of my shirt. I cried without inhibition, as though a child. My world was a poorer place. I knew that perfection existed and that I could never attain it, was unworthy of its attention.

Deep in a place I was afraid to look, a part of me contemplated the horror, which had regarded me and found me wanting. That small part of me shuddered and looked away before the realisation shrivelled hope.

The door opened. I sensed someone watching me. I ignored them and continued crying. The person placed a hand on my shoulder. "You okay?" The voice was a man's. It contained genuine concern and compassion for which I was grateful.

There was comfort in that human contact. I wiped my eyes and cheeks on my sleeve and turned to face him. It was Andy, whose careless shout led me here. A final sob racked my body as I dampened my emotions, pushed the pain into that place I was afraid to look, where it could wait, feeding on other, weaker, older siblings while the scars on my soul healed over or until it festered and burst forth in a gout of pus-like terror.

"You okay?" Andy repeated.

"I'll live," I said.

If you can call it that.

THE STEPS WHERE I SINNED
J G CRAIG

This is where I am now, neither dead nor alive, but existing, and aching for a salvation which I know might never come. I am just a man, I tell myself.

A special man.

I stroll down these steps, one at a time, running my hand along the sleek, black banister and occasionally running ragged fingernails along the cold, granite walls of the buildings on either side. They lead down from the cobbled, ancient streets of a city long destroyed by glass and steel, to the monstrosity of a dual carriageway at the bottom. Two hundred and forty three steps in all.

I counted once.

I'm sure I'll count them many times.

I had too much time on my hands one night, and so I began; one, two, three… and I never stopped from then on. It was my favourite place; deep in the shadows of the bricked-up alcoves that were positioned at every landing; the old lamps casting not a shred of light on my sanctuary. Deep in the night whilst patrons patronized their favourite haunts and the theatre nearby buzzed with an excited queue. Drunken laughter would fill the air, and bombard my mind with snippets of jealousy and bitterness.

I would stand there, watching the traffic rush by at the bottom of the stairwell. I often wondered where these steps had led to, before the new roads had been built and congested the city even more with noxious fumes and blaring horns.

I was standing at the bottom on the pavement one night, after having counted the steps once more, just to be sure that the count was right. I was illuminated by the lights from the passing cars; I had grown weary of hiding in the shadows and needed the excitement of streetlights and moonlight and fast-flowing vehicles. I heard her skipping down the stairs before I saw her, and knew it was a drunken girl by the beat of her steps: when you live in shadow and darkness you learn to appreciate the simpler sounds the night makes.

I turned and watched her; aware that she hadn't noticed me and was oblivious to the beauty of the staircase she now descended. She was no more than twenty years old but the worries of the world had rested themselves on her small, dainty shoulders.

How divine she looked. How utterly innocent and transparent were her thoughts that I wanted to call out to her, to beg her to share those thoughts with me. I was finished with memories of darkness and shadow.

I wanted moonlight and dancing. But the turmoil which fluttered around in my head like so many loose, crawling things prevented me from acting on my new-found impulses.

I said nothing, and she reached the bottom of the stairs and turned away from me without the slightest evidence she had noticed I was there. She hummed a tune as she made her way round a corner and under the bridge a few yards up.

She was gone.

I returned the next night and stood in the same place, watching the cars as they went about their busy journeys. I waited until the clock on the nearby church chimed four times and then headed back to my shadowy room, where dreams of the innocent girl lit up my subconscious ponderings like a rainbow of hope.

I wanted to invade her thoughts, to take what I could and be done with the remainder of her useless remains. In one, singular moment I wanted to be part of her; her desire, her need to be part of something more elaborate than she could conjure up on her own. I wanted to rape her emotions as the city around us had been raped in the name of progress.

I wanted to show her what I was.

Or maybe it was the other way around?

Perhaps the need was for me to feel part of something else; of someone else. To discard this feeling of detachment I felt for the people around me. To prove I was different and therefore worthy of notice.

I slept for most of the day, occasionally waking to the sound of a blaring horn or a screech of tyres from outside. But throwing the blankets over my head sent me back to sleep. Back to my dreams where darkness became light and banished shadows became joy.

I waited for nightfall, and as soon as it was dark enough, I returned to my staircase, where only I appreciated the contours of the heavily worn steps and the old, Victorian lamps that protrude from the granite walls.

I waited in the shadows this time, eager not to be seen lest I attract drunken squeals and comments.

She came a little after midnight, as I was sitting on the middle landing, head in my hands and thoughts of shadows returning to goad me. Her clumsy footsteps brought her stumbling into my arms as I stood up and turned. She giggled into my ear, the cloying stench of alcohol emanating from her small, perfectly formed, red lips. Her head lolled to the side and for a fleeting moment, the pale, smooth whiteness of her neck was illuminated in the moonlight, and the blue, throbbing vein begged me for attention.

That image was just as exciting as I had always hoped it would be. To see it there, in flesh and blood, and not some carnal craving nestled in the back of my mind, was to let the lion free of its cage and bow to the whim of my desire.

I could hold myself back no longer.

I opened my mouth as though to yawn, and bit down, the small incisors doing their work as they pierced the perfumed flesh and brought a warm rush of blood to my mouth. She groaned in pleasure, or misery - I will never know which - and slumped against me as I drained her existence from her. She muttered, and instantly the guilt welled up from the pit of my stomach and brought small tears to my eyes. I hugged her close; fearful I would lose that moment of bonding forever, and never be able to feel that kinship again. Her heartbeat slowed as I drank my fill, and when at last her hot breath came no more, I laid her to rest on the steps where I sinned.

And sinned again.

ALL SALES FINAL
PHILIP TINKLER

"Attention to all customers, Greenforest Mall will be closing in one hour. That's one hour, folks. The staff would like to thank you for your custom over the years."
Hurry up, fella. What have you got in there? A Cadillac?
Through the straining he heard a plop followed by a splash.
Finally, he's parked his load, Brian thought, standing at the urinal and faking a piss.
Hurry up and wipe your asshole, asshole and let me in there before...
The strainer stepped out, red-faced and relieved, as Brian squeezed in. For a second they looked like a pair of before and after shots. He threw his gift bag in the corner and yanked down his pants.
Oh man, remind myself to never eat Mexican in a food court again, he thought, pulling down his boxers. *Oh Jesus.* He lifted his face up; *I do not envy the cleaners tonight.*
The flood showed no signs of stopping, every time he wiped, the gripe struck again, forcing him to drop and take aim. He laid his sweaty forehead on his suit arm and closed his eyes, exhausted.
When he opened them the bathroom light was off.
I was asleep *in here?*
He checked his watch.
Over an hour had passed.
Worse, the muzak had stopped.
He cleaned up, stuffing a nest of toilet paper in his boxers just in case, grabbed Anne's gift and stepped out.
Stretching ahead thousands of closed shops. The only light remaining in the mall were the tiny bulbs illuminating window displays. Brian cupped his hands to his mouth.
"Hello, is anyone there?"
Yeah dipshit, everyone's here. Playing the world's biggest game of hide and go peek, don't ya know?
Half-remembering the location of the exit, he started forward. His footsteps echoed large and unwanted in the open space. It would be locked of course, no secret doors in here but he had to do something.
Here's a new tale for those non-existent cocktail parties. Locked In A Shopping Mall: The Great Escape.
He reached the end. Left or right. *'Urban Threads'* or *'Baby Blues'*.
He eeniemeenied it, feeling like the chubby kid he'd once been. He landed the *'Threads'* side. He jogged to the end.
"Sweet fuckin' *salvation.*" His voice rose on the last syllable as his boot connected with the steel shutter. He crouched and tried to lift it.
Not a chance.
Wonder where the candy shack is, I'm going to need some marshmallows if it's a sleepover.
He walked back the way he came, thinking how different the place looked empty. It was quite enjoyable, well, as much as being imprisoned in a ghetto mall could be.
No wailing kids in your way or old folk, staggering left and right as if drunk.
His stomach rumbled. *Don't know when to quit do ya?*
Well, he wasn't going to break into the food court just yet.
Won't look too good in the morning when they find me pigging out on the stock. Shit, what will I say when they do *find me? Sorry, I was just taking a dump and nodded off from the strain of things? Why didn't they find me? Cleaner's day*

Thirteen

off, I suppose.

He walked to the center of the mall and sat on the cement wall surrounding the fountain; its unappreciated spurting finished for one day.

Across from him another menswear store, a tad more fancy than *'Urban Threads'*. Five mannequins lined the storefront, each sporting a smartly fitted suit, each in a slimy over-casual pose. The curlicue script read *'Vestito Per Uccidere'*. Italian, Brian guessed. The middle mannequin was different. Bored, he walked over for a look.

The four dummies flanking the middle had modernistic heads, an upside down tear shape elongated at the top. Inscribed in the face were two C shapes. Eyes. An L made the nose, and O the mouth. They looked surprised why their compatriot was such an outsider. Instead of a head that resembled a surprised alien, the middle's was lifelike. Its facial features as human as molded plastic could be.

The sly face, narrow painted eyes and thin lips reminded Brian absurdly of a gangster. Looking at its coloring and hairstyle it had probably come from around the 1930's. Most of the paint had chipped away, leaving an elephant gray pallor. It wore a smart black pinstriped suit; a blue and purple striped umbrella lay over the shoulder.

Gray Ray, the mob mastermind of the mannequin world, Brian thought.

"Why you here with these aliens, Ray? Busted for counterfeiting fancy suits? And where did you get that *darling* bumbershoot?"

Ray didn't answer.

Just looked through the glass with sleepy-eyed smugness at Brian.

It was starting to creep him out, the way he felt with paintings of long-dead dudes in wigs, their eyes following his every move. Brian turned on his heels then swung back, drawing his finger as a gun.

"Gotcha!" Ray continued beaming his knowing smile, never flinching.

"Well, I'm gonna turn in for the night if it's alright with you boss."

Brian headed towards the food court. There was a plastic chair with his name on it.

Ray watched him walk out of view and continued watching long after.

Two hours later and Brian was awake. It was so damn *cold* in here. He sat up, shook out his suit jacket he'd been using as a pillow and slipped it on. He pressed the light on his watch. 11:40.

When does this place open? Six, seven? It's going to be a long assed night.

He walked around, trying to warm up, while his tired mind rambled.

So many shops selling crap people need to complete their empty lives. Without their piss-wash jeans, Ultimate Deluxe Special Edition Directors Cut DVD's and cell-phone accessory fun-packs they just couldn't *function.*

Brian wasn't a materialistic person, hell, he despised shopping but he'd gotten himself a girlfriend at the sprightly age of forty-three. Her birthday was approaching and here he was, in the cheap mall picking out a gift. He'd selected a pink fluffy scarf, on sale, like everything else. The place was to be demolished next week for a bigger, more beautiful mall. They'd even taken out the condom machines and public telephones. *There's gratitude for ya,* he thought, smiling an idiot grin.

Another hour passed as he checked the map, taking note of emergency exits. He sought out every one, hoping he'd be lucky. No such luck. All locked of course, there was no one to burn In Case Of Fire.

Well, except me, he thought, feeling mad at Mexican food all over again.

He looked at the alarm over an outdoors shop called, predictably, *'Happy Campers'*. He could break a window, but that would raise suspicions. What

Thirteen

would he say?

*I wasn't breaking in, seriously. I was just calling for help...*Nope, wouldn't work. They'd have him in jail faster than spicy food passed through ones body.

He stood staring through the window display, not seeing it. He was hungry, cold and sleepy. Before 7am (or 8) he'd have to re-enter that stinking restroom, emerging only when enough shoppers arrived to blend into without raising suspicions.

Suspicions. What was he going to say to Anne, his parting words being: *'Love you too, babe, see you around nine.'* She'll think I've been drinking with John again. Great. Well, that's a problem for...then he noticed.

Poking out of the tent in the window display a blue and purple umbrella.

He walked over and pressed his face to the glass.

That's one popular bumbershoot for such an ugly color-combo. It started to twirl, the colors mixing to a harsh bruise. He leapt back, heart hammering. He dragged his fingers across his tired eyes. The umbrella was dead still. He let out a tired, nervous laugh, s*leep-deprived hallucinations: fun for the whole family.*

He made his way to a cluster of shops with the brightest window displays, telling himself the light would keep him awake. It would look bad to be found sleeping like a bum by some curious cleaner or worse, security guard. In truth he was petrified. He'd heard footsteps ten minutes ago, even shouting out *"Who's there?"* like the bimbo in some slasher movie. He ran towards the sound, feeling scared and stupid, but found nothing stranger than another dark hangar of shops.

Curled up between an electronics store and garbage can, he thought the smell of junk would be the closest to people he'd be till morning.

Whupwhup... Whupwhup... Whupwhup...

Whispering. Flapping. He was being chased through the mall by a moth the size of a garden shed; it's velvety brown wings whapping down at him, scratching his face. He woke with a start, swiping his nose. A chip packet lay between his knees and nose, tickling it.

Chig Chigaba Chig Chigaba

What the...?

Whispering.

He got to his knees and cocked out his head, trying to make out the words. On the second level something flapped. *The moth is up there,* he thought, still scared enough to half-believe this. He didn't call out this time; he had to know what was up there, and that required stealth. He took of his shoes and crept to the escalator, stepping on with an awkward stutter having spent a lifetime being magically transported up and down.

When he reached the top he looked around, widening his eyes as if this would somehow make them telescopic. All he saw was more stinking shops.

There's probably a loose layer of tarmac on the roof, flapping in the wind. But the day had been calm, sunny. Yeah, but the night might be windy, could be a fuckin hurricane out there for all I know.

Chigaba

Brian spun around. Someone had whispered chigaba, whatever the hell *that* was, and loud enough to echo. More footsteps, this time closer. He crouched and for a man his size, crept silently to a seating area.

He slid his body under a bench and waited.

The footsteps came from the direction of a bookstore. Several times they stopped. Brian sweated it out, trying different reasons for this phantom shopper's appearance. From the unsteady beat, Brian imagined a cripple. Too slow to reach the malls exit before closing time, he was left stranded.

Before he could shit over this logic, the shadow appeared.

His heart plummeted like a body thrown down a well. Silhouetted in a dim pool of light in front of him stood a man holding an umbrella over his head. It lurched forward, twirling the umbrella as if casting auditions for 'Singing In The Rain 2' were being held next door.

No way, oh no fuckin way. That is not that mannequin, please God don't let it be... it came into view; face half-obscured by the umbrella and bad light.

There was no denying it. Gray Ray had escaped his display and was staring directly at him.

He shot up, smacking his skull on the wooden bench. Ignoring the pain, he lifted, looking like some strange species of tortoise. The bench slid off with a loud thwack, while Ray continued swirling and watching, his fixed sneer impartial.

Brian ran.

Chigaba

It echoed, surrounding him with its nonsense threat. He glanced to the side; the window of *'Vestito Per Uccidere'* was unbroken. The other dummies were staring at him with blood thirst, like drivers passing a car wreck hoping to catch a glimpse of red. In shock, his left foot slipped out from under him, his unprotected ankle twisting spastically.

He fell with a scream.

The tiny part of his mind still sane distantly heard the fountain and muzak kick back in. A mellow version of Mozart's Requiem played over the upward gush of water, now reaching the dizzy heights of second level shopping.

Shit, oh shit, he pulled off both socks, tying them tight around his ankle, hoping to stop the swelling long enough for him to put a garbage can through the window of *'Happy frigging Campers.'*

Clunk. Clunkclunk. Clunk. Clunkclunk

The escalator. He's gaining his sea legs while I'm losing mine. Brian stood, baring his teeth at the thought-destroying pain in his ankle and limped towards the dome shape ten feet away.

A vein the shape of forked lightning bulged out from his forehead. It was too heavy; he released his arms. Candy wrappers and cans poked from the garbage cans flap of a tongue, mocking him. He spotted a cart up ahead; its bright red sign advertised *Badges, Patches, Locks & Latches!*

He hobbled over, meaning to cower behind it.

He sat on the cold tiles wishing he were at home, wishing he hadn't made fun of Ray. But wishes were an illusion for kids. He threw back his head.

Oh god, oh what a... shaft. He grabbed his tie, feeding the end into his mouth to bite back the upcoming pain.

He could see Ray leaning casually on his umbrella, staring at the garbage can he'd tried to lift. Standing precariously on the cart, Brian reached up and pushed the vent grille aside. This was it; if he fell he was dead.

He jumped, managing to prop his elbows inside the vent, as his feet slid off the cart, swinging underneath him like those of a marionette. His heart was plummeting towards a stroke but the thought of Ray's painted on murderous eyes watching propelled him to pull his ass up to safety.

Darkness surrounded. *No display lights up here.* Brian replaced the grille not knowing if Ray could climb, not wanting to. He scrambled forwards until his knees were numb. Directly underneath a pair of brown eyes followed his progress.

He ended up above a sporting goods store. He didn't know its name.

Go down or stay up, which is safer? He didn't know so put his life to eenie meenie miny moe and ended up removing his second grille. He held his feet over the edge and lowered himself down, hoping his elbows held. They shook like a victim of palsy. His feet swung over the cashier's desk, skimming the surface. The landing could be bad, but he couldn't pull himself up even if he wanted to.

He let go.

Thirteen

"Aargh! Fuck!" Oh *fuck.*'

His leg bent like a plastic straw. The crack of his anklebone was the sound of a bat striking a homerun. He rolled off the counter, belly flopping three feet to the carpet.

'Umph!'

He turned on his back, sucking air back into his lungs. Baseball bats spun across his vision in a dark kaleidoscope. He raised his head and saw his foot now pointed off to the side at a rebellious angle. Groaning, he dropped his head back to the carpet, noting the sluggers a final time before passing out.

eeeeeee, eeeeeeee, eee eee eeeeeee.

Fingernails across blackboards, knifes across plates. It brought him back to consciousness with its high piercing whine. He turned his head to the window and watched an open umbrella with trouser legs walk by outside, the metal tip scratching the glass.

For a second Brian just stared, fascinated as if watching a great movie. Then his senses kicked into gear and he pulled himself behind the counter hoping he hadn't been spotted.

He could have been watching this whole time, while I slept, this whole goddamn time...

He checked his watch. 3am. He peeked over the counter, the front window was scratched to hell but no sign of his little Ray of sunshine. He reached around the counter, pulling a bat free from its bin.

He heard it, but didn't. *Maybe just rain rattatatatting on the roof, maybe the vents working out the dents my knees put in, maybe...*

Chicaba

Ray poked his paint-chipped head down from the place Brian had fallen.

Brian pulled himself away from the counter, bat held firmly across his chest, some small comfort against sound of plastic joints creaking. He watched numbly as Ray swung himself down with relative ease. To his horror Ray was wearing Anne's gift, the pink fluff hiding the neckline connecting head to body.

He pointed the ugly umbrella at Brian and continued smirking.

Laugh at me now, why don't ya? the look said.

The mannequin approached.

The faces around the monitor might have been watching live footage of the apocalypse. It would have been more believable than what they were now seeing. On fast forward they watched an overweight guy run around their mall. How he got in here was anyone's guess. The staff looked puzzled; every few seconds he glanced around as if some invisible pursuer was chasing him.

Though no sound was available, the look on his face suggested screaming. They watched him climb onto a red cart and stare at a garbage can he'd just been hugging. They watched him disappear into the ventilation shaft.

A security man, his name Jed tagged to his chest, spotted it first.

"Hey, who the hell's that?"

They all looked at the live feed camera. A man dressed in a dark suit walked towards the mall's exit, umbrella swinging to the side like a walking stick.

"He shouldn't be in here!" Jed said, and ran down the stairs to apprehend him.

Jed stepped out into the morning darkness. Between two rows of arc-sodium lights he spotted him. His walk was that of a toddler, a wobbling strut.

"Hey! Hey you!" The guy turned.

A gray waxy face fixed with the grin of a suicide-bomber was the last image Jed's brain received before he collapsed.

A shopper was the first to notice the change in the window of *'Vestito Per Uccidere'*. The new mannequin was suspended with wire like a puppet, face as

Thirteen

white as a china doll, so *lifelike*. As he drew closer to the dummy sporting the latest casual red number, he let out a scream that turned every shoppers head.

The shirt was soaked.

A NEW LIFE
STEPHEN TYSON

Stefan Markovic stepped from the train, pulled his scarf up, and pushed through the throng of commuters on the platform. At the top of the stairs, he placed his case on the ground, gripped the edge of the cubicle, and picked up the phone. As he fumbled for change, he looked round. The coin disappeared into the slot, and a woman's voice answered.

"Hello."
"This is Stefan."
"Mr Markovic, you've made it."
"All my papers were in good order."
"I believe you are going to stay at your Fiancées?"
"Not yet."
"We will need to contact you."
"I will ring."

He placed the phone down and didn't look up until he was out of the building.

The private hospital was on the outskirts of the city. The chauffeur pulled up outside the main entrance. Sandstone columns rose either side of the front door. Stefan watched, as the car pulled away. As he turned, the gravel crunched under his feet.

His room had a view of the garden, a shock of yellow on account of the daffodils. He guessed that Geoffrey Randolph would be in one of the adjacent rooms.

At three-o clock, he heard a knock on the door.

"We're ready, Mr Markovic," said the nurse.

When he woke, the room felt different, as though someone had been in during the night and stuck ice on the walls. He shivered, and a molten pain tried to burst out from under his skin.

He didn't look down that day or the next.

On the third day he lifted the cuff of his pyjamas. The artificial hand was plaster pink. He couldn't see the join because of the bandage around his wrist.

The tears came.

As the nurse pushed open the door he hid his head under the sheets. She rolled back the bandage, and grief skewered through his bones. When he stopped shaking, he felt as though his skin had split down the length of his spine. He closed his eyes, and there was nothing but red, moving in waves. The nurse rolled him over onto his side and jammed the syringe into his arm.

Geoffrey Randolph's aide came in carrying a briefcase.

"There will be a further payment, later, when it is certain the operation has been a success," he said.

All the notes were neatly bundled and tied with elastic bands. They looked as though they had been ironed.

"Ask the nurse if you need anything," the aide said, and left.

Stefan sat on the edge of the bed, stared out of the window, and thought that the sky looked the same.

Stefan placed his bag on the table in the centre of the room.

"Mr Markovic, I'm afraid there's going to be a slight delay," said the woman.
"Please, Stefan."
"I'd prefer it if we could keep things on a formal footing. Geoffrey has phoned and said he will do everything in his power to get here by eight. I understand the

Thirteen

last train leaves shortly after nine, so it should leave you plenty of time."

"Did he ask... how I was?"

"Your welfare has always been uppermost in his mind."

The woman came back with a tray.

"If you want something stronger, help yourself," she said, and pointed to a small glass fronted cabinet in the corner of the room.

"Tea is fine."

"I'm afraid you won't find Geoffrey very forthcoming. I appreciate that the operation can't have been easy, for you, but it wasn't easy for him either. He is not a young man."

"Marianne left me."

"Sorry."

"My fiancée. She has known too much pain."

"I better try Geoffrey, again."

She sat in the hallway. He could see her from the lounge.

"Well how much longer?" he heard her say.

Something was wrong - worse than when the nurse had pulled back the bandage. He could feel it seeping through the house. It was all over her now, crawling across her skin and coming out of her mouth.

"No Geoffrey, surely not!"

Stefan walked into the hallway and took the phone from the woman's hand.

"Hello."

The line went dead. He stared at the woman.

"What is wrong? Tell me, what is wrong?"

"He's bleeding. His hand."

Stefan slumped on the settee. The woman took the empty glass from him.

"I'm sorry, Mr Markovic. But, you knew the risks. If it is not serious we will contact you."

"And if it has not worked?"

"I'm afraid, we won't be in touch. You must have some of the money left."

"Very little. I invested it in a small business."

That night, Stefan wrote to his niece. He told her of his trip to England and promised he would send for her. He told her of the elderly man who loved music, and played his cello in the garden beneath the apple tree. How the old man's hand became arthritic, like the branch of a tree bent by the salt-wind. After he finished writing, he wondered what to sell in his shop.

Thirteen

ONE NIGHT STAND
MICHAEL O'CONNOR

She has long red hair, my date for tonight. That makes a change. I usually go for blondes. But she was so right for me that I could not resist her. Tall, leggy, a bit on the plump side, enough freckles to stop her thinking herself attractive. And, of course, she can't resist me. Plain women never can. They like a bit of blarney, a bit of blatant flattery, because they don't get much of it. But you have to show them that you're still a real man. None of this namby-pamby equality crap. They like someone who dominates them. But you have to do the romance stuff first or you never get anywhere.

"To all the girls I've loved before ..." I sing. She giggles at my breathless voice. She recognises my excitement. It must be through instinct rather than observation. She is not a dumb blonde but she is not very bright. Women never are. They are only good for two things, and I don't need anything cooked at the moment. That's a joke I never say to a woman.

"When you're in love with a beautiful woman, it's hard ..." She had a lot to drink in the bar where I picked her up, and now we have just finished sharing a bottle of Californian wine. We are sitting on the double bed in a shabby and otherwise sparsely furnished hotel room. I booked it this afternoon under a false name and I kept my face hidden behind a long scarf when I picked up the room key. I like my liaisons to be discreet.

I lean forward and kiss her fleetingly on the cheek.

"You said you were a gentleman," she says, feigning indignation. But her face is suffused with blood and her pupils have dilated and she is breathing heavily. Beneath the cheap little dress she is wearing it is clear that her nipples have hardened. I can tell that she is ready.

"You're a lady, I'm a man ..." I like singing. Songs have all that garbage about feelings in them already, so you don't have to make it up yourself. Women like to think you have feelings for them. They'll let you do anything once you convince them of that. And then you can show them who's boss. I kiss her again, two or three times quickly, and stroke her breasts while I am doing it. She resists for a moment, then her body goes limp and she falls back on the bed. Now I will be able to do whatever I want. I keep stroking her and kissing her on the neck and ears.

"Tonight's the night, it's gonna be alright..." I knew she would be easy. I am good at picking the easy ones. It got harder when Aids arrived, but you can still find brainless women willing to risk going home with a strange man if he knows how to sweet talk them. Of course I don't have to worry about Aids.

"My love for you is way out of line..." It helps if they are drunk, of course. Women get really randy when they're drunk. Probably anyone could pull them then. But I am good at pulling. I can do it even when they're sober. But it saves time if they're not. And I am in a hurry today. I have the urge today and I know there's no point trying to resist it. It gets stronger as I drag my big hands all over her body, listening to her moan with pleasure.

"On the day that you were born, the angels got together and decided to create a dream come true..." I whisper into her ear. She writhes enthusiastically.

"Please," she whimpers. "Don't..."

"Do you know what I'm going to do now?" I ask her softly. I don't need the silly songs any more. They have served their purpose. She just stares at me, her eyes misty and her lips red with anticipation. "I'm going to get my little pricker out and then I'm going to stick it into you over and over again until I'm satisfied." She thinks I'm being crude. Women like dirty talk when they're aroused. Her breathing becomes heavier and more rapid. She was a very good choice. Even for me,

Thirteen

women don't usually get going this quickly. Perhaps I'll try more redheads in future. People say they are passionate by nature.

I push her skirt up to her waist and pull down her damp knickers. Now I get out my little pricker. I had hidden it beneath the pillow when she went out to the toilet. Her eyes flare open as she feels me sliding it along her narrow thighs, and she opens her mouth to scream. But I force it shut with my left hand and gently slip my pricker between her legs and inside her. The warm delicious blood gushes out and she begins to twitch uncontrollably. It takes all my strength to hold her down, while I slide it back and forth, sawing into her filthy whore's body while the ecstasy within me rises and rises until I can no longer bear it and I give one final shuddering thrust which rips her belly open to her throat and spills her guts onto the bedclothes.

I am satisfied. The grinding ache in my mind has gone, for a little while. I carefully wipe the bloody entrails from my little pricker and put it back into its leather sheath. I will have to lie down for a little while. I'll sneak out later on, when it gets dark. But now I'm just going to roll over and go to sleep. It's what real men do.

Thirteen

ALONE IN THE CATALOOCHEE VALLEY
LEE CLARK ZUMPE

...the dark places of the earth are full of the habitations of cruelty
   Psalms 74:20

Joe stared up into the night sky while the balsams bowed to an early autumn breeze. Tonight would be cooler than last night; tomorrow night would bring frost to the higher elevations. A Cherokee had warned him this would be a bad winter. He felt it now, too.

Joe watched the last few fingers of flame shilly-shally amidst the charred remnants of knotty logs. He would let the campfire wane, knowing the cinders would stay warm through the chill of the backcountry night.

Far behind him, Fort Caswell seemed a distant, fading memory. His abrupt departure ended a promising military career; but, under the circumstances, he doubted any one would fault him for it – the Great War had ended almost a year earlier, and the need for soldiers and officers had been diminished. His superiors did not question his decision.

His long trek had taken him from the Carolina lowlands all the way up through Maggie Valley and across the Cataloochee Divide. The rough and rutted mountain roads crept sluggishly over the landscape, twisting and turning like a wounded copperhead writhing in agony. Sprinkled along the route he found only a few marks of civilization: A wide array of trading posts, logging camps, and remote pastoral communities carved out of the bitter and implacable Appalachian backdrop. The land never seemed willing to surrender itself, and it grudged every inch it lost to ranchers and loggers.

The forests grew thickest along the perimeter of each tiny village, as if mounting resistance to force the pioneers out of the mountains and back into the foothills.

Half a world away, the war left a different countryside scarred and defaced. Armies had gutted the ancient fields and primeval forests of Europe. Fierce combat had fouled the air with mustard gas, and with the screams of the dying. Joe had not seen it for himself – but he had lost his two brothers in the trenches of France.

Sometimes Joe found it difficult to believe they were gone.

News of their deaths at the Battle of Cantigny had arrived almost simultaneously. The heartache proved too much for his mother to bear. The doctors watched impotently as the colour drained from her face, the courage from her voice, and the vigour from her breath. In the end, she had shrivelled like wilting trillium, curling up into herself – her once-soft skin yellow and desiccated.

Joe carried with him a few last notes she had scribbled in her unsteady hands, observations for her only daughter and the two grandchildren she never met.

Before drifting off to sleep beside the embers of his campfire, Joe traced the path of a falling star as it sped across the twilight, dislodged from its family and sent spiralling through the void without apparent destination.

Some time long after sunset Joe awoke. Dawn seemed distant and inaccessible. The wind still stroked the treetops and the chill on the air had grown more perceptible. Joe could hear the rushing waters of a nearby stream where he had refilled his canteens earlier that evening. Beyond that, though, he could hear other sounds – less palpable but no less real.

The moon bathed the forest in a bluish-grey tint so that shadow concealed little more than natural hues. The mountains themselves glowed with an uncanny

Thirteen

radiance. Joe felt a low rumble unsettle the ground beneath him, and he heard the clang of pickaxes striking stone. The mountain seemed to cringe with each blow, recoiling in pain.

Joe shivered in spite of himself.

He lay awake, wincing with each perceived blow, imagining the arch of each pick, and the coal-black fingers coiled around each hickory handle.

Then, he heard a scream.

Joe scrambled to his feet, searching the shadows for signs of life. The bulk of the Cataloochee Divide pitched itself against the twilit ceiling behind him, the Balsam Ridge lumbered grimly to the west, and Mount Sterling ascended from the boulder-strewn banks of Cataloochee Creek. The recurring collision of metal and stone intensified, and the valley floor throbbed with inexplicable misery. Joe felt the sharp tooth of each pickaxe, felt the earth tremble beneath man's instruments of torture.

In the next instant he believed himself overtaken by madness: Joe heard another scream...and another. This time it was not a not a single, solitary scream piercing the dusk – this time, Joe heard a symphony of grief-stricken cries. The basin buzzed with disembodied shrieks and howls.

Then, silence.

Above him, the celestial sphere crept slowly toward the distant dawn. The forests huddled in their self-authored shadows, seemingly oblivious to the entire event. Joe reluctantly dismissed his apprehension as calm slowly returned to the valley. Knowing sleep would not return soon, he took up a spot on the ground close to the remnants of his campfire and prodded the cinders with a short twig.

A sooty appendage burst forth from the crimson embers, thrusting up into the air, desperately searching for something solid. Barely recognizable as a human arm beneath the charred and blistered flesh, Joe cringed as it flailed about – black fingers squirming pitifully in the moonlight. Before he could fully react, the seared hand had found him, violently clutching at his flannel shirt, tugging furiously.

Joe grunted and gasped as he struggled to his feet. He grasped the mutilated arm, pulling with all his strength. Orange sparks erupted into the air. In an instant, he had hauled someone – something – out of the remains of his campfire and onto the forest floor. There before him lay a thing so disfigured, so tormented and scorched and abused, that it had ceased to be human. Tattered skin and jutting bone and unhealed wounds comprised this victim of unearthly torture.

"Please," the thing whimpered. "They'll find us if you don't hurry."

Joe knelt by the suffering man. The wretch was so close to death that Joe had nothing to fear, and he found himself offering the man water from his canteen.

"No time," the man said. "Don't you see? You've got to get him out."

"Get whom out?" Joe said, fighting back waves of revulsion and nausea. "Where were you – where did you come from?"

"Below – the tunnels – they're everywhere, beneath every city..."

"Was there an accident?" Joe eyed the dying man's twisted, gruesome body – recognized the telltale signs of torture. The broken shackles on his blackened legs confirmed his intuition. "Who did this to you?"

"Them... Les Habitants des Endroits Sombres – the Dwellers of the Dark Places. They've always been there, below the surface." Bloody tears cascaded down his grimy face, scabs wept and slivers of burnt flesh fell to the ground. "The Frenchmen warned us about them...they came in the night, took us from the trenches." The man lifted a hand to wipe the tears from his checks. "God, Joe, you've got to hurry...Josh was right behind me – get him out, Joe – get him out."

Thirteen

At that moment Joe trembled. He cursed himself for not seeing it earlier: This miserable thing barely clinging to life had once been his brother.

"Jonathan?" Joe slipped a hand beneath the man's head, lifting it gently from the ground. "Oh God, Johnny?"

"Joe, get in there...they'll find him – they'll find all of us."

Joe did not hesitate. First, he thrust an arm into the embers – and, finding no base, he dove in headfirst. The warmth of the coals in the fading fire stung as he passed through the portal, but the heat he faced on the other side surpassed any pain he had felt in his lifetime.

Below ground, he found himself in a cramped tunnel vaguely lit by distant, raging fires. Instantly, his flesh roasted on the bone, singed by some far-off conflagration. Joe's eyes burned and his desiccated lips blossomed with scabs. Unseen flames sent short-lived sparks of light through the passage, crafting long epochs of darkness punctuated by brief moments of illumination.

"I'm in hell," he muttered, struggling to keep his sanity.

"No," a voice answered. Joe circled around on his heels, scanning the ephemeral radiance and the pools of pitch for signs of life. For a moment, the shadows slithered aside, revealing a crouching form. "This is not hell. You'd have to be dead to be in hell."

"Josh?" Joe started to move toward the sound of his brother's voice.

"No – don't come closer. You'll lose the portal. I don't know how John found it in the first place." Josh – five years older than Jonathan and Joseph – strained to his feet. He inched out of the shadows awkwardly, grimacing with each arduous step. "You two always had a gift, though – you had a connection that went beyond blood."

"What is this place?" Joe glanced toward the ceiling of the tunnel. Only a faint, crimson ring set apart the portal from the rock.

"Another world – a world within a world." Josh shook his head. "The Underworld of mythology. Only, there are no gods down here – just men and monsters." Josh paused a moment, then murmured "Monsters and slaves."

"We have to get out," Joe said, tugging on Josh's arm. Though still cloaked in shadow, Joe could feel blisters and lesions peppering his brother's flesh. "We have to get back home – Johnny's waiting for us."

"You'll have to help me," Josh finally slumped forward onto Joe. "My leg's broken – I can't..." Joe quickly adjusted himself so he could lift Josh up into the portal. As he steadied himself, Joe heard the sound of pickaxes break the long silence. Distant screams echoed through the caves. "So many men," Josh said, gazing down the passage. "They used the cover of the war to take as many of us as possible – to carve out their tunnels, to work in their mines, to forge their weapons. To them, we're no better than beasts. Our lives mean nothing."

"What if they follow us?"

"Don't worry," Josh said, his arms stretching toward the ceiling of the narrow passageway, "I think we're safe now...I haven't seen any signs of them since we escaped."

Even as the words whispered over Josh's tumescent lips, something wormed through the gloom farther down the tunnel. Joe could hear it hissing above the hammering clatter of enslaved, wailing workers.

He thrust his brother through the portal, sending a shower of embers cascading down into the tunnel. In the sparkles of glistening orange light, Joe saw something peel itself from the shadows – something impossibly reedy and sheathed in husk of emerald scales. Frozen in horror, air caught in his lungs, he waited anxiously for the next flicker of light from the distant raging fires to expose the face of this underworld atrocity.

Only its eyes slipped from the shade: Narrow, askew, and hideously scarlet

Thirteen

in hue, the shimmering orbs pierced the darkness and scrutinized him – examining him from head to toe.

Joe felt his brother seize him by the collar – felt his own legs push off the floor of the tunnel. Beneath him, the serpentine beast coiled against rock. It hissed and thrashed its long, tapered tail as its two skeletal arms clawed at the darkness. Joe flinched as he passed through the circle of cinders, shook as the frosty air of the Appalachian night bit into his flesh.

"Christ," he yelled, crawling back onto the valley floor, "What is it?"

Josh was too busy to answer him. He pried the canteen away from his brother's rigid fingers. Jonathan stared grimly at the heavens, his eyes now void of life.

The reptilian beast burst through the faintly glowing ashes of the campfire, hissing and growling. Its scrawny arms scratched the ground as it strived to pull itself out of the underground passage. Joe kicked dirt and rock in its face hoping to drive it back into the bowels of the earth, but the beast only grew angrier.

The torrent of creek water gushing from Joe's canteen cooled the embers in the fire pit, blotting out the orange and crimson specks glowing in the coals. The creature shrieked in agony, first pulling, then pushing itself into the ground. The portal solidified as the water extinguished the vestiges of the fire, and the reptile-like thing finally collapsed.

Cut in half, the beast twitched dreadfully until the first light of dawn crept into the valley. Beneath the sunlight, the thing's scaly hide sizzled and cooked.

Josh finally fell to the ground, all his energy depleted.

"Is it over?" Joe watched as the beast dissolved into a tarry heap of bones. "Will they come back?"

"No, not for us, not here..." Josh sat up, gazing at poor Jonathan.

"The war is over," Joe said. He suddenly realized how long his brothers must have suffered in servitude. He remembered the Battle of Cantigny, wondering how many of the casualties had actually been snatched by the Dwellers of the Dark Places – how many other soldiers in other battles had been lost to the underworld beings. "Some say it was the war to end all wars."

The sun hovered over the slopes of Mount Sterling, chasing shadows across the basin. The brothers would have dig a grave for Jonathan before they could move on toward the next settlement, and it would be slow-going with Josh's leg. They would have to hike all day and well into the night, but Joe knew they would keep moving.

Neither one of them would want to spend another night alone in the Cataloochee Valley.

FAUX PAW
NANCY JACKSON

She lay on the bed, the light of the afternoon sun draping over her naked body. The red highlights in her hair reflected delicately, as she twirled a strand between her fingers. Reaching over she grabbed her stuffed teddy, the one she'd had for over twenty-five years. Its fur wasn't as soft and one eye had been sewn on more times than she cared to remember. Still it was a comfort, and that was what she needed right now.

"Two wasted years," she sighed. Hugging the bear close to her chest she glanced up at the ceiling, watching it churn and sway. One too many bottles of wine were catching up with her fast. Objects swam together in a bevy of brilliant colours.

"I should have known," she said. "I was much too wild for him."

Leigh wiped away the tears, mumbling her stupidity of falling for a married man. He had been turned on by her carefree style, until his bitch of a wife got knocked up with some demon spawn. That changed everything. When he left this morning she swore it was over, he'd had his last anal fuck.

"Asshole," she said. It was liberating to call him names, almost empowering and erotic. A breeze played at her body, invading every crevice.

"Oh well teddy," she said. "It's not like I could be tamed anyways, I'd need a beast for that."

Closing her eyes, she followed her fingers down between her thighs. Damn, just the brief thought of him banging away in her ass turned her on! With a flick against her swollen nub her back arched and the adrenaline flowed. The fantasy was interrupted by a heavy weight pushing her deep into the mattress, almost crushing her chest. Growls echoed around the room like rolls of thunder. Matted hair turned razor sharp, fangs protruded from a snarling mouth.

"What the hell?" she cried. The bear grew to full size, a long snout extending before her face, its breath impure and scathing.

"Christ I'm seeing shit," she muttered out loud.

"Thought you liked it wild," it said. The massive beast turned and sniffed between her legs. Its tongue slithered and rolled inside her snatch, and lapped at the dampness. Part of her was in denial, either the alcohol or a twisted dream was messing with her, but there was no possibility of the thing being real.

Her nipples stood erect as its tongue sought out her G-spot, its teeth gnashing against her pubic bone. Thick liquid warmed her thighs, a welcomed heat to her bewildered mind. She tried to steal a look but the beast was too big, its body covering hers. Leigh fought to ignore the stabs of pain emanating from her abdomen.

The bear turned with blood dripping from its mouth, her blood he had feasted lavishly on. Her lower half was coated in crimson, soaking the pale satin sheets, a thin maxi pad caught during a strong menstrual storm.

Screaming she tried to move her numb and severed limbs. The thing lapped at her breasts, circling her nipples with the rough texture of its tongue.

"I need to wake the fuck up!" she shouted. The bear opened its mouth, rows of daggered teeth glinted against the sunlight, and drops of saliva pooled around her neck. Its breath was raw and foul.

"No!" she cried.

"You said you liked it wild," it repeated. She watched its nostrils flare, red eyes piercing deep inside, mentally aborting her soul. A sickening sound of her flesh being torn caught her breath. In his jaws he held her pale breast, undulating it back and forth from the tip of her nipple. Blood splattered all over the bed, floor, walls and nightstand, a splatter punk art show. An eruption of thick red liquid

Thirteen

streamed from the open wound, exposing her cartilage and bone, muscle and veins. The bear spat her breast out, sending an empty wine bottle crashing to the floor. Turning its attention to her other breast, it played with the nipple between bloodstained teeth, manipulating it until hard as a walnut.

"It's a fucking dream," she chanted over and over. The pain was excruciating as it dislodged her final component of womanhood. Its claws buried deep in her skin, producing a multitude of slices, cuts, and abrasions all over her frail body.

Strings of her blood and gore hung from its jowls, as he chewed up flesh. His nose buried deep in her chest cavity, hunting for something more appetizing. The sound of bones snapping gave her the final answer; she was wide-awake, and this was far from any dream she could ever imagine. Leigh grew weak and despondent, removing herself from the ghastly scene before her eyes. Pieces of her were flung in every corner of the room, her body floating in a tributary of blood and organs.

"Looks like I tamed your ass," said the bear. The room swayed above her as she listened to the tempo of her pulse beat sluggish and faint.

"What the hells is going on here!" cried a familiar voice. She looked up into his eyes, the man who had ruined her life.

"How did you get in?" she whispered.

"I came to return your key," he said. "I figured you wouldn't answer the door. What have you done to yourself?" Reaching down he picked up a jagged piece of the broken wine bottle.

"I didn't," she murmured.

"Is this because of me? You would actually kill yourself because I won't leave my wife!" he cried. Kneeling he buried his head between her mutilated breasts, his cheeks lying against the chamber of her bleeding heart.

"No," she replied.

"I'm going to call the ambulance, I can't leave you like this," he said. Leigh shook her head; she was beyond repair at this point.

"Take the bear," she said.

"I couldn't possibly," he said. "It's your favourite."

"Take it to remember me by," she said. He stood and stared into her eyes.

"Maybe it's better this way," he said. "I won't have to explain things to the wife." Picking up the stuffed animal, he held it at arms length.

"I won't be needing this filthy old thing," he said. "It's better that I forget you." Tossing it on the bed he turned to walk away. The bear came alive and lunged, swiping the side of his face clean off with his paw. Blood spurted, a ruby fountain raging down his body as it crumpled to the floor.

"You won't have to explain a thing to the wife," it said. Leigh smiled; her teddy made her feel safe and content after all. Closing her eyes, she welcomed the sweet scent of death, and counted down to her final drop of blood.

Thirteen

GORDY STARTS ON DAYS
LEE BETTERIDGE

That first morning I felt extremely tired and groggy from having a crap night's sleep and my head felt heavy and thick. Switching from the night shift on to days in one weekend had proved more difficult than expected. I just hadn't been able to drop off through the hours of darkness, although I was sure that after a full day's work and the half-hour driving on both ends of the day, I would have no problem sleeping that night. I'd be knackered.

I picked up Cledwyn on the way as we'd organised the Friday before, pulling up at his wrought-iron gate ten minutes after leaving my house. Cledwyn Neal was stood there waiting, an old rucksack slung over his shoulder and a flat cap pulled over his tangle of black hair. The morning was nice and bright and the sun shone blindingly through the trees and yet he wore a scuffed leather jacket that looked like it could possibly weigh more than me. He climbed into the car, the poor thing rocking under his weight, although he isn't particularly fat, just damn big. When he'd come up to the office on Friday and asked if he could cadge a lift off me I'd had to look upwards to talk to him, and I'm over six foot. Although the mass of uncontrolled black hair, the heavy handlebar moustache and the biker's leathers do add to the illusion of him being bigger than he is, there is no denying that he is damn big.

"G'morning Gordy!" he chimed cheerfully as he tried to get himself comfortable in the Fiesta's passenger seat. His legs looked cramped in the foot-well even though I'd been considerate enough to push the seat back as far as it would go before I set off.

"Morning," I said, pulling the car back onto the winding road and instantly being dazzled by the slowly rising sun. I pushed the visor down, which relieved my eyes for a few seconds, but there had been something wrong with the thing ever since I bought the car and it sprang backwards again. I pushed it back to the ceiling and sat higher in my seat.

We didn't talk much. I'm mostly quiet around strangers, especially big scary ones, but that isn't to say I was scared of Cledwyn, I just figured if he wanted to talk I'd let him start the conversation. Hell, I felt so sleepy that I didn't think I'd be able to speak coherent sentences anyway. I just drove, concentrating on the snaking concrete strip in front of me and trying my best to shield my eyes every time the road turned to the east and the sun stabbed at my eyes. A couple of times I pulled the visor down automatically but it kept springing back and pointing at my face, causing me to push it to the ceiling again.

My passenger just looked out of his window, perhaps thinking of the concrete he'd be working with that day. I doubt it though; that would be quite boring. He was more likely thinking of naked biker sluts straddling stripped down Harleys and knocking heads together. Hell, what I know, he could have been thinking about flower arranging and cross-stitch patterns. I didn't ask him, I just drove.

Even though I'd driven this road countless times the scenery looked surprisingly picturesque, this being due to fact that before today I was always driving in the dark. The trees were so green they didn't look real, and the grass was the same. I'm not very poetic but as far as I could tell, the landscape looked extremely pleasing to my inexperienced eyes. Fields and hedges holding back fat cattle on one side, rambling overgrown woodland overhanging on the other.

I found myself feeling disappointed that I was having to go to work and wouldn't be able to go for a leisurely walk through the woods on such a beautiful morning. Then it occurred to me that if I had been off work there would be little chance of me spending my time in the great outdoors. TV, Playstation, music and fiddling with my car; that's how I spend my spare time. Oh, and Claire of

Thirteen

course. Can't forget her. She's the reason I switched to days after all. I wanted her to move in with me but she said it was a waste of time if she was at work all day and I all night. We'd see each other just as little as we do now. And so I'd switched, even though it meant dropping a few quid in my pay packet. What a guy!

I rounded another bend into the blinding sun and pulled the visor down. It sprang back up and then there was one hell of a smash as something that had stumbled out of the forest bounced off my bonnet. I slammed my foot on the brake causing me to pitch forward, the seat belt to dig painfully into my neck and the sun visor to hit me right on the bridge of my nose.

Stars and psychedelic patterns burst into my vision as the thing I'd hit slid across the road in a blur of brown and Cledwyn said in a flat voice, "Oops."

As I waited for my eyesight to return to me Cledwyn swung round in his seat, mumbled something about a side road and climbed out of the car. I took deep breaths, trying to slow my heart, and rubbed at my nose with a hand. Without really wondering what he was doing I vaguely watched Cledwyn as he picked up the thing in the road and carried it past my window. Turning hurt my neck so I glanced in the side mirror and saw him disappear into the side road he'd evidently been mumbling about.

I started the car again, as it had stalled when I slammed on the brake, and after checking there was no cars behind me I reversed into the little farmer's lane that had swallowed Cledwyn. Once off the main road I turned off the engine and got out. Cledwyn was a few feet behind the car with his back to me. His broad shoulders strained his leather jacket as he struggled to do something with the thing I'd hit.

"What was it?" I called.

"A deer," he said without turning and without letting me see it.

"Did I kill it?" I asked.

"No," he said. "You just caved in its skull and snapped its back. I killed it. Just broke its neck."

"Oh!" I said and walked round the front of my car to see what the damage was. As I got there I heard a thud and turned to see that Cledwyn had dropped the dead deer in a tangle of greenery at the side of the lane. I could see a patch of brown fur and the tinniest bit of yellow, bright yellow, which I guessed was a crisp bag or something. The big man was walking towards me.

"What's the damage?" asked Cledwyn.

"Oh," I said and looked at the ruined front of my car. "Cracked bumper, bonnet dented to shit, number plate totally gone." I bent over. "Smashed headlight and indicator as well. Jesus, was that a frigging Terminator deer?"

I'd seen the signs warning of deer along this stretch of road countless times before but I'd never really thought I'd hit one of the things. Of all the deer and all the cars, what were the chances of it being mine that came into contact with one of the dozy creatures? Much higher than I'd have guessed, obviously.

Cledwyn smiled, looked through the back window and said, "You were lucky. We both were. It tripped as it came onto the road. Can I use this?" He pulled the blanket off the back seat.

"Yeah," I said. I only have it in there because my dad always has one on his back seat and I grew up thinking it was a necessity, like seat belts and insurance. Oh shit, insurance. It suddenly occurred to me that I was going to have to pay out for this bloody deer with a death wish. I rubbed a shaky hand down my face.

Cledwyn carried the blanket back towards the deer and said, "When it stumbled it made its body lower and that's what you hit. If you'd have hit it in the legs the thing would have flipped up and come through the windscreen most probably."

Thirteen

I imagined what scenario that would lead to but stopped when an imaginary hoof crashed through my skull at high speed, and I started wondering if deer had hooves. It's something I'd never thought about. Meanwhile, it looked like Cledwyn had wrapped the animal in the blanket because I noticed he was on his way back to the car carrying something wrapped in the blanket.

"Is it in there?" I asked.

"Yeah," said Cledwyn. "Open your boot."

"What? Why?"

"I know a butcher who'll pay good money for this," he said.

"What? A deer that's been smashed to shit by a car? Is it worth much?"

"Well it's a bit bruised I'd imagine," said Cledwyn. "But I'm sure he'd get some good meat off it. I'd share the money with you, of course. Go towards the bill for that." He nodded towards the front of the car. I thought for a second, then climbed in behind the wheel and popped up the boot. I felt the thump more than heard it as he dropped the dead beast into my boot, then he was climbing in next to me and rocking the car on its axles again.

"It won't bleed all over in there, will it?" I asked.

Cledwyn turned to me and said, "I hope not, for your sake," but I didn't quite get what he meant.

We got to work without a problem, although I was constantly waiting for the engine to blow up or something because Cledwyn had nicely pointed out that the car's radiator could be damaged. The security guy on the gate let me in without stopping me, and without even asking why the hell it looked like the front of my car had been sat on by a hippo.

I pulled up to let Cledwyn out at the mess cabins where the 'real workers' get changed and have their bate.

He said to me, "Now if I were you I'd try and park in the shade. The suns going to be out all day and its going to get warm." He jabbed in the direction of the back of the car with his grubby thumb. "It'll bloody stink if that thing starts cooking, know what I mean?"

I nodded and he got out. "See you tonight," he called and walked off.

Well, from then on the day got progressively worse. My car was smashed to shit and might not get us home at the end of the day, I was going to lose my no-claims bonus on the insurance because, although there are a great many stupid laws in this country, there is none stating that deer should carry insurance. And on top of all that, there was a dead deer in my car that was liable to 'bloody stink' by the end of the day. I thought things could only get better from here. I was wrong.

My supervisor, who is the buyer for the construction company I work for, had chosen to be ill that day so his two assistants, Rajesh and myself, were called upon to do his work on top of our own, which, unbeknown to most people, is the only thing that keeps the stores and buying department running. Rajesh and I. And do we get all the credit as we should? Do we shite.

The fact that my boss wasn't in was a slight advantage because it allowed me to park the car in the small yard where our office cabins are situated instead of down the road. I pulled it in right next to the cabin, to try and get as much shade as possible, with the disgraced front pointed at the store building and the back facing the huge rubbish pile behind the gate.

Just before break time about 9:25, Cledwyn Neal made his way up from the building site. As he had predicted, it was getting warmer by the hour and in the cabin we had the fans on. He was wearing his hard hat and hi-viz vest over a Meat Loaf T-shirt that looked dripping with sweat, and when I saw him I left my desk and went outside with him.

Thirteen

After calling me an idiot for not opening the windows of my car a little to let in air, Cledwyn decided that it was getting too damn hot and the deer in the boot of my Fiesta was going to be ruined before we got it to his butcher friend. He informed me that you are really meant to drain animals of their blood as soon as they die, which was something I didn't know and could have lived without.

His proposal was to take the poor thing out of my car and place it strategically in the rubbish heap a few feet off, still wrapped in the blanket, perhaps with one of the discarded empty pallets laid gently over it. This plan would keep the deer in the shade and allow the air to get at it. He didn't ask for my approval, just took my keys off me and opened the boot. I stood guard, kind of, while he muscled the thing in the blanket out of the car and into the pile of rubbish. In the end he loosely covered it with a scrap pf tarpaulin in addition to the wooden pallet. Then he went for his tea and a sandwich, and I went to help Rajesh with some paper work.

As I worked I thought to myself, yeah, it's quite a good idea that, Cledwyn. And it's no problem. Nobody will know there's a dead body in the stores yard, nobody can see it, and he'd said he would come back up at the end of the shift and put the thing back in the car, if I didn't want to. I didn't. He said that was no problem.

Then at lunch time Mike, our stores man, came bustling into our office, blowing bad breath and sour body odour everywhere, and started to tell us how he'd had the idea that one of the site diggers could come and remove that pile of rubbish that had been behind the gate since time began and how he'd be able to fit his car there and that there was nothing the boss could say 'cos he wasn't in and if he was Mike would just tell him to piss off anyway.

Yeah, Mike.

Sure you would.

I tried to make him believe that his car wouldn't fit in the space taken up by the rubbish or that the boss would bullock him for having initiative beyond his mentality. Mike was having none of it and disappeared to organize it. Then, ten minutes later my phone rang and it was Mike telling me I'd better move my car 'cos the digger was on its way.

I all but shit my pants. What could I do? I couldn't go and tell Mike I'd stowed a dead animal in the pile of junk and I couldn't let the digger come and start shoving at everything and maybe pulling the deer in half or ripping a pile in its belly and spilling its guts all over the place

I went outside, opened the boot of my car, removed the broken pallet and the piece of tarp and took hold of the knot Cledwyn had tied in my blanket. As I hoisted it off the ground I learned it was damn heavy, much heavier than I'd expected. I got a better grip and the carried it over to my car, the whole thing swinging as I walked and bumping against my legs in a way that made me feel sick.

I couldn't see inside the parcel, Cledwyn had done the wrapping too well, but I decided that if the weighty feel of it brushing my legs made me want to throw up, not seeing the dead thing was probably a blessing.

I strained to lift it up high enough to drop it in the boot. I let go and dropped it in with a sickening crunch, and the parcel kind of lolled about, as though I'd put it in sat on its arse and it wanted to topple over. With a grimace I gave it a shove and it righted itself, collapsing into a heap that almost filled the small boot of my car. I slammed the lid shut at the same time as a digger rounded the corner and drove into the yard.

When Cledwyn came up to get the deer ready for its journey ten minutes before clocking off time I told him what had happened. He cracked up laughing and was

Thirteen

still laughing when he climbed into my car for the homeward trip. My two passengers and I headed home under a slightly darkening sky and a few grey clouds. I dropped Cledwyn off outside the wrought-iron gate and he got out, took the thing from the boot of my car and walked away with it slung over his shoulder.

Before I drove off he called, "See you in the morning, Gordy. I'll wash this blanket for you tonight."

"Ok," I called back, put the car in gear and drove home.

When I got home I checked my answer machine. There were two messages. The first was from Claire saying she wouldn't be round tonight because she was going out with some friends. The second was also from Claire saying she would in fact be coming round because her friends had cried off. I'd been home just long enough to take off my boots, flick on the TV and listen to her messages when Claire walked in.

"What the hell happened to your car?" she asked after kissing me on the cheek.

I told her the whole story, including the bit where Cledwyn broke the poor deer's neck to put it out of its misery and the bit when I had to heft the thing into my car. She hugged me and when I started to whine about the money it would cost me to get the car fixed and I how I was going to lose three years no-claims bonus, she brought it all crashing into perspective.

"At least you weren't hurt," she said.

Rubbing the bridge of my nose where a nice bruise had been blossoming throughout the day, I agreed with her. "Not much, anyway."

Claire asked if I'd had anything to eat and I said I hadn't. She kissed me again and said she'd make me something while I had a shower. Then she disappeared into the kitchen.

I was just heading out of the living room when something on the TV grabbed my attention. It was the local news programme, the one that looks so cheaply made I wouldn't be surprised if it was in someone's basement.

But to say it grabbed my attention was a total understatement. What the guy was saying gripped me by the knackers and swung me round the room. My jaw dropped like on a cartoon and a sickly feeling squirmed in my stomach.

I left the house without saying anything to Claire, only stopping to pull my boots back on. I climbed in my car and drove much faster than intended.

Shortly after I was braying on a PVC double-glazed door. For a while no one came. I knocked even harder and then the door opened. It was a large set woman with a pair of torpedoes shoved down her blouse and black jeans that looked as though they must be cutting the circulation off in her chunky legs.

"What d'ya think your doing?" she asked through brown teeth.

"Where's Cledwyn?" I asked, hoping I'd got the right house in the dark.

"Who's asking?" she growled, probably upset that I'd been unfazed by her first sentence. Normally, I'd have been fazed by it. But not today.

Tell him it's Gordon. I took him to work this morning."

"Wait here," she said, so I did. I hopped about from foot to foot, wracked with impatience and praying what I was imagining wasn't true.

"Gordy? What's up?" It was Cledwyn, stood in his doorway like a man mountain wearing a glossy black kimono and his hair tied back in a tatty ponytail.

"I saw the news!" I said.

He looked at me blankly. Then said, "Congratulations."

"I know what happened."

Still with that blank expression, Cledwyn said, "What happened where? What are you on about?"

"I said I've seen the news," I said, and my voice sounded a bit shrieky. "They said there's a boy missing. Went missing this morning, lives on our way to work."

Thirteen

Cledwyn grinned. "Well that's sad and all that Gordy, but what's it got to do with me?" He glared down at me, the height difference being exaggerated by the fact that he was on the step and I just on the path.

"They said he was last seen wearing a brown duffel coat and brown pants, Cledwyn, and that's fair enough, but they also said he was wearing a bright yellow T-shirt."

The big man stared at me.

"I saw it," I said. "You tried to keep it hidden, out of sight from me, but before you wrapped it up in the blanket I saw it. Lying in the long grass. All brown, yeah, and it was a bit away from me, but I definitely saw a bit of yellow. Oh God Cledwyn, what did you do?"

Cledwyn rubbed a finger across his nose, and then brushed at his handlebar moustache.

Finally he said, "So let me get this straight. You think instead of hitting a deer this morning, you hit a kid. And I broke a kid's neck, not a deer, and bundled it into your boot. And right now I have a kid, not a deer, in my freezer out back. Is that what you're saying?"

Having it spelled out to me matter-of-factly like that, I realized it did sound a little crazy. I mean, why would Cledwyn do all that. It didn't make sense. And the news guy hadn't said anything about the eight-year-old being hit by a car, just that he was missing. His house was near the woods so he was probably hiding out in there for some reason.

Then Cledwyn continued. "And I suppose your reason for me doing all this is...what? That I'm a nice guy and didn't want this nasty little accident destroying your life. If you'd ran a kid down then the payments to fix your car would be the least of your worries. You'd be going to jail, Gordy. Murder or manslaughter, it's just a toss of a coin really. Your whole life would be over."

He sighed. I just looked at him.

"Just forget the kid," he said. "It was a deer, Gordy, just keep thinking that. And don't worry about anything, life's too short. Go home, get your car fixed and, oh, I'd give your boot a good scrub if I were you. I'll buy you another blanket for your back seat. That OK by you."

My head seemed to be spinning. I told myself that it was a deer I hit, nothing more, just a poor deer, but the voice sounded riddled with lies.

"Go home, Gordy," said Cledwyn and with a swish of his black kimono he was gone and I was alone in his garden. I walked back to my car with a tear dripping off my chin. I felt tired, more tired than I ever had in my life I think. I had hardly slept the night before, switching from nights to days and all that, and although I felt weary to my bones, something told me I wouldn't get much sleep that night either. In fact, I wondered if I would ever sleep again.

PERHAPS I'M NOT DARK ENOUGH
STEPHANIE SIMPSON-WOODS

Nightfall was approaching as Joanie stared at the blank document on her computer screen. She was trying to write a scary story for a contest she had stumbled upon over the Internet. Not only would she gain recognition, but she would also win $100. It didn't seem like much, but it would definitely pay for a few months of Internet service. Her eyes fixed on the screen in front of her, she tried to dig deep into the darkest part of her mind. The more she tried to prod, the more distracted she had become.

Her mind dwindled to her cosy afternoon watching the birds from a paint chipped rocking chair on her front porch. She remembered a striking Blue Jay toying with a small Finch at a feeder she had put in her yard last spring. She also recalled watering the flourishing patch of flowers she had planted after the last winter frost.

"Hmm," she sighed, " Perhaps I'm not dark enough to write such stories."

Joanie looked through her office window, out into the darkness that blanketed the sky. She tried to visualize something grotesque and evil peeping in: a flesh hungry zombie or a moaning, white ghost. Instead, she noticed her neighbour, Mr. Williams, turning on the sprinkler system he had installed so his lush, untarnished lawn would get a refreshing drink of water.

An hour had passed by and all Joanie had typed were two words: *'Nightfall was'*. As much as she brainstormed, nothing more came to mind. Her inner darkness was about as evil as a beef stew simmering in its own juices for 7 hours on low in a crock-pot. "That would make a great meal for dinner tomorrow night," she said aloud as if it were the most brilliant idea she had come up with all evening. Sad to say, it was.

Slightly aggravated with her thoughts, Joanie went into her kitchen and fixed herself a cold glass of hand squeezed lemonade and grabbed a few of the chocolate chip cookies from a batch she had carefully whipped together the evening before. She took a bite of one and smiled. The cookie was still moist and chewy, just like she liked them.

Returning to her chair, Joanie continued to munch on the cookies while she poked her brain for a horrific story idea. She turned her eyes from the screen once again and looked at a picture of her boyfriend, Alex.

Alex and Joanie had met 6 months ago at a blue grass festival, which was held a few miles from her town each year. She pictured the two of them dancing to a local band they had gone to see a week ago in a small pub the two of them frequented.

"I haven't called him tonight," Joanie mumbled to herself, running her fingers through her short, blond hair.

Joanie shook her head out of frustration and looked down at her keyboard. She wanted to feel the light touch of the keys on her fingertips, but not one good, scary idea would push its way from her brain and into her thoughts.

Joanie left her station for the second time that evening and snatched her white, lacy apron from a hook in the kitchen. She figured she was wasting her time thinking and should go on with her nightly routine.

Apron tied snug around her tiny waist, Joanie walked down into the cold, dreary basement she visited nightly. Stumbling through the darkness, she finally found the chain to the lone light bulb that brightened the quarters.

"How are you tonight?" Joanie asked the strange gentleman she had gagged and shackled to the concrete wall that surrounded the basement. "I guess you can't talk can you? Silly me. I knew better. Now if I could only find that…."

Joanie removed the floral, cotton fabric she had spread over a card table in

Thirteen

the corner of the basement and picked up a small handsaw.

"Here it is! I bought this baby at a yard sale for $1 and it saws like a pro," she snickered, moving toward the bound gentleman.

Joanie pressed the sharp, tooth-like blades of the handsaw against his arm and smiled at the gentleman.

Squirming in the shackles, the gentleman howled through the cloth handkerchief Joanie had stuffed into his mouth earlier that night after she graciously invited him into her home when he stopped by to talk her into buying insurance.

"Oh. Don't worry. I will make this quick. I promise. I still have to go upstairs and find my dark side so I can write a story."

Once again, Joanie smiled at the gentleman, quickly sawing the blades back and forth against his arm until she got to the bone, the man's flesh splitting in all directions. "See! That wasn't so bad was it?"

The man screamed as his sweat dripped into the bloody wound on his arm. He looked down at the cut, his breath quickening behind the gag.

"Now, now, don't be such a big baby. I hope you have life insurance," she giggled, walking away from the man and taking hold of another instrument from the table: an axe.

Lifting it over her small head, she brought it down above him, chopping straight through the bone on his arm, it falling to the floor, his blood splashing up onto her apron. "I should start investing in red aprons. These white ones never last through the night."

She put the axe down and picked up her handsaw and then grinned at the whimpering gentleman. "Please don't cry. It's distracting. Besides, I only have one arm, two legs and your head left to dismantle. The less you distract me the quicker I can get back to my story."

Joanie spent the rest of the early evening removing the man's ligaments piece by piece. When she finished, she cleaned herself up and returned to her computer.

"Now then, where was I? Nightfall was.... approaching as Joanie stared at the blank document on her computer screen. Yeah, that sounds perfect."

Thirteen

SORRY, CHARLIE
GREG VEST

The realization that something was terribly wrong had been slowly dawning on me over the past few days, or had it been weeks. I had lost track of time somewhere, and no matter how I searched, I could not find it. Other things had slowly been dropped or taken from me along my path to the downtown Saturday market. My jacket. My wallet. My name.

I walked around from small tent to small tent on that early summer day in Portland, Oregon. The market was near the Willamette River, and seagulls spied down upon me from above. However, it wasn't the gulls watching me that gripped my every muscle with fear. It was the people waiting for me in and around the market that made me want to run desperately. Yet, where could I run to where they would not find me? I had no money, no checks, no bankcard. Just two dollars in change in my pocket. No, I was powerless to do anything but continue on. My fate had been sealed long ago, although I was only realizing this at that moment.

The road that had led me to the market had been marked with incredible highs and lows, significant smooth highways at times, other times I travelled on dirt roads decimated by potholes. I had done everything they had told me to do. I joined the military to serve my country. I got a college degree. I married for love, not money. I had a long list of achievements and was grateful for much, and I had slowly watched it taken away from me little by little. I realize now that that was just part of the torture process. You see I was not who I thought I was. I was obviously who they thought I was.

Now, as I amble aimlessly around the market, waiting to be taken, they slowly show me what's in store.

How do I know all this? They tell me. I know it sounds crazy, but it's true. Telepathy. A neat and insidious combination of abilities, I might add. Not only can they manipulate me to go where they need me to go, but I can't cry out or say anything, lost in their mind control. Soon, the worst of it is about to begin. The man who glares at me from a nearby bottled water stand nods his head. He knows my thoughts. I now know their intent. A woman coughs behind me, sending me a confirmation. They mean to slowly torture me to death. It's as simple as that.

"You got it!" yells someone on the other side of the market.

A man walks by, looks at me, making sure he has my attention and lights a cigarette. They mean to burn the flesh off my bones. I cringed. I try to walk the other way and stumble into a woman filing her fingernails. I shudder at the thought of them pulling mine out. I don't deserve this. I was a good person. Sure, I made my share of mistakes, but I never really meant to hurt anyone. In fact I was a relatively well-liked fellow. Or was I? I desperately tried to rescue my mind from their tendrils, going back. Remember, I pushed inside my brain. Remember who you are.

I grew up in a small town in Nebraska. My kind parents were humble farmers, and I was a good student, got good grades, a bit mouthy at times, I guess. I went to church on Sunday, and I tried to be nice to people. I didn't always succeed, but I never meant to hurt anyone. I never got in fights; I never made much trouble. I didn't taste alcohol until I was seventeen, and I didn't lose my virginity until I was eighteen. I even loved the girl I had sex with. Doesn't that count for something?

"Not at all," the woman behind the homemade jewellery stand said to a couple nearby, a message that I know is really for me. "Not at all."

I'm continued to be paraded around the market. Is this how they do it, make people walk around in a public place, showing their secretive superiority? How

Thirteen

ingenious and wicked. I was led to a booth about genealogy. A poster showing a family tree was prominently displayed, and I wondered what they were trying to tell me. Did this have something to do with my past, or perhaps something from a generation ago? It was as if a light had gone off inside my head. BINGO. Something I did a generation ago.

"Got any questions?" the girl behind the table asked me.

Of course I do, I wanted to scream. Instead, they held me powerless to speak. She frowned at me, and I moved on. I noticed a sinister looking man with these strange polished rocks massaging the back of a potential customer with a large, black stone. He pulled it back briefly, as he eyed me carefully. The rock looked like a hook. My back already ached. I tried not to think of what the sinister man was trying to tell me in his non-verbal way.

I GET THE MESSAGE, I screamed inside my head, hoping that the ones who could hear me would come to take me away.

"Quiet down," a woman yelled close to me, as if to a child.

I noticed a few of them looking in my direction. An old woman gazed at me with false concern. Another young girl glanced my way and smiled, but in a bad way. Something I did a generation ago. Was she a descendant of one of my victims? I was sure that they were around.

I realized that I had been led here very purposely. Had I been involved in something all those years ago that I couldn't remember? Were they keeping me from remembering? How is any of this possible, I asked myself? One of the telepaths was happy to answer. I heard laughter ring out across the market. The first real revelation to my exhaustive torment was about to be unveiled.

You're a clone, asshole, I heard one of the telepaths say in their silent way.

I nearly fainted. The thought was so shocking I had to sit down. I stumbled down the lane full of trinkets, art, and other exhibitions, seeking the bench near the closed-off street. I threw myself down on the rough stone seat and desperately needed to smoke one of the few cigarettes I had left in my crumpled back. My hands shook as I lit up, some relief coming as the smoke filled my lungs and helped calm me enough to attempt to think this through a little more. Stinking thinking. I had never heard that before. Or had I?

I was obviously not who I thought I was, so who was I? I gazed around, seeking clues and answers, scared of what I would find. Nothing stood out, and no one approached me at the moment. I tried to sigh, to breathe in enough air to relax the vice that gripped my ribs so severely. I wanted to cry, but my eyes felt like tiny balloons, full of nothing but hot air. I wanted to ask for help, but I knew no one would aid me. I was doomed. I had done something terrible in the thirties, no, forties, no, fifties, yes, and now, I had been cloned, given a good life where I could almost taste the sweetness of it, only to have it turn sour at the last minute.

I had done well in the army up until the last few months where I had been accused of distributing drugs. I almost ended up in jail. Instead, I lived in fear for three months until I hit my ETS. End of Time in Service.

I met and loved a multitude of women during my college years. All special. All wonderful human beings. All of them dumped me.

I had travelled to New York one summer as a camp counsellor, where I met the love of my life on the Fourth of July. She was a counsellor at the girl's camp nearby, and it was love at first sight. She was from Australia, beautiful, a gem. We married in her home country, moved back to Nebraska, where I got a teaching job in a great little town, full of fine folks. It was one of the best times of my life. Yet, my dissatisfaction grew after being lied to and manipulated by people I trusted. I left an otherwise great experience on a drastic downer. I felt tired and very used up. Perhaps that had been part of my torture. I had been a full-time teacher and a full-time student. I persevered through more education, got a Masters' degree,

Thirteen

and through that, an opportunity to work at one of the finest publishing companies in the land. That is what had brought us to Portland in the first place. The job had started off excellent. I was so thrilled to be there, working a job I thought was my dream. But the deadlines soon took their toll. I was asked to do more and more and more. The stress built into such a pressure that even a space suit couldn't have withstood. I crumbled. I went into my dream job one day, and I just quit. That had been a few weeks ago. That had been when THEY had taken over.

I suddenly realized with great fear I didn't even know where my gem was at the moment. That had happened a great deal lately. I would go for these walks, sometimes on hot cement with no shoes on, as if made to do so. I would drive for miles and miles with no particular destination in mind, knowing I was being led somehow, somewhere, for something. At first I thought it was to join the secret society that had been moving me from place to place, failure to failure, to my secret success, whatever that meant. Recently, though, it had become apparent I was going to end up destitute, abandoned, deserted, and ultimately destroyed.

My gem. My wonderful wife. I had tried to make her happy. I loved her with all my heart. Yet, I had betrayed her with another woman. I had broken her trust and destroyed my integrity. It only happened once. That had been once too many. Was the guilt from that stupid, destructive mistake, coupled with the stress I had been under the reason I was descending into...?

"You wish!" a teenage boy yelled out behind me to his Dad, although I knew that the message had been for me.

So some of them developed their abilities at a young age. Good to know. Perhaps I would overcome their control. Surely they were the evil ones, out to torment me. Perhaps . . .

"Knock it off!" a girl yelled at me while looking at her boyfriend.

Yeah, she was right. I could nothing. I moved when and where they wanted me to go. They had me, and we all knew it.

I was innocent. I had made mistakes, but I hadn't really hurt anyone. I had been hurt as well. What had I done to deserve this?

A cacophony of voices chimed in together, a chorus revealing to me what I could not figure out myself. I stood up immediately and began to walk around again, not caring where I went, knowing they were driving me around anyway. The horror. The horror of it all.

So I was a clone. I was cloned as a process of justice. I was cloned to be given a second chance, only to have it taken away from me as I had taken it away from my victims in the last generation. Had I really done that? How could this be?

Then, all the conspiracy theories I had read, all the secret government programs I had heard about, all of it made sense. This was a new brand of justice.

I was Charles Starkweather. I had shot and killed eleven people in five different states in December 1957 and January 1958. They had electrocuted me on June 25, 1959. They had cloned me a few years later. Now I was to face my own brand of terrible justice. They would torture me to death. And then, they would clone me, and do it again. And again. And again.

I realized this wasn't Portland, Oregon, at all, really. This was Hell. Eternal Torment. Forever. They could clone me forever.

I wanted to run, but there was nowhere to go where they would not be. I wanted to scream, but they would not let me. I wanted to cry, but they would not turn on the valves.

"Thomas Austin?" a voice rang out from behind.

I turned to face the large man in the policeman's uniform. This was it. My time had come. I swallowed hard. I couldn't speak, nodding my head, hoping that my time with them would be brief. I knew it wouldn't be.

Thirteen

Two other officers showed up on either side of me then. I was cuffed and taken to a nearby police car, everyone in the market glancing my way, some smiling, most frowning.

We drove a good distance through the city. I looked long at the setting sun, knowing full well I would never see it again. Not with these eyes, anyway.

I tensed up completely when I discovered our destination. This wasn't a police station. It was a hospital. We drove past a large sign read that read Portland General. We stopped right in front of the main doors. So this was where they kept the torture chamber, disguised as a floor in a hospital. Brilliant. No one would ever suspect. After all, who went into a hospital when they didn't have to? Even when a person did, they only went to the areas where they were instructed to go.

The large officer held my arm as I exited the patrol car and led me into the lobby, the other two officers blocking my escape from behind. We went into the elevator, the four of us, and I couldn't help but wonder if they were on the torture team. Would they be dissembling me in a few short hours, or would I have to wait? I felt hungry for the first time in days. Would I get a last meal?

We exited onto one of the upper floors and approached the desk at the nurses' station where an average looking man and a cute older woman were sitting.

"This is Mr. Austin," the officer said, completely devoid of emotion.

"Oh, yes," the woman said, a hint of glee in her voice.

"They'll be glad to know you're here," the man said evenly, looking me directly in the eyes.

My lips started to quiver then. The injustice of it all. I mean, what I did as Charles Starkweather was evil, true, but I never did anything like that in this life. I had changed. Or had I changed because they had been manipulating me all my life? My temples began to throb as the concepts of my existence overwhelmed me.

The police officer removed my cuffs, patted me on the back, and told me to take a seat. Would they pull all the hairs out of my body one by one or just burn them off? I thought about how I had recently been pining over my thinning hair, and now I wished it had all fallen out. I tested what I was about to face. Making sure they didn't see me, I pulled a single hair out of my arm. The pain was excruciating. The three policemen were talking with the male nurse. The woman had gone down the long, wide, white hall. I noticed a man shuffling up from the distance, dressed in a white robe, a blank expression on his face. I closed my eyes and waited. The pain in my back now lit up like giant, hot railroad spikes had been pounded in there by John Henry himself.

I thought about my oldest brother, a great family man, a railroad man. I thought about my older sister, an easy going gal, likeable. I thought about my younger sister, a strong woman whom I respected. And then there was my gem. My incredible wife. I could finally cry then. I knew I would never see them again. Pain was my future. I found it hard to breathe.

"Try to stay calm. Come this way, please, Mr. Austin," the male nurse said.

I looked at the three police officers as they made their way back to the elevator. Obviously, my mental reins had somehow been passed from the policeman to this nurse. The officers had done their duty and would now go back to the real world. I hoped they appreciated what they had. I wished I had, at least much more than I did. Maybe I would in the next go around. The next time they cloned me to be punished for my crimes. I resigned myself to my fate and followed the nurse as he took me down the hall and into a small room.

"You'll have to change into this," he said simply. "We don't allow street clothes on this floor."

Thirteen

He gave me a large plastic bag to put my clothes in and a gown to put on. He left the room, stating he would be waiting for me outside. Of course he would. It was nearly over. How much could one person take anyway? I knew I 'd find out soon enough.

I walked out of the room, where the male nurse was waiting.

"By the way, I'm Jim," he said in a friendly way. "I'll be your nurse during your stay with us."

Oh, no. I realized that they could probably keep me alive for a long time. My lips quivered again. God help me. Help me.

"Please," I said, finally starting to cry.

"It's okay, Mr. Austin. Come on. Let's get you to the waiting room."

"I need a cigarette, please. I need a cigarette first!"

"You can't smoke while you're on the mental ward, Mr. Austin. Try to relax. The doctor will be in to see you shortly. Okay?"

I just nodded and followed him as calmly as I could. Mental Ward? Was false hope just another form of torture for these people?

I didn't wait long in the small sterile room before a doctor came in, asked me a few simple questions, and left. The older female had entered with him and he gave her a few words and a chart before he left. She took me back to where I had first started, at their station, and told me to wait there. I sat down, still afraid, more confused, but calmer. She returned with a small cup of water and two very large pills. She instructed me to take them and asked me to open my mouth after I had. I even had to lift my tongue, so she could be reassured that I had indeed swallowed the pills.

Was I being shown mercy? Were they just going to poison me?

"Are you hungry?" she asked kindly.

I shook my head no, even though I was. I soon found myself in a small room with two beds. A handsome looking Asian youth was lying on one of them, reading the Bible. I fell onto the other one, exhausted, sleepy for the first time in . . . I had found at least one of the things I had lost. On the wall above the door was a clock. It was 7:05. I realized actually that it was the second thing I had recovered. My name was Thomas Austin.

I slept. Deep, dreamless sleep.

The next day I was served a bland, but magnificent in its own way, breakfast and then visited by my gem. I felt better. In fact I was overjoyed to see her. She tried as calmly as she could to explain to me what was going on. There was a mixture of sadness and anger in her voice that kept me quiet. It seems I had driven off again, and when I didn't return that night, she called the police and reported me missing. That had been three days ago. They had found my Ford Escort downtown and searched for me from there.

"Where were you all that time, Tom?" she asked, looking at me with an expression that made the question even more difficult to answer.

"I don't know, Pam," I said, not wanting to tell her where I thought I was.

The medication took its effect over the next week, and I felt better and better. I started to gain back a little of the weight I had lost, and I was overjoyed that perhaps I had not lost everything I had thought I had lost.

They diagnosed me as Bipolar, or manic-depressive as it used to be called, and that I had had an episode. I hated that thought as it reminded me of television episodes, of which there are more than one. I never wanted to walk through any of that ever again. It was just a delusion. I wasn't a clone of Charles Starkweather. I was just Tom Austin, human being with a mental disorder. It wasn't even an illness, just a simple matter that my brain did not produce a certain chemical, which causes an imbalance. Medication treats it as long as you stay sober and regular about taking your dosage. I was going to live. I was

Thirteen

thrilled. Even better, I was soon moved to the floor below, where I got regular cigarette breaks.

Another week went by, and I was soon to be released. Things were good. I walked down the hall, not knowing what time it was, and approached the nurses' station, an exact duplicate of the one upstairs, only behind this one was a severe-looking man, dark both in tone and attitude. I was going to ask him when the next cigarette break was when he piped up.

"Yeah, yeah, I know. You're wondering when the next cigarette break is, and you've still got fifteen minutes. You see . . ." he said, gazing at me too darkly, too deeply into my eyes. I could sense it. Something was wrong.

". . . I can read your mind. Sorry, Charlie."

Thirteen

LAST SEASON'S GHOST
MIKE BEEMAN

The Hunters knew the rumours well before they moved into the long abandoned house on Highland Street. They had heard the stories (John in the bar he frequented every other Friday night and Cheryl from the gossip circle of her teachers' lunch club) of the lights that played at night through lifeless rooms of the old Pike house. It was common knowledge in the small town of Plymouth New Hampshire that teenagers dared each other to creep into the house on Halloween as a rite of passage, although few had the courage to actually go inside. Between the two of them, the Hunters could piece together a handful of histories about the ancient house that were all sworn to be true.

"A man who once lived in the old Pike house was murdered by his brother one night in a drunken dispute over money. The police never found the murdered brother's body, but rumour has it he was buried, still half alive, under the kitchen floorboards. Now the man's ghost haunts the Pike house, and on full moons you can heard him banging on the floor and hollering as he tries to get out."

"Once a newly-wed couple lived in that house, until the wife caught her husband cheating when she came home early from a business trip. She waited until her husband and his mistress fell asleep and then hung herself in the hallway outside the bedroom door, making sure that her corpse was the first thing the lovers saw the next morning. On the anniversary of her death it's said you can still see her body swinging in the breeze through the open windows."

"Don't go near that house! Old Ms Anderson (some say she was a witch!) used to live there. She would sit on her porch all day long, knitting formless clothes even in the summer heat, until she went crazy one night and shoved both knitting needles through her eyes. Now she wanders that house blindly searching for trespasser, especially children, to come in so she can steal their eyes to replace her own."

"That house is evil," the older women of Plymouth would say as they passed the Pike house on their way back from church. "That's the devil's house," and they would make crosses with their fingers, saying 'Hail Mary's. "*Haunted*," they would whisper.

"Nonsense," John told Cheryl when she mentioned the rumours. "That's just superstition; it's fantasy. I'd as soon live in fear of the bogy-man, or believe in Santa Clause than be afraid of a house. Sure, I can see where children might make up some stories to scare each other, the place isn't in the best shape I'll admit, but once I clean it up and give it a fresh coat of paint she'll look as good as any other house on Highland street." "Besides", John would say to Cheryl with a smirk, "the price is to *die* for."

So when the Hunters moved into the house in early August, only a few months after moving to the country from Boston, they were given up for as lost by some of the more superstitious denizens of Plymouth.

"That's the problem with these small New England towns," John complained to Cheryl, "they have nothing better to do but gossip, make up stories, and let their imaginations run amok. These are the descendents of people who held witch trials, after all. It's in their blood."

Cheryl was persuaded by her husband's unwavering confidence, but even so she still felt uneasy in the house alone in the evening. Cheryl would still find herself holding in her breath at night, waiting for the noise she thought she had just heard to repeat itself.

They had been in the house for a full week before the warnings the townsfolk had given them began to resonate in Cheryl's mind. "On full moons you can hear him banging on the floor..." seemed less foolish when Cheryl heard a mysterious

Thirteen

thump somewhere in the house at night. But then again, that could have been the screen door or old shutters being blown about by the wind. "On the anniversary of her death you can see her body swinging in the breeze..." Cheryl remembered when she heard a creak in the hallway that could be mistaken for a knot being pulled tight. But that could have just been the old house settling as the temperature changes in the night.

"Ms. Anderson must be restless tonight," John often teased, "She'll snatch those pretty blue eyes right out of your head!"

"Stop! You're Terrible!" Cheryl would shout, fighting John off with a magazine or pillow as he stumbled after her doing his best Ms. Anderson impersonation. "I just want to borrow them," he pleaded," "Only for a minute or two!"

But at midnight it grew harder to for the Hunters to make jokes; their smiles came much more slowly and took more effort to maintain. The occasional noises grew more difficult to ignore until John began to wonder if something, a rat or squirrel possibly, had made a nest in some part of their roof or walls. John left out traps at night, and every morning he found them sprung, but empty.

Finally, John decided to sit up all night hidden in the hallway closet, armed with his best fishing net, to catch the intruder. "You're not leaving me alone!" Cheryl protested when John tried to convince her to stay in their bedroom, "Besides, I can help too. We can take turns sleeping." They set up two chairs, cracked the closet door open ever so slightly, and settled in for the long night. By midnight John and Cheryl were fast asleep, propped together in the cramped closet. Both of them awoke with a start when the rat trap snapped shut. The Hunters leaned forward, each holding their breath, to align their eyes with the slim crack of light that fell through the space between the door and its frame.

Out in the hallway they saw not a rat, or a squirrel, or a cat, raccoon, or any animal at all, but a white figure kneeling down by the trap with its back to them. Hearing a gasp and anticipating a scream, John clamped his hand over Cheryl's mouth although he barely managed to stifle a shout of his own. "Stop it!" Cheryl whispered sharply, pulling his hand down.

"Shhhhh..." John breathed back. "Wait."

The white figure, which appeared to be a young woman in a nightgown, was busy prying something out of the trap. She was so intent on her task that she didn't notice the closet door silently swinging open behind her, or see John creep out, brandishing his net menacingly before him. He continued to sneak up on her as she pried the candlestick she used to spring the trap free, until he was just a nets-length away from her. John set his feet, took a deep breath, and with all the authority he could muster demanded "Who are you and . . ."

The woman let out a shriek and half-turned, half-jumped away from John, falling over the rat trap. Cheryl, who had started out from the closet, shrunk back at the sound.

"You're trespassing," John asserted, "and no doubt forced your entry into out house. You're in a lot of trouble young lady. And what have you been doing to my traps?"

The woman's initial shock was wearing off as she collected herself on the floor, struggling to take even breaths.

"I repeat: what are you doing in my house?"

"It's not *your* house," the girl answered as she rose and brushed her self off, "this is *my* house."

"It most certainly is not!" John said, "I bought this house several weeks ago, I hold the deed. Who are you to break into my house and tell me you own it?"

"I am Emily Reardon!" the girl proclaimed. "This house is mine and I will defend it from anyone who tries to take it from me." Emily judged from John's blank expression that he was not suitably impressed.

213

Thirteen

"Haven't you heard of the spirit of Emily Reardon?" she asked, bewildered, "The ghost of Pike Place, the Haunt of Highland Street?"

"I can't say that I have..." John said, "I have heard of a Ms Anderson, a murdered brother, and an adulterous couple, but I don't believe in the whole "ghost" nonsense. If you are homeless you could have just asked for food or gone to a homeless shelter instead of trying to steal food from my traps."

"No, that's not what I was doing!" Emily protested, "I was haunting you to drive you out!"

"Why would you want to do that?" John asked. "You don't even know me, or my wife. You can come out Cheryl, it's ok." But as he turned to call her John saw that Cheryl had already stepped out of the closet and was standing right behind him.

"Well," Emily began, squaring her shoulders. "I am destined to haunt this house and anyone in it until my death is avenged." And with growing confidence Emily described her tragic fate.

"I was raised in this house, in the room that is now the guest room at the end of the hall. This house has always been my home since the time I was born. At first it was just me and my parents here, but when I turned thirteen things started to change. My father lost his job when the paper mill closed shortly after my birthday, and when he couldn't find work he began drinking. His constant drunkenness, many well-known affairs, and countless public humiliations took a heavy toll on my mother, and she tried to kill herself by over-dosing on painkillers. Luckily, my father found her in time and rushed her to the hospital, but my mother was never the same. She was considered unstable and admitted to a mental hospital by the time I was fourteen, and I never saw her again. For a time my fathers drinking continued, as did his string of mistresses, but then it looked like our luck was changing. A rich relative, who loved father dearly as a child, died and we inherited his considerable fortune.

"Encouraged by this good turn, father swore off drinking and began to manage his money by investing it in stocks and bonds with a friend from his college days. Father even found a respectable woman that he decided to take as his new wife, Melinda, who moved in with him along with her grown son named Jeffery. I was sixteen by this time, and just wanted a happy life with our new family, but the happiness I felt was short-lived. I heard Melinda and Jeffery talking in hushed voices in the living room late one night when they thought I was asleep and I learned Melinda's true intentions. I overheard their plan, which was to kill my father after Melinda married him but before I turned eighteen so Melinda would inherit all our money.

"The next morning I told all this to my father as he drove me to school, and he listened sincerely to every word. Oh I thought he would leave her! But later that same day I found him and Melinda sitting, waiting for me in the living room. My father had told Melinda what I had said to him, and he didn't believe a word of it! He thought I made the whole thing up! They said I needed some "counselling," especially considering our family's history of mental illness. I went to get help, but the counsellor wasn't any better: he smiled to my face and nodded at everything I said, but when I left he told my father he was worried I was "delusional." He thought the wedding could trigger a breakdown, so they decided to send me away on a 'wilderness retreat' while the wedding was going on. By that time I thought maybe I was going crazy, maybe I did make the whole thing up because it was all so confusing, so I went willingly on the retreat.

"Oh, but I wasn't wrong! On my way out to the country I found an article about the "black widow" killer in the back of a newspaper just over the New Hampshire state border. The woman from the article travelled the country with her young lover, who was masquerading as her son, and tricked rich bachelors

Thirteen

into marrying her. Soon after the wedding night each husband died mysteriously, and after the new widow was given his fortune she was never seen again. This caused suspicion and after comparing several similar cases the police realized that this was a serial killing. The wedding picture from each marriage showed the same woman, with different hair in each picture and slightly more or less weight, but it was Melinda! I knew I had to escape, and I did with a boy named Jesse who believed my story and wanted to help. We hitch-hiked back to Plymouth, getting there on the wedding night after the marriage, and I even made it into the house to try and warn my father before it was too late. It was stupid of me to go alone. Jesse said we needed to get help from the police and left to go into town, but I knew they wouldn't help. Jeffery caught me when I came in, and tied my to a chair in the living room. He called Melinda who came by before long, and told me that the police had caught Jesse and were sending him back to the retreat before he could warn my father. It was all over. She poisoned me after giving me the news, and I died without ever giving my father the warning. Soon after he must have died, and she is probably out there now, enjoying our money, and working on some other man to do the same thing."

She had been lost as she told her sad story, but now Emily came back to life. "But I won't let her get away with it! I'll never give up! I'll tell everyone my story until she's brought to justice, haunting them until they help me find her and I won't rest until Melinda is..."

"Only you didn't die!" Cheryl exclaimed, shocking both Emily and John, who had forgotten all about her. "You didn't die because Jesse escaped from the police and came back to your house! He overpowered Jeffery and captured him with a pair of handcuffs he had stolen from a police officer!"

Cheryl turned to John and grabbed his shoulder, her excitement growing. "And Jesse found the antidote and rescued Emily before it was too late! But it was too late for your father, I'm afraid; he slipped into a deep and mysterious coma on his wedding night. Jesse was eventually caught and taken away by the police, and you were actually turned over to Melinda's custody! She would have killed you, but that would have been too suspicious, and Melinda figured no one would believe a crazy girl like you anyways...and she was right! Your father had signed a living will in one of his moments of sobriety shortly after he inherited the money, and Melinda was legally entitled to the fortune after all! They were about to get it too, the lawyers met in your house to sign over the money, and everything looked its very worst. The paper was almost in her hands when who burst in the door?"

Cheryl looked between Emily and John, but neither of them offered a guess.

"Your Mother! She had been released from the mental institute a long time ago, but decided to get herself back on track before she could return to your family. News of your father's marriage had reached her, and she rushed back to town. She wanted him to be happy, even if it wasn't with her, and wanted to see her daughter after all these years. She had met Jesse in the train station as he was coming back to Plymouth to save you again, and recognized that his story was about her own family! Your mother had never signed any divorce papers, a detail your father overlooked in the tail end of his drinking, so his new marriage to Melinda was illegitimate and she wasn't entitled to a cent! She was, however, charged with several murders and the attempted murder of your father. After the poison was discovered in your fathers system an antidote was developed, and he woke up after Melinda's conviction to see you, your mother, and Jesse all with him around his hospital bed."

"It should have ended there," Cheryl continued, "You know 'and they all lived happily ever after,' but they never know when to let a good series end these days, and with Emily's future marriage and inevitable baby, there was still a few seasons left before viewers gave up their loyalty to the characters. After a while, thought, it just became too sensational, with secret twins and hidden pasts and plot holes that just didn't make sense, and the show was finally cancelled and replaced by a sitcom."

"What?" John and Emily asked in unison.

"Don't you get it," Cheryl asked John, "She thinks she's Emily Lawson from 'Turning Wheels,' the old soap! I used to watch that every day with my mother after school."

"No!" Emily protested, "No, that's my life, I remember all of it. That happened to me!"

"I'm sorry," Cheryl told her, "but it really didn't. I think I know who you are anyways."

"No..." Emily groaned, "I'm Emily Reardon, I always have been!"

"That last name sounded familiar," Cheryl continued, "And I know the plot by heart so I was trying to remember who Emily Reardon was while you were going over the first two seasons. My friend, Henry Reardon, your real younger brother, was in my grade in school. I remember hearing that his older sister had died when I was young, and he was missing from school for a couple weeks, but I forget what she died from. It was something unexpected and random, like a stroke or brain aneurysm or something, but anyway that's how you really died."

"No," Emily said in a hushed voice as she turned to leave, "it can't be, that's all I remember. I don't know any thing else." Emily walked out of the room. The Hunters followed her dejected form as it faded down the hallway.

"That's all I remember," Emily whispered one last time as she melted into the night.

"I don't remember anything else..."

Then she was gone.

Inside John stared open-mouthed, alternating between where Emily had disappeared and where his wife now stood with unabashed amazement.

"Some people," Cheryl said, shaking her head as she took John's hand to leading him towards the bed. "Some people watch entirely too much television."

HOW TO KNOW A BODY
STEPHEN FRANCIS DECKY

Jay is holding Jennifer's hand on the walking path through the woods behind the college. It's the last full day of their first real vacation together: 5 days driving up through the heart of New England in a rented car. Their final stop is here, in a little college town in Western Massachusetts, replete with a trendy downtown shopping area stuffed with students and other tourists. The walk is Jay's idea - he's had enough of shopping, and feels a need to stretch his legs out for a while.

They walk for nearly an hour, then turn back, with the intention of stopping for a coffee at one of the cafés downtown.

"I can't believe I gotta go back to school on Monday," Jennifer says. "I so totally don't feel like it."

"You're almost done, you oughta be excited. Alls you gotta do is finish this semester."

"I fuckin' dread it."

A few more lame consolations cross Jay's mind; he quickly discards them, not wanting to destroy the afternoon by sounding insincere. They are still a good 15 minutes from the opening of the walking path, but he is suddenly desperate for that coffee, and maybe a cigarette - he quit a few months ago but has allowed himself to splurge whenever a true craving hits. He's got one now.

Beside him, Jennifer opens up her purse and removes a pack. She lights a smoke, and is putting them back in her bag when he stops her.

"Hey, lemme bum one." he says.

"Go 'head."

Squirrels are hopping from tree to tree overhead. Birds are landing on the footpath, pecking around for a few moments, then darting back into the bushes. The sunlight is in motion, speckled on the fallen leaves kicking around beneath their feet.

"I gotta take a piss," Jay says. He moves a few yards off of the path with the lit cigarette in his mouth. As he unzips and begins to pee, he feels a massive headrush coming on: It's his first cigarette in weeks, and the kick from it - though brief - reminds him of the pot he's still got stashed beneath the bed at home.

Motherfucker, I can't wait to get home, he thinks.

He is just zipping back up when Jennifer lets out a high-pitched squeak, the equivalent of a cut-off scream.

"Jen?"

"Oh my god."

He takes a branch to the head on his way out of the bushes, a stinging THWACK that leaves an inch-long cut across his forehead. The blood begins to trickle down to the side of his left eye. His hand goes to the cut to feel it; an instinctive, subconscious sense of relief washes over him: It's not as deep as he'd thought. *It'll stop bleedin' in a minute*, he tells himself.

Jennifer is standing a few yards down on the path, leaning to the left with her right hand covering her face.

"Jen, what is it?"

"Jay, please tell me that's not a girl."

"What's not a girl?"

"Oh god."

He wipes his forehead with the palm of his hand and approaches her side. The moment he touches her shoulder, her arm straightens out, her index finger pointing to the ground a few yards into the woods, where what looks like a dead body is lying in the dirt. They'd passed this area once already without seeing it, a fact that makes Jay's stomach leap. They'd enjoyed their walk. They'd kissed

Thirteen

and held hands.

"Jesus Christ," he mutters. Jen shivers and makes another squeaking sound as he takes a step toward the body. The blood looks bright and fresh, but a covering of leaves across its back and ass - it's lying facedown - makes him wonder how long it's been here: A couple minutes? A few days? He has heard there is a certain stink that dead bodies carry but as he sniffs the air he can only detect the smell of trees and dirt.

"Wait a minute," he says. His eyes re-focus on the body: The legs are out at impossible angles. The hair is shiny, a pitch-black colour with a sheen that seems, at one moment, otherworldly. In the next, however, it appears somewhat fraudulent.

A fake, he thinks. *A dummy.*

Jen grabs for his arm as he takes another step forward.

"Jay, no."

"Wait."

He leans down and sniffs once more, then straightens up and delivers a kick to the side of the dummy's head. A sound like a snarl erupts from somewhere below him: His eyes, for a moment, have turned skywards, half-expecting to see the head sailing off like a drop-kicked football over the treetops.

He misses the quick flash of teeth that sends Jennifer flying toward the opening of the path, too shocked to scream or do anything but run.

When he does look down, the body is squirming in an attempt to stand. One of its hands is pressed to the side of its skull that Jay has just kicked. Its legs - covered in a slick, filmy material that resembles, more than anything, a melted skirt - shake and tremble for a moment before settling into a kneeling position. From here, it turns its face toward Jay.

For a few seconds, he can't breathe.

Tell me it's not a girl, is what he's thinking: There is a gaping hole where its nose should be, splintered by protruding bone-splints. The eyes are white, full white; a smear of blood circles the right one, and the mouth is split apart by cracks through which a mess of gnarled, yellow teeth can be seen. It's wearing a rotted sweater, and both dried and fresh blood is caked in splotches all across its frame.

"Hey," Jay says: Weak, lame, and scared as he backs up, this time taking a branch to the back of his head, which flicks off of his right ear, breaking the skin, and causing a sharp stabbing pain to split through his veins.

His hands stay by his sides: He has already considered running, but the thought of the body following him has left him paralysed.

"I didn't mean to do that," he says. Lame. "I thought you were -"

Another snarl stops him in mid-sentence. The body stands abruptly, and moves on twisted legs across the dirt and dead leaves. It stops directly in front of Jay, and places a pair of damp hands on his shoulders while staring white-eyed into his face.

She's alive, he thinks.

She's not a girl.

Her hands slide weakly down his shoulders to his chest.

She screams: An ear-splitting burst that makes his eyes go blank momentarily, his body on the verge of fainting.

When she stops screaming, she begins to cry.

Hyperventilating, Jay attempts to back up, but finds himself still frozen by the girl's proximity. Her hands are sprawled out on his chest; her face comes forward now, pressing up against his heart, while a series of hoarse, guttural sobs makes her body shake uncontrollably. Jay suddenly remembers Jennifer, and wonders how long it's been since they first spotted the body.

Thirteen

A line of smoke rising up from his right answers his question: He's still holding the cigarette, the tip burning steadily a good inch above its filter.

"Hey, listen," he says, the sound of his voice echoing above them. The girl's hands have now come down from his chest and wrapped around his ribcage. Jay hears footsteps tramping through the leaves, and feels both a quickening of his heart and a sense of relief. *Jen*, he thinks, but when he looks back toward the path, he sees only an elderly couple, moving quickly, oblivious to the sight of Jay and the girl.

"Are you okay?" Jay whispers a moment later. He is just now picking up a scent from the girl: It is dirt-like, blood-like, a smell not unlike the forest itself, only stronger, more condensed. "I'm like totally sorry I kicked you. I really thought -"

"Muhhnn," the girl groans, stepping back suddenly, with her head down and her hands coming up to block the sight of her face. "Umm-muhhhn."

She turns and begins hobbling away, still crying, her arms lifting up from her sides once or twice, a sign of inconsolable despair.

Jay feels his heart drop. He straightens and reaches up to the cut on his forehead, then the one on his ear: The blood has already begun to coagulate. He watches the girl's hunched, drooping figure until it either vanishes or disappears into the mass of trees and bushes before him.

Eventually, he returns to the path, and begins walking back toward the college. He is within earshot of the city's traffic when he spots Jennifer leaning against a tree, smoking a cigarette, her face coated with tears.

"Jen?"

She doesn't speak. Even after he kisses her, and helps her stand. Even after he's walked her back to the hotel, and laid her down upon the bed, and watched her staring at the wall beside her head for nearly 45 minutes. When her eyes finally close, he stands up and is surprised to find that darkness has fallen outside the windows. He's hungry and also badly in need of a drink.

He is sitting at the hotel bar a half-hour later when the scent of the woods hits his nostrils and forces him to turn his head left and right. There are 2 couples sitting at tables near the bar, and a group of college-aged kids standing with beers in their hands in the corner. Jay sniffs the air and realizes abruptly that the smell is coming from his jacket.

The bartender steps out of the kitchen with the hamburger Jay ordered in his hands. He places it on the bar in front of Jay and asks if he'd like some ketchup.

"Hate to be an asshole," Jay says, "but do you think you can wrap that up for me?"

The bartender disappears into the kitchen once more.

Jay leaves him a fat tip, and is about to head back up to the room when he turns and steps out into the night time air. He tosses the boxed-up burger into a trashcan and stops at a drugstore for a pack of cigarettes and a lighter. He grabs a coffee from a café up the street, and drinks it while smoking on a bench outside of an ice cream shop.

He's chilly: His jacket is still sitting on the stool back at the bar.

A short while after deciding it's time to turn back to the hotel and get some sleep, he feels his head begin to swim and awakens at some point afterward on the footpath behind the college. He is barely aware of his own body, let alone the sound of his own voice calling into the trees. From time to time, he stops for a smoke break; aside from the light of the cigarettes, he can see nothing, but it's not until he literally walks into a tree that he realizes he has ventured off of the path and is now lost.

He is tempted to lie down and close his eyes for a few minutes, but instead begins flicking his lighter in an attempt to re-find the path. It takes him only a few

Thirteen

minutes, but at the moment he spots it, a rush of panic rolls up his spine.

Behind him, something begins moving through the trees.

Jay starts to run, then stops after a few steps: The sound is in front of him now, and on both sides of the forest. He flicks his lighter and sees a branch moving directly in front of his face, with the faint outline of a drifting shadow behind it.

"Hey," he whispers.

A branch cracks and Jay turns toward the source of the sound. At the same time, something damp brushes against his face, then his neck. He is sure it's only a leaf, but as he attempts to lift his lighter, another leaf slaps against his hand; the lighter falls away into the darkness. His eyes go down to the ground, then up as a set of wobbly footsteps crosses the path close enough for him to feel the vibrations in the dirt.

He is next aware of running, with his hands in front of his face to block the damp limbs surrounding him on all sides. He is not sure whether or not he's even running in the right direction, but for the moment he is unable to stop or do anything but focus on the sight of his own feet pounding steadily against the path.

The sight of a streetlamp overhead is a shock.

He stops in place, breathing heavily, while his eyes focus on the silent street ahead.

A shadow crosses the path, coming toward him.

Jay holds out his hands slightly, his mouth opening as the shape points toward him.

"What the hella ya doin' here?" a voice asks.

The shadow continues approaching, growing brighter beneath the streetlamp. Jay makes out the dark uniform, the cap, the holstered gun of a local policeman.

"I was ... takin' a walk," he says.

"This path is closed at night. I oughta give you a fine. You been drinkin'? Doin' drugs?"

"I had a drink."

The sudden beam of a flashlight blinds him, while the crackling of a walkie-talkie breaks through the rustling of nearby leaves. The cop checks his ID, asks some more questions, then tells him to get the hell back to his hotel.

Jay obliges, without complaint.

He falls asleep easily but awakens less than an hour later, in total darkness, with his heart racing and his skin crawling. Beside him, he can hear someone breathing: He knows it's Jennifer, but for a few harrowing seconds he is unable to remember what she looks like. It takes a sudden rush of courage for him to jump up and flick on the light switch by the door.

Jennifer is wrapped up in sheets, facing away from him.

"Goddammit," he whispers, staring at her, then focusing on the darkness outside the window. A sudden but powerful urge to dress and return to the woods shivers through him.

For what? he asks himself. *To say I'm sorry? I already said it.*

Sleeping on the bed is impossible. For an hour or so, he remains perched on the edge of it with the smell and heat of Jennifer's body filling him with a vaguely familiar sense of terror and repulsion. When he can't take it anymore, he gathers an extra set of sheets and a blanket from the closet and curls up on the floor by the window. He falls asleep only moments before sunrise.

In the morning, they eat breakfast in the hotel's restaurant. Jennifer has a

Thirteen

headache, and looks ill.

"You gonna be alright for the drive?" Jay asks.

"I just wanna go home," she replies.

He collects his jacket from the bar before leaving. The smell is still there: blood, dirt, and the forest. He clutches it to his chest instead of putting it on, and walks like this through the parking lot, several steps behind Jennifer.

On the way out of town, Jay makes a wrong turn and finds himself heading back up Main Street toward the college. Jennifer slinks noticeably down in her seat.

"Are you crazy?" she asks. "Where the fuck are you going?"

"Relax," he replies.

He stops at a red light just a few feet from the path and the woods beyond them. Jennifer's eyes are closed, her fingers pressed up against her temples.

"I'm gonna fuckin' scream," she says.

Jay stares out through the window, almost overcome by the longing to jump from the car and run headlong into the trees.

"Go ahead, scream," he says.

Jennifer hesitates then turns suddenly with both arms swinging, smacking and punching at his face and chest while howling unintelligibly, her cheeks smeared with tears. One of her fingernails scrapes a patch of skin from his forehead, and the blood spills down over his right eye, momentarily blinding him. His lip begins to swell as well, and his nose has gone suddenly numb with pain.

He's tasting blood.

Jennifer is still pounding him when the light turns green.

Gently, he pushes her back into her seat then squints the blood from his eye. Jennifer collapses with a long, terrible wail.

Jay keeps his eyes on the path until the cars start honking behind him and there's nothing else to do but drive away.

Thirteen

BY THE SHORE
MATTHEW BROLLY

It had to end here. A less than perfect symmetry, I guess, but in some ways it started here, long ago. Anna's body is heavier than I would expect. It would be easier if she was awake but the drugs won't wear off for some time, and I'm not yet sure she would appreciate the necessity of what we are about to do.

Already I can feel the rush of the sea. It is clearing my thoughts rapidly as if they were made of dirt. Anna's troubled dreams are becoming clearer in my mind and it is this, which drives me on. The water will soon cleanse us as it did that glorious day in childhood. We will be baptized together again, for a final, eternal time.

I can see the boat in the distance, hidden behind the rocks. Moments later and the opportunity would have been missed, as the sea is only inches away enticing the small craft into its depths.

Anna falls heavily into the boat but she doesn't wake, only a brief silence in her dreams as her body adjusts itself to its new position. The boat struggles as I drag it from the shore and it is a long time before I feel the icy touch of the water on my shoes. Briefly I wonder if the coldness of the sea is some omen, and for a wild moment I am a doubting Thomas. Yet the alternative is unbearable. Better to let the sea decide.

I have to fight the sea as we fall over the waves but soon it succumbs and we begin to drift. My head is almost completely empty – only the wonder of my own thoughts, Anna's dreams, and feint echoes of those unwanted sounds present – and I have time to gaze into the night sky and wonder at the miracle of the stars above me and the greater marvel below the boat and its particular significance to me.

The peace in my head is overwhelming and I let myself cry. If only this silence existed perpetually then the world could be as noisy as it liked. I would embrace the screaming Mothers and their tearful offspring, sing along with the machines of road workers, the chants at football matches, would revel in the company of nightclub goers and bypass demonstrators. I would accept the song of this wondrous earth if only there was quiet in my head. If, like before, the voices would all but disappear then I would have no need to commit these unforgivable deeds.

Anna stirs next to me and I can hear her confused thoughts. I wonder how I can explain and pray she will understand. Either way, it won't be long before she knows and we can embrace peace together.

Not long now, Anna. We can drown those crazy thoughts together. There is peace where we're going. A peace we've only dreamt of all this time. If you were awake now you would see the irony. You'll wake before the end, I know. One last time. One last kiss. Soon, Anna Darling. Soon.

I have a talent. We all have some sort of talent I guess, however minor. Mine is not a minor talent. It is not a talent I wish to have. I became aware of it at a very young age but have only shared my secret with one other. Until now.

The first time? Aged three, perhaps as old as four. I was misbehaving as usual when I heard a noise. It was my Father's, but he wasn't there. *I'm going to kill him if he's messing with my work again.* My father was a gentle man but at a young age such a threat, however idle, was enough to scare the hell out of me. My Father was an architect and I loved nothing better at the time than sitting at his easel and making my own recommendations on his working plans, usually with the help of a set of bright crayons. When I heard his voice, I immediately suspected trouble. Fortunately, I hadn't begun my latest design and quickly fled

Thirteen

his studio before I was caught in the act.

For those formative years my talent was a beneficial one. I could hear the voice, or as I learnt the thoughts, of my parents without them having to speak. It was a very imprecise science, one I was unable to rely on. Some days I could hear full streams of consciousness from my Mother and Father, usually mundane contemplation littered with feelings and thoughts I was unable to comprehend; other times, I could only make out occasional sounds, fragmented sentences and sharp, obscure words.

My talent led me into innumerable trouble. It took me sometime to learn that what people were thinking did not necessarily equate to their actual wishes. When misbehaving, I often heard my parents laughing in their thoughts at my antics. Naturally I continued my behaviour, happy to be making my Parents laugh, only to find out to my surprise that I was to be reprimanded for my actions.

More troubling was hearing the thoughts not meant to be shared. Now, I understand this. But then... Imagine everyone could hear your everyday thoughts. What would your lover think of your hidden desires, the others you are attracted to? How would the strangers you pass in the street react to your opinion of them? Have you ever secretly wished someone dead? Planned a murder in your head? Could you honestly say there is one friend in your life you have never wished wasn't there, even for the briefest of moments? Would shut up? Would do something with their useless lives? Imagine then that you alone could hear these thoughts from others. Imagine the pain even the most innocent of comments could inflict, especially to one so young. The truth is not always our friend. Mostly we avoid it if necessary, if it causes upset to others; sometimes we use it to our advantage, to cause damage. We rarely mean what we think, almost never act out the fantasies which swim through our head. I know that now, but it was a hard lesson to learn.

As I grew older, my talent developed. I say developed, but it grew out of control. It began to become unbearable once I hit puberty. It was the last thing I needed to contend with during that mysterious period. If you think the thoughts of adults are puzzling, try to listen to the wild musings of young teenagers: the insecurity, the bitterness, the petty complaints and hate, the uncontrollable longings... the fear. Added to this, my own confused feelings and thoughts. It was not a happy time, but if I'd known what would come later I would have accepted it.

I could hear more and more. During lessons, the worthless thoughts of my classmates would fill my head. They were just as bored as I; usually the teacher was more so. I was unable to concentrate. Double French Monday morning was bad enough without listening to Maria Pelinski's thoughts in a half-English, half dodgy French accent telling me she had two brothers and a budgie called Joey and lived somewhere in South-West England.

My evenings were spent alone in my bedroom, usually below my sheets trying to dampen the words bombarding my mind. Even from my attic room, thoughts found me. Streets away, I heard family arguments, guilty secrets, critical appreciations of the latest soap opera. It was as if the more I tried to drown out the words, the more they would try to haunt me. There was simply no escape. They began to take over, so I was unable to hear my own thoughts; literally.

I started to deteriorate in front of my parents and they had no idea why. I couldn't tell them now, not even if I wanted to. I had trouble forming words, and was far from being able to express myself adequately. I guessed they thought I was crazy – I had similar doubts. They tried to help me - urged me to be active, encouraged me to be sociable – but their efforts always backfired. They soon accepted my need to be alone, if far from understanding the reason why. Then one day, accidentally, they found a cure.

I don't remember the exact details. A vague picture of my Father comes to

Thirteen

mind. It is a blazing summer's day and he is smiling, telling us to pack. We are going on holiday the next day. I remember the journey, though. Sitting in the back of my Father's car, a million thoughts, none of them mine, rushing my mind as we journeyed from a small house in Swindon to an even smaller caravan park in Cornwall. I tried to sleep, to prevent the thoughts from hurting me, but was unable. We were stuck for hours in endless traffic jams, thoughts rushing in and out of mind like swarms of insects as we passed vehicles full of mundane boredom. I started crying but still they attacked. My parents tried to comfort me but I couldn't hear them, couldn't even decipher their thoughts as they rubbed my head or tried to hold me in their arms. I truly thought death could not be far away, and it was his dark arms I wanted to embrace me. I was shaking, watching my Mother's puzzled face, her own fearful hysteria and my Father's eyes in the rear-view mirror, narrow and scared when it began to ease. Not greatly, but significant enough to hear my Father's clear thoughts. *Thank Christ, we're nearly there.*

The caravan park was amiable enough. My parents looked delighted with their abode, and I was content enough to bask in their happiness though I was more enamoured with the sea-view. I had never seen the sea before, and was hypnotized by its presence. It called to me like nothing before and I couldn't wait to dive into its depths, even though I had no idea how to swim. My Parents were delighted at my enthusiasm, and soon we were heading down to the shore.

I can only describe that moment as an epiphany. It's a word too easy to abuse. But as I crept nearer and nearer to the shoreline, the feeling was so profound: I had some glimmer of a future.

The thoughts were slipping away. The sea was drowning them as I had tried to do a million times before. Some still struggled through – I could hear the amazement from my parents at the change in me – but I could battle against such mediocre numbers. The sea had freed my mind, and I would never forget.

I spent every waking hour during that holiday by the sea. My Father taught me the basics of swimming, and I would stay in the water until my skin became wrinkled and chapped. At last I was free. I didn't care how it worked; all I knew was the sea blocked out the thoughts reaching me, and that was enough for me. They were still there waiting when I returned to the caravan, but they were dulled as if I was a child again and the talent was more a blessing than a hindrance.

Two blissful weeks rushed by before my parents announced we were staying for good. I cried that day as they showed me around my new home; a simple abode, it didn't overlook the sea but you could hear the distant sound of the water from the window in my tiny bedroom. I'll always remember the look - not the sound nor the thoughts, but the look – from my parents as they showed me around that house. They still didn't understand the change in me but they didn't have to. It was enough for them that I was happy; I saw it in the curious smiles on their faces, the stunned glances they gave each other when they thought I wasn't looking.

For once I was normal. I flourished in this new environment, if not living a completely normal life then living as close to one as was possible for me. I started a new school and even managed to strike up some rudimentary friendships. I could still hear the thoughts but they were tamed by the background presence of the sea. If I concentrated I could forget they were even there for minutes at a time. I thought I could never be happier. Then came the second epiphany.

I heard Anna hours before I ever saw her. This was not that unusual - I'd heard the voices of thousands of people I would never meet – yet the first time I heard her voice in my mind I knew my life was to be changed irrevocably.

Each time she spoke in my mind it was as if someone had turned a radio on inside my head. As her words floated into my brain, a hundred other sounds, minute and distant, would accompany her. It was as if a heavenly choir had filled my head and I remember having to sit down to let the wondrous sound overtake me.

Within an instant I knew everything about her: her history, her friends, her dreams and desires, her favourite colour. I could smell the fragrance on her neck, taste the breath from her mouth. I had a complete mental image of what she looked like as if she was somebody I'd known all my life. The only thing I hadn't anticipated, the thing that made complete sense when I looked back on it later, was the greatest miracle of all.

I waited for her on the beach knowing the exact moment she would arrive. She looked so innocent as she turned to look at me, a slight sense of unease on her full lips. I realised then what I had never dared dream of before. I told her as much and she smiled. Then she ran to me and we embraced.

In the years to come we tried to analyse that moment. The closest we came to finding any comparison to the wonder we shared, continued to share, came from the testimonies of identical twins. Even then only a few cases came remotely close to what Anna and I had. The truth was that no one else could possibly be as close as we were: Anna and I shared the same gift.

The sounds I heard when she spoke in my mind were the echoes of the thoughts swarming in her own head. Who could tell what turned them into the extraordinary cacophony, but neither of us cared. Anna told me she heard exactly the same sound in her mind when she heard my thoughts.

We spent the first week of our friendship recounting our memories, sometimes in words sometimes just by thought. Anna had always lived by the sea so didn't take as much comfort as I did form its calming presence though she admitted she rarely fared far from the coastal town. At night we would talk each other to sleep even though we lived two miles apart. Hearing each other's thoughts was the perfect antidote to the unwanted sounds, which had plagued us all our lives.

It was only natural that we became lovers though through some sense of respect we waited until we were sixteen. Anna is the only woman I have ever made love to so I have no comparison but I can't imagine I could have ever felt the way I did with her with anyone else. It was more than the physical: as we made love, we shared each other's joy in our minds, experienced every tiny and intimate emotion we were experiencing.

Paradoxically, it was this intimacy that often threatened to drive us apart. It was hard for us to understand the emotions we arose in each other, and listening to the unbridled confusion in each other's minds had the potential for conflict. Furthermore, we had no secrets from each other; were unable to hide the darkest parts of ourselves. We grew up fast learning to trust one another explicitly, knowing one another like no two other human beings could ever do.

Both our sets of parents surprised us by welcoming our union. With their help we moved into together before we were eighteen though we waited a few more years before we were married.

Alone together, we learned to harness our skills. Anna taught me how to block out some of the sounds I heard in my head by concentrating on one particular thought. We even learnt to block out each other's thoughts with a modicum of success that was handy when Christmas and birthdays came around. We discussed children but knew it was not realistic. There was too little we knew about our gifts to risk inflicting them on someone else. But we were happy enough in our own little world. So much so that it was inevitable it couldn't last.

One February afternoon I heard Anna crying in my head although she was a mile away shopping in the local supermarket. I had been sleeping when her scream pierced my dreams. Within seconds of pulling myself from my slumber I understood her pain.

Thirteen

Earlier that day both our sets of parents had taken one of the local boat trips to a seal island a few miles off the coast. It later transpired that a freak storm had dragged the tiny vessel against the rocks of the uninhabited isle killing all but two of the people on board. As Anna's tears rushed through my head I already knew that only my Mother remained alive out of our parents.

She was trapped in the boat and water was filling her space fast. I could hear her wild thoughts as she struggled to comprehend what had happened, what was happening. Anna could hear them too and they magnified in my head until it felt as if it would burst from the pain.

I never found out my Mother's physical reaction to what happened to her. I don't know if her body panicked as the boat filled with water, as the corpses of people she loved floated by her. What I will always remember is the calmness that finally overcame her thoughts; the weary acceptance that her husband had died and that she would soon join him.

I ran against the wall trying to knock myself out as I heard her recount the water filling in, covering more and more of her body. She thought about me as it finally covered her face, a silent prayer that my life would be fulfilling and happy. I can't describe the anguish as I felt her mind go silent. Little did I know that I would hear her thoughts again.

We never recovered from that horrific day. I replayed the incident thousands of times in my head. Each time I thought of it I could hear the thoughts of my Mother as if she was standing right next to me; guilt overwhelmed me every time I thought of her dying thoughts.

For Anna it was worse. She used one of the tricks we had developed to try to hide it but I knew that whilst I had been asleep she had experienced her own parents' death as well as all the others on that feted trip. Her life became full of anguish and bitterness and I felt less and less able to help her; especially so when the thoughts began to return.

It was like being young again, the sea being no protection, – endless voices and thoughts filling my head confusing and disturbing me, leaving me in no state to live a normal life – except this time the thoughts sounded different.

At first this was of little concern to me as all I cared about was banishing the voices from my head. I used our life savings to buy a small boat which we moored in the marina, hoping that the closeness to the sea would ease the pain in my head but it was of little use. The sea was not the ally it had once been. Its only effect now was to clarify the thoughts I heard in my head, so that I heard tiny snippets of clarity from the multitude of voices I shared my life with. Only then did I realise whose thoughts I was hearing.

Who knows how it happened. Maybe it was hearing my Mother as she slipped from this world, maybe it was another, latent, talent I never knew I had. Either way, the dead had started to speak to me.

They were tragic stories; what else would you expect from the dead? The more I heard their thoughts, the easier it became to put together the fragments they offered into a cohesive narrative. I was hearing the pain of those unwilling to give up their hold on the earth. They chastised the living for giving them up, complaining that the time was not right for them; that they had too much to offer life to let it be taken from them.

I sympathized, but not enough to stop wishing I could banish them from my head. I couldn't sleep, the voices intensifying every time I shut my eyes. My gift, my burden, was twice as great as it had been when I was a child. The thoughts filled every moment of my life; there was no escape.

Fortunately the dead never reached Anna; at least she never let on, grief was her only burden now and it ate away at her more than the voices ever could. We made a woeful pair. We wasted away in our tiny boat, refusing to eat and

Thirteen

struggling to sleep. Anna refused to discuss anything with me and my mind was so full of the ghosts that I was unable to search her thoughts. It was this which finally made up my mind. I couldn't tell her my plan out loud – it sounded almost ludicrous when voiced – but I sent her enough thoughts to let her know; I allowed her silence to become my consent.

I stashed the boat in a little inlet I knew the sea wouldn't quite reach by the time I needed it and waited for night to come.

Anna dreams of her parents; of all those that died that horrific day. I hear her thoughts clearer as she approaches the waking world. She recounts her parents' thoughts as the rocks rip into the boat: the fear, the remorse, the final questions. Hopefully for the last time, she curses her gift: how it has destroyed her life; how she thinks it has destroyed the lives of others.

I hear our parents calling for us, pleading us to set them free. *We'll be there soon* I think back to them.

I place Anna's body in the sea and the coldness drags her from her sleep. I slip in next to her and push the boat away. Anna holds onto me as the boat drifts, a confused look on her face. *Why?* She asks

It is the only way I reply

'But I don't want to die,' she screams into the air. 'What gives you the right to choose?'

'I told you,' I try to explain, but she is panicking, flailing at the water that will soon take her captive.

Anna swims for the boat fading in the distance, but her body is too weak. She mouths something to me but I am unable to make it out. Her mind is silent, her thoughts blocked.

I swim towards her but she tries to pull away. 'You're crazy,' I think I hear her say as the water swallows her up.

My Mother cries in my thoughts welcoming Anna to her side. I hear Anna's parents as well, overwhelmed at being reunited with their daughter.

And you my son? My Mother calls.

The water is taking me now and there is a blessed silence as the thoughts drown with me.

Soon, Mother. Soon.

Thirteen

DEATH OF THE APOSTROPHE
PAMELA K. KINNEY

"You need to have more conjunction between sentences before this story is right," said the first sentence.

John slammed his fists down on the desk. "Shut up! This is my story!"

"Yeah, like you can write," giggled the word count.

"Wasn't your last novel a flop?" asked a comma.

"I heard his agent say that if he doesn't do a bestseller this time the agency's through with him," whispered an adverb to a pronoun. "Look, guys, let's write the story my way this time, and the next one's yours. How about that?"

"Shit!" growled the last word. "I'm at the end of this miserable mess and to tell you the truth, there won't be a next novel – it's that bad."

"Yeah, like a penny awful," agreed the title. "Even I'm pathetic. *Blood of the Vampire.*"

"Sounds like something a five-year old thought up!" piped up an exclamation point in a bored voice. For an exclamation point to be bored was the last straw for John.

He raced out of his office and grabbed a hammer in the laundry room. He carried it back to the office. Raising it up high and ignoring the screams and yells, he brought it down hard, smashing a hole in the screen. Sparks and crackling sounds filled the air as the monitor went dead.

"That should shut you all up!" snarled John.

The printer whirred to life and began printing up pages of the novel, shooting it out. Shocked, John stood there for a minute, just watching it. Then he blinked and slammed the hammer down on the printer. Down and down again, until he had broken it into pieces.

A shit-eating grin on his face, John sat down in his chair and dropped the hammer onto the carpet with a soft thud.

He leaned back in the chair and surveyed the damage.

"Guess I'll have to get a new monitor and printer, but hell, it's so peaceful," he said with a laugh. He closed his eyes, savoring the quiet.

Something blipped on the monitor and a picture came onscreen. It was a page from his novel, some of the words missing from the hole in the middle of the screen.

John jumped up and grabbed the sides of the monitor with his hands. "I destroyed you! There's no way you can come back on–not with a hole in you!"

"Well, it looks like you don't know everything. Just like you don't know how to write a good story either, dingleberry!" snorted a period. "Gosh, but I am so ashamed to be a part of this manuscript."

"What the hell kind of software did my wife pick up for me?" yelled John as he pushed the monitor off the desk. It landed on the floor with a thud, sparks flashing out of the hole. He picked up the hammer and turning to the case, slammed the head down on it over and over. "I'll stop you! Do you hear me?"

Screams and yells drifted up from the monitor, with some voices mocking John, telling him not to blame them but his wife for charging the software on his credit card, along with that butt-ugly lamp she got for the living room. John banged harder with the hammer when he heard this. He hated that lamp!

The yelling finally stopped. John stood there, the hammer clutched with a death grip. His chest heaved in and out, the breathing raspy. Sweat beaded on his face, with one drop of it dripping off his double chin.

"What is going on – " It was his wife. Lily stood there, her mean little eyes, which he always thought was the color of shit, darted from the wreckage to him. Her mouth opened and closed like some fish. John saw something stuck

Thirteen

between her tobacco-stained teeth, most likely from the dinner she had just came back from with the 'girls'. Girls, shit! A bunch of old hags, who gossiped like the nasty hens they were!

"Hello, sweetheart," he said, walking over to her and giving her a peck on her cheek. Makeup came off onto his lips, makeup she used to cover her doughy complexion. "Did you have a great time?"

Lily's eyes shifted to him, a suspicious glance in them.

"Forget my night out. I can see that you were busy while I was gone."

John shrugged. "Oh, you mean all this?" He gestured a thumb at the damage. "I had to destroy them, or they would have went on and on."

"Who was going on and on?" Lily took a couple steps away from him, eyeing him funny.

"The novel. It was trying to tell me how to write the storyline."

"Uh huh. I see . . ." She took another couple of steps back.

John frowned. No, she obviously didn't see. Lily looked at him like he was crazy or something. He stepped toward her.

"Honest," he said, "they were talking to me. I think it has to do with that software you bought – you know, the new writing program."

"John, your novel can't speak. Software doesn't cause the computer to make your story communicate with you."

He grabbed her arm, his fingers digging into her skin and waving the hammer in the air with the other.

"I swear to you, they did! It's that Goddamned software you bought me! Thinking that since I'm such an awful writer that some stupid CD for the computer will make me better!" He brought her face close to his. "Well, I'm not such a bad author and you're nothing but some old bitch with menopause who thinks she's better than I am!"

"Honest, I don't think I'm better than you. John, I love you." Lily's voice had become high and hysterical, like some screeching bird.

Lily began to tug her arm out of his grasp, her face wan and her eyes dark with panic. As if suddenly he had stepped out of his body John watched her frantic attempts to free herself with a detached air. He saw the hammer rise up and descend down upon her head, smashing like an egg cracking in half.

With the same detached air John saw the hammer with Lily's blood and bit of brain on it fall onto the carpet. He saw himself looking down at her body, which lay on the carpet like a broken doll, her limbs all askew. Blood seeped into the carpet, turning it from a golden color to a rich red one. He found that he actually like the red color much better.

"Boy, you couldn't even kill her right!"

John turned and saw the monitor had come to life again. On it, the words were jeering at him.

"Can't write a novel and he can't kill his wife properly," remarked one apostrophe. "The man's an idiot!"

"Nonononono!" screamed John, picking up the bloody hammer and hammering away at the monitor and other parts of the broken computer. "I killed you so stay dead!" He kept at it, screaming insanely, until the neighbors hearing ruckus came over and found him. And Lily. They ran back to their homes and called the police.

The police found John still hammering away at the computer, screaming, "You're dead, you hear me, dead!" over and over. Their guns trained on him, the police managed to get him to put the hammer down and allow them to handcuffed him. John let them lead him away, as tears rolled down his cheeks.

Deemed insane at his court trial for the murder of his wife John was sentenced to a mental institution.

Thirteen

Percy, one of the male nurses at the McCutcheon Mental Institution gave his co-worker, Sherry, a strange look.

"What's John doing, Sherry?"

"Well, Dr. Thomas said that after months of therapy he seems to be better. That to go ahead and let him write if he wants to. So I gave him some paper and a pen."

"Do you know what he's writing?" asked Percy. "I mean, he did write some bestsellers once upon a time."

"I'm not sure, but I think he said he's calling it *Death of the Apostrophe*. Or something like that anyway." Both nurses turned away and left the room. "Besides what harm can writing on paper do?"

"Hey, John, you think you're going to kill us with this new novel?" asked the title with a laugh.

"Yeah, he might," said an apostrophe. "It's such a stinker that it'll kill us to be the words for this trash!"

They laughed, but John ignored them as he continued writing. Besides he knew where the nurses kept the scissors in this place.

THE LIDENBROCK DUTY
MARTYN PRINCE

Death wasn't at all how I expected. He was much taller for a start. Thinner too, I fancy, with narrow shoulders and a frame scarcely thick enough to hang his waistcoat from. A pocket watch would have surely unbalanced him and sent him toppling. And no scythe either, as I noted with a curious sense of disappointment. Instead he carried a notebook, of the type favoured by collectors of taxes, with a curious pen clutched grimly between long and angular fingers. Yet, for all my earnest description, there will still be many among you who think me mistaken, that this clerk of a man, this wretchedly serious individual, was no more Death himself that I am flesh and blood, of which, I can assure you, I am neither. But let me say this: no other than Death would have tipped his top hat toward me in passing, conveying in a singular glance the twofold apology that was due. One for the visit he paid my earthly body not a day earlier, and one for the predicament of lingering existence with which I am so evidently accursed. And both of these I intended to address!

For the record let it be said thus: in life I shirked no duty, and as a husband and father there were many; so as ghost or spectre I would offer nothing less, even if Death himself be my taskmaster.

The high street on which I found myself was a bustling thoroughfare indeed, much more so that I was accustomed to. During those first ghastly moments, during the realisation of my own demise, I remember thinking just how crowded the King's highways were becoming in these modern times. And such crowded byways made for strangely tough going that day, despite the insubstantial nature of my person and its inability to either barge or be barged. But something of my daily life must clearly have remained intact. A preponderance of good manners, I think, for there must have been a dozen people that morning who received the tipped brim or tugged forelock of a gentleman trying to make his way through the throng. Yet my persistence in direction eventually rescinded all politeness in favour of decent pursuit, and if man or woman on that busy road were aware of my inhuman quarry then they would surely have cleared my path without question.

I admit I behaved like a common vagabond as I made my way with haste through the crowd, but on several occasions this tiresome rabble caused me such concern as to almost lose sight of Death in favour of closer inspection. Seemingly there had been many changes this day, or since my last visit to town, and all were to the people themselves. What mysteries were at work in modern London? Did my eyes deceive me or had I stumbled upon some foreign land, where clothes were scarcely fit for decent folk about town? Even on the finest, warmest day in an England one might expect more conservative apparel. Not one man in ten had on a decent collar, and he that did wore such contrivances about the neck as to render it entirely ineffectual. And as for the ladies, I have seen more appropriate dress on the seaward side of a Brighton bathing machine!

But let enough be said on the matter, for my astonishment detracts from the narrative in hand!

Death moved quickly. That much was certain. But in life and duty I had shirked no exercise and could hold my own against many a younger man. With this in mind I would not be outpaced by one whose more common countenance was mere bone and crevice. Within minutes I had come within reasonable distance – close enough, I fancied, for my voice to be heard. Drawing breath enough to counter my racing heart, I shouted across the street. "Death, sir! Cease your flight and speak with me, for I cannot maintain this pace all day!"

Thirteen

My voice had, for all its breathless volume, found the right ear in the crowd, for at that very moment he stopped. Yet he did not turn to face me, and I realised that there was another purpose to this sudden halt. That purpose filled me with dread.

Not ten yards away there stood a small boy, not more than eight years old and dressed in brightly coloured clothes with the queerest peaked cap turned backwards upon his head. I stared at him for a moment, fancying that he returned my gaze and saw me as a living being. I felt a certain foreboding about this child, something akin to an unwelcome familiarity. And as Death stood watching, I knew some terrible fate awaited him.

It was at that moment he broke hands with the young woman at his side, tearing from beneath her skirts. He broke well and ran swiftly, with a turn of speed to outpace any parent.

I have already remarked upon the busy nature of the street on which I stood, but at this point I must stress that my observations had not taken in the carriageway itself, nor the monstrosities which it conveyed before my eyes. For on that road the most unholy tide of steel and glass did thunder along its length; a molten magma of noise and confusion, the likes of which no mortal's wickedness might conjure. And it was towards this cacophony the child ran, lost in a world of fearless wonder, unnoticed by all but Death and I!

No stranger am I to physical exertion, so it was before the young lad's feet had touched the carriageway that I was running at full pelt in his direction, caring little for those in my path and even less for the disturbing way in which my body passed straight through them. Onwards I flew, gathering pace with every stride. Onwards, with my heart a resounding tattoo, until I came within reach of the boy and flung myself forwards with one enormous stride...

Alas, it made little difference. I passed right through him. I may have gained more ground in two strides than the average fellow would cover in six, but with substance sorely lacking my efforts were as an infant's breath to the wind. As I lay sprawled across the floor, recovering what energy I might, I could hear the sobs and screams of the child's poor mother, her heart broken. Yet my vision of this distressing scene is largely confined to imagination, for my eyes were fixed upon the willowy frame of Death himself as he scribbled in that infernal book.

"Good God, man!" I cried. "Would you stand there and do nothing to save him?" My temper was aflame; my blood, such as it was, boiling.

Death gave me no answer, save for a gnarled finger held to his lips that bade me quiet with a single gesture. Despite my temper, despite possessing a more than forcible nature, at that single motion I quieted as asked and noted all the more how this unfeeling fiend continued to scribble.

It had been my intention this day, on this morning of my passing, to seek out my unearthly slayer and question his motives. To make sense of a death so untimely, with the indulgences of later life laid before me like fruits for the picking. To ask why I should be denied the pleasure of watching my children go forth into the world and raise children of their own. And to ask why I, a man not ready for death, should succumb so easily to the reaper?

And so, despite the horror around me, despite the carnage of the street, I tasked him on the matter as I had originally intended, for I feared having no second chance. "Sir," I said, "I must insist you hear me and cease your infernal scribbling this instant!" I had all but lost my self-control. My voice shook with rage. "Sir, I insist on knowing the reason for my arrival on this deathly plane and my apparent lingering within it!"

Another gnarled finger was raised to the lips to hush my outburst, but this time it was followed by another skeletal digit pointing over my shoulder. Faced with such an absence of common courtesy you would no doubt forgive further aggression on my part, yet for some reason I had no such inclination. Instead I turned and saw, to my surprise, the very lad whom moments before had been struck down!

Instinctively I reached out to him and with a fatherly hand upon his shoulder enquired as to his health. Of course, my hand upon his shoulder told tale enough of what had happened. Only a companion in death might offer the touch of comfort.

Turning back, I asked Death in a quieter tone, "If you will not offer me any words of comfort, surely the lad might receive some kindness?"

Death said nothing, though by now he had ceased to write in his notebook and had turned the pages towards me. There I saw a script penned by an educated hand and listing points from line to line. The language was obscure and meaningless, but at the top of the page a simpler, bolder hand had been used. It read: Thomas B Lidenbrock. It was a name with which I was familiar, for in all but the middle initial it was my own.

For a moment I was taken aback, thinking that for my torment this creature from the grave was showing me my own epitaph for the spirits. At that moment my shock ignored the errant letter in favour of a personal horror. But this shock soon passed. Before long that gnarled finger was pointing again, and once more it was levelled at the young lad.

And then I understood.

So it was to be that my death had more purpose than merely a passage to the grave. And, for all my certainty of time, this day was far removed from the day of my passing. In truth there had been many such days; and weeks, months and years too. Who knows how long my passing had been held in abeyance for this greater calling? What changes had occurred that had led, step by step, to the child at my side? And this child was no mere child of time but flesh of my own. Grandson? Great grandson? That much I have yet to understand. But my duty to him is plain, as plain as a duty I had in life.

For the record let it be said thus: in life I shirked no duty, and as a husband and father there were many; so as ghost or spectre I would offer nothing less. Nothing at all.

THE BED
KELLI LOWRY

She was recently employed at an antique store on the waterfront. Taking care of the furniture was slightly overwhelming in a nerve-racking sort of way because some of it was so old.

Being left to lock up for the first time made her feel as if she had a great responsibility. After all, one headboard on an antique bed was thirty thousand dollars, and that was just the tip of the iceberg in terms of items and prices. Yes, this was of utmost importance that she do everything right. Everything from straightening the bed covers on the antique beds on display to dusting the matched oak hand carved sideboard and cupboard that was being sold as a set to the Royal Maundy money from 1678 to setting the alarm as she left the premises upon completing her closing up shop duties.

Walking past the one bed that fascinated her since the first time she walked in, she could have sworn she heard someone calling her name. She'd long since locked the door to do the few things, which needed done before leaving for the night and she knew she was alone.

But yet, there it was again when she stopped to listen. Noticing something different about the intricate carvings on the bed, she moved closer to look. What had once appeared as harmless and bucolic scenery carved into the headboard was now a grotesque and perverse tableau.

Sitting down on the side of the bed, she leaned closer for a look. The depraved and deviant acts that were being depicted were anything but heart warming. If anything, it was blood curdling and bone chilling. Feeling as if something were pulling her closer to the mattress, she curled up and edged closer to the headboard.

Abruptly, an uncontrollable exhaustion overpowered her. Lying her head down on the finely woven cotton pillowcase, she closed her eyes, slowly losing consciousness.

Breathing now slowing down, her body slowly melted into the mattress, her soul absorbing into the scenery carved in the wood.

Thirteen

FAMILY TIES
LAVIE TIDHAR

My uncle Oren was sitting stoop-shouldered on a chair in the kitchen. His face was a mask of blue and green and his skin was flaking all over the floor. A small pile of multicoloured flesh lay at his feet like a tombstone.

"Gevalt," said my Aunt Lily. We nodded in silence.

"The shame." Said my cousin Avi, who is only twenty-seven but thinks he can talk because he works in a bank.

"Who would have thought," said his sister Tali. She stared at my uncle's hands, which were clenching and unclenching periodically.

"*Nu*," said my cousin Gidi, who is from Uncle Dave's side and who doesn't like either Tali or Avi very much, 'who would have thought you fancy women?'

I looked at Tali with renewed interest. I never thought she was very interesting, certainly not enough to be a lesbian.

"Gidi!" Aunt Lily's voice sounded like the baying of hunting dogs, waiting to be unleashed.

"Or that you're –" his next words were silenced by my aunt's frantically waving hands, moving through the air like two well-honed blades. "Not in front of grandma!"

"WHAT?" Grandma wanted to know. She reclined on her armchair, checking the time sporadically on one of her three watches.

"Nothing mum, nothing."

"WHAT?"

"We're just talking about what to do with Oren mum!" shouted my aunt.

"Don't shout, I'm not deaf," grandma snapped. "What's wrong with him?"

Her words were welcomed with more unhappy silence. Uncle Oren's mouth made random snapping motions in the air. Grandma straightened with some difficulty and rummaged about for her glasses.

"On your head, mum."

"WHAT?"

"On your head!"

"Don't shout dear, you're giving me a headache." She peered at uncle Oren intently. "The boy looks like death," she finally pronounced. She sank back into her chair.

"That's because he is," muttered my dad. Uncle Oren's mouth gaped like a gefilte fish, his lips pink and colourless.

"WHAT?"

"Nothing mum!" Aunt Lily quickly said.

"Enough of your cheek," said grandma. She checked the time on the left-hand watch. "Don't know why Sarah had to marry you. Told her she was making a mistake." She fished a mint out of her cardigan pocket, unwrapped it and sucked on it happily.

Uncle Oren rocked in his chair. His teeth shone wetly in the electric light.

"We should blow his head off," I said. "Like in that movie." I pretended to shoot one of those double-barrelled guns. "Ka-boom!"

"Danny!" It's good parents are not allowed to kill, otherwise mum's look would have nailed me like a butterfly in a museum. Uncle Oren looked on, blinking rapidly. A yellow fluid oozed out of the corner of his eyes.

"Whatever the matter with him," my uncle Dave said quietly, "we can't throw him out." He looked around the room, watching our faces. "He's family."

We all nodded again. "Family is family," said cousin Avi.

"Pretentious prat," cousin Gidi whispered to me and winked. I laughed. Aunt Lily's face took on a dangerous aspect, like a fog hiding a nest of bees. Deadly. I shut up.

"How could this happen?" Aunt Shoshi stood up and waddled across the room. "We buried him in the best place. The best plot!" She was rubbing her hands together in nervous, jerky movements. "I thought this only happens to the *goyim*!"

"Maybe they buried a *goy* next to him, and he infected Oren," suggested Uncle Jordan. He pushed his sliding glasses back up the large ridge of his nose. "I never did trust that undertaker," he added.

"I know!" I said. They all looked at me suspiciously. "What we need to do is get a barrel of acid and *dissolve* him."

"Who let the kid in?"

"At least the kid has some ideas!" snapped Aunt Shoshi. "We have to do *something*." She paced to the wall and back. "It's so, so... It's just not Jewish!"

"He can't stay!" wailed Tali. She looked at us with wild eyes. "He's a *zombie*."

A deadly silence descended. The word was out. Uncle Oren was a living dead. A walking corpse. A zombie.

Aunt Shoshi held her head in her hands. "The shame."

"A *Dibbuk*," said uncle Dave reproachfully. "I'm sure zombies are of a different persuasion."

"Or cut him up with a chainsaw," I said, still absorbed in that line of thought. "First the arms, then the legs, and finally..." I paused for dramatic effect. "The *head*."

"Shut up Danny." Mum stood up. "Show some respect to your uncle." She walked to where Uncle Oren sat and examined him for a long moment, holding her face close to his. I kept expecting Uncle Oren to open his mouth and bite her throat off, but he just sat there looking dejected.

"He's family," said cousin Gidi.

"Dead, shmed," said uncle Jordan. "Oren is a good man."

"Was."

"Was shmoz." Uncle Jordan sat down like a man whose mission was successfully accomplished. There was an expectant hush.

"So *nu*?"

Then mum straightened up. "He's staying," she said.

Dad nodded his support.

Then, gradually, everyone else did. Even Tali.

And that was that.

It didn't take him long to settle back in with us. Uncle Oren moved to the basement, where the fresh ground, the damp and the dark did wonders for his skin. Dad and I even suspected he had a lady friend who came to visit him some nights, burrowing underneath the soil to keep him company. There seemed to be a lot less mice and frogs and flies than usual, and virtually no door-to-door salesmen. No Jehovah's Witnesses either, for that matter.

After all, as Uncle Dave said, family *is* family.

THE MAKESHIFT
GARY MCMAHON

The day I first saw her I was returning to work at the end of my lunch hour. It was Monday. Rainy. Dark clouds hung in the sky like fat, dirty airborne sheep. Other worker ants shuffled along beside me, covering their heads with big umbrellas, plastic carrier bags, newspapers. The face of one man who barged past me resembled that of a grotesquely made-up clown; newspaper ink had run and smeared across his features, rendering them nightmarish.

I was passing the huge display window of some generic department store, depicting a heavily romanticised domestic bedroom scene: King Size four poster bed, hanging drapes and laces, fake fur rugs, a silently roaring fake fire…and there she was. The girl of my dreams. The one I'd been (admittedly passively) searching for my entire life.

She was clad in an ankle-length silk negligee, bare shoulders peeking out from the wide neck of the garment like glimpses of some miniature alabaster landscape. In her pale and dainty hands she held a gossamer housecoat, as if in the act of discarding it in preparation for retiring for the evening. Her face was hard, smooth, a pure vista of symmetrical angles. Her eyes were blank, staring, but I knew that they saw me as I stood watching her through the drizzle. The hair was all wrong, of course; some fool had plonked a ginger fright-wig atop her perfectly oval head. But that could be changed.

She was beautiful. Exactly how I'd always imagined her in my guilt-ridden wet dreams and twitchy daylight fantasies. A dream woman, a synthetic goddess, a perfect partner sculpted just for me.

The crowd buoyed me on, carrying me through the sodden city streets, and I was borne away from her. But she remained in light, dazzling and beatific, a personification of every woman I'd ever put up on a pedestal and idealised. Except that this one would never let me down, never leave me. Never take me for what little I had.

I decided there and then that she *would* be mine.

The following fortnight was one filled with despair. We were so busy at the office that I was forced to work through my lunches. I imagined her standing there, straight-backed and immobile. Patiently awaiting my return. But my boss worked me like a dog, constantly placing more dull paperwork in my in-tray, insisting that I hit increasingly impossible targets before finishing for the day. So by the time I left the office and headed home, the shops were all closed. And crude steel shutters barred the way between me and my bogus babe.

By the time the weekend limped round I could hardly contain myself. Saturday morning I dressed in my best bib and tucker, and set off on the tube for central London like a lovelorn fool. I carried a small bunch of flowers and a copy of Kafka's *Metamorphosis* – I knew instinctively that she adored lilies, and I felt the title of the novel highly appropriate.

But when I got there she was gone. In her place stood a nude male impostor, stripped of all identity along with his borrowed clothes. The bedroom display was gone, too; they were obviously in the process of designing and creating another.

I could've wept. I ducked into the nearest pub instead, and drowned my sorrows with strong lager and idle chat with strangers.

When I finally left that place, pockets empty and bloodstream toxic, I had formulated a plan. I would liberate my love, by force if necessary! I knew a place where I could get a gun – a grotty little workingman's club south of the river, where an old college friend slowly drank himself to death every night of the week, working through his dole money as if that was all there was in his tired world.

But it turned out that no weapon was necessary.

Thirteen

Badly in need of solitude (and a piss), I entered an alley that led down the side of the department store building. It was littered with empty cardboard boxes, discarded fast food wrappers, and empty beer cans. Rats scampered across my path, clutching morsels between vile yellow teeth.

There was a tramp curled up in a recessed doorway, covered in a ragged blanket. He was embracing someone, and crying into the nape of her neck. The woman was naked, and stiff as stone.

It was her. The object of my desperate affections. Unceremoniously dumped, thrown out with the garbage...discarded and left to rot in the open like an unwanted pet.

I stormed over to the vagrant, fuelled by booze and indignation. When he saw me approach his eyes widened, and his mouth dropped open in readiness of a scream. But I stuck my toe-end into the orifice, filling it with my size tens. I beat that man until he stopped moving, and his blood leaked into the slimy gutter that ran up the middle of the lane. His face was a raw mass of pulped meat, and one of his eyes was bulging far too much from its cracked socket. But she was safe. My makeshift mate.

I picked her up and covered her with my jacket. Swept her away through streets that now seemed alive with malice.

She said nothing; didn't even thank me. I didn't care. Her weight in my arms was thanks enough.

Once back home I closed the curtains, turned off the lights, and placed her in a hot soapy bath. I scrubbed her clean of the filth of the city, the sludge of the streets. When I was done she was pure once more, and ready for my long-planned seduction.

At first we simply sat on the couch and watched TV. She wore some cheap mail order underwear that I'd bought for her long ago, before we'd even met. I preferred to sit in the nude, her hand in my lap. Teasing. She didn't attempt to move her fingers; to do anything sexual. Not yet. She wasn't that kind of girl.

Soon we would move onto the next level, but I was in no rush. I'd waited this long, so what harm would another few days do? I actually found her chasteness more of a turn-on than the blatant sexuality demonstrated by women in films, and on the street. They were crude, ugly; she was coy, slow to give in to the pressure of the chase.

Over the following hours she fell in love with me. I already felt those deep emotions for her, and had done for my entire life. To my new girl, it was all new, fresh, and wonderful.

By dawn on Sunday her barriers had crumbled, and I led her into the bedroom. I lay her down on my bed, and pressed my body against her. I won't lie: our first time together wasn't very good. It was clumsy, indelicate, but we eventually got where we needed to be. I wiped her down with a wet sponge, and we tried again. This time, it was slower, more loving. A long and filling meal, as opposed to the quick and unsatisfying McDonalds snack that had gone before.

We stayed in bed for a week. I only ever stirred from the mattress to prepare food, or use the lavatory. Every other moment was given over to desire. I ignored the telephone when it rang, and when someone banged on the front door, yelling at me through the letterbox, I just smiled at her. She gazed back into my eyes, empty as a room full of fashion models.

The first time she moved, it was during a particularly complex manoeuvre. She was on her knees on the floor, her arms locked out before her, one leg cocked up and out like a dog urinating against a tree. I was kneeling behind, pushing myself against her cold, lineless backside, probing, as always, for a way inside. She jerked suddenly, as if in shock. Then her head slowly turned, moving round through 180 degrees until her eyes were looking directly into mine. She

Thirteen

was smiling. And it was like heaven was looking through a window into my soul.

I felt my limbs go stiff, as if freezing, or turning to stone. Her mouth opened, and I could see a tongue wriggling in there like some big slow snake. Then she stood, graceful as a ballet dancer. Backed away. Still smiling.

I couldn't move, couldn't speak. Couldn't breath. But I didn't have to anymore.

The girl of my dreams wrapped me up in a blanket, and carried me outside. She hailed a cab at the side of the road, and bundled me onto the back seat. She sat up front, flirting with the driver; touching his knee and laughing at his shitty jokes.

The bastard even asked for her number, and she gave him mine. Told him that she was at home all day while her husband worked in a department store in the city, and he was free to call round for lunch. Her hand strayed to his crotch, squeezed. He looked at her like a starving man, his lips wet and quivering.

We got out of the cab beside the store where I'd found her, and she hauled me out onto the pavement. I tried to call out, to beg, to plead…but my mouth wouldn't work, the words refused to come.

She dragged me along that same alley, bouncing my head off the hard ground. She didn't' care for me, not at all. She'd merely been using me all along. All I'd ever wanted was her; all she'd ever desired was freedom. It must have seemed like a marriage made in heaven.

The tramp I'd beaten half to death was squatting in his customary doorway, balled-up against the cold. She called to him, asked him if he'd like some company. Then she gave him the bottle of whisky she must have taken from my drinks cabinet, and placed me down next to him. His grubby hands strayed over my body, rough pads of fingers caressing my every sealed crevice.

Before leaving she laid a kiss on my cheek. Her lips were soft now, gorged with blood and heat and passion.

My new friend drank the full bottle before he began. Then, hitching down his pants, he straddled me, bucking like a shot horse and chuckling into my ear. As he slept I felt his thick ejaculate cooling on the inside of my thighs. I felt sick. Defiled.

I've grown used to it now. He treats me well, other than the nightly rapes. Keeps me warm, and often kisses me tenderly when he's done.

She comes to me sometimes, the girl of my dreams. Flaunting new lovers, laughing as I plead with her through black button eyes that show nothing but the emptiness that I hold inside like a promise of something better.

Often she brings her friends. Others like her who she has managed to set free.

They stand and they stare, and they fondle one another's warm malleable bodies. Hating my inflexibility, my hard and brittle shell.

Soon everyone will be like her. The rest of us will have been replaced, usurped. Perhaps it's for the best; we didn't really make such a go of things did we? Maybe they'll do better, when they finally get over the thrill of their new flesh.

Then again, it's probably been happening for a very long time. Wooden actors, plastic politicians, false dawns, fake plastic trees and empty promises. There's a good chance that they've been ruling us all along, softening us up, preparing the way. Biding their time until the scene was set for their comrades to follow.

Maybe it's we who are the dummies after all.

Thirteen

DEADLINE
JOSEPH PAUL HAINES

It was in January of 1900 that my business brought me to Boston during the cruellest part of the year. A new century was upon us and there was optimism in the air that the lean times of the past might soon get behind us. I had finished up my dealings with a certain European count in search of an estate in the Massachusetts countryside and I had a number of days at my leisure until I needed to once again head south to the warm environs of Florida.

So it happened that I found myself at the estate of my good friend and writer of some renown, Charles Bekeley. I had a standing invitation to make room with him whenever I was in the area, and I called upon him the very moment I was available.

I had no idea that I would learn a secret that I would carry with me lo these fifty-odd years.

The two of sat in his study, enjoying our third snifter of Napoleon Cognac. Truth be told, this particular room in Charles's estate never brought much comfort to me and I avoided it whenever possible. Do not mistake me here, as the room was as comfortable as Charles's hospitality with its high stone walls and solid wood floors. Only the best of literature found refuge here amongst his bookshelves and any cigars not hand-rolled by the masters of Cuba were strictly *verboten*.

It was the décor that set my apprehensions at large. The fireplace consisted of a single piece of alabaster carved into the hideous face of a gargoyle; the fire contained within his gaping, fierce maw. Two-foot incisors, both stalactite and stalagmite, held the burning logs in place. At the far end of the room, a single door, banded with iron and no more than thirty inches in height, sat in silent foreboding. A great iron chain and lock secured whatever lay behind.

It may have been the drink, what that rendered my nerves immune that particular evening to this macabre spectacle; or I may have grown accustomed to Charles's odd taste in furnishings, but I was at ease therein for the first time in memory.

His writing desk lied behind our great, leather armchairs.

"Did I ever mention," Charles said, swirling the cognac in his snifter, "that my desk once belonged to G.D. Heartwell?"

"Whom?" I asked. The lateness of the hour was upon me and my wits were not as sharp as they might have been.

Charles smiled at my ignorance. "I'm not surprised your readings have not taken you to that particular stretch of the literary forest. He was a rather troubled fellow who wrote tawdry little tales of terror. Most likely he won't be remembered ten years hence."

I have never been one to hide my emotions well, and I'm sure my distaste showed in my countenance. "Well I should say not. Who wants to read stories like that?"

Charles wrapped his lap blanket tighter around his legs. "Poor chap actually died at that desk. Oh, others say differently; but I found his diary whilst clearing out the house. This used to be his office."

In spite of the fire, I found myself chilled. "My God, Charles. Why do you insist upon working in here then? That's perfectly morbid of you."

His gaze fell to the floor as he cast about for an answer. He mumbled, and I still to this day believe he said, "I don't have a choice."

"What was that?" I asked, but I was denied the satisfaction of an answer as a hideous squeal of what might have been bending metal echoed throughout the chamber.

Thirteen

Charles shot out of his chair, the fine crystal of his snifter shattering against the stone face of the fireplace. He grabbed my arm in a fierce manner.

"Now what's this?" I asked, abashed by his sudden, violent outburst.

His eyes were wide and he trembled; by God yes, he trembled this mountain of a man, and he shoved me toward the exit to his chamber. "Get out!" he shouted. "Get out and do not return until I seek you out! Go to your chambers and stay there."

"Charles," I said. "I don't underst – "

"If you value our friendship you will do as I say!"

I didn't understand what had so possessed him to act in such an extraordinary manner, but he was my friend and I was obliged to him his hospitality. I turned to go, and that was when I saw it.

Or, that was when I think I saw it. I'm not sure even to this day. The cognac flowed freely through my veins and the chill of the room's mysterious origins ran throughout my subconscious, but I saw, or believed I saw, the most incredible sight.

The small door at the end of the room bowed out from its centre and I heard the rattle of a heavy iron chain against the bands of steel. My stomach threatened to empty itself and I felt beads of cool sweat form upon my brown.

"My God," I said.

"Get out!" Charles yelled. I looked in his eyes. Rationality had fled his gaze along with his manners.

I turned and fled to the confines of my chambers.

That night passed more slowly than any other in memory. The snow shower heightened in intensity and entombed us in the estate as neatly as the pyramid in Giza did Amen-Ra.

I ensconced myself under the heavy goose-down comforter upon my bed and stayed there as quietly as I could. My bladder felt stretched to its limits and the pervasive chill in my chamber did not to alleviate my discomfort. As time passed with no ill-bred creature of night come to call, my rationality slowly returned along with a bit of my courage. I feared for my friend's sanity, and my concern for him slowly overcame my fear of the earlier proceedings in his chambers.

I left my room, and made my way to his chamber door, where lamplight spilled from beneath its heavy wooden frame. I lifted my fist to knock, then stopped when I heard a noise from within.

I placed my ear to the wood and listened. I heard a quick series of scraping noises, which, after a few moments time, I identified as the sound of a quill upon paper. He was writing. My mind somewhat appeased, I started to step away from the door when I heard something else, something I still to this day tell myself was a trick of the imagination.

I heard a door creak upon its hinges. And then, then, I heard scraping upon wood, as if tusks of bone were being dragged along the floor.

The scratching of Charles's writing intensified, quickened to a frantic pace and I could hear the laboured breaths of his effort as clearly as if I had been in the room. He sobbed once, a baleful, lingering moan of overwhelming horror.

The bone upon wood sound multiplied, the sound emanating from multiple locations within Charles's chamber. My curiosity could no longer be contained and I reached for the doorknob.

The noise stopped.

Just as suddenly as it had come, it vanished.

"Charles?" I said. "Are you well?"

A moment passed where I began to have serious doubts about my dear friend's condition and just as I was once again about to enter, he said, "I'm fine

Thirteen

now. I will see you in the morning."

Reluctantly I returned to my chambers. I don't believe I slept that night.

The sun came up the next day and brought with it a break in the storm. The countryside lay blanketed beneath five feet of snow and nothing, neither man nor beast, stirred upon its surface.

Charles met me for breakfast soon after, looking none-the-worse for the prior evening's phantasmagoria. He smiled at me over a steaming cup of tea and said, "I finished a new story last night."

"Did you?" I replied, peering over the edge of yesterday's edition of the Boston Globe. "I'm surprised you could work at all."

"Well," Charles said, his smile suddenly enigmatic, "you have to write when the muse strikes."

There was nothing in the world that could have made me pry any further. I raised the newspaper once again in front of my face. "Indeed," I said, and we never spoke of it again.

Thirteen

A MOTHER'S LOVE
ANDREW HAND

Helen wanted a drink, but more so she wanted to believe her was innocent. However, after nearly four years in the courts and three appeals, it was to time to face the fact that Walter was guilty of several murderers and was slated for execution in a week's time. Tomorrow would be her last chance to visit her son before the execution. She would not be allowed to view her son's death. The warden said the victims' family would attend and that it wouldn't be "comfortable". This was fine by her; she remembered when they electrocuted Ted Bundy. There had been hundreds of people: media, protesters, religious freaks.

    She lit a menthol with a shaky hand and took a long drag. The smoke did nothing to calm to her nerves. She felt so helpless; she couldn't let her son die at the hands of those bastards. She gazed lazily around her filthy kitchen, letting her mind wander. The idea came to her somewhere between the pack of cigarettes and the fifth of gin. It came all at once in a flood of inspiration. She rose slowly from her chair, the alcohol rushing to her head. She took a stained apron of a hook off the wall and lit the stove. She forced her tired face to form a smile. Pulling her cookbook off the shelf and set her plan in motion.

Helen stared at the kitten's broken corpse. It lay on its back, patches of hair missing from its belly, its neck at an impossible angle. More disturbing than the tiny victim was the smiling face of its killer. Walter sat beaming, dried blood on his dirty chin. He was giggling, giddy.
    "What the fuck did you do?" Helen asked.
    "I wanted to hurt something cute," Walter confessed proudly.
    Helen struck her son hard across the side of the head with the back of her hand. "The hell is wrong with you boy?" "Wipe that shit eating grin off your face."
    He looked up, his hand over the red patch spreading across his right cheek. "What you hitting me for?" "It wasn't nobody's, I found it momma, honest."
    The bus struck a pothole and pulled Helen from the daze she had drifted into. She lurched forward violently, almost dropping the package on her lap. She lifted the lid and peered in, the cake was undisturbed. She replaced the lid and adjusted in her seat, careful not to shake her son's gift. It was only now, years latter on the long bus ride to the prison that she could clearly recall the event. She remembered how hurt he looked after she hit him. He never saw the wrong in what he did. In hindsight, she could have handled the situation better, got him in to see a doctor or a preacher. Instead, she did nothing and eventually forced herself to forget the whole thing. "Shoulda wrung his damn neck."
    The bus driver came in over the intercom to announce that they would be arriving at the prison shortly. Helen's head was still throbbing from the night before, the bittersweet pain only cheap gin could deliver. She didn't mind though the headache it was change from the numbness she normally experienced.
    She settled back in her seat and sighed. She never caught him hurting "anything cute" again, but that didn't mean his wasn't doing it in secret somewhere. He would disappear into woods for hours. Always alone, she didn't think he ever had any friends. He came home one day his face covered in tiny scratches. He claimed he got them playing in a briar patch and she let it go. She was beginning to realize that she let many things "go". Still he was her only child and she loved him.
    The bus made a left turn onto a gravel road flanked on both sides by chain-linked fence topped with razor wire. It was several minutes before they could see the prison. It was an ominous brick menace. Helen thought it looked like a castle she'd seen in a movie once. For the first time since she decided on her course of

Thirteen

action, she got very nervous.

The bus came to a stop in a large parking lot. The thirty or so passengers filed out into the cool November afternoon. Helen was the last to exit, walking slowly carefully clutching her cake box. The brisk autumn air quickly found its way under her dress and forced her to shiver. A guard tower stood off to one side of the lot. She couldn't see his face, but Helen was sure the rifle wielding guard was watching her, his face concealed by mirrored sunglasses. Did he know what she planned to do? No, it was absurd to think anyone knew about her plan. She had only developed it herself last night. She dismissed her fear and hurried to catch the group.

An overweight man in blue uniform led the visitors. He introduced himself as the head of security and began to instruct them on proper visitor etiquette. Several guards wearing latex gloves stood on the other side of a metal detector to inspect the visitors. Sweat poured from Helen's palms. She was beginning to realize that hers was not a well-developed plan. She hadn't thought of what she would do if anyone found her "gift".

The large guard spoke in a commanding voice, "those of you with loved ones in the general population make a line up along the wall."

Once the visitors were in a line against, only Helen and one other woman remained. A Hispanic woman in a faded sundress stood staring at her feet. Helen recognized the look of pain on the younger women's face. It was the look of a mother wounded by her child. It was guilt, shame, and hurt rolled together. Helen knew it all to well. She was about to ask the woman her name when a grey haired man in a black pin-stripped suit approached them.

"Good afternoon ladies", he said extending his hand first to the younger woman than Helen. "James Chapman, I'm the warden, but you can call me Jim." The warden eyed the box suspiciously. "I called yesterday and they said I could bring my boy a cake, considering" Helen lied.

"Considering what?" the warden asked.

Helen eyed the warden coldly, "considering you're going to kill him next week."

The warden looked only mildly insulted, she would try harder next time. "You must be Walter Beck's mother," he said. "You have my regrets". Walter had only been recently been moved to Woodall for his execution, so Helen had not yet met this warden. She assumed he was like all the rest. He led them to metal detector and Helen froze.

"Is something wrong ma'am?" the warden asked.

Helen tried to look calm but her heart rate had doubled. "Is that going to mess up my cake?"

"It won't hurt it a bit, ma'am", the warden assured her. "You didn't bake a file in there, did you?" The warden smiled. "Sorry, bad joke."

Helen mustered her best fake southern belle smile and reluctantly set the box on the conveyer belt along with her purse. She stepped though the metal arch without setting off any annoying alarms. She collected her pocketbook from the belt, and looked about for Walter's cake. The cake was in the hands of a young dark haired guard its lid peeled back, its secret about to be discovered.

Helen used her best "irritated mother voice", "don't you go messing with my cake son." "I was up all night baking that and I don't need you poking you nose in it." She snatched the box from the young man's hands.

His face was a dark red. "Sorry ma'am". He said backing away.

Helen said it was all right, and followed the warden and the Hispanic woman down a long hall. He led them though several locked doors and several security checkpoints. Helen made a mental note of all possible exits. Finally, the warden placed them in behind separate doors.

Thirteen

The room was Spartan having only a stainless steel desk and two chairs. The three walls were painted a boring off white, and the third wall was replaced by two-way mirror. She sat for several minutes in silence waiting for Walter. She hadn't seen him since the trial, since they found him guilty of killing those three girls.

He came in then, his hands and feet shackled, clad in an orange jump suit. He was escorted to his seat by two armed guards, taking small awkward steps. His head was shaven, several tattoos visible on his arms and head. "Hello Mamma" he said. He seated himself in the metal chair and the guards exited.

"Why the long face?" he asked.

Helen stared at her son for some time "I don't know Walter, there's just something about my son being found guilty on three counts of murder that puts me in a foul mood."

A smile spread across his face "More like twenty counts, truth be told". The odd little smile reminded her of the time he killed the kitten. Nothing had changed. Nothing ever would.

Helen fought back tears, "Momma brought you a present". She reached a shaking hand under her seat and produced Walter's gift. She set it on the table and slid it toward her son. He reached out his cuffed hands and opened the box.

He looked up at her and smiled "thank you mamma is it chocolate?"

"Guess you'll have to try it and see" she said. They wouldn't let me bring you a fork. "So you'll have to use your hands".

Walter was already digging in, pulling free a large chunk of cake, licking frosting off his fingers. Helen gasped, "Lord forgive me."

"The cake's not that bad momma, but I think the eggs may have gone bad" Walter joked. He stopped laughing and filled his mouth with death. Only after her son finished his gift and sat wiping his mouth on his hand, did Helen began to lose composure. She covered her face with her hands cried.

Walter started to ask his mother what was wrong, but stopped. A sharp pain in his abdomen doubled him over. The cramping became more intense and his face reddened. He looked up at Helen in disbelief, the same hurt look on his face as the time she slapped him for killing the kitten. He attempted to say something but only gurgled, thick white foam forming in the corners of his mouth. He bucked in his chair and fell to the floor convulsing. He made a vain attempt to gag himself but his jaws were pulled together, immovable. He was jerking violently when the guards rushed in.

The first guard a blonde kid of about twenty yelled for his partner to go for help. He knelt beside the twitching prisoner unsure what to do. He looked at Helen, "what happened?".

She stared down at the animal she once carried.

"What should have happened years ago."

Thirteen

CALENDAR GIRL
ROBERT BELL

I didn't react at first.

I just stood in the alleyway, rubbish bag in each hand, and watched the two teenage brothers assault the old black lady. The bigger of the two punched her in the face while the other one tried to yank her to the ground. Their laughter bounced off the walls.

"Hey! What the hell're you two doing?"

Even though I sounded convincing, and even though I was ten-years older than the kids, my mind told me to run away – their father, Pete, would hear about this. What then?

Hands balled into fists, they gave me the same look Pete had given me on numerous occasions. The bigger one rolled up his left sleeve, displaying the old South African flag that Pete had tattooed onto his bicep six months ago. "Fuck off, you cunt," he said.

"Yeah, go back inside the fucking shop," the other one said, referring to the liquor store where I worked as a cashier.

Letting go of the rubbish bags, I rushed forward. They scampered backwards, almost falling over each other. That gave me a confidence boost, just when I needed it.

"Get out of here. Now," I said.

They glanced at each other, smiling.

"Fine," the bigger one said. "Dad's gonna fuck you up for this."

I said nothing.

After a few seconds, he motioned for his brother to follow him out of the alley.

I knew the reason for the attack. Shortly after Apartheid ended, a black family tried to move into Marble Hall, the rural town I lived in. The white farmers stopped them by buying all the available houses. Two days later a nearby township promised to attack us 'until the racist beasts changed their ways', and when our village suffered a spate of robberies, assaults and even rapes, the locals responded the way the kids just had. Few black people wandered our streets at night.

Once I was sure the boys weren't coming back, I knelt alongside the woman.

"Thank you very much," she said in a heavy African accent. She pushed herself up off the floor, and wiped her bleeding nose with the back of her hand.

"Are you all right?"

"Thank you. Thank you very much."

Geez, language barrier.

"Do…you…need…a…doctor?"

Smiling, she walked to a trolley parked against the wall. After digging through one of the many bags inside the cart, she returned clutching something, and gave it to me. It was a hand-drawn calendar. Her face was at the top, with each day of January pencilled in below her. I flipped to the second page, where February waited. Each month had her face.

"Uhmm, thanks, but are you all right?"

She returned to her trolley, humming a tune. That's where she was when I walked towards the exit. As I reached the corner, I remembered the black bags. In the past I'd been rapped over the knuckles by the store owner for not putting the refuse into the bins. I turned back, hoping I wouldn't frighten the old lady.

She was gone. So was her cart.

The good thing about a small town is that home and work are never far apart. In my case, the apartment I shared with my mom was across the road from the

Thirteen

liquor store.

That night, I ran home.

Mom was sitting on the sofa when I walked in, talking to someone next to her. Gooseflesh shot up on my arms when I saw who it was.

"Hello, Dickface," Eugene said, sitting with his legs spread, a beer in his hand.

Mom playfully smacked his forearm. "Babes, you said you wouldn't call him that."

Babes?

Mumbling hello, I walked to my room.

"Will," Mom said, following. "Let me explain…"

I waited for her to come into my room before shutting the door. "Of all the people, ma, why him?"

She closed her eye for a second. I use the word 'eye' because her other one was swollen shut, courtesy of her last boyfriend. "Honey, Eugene and I've liked each other for ages. We've just never been unattached at the same time."

After my father left us seven years ago, mom's subsequent thirty boyfriends were either co-workers or customers of the video store where she worked. Except Eugene. He was the current owner.

I said, "He's barely five years older than me—five years."

"Honey, love is a river that carves away all that stands before it."

"Don't use the poetry crap on me, not this time."

"There's nothing wrong with expressing your feelings."

"I am expressing them. I'm telling you I don't want him here."

Twelve years ago Eugene gave me my first black-eye when he beat me up in front of the whole school. He'd arrived a week earlier, and I guess he decided the best way to make his mark was by bullying someone younger. Either way, the beatings continued until he finished his education.

She patted my head. "Things'll change on Wednesday, trust me."

"Don't tell me you bought… Ma, you promised you wouldn't."

I was talking about the National Lottery, on which mom had spent half her salary for the past seven years.

"Calm down, this week is different. I consulted a psychic lady."

"Don't you think she would use the numbers herself if she knew them?"

"Honey, she doesn't care about money."

My mobile phone rang before I could reply. It was Tracey.

"Hey babe," I answered.

"Hey gorgeous, listen, can't speak long, driving home. Just called to tell you I can't make it tonight. Sharon wants to divorce Ian again, so I'll have to play peacemaker.

I sighed. "I had a run-in with Pete's kids today."

"What happened this time?"

She stressed the final two words, referring to three years ago when Pete got into a fight with another customer in the liquor store. Because I was the only eye-witness, and because Pete was already on parole for attempted murder, he tried to make me forget the incident. I didn't. Pete got two years in jail.

I told my girlfriend what had happened in the alley, leaving out the calendar.

"Geez, Will. Take a few days' leave."

"I'm not going to hide from him again. Where are you now?"

"Just outside Marble Hall. Listen, need to go."

"Okay. Love you lots. I'll see you tomorrow?"

"You bet ya. Mwaaa."

The sound of the doorbell awoke me at one a.m. later that night. As soon as I

Thirteen

opened the door, mom stumbled inside, reeking of alcohol. She sat down on the couch, her eye bloodshot and full of tears. "Thanks, honey, couldn't get the key into the lock." She opened her purse and took out blank lottery tickets, as well as a piece of paper that I guessed had on it the Guaranteed Winning Numbers from Psychic Lady.

"Ma, why's your hand swollen?"

For a few seconds she stared at the tickets. "He didn't mean to, honey, it was my fault. I should've asked him before I tried to take away his drink then he wouldn't have punched my hand..."

Then from outside: "Sylvia!"

Her head whipped towards the window.

"Ma, he's drunk and horny and couldn't pick up anything else."

"You don't know him like I do. True love lies buried within him like a diamond in the earth. I just need to find it."

I felt like saying I'd gladly ram dynamite down his throat and blow the precious stone out of his body. But as she walked towards the door, I did something I'd never done before.

I got involved.

I rushed round her, jamming myself between her and the exit.

"William, get away from the door."

"Not until he's gone."

Eugene shouted: "Woman, you coming or what?"

She ran for the window, but I got there before she did. "I said no, ma. For your own good."

The look on her face soured. "So this is how you repay me for all the years I sacrificed for you?"

"Just let—"

"Oh fuck off," she said, sitting down. "See if I give you one cent on Wednesday."

I stayed with her until she dozed off, by which time Eugene had gone. After carrying her to bed, I paced up and down in my room. Even though an hour had passed, my anger had not dissipated; she'd never sworn at me before, not when I was ten and set her hair on fire, not even when I told her I'd failed my final year at school. But tonight she had, and the reason for it was the same reason why I never had the courage to leave this town: Eugene.

I had to do something about him. Yeah, I thought, put on some muscle, maybe even learn karate. Get even for all those years.

I remembered a story about an actor who wrote himself a cheque for twenty million. He'd promised himself he would collect that money in ten years, regardless. I needed something like that, to remind me of the pledge I'd just made.

My calendar. I picked it up, took four pins from my cupboard, and nailed it to the wall. The old woman of earlier—my Calendar Girl—stared at me as I paged ahead six months. On the twenty-second of October, I wrote: BREAK EVERY BONE IN EUGENE'S BODY.

Seeing the writing gave me a warm, tingly feeling. So I repeated it over and over. By the time I'd finished, Eugene was due to have every bone in his body broken on a daily basis.

Then I had a darker thought: why not write something more threatening—and why wait all that time? Nobody would ever see the calendar, after all.

I let the pages fall back into place, and wrote in today's box: KILL EUGENE. Before I could take my hand away from the page, my conscience got the better of me and I crossed out the words. But, hey, I was only fooling around, and since tonight would not be the last time he beat mom, I wanted to write something more menacing. Above the crossed-out words I scribbled: EUGENE DIES IN CAR ACCIDENT.

There. That achieved my goal without involving me directly.

I was still smiling at my pathetic joke when the words started to move. The ink moulded together, slid down the page, to the bottom. There it split in two and made its way up the calendar, zigzagging like a snake up a grapevine. When it reached the top, the Calendar Girl's eyes moved, left eye to the left, right to the right. Her lips parted, and the lines slithered into her mouth. She closed her eyes.

I stepped back, wondering if my tired mind was playing tricks on me.

Then her hair changed. Peppercorn-like before, it grew out in long strands, the tips of which flapped around the page. I leaned closer. Her eyes shot open, cut through me like broken glass. I tried to pull my head away. But her hair leapt out of the picture and coiled around my neck. My greasy palms slipped off the wall as I tried to push away. Nothing helped. Her strands of hair were as strong as steel cables.

I felt my forehead touch the wall, and expected my skull to be crushed. Yet the wall gave way; my head entered a dark, silent world.

That's when I passed out.

I awoke in bed the following morning. I felt the slight bump in the top corner of my mattress, and using my left hand, pushed against the headrest, which moved every so slightly.

Yup, I was in my bed.

The calendar was on the wall. The old lady gazed ahead as I searched for the ink I'd put onto the paper yesterday. Nothing. Gone were the words.

All a dream?

There was one way to tell: check for the other writing. I lifted the paper... nothing there either. Shaking my head but smiling, I went to the kitchen and made breakfast.

I was still thinking about the calendar when I walked into the liquor store.

"Have you heard the news?" Booger asked.

There were ten minutes to go until opening, so the two of us were alone in the front while Michael, the store owner, fetched the tills.

Booger, real name Richard Brewster, had on a white shirt with the slogan PORN TO DO IT written in red. He'd been my friend since junior school, and since watching his first adult movie, he'd wanted to be a porn actor. Four years ago he went for his first—and last—audition. He phoned me minutes before he was due to perform, and described the previous guy's audition with two stunning woman. Booger was not so lucky, as the director wanted to couple him with a seasoned male actor.

End of porn dream. Beginning of career as cashier in liquor store.

I sat down behind my till. "What news?"

"The latest attack from the township."

Booger always started the day off by talking about the racial war in Marble Hall; today being no different, I hummed a yes, picked up the newspaper and started reading.

"Yeah, Johan came in here ten minutes ago, asked if he could buy a few beers."

Johan was the chief of police.

"Really..." I said, scanning the back page.

"Get this, there were thirty call-outs last night."

"Come again?"

"Thought that might get your attention."

"What happened?"

Thirteen

"No, no, please—read your paper."

"Booger, what happened?"

He delayed his answer for a while. "So yesterday Johan caught an old black lady handing out calendars."

"Okay."

"So he didn't think too much of it, but get this, all thirty people who made call-outs had one of those calendars."

"Meaning?"

"Johan he said he thinks..." He shook his head. "No, it's stupid. I'm sure he was just tired."

"Booger, what the hell did he say?"

"That the old lady was a Sangoma."

I crinkled my face. "Sangoma?"

"Yeah, you know, Witchdoctor, Black Magic, that kind of thing."

"Yeah, yeah, yeah, I know what you mean. Why did he think that?"

"All thirty people said the trouble started when they wrote something on the calendar—you wanna know the freaky part?"

"Yeah?"

"What they wrote came true."

The sign on Eugene's video store read: CLOSED TODAY

Upon seeing those words, I raced home. Wind rushed through my hair. My knees jolted with each step.

In my room, I stopped in front of the calendar.

"What the hell are you?" I said, understanding that I was now speaking to an inanimate object. I put my hands alongside the calendar—

The wall was boiling hot. Condensation popped through the paint like sweat popping through pores on human skin.

The front door opened, and I heard mom's heels click-clack on the floor.

I found her sitting on the edge of the couch, a scratch card clutched in her left hand. Attached to the card was a line of more cards. Scratching the card with her lucky two-cent piece, she moved her right hand in such rapid bursts her arm appeared to be shaking violently.

"Ma, I'm—"

"Not now William." Her body jerked when she said the words. "Leave me alone." She finished scratching the card, which had not been a winning one. She covered her mouth with the back of her hand. "Why can't I just win it for once?"

Seeing her in that state, I decided not to ask about Eugene. I went back to my room and paced up and down in front of the calendar, trying to decide whether or not to write something else on it. What if it did work? Would I write on it everything I wanted? I knew from studying Economics at school that man would never be without needs or desires. More importantly, he would never be without conflict. Would I write down the name of every person who wronged me?

But this time I could forget reason, for mom's sake. If the calendar really did work, and we won the lottery, I would sit down and think through my options.

On today's date, I wrote: WIN LOTTERY.

Within seconds the words melted, as they had done the night before, moved to the bottom, then up the calendar. This time the old lady opened her mouth so wide I could see her teeth.

When I left the lounge, mom was busy filling in lottery tickets. Used-scratch cards littered the floor around her, some scrunched up into balls, others torn into confetti-like pieces.

"Will, where'd you go to?" Booger asked as I walked back into the store. He had a

Thirteen

lottery ticket in his left hand and a pen in his right hand.

I noticed he wasn't filling in the ticket. "What's wrong?"

Booger averted his gaze. He'd only done that to me once before—one of his traits is that he stares at you without blinking—and that was the time his dad ran over my dog.

"Booger, what happened?"

He put down his ticket. "Why don't you sit down?"

"Why don't you just tell me what happened?"

"Tracey died last night."

I can't believe my reaction to such news was to smile, but I did. I walked to my seat and sat down.

"Will, I'm sorry, man. I only heard a few minutes ago—"

"How'd it happen?"

"Car accident."

"What? Was she on her own?"

"What do you mean?"

"Did she drive into another car?"

"Will, you're shouting."

"I'm not fucking shouting, just tell me, did she crash into someone else?"

"I'm not speaking to you until you stop shouting."

Through gritted teeth, I said. "Did she crash into someone else?"

"Yes." He ran his hand through his hair. "Eugene."

I punched the counter in front of me. Two bottles of vodka rattled against each other.

Right then I knew how it would happen: I would win the lottery, in exchange for mom's life.

"We'll see about that," I said, stepping out from behind the till.

"About what?"

"I need to get home. Be back later."

I went from standing still to running flat-out in a matter of meters. By the time I exited the store, my legs pumped and my arms flailed.

That's when something hit me from side on.

The next thing I knew, my head hammered the pavement.

"Fuck him up, dad!" I heard the voice of one of the brothers.

Pete. That's who was on top of me. Left arm clutching my neck, he drew back his right arm. Light flashed as he rammed his fist into my chest, again and again. Wind escaped my lungs with a whoosh. A spear of pain shot through my body.

"You feel like fucking with my sons this time, hey."

I braced myself for more blows. But instead I felt Pete's weight lift off me.

"That's how it is, hey!" Pete shouted, now next to me.

Head spinning, I rolled away and pushed myself up. Booger had replaced me. Pete was now on top of him, clutching Booger's neck, as he had mine.

"Will," Booger shouted, wriggling around. "Call the cops."

Cops. Good idea. I could phone from my apartment. That way, I could make sure mom was safe as well.

Ahead the teenagers stared at me with rounded eyes. One of them had a knife; the other stood empty handed. I ran towards him. Thankfully, he moved out of my way.

I was inside the flat in less than a minute.

"Ma!" I shouted, kicking open the door. I paused for a few seconds, hands on knees. The past few minutes had taken their toll.

But I had to find mom. I had to make sure she was safe.

"Ma, where are you?"

Thirteen

I was betting on Michael, the store owner, helping Booger. Otherwise my friend would be in trouble.

I walked to mom's room, where the phone was. I opened the door, flicked on the light.

What I saw stopped me immediately.

Nailed to her wall, above the phone, was a calendar exactly like mine.

Sitting alongside the phone was the piece of paper on which she'd scribbled the Winning Numbers from the Psychic Lady.

22-5-1-9-7-8. Those numbers meant something to me: 22nd of May, 1978—my birthday.

I looked down at my shirt, where I thought Pete had only punched me.

It was soaked in blood.

Thirteen

FREEING THE PRISONER
DARRYL SLATER

The olive green Land Rover rumbled through the sodden dusk. The headlights, switched to full beam, lit twin halos of fast falling water droplets.

The rain had come on quickly, and with a vengeance. Each of the vehicle's wheels left a spreading wake as they pushed through stubborn standing water.

Then, within moments the rain transformed to hail.

Icy bullets thrummed down onto the Land Rover's steel roof.

Leo had to raise his voice. "Can you believe this fucking weather?" Using the steering wheel, he pulled his scrawny frame forward until the seat belt pulled tight across his chest. Even so, he could see little further than the end of the vehicle's bonnet.

His eyes were drawn to the lethargic windscreen wipers as they flapped pathetically at the torrent of ice and water that sluiced across the windscreen.

Gordy sat in the passenger's seat; his hairy arms crossed against his D&G tee-shirt. A pissed-off look had set up base-camp on his thickset face.

A trickle of water leaked past the perished windscreen seal. It spattered onto Gordy's jeans.

"Tits on a bloody turnip! Now my new jeans are getting soaked. The wife's going to do her nut."

Leo shook his head. Lank greasy tendrils of hair swayed lazily. "You prick," he whispered.

"What?"

"I don't know why the hell you're wearing your new jeans anyway. For a start, they make you look gay, and what if we find someone?" Leo made a pistol with his fore and index fingers. He placed the pretend muzzle against Gordy's temple and fired a couple of imaginary shots. "You know what blood's like; it gets everywhere."

Gordy swatted Leo's arm away. "OK, so what am I supposed to tell Becky? 'Bye dear, I'm going out wearing these shitty old clothes 'cause If we get lucky and nail some scum-bag, I don't want blood all over my best clothes?"

Leo flicked Gordy a glance. "Up to you ain't it. But if you go out done up to the nines, she's only going think you're after pulling some piece of shag anyway."

Gordy shrugged. "Suits me, it'll keep the bitch on her toes."

Leo shook his head but said nothing.

As quickly as the rain had burst from a dull afternoon, then transformed into hail, it stopped. The headlights pushed their beam deep into the distance.

"Finally," Leo said. He stomped on the accelerator before making a notch-rattling change up into second gear.

"So, where we going to look first?" Gordy asked.

"Apparently, some scummers have been bedding down under the old railway bridge."

"The one at the end of Norton Woods?"

"That's the one."

Beneath the crumbling Victorian brickwork of the disused railway bridge, Milo scratched at the crotch of his third hand trousers. Sighing, he fed the fire with broken pieces of discarded furniture. The flickering yellow light played back and forth across his craggy face.

Nearby, Eddy, a younger tramp sat cross-legged. He split open a packet of Golden Virginia and exposed just enough dusty scraps of tobacco to roll two straw-slim cigarettes.

He passed one to Milo.

Thirteen

They both watched the fire but smoked in silence; neither of them willing to waste the precious smoke by talking between drags.

Milo finished first. He flicked the butt into fire. "I haven't see Pee-Jay this week any idea…"

He was cut short; out of the corner of his eye, he saw a stranger enter the shelter of the tunnel.

The stranger tossed a shabby green rucksack onto the soil. He was sodden from the downpour; his face was young, but long hair and a heavy stubble added undeserved years. His plain white tee-shirt and dark denim jeans dripped rainwater onto the soil.

But his appearance was not the main issue; what hung from his left arm was. A heavy steel chain, looped twice and long enough to reach the floor, hung from his left hand.

Milo and Eddy stood. They had the common sense to fear strangers, especially those that actively sought them out.

"Listen Mister, we don't want no trouble; and we sure as hell ain't got nothing worth robbing," Eddy said.

The stranger smiled. "I kind of guessed that." He ran his hand though his sodden hair and dried it on his tee-shirt. "Thing is, I need a favour. And, I've got the cash to pay for it."

Milo and Eddy exchanged an anxious glance.

Milo shook his head. "Look," he said. "I doesn't matter how much money you've got, you've got a bloody nerve coming down here looking for some freaky pervo-sex in exchange for a few quid. Go on, piss off."

The stranger's bottom jaw dropped open. "What, you think I…" He laughed out loud. "Sorry boys, but you're not my type, really you're not."

Eddy blew out a sigh of relief. "Ok then, what is this favour, and how much you willing to pay."

"Hang on a sec'." The stranger felt along the crumbling old brickwork. "There we go," he said, pointing to a steel ring that hung from the wall. "I want you to chain me to this ring, and no matter what I say or do, refuse to let me free before morning. And that sounds about…" He felt the rear pocket of his jeans, retrieved a padlock, a pair of handcuffs and a damp roll of ten-pound notes. "Fifty quid's worth of work. What do you say?"

"Fifty each, and maybe," Milo said, stroking his chins' thick grey stubble.

The stranger sighed. He placed the chain, padlock and cuffs on the floor. He counted the roll of notes.

"Look, all I've got here is eighty. But, maybe this will change your minds." The stranger opened the rucksack. He lifted out two six packs of Kronenburg, a fifty-gram packet of Old Holborn and two wrapped paper packages.

Milo was about to ask about the packages, but the pungent scent of chips, and of salt and vinegar answered the question.

Eddy and Milo shared a nod. Agreement was reached.

The stranger instructed Milo and Eddy on how best to restrain him. Once satisfied with the steel web of chain, the locks were clicked into place.

Milo kept looking over his shoulder at the chained stranger as he shovelled the chips into his mouth. He kept expecting trouble, but the stranger just sat there, watching them quietly.

"Fuck me," Eddy said, washing the chips down with a glugging swallow of the strong lager. "No one can tell me there's a better meal than this. No sod."

Milo smiled. It was nice to see the lad happy.

Later, when the chips had gone, but plenty of lager and tobacco remain, Milo heard the stranger chuckle to himself. He turned "What?"

"What exactly is freaky pervo-sex anyway?" The stranger asked.

Thirteen

Milo put on a deadpan look. "If Eddy's in the mood after a few more beers, you might get to find out."

An expression of uncertainty passed across the stranger's face.

Now, Eddy laughed. "S'Ok, mate. You'll be safe, you're not my type either."

Leo yanked the steering wheel hard to the left. The Land Rover bumped up onto the verge. He pulled hard on the handbrake lever, it engaged with a dry screech.

Climbing out, he and Gordy walked around to the rear of the vehicle. He opened the tailgate, leaned inside and slid a heavy holdall towards him.

"Toss a coin?" Leo asked.

Gordy's eyes rolled skywards. "Look, I'm sick to death of being 'Mr F.' Can't we choose? Just this once?"

Leo shook his head. "No we bloody can't. Every time we've done this shit, we've tossed a coin; *and* we've got away with it. It's a lucky ritual; we can't risk changing it."

Gordy looked up at the full moon. "Yeah, but every bloody time I've been 'Mr F'. Fucking mask chafes me up something chronic; and you always get to use the shot gun."

Leo fished into the rear pockets of his scruffy grey cargo pants and fished out a pound coin. "Grass is always greener with you, ain't it? Being 'Mr D' has its drawbacks. At least with 'Mr F' you only have to carry the Glock around." He flicked the pound coin up in the air. They both watched it spin and flicker in the moonlight.

Leo caught the coin and slapped it hard down onto the back of his wrist. He looked at Gordy, raised his eyebrows.

"Tails," Gordy said.

"Yup, have a winner; tails it is. So, I guess you want to be 'Mr D'."

"Too bloody right I do," Gordy said, smiling and rubbing his hands together. "Come on, dish up the equipment."

Leo reached into the holdall. He passed a rubber Dracula mask to Gordy; and stretched the Frankenstein one over his own head. He gave Gordy a handful of shells and heard the waxy thunk-thunk as two rounds were chambered. Leo slammed a clip into the base of the Glock and pocketed a spare.

"Right, let's go and kill us some fuckin' scummers." He said.

They walked down between the trees heading for the disused railway bridge.

Eddy sucked hard on the roll-up; he savoured the smoke for as long as he could before breathing out the swirling twisting cloud.

Milo's mind was elsewhere. He'd begun to see a change in the stranger. The quiet watchfulness had long since disappeared. Now he seemed nervous. His skin had become pale and shone with cold sweat.

"You Ok?" Milo asked.

The stranger blinked three times before nodding. "Just don't let me go."

"That's what you paid us for," Milo replied.

The stranger hung his head; his long hair swung forward and covered his face.

Milo caught Eddy's concerned gaze. He shrugged. "Let's just do what the man asked."

Eddy threw the empty chip wrapper into the fire. "I just don't like it. What if he dies? It'll look like we kept him prisoner."

"No-one's going to…"

A voice came from the north end of the tunnel.

"Die?" Said the man in a Frankenstein mask. "I think we'll decide if anyone's going to die here." He gestured towards the guy wearing the Dracula mask. "Right

Thirteen

Mr D.?"

"Fuckin' 'A'," said the shorter man, the one with shotgun.

Milo felt his stomach sink. He wondered why the God in charge of luck had dealt him such a shitty deck. "Look guys, we're not doing any harm here we're..."

"Shut the fuck up," the Frankenstein guy said. His pistol made an oily snick-snack as he chambered the first round. "In fact," he continued, "next shitter to utter a fuckin' word, dies. OK?"

The chained stranger groaned.

"What the fuck," the Dracula guy said. "I totally do not believe this. Looks like these two tramp scummers have got a bloody hostage." He waved his shotgun in Eddy's direction. "You got a name, shitter?"

"It's...It's Eddy."

"What the fuck did Mr F. just say about the next person to speak?"

"I didn't..."

Milo covered his ears as Mr D. loosed off both of the twelve gauge's barrels. He felt a damp spatter across his face. It was like some harmless optical illusion. Eddy's head vaporised, leaving a faint cherry mist. After a confused moment his body slumped into the fire. Milo could hear Eddy's blood fizz and spit as it pumped from his neck onto the burning embers of the fire.

Mr D. gave Mr F. a high five. "Nice fuckin' shot."

Milo felt his gorge rise and the room began to spin about him. He was assisted into unconsciousness by the butt of Mr F.'s Glock, who then began checking through Milo's pockets.

Mr D. knelt by the chained stranger and pulled at his restraints. "Bastards chained you up eh?"

The stranger said nothing. He seemed out of it.

"Don't worry, matey, we'll soon have you free."

"No, not free." Came a hoarse whispered response.

Mr D. shook his head. "What have these bastards done to you? No need to worry now, one of the scummers has been sent off to the great squat in the sky, and the other one will be joining him shortly."

Mr F. retrieved a bunch of keys from Milo's pocket. He jangled them, then tossed them to Mr D.

He quickly unchained the stranger. It took both of them to lift him to his feet and support him.

"Come on," Mr D. said. "Let's get you some fresh air. The stink of piss in there is enough to make any sod queasy."

They took the stranger out from beneath the tunnel. They sat him up against a tree stump.

"Back soon mate, sit tight," said Mr F. "We're just going to deal with that other scummer."

Regret at being set free lasted no more than a second, the light from the full moon bathed the stranger; against his skin it felt like sherbet on the palate.

Upon hearing laughter and a scream of pain from beneath the bridge, he felt the change come upon him.

All over his body he felt his muscles become dense and powerful. The change flooded his system with adrenaline. He felt a need, a hunger to run and hunt. Stalk and kill.

The final part of the change, the part he dreaded most started to take place. He felt his jawbone shatter then grow, his teeth sheared through the gum-line as they grew and changed position.

Fully metamorphasised, the pain of change began to fade. The stranger tried to laugh, but all that exited his muzzle was a menacing snarl.

Thirteen

He stood and walked back beneath the bridge.

Laughter stopped, the older tramp, face bloodied, was dropped to the ground.

The stranger felt his pelt pierced by a number of bullets, but it made no earthly difference.

He killed Mr D. with a lightning strike to the jugular. He took more time over Mr F. He savoured the sensation of the skull collapsing beneath his teeth and was pleasantly surprised at how long it took Mr F. to die. He liked his prey warm. The warmer the better.

Later, the Werewolf checked on the older tramp. He was badly beaten and had passed out.

Somewhere deep in his subconscious, a tiny glow of compassion flickered in the Werewolf's mind. He dragged the tramp near to the fire so that he wouldn't be too cold as he slept off the worse of his injuries.

With that, he ran from beneath railway bridge; he wanted to bathe in what was left of the full moon's glow.

JUST IN CASE
EDWARD RODOSEK

An endless, completely flat, glittery white plain extends to a horizon that trembles in violent heat. The glaring, violet-white sun, half the size ours on Earth, now shines nearly directly overhead. Its sharp rays dazzle my eyes and burn my forehead in spite of the visor I've lowered on my helmet. I look round, at first only hastily, and when I'm sure no immediate surprises are in store for me, I plot the most promising course with my binoculars. Well – there is only one course I can take because everywhere else is nothing but empty bareness.

Only in one direction, not too far away to the right, the plain is strewn with a number of huge rocks; some as big as houses. Most of these boulders are jagged, irregular in form, and the night-black shadows among them contrast sharply with the absolute whiteness that surrounds. I carefully check my oxygen supply, the pressure in my space suit, the external temperature and the other most significant things. All the indicators are green, all the values within the limits. I move on to inspecting the arms, attentively verifying what they've given me from the arsenal before the campaign: a blaster, a nerve paralyser, some micro-grenades, and a set of capsules with poisonous gas. Enough arms for all possible cases and for any conceivable enemy.

Finally, a forefinger reaches down to the cuff of my left boot, extracting my old, faithful knife. It is made of cold-forged steel; its sharp, glittering blade has been hardened with a laser beam. The slightly curved point and jagged edge of the knife are filling me with unshakeable trust. It is hidden in my boot because one's not allowed to carry any weapon not supplied by the armoury. But this knife is the only thing whose efficacy I really believe in. It was with me in the last war and helped me through countless dangers.

I adjust both straps of my heavy rucksack and start marching in the direction of those huge rocks. Now and then, I lift my binoculars and eye them. But I still can't distinguish any details among those dark shadows. When I reach them, I'll have to be extremely careful. As soon as I get there, I must immediately -

A sudden, violent blow knocks me to the dusty ground with such force that I roll several yards away. Only the long training drills of the past save me from fainting, the imparted reflexes enable me to bow down in combat position with my blaster aimed ahead and up.

Just above me some huge beast, a monster as from a nightmare, is flying in wobbly circles, watching me with hostile eyes. It's like those pterodactyls from Jurassic times, but this one is the size of a training plane. The monster glides above me, examines me - a welcome lunch that has been kind enough to offer itself to him. And then, suddenly, the monster begins to throw himself down, his colossal wings are now a dark, swelling shadow. I aim my weapon, the blaster throws up a blaze of hissing hotness; but the silhouette of the monster grows and grows, like a rushing locomotive, my finger on the trigger is paralysed...

The next instant, the monster slams down close to my feet on the stony ground that trembles from the stroke. The tip of the monster's wing strikes my shoulder so I fall again. Still, I'm on my feet again in a flash, the barrel of my blaster is aimed at the horrible dark mass in the middle of a cloud of dust. The dreadful bulk now lies motionless, a stench smell arising from it penetrates even through the special filters in my nostrils. I poke it most carefully with the tip of my boot, twice, three times. I don't want any more surprises. Yet, I could have saved myself these tests. The monster is dead, about this there is no more doubt.

I sit down on the dusty ground, for my knees are still very uncertain. Only now do I perceive some odd, salty taste in my mouth: my saliva is slightly coloured by blood. My shoulder hurts, and there I discover a long gash in my

Thirteen

thermo suit. I have to find the silicon spray and some plastic yarn in my rucksack to try and repair that damage. And this as soon as possible, before this hellish heat singes my thermo suit.

Hours later I move on. My thermo suit is stitched together. However I had to take it off during patching, so now I'm gasping from the unbearable heat. Fortunately the air here is all right, I don't even need to use filters any more. The sweat trickling from my forehead into my eyes almost blinds me, and I can hardly wait for the thermostat in my suit to cool me down again.

I still can't see anything suspicious or even odd either in the air or between the boulders on the nearby plane. Nothing dangerous anywhere, no movement at all. Still, I don't believe my senses, not quite. Just recently I've been taken in by a similar feeling. But I won't anymore, ever. No, sir.

Systematically, I examine a circular area the size of a football field in front of me. Repeatedly, I take only a couple of steps, then I stop, watching in all directions, listening carefully, distrustfully smelling the air.

All around me there are white, toothed rocks with sharp edges and dark depressions among them. Not until I'm entirely close to them do I see they're dusted with rubble and sand. I can't see any traces, footprints, or scents of paws or ruts. Nothing of the kind. Now I have to fix in the ground five or six sensor sticks near the boundaries of the covered area. They'll warn me of every possible change in surroundings – at every movement, at the merest shake of the ground, they'll amplify even the weakest noise, sending it all to my earphones. I must be completely safe at least for the next half hour, so I can take my lunch and maybe also take a little rest.

During my break nothing occurs. I rise, stretch out a bit and set forth. I've no idea in which direction I should go. I haven't the slightest clue who or what I might encounter. The only thing I do know for sure is, anybody or anything that comes across me would be my mortal enemy, a lethal threat to my life. He or it will all try to kill me if I don't kill him first. Therefore I mustn't hesitate, not even for a fraction of a second. That would be fatal for me. Every stupid tarrying of that kind would mean the difference between life and death - *my* life and *my* death.

Suddenly I hear a slight sound in my headphones. I instantly bow down, my eyes scanning at all directions, my hardened body a taught steel spring, all my tensed muscles tough, tenacious, prepared for instant, effective action. I'm turning into a wild beast, a dangerous predator, into a machine, programmed for slaughter.

I take a couple of quiet, stealthy steps along the narrow fissure among the rocks. Then I rise slowly, by inches, and try to get a peep over a low ledge overgrown with thin, dry grass.

After a few moments I can, finally, catch sight of them. Three deformed creatures of malicious appearance, resembling a combination of hyena and gigantic octopus. A fire burns in their midst. A whole collection of weapons hangs from them, with more on the ground around them.

Although I'm standing completely immobile, one of them looks towards me and reaches, lightning-like, for his belt. My trained reflex orders my arm to fling a hand grenade among them and to press my body at the ground. A horrible bang, a searing flash. Not until the hail of fragments stops do I dare peep out again over the rock.

Two of the disgusting creatures are lying motionless on the ground, but the third one, although bleeding, aims his weapon on me. His shot strikes the ledge just above my head and a few drops of molten stone drip on my helmet. I exterminate him with my blaster.

It's over. I can draw a deep breath again. I sit down on the ground and wipe some cold sweat from my forehead. My palms are damp, one of my eyelids is

Thirteen

twitching nervously. Nevertheless, everything is all right. My quick reactions have saved me once again. Otherwise, I would now be lying on the dusty, rocky ground, with those space monsters trading jokes over my corpse.

A bit later, I stand up and decide to move onwards. It doesn't matter where to. Simply forward. Now the sole important thing is to stay alert. I must remain a predator; not prey, a predator.

Suddenly, a wall emerges just thirty steps in front of me. How in heaven could that have happened? Why didn't I notice it much earlier? How had I overlooked such an obvious thing despite my incessant watchfulness? I reproach myself. Apparently, my double success in the last conflicts has soothed, made me weak. And that is dangerous. Such behaviour might be lethal for me. I swear to myself that this will never happen again. From now on, I have to be quicker still, even more resolute, even more prepared to kill. Otherwise, I won't survive.

The wall is vertical; its surface is smooth, planed, almost polished. No doubt an artificial object. When I approach, I can observe a tiny, rectangular break in it. It's like a barely visible frame, a bit higher than me. From somewhere behind the wall a high, harsh sound utters forth. Three times, every time only for a few seconds. What could this be? Probably, a new trap for dupes. But now I'm prepared for everything, even the most unexpected possibilities. I squeeze my blaster in my right hand, a paralyser in my left hand; a few micro hand grenades hang from my belt. I make a careful step forward -

At that moment that frame on the wall slides sideways and an opening appears, in it a uniformed human figure. Yet another new guise of a space enemy! Simultaneously with that thought, my right forefinger squeezes the trigger. But my blaster remains mute, and the alien at the door grins scornfully at me. I jerk him with my paralyser, but this also fails. Then, despairingly, I reach for my micro hand grenades - though I've a premonition these wouldn't go off at all.

And they don't. My entire stock of weapons, all these wonders of cutting edge technology prove to be useless, and all my efforts to fight are in vain. And this mocking alien knows that all too well. But... he doesn't know the whole truth.

He doesn't know about my own knife.

In a split second I pull it out of my boot and fiercely stab it into the alien's abdomen. I observe how his haughty smile freezes on his face, then fades to an expression of enormous astonishment. He collapses limply, like a rag-doll, in front of my feet. Even now someone violently slams my head, three other aliens jump on me, wrenching my arms behind my back, then knocking me down to the ground and pinning me there.

So, that's the end, definitely. I'm aware that I'm beaten. Still I haven't simply surrendered to them, those sons of bitches! I've made them work for it. Let these bastards see what we Earthlings are made of. No doubt they'll think twice about whether it pays to invade our planet.

As they push and pull me away I glance backward, and my eyes drift over to the large, shiny inscription about the door they hustle me through:

PSYCHO – SIMULATOR
Authorized Military Personnel Only

Thirteen

FALLING IN LOVE AGAIN
DAWN WINGFIELD

It was absolutely terrible, what happened to my poor husband Tony. He still wakes up at night, all sweaty and shaking. I hold him and tell him it's okay, that poor Peggy is at peace now.

I'm getting ahead of myself though.

It all began one quiet afternoon when I was puttering around my gift shop, dusting the stock and having a tidy up, wishing summer would hurry up and come. The bell over the door rang and I glanced up with a smile. A man came in and said hello before starting to look around, picking up figurines, putting them down again, then pausing to admire a shelf of teddy bears. I kept my eye on him, not because I thought he'd nick something, but because he was rather an attractive man. In his fifties, with distinguished wings of grey in his hair, and lovely blue eyes surrounded by sexy crinkles.

"Can I help you?" I finally asked, coming to stand in front of him.

He gaped at me in my black leggings, ankle boots and clingy orange top that showed a generous amount of cleavage. I'm fifty-two, but if you've got it, flaunt it, is what I always say.

"I'm looking for a present for my wife," he spluttered.

I hid my disappointment with a smile. "Maybe I can make a few suggestions?"

We decided on a china dolphin and a box of chocolates. He paid with a cheque, and I handed him the wrapped gifts in a pink carrier bag. "Goodbye, Tony and thanks for stopping by."

"Thanks for the help," he replied, and left, as I stared after him, then looked down at the cheque in my hand. Tony Henderson. I couldn't help thinking how well my name, Viv, sounded with his last name; Viv Henderson, Vivian Henderson, Mrs. Viv Henderson. Silly, I know, but I was lonely since Reg died. I longed for some love in my life, someone to care for, who would love me in return. I saw that Tony lived in Cornwall Gardens, a street of large Victorian villas on the edge of town, and I couldn't help feeling a pang of envy. I lived alone in a one bedroomed flat.

I thought I'd never see him again but a few weeks later I was having a sandwich in the leisure centre next door to the shop and there he was. I went over, wondering if fate was finally on my side.

"Well, what are you doing here?" I beamed.

"I'm work here." He looked at me blankly.

"I'm Viv. From the gift shop," I reminded him. "Did your wife like the presents?"

He nodded as he recognized me. "Why don't you ask her yourself?"

For the first time I noticed the plump, matronly woman sitting at his side. She was swathed in a pink cardigan and a flowery tent of a dress. Her short hair was coarse and grey and a pair of glasses perched on her pink snout of a nose.

"This is Peggy, my wife," Tony said.

Peggy smiled and invited me to have lunch with them.

I think it's such a shame when a woman lets herself go. How on earth can you expect a man to stay interested when you resemble a lump of lard in a sack? I could see Tony stare at the two of us as we chatted, unable to resist a comparison. Peggy looked like something the cat dragged in and I was in a red pencil skirt, black stilettos and a low cut black silk top.

I wasn't a bit surprised when Peggy told me she was a housewife, and loved cooking. The most exciting thing she ever did was crochet toilet roll covers for the annual church bazaar. Poor Tony.

Thirteen

"Are you married, Viv?" She asked.

"I'm a widow," I replied, with a brave smile. "Reg died two years ago this Christmas."

Peggy's myopic eyes widened in sympathy. "Oh, you poor thing. It must be hard, coping without him."

I nodded, tears welling up.

"And your poor husband, he couldn't have been any age at all…"

"He was forty-nine," I sniffed, fishing in my bag for a tissue, thinking of the awful pain Reg had endured. It had been so hard, watching him die, even if the love I'd felt for him had faded to nothing. Reg hadn't a shred of ambition, and he hadn't made me happy.

"You're spending Christmas with us," Peggy said firmly.

"Oh, I couldn't…" I murmured, seeing Tony's expression of surprise.

Peggy looked at him. "Right, Tony?"

"Er… right," and he grinned, leaning over to kiss his wife. "Consider yourself rescued, Viv. My Peggy can't bear to think of anyone alone, especially at Christmas."

He was right about that. When I turned up on Christmas morning there were two ancient old ladies sitting in front of the television and a rather smelly man Peggy had brought back from the homeless shelter was tucking into a plate of mince pies. It was a wonderful day though, and afterwards, Tony, Peggy and I became firm friends. I'd pop in to see Peggy regularly and sometimes Tony and I would have lunch together at the leisure centre. Just a sandwich and a cup of tea, but those times were magical. We were in love, although as a married man, Tony was far too decent to bring it out into the open. He didn't have to. It was plain from the way he smiled at me, and the way his eyes kept straying to my breasts.

One spring afternoon, I decided to go and see Peggy on my day off, knowing I'd end up with yet another stodgy recipe tucked into my bag when I left. I felt sorry for her really, but I kept up the visits so I could learn more about Tony. I discovered that he loved golf, and that they visited the Isle of Wight each year.

Peggy put the kettle on, much less chatty than usual, dressed in one of her floral polyester ensembles.

"Is everything okay?' I asked.

She didn't answer at first. Silently she pulled two mugs from the cupboard and opened the teabag tin. "I know what you're up to, Viv!" She suddenly choked.

"I stared in amazement. This was so unlike Peggy. "What are you talking about?"

"You're after my husband!"

I think I went red, because my face suddenly felt hot.

"Well, you're not going to get him," she continued, all agitated and looking uglier than ever. She took milk from the fridge and slammed the fridge door. "We've been married for thirty years! Tony loves me!"

I smiled at her gently, feeling pity. "Of course he does."

"If you think my Tony could ever fancy an old tart like you, mutton dressed as lamb, going around with your boobs hanging out, you're sadly mistaken," she screeched.

I stared at her, speechless. Her spiteful words really hurt.

"I know how you're always popping into my husband's office," she snarled. "It's got to stop, do you hear me? Get out, Viv! Get out of my house!" She turned, leaving the two cups of tea on the table and ran upstairs.

I buried my face in my hands, shaking, wounded. Never in a million years would I have thought Peggy could be so vicious. I had done nothing wrong. All I

Thirteen

was guilty of was befriending her, a boring and unattractive woman. Tony and I had fallen deeply in love, true, but that wasn't exactly our fault.

I poured the tea down the sink and washed the cups – which were floral – then carefully dried and put them away. I opened Peggy's cutlery drawer. All her spoons, forks and knives were laid in obedient, gleaming little piles, with larger utensils – potato mashers, egg slicers, carving knives, off to one side. I found what I needed and followed her up the stairs, noticing the expensive, subtle grey carpets springing beneath my feet. I'd never been upstairs in the house before, but Peggy had left the main bedroom door open and she was lying on the bed having a cry after her little outburst. She didn't hear me go in.

It was a huge peach-coloured room with an en-suite bathroom – something I'd always fancied. Peggy opened her eyes as I approached and began to sit up, groping on the pillow for her glasses. I did get a bit carried away, and I admit I shouldn't have cut her head off, but then she shouldn't have said such horrible things, should she?

There was an awful mess and I knew the carpet was ruined forever. The wallpaper would probably have to be replaced too, but it was rather old-fashioned anyway, with all those overblown peach roses. I stripped out of my sparkly pink cotton top and leggings and rummaged through Peggy's wardrobe, tutting in disgust at how huge and flowery everything was. By some miracle I found a plain royal blue thing and slipped into it, stuffed my clothes into a plastic bag I found in the kitchen and left the house. It was the middle of the week, early afternoon, and there was no sign of activity in the street, thank goodness. I started up my car and drove away.

Of course it was in all the papers; the town had never seen anything like it. Police thought it might have been one of the vagrants Peggy was always so kind to, and they arrested the scruffy man she'd invited for Christmas, but in the end had to let him go.

Tony has said he couldn't have managed without me during those awful days after he discovered Peggy sprawled on their bed, stabbed over fifty times and decapitated. I was there for him, as he cried and poured out his grief. I helped him arranged the funeral and persuaded him not to put the house up for sale. I had the bedroom professionally cleaned and decorated – this time in tasteful subtle shades of cream. I did a lot for Tony, and our love blossomed. We were married six months after poor Peggy's funeral.

That was two years ago. I understand that Tony suffered a terrible shock, but you'd think he'd be over it by now. He's still on anti-depressants though, still disturbing my sleep by waking up in the night and shouting his head off. He sobs uncontrollably while I hold him as if he were a small child. Quite frankly, I'm exhausted by it.

I still have the gift hop and recently a used car salesman from the new place on the High Street has started coming in. We talk, and Bob is so sweet and understanding, not to mention attractive. I seem to be falling in love with him. I'm not sure what will happen next, but poor Tony is so depressed. I wouldn't be at all surprised if he took an overdose one of these days.

Thirteen

THE ACCIDENT
LEISA PARKER

And as the vehicle suddenly stopped, with its flashing lights, its high pitched wail, the EMTs were out and running. Running as fast as they could, as fast as their legs would allow. And Rico, the smaller of the two, a bit lighter, a bit faster, was almost there, to the scene, to the cliff. And Lido too, not far behind, lumbered along, with his large bulky frame, his bag of supplies. And as they neared the scene, they hurried that much more, for they knew it was critical, there wasn't much time. For the car, the wreck, it was swaying a bit. Ready to teeter, to slide, to plunge...

And as Rico finally reached it, the crumpled bunk of metal, his eyes, his greyish-greens, they began to dart and to dart. To search and to search. Scanning... scanning. Taking in the whole of the car, any possible survivors. And his eyes did find one. The driver. His head slung forward across the fur-lined wheel, a bright canary yellow. Or, what used to pass for a bright canary yellow anyway. For the man, and the wheel, were now a sloppy, dripping mess, of red and clear liquids, fluids and blood. For the back of the man's head bore a wound, though not untreatable, of shattered skull and matted tissue. Almost a dent. Like a punched-in football. And as Rico's brain raced and computed, he moved quick. Quick, yet calm. As he stuck one thin brown arm in, straight through the driver side window, careful to avoid the sharp pointed shards, the glistening broke glass. And as his thin fingers reached the man's flesh, his neck, they began to scope and to scope, to probe and probe. Searching for a movement. A beat. Some kind of pulse. And then it was there, slow but steady, and his face turned to Lido, crouched on the ground, unbundling supplies, bandages, needles, morphine...

"I've got one man, I've got a pulse. Get the..."
And then the driver moved. His neck, his head, beginning to loll about, from one side to the next. Like that of a newborn. Helpless. Weak. And then it fell backwards. Slumping unto the bloodied headrest behind him. His face aimed at the mangled car roof, the sky. His features exposed. And Rico shrieked, loud and shrill. Drawing his hand back quick. His arm, his skin, scraping against the shards of glass, the awful thin points. His blood beginning to surface, to appear, to drip, drip, drip.

Drip,
drip
drip.

And Lido's head snapped up, his eyeballs bulging, his skin pale. For Rico was a guy's guy, one of those tough macho deals. And Lido had never, in all his days, heard him make anything less than big tough manly noises. Let alone a shriek. And so it was a shocking thing to hear, it was a heart-stopping thing. Creepy actually. But not as creepy as something else. Rico's face. For as Lido's bulging eyes flashed upward from his bag, his gut wretched a bit, and his blood ran cold. For Rico's face, his features, they were nothing but a canvas, a landscape, of disgust and distaste, repulsion and shock. As if he'd just came across a 75-foot rattlesnake that had shit all over itself. And then rolled around in it.

"Look at him man - it's him, it's him!" Rico practically hissed, as he stepped back, quick and sharp, his boots scuffling in the gravel, kicking up small bursts of dry white air.

"Gawd, who Rico, who? Who is it?" Lido practically shrieked himself, as he got up and hurried over to the mangled car. A rash of chill breaking out across his flesh; a rash of goose pimples. And as he leaned in close, close but cautious, to the driver's side door, he swallowed hard. His eyes taking in the view. The view of

Thirteen

the man: the driver. And Lido's eyes turned into mere slits, his brow frazzled, as he took inventory of the driver again and again. The thin tight lips, the spot of a nose, the massive scars and pits from full blown acne, the birthmark.

And then Lido jumped, crawling in his skin, as the car creaked and moaned, loud and metallic, beginning to teeter again, to dip, the white waters crashing below, the jutting rocks.

"Man Lido! Don't you recognize him... don't you?"

And though Lido said nothing, he did recognize the man. Fully. Completely. His lips dipping further downwards.

"I mean... I know you don't watch 'America's Most Wanted' or any of those true life killer dramas but it's him. It's him. That fucking serial killer that's been all over the news, all over those posters that are plastered everywhere. I mean you had to have seen some of them, somewhere. Even someone like you, Lido. Someone who squirrels away most of the time, hiding in his apartment. Even you've had to have heard about that birthmark, that crescent on his cheek. You've had to at least heard about that...and it's there Lido, it's there!"

But Lido only stood, staring at the car, the cliff.

"Well don't you see it?" Rico practically screamed again, as he stepped closer to him. To Lido and the car. His face eager and searching. Growing a deep, deep red, almost purple.

"Yes, yes" Lido replied, calm, but firm. "I do, I do... I do see it. But there isn't time for all of that right now." And he spun about then, to face Rico. "I mean we got to get him out of there Rico. This car's going to go, and go soon. Smash into the rocks. Break into a million pieces..."

"Fuck it... didn't you hear me? *Serial killer.* I say let him go, let the rocks eat him, the fish nibble. Hell, I'll even do it myself if I have too. Give the car a push. I mean nobody's around here Lido. Nobody. I mean look around you, it's the middle of nowhere and the scene of a gawddamned accident Lido. An acciden - "

"Listen to yourself," Lido replied, soft, yet even, and under his breath. "I mean I think it's disgusting too, but still. It's our job to save people, not to kill them. We can still pull him out of the window, break out the glass..."

"Fuck it, Lido. Fuck it," Rico practically screamed, his voice pitching. "Have you gone loco or what? I mean, since when did you become such a bleeding fuckin' heart? Didn't you hear what this guy did to those people? Those people he just snatched off the streets. Out of their homes. He tortured them for days, you know. He strung them up like cattle, like hogs, like sheep. And then he beat them. He whipped them. He starved them and burned them. And then he raped them. Raped them all. The men anyway. Bent them all right over those pipes in that dank black basement, that basement filled with rat droppings, with stool, with..."

"I don't care," Lido snapped. "That's not what we're here for. That's not what we're trained for. Now let's get to it." And Lido turned, swift and deft, away from Rico, and back to the car, to the man.

"What?" Rico yelled as his lips pursed, and his hand shot out, grabbing Lido by the arm. "What if he had done that to your brother man, your sister?"

"That's sick, asshole, really sick. Now let me go." But Rico wouldn't, his grip like a vice. And though Lido didn't want to, they both knew, that if push came to shove, Lido would walk away from it. Hands down. But that really wasn't what Lido wanted, it wasn't his way.

"Listen Rico." Lido said, his voice as soothing as possible. "I can understand what you're saying, but all it comes down to is this. That we aren't judge and jury here. It's not our right. Let the courts do that. I mean the guy will pay for what he did. I can't just stand here and let you murder the guy just because you carry a personal disgust for the guy. Want to carry out some kind of personal vigilante

Thirteen

justice."

"Hey, it's not just me man. It's the world too," spat Rico. "And anyway, killing this piece of shit would be a gawddamned public service. It would prevent future rapes, future murders... plain and simple..."

And then the car creaked again, louder this time, the metal straining, beginning to teeter again, steeper, stronger, back and forth, back and forth. And now, there was something else. Something new. A smell. A strong smell of gasoline, of thick black fuel. And then something else. For the man inside, he moaned, soft and slight. His eyes beginning to move, to flutter, beneath his blood soaked lids.

"Ah, gawd, " Lido said, his stomach beginning to churn, to knot. "Come on, Rico, the guy's regaining consciousness now. Come and help me get him out of there." Lido felt almost on the verge of tears, a full-blown gush.

And then, thankfully, thankfully, it happened. Rico softened. His hold on Lido released. His features beginning to contort from those of keen sharpness, to softness. Defeat.

"Fine," he whispered, low but resolved. "Fine." And Lido breath gave out, relaxed, calm. Anxious to get the man out, knowing the clock was running, and running fast. And as Rico stepped back towards the car, reaching an arm towards the window, the glass, his fingers began to ball, to fist, and then he was swinging, full force, towards Lido, his side, his stomach...

And Lido gasped. Trying to move, to avoid the blow. But it was too quick, too out of the blue, and so it caught him, straight in the gut. And the pain was instant. Both the betrayal, the belly.

And as he swooned to the ground, his face distorting into that of a grimace, his arms clutching his stomach, he began to mumble "No Rico, don't."

But Rico was already there. In action. Doing. Both of his palms slammed unto the twisted metal, the car, and then he pushed, he shoved, with everything that he had. Until the car, it moved. Slowly at first, as if in protest. As if fighting for its life. Its weight barely shifting above the white rocks, the pebbles, the gravel, the greens. And then it gave, lurching downwards. Beginning to slide, to shift, to fall, and then it was gone...

Almost...

For the upper corner of the car, the driver's side, the tire had caught. On a snaggle of stump, of root. Entangled within the earth, the soil, for perhaps thousands of years, possibly more. And as the car, most of it dangling over the narrow edge, began to sway and moan, Lido stared. His eyes wide and bulging. Gawking. The scene reminding him of a cat hanging from a shelf, one paw gripped for dear life. For survival. And then the driver, he moaned louder. A sound of pain, of ache.

And Lido jumped to his feet, still clutching his bruised stomach, his eyes staring into the corner of jutting metal. At the man trapped inside. And then he watched as his eyes, the driver's, they opened. Sleepy at first, puzzled, and then bulging. As the car suddenly lurched, and there was a crunch of metal and the scratch of leaves, the sound of girth and strain. Of loss. As the roots, and the stump, the edge of the earth, the cliff, it gave way.

Fully. Completely.

Dropping and dropping.

Falling and falling.

Soundlessly. Quietly. Except for Lido. Who shrieked loud and wide, his cries filling the air, the dust. As he rushed, half bent over, to the just borne edge, the scatter of falling pebble and rock, root and earth. And as he stared downwards, his mouth open wide, he saw the car flip and flip. He saw something within it, the driver, bouncing about. And then a horrendous sound, a sickening sound. Of

Thirteen

screaming metals and screaming flesh, as the car smashed into the sharp hardness below, the crashing blue-white waves. Then a burst of fire, of flame, of red-black heat. And tears sprung to his eyes, as Lido thought of the man. The man he had only just met, and the fear he must have felt. The fear he must have known. And now, now, as he watched. The body parts, of both man and machine, began to lap and to slap about the open wide sea, the soft harsh blues. And Lido, letting his own waters stream, whispered to himself. The only word that he could, the only one that was right. The only one that, despite the long years and the longing, the wishing and wanting, had never before crossed his tongue, his lips, his thin tight mouth.

"Pops."

Thirteen

GRALLABELLE
PHILIP TINKLER

The station wagon bounced across the road like an old whore turning her last trick. Its torn backseat held memories of girls, wide-eyed and braless under the stars. Its trunk had been home to Wes after Terry locked him in for swiping the last beer one crazy summer.

Al would graduate soon, college friends would vanish and today he was intent on making a memory to savour in their potbelly years. Joe had inspired this evening's trip. Sitting there in the retirement home, taking mental vacations to times when his hair was full and life fuller. He'd been Al's neighbor growing up and treat him like a grandson.

'Went to see Joe today,' Al said.

Wes and Terry exchanged a look Al caught in the rear-view.

'Think your buds turning into a tea doily? Joe's eighty, but the stories he tells! Fuck, he's not some piss-soaked curmudgeon. He's a *man*, not an age. Slaps nurse's asses, drinks Skogsra beer...'

'Okay, Jesus Al, we get it!' Terry piped.

'Joe was different this morning, far away. I was telling him what styles the girls are wearing this season when he starts clenching his fists and grinding his dentures. I thought: Shit, I've over stimulated his mind.'

'Outta the blue he starts talking about life in the forties, before fun was invented, as Joe put it. He'd heard tales from drifters and local loonies about an abandoned village called Grallabelle. Joe and buds hiked into the woods to see if the tales were true.'

'Tales...?' Wes asked.

'Strange lights, children singing, creatures...they saw a man with the legs of a chicken walk across the balcony of a house there. He tipped his cap and strutted inside. They high-tailed it home scared shitless.'

Terry broke up. 'Did that old fart get you! Cock with legs!'

'That's where we're going campers,' Al said.

'What else did Joe see?' Wes asked in a polite choirboy voice.

'Things you couldn't imagine,' Al said, trying to sound mysterious.

Al didn't believe Joe. *Chicken Men* – what bollocks. But for a goodbye present to his mates, he'd buy it. He already had Wes, who never missed an issue of UFO Monthly. Terry, who suffered BS lightly but dealt freely, would be tricky.

The roads fed through forest like tangled electrical wires. They'd been driving three hours, any sense of adventure leaving the trio as day seeped into evening.

'Hey *Aaaaaal*,' Terry whined in perfect nasal imitation of Peg Bundy, 'I think we're lost.'

'Get ready to be shocked - think ya right,' Al admitted, then noticed the man on the pushbike. He was dressed like a rebel Quaker, his raggedy beard and faded green cape billowing behind him. Al slowed, cocking his head out the window.

'Hey buddy, we're lost! Which way to...'

Surprise cut him off as the Quaker veered sharply into the woods.

Before disappearing from sight, he shot Al a knowing look.

'Ha. Ha,' Terry said, 'Real fucking funny.'

Honestly confused, Al glanced back.

'Maybe we can stop at this invisible McDee's up ahead for Phantom Burgers,' Terry said.

'You didn't see him!' Al shouted. 'He was right there... just steered into the

Thirteen

sticks! You saw him, Wes... *right?*'

'Al. I could be with my girl right now. Save this shit for Halloween.'

'He was there, not fuckin around!' Al protested.

Twenty uncomfortable minutes later they arrived at the forgotten water tower where the path to Grallabelle supposedly began. They shouldered their backpacks, Terry handed out beers and soon the combination of alcohol and fresh air killed any animosity.

The path winded deeper into the forest past red oaks. *Sentries of nature*, Al thought. Without notice, Terry ran, dropped to his knees and started sniffing.

'Aw, put em down. Could be poisonous and I'm not dragging your dead ass back to the car,' Wes said. Not listening, Terry continued carefully laying the mushrooms inside his pack, next to pussy mags and MP3 player. Paul Bunyon he was not.

'Look at the size of these!' he squawked. 'Bet these beauties...'

Al's boot plummeted down, crushing the 'shrooms and Terry's grin.

'Zat for!' Terry spat.

'Daylight's wastin,' Al said simply, walking away.

They'd lost the path. They sat on a deadfall, exhausted from doing what cars had eliminated from their lives. Somewhere an animal called.

'What was...?' Al began.

'Bobcat maybe, or Red Fox,' Wes offered.

'These woods are sure full of comedians,' Terry quipped.

'Too full,' Wes said, laughing. Al joined in.

Frowning, Terry popped another longneck.

'Come on boy scouts of America, its getting dark. If there is a Grallabelle we best find it or we'll be sleeping with Sasquatch,' Al said, getting up.

'I did that once,' Terry said seriously, 'balls were blue for a week.'

Laughing, they hiked on.

An hour later they were stopped again, flashlights hanging limply from their hands.

'Wes, man, what is it?' Terry asked.

'Not sure. Would've said St. Elmo's Fire but that needs a conducting service and strong electrical field. This has neither.'

'Corpse Candles,' Al muttered.

A series of translucent orbs hovered before them like overgrown fireflies. In the centre of each a ball of pale changing colour. Lilac faded to yellow; yellow to pink; pink into lilac. Slack jawed; they watched the orbs gel together into a milky-green, vaguely human form, its top ending in a misty upside down T-shape. *Like an Amish hat,* Wes thought.

'Must be swamp gas or some shit, right?' Terry asked, urgently.

'It's signalling us!' Al yelled.

The form rose above them, one smoky arm pointing left in a *walk on by* gesture before floating away into the dark.

'Let's follow it,' Al said, already jogging.

'Naw, man. Naw,' Wes said in a strangled voice, but he and Terry were already chasing Al, flashlights bobbing and illuminating eyes of curious squirrels.

'Ah *fuck*. Oh *fuck*.' Al and Wes stopped running, turned to see Terry sprawled to the ground clutching his nose. Dark syrup leaked between his fingers.

'You okay?' Wes asked.

'Peachy, thanks. Ran into a bastardly tree.'

Al was already examining the "tree" with uneasy eyes.

'Not a tree. Look,' he said. They came over.

'The golden oldie wasn't yanking your pisser,' Terry said, studying the sign

Thirteen

he'd crushed his nose against.

The signpost stood six feet high, moss coated and ancient. Five oak markers were nailed around it, carved on each the name of a town none of them had heard of...

...except the topmost.

Al read them out.

'Vilcakis, Tybeloney, Bryemurgh, Frithsville, Grallabelle.'

'What's that number Al?' Wes asked.

Al placed his finger against the number scratched under Grallabelle.

'88 steps...they marked the distance in *steps*?' Al asked, and then felt something huge crawl over his hand.

He leapt back, arms flailing like The Scarecrow. The flashlight flew loose, momentarily shining his disgusted face before thumping to the canvas of dead leaves underfoot.

Terry trained his flashlight at the fist-sized insects crawling over the sign. Beetle-like but wrong somehow. Wes realized first. 'No heads. They have no heads but they're crawling.'

Marking their backs, were four red circular markings. *Eighty-eight*, Al thought sickly.

'Guess we'll follow the sign,' Al said. Terry followed, holding bloody nose to shirt-sleeve. Wes stayed, wondering why nobody knew of these lost places.

Who lived there? Were they abandoned? Why?

He illuminated the middle marker. *Bryemurgh - 562 steps.*

Softly, as if from a great distance, a sound like bagpipes drifted over.

Wes shuddered and left.

Two imposing hickories stood before their exhausted faces and beyond them lay a large circular grove. Moonlight struck off outlines of buildings dotted randomly in the clearing.

Like a shared illness, their minds whispered *Grallabelle*.

They entered the village.

'Stick together,' Wes said. No one argued.

'Who would build a village out *here*?' Terry asked.

'Maybe we'll find out,' Al said, praying they wouldn't.

They walked to the centre, sat on their backpacks and looked around like rabbits surrounded by unseen pray.

'Fucking *stinks* here,' Terry said, 'those Pineland Scent air freshener assholes should get a whiff of this place for their next turd spray.'

'Anyone bring any extra batteries?' Al asked and was shot back with a double no.

'Useless. Think we can make a torch out of Terry's jerk mags?' Al asked.

'There's something hanging on that tree,' Wes said, 'something swinging.'

Al and Terry's weak lights joined Wes'. The silhouette gently swaying from the lower tree branch looked like a hanging midget.

'Should we...' Al started.

'No way, let's go back. This place stinks and I'm *tired* and *cut*...'

'Chicken?'

'Not funny Alan,' Terry said, close to tears.

Suddenly, Al sprang up and ran to the tree. A minute later he shouted back:

'Chicken legs!'

Wes's mind filled with the awful image of the Chicken Man running towards him, grinning as his head ricocheted back and forth, carried by thin, powerful legs.

'Come over!' Al yelled.

Eyebrows raised, Wes looked to Terry who only shook his head like a petulant child. Sighing, Wes jogged over before his temporary beer-induced

Thirteen

bravery whittled away.

The branches were covered with severed chicken legs, hung by yarn like strange fruit.

'Jesus,' Wes gasped.

'Yeah,' Al agreed. 'Who would do this? Some are twenty feet high.'

'Doubt kids,' Wes said, 'too much trouble.'

'Where's Terry?' Al asked. *'Terry! Come over you chicken shit!'*

Wes swallowed at the bad joke.

'Let's go. Terry's already freaked out enough without this,' Wes said.

They started back.

But Terry wasn't there.

Where he'd been sitting only minutes before was a mouldy plastic doll. A parade of earwigs and centipedes crawled inside the cavity of its rotted head. It grinned up at them: *I know something you don't know.*

Al picked it up. A limp string ending in a plastic loop hung from its back, curious, Al pulled it. A gurgled babble came from the doll, reminding Wes of back masked messages on rock songs. He grimaced at the nonsense words.

Ifac yougla lykt gubbe meata chigaba lorst huldra!

Frowning, Al threw it to the ground and cupped his mouth.

'Terry Come here ya fucking clown, we're going back!'

Silence mocked him. Wes looked at Al like a kid lost from his parents.

'Come on, Wes. We have to find him...meet me here in twenty minutes, okay?'

'Split up?'

'Bingo. You take that side, I'll take the other.'

Al disappeared to the left behind a cluster of wooden buildings. Wes eyed the doll. Its glass eyes stared back unfazed, its grin seeming stronger now they were alone.

Wes smacked his palm against the dying flashlight, something that would cause a dazzling beam to burst forth in a movie, but it remained dim.

Wes set off for the brick buildings to the right. Half expecting that numbnuts Terry to leap out, his heart skipped three beats when something spoke up in a cracked voice.

'tay a while, stray Wesley, ave a tay.'

Jesus, the doll, that was the doll, oh Jesus, his mind cried in an idiot mantra.

He ran to the nearest building, throat too strangled with fear to scream.

When he got inside he wished he hadn't.

The houses on the left reminded Al of cottages mental defectives kept on the coast of insanity for muggy summers. The doors were seriously messed up. Some were nine feet high, others three. One was hexagonal, as if the carpenter had been on a steady magic mushroom diet since the age of six.

But the windows were the worst. They were boarded up, but each board had been painted with a little "scene". Crudely painted curtains, painted flower vases, painted shutters. One even had a painted cat, its black eyes wisely ignoring the stranger in town.

Dear Terry, you have been cordially invited to get your ballsack stapled to your asshole for making me search such a quaint little village such as this. Dress is casual and loose to accommodate for swelling...

Al stopped. A house that wouldn't have looked out of place in a Deep South plantation lay ahead. A rotted balcony entwined with creepers ran around it.

Chicken Man's house, Al thought, and stomped something metallic.

Thirteen

He bent to pick it up. A beer can. Time had bleached all life from the colours but Al could still read the label: Skogsra. 'Joe' Al muttered.

Behind him, someone giggled. Al spun, catching a glimpse of tiny shoes vanishing behind a house. *Peek-a-boo Terry!* Grinning, he went over.

Wes leaned against the door, heart pumping terrified blood. He took five undulating breaths, opened his eyes. *Dark as death in here,* he thought. Not wanting to bump into something (*someone*) he dropped to his knees and felt his way across the room.

Four legs, wooden, that's a chair then, long, waist-height, a table. He felt over the table, hoping there'd be a... *ashtray bottom, waxy finger - candle.* He reached into his jeans pocket, brought out a match and lit the candlestick.

The room was tiny, decorated with two chairs, table and dresser. In the corner hidden away like an unwanted Mongoloid child was a narrow staircase.

Smells so sad here, Wes thought, *like damp rot of the soul.*

Wes walked over to the dresser, the doll forgotten as if in another time.

He pulled open the first drawer. *Shoes, tiny shoes, the type babies wear.*

He opened the second. *Broken mirror glass. Glimmer of secrets unknown.*

He opened the third. *Fine length o' rope, grand fer hangin is that rope.*

He opened the fourth. *Bones, yellow. Oh Wil, what've a done...?*

Screams from upstairs pulled Wes back into the slippery reality of now.

'It hurts, *oh God it HURTS so much, so* much, *make it stop. Stop! Please won't you...make it...*STOP THAT! *Why are you, Wil please, it huuurrrts...'*

The voice trailed off in screams not of man or woman but only mortal agony.

It's Terry, oh shit, oh Jesus, Wes' mind yammered. He ran upstairs.

No, his mind proclaimed, *that's not possible.*

Around the corner of the house, Al gaped at another boarded up window. The flashlight, now a thin queasy orange, jittered from his shaking hand at the painting.

Two black curtains hung aside a familiar figure, hands plastered to glass that never was. The open mouth screamed its silent nightmare at the village maps denied. Al reached out to touch the bright red straps of Terry's backpack. The paint was still wet.

Al turned and ran, getting almost ten feet before crashing through the rotted trapdoor of a root-cellar. Darkness swallowed.

'Terry, I'm coming man! Hold on...'

Wes reached the top of the stairs and stopped dead.

Lit by golden candlelight, the bedroom was like something out of a fairytale. The bed was an inviting structure of thick oak and satin sheets. The hand-polished wooden floor reflected the imposing wardrobe, the fine chest, mirror...*the mirror.*

Wes walked over to the mirror, its curvaceous frame drawing him. He set down his own candle and looked in. His lucid reflection hung like a half-truth in front of the cozy room. A ball of liquid excitement curdled in his stomach like a child's wonder.

Lying naked on the bed was the most breathtaking woman Wes had ever seen, dreamt or imagined. Her legs crisscrossed slowly over the sheets, making whisper sounds. Her breasts stood pert in the flickering mellow light, causing Wes to grow where it counts.

The most amazing thing was her hair. Long and coarse, it trailed down to her calves in a moss-like shade of green. Wes watched the reflected woman stand and walk over to him, noticing her bush was indeed a bush. Green and leafy, it rustled between her thighs.

Then her hands were caressing his shoulders, her impish lips against his ear.

Thirteen

Wes closed his eyes.

'Who are you?' he asked. She smiled sadly.

'I was *life*. I was...*here*.' She sighed, coating his skin with gooseflesh.

'Wesley, you must leave. This was...' her hand gestured towards the room, Grallabelle, the woods, beyond.

'This *was*.' She said with finality.

Coldness swept over Wes. He opened his eyes to a shattered mirror hanging over torn wallpaper. Accusing faces in mildew stains seemed to jump out at him. He turned. The candles were gone, wardrobe, bed, even the ceiling. The room was decrepit.

Wes looked up at the lavender sky. Dawn was coming. He walked over to where the bed had been and squatted. Next to a pile of bones lay a single green hair.

Crying, Wes pocketed it and ran.

Al came round to a punchy egg smell mixed with hay. He was in some sort of cellar and his left leg wasn't right. It took an extravagant turn at the knee, pointing off in a new and exciting angle. Crying, he forced himself onto his elbows.

So Terry, enjoy the trip? Grallabelle was fuckin kick-ass, right? Yeah, scary shit there. How bout you Wes? You had a hoot? Well, I'm glad. Thought you'd dig it. Good times.

Fuck you, mind, Al told himself. *Broken leg, bleeding head, soon be dead, great,* he thought, looking around his tomb. Blackness, except the square hole he'd fallen through.

'Whoopsy daisy,' a drawling voice said.

Al yelled with surprise, his eyes straining to see the tall shape standing in the darkness.

'Now, what'd a young man want ere?' it asked. Al remained silent.

'You know, you can tell where a body comes from by their eyes, on em, *in* em, light beyond the light. I see great sky-scratcher lights in yours, boy. Come from that new city over yonder, eh? Aye.'

The shape leaned forward into the light.

'Where would ya say *I* came from?' it asked.

Al looked into beady eyes as deep and empty as a well that dried up centuries ago. His eyes broke free like escaped convicts, looking down at withered drainpipe-thin legs the colour of rotten tangerines, then up at the potato-sack face and maniac grin.

'Who are you?' Al asked.

'You know. But tell me, who're *you*?' Chicken Man returned, ending all questions.

He went for Al, clucking and tearing. Al went kicking and screaming.

Trees whirled by Wes, their wooden arms reaching, scratching. He ran by the signpost, the miserable bagpipe sound to his left, then behind, fading like a waking dream.

The swimmy-green swamp gas hovered in front, splitting off in eight separate directions. A signpost of sorts – one that leads to places where the town slogan is "Why".

The steady thump of his shoes lulled him to an open-eyed half-sleep.

He turned at the sound of voices. To his right sat a circle of cross-legged children having a three a.m. campfire sing-song. They looked over with featureless faces the colour of old scar tissue, laughed hollowly, then returned to their song.

Wes joined in as he sprinted by.

Thirteen

Ring a ring o' roses a pocket full of poses, A-tishoo! A-tishoo!
Wes fell down.

Sunlight penetrated through his eyelids casting the world pink. He sat up, peeling his stiff body off the baking road. *Road.* He looked down at his scratched hands, concentrating on not thinking. He waited. A car would come, take him home.

He heard it before he saw it, coughing and spurting like a heavy smoker. Even in his present mental state, he was still stunned at what he saw. A black 1920's Model-T pulled into view. *Looks sorta like Laurel & Hardy's rustbucket,* Wes thought.

He poked out his thumb. The car slowed in fits and jerks. A sun-wrinkled bearded face poked out the window, giving Wes the once-over with a crooked, wry smile. The man was dressed in a leaf-green suit, the type a farmer wears to market.

'Say! Look worse for wear boy, been wrestling with thornbushes?' the man asked.

'Something like that... thanks for stopping man... erm, mister,' Wes said.

'Aye, look a merry old state! Hop in, lad.'

Wes crawled in the passenger side with a sigh, body aching, mind reeling. The car coughed and pulled away. The man looked over and winked, licking the tip of his nose with his tongue.

Whafuck? Wes thought. The silence dragged uncomfortably. Wes forced some small talk.

'Nice car. Real antique, where'd you get it?'

'Antique, he says! Traded in me bike for this machine. Aye I did!' he shouted indignantly as if Wes had disagreed.

'Gets me around lickety-pip!' he finished, minutes later.

The man spat a huge, amber gob in his right palm and offered it.

'Wil, pleasemeetcha,' the man said.

Wes stared at the dripping palm, hoping he would retract the handshake. He didn't.

'Wes,' he said, feeling slimy phlegm grease the introduction.

'Where you headed, Wes? Me, I'm away to Bryemurgh. Dwarf there that does things you couldn't imagine if you grease her palm just right.'

Shock ran through Wes like a wrist-thick catheter insertion.

He grabbed for the door handle but felt only smooth panelling. Yelling, he drove both elbows into the window and both feet into the windscreen. Nothing so much as cracked.

Wil ignored this behaviour as if it were nothing more than thumb twiddling.

The car swerved left into the woods.

'You'll enjoy Bryemurgh, oh will you ever! Toffee Tortoises, many Chip-Chop rides as ya please, Sarsaparilla Fuck-Hermits and all the bagpipes your ears can drink, m'boy. Be there soon, Wes,' Wil said, reaching over and pinching his cheek.

Conscious thought grew lost in the mad funhouse world Wil spoke of. His raspy voice bringing to life the Bryemurgh Towne Fair, where men and women threw blunt knifes at passing clouds, sang nursery rhymes of Limbless Lenny, lashed their pale skin with hickory sticks and posted blank postcards to dead siblings.

The old car bounced over bumpy soil, trees rushed by in a sickening blur as they drove in large circles. But they would be there soon. Wes closed his eyes and listened to Wil, losing himself in a cul-de-sac of sanity with each passing word.

They would be there soon and they'd have a stay.

Thirteen

IN YOUR GROCER'S FREEZER
ROGER DALE TREXLER

The daily regulars had dwindled away to nothing since the big Super Food Giant had come in on Borton Street. The customers that Jose Fernandez had served with a smile and a promise that he had "the best selection of meats in town" were discovering that his boast was far from the truth. Jose had a wide selection of meat, to be sure, but the low prices of the food chain enabled them to buy ten times the variety, and maintain lower cost. In short, they were cutting Jose's throat with a dull knife, making the agony linger.

What can I do? he asked himself. The Gringos, they don't know loyalty. It wasn't that way back in Mexico. In Mexico, people understood the importance of the services a shopkeeper offered. They took advantage of them. They were faithful. He shook his head as he walked to the door. There, if he peered to his left far enough, he could make out the sign that read: SUPER FOOD GIANTS PLUS! WE WILL NOT BE UNDERSOLD! His days as a businessman were numbered. He was being swallowed up by the system, spat out by corporate conglomerates that dealt more with ledgers than people.

What happened to the personal touch? he asked himself as he locked the door after his worse day in years. What happened to service with a smile? Once again, he shook his head and went back to the cash register to count out what little cash he had taken in for a deposit. At this rate, the creditors that had been hounding him gently for years would soon become fiercer. He only hoped he could bring himself out of this emotional slump before the decline in sales reached its apogee. He hoped. But he doubted it would come.

The next week showed a more drastic change than he was accustomed to. Before, he had a customer or two (usually more) in the store at all times. Now, he was lucky to have one every thirty minutes. It was enough to drive a man insane, and Jose wanted nothing more than to wrap his hands around the owner of the Super Food Giants and squeeze ever so gently. He wanted to make the man suffer as he had; Suffer the humiliation of business dropping off to nothing. The agony of trying to make it work when it couldn't possibly work. The pain of knowing that he was a failure. For that week, Jose's wife, Maria, had notice a considerable change in her husband. He was more eager to start a fight and, although he never stuck her, she could tell that he'd wanted to. Several times. His sleep was in short cycles, up three hours, sleep three hours. He was a man on the edge, and she knew that he would slip over the side without her knowledge. That frightened her, but not Jose. He was a warm, loving husband; he would do nothing to harm her. Or so she thought.

Ten days had slipped by. Business was now nothing more than a trickle; people needing this or that, not wanting to transgress the city block to the Super Food Giants to save ten cents. Those people, the ones who still made his livelihood, Jose despised. But he tolerated them. It wasn't until the twelfth night, when Jose was too exhausted from worry to carry it farther, he fell into a fitful sleep. It was no surprise that, when the brilliant lights flooded in through the bedroom window, he thought he was still in a dream. The glow was sort of like neon, but not exactly. There was a warmth, a heat to it. Also, there was a sentience within the light.

And that mind was trying to make contact with him.

Jose stood there, frozen in his spot. The light faded after awhile, and it was then that he saw the spaceship. Even though he had never seen such a vehicle before, he could tell that it had been damaged somehow. The whole front quarter of the craft was ripped open and charred. His wife walked up on him and said, "What in the....?" Jose jumped. He had not heard her. He turned and saw the

Thirteen

panic in her eyes. They lived well outside of the city on a modest ten acres of land. The nearest house was four acres away, and screaming would not bring help. The ship's glow faded. "I'm going to get the gun," Jose told his wife in a shaky voice. He stepped back inside the house, and she followed him. He went to the gun cabinet that held his Remington 12-guage shotgun and .30-. 30 rifle and opened it. He took out the 12-guage, thinking to himself that it would have a wider spread. He didn't know what to expect out there, but he wanted to take as many of them out with one shot as he could. He took a handful of shell and put them in his pocket. Then, he reached back in and took out another, handing them to his wife. When they came back to the door, the alien spacecraft was silent.

No noise whatsoever came from the vehicle. Reluctantly, Jose walked toward the spacecraft. He wasn't an idiot; he'd had plenty of time recently to read through those tabloids that decorated his counter. Aliens in those magazines weren't friendly; they wanted nothing more that to stick needles in his brain and impregnate his woman. He would not allow such a thing to happen. Not as long as he had a gun and his senses about him. He stepped closer to the spacecraft. Nothing came to greet or assault him. He moved in closer yet. He was finally able to reach out and touch the ship's hull. It was still warm from entering the planet's atmosphere. Jose glanced back at his wife. She was standing in the doorway, her hand in her mouth, biting a finger in nervousness. He turned and stepped inside the spaceship. And his life would never be the same again.

Six months later, Jose's business had quadrupled what it had been. What it had been before the Super Food Giant went in on Borton Street, that is. He had to hire on extra help to fight the increased workload, but that was nothing that he could not handle. "Ms. Griffith," he said with a smile as the old woman walked up to the counter. "How are you today?"

"Okay, I guess," Ms. Griffith replied. "My intestines and bowels, they've been bothering me lately."

"Well," he said with absolute sincerity, "that's too bad, have you tried our specially cured meat? It's good for what ails you."

"Ain't no meat gonna loosen by bowels," she replied, sarcastically.

"Pardon me," a voice from nearby interrupted. "But, you should really try the ribs. They helped me."

"Unsolicited praise," the old woman said sarcastically. "It's enough to make you sick."

"Wait a minute, wait a minute," Jose said as he walked around the counter.

"What you want me for, young man?" He walked back toward the rear of the store. Reluctantly, the old woman and the girl followed. "The proof is in the pudding," he said as he walked. "And, just for that reason, I've set up a taste test booth in the rear." The taste test booth, as he called it, was nothing more than a table with a few plates of select meats before it. Another young woman sat in a chair behind the table. She stood when she saw them approach.

"Would you like to sample our specialty meats?" the girl asked the old woman nervously. She failed to see the boss coming; she had been daydreaming.

"Ms. Griffith would like to sample this meat," he told the girl.

"Oh," the young girl replied. She bent and picked up a slice of meat on a toothpick, offered it. Ms. Griffith looked warily at them.

"This ain't dog meat, is it?"

"No, Ms. Griffith," Jose replied with a smile and a laugh. "No, it's not."

Slowly, the old woman lifted the piece of meat to her lips and tasted it with her tongue. "Ummmmm," she said, creasing her brow. Then, she popped the entire chunk into her mouth, groaning with pleasure as she chewed. The flavour was mildly salty, but not salty. There really wasn't a comparison for it. It was the seasoning, she reckoned in her old-fashioned mind. The curing. The meat was so tender and delicious that it melted in her mouth. She grabbed up another sample almost before the first was ingested.

"This is delicious!" she said with her mouth full of meat.

"Then you're sold?" he asked.

"Yes."

Jose smiled. "How much would you like?"

"Ten pounds," she replied. "No, twenty." She looked wild eyed and delighted with herself. "Hell, make it a hundred pounds." Jose nodded.

"I'm sorry, Ms. Griffith, but I can't part with that much meat for less than, say, one thousand dollars."

"One thousand dollars!"

He shook his head. "That's right." He turned and looked away. "You see, the meat you've tasted is imported. It's not from this country. It's a delicacy in other parts of the, um, world, but it can not be imported by conventional means."

"Why," the old woman snapped. "Is it diseased?"

"On the contrary," Jose replied. "It's the cleanest, freshest meat you're likely to find this side of... well, Mars!"

"What?"

"Let me explain," he said. "This meat does not come from this country. It's not beef, poultry, pork or whatever." He smiled. "You might say that it's out-of-this-world!" The conversation continued in that vein. Yes, the old woman wanted some of the delicious meat. No, she didn't care if it was kangaroo meat. She didn't care if it was sea turtle - she loved it and she had to have it. Now! She wrote out a check - cleared by Jose through the bank, of course - and Jose had his delivery boy haul the meat to her house.

"Hmmmm," he sighed. "Another satisfied customer." After Ms. Griffith left, Jose walked back into the freezer with his electric knife. He chose one of the two dozen aliens and put the knife to a tentacle, started carving. "It's a shame you guys can't understand English," he told one of the cadavers. "All a guy's gotta do is stand in front of that view screen on your ship and smile, and another ship comes." He sliced off the snout, the rich meat falling limply into his hand. "And it's doubtful you ever heard of free enterprise," he said with a smile.

APPENDIX
SARA JOAN BERNIKER

"It's gotta come out, okay? I can't just leave you like this."

The girl was past the point of responding. Lying on her back, blouse hiked up over her breasts, she clutched at her stomach.

"It's gotta come out," Jake said again, as if to reassure himself.

He stood up and steadied himself against the grungy wall, half-wishing he'd done ecstasy and speed like everyone else at this crazy party. If he had, then the girl on the floor wouldn't seem so important. Better to be spinning on the dance floor then to be in the grips of this grinding terror that told him he would fuck up, and fuck up bad.

So that he wouldn't have to look at the sick girl, Jake stared at the people who had brought her here. He'd seen them around campus and on the school bus during the trek up to Deep River, but didn't know their names. Didn't know the sick girl's name either, but that didn't change anything. Her appendix was swollen and about to burst. Either it came out, or she died. There was no time to get a real doctor.

Outside the bathroom, the party pulsed on: music and sex screams and laughter and people kicking the shit out of each other. Everyone was so messed up. Hardly any of them had noticed the sick girl crouched and heaving among the blissed-out throng on the dance floor. If that girl hadn't seen her...

He gave himself a shake, trying to focus. "What's your name?" he asked the redhead in the black dress who'd found the girl.

"Annie."

Jake glared at the two guys in baggy pants and tight t-shirts who were inching towards the door. "Where the hell do you think you're going?"

"Bad scene in here, m'man," the blonde said. Sweat streamed down his face, and the pouches under his eyes made him look like an old man--speed would do that to you. Track marks ran up and down his arms like battle scars.

"There's nothing we can do. You're the doctor," the other one said, slipping out of the bathroom in a wave of patchouli and B.O.

"Yeah, Doc. You fix her," the blonde added, and then he was gone, too.

Doc. Yeah, right.

Jake could tell himself that this was an easy operation, one he'd read about in textbooks and seen performed on the Discovery Channel, but that didn't make him any more competent. He was pre-med, for chrissakes. That was about as close to being a real doctor as a farmer was to being a veterinarian. Less. At least the guy in rubber boots, overalls, and a John Deere cap had the practical experience that came from being around animals.

He was dead.

No, Jake corrected himself, he'd live. It was the girl trembling on the dirty tile beside the bathtub who was in trouble.

Annie pressed herself against the bathroom door and fumbled with the knob.

"You her friend?" he asked to keep her from bolting. "Know anything about her?"

"No, I don't even go to Brandeis. I came up from Boston with some girls I know from high school. Y'know, thought we'd go to the mega-rave, see what it was all about. It's pretty lame, though, just a bunch of freaked-out assholes. I could have seen that in the city."

Jake nodded, almost smiled. "Yeah, take people out of their normal lives and they think it's so fucking special. Like being out here in the middle of nowhere is really any different from dorm parties or bar crawls." He heard what he was saying and winced. What was he doing making like this was some normal evening that might end with getting laid?

The girl on the floor began to convulse, her feet tattooing a panicked rhythm against the tile. After a few terrible seconds, she grew very still, her face white and waxy.

"Do you know anything about medicine?" he asked Annie. "CPR, first-aid? Anything?"

"No," she whispered, her dark eyes not straying from the sick girl. "I'm an English Lit major. I don't know shit."

"You need to go find me something I can cut her with," Jake said. "I have to take it out before it bursts."

"Like what?"

"I dunno. Something sharp. Look around. Ask people." Jake knew that most of the partygoers were beyond simple conversation, but maybe Annie could rifle through their purses and knapsacks.

She nodded and ran out the door. He wasn't so sure that she'd be coming back.

Jake knew that he should comfort the sick girl - he could practice his bedside manner, if nothing else - but he didn't want to touch her again. It had been bad enough to smell the stink of cigarettes and perfume and rot that had risen from her lips, like the gases of a corpse, when he'd first pressed his fingers against her hot, swollen abdomen.

The blonde had called him Doc, but it wasn't true. An hour ago, busy having a bad time, Jake had been pointed out to Annie and the two slackers carrying the sick girl by a guy he knew vaguely from Psych 101. "Talk to him. He's a doctor," the guy had yelled before stepping back onto the dance floor.

It was just Jake's luck to be at a party populated solely by English Lit, Cultural Studies, and History majors. Not a science student among them; even the drug dealers were studying Proust.

The door banged open and Jake's heart leapt with a mixture of trepidation and dismay. "That was so fast," he said, expecting Annie.

A couple tangled up in an embrace pushed their way into the tiny bathroom.

"Want you so bad, baby," the girl said, thrusting her hand into the waistband of her skirt and pulling it partway down to reveal pale belly and pink underwear.

"Me, too," the guy replied. He was grinning like a fool.

Jake watched them for a scant second, then lunged at the door. "Get out!" he screamed. "Get a room!"

"Screw you," the girl said, leading her guy back out into the smoky fray.

When the door swung open again, a moment later, Jake wished he had something to throw at them. Maybe a hose so he could spray the horny couple like the rutting dogs they were. "I told you to get out - "

"I found it!" Annie's eyes were shining, and she no longer looked so frightened. Holding her hands behind her back, she said, "Guess what it is."

"I don't have time for this. Give it over."

"C'mon, guess!"

With dull horror, Jake realized that this girl, in her short black dress, sensible heels, and pearl earrings, was very, very drunk. "Okay, I'll guess. A knife?"

"Nope. Try again."

On the floor, the sick girl moaned softly, as if she knew that she was doomed. Jake saw a dusty boot print on the sleeve of her blouse, and his heart clenched with pity: someone had stepped on her, out there on the dance floor.

"Guess, asshole!" Annie said.

"A scalpel?" Like he'd ever be so lucky.

"That's the same as a knife. That guess doesn't count. You're never gonna get it!"

Thirteen

"Then just give it to me. Please!"

"Fine. You're no fucking fun." She held out her tanned arm, dangling something small and shiny between her thumb and forefinger.

Jake stared at the razor blade feeling as if he'd been granted a reprieve. "Hey, that's not bad," he whispered.

"Yeah, this chick was cutting up lines on the coffee table. Should have seen the look on her face when I snatched it. Bitch almost cried."

"Okay. Hand it over."

Almost gently, she placed a warm hand on his chest and pushed hard, knocking him against the cracked sink. Straddling the sick girl, Annie said, "I'm gonna try to fix her. I'm gonna play doctor. Bet I'll be good at it. I used to like to cut things. Myself mostly. Could use that kind of release now, that's for sure. I feel so damned crawly. Like my insides want to become outsides."

What the hell was this chick on?

Jake crossed the bathroom in two steps and crouched beside her. "You don't know what you're doing," he said. "Give it to me."

"Okay, Doc. Here you go." She made as if to hand it over, then slashed hard with the razor, opening up an eight-inch gash just below the sick girl's small freckled breasts.

"So much blood," Annie murmured, tracing her finger along the gaping wound. She tossed the razor at Jake and stood up. "It's your mess now."

"Aren't you going to help me?" he asked, pulling his shirt over his head and using it to staunch the blood. "Please, Annie!"

"I'm sick of this crazy buzz-kill shit," she said, her voice so flat that Jake wanted to scream. "I'm gonna go dance." She paused at the door and smiled. "Don't worry so much. If you fuck up, you can always slit your wrists."

But Jake wasn't listening to her anymore. He was bent over the sick girl, who no longer even trembled, trying to remember just where exactly the appendix was located. Every single thing he'd ever learned in school was gone. He was lost.

Gingerly touching her swollen belly, Jake found the spot that seemed the hardest and the hottest. The first incision was always the most difficult, one of his professors had liked to say. Sweating, maybe crying, the music of the party worming into his skull and pushing out all coherent thought, Jake raised the bloody blade and brought it down in a smooth, glittering arc.

451208: A MAN LIKE ANY OTHER
LEE BETTERIDGE

I was sat at the back of the cool church; the area where, during a funeral at least, the people gather who feel that maybe they don't belong. I shared a pew with an elderly gentleman whose neck was red and ruddy and whose knees crackled when he knelt to pray. I didn't pray. I'd have felt like a hypocrite if I had, so I just gazed down at my hands, one gloved and one not. The old man sat next to me, close enough to touch with an outstretched hand, but I don't think he even noticed I was there.

The funeral was for a man who had died after fighting cancer for over sixteen years. His death, however, was not due to the cancerous cells eating away at his body, but more to do with the piece of cheese-on-toast he'd been eating in his office when he choked to death. His name was Larry Joseph Trevelyan and he had been fifty-seven years old. To me, however, he was 451208. That was his number.

During the funeral I learned a lot about the man I knew as a number. I learned he was married and had been for twenty-seven years and that his wife was called Pearl. In those twenty-seven years he had fathered three children, two girls and a boy, called Amy, Karen and Adrian. I already knew he worked as an Estate Agent as I'd been in his place of work, but the fact that he bought and renovated old, classic cars in his spare time was new to me. And he preferred to go by 'Joe' and not Larry or Joseph. The priest didn't mention cheese-on-toast once, however.

Unfortunately I hadn't seen the person at the funeral whom I'd hoped to meet, and I was disappointed about that, but had I not come and sat at the back of the church with a draught tickling my neck like the hand of a ghoul, I would never have known any of this. And as 451208 – Mr. 'Joe' Trevelyan – was carried past me and the other mourners by the pallbearers and followed by his distraught, weeping family, I realized that I was glad I'd come to my first funeral.

The church was small and humble, sat among chestnut trees and surrounded by the markers of the dead. Hundreds of graves and hundreds of people. Hundreds of numbers. The day outside was bright and fresh with a chill that only surfaced when the wind blew. I found a wooden bench away from the mourners gathered to watch 451208 lowered into the ground. I sat, pulling the tails of my coat up over my thighs and resting my hands on them.

Across the churchyard I could hear the vague mumblings of the priest and the wet sobs of the widow as the prayers were read out. I'd never been to a funeral before so this I can only presume, but I'd watched enough TV to make an educated guess. From where I sat, I couldn't quite make out the mound of freshly dug earth that would inevitably be there, no doubt thoughtfully covered with a sheet of green material.

A sound to my right caused me to turn in that direction and I watched as a pretty-faced woman walked towards me. This was her, the only reason I'd come to this funeral. The woman whom I'd come to try and get a glimpse of, I was sure of it. I'd only seen her once, in 451208's office, in a photograph on his desk, but I was sure this was her.

She had the most striking eyes I'd ever seen: a pale, steely blue that seemed to radiate light somehow. Her hair was different from the photograph. It was still a golden blonde but where it had been long and wavy was now short and almost boyish. Not manly though, still feminine, just boyish. I thought perhaps it was a style that was a little young for her as she was probably in her early forties, but who am I to say. I'm no authority on style of any kind; I just learn what I have

Thirteen

from the TV. She didn't speak or nod or do anything to acknowledge me but sat delicately on the bench where I sat and gazed into the distance. She probably hadn't even noticed me, like the elderly man in church. People rarely notice I'm there.

As the lady watched the funeral service winding to an end, I watched the profile of her face. She had what I think are called 'crow's feet' or 'laughter lines' at the corner of her eye and I believed that when she laughed, as in the photograph she had been on the verge of, her face would light up with the most sheer, brilliant beauty anyone had ever seen. Now, however, there was no laughter or happiness of any kind in the lines of her face. I watched as tears ran down her cheek.

"Did you know him?" I asked, and she physically jumped, spinning her head and clapping a hand to her mouth.

"Ooh," she said. "You made me jump. I didn't see you there."

"Sorry," I said.

I waited for her to answer my question, leaving it her decision if the conversation was to go any further.

After what was surely a full minute she answered, "Yes, I knew him.

This was obvious to me as I'd seen her picture in the man's office, but I had been somewhat confused by her not being in the church during the service and the fact that she wasn't with the others now, around the grave. I'd presumed she was his wife. Widow, now, I suppose, but I was wrong.

"I was his lover," she said and looked at me with sad eyes, as if looking for judgment. I gave none either way. "I know that sounds sordid and cliché," she said. "But it was nothing like that. I loved Joe with all my heart and now...now..."

She sobbed for a while and I turned away and watched the mourners. I could hear a faint mechanical buzz coming from that direction and supposed it was the coffin being lowered into the ground.

"Did *you* know him?" she asked after regaining control of herself again.

"Not really," I said, without elaborating.

"Are you with the funeral directors?" she asked.

"No, why do you ask?" I said, and she nodded to my clothes. My long black coat covered black trousers, black shirt and black tie.

I smiled, "I always wear black. Old habits die hard I'm afraid."

She took that as answer enough, then introduced herself.

"My name is Caroline December, by the way."

She held out a hand and although I was reluctant to take it, I gripped it softly with my gloved right hand and shook it.

"Vaughn."

She said, "Vaughn...?" leaving a space for me to fill in my surname.

"Vaughn's enough," I said, and released her from my grip.

"Why do you wear just the one?" she asked, meaning my leather glove.

I didn't really know what to say, but I quickly came up with, "I have a skin condition."

We both looked away towards the priest and the others and it looked as though they were taking it in turns to drop handfuls of dirt into the grave, and below such a bright blue sky the scene seemed extremely sad.

"Death is such a waste," said Caroline December. "Don't you think?"

I was quiet for a second, and then answered, "Sometimes."

"Well in this case it most definitely was. Poor Joe never hurt a fly and he's had a goddamned dog's life." She looked at me with those steely blue eyes brimming with tears. "Vaughn, he'd just got the all-clear from the cancer. He was just about to start living again. It's just such a damned waste."

I said, "Death can be a lot of things: a curse, a blessing, sometimes even a

Thirteen

travesty, and yes, even a waste, but none of that matters. It's the life that went beforehand that is of consequence. And surely that wasn't a waste."

She thought about this, and then said, "You speak a lot of sense for someone of your age."

"I'm older than I look," I said. "But I have seen enough of the world to make a few judgments. I would very much like to share some more with you, if you were interested."

Caroline December looked at me with a half-smile on her mouth and a surprised look in her eyes. The thought of a woman in her early forties going out in public with a man who appeared to be barely past twenty was obviously amusing to her.

"What?" she asked. "Like a meal together or something?"

"Yes," I said. "Or coffee." This was an expression I'd picked up from the TV.

I was getting ready to sound not-bothered after she turned me down when she surprised me by saying yes.

"OK Vaughn," she said. "I like talking to you and although this is a bit strange for me, talking will no doubt do me good." We arranged to meet at a coffee shop in about an hour's time, giving us both time to get changed.

"You can tell me more of what you think about death," she said as she stood. "In all its guises."

The people around the graveside were dispersing now and I figured the funeral was over. Everyone would be going somewhere for either tea and sandwiches or beer and sandwiches. I, however, would have to go back home and see if I had any emails.

"See you later Caroline," I said as I watched my only reason for coming to this funeral walk away.

As I walked home through the bright, crisp afternoon with my hands clasped behind my back, I watched the people I passed with great interest. They were all just going about their business - be that nipping to the shop, picking children up from school, having a quick smoke before the boss came back to the office – and I found myself thinking that although everyone is different, everyone is also very much the same. The funeral I was walking home from could have been any one of these people's goodbye to the world. 451208 was just a man like any other, just going about his daily business when the cold hand of Death crept up on him. That could have been anybody. Any one of these people, any one of these numbers.

I live in a flat above a newsagent called Goodall's on the High Street. Mrs. Goodall, the owner, is a nice old lady who smokes about eighty cigarettes a day and coughs up huge amounts of phlegm. Her son Desmond sometimes helps her out in the shop but he is fat and lazy and I often help her to lift heavy boxes of sweets and bundles of papers if she needs me to. I don't mind because Mrs. Goodall is very nice and pleasant with me, unlike Desmond who calls me things like 'Lurch' and 'Creeping Jesus' when he thinks I can't hear him.

When I got home I went into the shop first and bought a bag of chocolate-covered raisins. Desmond wasn't about so I asked if Mrs. Goodall needed a hand with anything. In between dry coughs she said she didn't, so I went round the back and up the stairs to my flat.

As I shut the door the alarm started to make its monotonous err-err-err noise and I swiftly stepped over to the keypad and typed in the PIN number to shut it up. I looked around the room, my living room and revelled in its bleakness. White walls, white-washed floorboards, one white leather armchair and a black TV set. I have no pictures, artwork or ornaments as I deem such items to be for sentimental people who believe in happiness ever after, life after death and fat-

Thirteen

free diets.

I crossed the room and entered the kitchen where I opened the refrigerator and grabbed a can of Coca Cola. Popping it open and taking a long prickly slurp I surveyed the room and was pleased to see that I hadn't left any dirty crockery in the sink. I hate coming into a dirty kitchen; it makes me feel unkempt and idle.

In the corner of the small kitchen is a sickly green drop-leaf table that I have never once sat at to eat. In my view, that is what armchairs are placed in front of TVs for. I do sit at this table at other times though, and this was one of those occasions. I sat, flipped open my laptop computer that had been laying there like a slab of grey slate and switched the power on. As the thing booted up I ate a handful of chocolate-covered raisins from the bag in my pocket and washed them down with cola. I never fail to feel content as I feel large amounts of sugar coursing through my body. It's a wonder I don't look like a walrus.

Once the life had beeped into my laptop I used my left index finger to take the pointer to my email Inbox and opened it up. I had three unread messages. All three had Vaughn written in the To column but nothing in the From column. That was nothing unusual. I opened the first message and was confronted by a window with a seven-digit number:

1215225

and nothing else. Just stark black figures on a stark white background. I opened the other two messages in turn and they also contained a number each; 165135 and 12965. I left the Inbox open and entered a database I have saved to the hard-drive of my computer.

Once this file was open I clicked the Search icon and typed in the first number I'd been emailed. I could have scrolled through the fields of the database manually as it is all in numerical order, but there are so many individual entries that it would take ages, especially with three to find.

The laptop found the name that referred to the number 1215225 and I wrote it down on a Post-it along with the address. I did the same with the second number, and jotted down the name and address I was given. The third number, 12965, came up with something that couldn't be right. I retyped the digits into the space in the Search window and it came up with the same result. The address I was given was my own, and the name was Elisa Jane Goodall.

"No!" I growled, surprised by my own anger. I hit the table with my gloved fist and the can of cola fell to the floor, its sugar-laden nectar glugging onto the floor.

"Not Mrs. Goodall," I said to the empty room, feeling the despair and futility that is inflicted on thousands of people every day. "I like Mrs. Goodall."

My laptop beeped and the icon popped onto my screen that meant I had a new email message. It was to Vaughn, with the From column left blank.

I opened the message and this is what it read.

Do your job and don't get emotional.

In frustration I reached over and roughly clicked off the laptop without shutting it down first, realizing this was a pretty dismal attempt at rebellion and not caring.

I stood and strode through the living room, kicking the drinks can as I went and spraying my legs and the skirting board with cola. In my bedroom I looked at myself in the mirror and glared at my reflection. My brown eyes seemed to enrage me and my jet black hair felt like an abomination; a falsity somehow. I didn't feel that I should be allowed to be human. Then I thought of the last email I'd received and recalled what I'd said to Caroline December about death being not about actual death, but about the life that went before. I had to think of Mrs. Goodall not as a person, but as a number.

To prison wardens people are just numbers, as they are with bank managers, telephone sales companies and the National Insurance people. It is

Thirteen

the same for me. People are represented by long strings of digits that have no connection with the individual to whom they belong, other than the fact that they have been allocated to them. I see the faces and learn there names, but only at the very end. During their association with this world and my self, they are but another number in the list. All except Mrs. Goodall, who had always been a good friend to me. But life had to go on, and there had to be something at the end.

I left my flat without clearing the mess up in the kitchen. I would be back in a few minutes, but I had to do what I was about to do immediately, or else I might lose my nerve, and goodness knows what trouble that would cause.

As I walked in through the shop door someone rushed outside right past me, without noticing me. People rarely notice me. Inside the shop was a scene that disturbed me greatly. Several glass jars of instant coffee had been smashed on the floor and the fragrant brown granules surrounded two figures. One was Mrs. Goodall, and she was lying on the ground, flat on her back, while the other person, Stan Baxter from two doors down, was performing mouth-to-mouth resuscitation and cardiac massage. Mrs. Goodall's skin looked waxy and pale, and it was obvious to me that all those years of abusing her lungs with cigarettes had finally paid its toll, but I knew she wasn't dead yet.

For a few moments I watched as Stan Baxter pumped away at the old lady's thin chest and blew his life's breath into her lungs. I stood next to Mrs. Goodall's head and looked down at her. Stan Baxter didn't see me there. Even when he stood, whispered under his breath "Where's that bastard ambulance at?" and ran from the shop, no doubt to locate the person meant to be calling 999, he wasn't aware of me there, between Mrs. Goodall and the magazine shelves.

Alone in the shop now, I crouched next to the vulnerable old lady whom I knew more than anyone in the world, the lady who'd smoked so many cigarettes for so long that two fingers on both hands were yellow. I smiled down at her and pulled the glove off my right hand. The sight of my withered and emaciated appendage struck me as grotesque, as it always has and in all probability always will. The shrivelled skin barely wrapping the jutting knuckles and bone, the hand is not quite skeletal but it is only a layer of grey, papery skin away from it.

I lay my hand on the Mrs. Goodall's soft cheek and shivered as the raw, icy power buzzed in my hand, causing the hair on my neck to stand up and a faint blue glow to illuminate my knuckles.

I said, "I hereby give you leave of this world and consent to enter the next."

The glow faded and I covered my wasted hand with the glove once again. Mrs. Goodall, or number 12965, was dead.

I left the shop and heard the sound of an ambulance's siren as I entered my flat. I had to get changed so that I could go and meet Caroline December. Plus I had two more visits to make; one for each of my emails.

I couldn't wait to talk with Caroline and feel her steely blue eyes on me. I don't know why, and I don't know what the feeling is when I think of her, but I know I like it. I don't think its love, or even lust for that matter. Maybe the feeling is just... happiness. I'd settle for that.

And what was it she'd said we could talk about. She said I could tell her more of what I think about death.

Well, the thing is, I don't think, I know. Everything there is to know about Death. His name is Vaughn and he lives above the newsagent. Goodalls. He likes watching TV and eating sweets and drinking sugary drinks. That's Death here, anyway, in this town. In the town just north of here he's a man named Lawrence who works for a bank. South of here, Death is an old woman called Annie who pushes all her belongings round in an old Silvercross pram.

But that isn't what poor Caroline wants to know, I'm sure. She has just lost a loved one and wants to know all the enlightening stuff, all the deep, meaningful

Thirteen

things that don't really exist.

What do I think about Death?

I think it all comes down to this. Whoever you are and wherever you might be, when your number's up, it's up, and it's as simple and as frightening as that. There's nothing you can do about it and there's certainly nothing I can do. My orders come from much higher up. And when your number comes out of the hat, or the Inbox, and you choke on your cheese-on-toast or your heart fails or a piano falls on your head, it is inevitable that one of my kind will be there. Nobody will see us; people rarely do, but one of us will be there to lend you a hand into the next world. A cold, wasted hand.

DEATH TO THE SWITCHBLADE QUEEN
JAMES BENNETT

The day Margaret Fellows tore off her face was one of those days when anything can happen. At least, that's what the other students said when they talked about it later. There'd been an atmosphere to the preceding week before the accident. It had been prom week. There was magic in the air.

Ever since she'd won the '58 beauty pageant at Arrowsbrook High, Illinois, the female members of the Orchard gang had found her unbearable. She'd always been slightly unbearable, of course – slim, attractive, blonde, well spoken, rich – but for some reason, her airs and graces had been easier to ignore before. Maggie's shyness and politeness may have won over the judges, but not her rivals.

Under the autumnal sun, jealousy congealed in the other girls' teenage hearts like rotting fruit on a compost heap.

"Just look at her," Cynthia Orchards said to her female colleagues as they waited for art class on the school steps. "Butter wouldn't melt. She walks around like she owns the damn school."

"Stuck up bitch," Rhonda Williams agreed, then popped her gum bubble sharply, leaning forward as the pigtailed object of their disdain passed. The other girls laughed as Maggie Fellows jumped at the sound, and hurried off towards the double doors with her books clasped firmly to the front of her pink cardigan.

"Apparently, Bobby Rose has asked her out on a date," Poppy Martins volunteered nervously (she was still a first year initiate of the Orchard Gang). "I saw them talking in the gym together on Monday..."

"No fucking *way*!" Cynthia roared, shaking her dark tresses in irritation. She (like several other girls in their small society) had shared more than a fumble with Bobby Rose in the Wickling Woods the previous summer break. The brief spell had been broken later, however, leaving Bobby free to continue his adventures into girl-land, and leaving Cynthia with a sore pussy and a ten-foot high grudge.

A grudge not assisted by the fact she'd lost the Arrowsbrook beauty crown to a girl she couldn't stand.

"It's true," Poppy insisted, glad of the way Cynthia now noticed her over the other gathered girls, her dark eyes narrowing into slits of interest. "Bobby told me so. Bobby's taking her to the Washington Empire!"

"It's only because she's the queen this year," Rhonda chipped in, chewing loudly. "Bobby always dates the queens. It's, like, tradition or something."

Cynthia pushed her ample breasts out at her gathered flock in a gesture of defiance.

"They won't make it to the prom," she told them grimly. "Come on girls, you know what to do..."

Bobby Rose picked Maggie up at six o'clock from her father's house on Lincoln Avenue. His red Cadillac seemed to dwarf the narrow road as she looked down at him from her bedroom window. She'd been getting ready, squeezing into a white blouse and pleated skirt, fastening a scarab broach to her woollen cardigan, which she'd thrown casually over her shoulders.

He beeped the horn, and she saw her father walking down the garden path to meet the youth in the leather jacket, who sat behind the wheel smoking a Lucky.

Her heart quailed.

Oh no.

Daddy wasn't going to be very polite. She could tell by the way he placed his heavy hands on his wide hips, and the way his head swept back and forth, taking

Thirteen

in the body of the Cadillac as if it were an enemy vessel.

She opened the window a crack to hear their conversation.

"Now look here son, I don't want no funny business," her dad was saying, speaking round his pipe as if addressing the troops. "Maggie's only sixteen, and I want her back home by nine. Is that understood?"

"Yes, Mr. Fellows sir, loud and clear," Bobby Rose replied in his permanently laconic drawl. He held up his open palms. "She couldn't be in safer hands. None of that old voodoo."

"Don't know 'bout that," her father replied, but seemed satisfied momentarily, before he spoke up again with "Say, sonny, you gonna join the army...?"

Maggie took this as a sign to leave. She was out by the Cadillac before her mother had a chance to say goodbye, jumping into the passenger seat and blowing her father a dismissive kiss.

"Night, daddy," she cooed with a wave, leaving the bewildered man shaking his head in a cloud of tobacco and exhaust smoke as they roared off into the night.

The Washington Empire was the only movie house in the small farming town of Arrowsbrook, but it was majestic nevertheless. Rows of coloured light bulbs glittered in sequence around the hoardings announcing that week's show.

Tonight, Bobby Rose was taking Maggie to see '*We Were Teenage Aliens*'. Everyone at school had been talking about it, and the queue outside the Washington already proved it was going to be a big hit.

As Bobby and Maggie crossed the car park and joined the crowd, they became suddenly jostled by a group of girls. One of them shouldered Maggie so hard she nearly fell, and Bobby had to support her under one arm, his other hand lightly squeezing her breast as if this somehow helped.

"My broach!" Maggie cried, dismayed, her eyes searching on the ground frantically for the ornamental scarab her mother had given her last term. "I've lost my broach!"

"I'm sure that was Rhonda Williams," Bobby said thoughtlessly, looking back over his shoulder and ignoring her plight as she searched the ground desperately, then he turned back to Maggie and his eyes widened. "Damn, you're hurt!"

She looked down. The front of her cardigan had become ripped where the broach had come free, and a few spots of blood now speckled the pink wool where the pin had scratched her chest underneath. Leaning in for a closer inspection, (an excuse to take in the beauty queen's curving bosom) Bobby cooed gently and began to dab at the wound with a handkerchief.

She pushed his hand away.

"It's ok, Bobby," she told him. "It's just a graze."

He hid his disappointment behind a cocky grin.

"You sure are pretty Maggie," he said.

She blushed as he took her hand and led her across the road to join the queue outside the Washington picture house.

The movie was good. He bought her ice cream and kissed her in the Cadillac afterwards when he'd driven up to Blake's Point overlooking the lights of the small town. He'd tried to undo her bra, then to push up her skirt, despite her quiet refusals. He'd thumped the fur-covered driving wheel after his third attempt was met with another soft denial, and she'd become terrified of the bulge distending the front of his jeans.

He'd grinned when she started to cry and drove her home.

On Lincoln Avenue, he'd apologised.

"I'm a man, Maggie," he explained. "It's just the way things are done around

288

Thirteen

here."

"I'm sorry, Bobby. I wasn't brought up that way."

"No shit."

"You still gonna take me to the prom?" she asked hopefully.

"Yeah," he replied, then took in her pale oval face in the moonlight and sighed. "You're the beauty queen, ain't ya."

It wasn't a question. Bobby knew what belonged to him. The beauty queens always wanted him to be their beau. It was tradition; as unbreakable as law.

The next day at high school, Maggie lost her hairbrush after gym class.

She'd been looking for it in the locker room when Cynthia Orchards and two of her cronies pushed their way through the doors and leant against the wall, blowing gum and regarding her with utter contempt.

Maggie forgot the brush and tried to leave, but Cynthia blocked her way.

"Well, if it isn't Bobby Rose's new sweetheart," the dark eyed girl said in a sing song voice. "Treating you good is he, Miss Illinois? Taking you to the movies, an' all? Why, it'll be marriage next..."

"I don't want no trouble," Maggie answered with trembling lips, intimidated by this tall brunette with the obvious chip on her shoulder. The two other girls tittered cruelly.

"No trouble for the beauty queen," Cynthia said, and reached out to stroke Maggie's cheek. "It's such a shame to see tears in those pretty blue eyes. What would daddy think?"

"I... I know you wanted the crown," Maggie replied, trying to sound kind, "but sometimes, it's just down to luck, Cynthia. If it wasn't me, it would've been somebody else!"

"It should've been me!" Cynthia yelled, and punched the locker next to Maggie's head with a loud clang. "Not some stuck up little popinjay from the rich side of town! You just watch yourself with Bobby Rose, ya hear?"

"Especially if he wants to take you out to Wickling Woods!" one of the girls chimed in, and all three of them giggled horribly as Maggie fled.

Prom night was only three days away.

Maggie's mum had been busy preparing for her daughter's 'big night' as if American lives depended on its success. Maggie wondered if her father's military work had somehow filtered down into her mother's personality, making the prom into a battleground where only the best dressed could win. The stealing of the Arrowsbrook beauty crown was her mother's success too, that was painfully clear.

Maggie had caught her polishing the silver crown at the dining table after school, and she'd splashed out on a genuine Christian Dior nightgown for her daughter, much to Maggie's pleasure and her father's disapproval.

"You'll be like a princess," Mrs. Fellows announced happily when Maggie first tried the dress on, the blue satin clinging tenderly to her lithe young form.

"She's the damn queen," Mr. Fellows grunted from the living room armchair where he was watching the news. "Now all she needs is a king, instead of prince god darned charming in that red monstrosity..."

Their banter did nothing to upset Maggie's radiant mood. She was going on the arm of Bobby Rose, as queen of Arrowsbrook.

Cynthia and the Orchard gang could just go swing.

The night before, the Orchard gang all met up in the disused store shed on the edge of Wickling Woods. They weren't supposed to be there, as Poppy Martins reminded them as they all clambered out of Rhonda's convertible, but they ignored her whining like they always did.

Thirteen

Soon, the five of them were gathered around the small wood-burning stove in the middle of the littered floor, having jacked the lock again with a crowbar. Just like before. Just like when they'd come here to 'do' Bobby Rose.

The fire under the stove glowed scarlet, warming the girl's skin.

Rhonda lit fat wax candles and placed them around the large rickety chamber. They fluttered in the breeze coming through a section of collapsed roof. One of the candles she kept, and held over the fire, drawing it back to her bosom before it melted and dripped into the flame. She sat there, moulding the substance between her long fingers.

"Did you bring the stuff?" Cynthia asked, holding out her hands.

"I got mine," Ruby Rockefeller announced and shoved a hairbrush into Cynthia's hands. In the light, the stray blonde hairs there looked like gossamer on a fresh spring morning.

"Give it to her," Rhonda instructed Poppy, and Poppy reached into her coat pocket and brought out the broach.

"It sure is pretty," she said as she handed it over.

Cynthia grinned like a drunken demon.

"And I got *mine*..." she said.

The sound of the switchblade opening in the girl's fist was sharp enough to cut the night.

Prom night.

Maggie swept down the stairs to meet Bobby Rose on the doorsteps as her parents looked on adoringly. He wore a white tuxedo, and his clean grin and Brylcremed brown hair gave him the appearance of a gentleman, which even his past conquests might have momentarily fallen for.

He breathed in audibly at the sight of his date in the blue satin dress, her blonde locks curled back underneath the silver Arrowsbrook beauty crown. Her pale cleavage snaked up to her long neck, and her rouge lipstick lit her smile like a neon sign as he approached her to kiss her cheek and fasten the corsage to her wrist.

"You look beautiful," he breathed into her perfume.

"Well, of course she damn well does," barked Mr. Fellows, the romance of the occasion already passed for him. "She's the god darned beauty queen, not a land girl!"

"Oh, George, don't make a fuss," Mrs. Fellows tutted, and ushered the young couple onto the porch. In a hurried whisper behind her she hissed, "Can't you see they're in love...?"

George Fellows gave a 'humph' and retreated back into the house.

Mrs. Fellows waved them goodbye as they set off in the red Cadillac, all her romantic ideals following behind them, before she turned back inside to make dinner for her grumbling husband.

In the parking lot behind the basketball courts, where the high wall of the Arrowsbrook High School gymnasium muted the music coming from inside, Cynthia and the Orchard gang sat in the convertible and waited.

The little waxen doll in Rhonda's hand had been dressed in a blue Barbie doll dress. The little crown upon its head had been made out of tin foil, and Rhonda felt rather proud of the way the real blonde hairs spilt over the moulded face like a shroud.

"Come on," she said to Cynthia impatiently. "They must be on their way by now!"

"This isn't the same as what we did for Bobby Rose," Cynthia snapped back

Thirteen

from the driving seat. "It takes more concentration. Love spells are easy."

"Let's just get on with it," Poppy said, feeling nervous and already regretting ever having become involved with the gang. She didn't think they'd ever take it this far.

"Let's do it!" Penelope Smith whooped joyously. She'd been dumped by Bobby last semester, after her term as beauty queen had ended, and seeing the object of her affections mooning around the school grounds after Maggie Williams had been keeping her up late most nights.

"Alright already!" Cynthia replied tersely. "Hand me the broach."

Poppy leant forward and placed the scarab broach in Cynthia's waiting hand. The pin stuck up from the crystal design like a finger pointing at heaven, and in the light thrown from the gym's high window by the disco balls within, the dried blood on it looked as black as a moonless midnight.

The first thing Bobby Rose noticed, when Maggie started screaming, was the blood.

One minute they'd been driving down Abraham Drive in the moonlight on an empty road, the trees flashing by in the misty light of the Cadillac's headlamps, the next, chaos exploded all around him.

One minute, they'd been making idle chat about weather, exams and whether Maggie would make it as cheerleading captain next term (*boy, but he was going to poke her tonight whether it killed him*), the next, her throat was ripping the air with an ear splitting wail.

He'd jumped, glancing over at her in alarm, his cool evaporated by the sight of her.

The blood came in a flood from behind Maggie's hands, which were clamped tightly to her face, her gloved palms open wide enough to allow her red circle of a mouth to continue its hollering. Now blood fanned from there as well, a long, thick dribble ejected onto the dashboard, splattering the windshield in scarlet globules.

Blood trickled down Maggie's neck and into her cleavage, a crimson river snaking onto the satin fabric of her evening dress.

"What's happening?" he cried dumbly, his eyes flicking back and forth from the road, the Cadillac swerving dangerously close to the verge.

"My... face!" Maggie yelled insensibly. "My face..."

"What's wrong with your fucking face?" he yelled back, his heart shuddering with panic.

"It's burning!" she yelped, and grabbed the lapel of his tuxedo with one hand, as if somehow this act could make him understand the pain.

Behind the gym in the convertible, Cynthia twisted the little doll on the broach pin above her cigarette lighter.

The girls chuckled as one.

"It sure is gonna be one hot date!" Rhonda exclaimed in wild jubilation.

Bobby Rose couldn't believe her hair was on fire.

When it began to smoulder, he'd had to blink to make sure his eyes weren't deceiving him, but as the first flames blossomed with a loud whoosh and the cab of the Cadillac became illuminated with the glow, he knew it was so. Her pageant crown blackened above the inferno of her hair, blonde and silver wreathed in foul smelling smoke.

Desperately, he struggled out of his jacket, keeping one hand firmly on the steering wheel, and then flung it around Maggie's head. Her screaming penetrated his skull like a jackhammer, and he wished he hadn't indulged in beer earlier – these stupid thoughts circled his brain as he struggled against Maggie's

Thirteen

flailing arms.

"Do it!" screamed the girls in the convertible. "Do her good Cynth!"

"As you wish, ladies," Cynthia said, opened her switchblade and plunged the blade straight through the little doll's face.

Maggie tore at the skin of her face with painted nails.

The tuxedo jacket fell in her lap, and Bobby was treated to her exposed skull as she turned towards him with beseeching eyes. The lids of the eyes became scratched away with one single frantic movement of fingers over the skin.

Skin, which Bobby noted in shock, now bubbled and ran like red lava. Fleshy blobs of the stuff fell onto her bloodied dress with a dreadful wet sound, and he reached out to try and prevent her from further damaging herself.

"*Bobbbbbyyyyyy...*" she keened at him, her lips cracking open to reveal her sizzling gums. One of her eyeballs exploded suddenly, splashing him with hot fluid.

He yelped in horror.

The Cadillac swerved again in a wide arc.

He didn't see the tree. His rigid legs had depressed the accelerator to busting point and in the distraction of his fear, he hadn't even realised.

The tree met the Cadillac with a horrific crunch, and all was silent.

Bobby Rose and Maggie Williams stayed silent.

Forever.

In the back of the convertible, Rhonda laughed.

The other girls joined in apart from Cynthia, who simply regarded the mess of wax on her jeans and smiled to herself as she gazed out the windshield. She threw the broach over the side of the car door and it shattered on the tarmac with a small tinkle.

"Told you they'd never make the prom," she said.

Thirteen

THE HEALTHY MAN
JANE MACKENZIE

The healthy man does not torture others—generally it is the tortured who turn into torturers.
   - Carl Jung

Flexing stiff shoulders wearily, Sadovy Mildmay steps into his office and allows the door to close behind him with a firm click. All sound from the rest of the facility vanishes instantly and for perhaps the thousandth time he gives silent thanks for the expensive sound-proofing.

He rips the lid off a carton of juice he grabbed on the way to his office and collapses into the black leather chair at his desk. The chair whirrs a little as it automatically adjusts, correcting his posture and providing just the right support for his aching muscles. The computer on the desk blinks into life.

Sadovy takes a large swig of the juice, enjoying its coldness even as he gags at the saccharine artificial fruit taste, then he clears his throat. "Open today's report."

The machine complies.

"A breakthrough with subject 5788Y3..." he pauses and pulls the keyboard towards him, desiring the impersonal clickety-clack of typing rather than the sound of his own voice recounting the day's events. Getting technical services to fit the keyboard in his office had been a bureaucratic nightmare, but it had been well worth it. It is an old-fashioned way of doing things, but then Sadovy is old-fashioned in many things.

It has, overall, been a good day. 5788Y3 provided information that could prove invaluable to the military planners. The location of the Kobya Base has already been sent to the counter insurgency ministry. All that really remains to go in the report is the detailed analysis of the methods used.

Simple really. Pain. Fear. The fear of pain and the pain of fear.

In the end that was all it took.

Oh, there were variations. Lots of them. To date there are 107 different methods of torture recorded by Sadovy, who keeps detailed records of the effectiveness of each and every one. Eyes, knees, teeth. The soft skin under the fingernails. Mild poisons that caused agonising stomach cramps. Electrodes attached to the genitals. Each technique was documented, with careful notes on what was effective and what was *too* effective.

Of course, it isn't all about physical pain. Solitary imprisonment, sensory deprivation and deception – these all have their place in interrogation. The files filling the bookcases along the wall above Sadovy's head are a connoisseur's library of torment and suffering, a litany of agonies, set down in exquisite detail.

It would be wrong, however, to suppose that this man is a sadist who takes pleasure in watching other human beings suffer. Those who know him outside his work would call him kind and generous, a sociable, likeable, family man. His employees consider him to be an excellent boss – he is encouraging and attentive and does not play favourites.

His work is not about revenge or some personal grudge. He has not lost some favourite son to an enemy bomb. Nephews and nieces, yes, but then, these days, who hasn't?

He hopes, as almost everyone does, that one day all of this will be over. That the war will end with victory and he can go back to the work he prefers - teaching and researching microbiology. But he does not think of his work as any worse than that of anyone else involved in this painful war. And certainly if he did not do it – someone else would.

Thirteen

This is how he might rationalise his job to himself - if he thought about it at all.

It has been three years since he last thought about it at all.

Three years in which the world around him has gradually collapsed into chaos, sound-tracked by the constant wail of sirens. A conflict that once seemed distant, now rains destruction on familiar places. The streets mentioned on the evening news are places where he has attended dinner parties or joined friends to watch a sports match.

So for now he is just a busy man, with a report to finish and a home to go to. He does not expect to be troubled by nightmares tonight, nor is he plagued by memories of the terrified young men and women in the cells below him. He plays the linguistic game of thinking them merely subjects, cultures in Petrie dishes. He has replaced their names with numbers and that is what they have become to him.

Every day he plays the delicate balancing act of breaking the spirit without breaking the mind. He has become very good at it. Information gleaned by Sadovy is more likely to be correct than information from almost any other source. He genuinely has no idea of the awe his name inspires in certain circles.

Tonight he plans to go home, pour himself a glass of brandy and put on an old romantic comedy. His wife is likely to be working even later than he is. Given the most recent news from the front, things will be frantic at the hospital tonight.

His fingers finally finish their complex dance over the keyboard. "Close," he commands, and the bright computer screen blackens instantly.

He rises to his feet and gives a tentative shrug, finding to his satisfaction that the ache in his shoulder blades has gone. As he pulls on his grey woollen coat, he remembers noticing earlier that the straggly office plant was looking a little dried out. He pours the remnant of the revoltingly sweet juice into the soil – unsure as to whether it is really the best thing for the half-dead plant.

The director of Interrogation Camp Gamma walks down the clinical white corridors with a spring in his step. He bids farewell to a stony-faced cleaner and suppresses a chuckle at the fact that her auto-mop is disobediently fleeing from her around a corner.

Outside he takes a deep breath. There is a faint bitter tang of explosives in the air – but that has been there a long time. He wonders a little that he should notice it tonight, then shrugs and walks to his car.

Less than two hundred miles away, the pilot of a Zikobomber flips a button, then watches on his targeting screen as Kobya Base is swallowed by dust and flames. It is an awesome sight and a significant tactical victory.

HER LITTLE SECRET
WILLIAM I. LENGEMAN III

They shot my father when I was five years old. They say you don't remember things that happen when you're that young, but I do.

Everything is a blur - until the doorbell. I liked it when the doorbell rang. I always dropped what I was doing and ran to the door. Sometimes I yelled. My father always got mad when I did that and my mum looked worried, but it never stopped me for long.

I ran into the front room as my father was opening the door. I remember him looking over his shoulder at me. He looked mad. He told me to go back to my room. I didn't listen. I went and stood right behind him.

I didn't know the man on the porch, but that wasn't unusual. Lots of strange men came to the house. Most of them were really nice. They gave me money and joked with me and noticed that I was there, something my own parents didn't do much anymore.

I knew what guns were. My father always had one with him, but so what? I always thought everyone's dad carried a gun. The man on the porch had a big gun. I was thinking too slow to figure out what that meant. My father was thinking faster, but not fast enough.

Dad reached for his gun. It always stuck out of the back of his pants. I never understood why he kept it there. He grabbed it just as the other man shot him. I never heard a gun before, except on TV. It was really loud.

I felt something wet and sticky on my face. I tried to rub it off, but I just smeared it around. My mother was screaming as the man shot two more times. I was crying. My father stumbled back and fell on me. He was really heavy. I knew he was dead, even though I didn't really know what that meant.

Things were different after that. Mom was upset and cried a lot. She drank lots of beer and never paid attention to me. I tried to talk to her, but she didn't pay attention, except on that night when she woke up and saw me and started screaming. That scared me so bad that I went away for a long time. When I came back, mum was gone.

I stayed in the house after mum left. The new people don't pay much attention to me either. There's a mum and a dad - he doesn't carry a gun - and a baby and a girl who is a little bit older than me. They are nice and they laugh a lot. I wish my mum and dad had been more like them.

The only time the new mom and dad get mad is when the girl tries to tell them about me, but she knows they don't like that now and she doesn't talk about it. She says I'm her little secret.

Thirteen

POSSESSION
STEVEN SOUTHWORTH

Trevor screamed as Irene doused him with water, squeezing every drop from the two-litre bottle.

"I knew it. I knew it. The holy water burns. The dark one has taken you." Irene grabbed the crucifix from the bedside cabinet and held it to her heart. She turned away from Trevor, fearing that he was about to take on another form.

"It didn't burn me, you lunatic. It's freezing! I asked you not to put it in the fridge." A track of chilled liquid slipped under the collar of Trevor's pyjama top.

"Are you sure?" Irene said, glancing at Trevor. "It didn't even hurt a little?"

"No. Not until you threw the bottle at me. Come on, Rene. You can't keep me like this forever. You've tried the cross, the bible and the holy water. I'm not possessed. Why don't you undo these chains and we can go and have a nice cup of tea? Please, love. Please."

Irene tested her crucifix against her husband's forehead one last time, and then began to unbolt him from the bedroom wall.

"I was so certain," she said, shaking her head as she opened a padlock. "I could feel it on you. And smell it and taste it and... and..." She fumbled with the padlock, clicking it closed again. "I still can."

Trevor groaned and dropped his chin onto his chest. "What are you going to do now? Call the priest?"

Irene ran from the room and reappeared two minutes later, her face fixed with stony conviction.

"Irene?" Trevor started. "What are you - ?"

She silenced him with a raised finger.

"They say the devil can resist fire." She stepped towards Trevor, a can of petrol in one hand, a lighter in the other.

"I think it's time to test that theory."

Thirteen

HELL INSIDE
NATE SOUTHARD

They had only asked for help.

Now, as Tucker waited with his hands tied behind his back, the thought skipped through his mind like a record with a bad groove.

They had only asked for help.

It was Henry that had needed attention, not Tucker or Conrad or even Suzanne. It was Henry, who had broken his leg in at least three places when they had stopped to put gas in the station wagon. For whatever reason, they hadn't bothered to check if there were any zombies in the area first. A pair had appeared out of nowhere, lunging for Henry, and Henry had fallen over the self-service island as he tried to get away. Tucker and Conrad had taken care of the zombies, but Henry's leg had already snapped, the sound of cracking bones as loud as gunfire.

Tucker heard Suzanne crying next to him. He turned to her, trying to think of something to comforting to say. When nothing came, he settled for a sigh. He knew what was coming, and there was no way to sugarcoat it.

"They can't do this," Suzanne managed to whimper between choking sobs. She had been repeating the phrase since the guards had dragged her twisting and screaming from the station wagon. Tucker couldn't tell if Suzanne believed the words or if the mantra was the only thing keeping her sane.

"There doing it," Conrad said. His voice had the same matter of fact tone it always had. "Better get used to it."

"Quiet," Tucker snapped.

"I'm just saying."

Tucker stared at his feet and listened to the sounds coming from the main tent. There were curses and shouts, screams and cheers. There was an especially loud roar, and one of the two guards chuckled.

"Betcha that one hurt."

Conrad spoke up. "Say, can you tell them to hurry it up in there? I'm getting anxious."

One of the guards waved his Mac 10 in Conrad's direction. "Want me to hurry you up?"

"That's okay," Conrad said. "Guess I'd rather you take your time."

A moment later, the man Tucker had learned to call Bridges pulled open the tent flap and stepped inside. He wore a faded duster and a bowler hat that looked like it had been dragged behind a car. His eyes met Tucker's. Bridges smiled, and Tucker thought about how it would feel to cut the man's lips off.

"How we doing, folks?"

Suzanne leapt to her feet and charged. "You can't do this!" she screamed as she bore down on Bridges, but he stepped to the side at the last minute, sticking his foot out. Suzanne tripped over it and landed face down in the New Mexico dirt.

Tucker started to get to his feet, saw Conrad do the same, but an instant later he saw the guards wave their guns, and he and Conrad both sat down again.

"You can't do this!" Suzanne shrieked.

"It's done," Bridges said. "Don't know why you're still in denial."

"Up your ass," Conrad said.

Bridges took the bowler off his head, slapping some of the dust off of it. "Calm down, son. Fair is fair. You pulled in here looking our help. You have to pay for that sort of thing, y'know?"

"This is barbaric," Tucker said. He was surprised he could still talk, he had

Thirteen

been silent so long.

Bridges shrugged, then stooped to pull Suzanne off the ground. She twisted against his grip, and he shoved her toward Conrad. "Some might say it's a barbaric world now, most of it being dead and all. You got those things running around out there, munching down on the survivors. You ask me, I'd say that sounds barbaric as hell."

Conrad spit. "How do we know you'll live up to your end of the deal?"

"You don't. Guess you'll just have to survive and find out."

"What a comfort."

Bridges smiled again.

There was another roar from the main tent, louder than all the others, and a small man wearing glasses poked his head into the tent.

"Next up," he said.

Bridges clapped his hands together. "On your feet, ladies and gentlemen. Your public awaits."

Suzanne's sobs grew more intense as she stood up again. Tucker stepped next to her.

"Stay behind me," he said.

"They can't do this," Suzanne moaned.

"Listen to me," Tucker said. He heard Suzanne's breath hitch in her chest, and he knew he had her attention. "You stay behind me, okay? If I'm out, you get behind Conrad."

"Okay."

The guards approached them, waving their guns toward the exit. Conrad stood at Tucker's side. He tried to twist free of his bonds, but the rope was too tight, too strong. He looked to Tucker.

"Any idea how we're going to do this with no hands?"

"Try to get them off their feet. They have soft skulls. You should be able to stomp their goddamn brains in once they're on their backs."

"Sounds too good to be true."

"I thought so, too."

The guards led them out of the smaller tent and into the open space that led to the big top. Tucker felt the hot wind blast his cheeks with dust, felt the last light of the sun bake his skin. He closed his eyes and tried to savour the feeling, but the barrel of a gun poked him in the kidney and ruined the moment.

Bridges stood at the big top's rear entrance, the man with the glasses at his side. To the man's left, Tucker saw two words painted in block letters on the tent's canvas. They were big and red and easy to read.

HELL INSIDE

"How appropriate," Tucker muttered.

Then the cheers hit them.

The crowd was wild even before Tucker and the others were led into the makeshift arena. The thunderous sound of applause was frightening, and when the crowd saw them walking down the aisle it became downright terrifying. Tucker saw Conrad's lips move, but he couldn't hear a word his friend had said. Tucker found himself thinking again.

They had only asked for help.

Tucker studied the arena. It was a dusty pit a little larger than a tennis court. Walls had been built out of cinderblocks on all four sides. They couldn't have been more than twelve feet tall, but they towered over those who might try to escape. Each wall was topped by a crude, rusted metal rail, and row upon row of spectators rose beyond the walls. They yelled at Tucker and the others, some hurling insults and others offering words of encouragement. Tucker saw a woman the size of a commuter bus wave a pair of shredded cotton panties in the

Thirteen

air. Tucker turned away, sickened.

There were two entrances, each on opposite ends of the arena, and both were sealed with iron gates. A pair of armed guards stood at each gate. They looked eager for somebody to make a run for it, like they hadn't been given enough chances to prove their worth. Maybe they just wanted a chance to use their weapons. One smiled at Tucker, a toothless grin that seemed less human than any zombie, and Tucker dropped his eyes. The dirt floor was dark, wet in places. Tucker didn't have to ask what had stained the ground. He could still smell the blood in the air.

Bridges stepped into the middle of the arena. He held a microphone in one coiled fist. The crowd fell into an anxious silence.

"Ladies and gentlemen," Tucker said. "We now bring to you tonight's main event!"

The crowd erupted with applause. Tucker flinched. Behind him, he heard Suzanne squeal in terror.

Bridges continued.

"Three survivors, three noble souls, came to us this morning seeking medical attention for their friend, a man that may be mortally wounded."

"Bullshit," Conrad mumbled.

"Now I ask you folks, are we not civilized?"

The crowd cheered.

"Are we not loving and kind?"

The cheers grew.

"Are we the kind of down and dirty folks that would turn their fellow man away in his hour of need?"

The cheers swelled to a deafening roar.

"Hell no, we're not!"

Bridges threw his arms wide and soaked up the crowds adoration. Tucker found himself thinking that Bridges might have made a good politician if the world hadn't ended.

"So we're gonna give these folks a chance to save their friend. If a single one of these three fine friends survives what they are about to face, we will treat their wounded friend with the best care we can provide. If none of them survive, however, then I will personally put a bullet behind the bastard's goddamn ear!"

The crowd went wild. Tucker was reminded of evangelists and tent revivals.

"And I'll wheel him right out here and let you fine folks watch!"

Conrad spit at the ground, disgusted.

Bridges motioned for the crowd to quiet again. He hunched his shoulders and put the mic to his lips, letting the crowd in on a big secret. "Now, ladies and gentlemen, I know what you're thinking. You're wondering how many of those vile, undead, flesh-eating bastards these folks have to face."

Tucker saw the crowd shift forward in their seats. Their anticipation filled the air with something that was thick and ghastly. Tucker thought he might swoon from the power of it.

Bridges continued. "Well, I thought long and hard about that myself. One of these folks is a woman, and she's a dainty little critter at that. She has two strapping young bucks with her, though, and that does even up the odds some, so after some careful deliberation, how many do you folks think I decided on?"

The crowd called number after number into the air. Tucker heard every possibility between one and one hundred in the matter of seconds. He never took his eyes off of Bridges, not even as he worked his wrists in their binds, trying with all his will to twist free of the ropes. His wrists burned, and he felt the first warm trickle of blood creep down his hands, but the rope held him tight.

Bridges stood in the centre of the arena and laughed. "To tell you the truth,

Thirteen

folks, I thought long and hard, and I realized that these three were some true-blue lucky people. To have made it so far, and to have found folk like us - folk so willing to help their fellow man - you'd have to be one lucky son of a bitch."

Tucker noticed movement behind Bridges. The second gate opened, and a pair of guards wheeled a cage into the arena.

"So I decided on a lucky number," Bridges said. "Tonight, in this very arena, in front of your live, steaming eyes, these three will face seven flesh-eating zombies!"

The crowd roared with approval.

Bridges stepped out of the way, and Tucker got a good look at the cage. Sure enough, seven rotted creatures waited behind its iron bars. Four had once been men. One wore overalls over his mottled and broken skin. Another must have been over three hundred pounds, his flesh grey and sagging. Two more had once been women. Tucker almost smiled as he noticed that one was still wearing an evening gown. The last, the one that snarled the loudest and hurled itself against the bars again and again, fighting to free itself and attack, had once been a boy of no more than twelve.

Tucker heard Suzanne scream behind him. She screamed again, and Tucker heard her collapse to the ground. "Get up!" he told her, but she did nothing but curl into a ball and shriek.

The crowd laughed.

"Go to hell!" Conrad roared. "Every last one of you bastards can go to hell!"

Bridges stepped up to him. "Sorry there, son. You're the one in hell." He smiled. "Didn't you read the sign?"

Bridges stepped to the arena's centre again and put the mic to his lips. He threw one arm wide. "Ladies and Gentlemen, let the entertainment begin!"

Bridges jogged out of the arena, dragging the microphone behind him. The gates slammed shut, closing off the aisle as a means of escape. The crowd hushed with anticipation.

Tucker and Conrad shared a look.

Suzanne cried. She began to climb to her feet.

There was a low hum followed by a metallic popping sound, and the cage door swung open. The crowd screamed with delight as the zombies burst forth, crossing the arena toward Tucker and Conrad. The child led the way, jaws opening and snapping shut, licking its cracked lips with its rotted, black tongue.

"Remember," Tucker shouted, "get them off their feet!"

Conrad nodded.

And then Suzanne rushed passed them.

Tucker tried to call out, tried to stop her, but she charged past like a freight train, screaming in a way that told Tucker she had insane long ago. She ploughed into the zombies at full speed, knocking four of them over. She tumbled into the rest, and they fell upon her in a voracious frenzy.

Tucker knew what he should do. He should charge after her and kick in the skulls of those that Suzanne had knocked down. They were slow and clumsy and had trouble getting off the ground. It would be easy. Tucker couldn't seem to make his legs work, though, couldn't move at all. He could only watch as they tore Suzanne apart. Those on the ground, the two women, the child, and one of the men, attacked her legs instead of trying to right themselves. Tucker saw the child bite down on Suzanne's calf, his teeth gnawing through the denim of her jeans and drawing blood beneath. He saw the women rip at Suzanne's other pants leg, exposing the pale skin of her calf and thigh before sinking their teeth in and tearing her flesh away.

Suzanne's screams crescendoed, becoming a wail of agony. The fat man bit into Suzanne's neck, and the wail became a gurgle. Blood burst forth and

Thirteen

washed over his diseased face.

Tucker heard Conrad gag and vomit.

When the remaining men tore off Suzanne's shirt and dug into her naked flesh, Tucker found the strength to move again. He ran forward, legs picking up speed as he went. He had just enough time to pray that Conrad was behind him before he cocked his leg back and swung it forward with all his might. It connected with the one of the women, the one in the cocktail dress. The toe of Tucker's boot slammed into her temple, and her head exploded like a melon hit with a shotgun shell. Bits of bone and wet grey chunks of what might have once been brain splattered against the ground. Tucker saw skin and bone stuck to his boot and shook it loose. He turned and kicked the other woman. He missed and hit her in the neck. His boot cut through her soft flesh and burst through the other side. Her head lolled back on its spinal cord, and she fell to the ground, arms and legs writhing in the dirt. Tucker stamped on her head and crushed it.

He turned to look at Suzanne.

She was gone. In her place was a bloody ruin that might have once been a body. The zombies swarmed over what little was left. The fat one had her head in his hands, his mouth pressed against the pulp of her severed neck. The men had ripped her torso apart. Tucker watched the three of them pull at her intestines, cram them into their mouths with greedy gluttony. The child had Suzanne's leg cradled against his lips, his mouth, chin, and chest streaked with her blood.

The crowd roared, but Tucker could still hear the sounds of chewing over the noise.

One of the zombies looked up, and its dead eyes seemed to lock onto Tucker's. It let Suzanne's intestines slip through its fingers and stepped toward Tucker. Tucker backed away, now unsure of what to do. There were still others on the ground, but this one stood in the way. Tucker felt his stomach roll as the zombie's blood-smeared tongue flopped out of its mouth and licked at its chin.

Tucker backed against the arena wall. He was cornered.

The zombie closed in on him, its eyes gleaming with hunger.

Tucker sucked in a breath to scream when Conrad came out of nowhere. He kicked the zombie in the knee, and Tucker heard a wet crunching sound as the knee buckled inward and the zombie crashed to the ground. Conrad leapt into the air and came down with both feet on the zombie's head, splattering it like a fly on a windshield.

Tucker breathed deeply, the rank air somehow sweet in his lungs. "Thanks."

Conrad nodded, but he didn't say anything.

Tucker stepped away from the wall and approached the remaining zombies with Conrad at his side.

The men didn't see Tucker and Conrad coming until it was too late. They looked up from the viscera in their laps in time to see boots flying at their faces. One let out an angry hiss before its head burst. The other made no sound. The air filled with the choking stench of rotted flesh and tissue. Tucker felt his stomach roll again, then lurch. He turned his head to the side and vomited, the feeling hot and sharp in his throat.

Then something hit him.

It was the boy. He struck Tucker behind both knees, and Tucker fell forward. He landed in the pile of organs and flesh that had once been Suzanne and felt warm blood streak his face and hands. He tried to push himself up, but the kid pounced on his back. Tucker felt fingers twist themselves into his hair and pull. He screamed. More fingers tried to wrap around his neck, but they were too small. Instead, they tried to tear at his flesh.

Tucker heard a war cry, and then the fingers were gone from his hair and

Thirteen

neck. He turned to see the child roll through the dirt and blood. Conrad stalked him, hunched over low and ready to attack with his legs. The dead child scrambled for an escape, but Conrad slammed a boot down on its back, and it collapsed into the dirt again. Conrad took a step and kicked the child's head as if he were trying to put it through a pair of uprights. Blood and brain and bone sailed through the air, peppering the ground and the arena walls.

Conrad turned to Tucker. This time he smiled. "Do I always have to save your ass?"

"Looks like."

And then the fat man fell on Conrad.

He latched onto Conrad's neck, same as he had with Suzanne. Crimson pumped from Conrad's jugular. Conrad's muscles seized with the strength only a man in agony can muster. Tucker screamed Conrad's name, but it was lost among the crowd's cheers.

Conrad sank to his knees. The fat man held on, gnawing at the wound he had opened. Tucker raced toward them. He saw Conrad's eyes flutter and close. The fat man let go, tearing the cords of Conrad's neck, and Conrad's body flopped to the ground.

Tucker kicked.

He saw something close to delight in the dead man's eyes in the instant before his boot caved the man's face in. Tucker screamed as he kicked again, and the head shattered. The fat man's body collapsed beside Conrad's. Tucker kicked the dead man's torso, and it burst open like a wet garbage sack, spilling rotted organs onto the ground. The stench choked Tucker, and he stumbled away before crumbling against the arena's wall.

The crowd went crazy.

The gate swung open and Bridges stepped into the arena, barking into the microphone as he came. "Can you believe that folks? Three against seven, and only one survives! Let's hear it for my man Tucker!"

The crowd chanted Tucker's name. Tucker looked up and saw both women and men leaning over the rails, trying to reach out and touch their new hero.

Tucker hated them all.

Bridges sauntered over to Tucker, gripped him by the shoulder, and helped him to his feet.

"Those were some mighty fine moves, son," he said through a smile.

Tucker spit a wad of blood in the man's face.

Bridges's smile never wavered. "To be expected. Guards?"

The guards appeared, still carrying their guns. One grabbed Tucker by each arm, and they led him toward the gate.

"What are you doing to me?" Tucker asked.

Bridges wiped the blood off of his face. "You're getting your reward, son. Enjoy it."

The guards led Tucker through the gate and out of the arena. Tucker heard his own name ringing in his ears, the crowd saluting the victor.

The guards led Tucker across the open ground. The sun had set, and the night air was cool and clear. The guards were silent. They didn't even look at Tucker when he asked what was going on.

It wasn't until Tucker saw the brick box they were leading him toward that he knew the worst was only beginning.

The brick box was bare inside except for a single dirt-streaked light bulb in the ceiling and a pair of iron manacles bolted to the wall. Tucker struggled in the doorway, thrashing and kicking against the two guards, but a hard fist to his kidney knocked him to the floor. The guards untied Tucker's hands and snapped the manacles over his wrists. In a way, Tucker was thankful. At least the

Thirteen

manacles didn't tease you with the possibility of escape.

A few moments later, Bridges appeared in the doorway. His smile was bigger than ever.

"What is this?" Tucker asked.

"You reward, like I told you," Bridges replied.

"What? I get to wait until tomorrow night? See if I can survive another round?"

"No," Bridges said. "We don't play that way, letting people fight until they lose. That's just cruel. Around here, we like to let our winners get their just desserts."

"What, I join the community? Do I get to watch others used for sport?"

Bridges laughed. "Heck, no! Think we got food to spare around here? No way. We have other uses for our winners."

Bridges stepped away from the door, and the guards entered with Conrad's body in their arms.

"No," Tucker said.

"Sorry," Bridges said. "Thing is, we get more survivors stumbling into camp than zombies, so we have to make our own, and we like to give our newborns a first meal. They're mighty hungry when they wake up."

"Bastard," Tucker spat.

"Nothing personal, buddy. Just the New World Order."

"What about Henry? What are you going to do to him?"

"Guy with the bum leg? He was fed to the zombies hours ago."

Tucker pulled at the manacles as Bridges and the guards left the box. He hurled curses at Bridges until his throat felt dry and sore. There was a sharp *clack!* as a bolt was thrown outside the door, and Tucker was locked in.

Tucker stopped fighting. He hung by his wrists, defeated and exhausted.

Then Conrad's eyes fluttered open.

And Tucker found the strength to scream.

SHELBY'S WITCH
KENNETH RYAN

I regarded the newcomer with contempt. He sat cross-legged in the folding chair, pale blue eyes flitting, unwilling to engage my narrow-eyed scrutiny; a nervous hand pulled through youthful curls. The others welcomed him, even mollycoddled him and served him coffee; but to me he was an intruder, a dim-witted hopeful, certain to desecrate our sacrosanct work by mere proximity.

Always, I bore this responsibility – the banishment of mediocre authors. As skilled and talented were my peers, they were also unusually forgiving and encouraging; not I. Writing has always been a sour and foul business where one's most personal accounts and vulnerabilities are exposed and weighed against the ignorant judgment of a dollar and its whimsical keepers. If fate determined only failure for this pretender, then I would be its clarion; with a few words of keen, steely criticism, he would depart. He might never write again; so be it, for better my quick mercy than years of his fruitless toil and the inevitable disdain and rejection of a merciless editor.

Mrs. Curtis announced, "Because our new guest must be at work by nine, he will read first." He started the story, reading his inept cursive from a yellow legal pad, while my peers feigned interest. He spun a horror story, a child's story, witches prowling a darkened wood, seeking tender human meat for their stew pot, oh dear. As he read, he glanced at his audience, taking furtive snapshots, and frequently lost his place on the page as a result. He tried to re-establish his pace; he kept his finger on the pencilled words, and brought his voice to tremulous breathlessness as he reached his self-crafted climax. He lowered the pad, grinned, as if I might nominate him for a prize, and wiped his forehead with that same shaking hand. Poor fellow.

Mrs. Curtis and Ms. Guss smiled and clapped politely as their sanguine inclination demanded. Mr. Turk grunted; Mr. Todd gaped; I grimaced.

The newcomer waited, fingers tapping a nonsensical percussion upon his knees, unsure of our protocol. As I sat diametrically opposite, his anticipatory gaze fell upon me, and the eyes of my reluctant peers followed. Very well. I rose, stepped outside the circle of chairs, and began my most thoughtful pace around the perimeter, that their heads might become more sensibly fastened to their necks as they followed my course.

"Firstly," I said, "unless your last name is K____, the horror genre is inaccessible to you, as to all newcomers. Abandon it. Even Mr. K____ has recently resorted to clichés. Witches, goblins, apparitions, all with murderous intent, are tired devices, even to the juvenile mind. Do not mistake what I tell you, sir, abandon this pursuit. The only worthy genre is literature. Now, before I lead you astray, I don't believe you have the natural talent to pursue the righteous course. I can forgive your split infinitives. I can neither forgive nor ignore your clumsy prose and plodding pace, your lack of narrative command, your bland descriptors, and two-cent similes. They doom your effort."

The heads of my peers followed me, swivelling in vertebrae-crackling satisfaction, but the poor sod simply stared at his pad, unwilling to accept the reasoned truth of my assertions. As it was for his benefit, and he must have surely been listening, albeit without acknowledgement, I continued. "Abandon your work, sir. You have no gift. Furthermore, witches are not scary because they are not real. Do you know what is scary? Real things, sir, are scary. There are many sinister things in our world. Have you ever considered the unblinking detachment and observatory judgment of a single bird on a phone wire? Has it ever struck you that doctors can be extraordinarily antiseptic and aloof even while rendering great pain upon a helpless patient? Real things, sir, that, with the application of even a hobbled imagination, might be made quite sinister indeed."

He fled immediately, straight up the library stairs, dropping his amateur scribble on the floor. I closed my circumference and drew tangentially toward the pad. I picked it up delicately, as if it were infectious, and tossed the horrid effort into the rubbish pail. Honest assessments never come without an ego-bruising price. My responsibility had been realized though; I had helped him. I resumed my seat and the others, unexpectedly, drew their chairs close in a screech of scraping steel.

Mrs. Curtis started, "Don't you think you were too hard on him, Chester?"

"He seemed like a nice man," Ms. Guss offered. "Timid, but weren't we all?"

"That poor man," Mrs. Curtis continued. "He didn't deserve such vitriol. The story wasn't so bad."

Mr. Turk then said, "Christ, Chester. That was really uncalled for." Mr. Todd shook his head in solemn agreement.

"Just one moment," I insisted, and stood. "Are you suggesting that you don't agree with my wholly accurate assessment? Did you like his work?" The group had never before questioned me after a banishment. I found myself defensive, at once prepared to thrust or parry. "We all know that my role as leader of this group is to weed out the hackneyed, to better ensure that our own efforts do not become polluted with the rot of the unskilled. Our efforts here are pure. The courage of candour that you lack is a mantle that I bear seriously. I do this for all of us, and for that pathetic dreamer, so that he might resume and redouble his efforts at whatever vocation he relies upon for subsistence." I awaited their meek response but still my limbs shook from the treachery of my group.

"What was his name?" Mr. Todd asked.

"His name? What bearing has his name on this discussion?" I asked.

"This isn't the first time," Mr. Todd said, "that you dashed a man's dreams with knowledge of nothing, not even his name, just a few lines of hastily cobbled prose."

"Chester," Mr. Turk said, "we discussed this amongst ourselves before you arrived. You are excused from this critique group. Good luck with your writing, sir."

"No," I protested. "This is my group. I am not excused. It is you who are excused. How dare you! You embrace hook-nosed witches scampering among the brambles and trees in a fit of human bloodlust and you discard my exploration of the human heart?"

"I find you have little understanding of the human heart," Mrs. Curtis said. "Please leave."

With no more dignified option, I turned my back to them and strode defiantly toward the stairwell. "His name," Mr. Todd called after me, "was Shelby."

I heard Mr. Todd's words as I ascended. Shelby, I thought, what bearing has his name? My group's calculated infidelity assailed my consciousness as I left the library and stepped into the dreary evening chill. That Mrs. Curtis' doting nature masked such faithlessness, that Mr. Turk's generous bulk concealed such perfidy, was beyond my faculty. Such was my torment that I aimlessly stepped into the road and immediately fell back to my seat and hands, flattened by the shock of a speeding sedan, but an arm's length from my chest, and its blasted horn.

I recovered, brushed the grit from my hands, but my arms numbly tingled of their own accord. My brain, wet with adrenaline and alert at its core, saw me safely to the opposite pavement. But, this newly activated and primitive core insisted on instinct over reason, and guided me to my daytime habit of the wooded path, a shortcut to my home, rather than the luminous safety of the sidewalk.

Thirteen

I scarcely noticed that I could not see the scarred tree trunks, their bare, wasted branches, or the pollution of their curled crisp brown leaves on the forest floor. That no protruding root or random rock impeded my step supplied my dormant consciousness the navigational reassurance that I adhered to the dirt path, even in the impenetrable black.

The shock completed its course as I walked, and the blood-engorged muscles of my arms and legs returned themselves gradually to the control of my sensibility. Here then, I first became fully aware of my place in the woods, my orientation shrouded, and the alpha of my blind entrance and the omega of my destination utterly concealed by the night. I paused on the path for an instant and considered my disconcerting situation. Logic insisted that I continue, that turning back would rob me of significant time that I might otherwise exploit in revising my manuscript. I resumed my pace, and that wash of adrenaline, as if the core of my mind found its first taste delicious, threatened to spill over the dam of my will.

The core, that frightened and cowering beast, the curse of an evolutionary defensive spasm that clung dumbly to modern man, found teeth-bearing courage and lapped yet more adrenaline when I heard the echo of footfalls behind me. Applying my fast-fleeing reason, I thought, an echo, an auditory trick, invisible waves and reflective mass. Yet, steps in concert with my own, a hush of foot upon earth, somewhere behind me, closed. When that animal drank its gluttonous gut fully of my hormonal gush, it cruelly projected its ignorance with frightening realism. Shelby's witch, the bloodthirsty, cackling hag, ridiculously clichéd, trod surreptitiously in my steps upon the path, fiendishly fixed on adding my meat to her stew. I could summon no reason to counter this vision so vilely and childishly posited.

I ran.

I ran, and my exquisitely attuned ears detected the increasing pace of, I imagined, curly-toed, brass-buckled shoes beneath determined, spindly legs, and the hushed, foul pant of breathless pursuit. My eyes saw nothing ahead or anything behind; I checked over my shoulder with every other step. My heart grew so bold in its work that its own bass rhythm masked my footfalls upon the path. That core of my brain, the beast that now owned each of my physiological functions, then, of its own animal ignorance, subverted itself by conjuring an image of a gnarled, clammy hand reaching for my shoulder. Hogwash. My resilient consciousness considered this notion, a creation of the Brothers Grimm, and firmly rejected it. The moment I calmed my legs and ceased my flight, the evidence of phantom pursuit ceased as well. This was, indeed, a proud moment, and I rewarded my newly assertive higher brain with well-earned and greedily inhaled oxygen.

I tamped my damp brow with my coat sleeve and then stretched my arms over my head to increase the capacity of my starved lungs. No footfalls threatened. As my reason strengthened and I nourished my body in sweet, redemptive pause, I considered my critique group, the catalyst for my unwitting detour. Was there merit to their disdain? Was my ouster justified by some unrecognised egotistical flaw? Had I so cruelly treated the untalented Shelby, and others before him? Perhaps I could have wielded a gentler criticism. Perhaps I could have even encouraged a study of the classics and then a resumption of the craft with a fresh perspective. Poor Shelby, I lamented. I revisited his face, his boyish curled locks of sandy hair, his earnest blue eyes glossed with dew. I had been unfair to the man; he was an innocent. I would rejoin the group, repentant and humble.

I resumed my walk through the woods and ignored the incorporeal echo of my steps upon the dirt, as if something approached from out of the shadow of my wake. So self-satisfied was I with the exploration and revelation of my own human heart, that I discounted the unreasonable creature who thirsted for yet another dose of empowering elixir from my taxed adrenal glands. Submissive, and bound within a cell of rational thought, it required only the slightest impetus to achieve utter emancipation and control.

A tick: the sound of a pebble striking another on the path, a tick of a pebble that my shoe did not raise. I stopped and turned fully in the opposite direction, an act in defence of newfound reason. I expected to see nothing in the black from where I had come, and I did not. There was no witch, no discernable tree, and no natural denizen of the nighttime wood. I stood firmly still; I even stopped my breath to best convince myself that the only sounds delivered to my ears were of my own blind and clumsy gait.

As I stood defiant, invisibly silent, I heard another tick of pebble striking pebble, then, another, from somewhere before me. At once, then, the dry-bone clicking of many small stones rattled within the space beyond my sight, as if a bag of marbles had been emptied upon the trail.

I fed the beast again of my own juice, turned, and sprinted blindly forward. In this flight, my reason conjoined with my subconscious and painted a rational scene of a delicate man with a shattered ego, pursuing his insensitive critic, weapon in hand, his own uncontrollable beast enraged and free to act with a blood and guts instinct. No longer behind me, but from my right, I heard the crunch of dead leaves underfoot, as if this thing were circling, bound to appear before me, and capture me in its frightful embrace. That, as it ran so indiscreetly upon the leaves and did not pause, as if there were no darkened trees that it must dodge, convinced my conjoined sensibility that indeed it was Shelby, and he possessed an undeniable supernal fury.

I did not note the discomfort of my rapid breath or concern myself with leaving the path. I gave every resource to my body and saved nothing for consideration; that I did, beyond what I might have expected, saw me to light, the weak light of a street lamp, so insignificant that it might have been a phantom itself.

As I ran toward it, it grew stronger, a sublime beacon, and I more determined to find myself awash in its clarity. My pursuer, perhaps now I pursued it, worked to contain me before I reached the street. I heard its thrashing atop the leaves at two o'clock, its own wheezing breath at one o'clock. The next sound I might have heard would be its victorious and vindictive howl at dreaded midnight.

At that point, nearly to the street and nearly captured, both my reason and my instinct abandoned me, each giving their essence and will to my flagging legs, a sacrifice for the preservation of the whole being. Due to this phenomenon, no doubt, I have only a shadow of a memory of the final moments of that ghastly episode. I reached the light. I reached the street. Something struck me.

When I opened my eyes, I recognized first that familiar reason and its logical inquisition firmly controlled my consciousness, its impulsive cousin safely stowed beneath my renaissance cortex, and satisfyingly bright light. My second recognition was that of pain in both legs, unparalleled in my experience, and a disconcerting notion that my jaw, somehow, sat askew on its hinge, pressured by bloated tissue. My eyes and nose also throbbed with unnatural swell.

I lay in a room painted in the colour of shrivelled peas. All else but the light remained hidden by virtue of my ungracious position of immobility. Still though, my reason sharpened; I realized that a doctor leaned in to me and grinned. I did not mistake him; certainly, I recognized that boyish curly hair and those pale blue eyes. He spoke to me about good fortune, that the charity of strangers saved my delicate body from expiration. I closed my eyes and reasoned that he would not know me, that my swollen and bruised features might yield nothing to spark his own recognition. If he were to somehow discern my identity, then surely he might

Thirteen

know by intuition, the redemption in my heart. Oh, that I could move my jaw, he would know my heart.

He gripped my shattered leg with insensitive force. Then, in a most practiced and banal tone he mused, "Oh dear, I've got to reset this bone. Where is my mallet?" With disinterest, he added, "This might hurt a bit, Chester."

Thirteen

PRESENCE OF MIND
JAMES LANE

The hulking form of the ancient Royal typewriter sat atop a writing desk that might have been an antique if it wasn't so scarred and stained. It almost seemed to be brooding, menacing in that peculiar way of long unused machines.

"Foolishness."

What emerged was far from the emphatic denial he had intended - little more than a forceful exhalation. He ran a sandpaper tongue over dry and cracked lips. His throat clenched with a sudden arid ache. The creak was almost audible as he swallowed. An age-spotted hand caressed the keys, trembling with reluctance and perhaps even fear. The pallid fingertips drew back accompanied by a sharp hiss. A flicker of disgust crossed his face as the offending hand dropped to his lap. The other hand began to scrub it unconsciously.

Mixed emotions warred across the heavy lines scoured deep in his thin, drawn face as he glared at the Jurassic device. Old and decrepit, the critics had said. A relic, an out-of-date affectation and affront to the dawning world of sleek modern efficiency. Critics said those sort of things all the time. They were paid to. He'd never paid attention to then before. Now, grimacing at the bulky machine with a bright amalgam of fear and loathing, he had to wonder if they hadn't been right.

It didn't matter. A state-of-the-art computer, winking and flashing, would have been no different. But the prehistoric monster on his desk made it feel worse – heavier in his mind.

He snarled, wrenching his gaze away. His hands snatched at the wheels of his chair, gripping with white-knuckled intensity. With a wrench that belied the strength in his wasted arms, he twisted the chair around. It lurched. He fought for control, teetered on the edge and just managed to right it. The left wheel thudded on the wooden floor. A wild grunt escaped lips twisted in a crazed grimace. He gave a single tremendous shove, sending him careening towards the door. The chair lost momentum, slowed, stopped. His hands settled back in his lap, returning to their unconscious wringing. Shoulders slumped. A blank and unseeing gaze rested on the door. A sigh that might have been a sob trickled forth and he slumped further into the chair.

With slow, mechanical reluctance, he looked back at the accursed typewriter. A bitter, loathing chuckle crackled up. No, not the typewriter - it was nothing more than an unthinking device. He was the problem - him – the user, the driving drone, the *author*. Another rusty chuckle spilled out, dripping sarcasm.

Go on. The frigid voice sliced across his mind, cutting like a glittering blade of ice. *Go back. You know want to. You have to.*

His head shook in denial. Bony fingers curled into tight fists and rose to hammer, once, at his temples.

"No..." he whimpered, pouring quiet terror and desperation into that single utterance.

Malignant laughter echoed through the chambers of his mind. *You cannot deny it.* The hissed words seared into his brain. *Don't forget, Arthur. You made the deal. Now it's time to pay the piper.* The mental insinuations roiled with gloating malice.

Arthur's upper lip curled in disgust.

"I... I don't w-want..."

Want? What you want does not matter. You struck the deal. You know the price.

The thin and sticklike man sat in stony silence. Absent of any sound but ragged breathing, the moment stretched out. The voice brain did not comment

Thirteen

further. Arthur broke the preternatural stillness, flexing his fingers to reveal the crimson crescents dug into the pale flesh of his palms. He reached for the wheels of his chair again. He rolled it forward, just to gain enough mobility to turn the confining contraption.

The door slid out of his field of vision. The chair rotated, bringing him to face the mahogany bookshelf that dominated one wall. His questing gaze ran over stacked books of grammar, literary form and style. He skipped past shelves of classic literature and contemporary fiction, compilations of literary and fiction magazines. Drawn inexorably upwards, his eyes came to rest on the novel holding the place of honour on the top shelf.

These books all shared one common aspect – the name A. E. Copeland embossed on the sides in gold gothic script. They represented the sum of his life's work over the past three decades. They were his passion, his pride – and his downfall.

Indeed, just what you always wanted. A dozen published novels, including nine best sellers. A wonderful collection, a worthy lasting testament to your life's labour.

There was a pregnant, knowing pause.

But not perfect. You might even say, Arthur, that it's incomplete – just like you.

He'd known what was coming, but Arthur still winced. His gaze slid from the bookshelf, coming to rest on his lap, dwelling on the fact that one half of said lap ended mid-thigh. The remainder of his left leg was simply non-existent. The amputated stump, covered by the empty fold of his pants, caused him to shut his eyes, warring against the urge to vomit.

The doctors had taken the leg six months ago. The strange virulent cancer that had just been beginning in his lungs had somehow spread to and flourished in the limb. The doctors couldn't explain it. By the time it had been discovered it was too late. They couldn't save the leg, so they removed it to try and prevent further spreading.

It didn't help. The cancer still in his lungs and resisted all treatment. Any effort to reduce or confine it met with failure. Within three months, it had spread its malignant reaching grasp to nearly every major system in his body. The doctors could not fathom it, but he wasn't surprised. He knew that his affliction was outside their science. This was not some mutated failing of his own body. This was more than that and worse.

He'd made a corrupt deal with something and now the corruption was being revisited on him. No medical science could save him.

He sent the last of the doctors away. Let them stew in their puzzlement. Turn a deaf ear to their warnings and dire predictions. He signed out of the hospital and returned home alone. He had no family and precious few acquaintances, let alone true friends. The success of his distinct and disturbing brand of horror had only served to further distance him from the mainstream of society and the people he knew. He returned to an empty house wanting only to set his affairs in order and die. He was surprised to find that he welcomed the thought of it. It would be better than this.

How touching. But you're not going anywhere just yet. You have work to do before you go.

Arthur reopened his eyes. Defeat creased his haggard features and tears streaked hopelessness down his sunken cheeks. The last vestiges of fight drained away.

"I know." He whispered.

Good. You know what must be done?

The slick excitement sickened him. He snorted.

Thirteen

"Of course." Despair welled up, black and clutching. He opened his mouth to continue, but gagged at the taste of coppery blood and vicious bile in his throat. In the end, he said nothing, just nodded. He took a deep shuddering breath and turned red-rimmed bloodshot eyes back to the monstrous bulk of the typewriter. He set his hands to the wheels of the hated chair and worked his way back.

He bit back a sob as he rolled a crisp, white sheet of paper into place. Fingers upon the keys, he could feel the presence lurking there. It coiled in his mind, leering over his metaphorical shoulder. It was not unfamiliar. Uncountable hours had passed like this. Sitting here, fingers flickering over the keys while gruesome and disturbing ideas into his head, filtered through his imagination. Like hot water being forced through dark rich coffee, they had brewed books. The feel of it disgusted him now, that slithering lurker. Never before had it felt so wrong.

Realization dawned. Arthur blinked, eyes widening.

"Leave."

What? What did you say to me, Arthur?

"Leave." Stronger this time - a command.

How dare you... The howl slashed a line of fire across his thoughts.

Arthur's face split in a genuine smile. "That's the way it has to be." The words were calm, serene. He felt the click of certainty. He was right.

Hesitation.

"You have to leave. I have to do this on my own. If you want your payment, you'll have to go until I'm done."

He knew that the presence could sense it too. He could feel the indecision, the gnawing doubt. He felt a brief thrill of private pleasure, but it didn't last.

"I can't choose not to write this, just like you can't slink out of my life without it. The deal was made and now the deal has to be done." That click again, and he was certain of that, too.

You think too much of yourself, Arthur, to think I worry of a betrayal from you. I know you too well.

But the agitation was there, Arthur was almost certain. Good. It was trapped now. Pride and vanity would send it away, just as would the knowledge that this last job must be done alone. To do otherwise – to protest - last job alone. To do otherwise would reveal it's uncertainty and weakness. It might even break the pact.

Then it was gone. Arthur was more alone in his own head than he had been in months, years.

He sank back with a sigh. Relief drained his tension and stilled his quaking limbs. A half-smile flitted across his weathered features, but dimmed as his gaze rested once again on the typewriter. He hadn't lied. He was compelled to follow through. There was nothing else for it. His reprieve was as temporary as his small victory. It all came back to the same thing. He remained a crippled, dying man, made old before his time, with no choice left to him.

Almost of their own accord, his bony fingers began to punch the stiff keys. The clacking thud of bars pressing inked ribbon to paper was intermittent, picking up speed. The clarion call of the bell rang out clearly in the silence of the room as the carriage reached the limit of its mobility. Arthur took no notice. On reflex, his hand snapped up to thrust it back so he could continue.

The thundering roar of snapping keys and ringing bells continued to build momentum. A smile curled the corners of his mouth. The smile grew as bold black letters spread like wildfire. Unfolding further, it took on a manic edge. He whipped the first complete page from the typewriter, the mad gleam in his eyes matching his grimace. Another sheet rolled up and the frantic typing.

The seconds ticked into minutes, minutes into hours. The rapid-fire sounds of typing broke only for a new sheet of paper, and once when a spasm of coughing seized him. He clutched frail arms around aching ribs, doubled over. The wrenching coughs tore at him for over a minute. When he sat up again, tears leaked from his eyes and a trickle of blood ran from the corner of his mouth.

Bloodshot eyes glazed with pain locked on the half-finished page protruding from the typewriter. Heedless of tears or blood, gasping for renewed breath, he reached for the keys. The typing resumed and the crazed look re-appeared, all the more disturbing for the damp tracks on his cheeks and bloody trickle on his chin. Fingers hammered keys, words imprinted on pages, and the stack of finished pages grew. With sudden finality the last period was thrust into place. It was complete.

Arthur gaped without comprehension at the final page, still poking out of the typewriter. Like a sleepwalker, he extracted it, laying it with something akin to reverence atop the sheaf of completed pages. He blinked. Like a patient rising from the depths of coma, he became aware of the world around him.

The setting of the sun had stolen the light from the room. A Tiffany's Banker-style desk lamp bathed the typewriter in a lambent golden glow. He had no recollection of turning it on. Sensations flooded to his brain from throughout his body. His hands and wrists were cramped, his throat dry and cracking, his bladder almost painfully full, but worst of all, the bitter coppery taste of old blood. He never kept a timepiece in his study but by all indications several hours had passed.

His immediate inclination was to wheel the chair away. Perhaps relieve himself, get a drink to wash out his mouth and sooth his parched throat, take something for the awakening pain in his hands and the subsiding ache in his chest. He curled his throbbing digits around the wheels as his gaze fell to the neat stack of pages that were his final story.

"No." The word cracked in his dry throat. "No more delays."

He picked up the slim sheaf of papers. There were fewer sheets there than he had thought. What he held in his hands was hardly enough to be a chapter in one of his novels. It didn't feel like much but it was all he had, all that was left in him.

"It's done."

He felt the cold rush of its return. Sickening eagerness nauseated him. His fists clenched. Pages crumpled with a dry crackle.

Stop. The cold command dropped into his head. His fingers loosened.

Better.

"No more." Arthur whispered. "I want to be done with this."

Fine. I tire of these games as well. Get on with it.

He nodded - a reflex. Drawing in a ragged breath, he lowered his eyes to the pages in his hands and began to read.

What is this? What are you doing Arthur?

He ignored the shrieking query and continued to read.

Stop. You cannot do this, must not. I forbid it.

The sound of rising panic brought a ghost of a smile, but the reading never faltered. The first page was flipped to the back. The second soon followed. The voice in his head continued to wail denials, but as the pages flew past it was joined, eclipsed, by a growing pressure. The words continued, coming with a life all their own. They fell from his lips with compelling strength. The end of the last page approached. The ringing force in his mind built to a crescendo.

Noooo... the agonized screech echoed in his head as the last word passed his lips. Blackness overtook him.

"oooo..." the trailing denial slipped from Arthur's mouth as the world returned.

Thirteen

He blinked, uncertain. The room looked the same. Almost no time had passed. Nothing had changed.

He glanced at the pages in his hands. The final words of his last story stood from stark white paper in bold black type. Laughter bubbled up, strained yet gleeful. It was shattered by the wracking cough that brought frothy blood to his lips. He raised his hands to wipe it away. Discarded pages splayed over the floor.

"Gone. No voice, no deal, no anything... never was... terrible stories, terrifying images... all me, just me... fractured mind... All gone... and it dies with me!"

The breathless whisper trailed into hysterical giggling. On the floor, the pages of the final tale bore witness, glaring words staring, unsympathetic, from the first page.

'The hulking form of the ancient Royal typewriter...'

Thirteen

THE MAGICIAN
GARETH FRY

There was a real buzz around town. An atmosphere so electric it could send a shiver down the spine and make the hairs on the back of your neck stand on end. He felt the power and drew it towards him, absorbing it, feeding off it and feeling his strength grow deep within. He was the great magician. The unnamed one. The masked one. Nobody knew his identity but everybody worshipped him. On his last television show he had made the moon disappear from the sky. He had caused the QE2 to rise above the water. The ratings had gone through the roof and the national grid recorded its highest ever output as kettles all over the country were switched on after the closing credits. Tonight was different though. Tonight he was back in the theatre. It was what he enjoyed most. The closeness of the audience. The sense of life that those few hundred people could inject into the show. It was what he needed most. His wife had died two days previously and the sadness blackened his heart. But the show had to go on and, with the help of those select ticket holders, it would certainly do that. This was to be his finest show, his finest accomplishment. His finale was to be a miracle.

He stood in the wings and looked on to the stage. His props were in place and he went over the act in his mind. He was always mute during his performance, preferring to use the power and raw emotion of heavy metal music to drive the show. The effect it produced was staggering when mixed with some atmospheric lighting and was the work of a very good crew. Yet, they were as much in the dark about his identity as the general public. He never gave interviews. His wife had been his agent, manager, publicist, and his communication with the world. He was a mystery and he liked it like that. It would certainly help after tonight. His act for this show was, for the most part, best described as routine. The almost obligatory cutting people in half, escaping from certain death, making wild animals appear from thin air and a few card tricks for a bit of audience participation. Sure everything had a bit of a twist, his own devious slant. The wild animals would appear in the auditorium for instance rather than in a cage ten feet in the air. But there was nothing that was going to stretch him or tire him out. He needed all his energy for the finale. It was going to be something that would be talked about for some time.

The show went well. The audience were stunned into a hushed silence in all the right places. They clapped and cheered right on cue. His volunteers, dragged out of the crowd, all had willing personalities and made the only unpredictable part of the show go without a hiccup.

All the lights went out, except for a solitary spotlight that shone down on the magician's form.

'Ladies and gentlemen.' There were surprised murmurings in the audience. 'I know that none of you has ever heard me speak before, but tonight is no ordinary night. I have a pain that I want to share with you. A problem shared is a problem halved somebody once said. Well, together we can do better than that. Two days ago my wife died.'

The murmuring in the audience subsided and the mood in the theatre changed noticeably. True it was still shock, but a different sort of shock.

'She meant everything to me and I can't bear to live another day without her.'

'My god, he's going to kill himself on stage,' somebody in the audience shouted.

'No, I'm not going to do anything like that,' reassured the magician. 'I perform magic remember. I can do something far more wondrous to alleviate the sorrow than kill myself. Ladies and gentlemen, tonight I am going to perform a miracle.

Thirteen

For the first time in my magic career this is going to be no trick, no illusion, this is going to be reality. Tonight I am going to do something that has only been done once before. I am going to raise someone from the dead. I am bringing my wife back to life.'

The silence was almost uncomfortable.

'I need your help though. I want you to channel all your thoughts and energies into what I am doing. I need you to give up your very souls to help me achieve the impossible. Will you do that for me? Will you give me everything you have to help overcome this tragic situation?'

The audience spoke with one voice and gave the magician the answer he wanted to hear. He had never doubted them. After all, despite his speech, these people would never believe that this was anything but another trick.

Music began to play, a slow haunting ballad, but still with those customary guitars powering away the melody. The magician stepped backwards out of the spotlight and into the blackness. The beam widened a little and then moved backwards along the stage. It encapsulated the magician once more and also threw its powerful beam on to a table covered by a black cloth. Upon the cloth lay the magician's wife. Those at the front of the theatre could see her face perfectly. She looked so peaceful lying there, her beauty almost sereneness. There were stifled sobs from the audience. This woman was a well-known figure and whenever she had given interviews people fell in love with her. She had that ability to capture people's hearts. It was one of the reasons that the magician had got his big break on television. Sure he could do amazing tricks, but the producers believed that his sort of entertainment was dead as a television spectacle. She had convinced them otherwise. The audience had said they would help the magician with his miracle and now that they had seen her face they actually believed what they said.

The magician sensed the emotions that were pouring forth from every person sat in the auditorium. He would need that and once more he harnessed them and drew them into him. Dry ice swirled on to the stage, masking him and his wife from the audience's view. A screen at the back of the stage flickered to life. It fired out rapid and variable images and all eyes in the theatre turned to it. The magician began to chant. They were not words anybody could understand, but the audience did feel relaxed and calm hearing them. They began to feel a loss of consciousness and a heightening of subconsciousness. In this hypnotic state they were open to suggestion. The magician changed his chant. Again the words were of no language these people had ever heard before but the voice was no longer calming. It was powerful, it was ordering, it was commanding. There was a strange sensation as the audience felt the air around them. It had a spirituous presence to it. A supernatural power was working on their bodies and their souls and they were helpless to stop it. Still the magician chanted, still he commanded, his voice crescendoing until it was almost shrieking. Then, abruptly, it stopped. There was a gasp from the auditorium as three hundred pairs of lungs simultaneously expelled air. Then there was silence.

The house lights came on. The magician took his wife's hand and she rose from the table. They embraced and then walked to the front of the stage. The magician looked across the silent auditorium and surveyed the peacefulness.

'Thank you my friends. I will never forget what you have done for me here today.' He led his wife from the stage and the two of them were never seen again.

The audience remained seated. Their lifeless eyes would never again witness such a miracle.

NIGHT TIGER
DONIA CAREY

"Whatsa matter Jimbo, can't take the heat?" asks Roy, and gives the girl a wink.

I can see myself in the mirror, that big fish eyeball we got over the counter, and it seems I'm a balloon floating on the ceiling. The girls look right through me, take their change with that vacant look behind the eyes. They piss me off because I see them all right, all jumpy when Roy's around, their asses twitching like kitten's whiskers at the smell of catnip. Roy looks like Burt Reynolds, only taller—and a good head taller than me. Big muscles. He works out in his basement apartment that's rigged up like a gym. He has these weird oriental weapons, swords and stuff, and knows how to use them all, he says.

Just look at him now. Face slick with sweat but still he's Mr. Cool. That moustache of his, even in this heat it looks alive. For a month now I've been trying to grow one, but it hasn't amounted to more than a couple of thin, droopy hairs that would shame a rat. It's like that with everything I try to do, and then guys like Roy—they don't even have to try!

Around ten o'clock there's a lull, hardly any customers in the store. I'm getting real nervous about Jill; she's usually been in by now. What if somebody hurt her? And me stuck next to the cigarettes and razorblades, trapped behind a counter I should be leaping over so I can fly, fly to her rescue, make her safe forever. And then I spot her coming in the door behind Mrs. Savitsky. Barefoot, wearing a pair of cut-offs and a faded blue T-shirt: Jill. My breath always catches when I see her, the long long smooth hair pale as a Golden Delicious apple, her skin all apple-speckled and smooth too. Tonight sweat clings to her face in little droplets as if she just came out of a cold refrigerator.

"The change. Just gimme my change," says a bald man with a carton of milk who looks as though he's been standing in front of me for a while.

When Jill comes up to the cash register with a raspberry yogurt and two cans of cat food, she gives me a smile. She's the only girl who ever smiles at me. Roy's at the other end of the counter listening to Mrs. Savitsky. Her head sprouts curlers like the coils of barbed-wire you see on tops of fences. "I had the landlord put safety locks on all my windows so they only go up so far," she's saying. "Can't be too careful with that maniac still loose."

"My locks are broken, been meaning to get new ones," says Jill. She has a chipped tooth in front, little-girl smile. She puts the yogurt on the counter, balances the cat food on top.

"I wouldn't broadcast it, honey," says Mrs. Savitsky. "Better go to the hardware store first thing tomorrow. He's nothing to fool around with." She lowers her voice. "My brother-in-law's on the police force, and what he told me--! Things the papers can't print. And there's more things only the police know—he's not allowed to tell anybody, he just says, 'Rita, watch out, this guy's a real sicko!'"

"I'm not worried about any killer," Jill replies. "If he's got any sense, he's home having a cold shower. Or he's in an air-conditioned bar somewhere."

"Want me to come up later, baby?" Roy says. "Put some nails in those window frames? I've got my hammer right here."

The way he looks at her! The smell of his Aqua Velva enrages me, and something in me starts to erupt. He'd better watch out, better leave her alone, the fucking animal! But I don't say a word, can't make a sound, because the pollution is back, filling my throat. I stand like a dummy as Jill looks right into Roy's eyes. "I'd sooner take my chances, thanks," she says, and goes out without looking at me.

After she leaves, I'm so jittery I can hardly stand being with Roy. He's in a good mood now, full of himself. "Wow, get a load of that red-head! Freckles turn me

Thirteen

on.... A night like this was made for passion—jungle love!—there's nothing like it! You ought to try it yourself some time, get your nose out of those books, get yourself a girl...hell! if I was twenty again...." He fixes himself a coffee. "But that Jill," he says, rolling his eyes, "she's really something else. Even you think so, am I right?" He laughs like an imbecile; I'd like to smash his teeth in. "You're sweet on her, aren't you, kid? Come on, I've seen you gawking at her. But Jimmy, she's not in your league—and besides, I think she's got the hots for me...."

"You lay off her!" I shout, butting at his chest with my head, only I miss him—he's moved aside, and I'm knocked off my feet, wedged between the counter and the trashcan. I flail around and Roy grabs my wrists and pulls me up. "Hey, hey, easy now, Jimmy, calm down. Can't you take a joke? Easy, easy, not so serious—that's it, relax." He laughs. "If you could have seen your face!"

Thirteen

THE TOWER
MATTHEW BATHAM

They had been walking for weeks. Neither sure where they were heading. Neither caring.

Andrew Mandrake yawned. It wasn't unusual for a manuscript to have this effect on him, but normally he managed to get past the first sentence. To be fair to the author, David Black, it was 6pm and it had been a very long day.

Nathan was tall and stocky. His face always flushed. He sweated a lot. His face was earthily handsome. Giles was smaller, wiry. His fists were permanently clenched.
They were on the outskirts of a small settlement when they found the body. It was clothed in symbols of wealth and gold coins spilled from its pockets. They leapt upon the treasure like hungry wolves feeding. "We're rich!" cried Nathan.
"We are my friend!" cried Giles. The world is ours for the taking."

"Oh please," said Andrew, yawning again. But he read on.

The story, littered with clichés, told how Giles inadvertently kills Nathan in a fight over the gold. Giles wanders on through the wilderness, wracked with guilt until he discovers a tower – a very gothic tower. As if by magic, thunder clashes and it begins to rain. Giles takes shelter in the tower. A ghostly voice speaks from the darkness. The owner asks him to follow and Giles is led up a winding stairway. "The master awaits," says the guide, an ancient man with a long white beard. Inside a room at the top of the tower Giles meets the master – a blob with wings the vomits a lot. The Master demands that Giles serves him in return for bringing his friend back from the dead – that and untold riches. Giles agrees, a pact is made. The floating blob keeps its side of the bargain; Giles doesn't, resulting in the evil blob cursing not just Giles but every first-born son in every generation of his family for eternity. Not the right evil blob to have crossed.

"I have condemned my son and his son and the son that he has and ever son of every boy in every generation to come!" wailed Giles, his fists clenched.

"Give me strength!" Andrew pushed the manuscript aside. He really didn't care about the exact nature of the curse and he certainly didn't want to plough through three hundred more double-spaced pages to discover the eventual outcome of *The Tower* by David Black. When would someone send in something half decent? Unless he discovered that literary light soon, *Seething Dread* magazine would be putting up the closed sign and he would be condemned to a life of writing for dull trade magazines.

"Home time," said Andrew, switching of his desk lamp.
He walked form the small desk to his sofa and reached for the TV remote.
"Home," he sighed.

"I read an appalling manuscript the other day," said Andrew, taking a bottle of wine from the fridge.

"Surely that's not unusual is it?" asked Catherine, depositing her dirty plate into the murky water that filled the sink.

"I'll wash that later," said Andrew.

"I'd wash the rest of whatever in there too." Catherine grimaced at the smell rising from the bowl.

"I work long hours and have a very demanding girlfriend who expects me to cook her romantic meals three times a week," said Andrew, kissing her. "Shall we drink this in the living-room?" he gestured to a sofa in the corner of the open plan studio flat. "Or in the bedroom?" He nodded towards a futon in the opposite corner.

"The living-room sounds fine," said Catherine, "I could do with a change of scene. So what was so awful about this particular manuscript?"

"It just really grated on me. I only read the first two chapters. It was about three hundred pages or more. I just can't believe someone with so little talent would go to so much effort."

"How many terrible manuscripts do you get sent to you though?"

"Loads, but most of them are about twenty pages long. This was probably six months work, or more and it was dire."

"I predict a standard rejection letter," said Catherine, taking the glass of wine Andrew offered her.

"I sent it the next day. He'll have read it by now. Probably cursing me as we speak, telling his friends he can't believe I could be so short-sighted as to reject his master-piece."

"I can't believe you're even thinking about it," said Catherine.

"Nor can I, actually. You're right, I read crap stories every day. But this one made me feel a bit dirty it was so bad." Andrew sat, stretching his legs across Catherine's.

"Make yourself comfortable," she said. "Don't worry about my legs going to sleep. I'll just hobble home like some old drunk."

"Why don't you stay?"

"Early start tomorrow. Lots of marking to do that I should be doing now."

Andrew pouted. "I like it when you stay."

"Don't be a baby! Mr Chuckles the Rabbit will keep the nightmares away."

"You promised never to mention Mr Chuckles," said Andrew.

"And I never will again," replied Catherine.

Mr Chuckles didn't do his job that night.

Andrew was in the tower – the tower from the terrible manuscript by David Black. He remembered the author's name even in the dream.

"Talk about taking your work home with you," he thought, climbing the stairway. He could just make out the servant up ahead.

"The Master is expecting you," said the old man, nodding solemnly towards a door with a handle shaped like a snarling dog.

"I think I'll pass," said Andrew. He had thought about forcing himself to wake up, but he was worried he wouldn't get back to sleep and he had another load of manuscripts to plough through tomorrow.

"The master is waiting," said the servant, and Andrew, deciding he had nothing to lose, opened the door and stepped into a vast circular chamber. The room was completely bare and icy cold. Andrew couldn't remember feeling cold in a dream before.

"Welcome," came a high-pitched, gurgling voice and Andrew looked up. There, floating just above him was the creature from *The Tower*.

"Grotesque," said Andrew.

"Charming," said the creature.

"Sorry," said Andrew, "I'm just a bit bored with this dream. I wasted enough time reading the terrible story without having to relive it."

"What?" the monster looked puzzled, or as puzzled as a blob with a head like a rotten jacket potato protruding from its chest can look.

"I may just wake up," said Andrew.

"I'm sorry," said the monster, bobbing up and down. "This isn't in the script. Why is he re-writing the script?"

"I have no idea," replied someone from the shadowy depths of the room.

Thirteen

"Who are you exactly? You're supposed to be Giles, but you look nothing like him. And what on Earth are you wearing?"

Andrew glanced down at himself. He was wearing a pair of boxer-shorts dotted with yellow ducks. Catherine had bought them for him.

A man wearing a pair of striped pyjamas and a red dressing gown stomped into the light. He was holding a manuscript in one hand and a pen in the other.

"Who are you?" he asked again, glaring at Andrew through a pair of black-rimmed glasses that made his eyes look enormous.

"Andrew Mandrake," said Andrew.

The man muttered the name under his breath several times. "Andrew Mandrake!" he suddenly blared. "Editor of Seething Dread magazine?"

"Editor, publisher, owner," said Andrew.

"And complete tasteless fucker," said the man.

"I beg your pardon?"

"My name is David Black," said the man. "And this (he flapped the manuscript) is *The Tower*, the novel you so stupidly rejected."

"This is too much," said Andrew.

"Oh I am sorry to waste even more of you precious time," said David. "I just spent a year of my life writing this and what do I get in return? Rejection letters from every publisher I send it too. You were my last resort."

"I don't actually publish novels," said David. "If you'd read the submission guidelines panel in the front of the magazine you'd have seen I don't publish anything over 8,000 words. I don't know why I even bothered reading the first couple of chapters of your book."

"The first couple of chapters!" screeched David. "The first couple of chapters!" he looked at the monster, still bobbing in mid air. The creature shrugged, or did whatever a blob with no shoulders does instead of shrugging.

"So you didn't actually read it at all then?" said David, taking a few steps towards Andrew. "You rejected my book without even reading it."

"Yes," said Andrew. "I don't publish novels, just short fiction… eight thousand words and under."

"You could have serialised it!"

"We don't publish serials, unless they're by a known writer."

"How am I supposed to become a known writer if nobody publishes me!" demanded David.

"Do you spend much time revising what you write?" asked Andrew, trying to be helpful.

"What do you think I'm doing now? I've spent every night since your rejection going over and over every scene."

"Chapter, you mean."

"I like to think of them as scenes. I'm a very visual writer."

"Fair enough. Look I hate to be rude, but I'm going to wake myself up now."

"Oh typical! Don't stay and listen to a bit of feedback from a disgruntled contributor will you! It's people like me that keep magazines like yours going!"

"It's people like you that close most of them down," thought Andrew.

"Go on then! Wake yourself up, but when you realise what a dreadful mistake you've made give me a call."

" I don't have your number."

David spat out a 10-digit number. "Write it down when you wake up and call me on it when you need to apologise."

"Will do," said Andrew and he screwed his eyes shut and heard the familiar buzzing in his head as real life seeped back, squeezing out the last remnants of the dream.

An hour later, while he was sitting at his desk reading the latest batch of

Thirteen

terrible manuscripts the phone number jumped into his head. He scribbled it down on a scrap of paper, smiling at his own stupidity and continued reading. Ten minutes after that he picked up the phone and dialled it.

"Hello," sad the voice at the other end of the line.

"Hi," said Andrew, feeling utterly ridiculous now. "Could I speak to David Black please?"

"Hello Andrew," said the voice. "This is David Black speaking."

Andrew slammed the received down and pushed his chair backwards as if the phone were contaminated.

"Something weird happened today," said Andrew, already drinking wine, even though it was only six o'clock. His usual rule was no alcohol until after eight.

"What?" asked Catherine, depositing a bag containing two chicken kebabs on the coffee table.

"I dreamed about that book last night – the one I told you about, the really awful one."

"Not that again."

"It gets better. The writer was in the dream. He had a real go at me about not reading the entire manuscript and told me to ring him when I realised I'd made a mistake rejecting it. He gave me his phone number. I don't know why but I remembered it this morning and rang it. He answered."

"Who?"

"David Black, the writer."

Catherine froze half way through removing her coat.

"What did you say his name was?"

"David Black. Why are you looking at me like that?"

Catherine slumped onto the sofa.

"I think I know him," she said.

"There was a boy at school called David Black that had a crush on me," said Catherine, clutching her glass of wine. "He was a bit of a geek – curly dark hair and glasses with really thick lenses. He bought me roses once and gave them to me in front of everyone in the sixth-form common room. It was awful. I walked away without saying anything and dumped the roses in the first bin I came to. I felt terrible but I was just so embarrassed. It was after that that the dreams started."

Andrew topped up her glass and filled his own. "Go on," he said. "I'm gripped."

"They were just really vivid dreams and he was always in them. In one of them I was trapped in a tower and he rescued me by climbing up the side like Spiderman. In another one we were floating down a canal in Venice and he was singing that song from the Corneto adverts – remember them?"

Andrew nodded, impatient for her to continue.

"The last David dream I had we got married. I was dressed in this hideous flouncey white dress and he was all tuxed up with his hair slicked back. He told me I'd make him so happy if I'd just say 'I do' at the appropriate point. Next thing I know there's a priest and he's asking me if I'll take David Black till death do us part."

"And did you?"

"It just slipped out. It was only a dream and he looked so excited, I couldn't bear to disappoint him. Anyway I woke up and the phone was ringing. It was David. "Thanks for making me the happiest man alive,' he said, and I just screamed the house down."

"What happened after that?"

"I tried to ignore him but he kept putting his arm around me and calling me

Thirteen

Mrs Black. He really thought we were married. Finally I snapped and told him exactly what I thought of him in front of quite an audience. He looked completely crushed. I thought he'd be popping up in my dreams for weeks making my life a misery, but I never dreamed about him again."

"Do you want to stay tonight?" asked Andrew. "You look really shaken."

She shook her head. "I think I'd rather be at home. "Andrew, the last I heard, David Black had been committed. He was a sick man – really disturbed. Be careful."

"But he never tried to get back at you for rejecting him?"

"No. But I think he's probably more upset by your rejection."

The elephant hadn't moved since Andrew had found himself staring at its leathery knee. He wasn't sure exactly how long that had been. In reality maybe no more than a few seconds, in dream-time it seemed like quite a while.

Beyond the stationary elephant stood a similarly static stag, with one antler missing and next to this a three-legged hippo.

A shadow fell across the scene and Andrew looked up to see a huge boy staring down at him through thick lenses.

"You again!" squealed the boy, his voice half-way through breaking. There was a massive spot on his chin.

"If this is a nightmare that spot will burst," thought Andrew.

"Why did you hang up on me?" the boy demanded.

"What are you talking about?" asked Andrew.

Oh grow up!" said the boy and Andrew found himself looking down into his magnified eyes instead of up. The animals, he saw, were made of plastic and arranged on the floor of what was obviously the boy's bedroom.

"It's me," said the boy. "David Black. I'm just in character. I play to boy from the book in this part. Not that you even bothered reading that far. The story goes on to tell about a boy, called David actually, who has inherited the curse brought upon every generation of first born sons by the murderous Giles."

"I see," said Andrew. "That sounds great."

"In a minute this beautiful female vampire will appear at my bedroom window. She's come to bite me and condemn me to a life of eternal misery like all the first born sons before me..."

"Jesus!" Andrew was staring at the window, or more specifically the stunning woman that floated outside. She was the archetypal female vampire – lush black hair, perfect white skin and the biggest pair of breasts Andrew had ever seen – in dreams or in real life.

"I've overdone it with the breasts haven't I?" said David.

"Not one bit!" said Andrew. "Give the punters what they want."

"I should knock a few inches off."

"No! Add a couple on and give us both a dream experience to remember."

"I'm a minor!" said David.

"Well close your eyes then."

"You would as well wouldn't you?" said David. "You'd come into my dream and shag one of my characters right in front of me after rejecting my novel without a second thought."

"Yes I would," said Andrew.

"Go on then, be my guest. Knock yourself out, have a field day. Fuck her senseless!"

The window blew open and the beautiful creature floated into the bedroom. She smiled at Andrew and cupped her breasts in both hands. "Come on," she whispered. "Come and taste them."

Andrew took a step towards her.

Thirteen

"Oh dear!" said David. "I think I can hear your alarm clock, Andrew."

And Andrew heard it too, the clanging of the big red clock he's bought from Woolworth's. And as the vampire reached out to pull him to her bosom he woke up to a dismal Wednesday morning and Mr Chuckles the Bunny clutched to his hammering chest.

"You don't remember exactly why he was committed do you?" asked Andrew, taking a bite from a piece of toast while he waited for Catherine to reply. The line crackled while she thought.

"No," she replied eventually. "I only heard a rumour, a couple years after I left school, that he'd had some kind of breakdown and been sectioned. All sorts of stories were flying around for a bit – that he'd killed someone, that he'd molested some child. I don't know whether I believe any of them, but I do think he's unstable. As for this dream thing he does, I don't understand that at all. I'd started to think I was the mad one."

"He certainly makes the most of his dreams," said Andrew. "The way he uses them to revise his stories."

"I remember his writing now," said Catherine. "He used to show me his stories sometimes. They were always a bit sick."

"In what way?"

"Science fiction and fantasy stuff, but always with a nasty edge. I can't put my finger on it – just sick."

"Maybe I shouldn't have rejected his novel so quickly, sounds just what I'm looking for."

Catherine made a non-committal noise. "I have to go. Sally's due in ten minutes and I'm still in my bathrobe."

"Okay, pet, I'll see you tomorrow."

"Don't call me pet, Andrew, it makes me feel like someone common from a soap opera."

Andrew laughed and blew a kiss down the phone before replacing the receiver.

He glanced at the pile of unread manuscripts on his desk and then at the scrap of paper with David Black's phone number scribbled on it. It would be so easy to ring it and arrange to meet with him. There was something fascinating about a man that could pull other people into his dreams.

He yawned. "Bed time," he said. It was seven fifteen.

He was standing in the middle of a cornfield that was dotted with enormous red toadstools.

"Hello," he said to David, who was sitting on one of the impressive fungi reading his manuscript.

The writer looked up from his revision. "What?"

"I just said hello."

"I'm busy. Why are you here again? I don't ask you to keep coming into my dreams. I just want you to publish my book."

"I don't publish books, just...."

"Short stories of no more than 8,000 words, I know." David's gaze returned to his manuscript.

"So," said. "Andrew after a tense silence. "How long have you been able to do this dream sharing thing?"

"Always," said David without looking up.

"I think you know my girlfriend, Catherine Healy."

"That bitch!" Now he looked up, face baring an expression like someone who has bitten into an apple and found half a worm.

Thirteen

"She is not a bitch."
"She was to me. We were married."
"She told me."
"Is she still as prissy as ever?"
"She's wonderful actually."
"I'd forgotten about her. It was a long time ago. I've been through a lot since then."
"Are you still...?" Andrew paused.
"What? Mad?"
"I was going to say in an institution."
"Sheltered housing."
"You didn't really kill anyone then?"
"Who told you that?"
"Just a rumour."
"No, I didn't kill anyone or fiddle with any kiddies or sleep with my mother. I just had a breakdown. I had a lot to deal with. Parents splitting up, being put in a children's home, stories being rejected, dragging people into my dreams all the time and having them treat me like a freak afterwards."
"It can't have been easy."
"Don't patronise me. The only thing I want from you is a publishing contract."
Something shrieked above them and a gust of wind blew several pages of the manuscript across the field. Andrew looked up. A thirty-foot long dragon was flying across the pink sky.
"Is that one of your creations?" he asked.
"Well it isn't one of yours is it."
"Is there a dragon in *The Tower*?"
"No. I'm writing something else. Something shorter. Around 8,000 words, or less. There's a dragon in that."
Andrew felt a burst of compassion for the man.
"I'll be glad to read it," he said. "But I can't promise anything. Dragons are a bit overexposed."
A second stronger gust of wind blew even more of the manuscript from the toadstool. David swore and jumped down to retrieve them.
"David, you are in control of that thing aren't you," said Andrew watching the dragon swoop down, seemingly towards them.
"I usually am," said David, grabbing pages from amongst the corn, "But I'm a bit distracted tonight. You'd better make a run for it."
Andrew ran. He could hear the great leathery wings of the beast beating and feel the draught they created on the back of his neck.
"Run!" screamed David and then he began to laugh. "Did I mention it breathes fire? Bit passé I know, but still deadly."
Andrew chanced a glance backwards. The dragon was hovering a few feet from the ground, its forked tail curled underneath it, front legs raised like a dog begging. It opened its cavernous mouth and took a long, deep breath.
"Shit," said Andrew as the flames burst forth.
He closed his eyes, squeezing until his head buzzed. Intense heat engulfed him.
He sat up in bed, gasping for breath. His skin still burning.
David sat up next to him.
"Jesus! What are you dong here?"
"It's my dream."
"This can't be a dream. This is my flat. How could you dream about my flat? You've never been here."
"Haven't I?" said David.

Thirteen

Andrew shuddered and shut his eyes again. This time he woke up to his real flat, still bathed in semi darkness and the realisation that David Black knew where he lived. That David Black had been here.

"Do we have to talk about David Black?" Catherine slumped onto the sofa and reached out for the mug of coffee Andrew was holding.

"I think he's been here. I don't like the thought of him knowing where I live."

"Don't you print your address in the magazine?"

"No, I use a PO Box number. Do you know the kind of people that read small press horror/fantasy magazines?"

"People like you?" ventured Catherine.

Andrew paced the length of the room, slopping coffee onto the laminate flooring.

"What if he is dangerous? What if he comes back and tries to kill me for not publishing his awful book. I don't even publish novels, just short stories 8,000 words and under."

"Calm down Andrew. I don't think he's a killer. He always seemed quite sweet really."

"He had me burnt to a crisp by a dragon."

"That was just a dream."

"It felt bloody real."

"I'm sure you've dreamed of killing someone before. It doesn't mean you'd actually do it in real life."

"Comforting. Very comforting."

"Do you want me to stay tonight?" asked Catherine.

"I always want you to stay, but not because you think I need mothering. Anyway, if he is planning to come back it might be better if you weren't here. He wasn't very nice about you."

"Why did you mention me?" Catherine slammed her mug down on the coffee table. "Thanks a lot Andrew. What's the betting he'll start dragging me into his dreams now?"

"He hasn't bothered to in about fifteen years, I don't see why he'd bother now. I think its me he's interested in these days."

"You sound almost happy about it. Maybe the two of you could become real chums and swap notes about me."

"Actually, Catherine, I'm pretty knackered. "I may turn in."

"It's nine o'clock!"

"Sorry. Been a tough couple of days."

"You actually want to go to sleep so you can talk to him, don't you?"

"No! If I wanted to talk to him I could just call him."

"That would mean admitting you wanted it. One minute you're saying you're freaked out by the fact he may know where you live the next your going to bed in the middle of the afternoon so you can be with him."

Catherine stood, drained her coffee cup and grabbed her coat from the arm of the sofa. "Sweet dreams," she said, heading for the front door. "Let's just hope your new best friend has turned in early too."

"Catherine, I didn't mean you had to leave right away. I just said I was tired. Stay and have a glass of wine."

Catherine closed the door behind her. Even her footsteps clattering down the communal stairs sounding angry.

For several hours Andrew couldn't sleep and when he did he slept dreamlessly. It was well into the night before he found himself in a David dream. The scene was a forest, a dense, dark forest that closed in around Andrew as he walked,

Thirteen

searching for its architect.

"Andrew!"

Andrew recognised David's voice, but couldn't see him. "I've got her, Andrew," said David, still just a voice. "I have her in the tower and I'm going to kill her unless you do what you know you have to do."

"Who have you got?" asked Andrew, still searching the gloom for a sign of David.

"You know who! The other great rejecter. The cock tease, the little Miss 'I can't stay the night, I've got marking to do!'"

"How could you know about that?"

"Lucky guess."

"What do you mean you've got her? Got her in your dream or in reality?"

"Both."

"Let me see her."

Catherine stumbled towards him. Her hands were tied, her hair tangled with leaves and twigs. She fell into his arms, breathing heavily, then stepped back and slapped him.

"That's for reminding the sick freak that I existed!"

Andrew rubbed his cheek and proceeded to untie Catherine's hands. She had a point.

"Where does he have you?"

"I was tied up in this tower and then I was suddenly stumbling towards you." Catherine shook her hands to draw blood back into them.

"No, I mean in real life."

"He has me in real life?"

"That's what he said."

Catherine looked pensive. "I remember leaving yours. Someone calling to me and then... being here."

"What do you want, David?" called Andrew. "Just tell me."

"Surely to God you don't need to ask me that. I want my work published and I've decided you're the man to publish it. I want *The Tower* serialised and I want every short story I send you given prime position inside that rag of yours."

"But *The Tower* was terrible, David," said Andrew.

"Careful," whispered Catherine.

"You didn't even read it."

"I didn't need to. The first two chapters were so dire."

The forest fell silent.

"You've upset him," said Catherine. "He better not take it out on me."

"David!" called Andrew.

"What?" David was standing just a few feet from them, still clutching his weighty manuscript. Two men stood either side of him – Giles and Nathan, Andrew guessed.

"Why don't you tell them you don't like The Tower," said David. "Tell them they're destined for a life stuck in a drawer gathering dust. And him....." David jerked his head upwards to where the hideous blob creature was floating, vomiting forth jets of what looked like custard.

"Good God," said Catherine.

"David," said Andrew, "Why are you writing all this stuff about monsters and towers. The first rule of good writing is to write what you know. Most writers have to interpret that advice loosely, but you could do exactly that and still write an amazing fantasy story."

"What are you talking about?" David clicked his fingers and the characters from his book disappeared.

"Think about it, David. Your dreams are so vivid it's like being part of a movie

Thirteen

and you can share them with other people. You use them to revise your fiction. Can't you not see a story there somewhere?"

David looked coy. "Isn't that a bit egotistical?"

Andrew laughed. "I'd forgotten about your insufferable modesty."

"And *The Tower*?" asked David.

"Put it in that draw and let it gather dust," said Andrew.

"And that's your final piece of advice?"

"It is."

Andrew woke up.

He tried calling Catherine all of the following day. She hadn't turned up for work and wasn't at home. Her mobile was switched off.

He thought about calling the police, but what would he tell them? That a grown woman had gone missing for less than 24 hours, after having rowed with him. That he suspected a crazed horror writer had abducted her, because he's told him so in a dream?

He didn't sleep that night. He was about to drift off early the next morning but was jolted back to consciousness by the intercom. It was the postman, with a recoded delivery.

Andrew ripped open the brown envelope, throwing the remnants onto the floor and reading the letter that accompanied the thin manuscript.

Dear Andrew,
Thanks for your invaluable advice. I wrote this the very next morning. Hope you like it. It is exactly 8,000 words long.

Yours
David Black

The story was called *The Writer Who Didn't Take Rejection Very Well*.

"Definitely autobiographical then," thought Andrew, and he began reading David Black's tale.

The first few paragraphs told of a torturous childhood, a violent father, an alcoholic mother, culminating in his being taken in to care aged nine.

In the children's home he was violently bullied and abused by one of the carers. It was around this time he began to escape into his dreams and learned that here he was the strong one. Shortly after this discovery the bullying stopped and the other children began to avoid him rather than taunt him. The bullies had all been plagued by vivid dreams in which David orchestrated terrible events, usually ending with the dreamer's violent death.

Aged 16 he met the lovely Catherine. Andrew smiled at the description of this beautiful vivacious girl, tinged with retrospective bitterness.

The bitterness poured onto the page following his rejection by Catherine, who became Catherine the bitch.

The story skipped events directly following school, perhaps these memories were too painful for David to draw inspiration from.

And soon the tale brought the story almost up to date, telling of David's desperation to be recognised as a great writer, his penning of *The Tower*, and efforts to find a publisher.

Soon Andrew himself made an appearance and the references were not flattering. Patronising, talentless prick being one description.

The story told of David inadvertently dragging Andrew into his dreams, and the discovery that the 'talentless prick of a publisher' was married to the 'whore, bitch schoolgirl'.

Thirteen

David managed to fool the patronising wanker into thinking he had been inside his home, when all he had done was recreate the idiot's own thoughts into the fabric of a dream. Discovering Andrew Mandrake's address hadn't involved any mysticism. David had phoned directory enquiries.

Andrew made a mental note to go ex-directory.
Catherine's abduction followed next - simple exercise involving chloroform and a van.

She wriggled and cried like a cat that doesn't want to picked up, until the drug knocked her out.

Next came an account of the final dream in which Andrew had passed on the advice – good advice judging by the improvement in David's writing.

David decided to take notice of the prick-publisher. He woke himself and set about writing something real – of 8,000 words or less. It went well until the last paragraph. How could he end his story? It needed a punchy ending. The prick teasing whore from school moaned from the sofa, where she lay bound and gagged, and David had his ending.
He used the chloroform to silence her and carried her back to the van.
He used the prick teaser's keys to enter Andrew Mandrake's pathetic little apartment and found him sleeping. A quick sniff of chloroform and David knew he would sleep for long enough.
He slipped back to the van and carried the still unconscious Catherine up to the publisher's flat, where he gutted her with the publisher's own bread knife. He though he would never be able to clear up the mess.
He shoved the dead whore into the publisher's wardrobe and pushed the door closed.

Andrew stopped reading.
He felt suddenly sick. He turned and stared at the door to his cramped wardrobe and tried to remember if he had opened it in the past two days.
He stood and walked on jelly-legs across the flat, gripping the wardrobe door handle.
He wouldn't!
He saw her, guts hanging from her stomach like butcher's offal, face fat and blue.
He yanked open the wardrobe door and screamed at the sight of his best wedding suit.
"Jesus!" Andrew sank onto the sofa, hugging himself and rocking gently.
Exhaustion finally got the better of him and he fell into a doze. Soon the doze became a dream and finally a David dream.
"Well?" asked David, once again perched on a luminous toadstool in the field of corn.
"It was better," said Andrew. "Where's Catherine?"
"She must be awake," said David. "Not that there's much difference between waking and sleeping when you're locked in a dark cupboard."
"She's alive then. The ending was just made up?"
"This time," said David. "But it was a very powerful ending, don't you think?"
"Effective in a primitive way."
"Don't like that tone," said David.
"Sorry."
"I'll let you have her back," said David. "But you know the condition."
"*The Tower?*"
"I'm sure you'll grow to love it."
"I doubt that."

Thirteen

"I'll expect to see the first instalment in the next issue. Once I do, I'll take her home and tuck her up in her own bed. I'd bring her to yours, but she doesn't seem too keen on sleeping there."

"Whatever!" said Andrew.

"Do we have a deal?"

"Do I have a choice?"

"Not as I see it."

"Then I suppose we have a deal."

A cheer rose up from amidst the corn and Andrew saw Giles and Nathan and the creature leaping (and bobbing) excitedly. There were others also celebrating that he didn't recognise, although he was sure he'd come to know them.

"Just one thing, that I won't budge on" said Andrew.

"What's that?" asked David.

"The length of each instalment – it can't go above 8,000 words."

Thirteen

THE SNOW CAME SOFTLY DOWN; OR,
THE KINDNESS OF GHOSTS
BRIAN SHOWERS

Chapter I: The Tale of the Hearth

The snow came softly down, covering the winter market and slowly filling tracks that crisscrossed the muddy field. Nicholas Goodrich carefully packed his purchases into a large burlap sack; a small, wooden rocking horse for his daughter, a set of blocks with letters of the alphabet engraved on them for his son and a new set of combs for his wife. He hefted the sack onto his shoulder and set off from the market to collect the rest of his belongings from his room at the White Oak tavern.

"It looks like it may come down heavier, Mr. Goodrich. Are you sure you won't stay another night?" The innkeeper looked up from washing dishes and out the window at the crisp winter afternoon, now marred by tiny flecks of snow.

"I'm afraid not. I've finished with all of my business and there's still enough daylight to make it home by tonight, though my family doesn't expect me until tomorrow afternoon," he said with a gleeful grin.

The boisterous song of a few Yuletide revellers, the centre of which was a large man with a thick red beard, rose discordantly over a feast of beer and beef, "O sing, all ye citizens of heav'n above! Glory to God, all glory in the highest!" Their voices roared drunkenly together.

The innkeeper smiled at Nicholas, "I suppose you'll be wanting to surprise your family too, it being Christmas Eve and all."

Nicholas patted the sack full of food and gifts, winked at the innkeeper, and made his way through the crowded tavern towards the door.

"What's this?" bellowed the man with the red beard to the innkeeper. "You're not letting one get away without a drink are you?" and then turned towards Nicholas and repeated his question as a statement, "You're not getting away without a drink."

"I'm afraid so," replied Nicholas. "I mean to return home tonight and I still have the woods to negotiate before nightfall."

The crowd of drunkards made a loud wooing noise at this and turned their attention to Red Beard, who was now wetting his throat with a great gulp of beer. "You'll not want to leave the tavern fire for the cold woods, kind sir, leastwise not this night." He paused with expert dramatics to take another swig of beer, allowing the listeners to gather.

Nicholas blinked almost as if in disbelief then a smile peeled across his face, "I suppose, if there's a quick story involved, it wouldn't hurt to stay for just one." The Yuletide revellers broke into a cheer and quickly hushed for the storyteller to continue. The innkeeper brought Nicholas a mug of beer, and then, as the men had already anticipated, Red Beard began his story . . .

"This town wasn't always here, you know. It is, in fact, a youthful cherub when compared to the hoary oaks of the surrounding forest; and only a simpleton would think that our town was the first babe to be born in these woods. The fact is, our ancestors built this town from the ashes of the previous village that stood on this very site. The men that lived here before us were driven out of the area with fire and cold steel. Those who weren't put to the sword were banished deep into the forest. You see, the men that lived here before us, they weren't proper God-fearing men like us. They practiced dark magics – and in those days it wasn't uncommon for newborns to go missing from the cribs of the neighbouring villages. These people worshiped the darkling spirits that lived deep in the forest . . . and in the very trees themselves!"

"Just like we worship the grain, ain't that right lads!" interrupted a man near the fireplace. Mugs were hoisted all around amidst a hearty cheer.

"Thank the Lord for that!" bellowed another.

"Thank the Lord indeed," continued Red Beard, "For it was a man of the Lord who purified this land after the heathens were driven out. Because when they left, their own holy men beset this land with a curse." The rowdy listeners hushed once more.

"A curse? What was it?" asked a man in a whisper.

"Now the first two years passed with the usual hardships, but on the third year there came a plague from the forest; a plague from the very bowels of hell itself! In the autumn of the third year a herd of wild swine, with mangy black hair and tusks dripping with foam, swarmed the fields. They ruined crops and scattered flocks. Groups of hunters went into the forest, but could find hide nor hair of the beasts."

"I would've found'em, the dirty buggers!" growled the man in the corner. Some of the other men nodded vacantly, confirming their comrade's sentiment, but most sat silently, too enrapt to comment. Nicholas too sat transfixed in his seat. Red Beard continued:

"The very same thing happened the next week. The boars returned from the depths of the forest, snorting and rooting their way through the fields. The men of the village drove them out again, but the damage had already been done. The yield at harvest that year was scant.

"The swine continued their raids, turning their attention from fields to food stores at the onset of winter. The devils'd claw and dig their way in, and sometimes chewing through the very walls of the silos. And no matter how many hogs they killed, there were always more. They tried using guard dogs, but those were only torn to shreds or simply gored by the marauding hogs. They even called upon the local parish priest who tried to exorcise the demon-swine, but with no avail. Fortunately, by winter the villagers defended their food stores well enough that nary a pig could get through to feed, but their shadows could still be seen lurking at the edge of the forest. The villagers, our God-fearing ancestors, prayed that the devils would starve and go elsewhere."

Red Beard paused to wet his throat with another beer. "What happened next," asked an eager listener? Red Beard licked the foam from his lips and continued.

"There were no attacks for many weeks, and on Christmas Eve the men let their guard down to prepare for the Yuletide festival. That night, the villagers drank and danced their way to midnight, but just before the clock struck the hour, a low rumbling sound reverberated through the church hall. One by one, the villagers stopped dancing as the rumbling grew louder. The villagers were already huddled together when the door of the church hall burst open with a torrent of wild pigs, all squealing and snorting. They knocked over tables and trampled the decorations. The evil marauders rooted through the food on the floor, slavering over boot-trodden mince pies and tearing apart whole turkeys in their filthy and unwholesome mouths."

The men around the fireplace laughed, whooped, and made pig noises at the climax of Red Beard's tale. They joked, snorted, and slapped each other's backs while Red Beard waited patiently, knowingly, for them to calm down. When the moment was right, he continued:

"Nine children were never found." A grim silence descended upon the tavern. "When the unholy swine finally retreated, and the villagers returned to their homes still shaking with fright, there were nine children missing from their beds. Nine children who were never seen again."

The tavern assembly was silent, their merry thoughts of partying pigs turned to those of children being torn from their beds by hungry swine and dragged,

Thirteen

screaming, into the forest where they were rended limb by bloody limb in those filthy and unwholesome mouths.

Red Beard continued his story I the thickness of silence, "The next day a party made up of local hunters went into the forest to search for any remains, but neither the pigs nor children was ever found. After that night, the wild swine were never seen again--but the curse was far from over. You see, every few years, someone still disappears in those woods. Sometimes hunters, sometimes travellers - but mostly children. And while there's not a single swine in that entire forest now, there's still something out there . . . waiting." Red Beard, finished with the tale, leaned back in his chair quite pleased with himself. The men gathered around all nodding in agreement as if they each remembered either a recent incident or a story vaguely recollected from their own childhoods. "They say," Red Beard started again with a mischievous look in his eye, "that the ghosts of the dead children become restless this time of year, Christmas Eve, wandering the forest where their mortal remains were spirited away. Look! There's two of them now!" barked Red Beard, as he leapt at Nicholas Goodrich.

Nicholas turned white, eyes glazed over in terror. He looked through the frosted windowpanes with the rest of the crowd. Pressed against the glass were two miniature faces, four grubby hands and two sets of beady black eyes peering into the tavern.

"Get outta here!" The innkeeper came out from behind the counter and banged on the glass with his meaty fist, "Get outta here! Bloody street urchins." As the innkeeper dispelled the ghosts, the whole tavern broke out in laughter with collective relief. All save for Nicholas.

"But you're a grown man, Mr. Goodrich, stout, and thick in the arms," said Red Beard brandishing his own muscles with a grin, "You're no child. You should have no trouble navigating the woods on this night." Nicholas smiled weakly at Red Beard as the rest of the audience broke into little groups, resuming well-worn conversations and half-hearted arguments.

Nicholas gathered his belongings and paid the innkeeper for the beer. As he laid his coins on the counter, the innkeeper leaned over and spoke to Nicholas in a low tone.

"It's just a story you know. And Red Beard, he sure knows how to tell'em, aye?" He gave Nicholas a weak grin, "Still, it gives me goose flesh, no matter how many times I hear it. I'm surprised you haven't heard it before. Are you sure you're all right?"

"Oh, yeah, it's nothing. I was just thinking of my own two children. At any rate, I'd best be off if I'm to get home in time." The two men moved towards the door.

"Give my regards to the misses, Mr. Goodrich, and a Merry Christmas to you and your family. Have a safe journey home."

"Thank you, sir, Merry Christmas to you too."

As Nicholas left the warmth of the tavern for the cold chill of the afternoon, the man in the corner of the tavern yelled after him, "Watch out for the pigs!" which garnered a round of snorting and rowdy laughter.

Chapter II: The Ghostly Waifs
The air was crisp and the sky a light grey, sunset still many hours away. Delicate snowflakes dropped lazily from the sky. There were few people left in the streets, most going home to their families or transporting goods from the market. Occasionally Nicholas spotted a large gutter rat. Each invariably had a fragment of unidentifiable vegetable or bruised piece of fruit in tow, presumably to feed their own families a Yuletide feast.

Nicholas trudged along the main street towards the edge of town. Soon he

Thirteen

found himself on the very outskirts, walking alongside the low cemetery wall. At the edge of the cemetery stood a church, whose tall steeple rose up into the flurried afternoon sky. It was along this vacant stretch near the cemetery gates that Nicholas felt a presence trotting along at his side.

"Can you spare a few bob, please, sir?"

Nicholas looked down to find the owner of the voice, a young boy, no older than nine, holding the hand of a girl who could not have been more than a couple years his junior. The boy held out his dirt-encrusted hand and repeated his question, "Please, sir, can you spare a copper?" Nicholas squatted down on his haunches and surveyed the pair. The boy, dressed in layers of torn rags, was unshod while the girl, despite the benefit of shoes, wore only a tattered, antique white dress. Most distressing, however, wasn't the state of their dress, but their visage. The topmost layer of the boy's outfit was dirt, from head to toe that gave him a swarthy countenance. The girl's was the opposite, though equally alarming. Her face was hauntingly drained of colour; a porcelain white that matched her dress. As strikingly as they contrasted each other, they had one feature in common: a look of extreme malnourishment. Instead of the full pink cheeks that children normally have, their cheeks were sunken like a beggar man in his twilight years, and they both stared at Nicholas with dull, black eyes.

Despite their ghastly state, Nicholas smiled as warmly at them as he would at his own children. "Where are your parents?" Nicholas asked. "It's Christmas Eve you know. Why aren't you at home?"

"We don't have homes, sir," replied the boy, still looking hopeful for a charitable donation.

"How long have you lived like this?" asked Nicholas.

"I can't remember, sir. Lucy here was already homeless when I met her."

Nicholas looked the girl in the eye and gave her a warm smile, "Hello, Lucy. My name is Nicholas." She stared at him vacantly, her sweet face expressionless. "Can you tell me how long you've been out here, Lucy?" She continued to stare out from her hollow eyes.

"She don't talk much, sir," the boy offered by way of explanation. "I do all the talking for both of us. My name is William," and he proudly stuck out a grubby little hand.

"It's good to meet you, William," said Nicholas taking the boy's hand in his, wincing briefly at its coldness. "Please, tell me, how did you come to live this way? Certainly you should have some place to go for Christmas Eve."

"It seems like such a long time ago, sir, I can barely remember," started William. "It used to be that I lived with my mama and papa. I didn't have no brothers or sisters, so I was often on me own. My papa, he always went out hunting on Christmas Eve to bring home a rabbit for the dinner. I remember mama saying, 'Go along with your father, now, to keep him company.'" William's eyes wandered to the opening of the forest up the road, beyond the church.

"We sat in the snow for ages, but never saw a single rabbit. I got bored and asked papa if I could explore. He said 'yes,' so I went deeper into the woods to find some playmates."

"Playmates? In the woods?" asked Nicholas, slightly perplexed.

"Yes, sir. A voice told me that there was a place deep in the woods, a warm place where there were many children to play with.

Nicholas was bewildered, though recalled the fantastic stories his son often told, and decided not to press William for an explanation. "Did you find the children?"

"I don't know, sir," said William with a sad and distant look in his eye. "I don't remember."

"What do you remember, William?"

Thirteen

"I remember walking home, sir, walking home all alone. But the funny thing about it was that it wasn't winter no more. I remember that because the moon was big and bright and I could see lots of flowers growing in the moonlight. And even though the night air was warm, I remember feeling very cold, like I had a fire of ice in my belly.

"My parents, they were already eating dinner when I got home. There was a place set for me, but there was no food on my plate. They were wearing black, sir, my parents were. And they wouldn't talk to me. They wouldn't even look at me!" William looked as if he were about the cry.

"They may have been upset with you William," comforted Nicholas, "but that doesn't mean they don't love you. I sometimes get angry with my children, but I still love them."

"It wasn't like that, sir," cut in William, wiping away a tear, "I don't think they were angry with me. They just didn't talk to me. Night after night was like that. That's all I can remember. Night after night I would sit there with an empty plate. But I never ate a thing."

"You didn't eat? Why didn't they feed you? Weren't you hungry?" asked Nicholas aghast.

"No, sir, I never felt hungry. I don't know why, but the only thing I wanted was for them to look up from their plates, to look up at me, and say, 'There's our boy Willie! Come give us a hug, Willie!' But they never did. So I yelled at them. 'Look at me! Look at me! I'm here! Why won't you look at me?' I shouted. Mama looked at me then, but only for a moment. Then she started to cry. Papa looked at me too, but he was angry. 'Go away,' he yelled at me, 'Haven't you hurt us enough? You're no longer welcome here. Be gone you devil!' So I ran from the house. That was the last time I saw them. I've lived on the streets with Lucy ever since. Lucy found me on the first night."

"That's awful, William. There must be some explanation. Where are your parents now?"

"They moved to another town, sir. They were angry with me, so they moved to another town."

"It's cold out here, William, how do you and Lucy keep warm? You don't have shoes and she doesn't have a coat."

"We live out here," said William, gesturing to the expanse of the graveyard, "But it's ok, sir, it's like we don't feel the cold no more."

Nicholas didn't know what to say. His own two children were similar in age and it pained him to think that parents could be so heartless. He sized the children up and then set down his sack. "I was going to give these to my own children," he said as he scrounged around in the sack, "But I think they will fit you just fine." He pulled from his great burlap sack a set of new shoes for William and a heavy coat for Lucy.

"Thank you, sir," said William with a spark of light in his deep, flinty eyes. "You're very good, sir." Lucy, however, said nothing and accepted the gift without response.

"You're welcome," said Nicholas. "And something else for you," he reached into his pockets and gave them each a handful of peppermint drops. At this, Lucy's eye widened in their deep sockets and she smiled at Nicholas. "Well, that certainly put some life back into you, Lucy!" said Nicholas with a broad smile.

"Peppermint drops are her favourite. I wish we had something to give you, sir," said William overjoyed.

"I think a 'Merry Christmas' would do nicely," said Nicholas.

"Yes! Merry Christmas, sir, and God bless," replied William. Lucy leaned in and lightly pressed her cold lips against Nicholas's cheek.

Nicholas rose to his feet. "Now I'm going to go into the church and have a word with the vicar. We'll see if we can't find you a place to stay."

He left the children standing at the entrance of the cemetery and hiked up the path to the church. He pushed on the old, oak door, but it was bolted shut. He banged on the door so loudly that an echo reverberated throughout the church hall, and then waited for a moment, but no one came. Nicholas scrawled a short note to the vicar telling him of the two vagrant children, and tacked it to the door. *The vicar must be at the market*, thought Nicholas as he walked back down the path to the cemetery gates.

When he arrived, the children were nowhere to be found. He stepped through the gates into the cemetery, thinking they may be just inside, wandering amongst the stones whilst waiting for him, but they were nowhere to be found. He scanned the road in both directions but could find no sign of the children. Nicholas shivered at the thought of the children seeking refuge from the winter in the cemetery; huddling together for warmth in a vault shared with occupants who would not mind so much the extra company. *I hope the vicar returns soon and finds the children before the winter chill sets in*, thought Nicholas. *I should probably keep going myself lest darkness catch up with me.* He hefted the sack on to his shoulder and set off for the forest.

And in the thin layer of powdery snow that lightly dusted the ground, Nicholas's were the only set of tracks leading away from the gates.

Chapter III: The Beast in the Holly
The forest was considerably darker than the day. Ancient oaks towered around Nicholas Goodrich and a canopy of skeletal branches crosshatched the sky overhead. The forest was silent, save for a thin layer of snow that crunched under his soles and the rustling of dry leaves stirred by his stride. Every so often Nicholas caught a quick scurrying movement from the corner of his eye, but would look only in time to see the underbrush gently disturbed by what was probably a stray pheasant or an evasive hare.

Nicholas plodded on through the increasing flurry of snow only stopping briefly to rest against one of the mighty trees. *These trees,* he thought as he ran his hand across the gnarled bark, *older than the town itself. And older than that, even!* He marvelled at the age of the forest and tried to imagine a time when the trees were still saplings; perhaps a time before man had first set foot amongst them. What sort of beasts stalked the forest then? A tiny clump of snow fell from the branches and onto the back of his exposed neck sending a wet chill down his spine. He quickly brushed it away and decided to move on to keep the cold from settling into his fingers and toes.

The path Nicholas followed was narrow, not much wider than a game trail. It was used primarily by woodsmen, hunters and those who lived on the other side of the forest and travelled on foot. Those fortunate enough to have transportation used the main road along the forest's southern border, which is more suitable for carts, wagons, and horses. But the southern road is nearly triple the distance, making the path through the arboreal deep, though unpopular, the most direct route. Despite this, most pedestrians still laboured the length of the southern road, shunning the directness of the woodland path. Though few would be able to say why, those who did did so only by the safety of a tavern fire.

Nicholas pushed on, deeper into the forest. The path, already quite narrow, became even harder to pick out, not only for the mounting snow, but because very few hunters ventured so deep into the wood pursuing game. The branches were thick and numerous enough that they nearly blotted out the glow from the soft, purple sky above. Nicholas stopped and hurriedly produced a small lantern and tinderbox from his sack. The first time he attempted to light the lantern a small clump of snow fell from a branch above him, extinguishing the struggling

Thirteen

tinder-flame with a sizzle. On the second and third attempts, the wind rushed up and eagerly extinguished the flame before he could light the lantern's wick. The fourth try brought success, and the lantern soon threw off a sphere of warm yellow light. He forced the thoughts away from the cold and darkening wood to the warmth of his cottage and the crackling fire therein; of the gifts he had for his family, and of the mulled wine and spiced cakes that awaited him at the end of his journey.

Rising from the ground to continue, lantern hoisted high, Nicholas found that he had lost track of the path. It was as if the forest had closed in around him while he was occupied with the lantern. Thick brambles and underbrush surrounded him with nary a path in sight. Slightly panicked, Nicholas methodically cast the light into the depths of the woods, hoping to catch any sign of the trail. Nicholas searched the trampled ground at his feet, hoping to find his own footprints in the snow, tracks that would lead him out of the tiny glade and back to the main path. But the wind and the weather conspired against him. The footprints had either filled up with or were drifted over by the snow, now falling heavily in big, fat flakes.

As he searched for footprints, Nicholas saw something. Shapes, large shadows, moving silently through the forest around him. Nicholas's mind raced as to the nature of the beasts that stalked the night just outside the precarious safety of his lantern. Probably wolves. So long as the lantern was lit, they would keep their distance. Just then a guttural snuffling followed by a high-pitched squeal issued forth from a thick mass of underbrush just beyond arm's reach - a sound no wolf would ever make.

Nicholas ran, abandoning his search for the trail. The beasts pursued, snorting and crashing through the underbrush behind him. He fled aimlessly through the forest, but no matter which direction he chose, the trees always seemed to move in on him blocking any escape after a dozen or so frantic strides. He changed direction and desperately tried again, pushing away branches to clear a path, praying that this new direction wouldn't lead him directly into one of the things that rumbled through the forest. As he ran, branches and thorns scraped and *clawed* at his arms and face. The sack of gifts he carried became a burden that he discarded in his wake without so much as even a glance.

Murderous squeals echoed through the hollow and seemed to come from neither near nor far, leaving Nicholas directionless in his escape. He paused briefly to catch his breath, his mouth tasting of sour iron and heart ready to explode under the pressure of sheer terror. Somewhere nearby one of the great beasts shifted on its haunches. Nicholas coaxed his legs to action. The hulking shapes kept pace with the terrified man, corralling him randomly amongst the trees.

Finally Nicholas hit his stride, dodging trees and moving quickly through thickets. He was so busy scanning the forest for his demonic hunters that he barely noticed a holly bush looming squarely in his path. By the time Nicholas was aware of the bush it was too late. Instinctively, he put out a hand to stop himself from crashing headlong into the thorny shrub. His outstretched hand plunged into the holly, the sharpened leaves ripping at his clothes and scratching his hand apart. But it wasn't the bush that stopped his momentum. What did was mercifully secreted away inside, obscured from this world by thorny leaves and red berries. Nicholas's hand came to rest on an oily and slightly malleable surface, thick bristling hairs entwined his bloodied fingers. The hulking mound within the shrub shifted, emitting a deafening squeal, and the heat from its ghastly bulk burned Nicholas's hand. His fever broke. Nicholas screamed, pulling his scorched hand away from the creature's flabby, searing flesh.

He ran from the accursed holly with its evil core. The creatures, squealing in

Thirteen

unison, thundered through the brush after him, snapping branches in their jaws as they advanced and closed their ranks. Nicholas was unable to run further. Sick with exhaustion and terror, he came to rest at the base of what looked like a tree trunk from far off, but proved to be a tall stone when he slumped weakly against it. From the dim radius of light that his lantern threw off, Nicholas could see the dark silhouettes of other stones, each the size of a menacingly large man, standing around a rough, circular clearing. Scant vegetation grew in the clearing, only becoming dense outside the congregation of the megaliths. Nicholas stepped into the stone circle. Within the circle was an enticing warmth and an unnatural silence. Without, the beasts snapped their jaws and closed in.

Slowly, Nicholas hoisted the lantern above his head and peered into the dense underbrush beyond the small clearing. Peering back at him, though concealed by undergrowth and darkness, were an uncountable collection of dimly luminous eyes. The bushes rustled and the eyes, murderous and blood-thirsty, leered at his very soul. Then, a cloven hoof at the end of a plump and bristly leg, protruded from the darkness, breaching the perimeter of the towering stones.

The mortal man opened his mouth, but could only mime a silent scream. He sank to his knees, a quivering mass of goose flesh, and awaited his fate. Nicholas dropped the lantern from his trembling hand. It smashed on the ground, extinguishing the light. What came after was a terrible darkness.

Chapter IV: The Footprints in the Snow
It first came like a cold pressure brushing lightly against his cheek, almost tickling as if a fat snowflake fell upon his face. Then there was a softly whispered melody in his ear, like when his daughter would climb onto his lap and quietly sing her nonsense songs to him. And then, over his lips and nose drifted the sweet scent of peppermint that, while faint, warmed him inside and out. He wiggled his fingers to make sure that they were still there. Revived, Nicholas Goodrich gradually opened his eyes to find himself lying in the snow.

Nicholas's first view was that of the black branches of the oaks against the night sky. He slowly sat up, head throbbing. A thick layer of snow clung to the sides of trees and blanketed the forest around him. The lantern, now in one piece, sat on a smooth flagstone, burning softly. The yellow flame struggled, almost extinguished, but still with life. The burlap sack lay in a heap nearby.

As his eyes focused, he found himself to be just outside the stone circle. Standing on weak legs, Nicholas surveyed the forest in the unearthly glow of a soft, bluish twilight. Whatever danger had lurked on the edges of darkness before had been chased away by the dim luminescence. The whole forest, as far as Nicholas could see, was immobile and frozen, yet pulsating in its still life. But the inside of the circle, despite the blue twilight, was still strangely dark.

Nicholas felt warm enough, despite the significant amount of snow on the ground, to continue searching for the way home - or a path that would quickly lead him to any border of the bewitched woods.

As Nicholas gazed into the forest, he felt a presence at his side. Upon looking down, despite what he sensed, he found that he was still very much alone. However, imprinted into the deep snow was a set of tiny footprints that began where he had been lying and lead into the woods beyond. Nicholas squatted down onto his haunches and surveyed the tracks. To his surprise, they were fresh, as if only recently imprinted in the snow's smooth, white surface. A brief glance around and he saw that there were no other tracks leading to or from where he presently stood. And then in the distance, carried lightly on the wind, Nicholas heard a child's song.

Snapping into lucidity, he cautiously called out, "Hello?" But the only reply was the faint melody, swirling around in the eddies and gusts of the wind. "I'm lost! Please help me!" pleaded Nicholas. The response was the same. At last a tiny, yellow light winked at him, as if someone carrying a lantern was ducking in and out from behind the trees. "Please, wait for me! I'm lost!" In an instant Nicholas found himself chasing after it, following the tracks, which always lead in the same direction as the light.

He followed the footprints for what seemed like hours, and even though it was still snowing steadily, they were always fresh, never filling up with snow. No matter what his pace, Nicholas never got any closer to the tiny lantern light that bobbed about in the distance. Occasionally, he fancied he saw the outlines, in the forest's darker recesses, of the terrible beasts that had given him chase, but like the lantern bearer he followed, they too kept their distance.

After a time, exhaustion set in. Nicholas leaned weakly against a tree watching the lantern in the distance. It winked at him for a moment longer, and then completely vanished into the darkness beyond. "Wait!" he cried. "Oh, please wait!" Nicholas stumbled to his feet and raced onward, still following the crisp footprints in the snow by the light of his own lantern.

It wasn't after much longer that the trees thinned and Nicholas found himself on the edge of a wide moor. With borrowed strength, he followed the tracks for another two hundred metres until he came to a small bridge that spanned a shallow creek not yet frozen over. The tiny footprints had led him faithfully for miles, but on the middle plank of that snow covered bridge, they abruptly stopped. Nicholas plunged into despair. He fell to his knees, weeping for joy to be free of the accursed woods, and then in sorrow for he was still very lost and very far from home.

Through bleary eyes, Nicholas saw a glimmer of hope. His luminous guide, answering his prayers, re-appeared twinkling in the distance. He rose slowly to his feet, leaving his lantern and sack on the bridge, and staggered across the field in pursuit, determined no to lose sight of his guide again. But this light, unlike the light he followed before, didn't bob about or wink at him. Instead, it hung perfectly still in the blackness of the moor. On the other side of the field Nicholas came to a long stone wall that he leaned on for support as he approached the light. The light grew ever larger as he neared it and soon Nicholas realised that it wasn't his guide at all, but the window of a small cottage and a lantern that hung beside the door. With his last burst of strength, Nicholas staggered through the hawthorn dotted yard, and upon reaching the cottage door, collapsed in a heap.

Chapter V: The Cottage on the Moors
"Drink this, dear," said an unfamiliar voice. Nicholas's eyes focused on a withered old woman whose wrinkled smile reflected years of kindness. He was sitting in front of a blazing turf fire wrapped in a large wool blanket, his head still throbbed, but his wounded hand was already dressed. The old woman offered him a small glass of brandy. He drank the liquor, choking on the vapours, and handed the glass back to her.

"You must have had quite a scare," she said taking the glass and going back to the large, iron stove in the corner of the room. "It's a good thing we found you when we did. You should have known better than to go into the woods on a night like tonight," she added almost scoldingly.

As she spoke the front door burst open, snow drifting into the room. An old man with a thick white moustache covered with frost came in carrying Nicholas' sack and lantern. "I found these down at the bridge," he said to the old woman as she scurried over to him.

"Our visitor's awake," was her reply. She took his hat and gloves and handed him a small glass of brandy. "Drink." After she made a minor fuss over the snow he had tracked into the tiny cottage, the elderly couple settled

Thirteen

themselves into chairs near the fireplace.

"The forest is no place for anyone on a night like this, you know. What were you doing out there?" asked the old man.

"I was on my way home from town, sir. I wanted to surprise my family on Christmas Eve. They aren't expecting me until tomorrow. I left town this afternoon, but when it started to snow I got lost. And then I was set upon by..." Nicholas hesitated and closed his eyes. He could see the cold outlines of the beasts imprinted on his eyelids. The old man looked at him curiously.

"Oh dear, you poor thing," worried the old woman without even waiting for Nicholas to finish his sentence. "Your family must be so worried. Do you have any children?"

"Yes, two. A boy and a girl," Nicholas replied distractedly.

The old woman looked very pleased, "We had a daughter once. How old are your children, Mr. Goodrich?"

"My son is nine and my daughter will be six this spring," replied Nicholas still under the old man's scrutiny.

"Six! That's how old our daughter is!" her face cracked with delight.

The old man cut in. "Tell me," he asked directly. "What were you chased by?"

Nicholas was silent for a long moment before finally deciding: "Wolves. I was chased by wolves."

"Well," replied the old man solemnly, keenly detecting Nicholas's half-truth, "those woods are a very dangerous place, especially with the snow coming down so heavily. Our daughter once got lost in a storm like this, but that was many years ago. And probably before you were even born." The old woman nodded in agreement.

"I'm sorry to hear that," said Nicholas thinking of his children. "And you're right, the woods are dangerous. More so than I ever would have thought before tonight. I hope your daughter was all right."

The old man shook his head. He stood up and retrieved a snuffbox from the holly-decorated mantle. "I'm afraid she was never found." He gestured towards Nicholas with the box. Nicholas declined. "We've never really given up hope, though." He lit the pipe. "Sometimes, on winter nights, like this one, we put a lantern out, just in case Lucy ever needs to find her way home. But tonight it looks like the lantern guided you here instead. And we can thank God and his angels for that, eh?" and he patted Nicholas on the knee with an old, rough hand and smiled.

Upon hearing the girl's name, Nicholas felt a warm chill, like a gulp of particularly strong whiskey. He smiled weakly at the couple; Lucy's now aged parents. He could barely believe it himself and for the sake of their old hearts, did not tell them how he was lead to their cottage. "Yes, it must have been an angel who guided me to safety."

"And now that you're safe and sound, dear, have a peppermint drop." The old woman offered Nicholas a jar. "I made them especially for Christmas, you know. They're Lucy's favourite."

Nicholas half rose at the offer. "My family," he remembered, "I'd still like to get to them tonight. Is there any chance you could…"

"I figured you might want to be off as soon as possible," said the old man, finishing Nicholas' thought, "and I think you're strong enough. I'll go out and hitch the pony to the sleigh and just as soon as you're ready, we'll be off."

"That's very kind of you," said Nicholas. "And please, if you would, stay the night with me and my family. Tomorrow is Christmas Day and we're very fond of guests."

The couple graciously accepted the invitation. The old woman packed a few belongings, taking care to pack an extra jar of peppermints for Nicholas's children, and they were ready to go. Soon the trio was huddled together in the sleigh, cutting across the frozen moor to the main road, and then onwards to Nicholas' house.

Epilogue

That night the Goodrich family and their guests rested peacefully; snug beneath heavy quilts on top of thick, comfortable mattresses. The embers in the hearth glowed orange, gently heating the home. The tiny cottage was silent; the only sounds that could even faintly be heard were snowflakes falling on the rooftop. Nicholas sat in front of the fireplace with only his hopes and fears to accompany him.

Before retiring to bed Nicholas went to the kitchen and filled a large wooden bowl with fruits, nuts, and peppermint drops. He crept to the front door and set the bowl outside in the snow. "Merry Christmas, William and Lucy," he whispered, and then just as quietly made his way to bed.

The next morning the fruits, nuts, and peppermint drops were gone, and leading from the forest to the empty bowl were two pairs of tiny footprints. That day the family would talk, sing and bake all day for the Christmas feast, but Nicholas never mentioned the children to anyone. And by mid-morning the footprints had already filled up with snow.

THE ART OF EULA MAE
BONNIE J. GLOVER

I dreamed I was young and Eula Mae was with me. We were running in the tall grass behind the house I lived in with Mama and Papa. Shoes off, hair riotous and nappy, caught with bits of twigs and leaves as we rolled down the small hills littering the property. It was changeling season, autumn, and we felt the cool wind on the backs of our necks and arms.

I was happy to be with her. She snatched me in her lap and braided my hair, all the while whispering secrets in my ear that made me giggle.

When she finished, I had a ginger coloured braid down the middle of my back. She pushed me away roughly, tugging the braid as we ran to the edge of the lake. We stopped and suddenly became silent. And still as the stillest night. She stretched her arms out to the water and I did the same. She turned to me, eyes serious and clouded black.

"When you are still young, I will be an old woman. Will you take care of me?"

I was barely five. "Yes." I said, solemn and eager to please. "Yes." I said a second time, nodding vigorously. And she smiled. In my dream she moved slowly, taking my hand. A knife appeared, sharp and gleaming. She cut my index finger and a drop of blood, perfectly fat and red, sat on the tip. I wanted to cry but before I could, her tongue was on the wound, flicking over it first, then her full mouth like suction, engulfed my finger, then my entire hand.

She began to laugh aloud, words tumbling from her lips, her laughter and my fear making them almost unintelligible. I thought I heard, "Remember what you have promised. Remember."

When I woke, I was bathed in cold sweat. I reached for the telephone to call Aunt Eula Mae. The vividness of the dream so disturbing that I needed to hear her voice across the miles that separated Alabama and Florida. I had to be sure there was a distance, that the smell of red clay dirt and grass that assailed me as I woke were but fragrant memories of my childhood, haunting me and not Aunt Eula, haunting me. I felt relieved when she answered the phone.

"Why, child, you musta read my mind. I was jus' thinkin' on you."

She was beautiful, Eula Mae, with clear skin and coal black hair that she kept gathered at the back of her neck. The old folks called her *mulatto,* her lightness attracting men from all over the county. I remember Mama watching Daddy watch Eula Mae as she sashayed into a room, seemingly oblivious of the fact that she was a magnet. But there was a knowing in her face. And I sensed that. Whenever I think of Eula Mae, I see her knowledge first, like a mask that has slipped off and then the smile appears, covering up everything else.

Aunt Eula Mae arrived on my doorstep one cold Sunday morning while the dark clouds threatened the sky and short gusts of wind made it unseasonably cold. I watched from the window. She was bigger, wider, and slower than I remembered but still my aunt. Her grey streaked hair was still gathered at the back of her neck, her skin now lined but blemish free.

Before her finger touched the bell I flung the door open to welcome her to her new home. I hugged her as my children clung to my dress. They had never met Eula Mae. Only spoken to her in fragments over the telephone. They approached shyly and cautiously, then helpfully, as we all moved her bags from the front steps to her newly decorated room.

After she rested I showed her the house. I tried to keep the swell of pride out of my voice. But she oohed and ahhed over everything, fingers trailing enviously over the damask silk of the curtains, the ivory and jade animals I displayed in the

Thirteen

curio. She tilted her head in my direction.

"You sure do have a fine house with all these beautiful things."

"Thank you Eula Mae. But you know that this is your house now too."

Our eyes met for a moment. And I felt a pricking in my heart. I was happy to be able to give her a home. But there was something else too. The way her hands lingered and touched my things. She seemed overwhelmed but delighted at her good fortune. Already covetous. I stopped in mid-thought, determined to be positive. Eula Mae was my new helpmate and I was going to appreciate her, appreciate whatever she brought with her, all the way from the back hills and dirt roads of Alabama.

Curiously, my husband, Ray, took an instant dislike to Eula. He stared at her rotund body and listened to her down home ways with guarded eyes.

"Honey, I know she's your aunt, but think of the children, this exposure..."

"Ray, there's nothing wrong with my aunt. She loves the kids and they're going to be fine with her."

He had a habit of raising his eyebrow whenever he was sceptical. He did so now and I felt an urge to scream. How dare he complain about Eula Mae? I supposed he would rather a stranger than a relative help with our children. As far as I was concerned, he would have to get used to her.

She began by sharing with my children her predilection for moon pies, pork rinds, ham hocks and fried spam. They sat at the table together, greasy mouths smacking loudly, their enjoyment of the food evident.

"Mama, Eula Mae fixed us some ham hocks. They's good."

Placing my briefcase on the floor, I leaned in and kissed my baby and then my oldest child, on the forehead. I kissed Eula Mae on the round cheek she offered me, careful to miss the greasy juice that dribbled from the side of her mouth. I wanted to say something, something about all the other types food we had. About how their near perfect diction had changed, reminding me of my young Alabama ways. But I managed to keep my lips closed.

"Look how they's eatin'. These boys cleanin' they plates. Knew some good home cookin' pick up them appetites."

I smiled and unbuttoned the jacket of my suit, a blue, double-breasted one with gold buttons.

Eula Mae nodded towards me from her stance at the built in kitchen table. She never sat. She claimed the chairs were too high for her short legs to reach with ease.

"I'se jus' too big."

Eula Mae wasn't telling lies about being a big woman. She was titless, which she said was a disappointment to her growing up, but she had a large butt that now rocked and swayed with her every move. I shuddered at the thought of carrying such a burden in my old age.

"Hard day at work?"

I shrugged. "Just like any other day."

"Want me to fix you something?"

"No thanks. Ray and I are going to dinner later."

My older boy, Jonathan, poked out his lip.

"Why you always going to dinner with Daddy? I could take you. I got some money." David, the baby at four, looked as though he was going to complain too but Eula Mae stepped in.

"Your mama jus' got home from a hard day at work. Now let her go on up stairs an' get outta them clothes 'fore you start on her."

I was relieved. I picked up my briefcase, took off my pumps and headed for the master suite upstairs. Eula Mae was clearing the dinner plates, wiping the table with a damp sponge and directing the boys into the family room for a short bout of television. Television, Eula Mae believed in, like pork chops covered in gravy and not taking a bath during your "monthly."

When I went downstairs, Eula went to her bedroom. I turned off the television and looked for some soothing CD to put on, the kind they liked to listen to and not dance.

They were asleep shortly and still Ray, had not come home. I knocked on Eula Mae's door. She sat on the bed, one short leg on the floor and the other stretched in front of her. One hand pushed at the elastic in her pants and cradled her large stomach. She appeared in thought.

I moved about casually, finally sitting at the foot of the bed. Her room intrigued me, filled with knic-knacs and candles. Candles of all colours, of all hues. Some lined her dresser, some on the floor. All unused. From the ceiling fan hung a small air deodorizer, an Indian head. "Big Chief" it read.

Ray didn't like the candles.

"Eula Mae, are you planning on burning the house down?"

"No siree. Not this beautiful house. I ain't gonna do no such thing." I winced. He couldn't help the pompous way he spoke or she the obsequious way she responded.

"What did you do today?" I asked.

She shrugged her shoulders. "Me an' little man went for a walk. Can't hardly believe it's November here. It's so warm."

"Yeah, it's great isn't it?" I heard the key turn in the lock. Ray was home.

"Eula Mae, you don't mind if we go out to dinner do you? The kids are sleep -"

"You know I don't mind. But make sure you bring me back something sweet – like that Key Lime pie you got me the last time. That sure did taste good."

Ray stood at the bedroom door. He filled a room up because he was tall and sure of himself.

"Hello, Eula Mae." Eula acknowledged him quietly with her eyes downcast, hands returning to the outside of her pants.

"How are the children?" He directed this at both of us but before we could answer he turned and walked to their room.

"I know your husban' don' like me much. I ain't gonna stay long. Just 'til the first of the year."

"Aunt, it's not that he doesn't like you. It takes him a while. That's all. He's got to get to know you." I tried to reassure her. I went back and ran my hand on her bare arm. Her small head remained turned from me. I knew her dilemma. Where would she go if she left us? Where would she call home?

She nodded to the wall. I didn't have a sense of what to say to make her more comfortable. It was an adjustment for us all. I could hide my feelings but Ray was a different story. Somehow his dislike of Eula Mae showed as clearly as her envy of my home and my possessions.

"I been meanin' to ask you something." Her voice startled me. My thoughts had drifted. "I sure would like to have a picture of you an' Ray." She smiled and continued. "I wants to be able to remember y'all when I'm gone." I nodded without thinking of the strangeness of her request. We had made no plans for her to leave and in all likelihood it would take months for us to make any arrangements.

"Take the one from the family room, you know, the one with me and Ray in Paris. But Aunt Eula, please stop thinking that you're leaving."

"Child, y'all don't pay me no never mind. Y'all go on out, have a good dinner." Her mood had changed swiftly. She bustled me out of the way, heading for the family room. Her smile was bright, unnatural.

Ray and I left the house. I waited until we had an uncomfortably long silence

Thirteen

in the car and to the restaurant. Until the pretty young waitress had taken our order with such a flirtatious grin at Ray that I countered with one of my own in her direction. Only she didn't get it and smiled back.

Ray leaned forward, face restless and newly lined.

"All right, out with it."

"Out with what?"

"Whatever it is you think I did wrong. I know I was late tonight but I had to meet with some people. You know how hectic it gets."

"It wasn't that you were late."

"No?"

"Nope."

"Okay, then I'm out of guesses. What did I?"

"It's Eula Mae."

He sighed deeply staring into his Chardonnay.

"Honey, I've tried to be friendlier, I just, you know it's only that I need more time, to get used to having someone else in the house. Her habits aren't like ours."

"They may not be, but she's part of our family now. Look, we wouldn't even be able to go out for dinner if it weren't for her. Jeez, Ray, at least try to be halfway friendly."

"Shit, it might help if she got rid of some of those candles. It doesn't make sense to have all those candles in the house with the children. What's she doing with them anyway?"

I shrugged because I didn't know. Together we sipped our wine and tried to keep the rest of the conversation light. I contented myself with admiring his slender physique and the way his fingers laced around the stem of the glass, delicate but sure in so many ways.

"You should have seen her, known her, when she was young. There was no one more beautiful than Eula. Even my father thought so. She would come to stay and Mama ended up asking her to leave a few times. Daddy paid her too much attention."

"Don't worry baby, you ain't gonna have that problem from me." Ray laughed, showing his white teeth against skin that looked merely tan, as if God had put a hint of coffee in the milk. "I ain't never been interested in no old, fat lady. Especially one without any ta-tas."

Leaving the restaurant, Ray grabbed me and pulled me close in the elevator, kissing my neck, bringing my fingers to his lips.

"For you I'll try harder. Just tell her to cook something Italian every once in a while. I'm sick of corn bread."

I laughed and pushed him away. "You just ain't used to real down home cookin."

When we pulled into the driveway, I knew something was wrong. Every light in the house was on. At a quarter past midnight, that only meant trouble. Before Ray could park, I was halfway out the car, running to the door. Eula Mae opened it.

She was wrapped in a heavy black shawl although the night wasn't cold, more spring-like than late fall. I searched her face and knew that she was disturbed. Her lips trembled and her eyes were watery. I grabbed her arm.

"Eula Mae, what's wrong?"

"Child, calm down. The baby woke up an' been screaming for you. I couldn't get him down again. He woke up Jonathan too. So we all sitting down in the family room."

Small feet raced across the expanse of the formal living room. He stopped

Thirteen

near Eula Mae, transfixed, until he figured out how to get around her. Ray came up behind us and reached long arms to pick David up. Eula Mae moved and we went inside.

"Hey guy, what's happening? Why are you still up?" Ray was talking to him as we headed towards the bedroom the children shared. David quietly laid his head on his father's shoulder as if calmed by daddy's presence. I was switching lights off and Eula Mae was silent. When I glanced in her direction, I saw her mouth, tight and thin as she made her way behind me. Slowly lumbering.

"He say he seen something. Say it scared him. I couldn't get him to go back in the room." Ray ignored her, too intent on getting David and Jonathan, whom he collected on the way, into their bedroom.

I knew something wasn't right. The image, the vague outline of Eula Mae and her thin-lipped sigh of resignation bothered me. I could not understand why David had been so inconsolable. He'd never had a problem like this before.

I smiled at Eula as I absently kissed her good night. Ray left the boy's room, closing the door behind him, finger to his mouth as though he had to cue me. Playfully, I rolled my eyes in Eula Mae's direction. She was standing at her door. She grimly nodded her head, as though agreeing with me that Ray was a problem. She closed the door to her room. That night I dreamed.

I was sixteen. Dancing in circles, happy. Mama and Papa were giving me a party and Eula Mae had come to town to help with my dress.

She was on my bed, hunched over sewing. When she spoke I had to strain to hear the raspy voice. But it was Eula, even though it didn't sound like her.

"Come here child, I have something for you." I floated to the bed, feet arching like a ballerina.

But she was no longer there. My hands ran over the coverlet, as if trying to feel her presence. It was so dark on this side of the room. Then I heard it, near my ear. The snip, snip of scissors. A faint rustle. Eula Mae was now at my side with a triumphant smile on her lips. Holding an inch of my hair with a pair of scissors.

"I've been wanting this for a long time."

I was confused. I woke with a question. Why did she want my hair?

The next few weeks were difficult. David barely slept and ate even less. My child clung to me when I got home every evening. Jonathan was fine though. Healthy, laughing and picking up weight. Eula Mae was as withdrawn as David, worried about his new disposition, his lack of an appetite. And leaving us.

"I'se makin' some plans 'bout leavin."

"Eula, I told you that this is your home now. You can't leave."

"Yes I can. It'd be better that way."

She refused to look at me. We were in her room. I noticed now that some of the candles had been used, the tiny burnt wicks bending towards the wax. There was also a scent, light and cloying. I sniffed.

"What's that smell?

"Oh, child, it's only some lavender."

"Lavender?"

"Yes, that lavender is good when you got some tension in you and you need to relax."

She sat in her customary position, fat legs swinging on the side of the bed, unable to touch the floor.

"We'll see what happens."

I left as she swung herself off the bed and walked slowly to her dresser. I saw her lighting a dark candle, one so dark that it might have been mistaken for black.

Thirteen

Home early the next evening I struggled with the key in the lock. Eula Mae opened it. The children had already been feed, bathed and put to bed. She smiled and said that David had eaten all of his dinner.

"I made his favourite tonight. You know your boys like them smoked neckbones with gravy and rice. I gave them each a moon pie when they was finished." She took my briefcase and I followed her into the kitchen that was spotless. For weeks now she had taken over the chores in the house as well as the children. My floors gleamed and everyday I found a pair of clean panties and a bra to wear to work.

"You jus' sit yourself on down. 'Fore you go on upstairs to take your bath, you relax here an' have a cup of this here tea I done made up."

I sat at the kitchen table, nodding at the thought of a hot cup of tea. The kettle let out a low whistle and she walked over, barefoot, reaching her thick arm to get a cup from the cupboard.

She spent a number of moments at the stove and I heard her speak, low, mumbling words I couldn't hear.

"Eula Mae, did you say something?"

"Oh honey, I'se jus' talkin' to myself. You know how us old folks are." But it seemed to me that there was something in her voice. She placed the tea in front of me and took her seat, opposite me.

"Well, what were you saying?"

"Oh, it was just a little prayer, you know, for you an' lil' man. When we was growin' up we did stuff like that. Blessed the food, prayed for peoples good health and for the things we wanted. Doncha remember nothing from when you all stayed on Limestone?" I shook my head. We moved when I was six. That was thirty years ago.

For the first time I noticed how her mouth curved downward in a mean smile. How her teeth glistened pearly white, strange for an old woman. Eula Mae reached across the table and put the back of her hand on my cheek, on my forehead. "Drink that tea up now. I think you got a fever."

That must be it, I thought, fever. Not anything she's done or said. Not that all of a sudden she looked like the wolf in Little Red Riding Hood. That her teeth appeared larger and longer than I thought they should be. The fever. I bought the cup to my lips and gulped down a mouthful, forgetting that she had just taken it from the stove. The liquid was wonderful, just the right temperature, with a sweetness I'd never tasted before. The taste encouraged me to drink more, faster. When the cup was empty I found my tongue licking the edges, following the smooth curve of the cup inside the lip, even touching the bottom, where the dregs collected.

Eula Mae grinned. "My, you was thirsty."

I felt heat from my feet to my belly. Surging.

When I woke up I was lying on the floor. Naked. A circle of lit candles surrounded me. There was a soft chanting, a steady drone. I could not move or speak. I heard a voice and I watched through frightened eyes as a shape approached me and moved into the light so that I might see. Only the it was me. Naked.

She moved closer, whispering, murmuring.

"Yes, it is you. I am you now, and you are me. Isn't that funny?" Gone was the southern drawl that I grew up hearing. "Look, look at your hands, look at your body. You're a fat old lady." As she spoke, I noticed her body trembled with laughter that she held in for fear of waking the children.

Able to move my head, I stared down at the atrocity that was now my body. My breasts lay small on my torso, flat and uninteresting. My stomach was bloated

Thirteen

and gorged beyond recognition. Wrinkles cursed through fleshy fingers, legs. I sagged everywhere.

I managed to speak. "How?"

"Oh, you're curious huh? You want to know how old Eula Mae did this to you? Oh but dear, that is such a complicated story. And I'm afraid that if I told you, you're so smart that you'd find a way to change us back. No, I don't think so. I'm not telling you anything. But don't worry, Eula Mae. You can stay on right here. With me and Ray and the kids." She bent to my ear. "I'm not that cruel. I'll let you stay near your children. But, if you tell, if you ever try to tell, I'll have you put away. Dementia. Breakdown. Or just plain old age."

My eyes were glued to her as she twirled her new body, my old one, around the room. Her breasts and butt high and firm. Running her hands through her new hair, caressing the inside of her new thighs. Touching the sparse hair on her new vagina. I felt a shiver of pure hatred run through my body.

After a while she started to blow the candles out, one by one. She picked up my clothes and put them on, then she stood near me again and mumbled a few words while waving a scented cream under my nostrils. I flared to life then, able to move but only slowly, the newly acquired girth hindering me.

"Why?" I asked this as I struggled into a house-dress. I did not want to remain nude in front of Eula Mae. Her triumphant eyes scanned my body too often as if she too could not believe what had just transpired. I couldn't bear her glance.

"Oh please, spare me. Isn't it obvious that I wanted what you had? Wanted it with every fibre of my body."

"Everything I had I was willing to share."

"No you weren't. And you couldn't. You can't share your youth. And that's what I wanted from you. That, and your husband. And your house. See, you go on and be Eula Mae. Do your job around here and I won't send you away."

We were both dressed when we heard the key turn in the lock.

"Eula Mae, you won't mind if Ray and I go out to dinner tonight, will you? I promise I'll bring that desert you like so much. I'll bring you a big slice." She flounced out of the room, throwing me an air kiss.

I sat still until I heard them leave the house, moving my new/old body to the family room and sitting in my rocker. I heard the patter of tiny feet and saw David as he hurled himself into my lap.

"Aunt Eula, I'm scared. I saw something, something with Daddy, I know it was a monster."

"Shh, shh, lil' man. No such thing as monsters."

I laid his head on my now flat chest and rocked him and rocked him.

I am looking for ways to thwart her, to change back to myself. But Eula Mae is a smart woman, demon smart. She is careful of me and rarely leaves me alone for long periods of time. She knows I will find the secret, the formula, the spell, whatever it takes to win my freedom from this old shell of a body.

She has quit my job. She knew better than to try to be professional. And Ray loves it. Dotes on her, the way she sleeps with him every night, strokes his body and presses against him every chance she gets.

I sit and wait and rock. Loving my children. Watching and ever patient. As she was, so shall I be.

Thirteen

VIGILANTE MAN
NIGEL ATKINSON

Ruby Wilson was guilty. Everyone knew she had poisoned her 78-year-old husband to end his suffering from Alzheimer's disease. People despised the Crown Prosecution Service for subjecting the frail old lady to the indignity of a trial. Taking its duty seriously, the jury deliberated for three days before finding her innocent. The next morning the Independent and Guardian newspapers ran identical front-page editorials calling for a change in the law on euthanasia.

Vincent Harris had watched the trial from the back row of the court's public benches. Moments after Ruby entered the court a vision of her kneeling at her husband's graveside, asking for his and God's forgiveness, flooded Vincent's consciousness. His body clenched like rigor, he watched the poor woman's contrition.

Vincent could see the future in perfect clarity, but only in very specific circumstances: whenever he saw a murderer, he envisioned the defining moment in the killer's future.

Two years earlier, Vincent was an ordinary man. In late middle-age, he was divorced without children. He lived a two-up-two-down terraced house in a small town in the north of England, and got on reasonably well with his neighbours. He watched football and soap operas on a portable TV, read historical novels, and waited patiently for his pension. On retirement he hoped to buy a small villa in Spain. Despite saving often as he could for years, he doubted he would be able to afford to the way prices were rising.

Then Vincent's world changed.

You probably remember the media circus when poor little Cathy Pallister disappeared. The six year-old lived two streets from Vincent and he, like every other unattached adult male in the vicinity, was a suspect. That Alan Fawcett, the proprietor of the town's one-and-only sex shop, fingered him as a regular customer with an interest in under-the-counter material didn't help. When the police picked him up, Vincent argued (truthfully) that he had only been in the place twice, and on neither occasion had he bought anything.

"I was curious," he told the hard-faced men of the CID.

"Did you like it?" they asked.

Vincent hadn't. Everything was plastic: the cheap shelves piled high with strange sex-aids, most of whose functions he couldn't guess at, the women in the magazines.

"So why did you go back?"

"I don't know," Vincent replied.

"What did you mean when you asked the manager if he had any 'special' stuff?"

"I don't know what you are talking about. I never said anything to the man. I don't know if I even met him," Vincent said. Under the table, he clasped his hands tightly to stop them shaking.

The police released him after three hours when his boss, Mr. Green of Green's department store, alibied him. Vincent, Mr. Green and several other staff members had been stocktaking the Sunday morning that Cathy disappeared. The detectives wanted to know why Vincent hadn't told them this at the start.

He avoided looking at their angry, disappointed faces. "I've never been in a police station before."

They threatened to change him with wasting police time, but didn't. Mr. Green dropped him off at home. Vincent could sense the curtains twitching and eyes boring into his back as he turned the key in the front door's lock. It was late

Thirteen

summer, and the sun was shining outside but the house was cold. He sat quietly on his sofa, his arms clasped around his knees, just listening. He could hear people talking in the street and cars driving past. The day fled by unnoticed. Just before his usual bedtime he stood up. His back ached as he reluctantly turned the TV on in time to catch the late local news. The newsreader, a blond girl with distressingly white teeth, looked serious as she read her autocue. The police, she reported, had interviewed a local man for several hours, but had released him owing to 'insufficient evidence'.

Shortly after Vincent climbed into bed, someone threw a brick through his front room window.

After a sleepless night spent clutching sweaty bed sheets to his chin, Vincent reluctantly went downstairs. The brick lay in the centre of the carpet, surrounded by glass. The cheap stained glass pane depicting a sunset that his ex-wife had given to him three Christmases ago, hung by a sticky thread to the shattered window. Then it fell with a soft clatter.

"Well, this isn't right, is it?" someone said.

Vincent looked up. His neighbour, Peter Briggs, was looking through the broken window from the street outside. He was several years older than Vincent, and had recently retired after a lifetime in the building trade. A big man, without regular exercise his muscle had quickly turned to fat, and his skin was mottled with liver spots.

"Listen, pal. I've still got my contacts. I can get this fixed today; good as new and at trade price," Briggs said.

"Well, that's kind of you," Vincent said. Without thinking about the shattered edges, he reached through the window to shake his neighbour's hand.

A giant hand grabbed Vincent and hurled him . . . somewhere . . . where colours burned with razor-edged intensity. Bright surroundings coalesced around him. He was standing on a landing in E-wing of Durham jail. Vincent had no idea how he knew this; he just did. A man wearing prison uniform was being escorted by two prison officers. It was Peter Briggs. He had lost several stones in weight, and his flesh hung from him like a shroud. Sudden angry shouts came from below. The guards left Briggs and looked over the railing. A powerfully muscled man, with the word 'scum' tattooed on his forehead, ran out of a nearby cell and buried something sharp and metallic into Briggs' chest.

"That's for Cathy, you bastard," the executioner screamed.

Briggs' face loomed over him. Terrified, Vincent realised his front door must have been unlocked all night. How else could Briggs have got in? He tried to scrabble away, but the man's strong hand on his shoulder held him down.

"Get away from me!" Vincent shouted.

Briggs stepped back, hands held high. "Hey, sorry pal, just trying to help. I'll be going. Let me know if you want the window fixed."

Cathy's body was found later that day. It was stuffed in a culvert adjacent to the town's long-derelict shoe factory. Vincent avoided the TV news after the first bulletin. The elliptical descriptions of her ordeal were irrelevant. His vision filled in his dreams and resonated in his waking life. With each reiteration, the icy precision of the killer's death was counterpointed with bloody overtones of his deed; as if Vincent had been cursed with a glimpse into Briggs' soul as it fled his body.

Mr. Green didn't hide attempt to his relief when Vincent called in sick. They both knew he couldn't face the public across a shop counter; at least until Cathy's killer was brought to justice. Vincent said he would be in later in the week. He knew that was a lie, and wondered if Mr. Green, an old-fashioned, decent man, realised

Thirteen

it too.

The day passed slowly. Vincent listened to the whispers of passers-by. He couldn't make out their words, but he could sense the accusations. Around teatime, the local evening paper landed with a thud on his doormat. Reluctantly, he picked it up and opened it. Someone had spat phlegm into its folds. He cleaned the mess away with paper towels, leaving a greasy smear, spread the paper out on his kitchen table, and forced himself to read the lead story.

A police spokesman was reported as saying that they had 'extensive' DNA evidence, and would be asking local men aged between 16 and 70 to submit a sample.

The next morning, Vincent was first in line to provide a DNA sample. He quickly realised that was a mistake. It was 8 o'clock and he was the only volunteer so far. His friends from the CID stood around and watched silently as the pretty technician swabbed his mouth. When she was done, he was quickly ushered out of the police station. He desperately wanted to stay, so that people could see him stepping forward.

"If, I mean when, I'm exonerated, will you tell people?" he asked the young constable who escorted him out.

"DNA tests are confidential, sir. We would never release that information."

Briggs was arrested a week later. He hadn't volunteered a DNA sample, but neither had most of the town's men. While driving his wife to the supermarket, a salesman who was too busy fiddling with his mobile phone ran into the back of his car. The impact popped the boot open, and the policeman who was taking details noticed a cardigan matching the description of one belonging to Cathy and missing since her death.

When Briggs came to trial three months later there was no mention of DNA, but there was the cardigan and extensive evidence from hair and fibres linking him to the crime. The defence tried to muddy the waters by claiming another person had been involved. The prosecution didn't dispute the claim, and the jury took under an hour to find him guilty.

Three weeks into Brigg's thirty-year sentence, Lucas McNish, serving multiple life terms for the torture and murder of rival drug dealer and his family, drove a sharpened fork under Briggs' sternum into his heart, killing him instantly. Next morning the first edition of a national tabloid called on its front page for McNish to be pardoned. Subsequent editions, under a new editor, led on the sex life of the England football captain.

Even after Peter Briggs' death the whispers continued. People crossed the street when they saw him coming, and moved when he sat down on buses. He dropped hints about his DNA test. It made no difference. DNA hadn't come up at the trial, and people remembered the defence's suggestion of an accomplice. He never returned to work, and rarely left his house. Things came to a head when blazing paper was shoved through his letterbox early one morning. He woke to the fire brigade kicking his front door in and choking smoke pouring up the stairs. The firemen were sympathetic until the police arrived and had a word with them. A week later Vincent sold his house for a fraction of its value and moved to a city a hundred miles away. He lived in a dingy flat above an Indian take-away whose staff played strange music too loud all day and most of the night, and practiced his anonymity.

To escape the noise, he wandered the streets whenever the weather was fine, and often when it wasn't. One day he found himself in front of the city's Crown Court; a huge, desolate building he decided must have been inspired by

Thirteen

Albert Speer's designs for the Third Reich.

He hardly remembered walking into the building, asking directions from a distracted woman at reception, and then sitting down at the back of the court where Dwayne Francis Hiller was being tried for the murder.

Dwayne had a reputation to keep up. At the age of eleven he had thrown a bottle of acid at a teacher, scarring her for life. He didn't go to school much after that but, fifteen years later, had made a success of his chosen field. He ran a third of the city's prostitutes, and had plans to expand his empire. His ambitions led to a shootout in a crowded pub that ended with rival pimp Eric Herbert dead, and two innocent bystanders badly wounded.

Vincent's heart clenched when Hiller was brought into the dock, handcuffed between two burly policemen. His second vision was worse than the first. Again it was set in a prison and involved an improvised knife. Hiller had shoved it between the ribs of Petie Fry. Foaming at the mouth and thrashing in the grasp of two court bailiffs, Vincent writhed on the floor. The killer's exultation twisted in him like a corkscrew. Hiller was the daddy now. No-one could pin this one on him. He'd do the business inside and keep control of business outside. When he got out he'd be set for life.

When Vincent woke up in a hospital bed, the nurse hovering over him was efficient but distant. She left quickly, and a young woman detective sergeant accompanied by two male constables arrived.

"We know all about you," the DS said. "We've got your files so you'd better watch your step. Any funny business and we'll have you."

Her voice had the local twang in it, but Vincent could hear the underpinnings of refinement she was trying to hide. He felt a pang of empathy with her necessary deceit.

"I haven't done anything," he said.

"Better keep it that way," one of the constables said. His colleague nodded and drummed his fingers on the handle of his truncheon. For a mad moment Vincent wanted to laugh at the predictability of their reactions.

The policewoman told Vincent he was banned from the Crown Court and, for a couple of months he stayed away. Fighting his growing agoraphobia, he frequented crowded places – shopping centres and cinemas, football grounds and public parks – his senses on edge. But, despite the lurid headlines, murder was rare, and murderers rarer still. There was only one place he could be sure of finding them.

The town's Oxfam shop supplied him with a remarkably smart suit of clothes, and a muted but elegant silk tie. With his newly cultivated, neat goatee beard he looked nothing like the wild-eyed man dragged from the court. He worried that the police might grow suspicious about his change of appearance; but he had to *know*.

Vincent found that he could stand the visions if he prepared himself. He took long, slow breaths and imagined surf climbing then receding an empty beach. Seagulls circled high above, and the sun was bright but not too warm. When the murderer was brought in, he focused on his perfect image, holding it for as long as he could as the dark percolated in. It was still hard. Other spectators watched his clenched form from the corners of their eyes, and edged away. He cut his fingernails regularly to stop them breaking as they dug involuntarily into the hard wooden bench. Over the next few months he shared the futures of a dozen men and two women. For most of them, the key moment was when the jury foreperson stood up and changed their lives forever. The verdict was usually guilty but, on two occasions, murderers walked free.

Thirteen

A year after he moved to the city, the noise from downstairs stopped. The takeaway business had folded. Vincent wasn't very surprised; it never seemed to have many customers. Relieved, but fearful of the other shoe dropping, he spent more time in his flat. He still attended every murder trial. After a few weeks peace, he was woken by the sound of hammering and electric drills. He dressed quickly and scampered down the narrow stairs. Workmen were hoisting a large plastic sign with the single word "*Adult-topia*" picked out in bright red letters. Above the shop door there was a smaller sign.

It read: "Licensed sex shop. Proprietor, Mr. A.K. Fawcett, esq."

The words hit Vincent harder than one of his visions. Alan Fawcett – the man whose lies had started Vincent's nightmare – had come back into his life.

"I'm sorry, sir, the planning application went through three months ago. There were objections, but none from people living nearby the establishment."

Mr. Blake was young. The index finger of his right hand flicked at a cat's cradle of wire and metal balls standing on his otherwise empty desk. The balls clicked as they swung back-and-forth.

"I thought you had to inform residents when people wanted to open places like that," Vincent said.

"Of course, any residents on the electoral register were duly informed." Click-click-click. "You are on the register, I imagine?"

"I haven't lived here long."

Click-click-click. "If you ask at reception, they will give you a form. Next time something comes up, we'll let you know. You'll get to vote as well. There's council elections coming up." He smiled for the first time. "Lots of overtime when they're on."

Peering through thick net curtains, Vincent watched the dark Mercedes pull up opposite the sex shop. The car door swung open. Fawcett was slim with neatly cut hair and wore an expensive-looking suit. He turned and glanced up for an instant before crossing the road.

Vincent fell to the floor, smacking his head against the window ledge on the way down. The vision was his worst ever – the ordeal of poor Cathy Pallister – the threats against Peter Briggs' grandchildren if he talked – money slipped to a copper who cared more about lining his pockets than finding a child killer -- Fawcett dying in tangled metal and fire -- and something else.

With a sense of wonderment, Vincent realised that he was seeing the deaths of not one, but two murderers.

Vincent had a few thousand pounds tucked away a savings account he had managed to keep from the DHSS. He bought well-cut clothes at Marks and Spensers and took up residence at one of the city's best hotels. The receptionist had looked strangely when Vincent declined to hand his credit card over (he couldn't, he didn't have one), but was mollified with a twenty-pound note. Another twenty secured a room on the fifteenth floor, with a southern view.

Vincent lived on room service (for which he always tipped generously). It was expensive, but he could keep watching through his powerful binoculars as he ate. For two months he watched Fawcett's comings-and-goings, taking meticulous notes of times and activities, looking for a pattern. After a month, he knew that Sunday morning was best.

But still he waited. He had to be sure.

A week before his money was due to run out Vincent spent a rare hour in the hotel's over-glitzy bar. He sipped poor quality champagne and thought about nothing. He was about to get up when a woman sat beside him. She introduced

352

Thirteen

herself and Vincent offered her a drink. About his age, she was called Sue, and was in town for a business conference. They chattered amiably. Vincent skated through his cover story about being a writer who needed to get away to complete his latest book. He felt foolish. Luckily she didn't press him. He was surprised when she invited him back to her room, and more surprised at how forward she was in their lovemaking. His ex-wife was the only other woman he had slept with, and she had never taken the lead.

Lying in bed the next morning, he was ashamed at how happy he felt, and almost sick with relief when Sue told him she was leaving later that day and probably wouldn't be back.

In any case, she was married.

The taxi driver seemed a decent man. He was a Hindu, and his dashboard was plastered with plastic icons of strange gods and photographs of his wife and three fat children. Vincent hated what he had to do next. He reached into the canvas bag on his lap and pulled the carving knife out.

"Get out," he said.

The taxi was parked in a bye-road two miles outside the city. Vincent hoped it would be at least an hour before the driver could report the theft of his vehicle. It would be all over by then.

"Get out," he repeated, pointing the knife at the man's throat.

The driver ran away across a field, and Vincent slid across into his seat. It was still warm. He started the engine and headed for the city. There were few other cars about, which suited him. He hadn't driven since his wife got the family car as part of the divorce settlement. Worried about his rustiness behind the wheel, he took a couple of driving lessons. He told the instructor he had been abroad for several years and needed to get used to driving on the left again.

Vincent parked at the top of the small hill overlooking his old flat. It was the perfect place. Demolition work on the side of the street opposite the shop had cleared his lines of sight to the traffic lights at either end of the street. The chances of someone driving past at the wrong time were small, but it was good to be sure.

At five minutes past eight, Fawcett pulled up his Mercedes and crossed the road. Vincent blessed the double yellow lines that stopped him parking in front of his shop and started his engine. *Adult-topia* was set back a little way from the street. To one side, a skip full of rubble from the demolition work blocked the pavement. A pile of black bin bags, filled to bursting, obstructed the other side. The sex shop was protected by steel shutters and heavy padlocks. It always took Fawcett at least five minutes to open up. Vincent undid his seat belt, let the clutch out and put the car into gear.

It rolled slowly forward.

Fawcett fiddled with his keys.

The car picked up speed as it rolled quietly down the hill.

Fawcett stopped for a moment and half turned around.

Vincent watched the speedometer climb past 40. With fifty yards to go he floored the accelerator.

"This is for Cathy," he whispered as he raced to meet the vision of his own death.

Thirteen

BALANCE OF THE DEVILS
CHRISTOPHER CATHRINE

Ted Jefferson lay in his deathbed. He harboured no delusions of pulling through, despite the encouragement from his doctor. He had been planning on running for Governor, and owned the largest railroad company in the territory. But none of that mattered anymore. Not lying here with a punctured lung, and Lord knows what other internal injuries. His breath was coming shallower and more painful by the day.

All that mattered now was revenge.

There was a dull wrap at the wooden door to his private residence. Nobody ever called on him here. He didn't keep personal friends. He hadn't seen the point until last Wednesday. All they could do was provide leverage for his rivals, he had thought. Now, lying dying, he wished he had at least one friend. Never having wanted children, he found it strange that he felt regret at never having had a family.

Jefferson listened as the door creaked open. He could just make out the murmur of Jeremy, his butler, but not the words.

The door closed with a thud, and after a moment he could hear footsteps on the stairs. Two people. One wearing the refined shoes of a man who never travels out of comfort – the other the clang of heavy leather and spurs whispering of years out in deserts and on the plains.

That would be the man he had been waiting for. The reason he was clinging on to the few frayed threads of life.

His door opened a crack, and Jeremy pushed his head through into Jefferson's luxurious bedroom.

'Boss?' he asked, quietly, checking his master was awake. Jefferson was known by most as Boss Jefferson, and he liked it.

'Yes, Jeremy? Is it who I sent for?' Jefferson croaked, this much an extreme effort.

'Yes, sir,' came the reply. The fear in the voice exhibited only as a slight tremor – testament to the high calibre of his servant.

'Well, let him in then! What are you waiting for?' Jefferson almost yelled – would have yelled, if he could.

Jeremy nodded, and disappeared.

A second later the door opened, and those boots announced the man's presence.

The bounty hunter enters the room. Standing in full light, somehow the man seemed to take the shadows from the hallway with him. His face is cloaked in the darkness cast by the brim of his hat. Normally Jefferson would draw attention to the breach of etiquette, but on this occasion he doesn't even notice. He is consumed instead by the twisted, cruel abomination that is the excitement of revenge.

'Ted Jefferson,' comes the introduction. '*Boss* Jefferson, as most call me,' he adds, a sickly sweet smile crossing his feverish face. 'Welcome, Mr...?' Jefferson prompts. However, the man remains silent, staring coldly at the crippled tycoon.

'Yes, quite, well...' Jefferson blubbers, not quite sure how to deal with this man. He had thought he would never be closer to death, before meeting its cruel embrace. Now he wasn't so sure. It felt as if Death himself were hovering around the man at the foot of his bed.

Or that the man *was* Death.

'I am sure you've been told, or heard, the basics of why I have called you here,' Jefferson began. 'And I am quite sure you know what you are to be asked to do.'

Thirteen

He had hoped to elicit some response with this – hinting at the man's career in dealing death – but he got not even a nod of acknowledgement.

Jefferson eyed the man, with a hint of fear creeping into his watery eyes.

'I did ask for you in particular,' he gulped, continuing. 'The contract is for not for anyone else. I need your special...' he fumbled for the correct word. 'Skills,' he used, in absence of a better option. 'And the insurance that I get from your reputation,' he added, warily. He didn't want to push the man too far, but he did want evidence that he was at least *human*.

Still, the bounty hunter gives no sign of interest. He merely shifted his weight from one foot to the other, with the creak of stiff, trail-worn leather.

'The basics do not likely give this story its due,' Jefferson pushed on. 'I want you to know why I want Sam Hall dead...'

The bounty hunter lifted a cigar to his mouth. Striking a match, the flare of the fire gave a brief clear view of the man's rough deadpan face. Seeing it in its full detail, it seemed plausible that the creaking sounds had come not from the man's boots, but his skin itself. The moment was quickly lost, the light dying to a hellish red glow, giving only the impression of a demon who had long since lost the last vestiges of humanity.

Standing there, the man listened as Jefferson recounted his story.

Jefferson had been sitting behind his desk that fateful day. He'd tell people he was working his way through paperwork relating to the new rail line he was supposed to be heading, through his company 'Jefferson Railroad Inc.'. The truth of the matter was he was looking through the different campaign posters and flyers he'd had drawn up by a local artist. He could see himself as Governor now. In truth, he always had done. Jefferson was no modest man, and he felt himself far above the local populace.

Lost in his little world, where he ruled supreme, he failed to notice the door to his office open. It was the hot breath of air on his face which made him look up.

Standing in the doorway, silhouetted, stood a dark figure. The coat hung down to the man's feet – that much he could tell. He wasn't the tallest man, but he had a hell of a presence.

Jefferson smiled.

'Sam,' he greeted the man gladly.

'Mr Jefferson,' came the reply. He'd never called Jefferson 'Boss'.

The small man swaggered into the office proper, his long leather drover swaying like a cloak. Small dust clouds rose where the corners of the jacket disturbed the gathered sand. No matter how much effort you put into cleaning, how much you paid people, the desert could never be fully banished from any building in town.

Sam Hall approached the desk, and stopped, standing.

'So, did you get it?' Jefferson asked, anxious.

Sam grinned, his long blond hair framing his sun-burned face. The small pointed beard he wore gave him a disquieting air when he smiled. He reached his hand into a pocket concealed in the inside lining of his open drover. When it emerges again, it is holding a beautifully ornate wooden box.

He proffered this object towards Jefferson.

Jefferson stumbled out of his chair. He couldn't stop himself from reaching out towards the box.

'You did...' he said, voice trailing off.

Sam jerked the box back, just out of reach.

He tutted. 'Mr Jefferson, I believe we had an arrangement,' the man said, his voice smooth, yet with a slight edge to it. 'The money, please,' he smiled, holding his right hand out, open.

Thirteen

'Of course, of course,' Jefferson breathed. He fumbled under his desk, and removed a small sack. He dropped it into the open hand with a clink. Sam had to lower his arm slightly, compensating for the weight.

'It's pure gold, unmarked, as per our arrangement,' the tycoon said.

Sam had smiled, a cold terrible expression. Jefferson had felt the warmth sucked out of the air by that grim smile.

'Why, thank you, Mr Jefferson,' he had replied, placing the sack in his left hand jacket pocket.

Sam had then placed the box deliberately in his pocket, also. This should have been warning enough for Jefferson, given Sam's underground reputation.

'Now, the my trinket?' Jefferson had managed to say, before he saw Sam push his coat back, revealing the six-iron.

He remembered being confused, briefly wondering why there was also a sword strung against the man's belt, under the long jacket, before it sank in.

Sam had drawn his gun, and taken two shots at Jefferson, knocking the man to the floor.

Lying there, on the warm wood of the floor, Jefferson watched as the man he had hired in good faith replaced his gun, and turned to leave. The hem of the leather brushed Jefferson's face. He could still smell the leather and sun now, and would remember that until his final breath.

His eye-glasses had been thrown off when he'd fallen, and the majority of the room was now a smudged pastel drawing to his mind. The blood trickling from the wounds in his chest promoted this impression, but before long he couldn't feel the wetness.

All he could see was the boots.

Those polished black shoes. The raised heels clicking against the wooden floorboards, as Sam Hall walked from the room. As they lost their focus, he heard the clink of shattered glass, and knew he would never use his eye-glasses again. Not that it mattered. He was sure at that moment he was dying.

It had been God's will that he lived though. God's, or Satan's. And he intended to use this gift to take his revenge on the man who had killed him. He knew this was to be his last act when he awoke in his bed, the doctor leaning over him explaining that he'd lost the use of a lung, and may not ever make it out of this bed again.

The bounty hunter had stood silently, listening patiently to the tale. The smoke from his burning cigar drifted around his head, adding to the ethereal sense of the man.

'He thought I was dead,' Jefferson finished. 'But I'm alive, one lung less. And I want him dead, the box in my hands.'

Jefferson wondered if this would induce a response. Others who he had discussed his plan with had pointed out that it would likely by to cold dead fingers that the box would return. Jefferson felt scared of this, but pushed the thought from his mind, forcing the strength everyone knew him for. He'd say he didn't care. But this man – this bounty hunter – didn't say a thing.

Instead the red-lit face seemed to be looking upon the dying man with contempt.

'I want you to kill him for me. The price is as agreed, Do you accept?'

The shadowed man nodded slowly, deliberately.

'Excellent,' Jefferson said, and laughed – a harsh sound. This laugh quickly degenerated into a coughing fit which lasted until after the hired assassin had left his home.

Charles Eldrich – 'Cheech' as he was known by the locals – wiped down the bar,

Thirteen

preparing to close up for the evening. There were only two people left in the saloon, other than himself. One was a regular drunk, a young lad who gambled away the day and drank away the night. If he could afford to, he'd try and talk some sense into Calum one of these days, but right now Easington wasn't raking in the rich, and he needed the boy's patronage.

The other man had just arrived in town three days ago. For some reason, the man seemed to insist on talking to him. As the bartender, he was used to talk from his regulars, but the Watering Hole was a small, dingy saloon off the back and beyond. There was a reason he'd set up business here, and it sure wasn't the conversation. Right now, all he wanted to do was close up shop, and head off to bed.

'...and you know I is the meanest due in these here parts...' came the slurred drawl of Sam Hall. The man just never shut up.

'Yes, so you keep saying, sir...' Cheech responded, putting emphasis on the 'sir'.

Sam may have been drunk, but he somehow managed to hear this subtle insult hidden in the barman's tone in a moment of clarity. Annoyed, he slammed his beer down.

'You don't believe me, huh?' he said, voice raised. ' Well, I'll tell ya somethin'. How'd ya think I afford stayin' here in... in...' The man frowned, as if trying to grasp for something he knew was there somewhere.

'Easington,' Cheech sighed.

'Here in Easington,' the man continued, more happily. 'No work, drinkin' and gamblin' all night?'

Cheech laughed, 'The way you throw cards? I honestly have no idea.'

He moved to the corner of the bar, and continued to clear up the sticky liquor spilt over the course of a slow day.

'D-d-don't ya wanna know?' Sam called from he other end of the short bar.

Cheech replied without even looking up, back turned. 'To be honest, I couldn't care less.' He raised his voice, adding a little force to it, so as the other barfly could hear. 'Closing time! You don't have-ta go home, but you can't stay here.' He hoped that Sam would get the message as well.

Calum certainly did. He gulped down his beer, and, staggering to his feet, succeeded in making a thirty second walk last close to a minute as he wound his way around imaginary objects, knocking over a table in the process. Cheech sighed, as the batwing doors swung, brushing the cool night air into the saloon.

'Wow, ain't we friendly in these here parts?' Sam managed, holding a belch which he now let out with relief. He takes a swig from his beer, and then raises his voice so as Cheech listens. 'Well, seein' as how I is in a good mood, I think I'll tell ya anyway.'

'Oh fantastic...' Cheech says, under his breath, still not turning to face this annoyance.

'Ya see, I'd been driftin' for a while. You know, the odd job here 'n' there. Mainly hired gun. I likes ma shootin'.' Sam dredged on with the determination only possessed by narcissistic drunks. He didn't care whether Cheech was listening or not. He just liked the sound of his own voice. But he also knew that he was so interesting that sooner or later the man *would* listen. 'Anyway. Along the way, I hear's this story in a bar. 'Bout some gold, and a man who's wantin' to hire someone ta get it. Railroad tycoon. Ya may've heard of him. Jefferson's his name.'

At the mention of Boss Jefferson, Cheech looks up sharply. He tried to feign ignorance afterwards, but the damage is done.

'Ah. I see y'do know 'im,' continued Sam, a smile creeping across his face. Cheech wiped his head with the cloth, annoyed at himself for having encouraged

Thirteen

the man. 'Well, he hires me,' the story went on, Sam's voice becoming less slurred as he got into it. 'Got a few good references, but no money out on me, so no picture. Nobody knows who I am. I go out an' get this gold. Had ta kill five men t'get it, but I did. An' I take it back ta him and he pays me. But instead-a givin' him the gold, you know what I did?' Sam squinted in a way that Cheech liked not one bit, and then burst out laughing. 'I shot that cowardly worm down dead! An' I took the gold for maself too!' Sam almost falls from his stool in the unhealthy laughing fit that followed.

Cheech had become a lot more interested towards the end of this little story.

'You killed Boss Jefferson?' asked the bartender, sceptical.

'Damn straight I did,' Sam says, matter-of-fact.

'He's dead?' Cheech asks, a little scared. Then his face lightens, and he shakes his head, letting out a small laugh. He couldn't believe he'd just been taken in by a wandering drunk. 'Na. You can't prove it. Nice story.'

He returned to gathering bottles from the bar, and wiping the rings left on the bar top.

Sam, however, has darkened at this show of unbelief. 'It's true damn it!' he exclaimed, a little uneasily, hitting the bar.

Calming slightly, he swallows the last of his beer. As if forgetting his previous outburst, he calls out to Cheech, asking for another. Surely, the half-Mexican though, he at least remembered the closing call.

'Look, I gotta close up,' he replied, trying to keep the irritation from his voice.

Sam was unfazed by the rejection. 'Just one more? C'mon,' he pleaded, his best smooth talking voice being dragged out of the depths of his dusty and inebriated brain.

Cheech placed his fists on the bar menacingly. He stood a good half foot taller than the small man who was refusing to leave his saloon. He may be a great yarn spinner, but Cheech was not going to let this man get the best of his mind again. He may be a petty criminal, but there was no way he'd done what he said, and he was not gonna be afraid of him. Besides, he kept a rifle under the bar. There wasn't gonna be any trouble.

The barman leaned forward, resting on his knuckles. He stopped inches from Sam's face, his shoulder length black hair falling forward, the grease that had held it in place, brushed back from his brow having long since given up the ghost in the acrid air of the saloon.

'No,' he said firmly, with a hint of menace. 'You gotta leave. Now.' The final word as a full stop, making clear that this was no request.

After standing like this for what seemed to Cheech as an eternity, and to Sam like a butterfly's wing-beat, the taller man broke off, feeling, wrongly, that he had made his point. He went back to cleaning up, this time concentrating on the dilapidated shelf holding the liquor bottles. Some of these were strangely expensive, one even having been brewed at the Glen Turret Distillery, in the highlands of Scotland and its oldest whisky distillery – if one were to believe the label. Cheech lovingly dusted these, wiping off sticky finger prints from a flurry of orders earlier that day, during the regular card game. He fully expected to find Sam gone when he turned back around.

He was sorely mistaken.

Instead of leaving, the man had removed a small wooden box from his folded jacket, which rested on an adjacent stool. Seating was never at a premium at the Watering Hole.

'I got the proof,' Sam slurred.

Cheech sighed, but found himself drawn to the box with its beautiful carving of a humming bird enclosed in an intricate carved ring.

'What proof?' he asked.

Thirteen

'The proof that my story's real, 'n' I killed Jefferson,' Sam stated, misunderstanding the question.

Cheech pulled himself from the force that was compelling him to believe this drunk. As a rule he never believed the outrageous stories he heard in here.

He smiled. 'You're drunk. Go home, get some sleep, come back tomorrow.'

'Look,' Sam says, simply, ignoring the previous statement, and offering the box. 'This is the box I was sent ta get.' He tapped it with his thumb. The sound gave away the high quality of the wood. 'Aztec gold inside.'

Cheech had almost dropped his jaw when he'd heard the tap on the wood. The box itself must have been worth a small fortune. But with gold inside – let alone *Aztec* gold...

'Show me,' he said, lightly, as if in a dream.

Sam opens the box, illuminating Cheech's face with the reflected light from the oil lamps.

'Glorious, ain't it,' came Sam's voice, but Cheech didn't hear.

Placing a new bottle of beer before the man absently he looked intently down at the wooden box. He was engrossed by the gold. Taken by the fires of hell which played on his face. Those same flames that had whispered of power to those whose greed had already led to death in pursuit of this prize.

The sign stood alone in the windswept dunes of the desert. A slight rise hid the buildings from view.

A single man sat on his horse, looking down at this decrepit wooden board sign. As if bored, battling with his better judgement, he paused ten feet from the plaque. The thorn scrub around the thing would clearly scratch his horse if he tried to battle any further off what laughably passed as a road. After a moment, his heavy boots hit the dust, and he strolled over to the town sign.

Stencilled across the wood in faded black paint was:

Easington Town
3 Miles
Population ~~112~~

The score through the population count was less faded than the rest of the sign. Scrawled next to it, in sharp contrast to the careful stencil work, was the amendment of: 99.

The man, wearing his knee length pommel slicker stood before the sign, as if considering some fundamental philosophical statement that was like to turn one's world perceptions over.

Turning to a post, or snapped tree – it was difficult to tell in the sun-bleached wasteland – were too planks of jagged wood. The first of these boldly proclaimed 'NO GUNS. REPORT TO SHERIFF JOHN BROWN'. The second had scrolled 'Saloon: The Watering Hole. Rest those weary feet and wash away the desert dust!' artistically, in what once had been red paint, now more an orange-pink.

The tall figure of the Boss Jefferson's bounty hunter walked back to his horse, thumbs hooked in the gun-belt beneath his slicker.

In the Watering Hole that morning, Sam had gone up to the bar for another beer. This was only partly because of wanting one. It was more because he wanted to escape from the table where a third terrible poker hand awaited him. There was a man in the corner strumming out a nice tune on a beat-up guitar. Listening to this, Sam didn't hear the batwing doors creak, announcing the arrival of a new customer.

The two card players did notice, however. They'd seen that face drawn on

Thirteen

posters back East. They followed the man, as he made his way directly for the bar, leaving dust boot prints across a straw mat.

Sam, however, merely lights up another cigar, and turns to take his dreaded seat at the poker table.

Not realising the man had was directly behind him, crossing to stand next to where he had been previously, Sam walked straight into him, spilling his beer down the larger man's shirt.

'Hey man, watch where you're goin'!' Sam yelled, looking up at the newcomer.

The man looked down slowly, brushing a hand against his shirt, opening the slicker wide enough to show the 'Peacemaker' in its holster by his hip.

'I mean, you don't know who I am, d'ya?' Sam continued. The man lifted his trail hardened face slightly to look at Sam, and lifted his eyebrows quizzically. Sam smiled, taking this look for concern. 'You better watch yourself. I'm a damn quick shot and I really don't like folks spillin' ma drinks. You get me?' he prodded the tall man in the chest, holding his cigar in his teeth.

To this the stranger said nothing, and again Sam misinterpreted this as definite fear.

'Yeah, that's right, man. You wanna watch out for me!'

Grinning, Sam danced around the tall figure, miming gun fighting with his hands, the remainder of his beer tucked under his arm. Brown liquid dribbled down his rough hewn cotton shirt.

Sam returned to his seat, laughing.

'Man, did you see that?' he asked the card players. 'Whoa! Did I scare him or what?'

The encounter had cheered Sam up somewhat since checking his new hand. Now, looking at the sullen faces of his companions, his mood dropped slightly.

Wayne leaned forwards. 'You know who that is?' he asked, conspiratorially, with fear dripping off his tongue.

Sam laughs again, trying to sound nonchalant, but failing pathetically. 'No... some drifter...' he offers, weakly.

'I've seen his picture on ma way out here, heard stories...'

'So...' Sam interrupted.

'Oh, nothin',' Wayne replied, annoyed. 'Just you made fun of one of the most ruthless bounty hunters around, 's'all.'

Sam felt his skin crawl. 'Yeah?' he asked, pitifully, as he glanced over his shoulder.

At the bar he saw the new comer – Boss Jefferson's bounty hunter, he was almost sure of it – talking with the barman.

'Yeah. I even heard he'd gotten himself in a massive gunfight with the Feds. Not just the local law. The big guys,' Wayne drank from his bottle, drawing out the suspense. 'Thing is,' he said, leaning forward slightly, voice lowered, 'Caught in a crossfire with those damned macaroni eaters out East. I'd ne'er heard anythin' 'bout him since. No one had. The Feds even say he's dead. Musta been layin' low...'

Sam took a gulp of beer, as Wayne trailed off.

'So, you guys gonna play cards?' he said to Wayne and Jim, the quieter of the two. 'Or y'all wanna run home to your women folk?' he added, trying to pull himself back from the brink of cowardice.

The other two looked at each other, their cards, the money, and then back at Sam.

'You know,' started Jim, sarcastically, 'I think the way you're playin' here – and I reckon I speak for the lot of us – we'd be plum stupid to quit now.'

They all laugh at this, although Sam's sounds hollow.

Thirteen

Wayne looked darkly over to Sam, after the laughter had run down. 'Unless, of course, you manage to get your ludicrous bets in early enough,' he said, his voice bitter.

'Hey, you can't blame a guy for bein' financially secure, now can you?' Sam asked, smugly.

'Yeah, but with that much money, it's a wonder you're dumb enough to lose any of it!' Jim put in, causing a second bout of laughter. Sam was beginning to think he'd misjudged Jim.

'Hey, ya can't choose your luck,' he defended himself, the hurt not at all hidden in his tone.

'No, but you can learn how-ta play!' Wayne pushed.

'Oh yeah?' Sam said, his voice slightly too loud. 'Shut up and lets just *play*, shall we?'

'That be your definition of play, or ours sugarplum?'

This last comment from Jim pushed Sam a little too far, and his face darkened, the blood rushing back to where it had vacated in fear only moments before. He moved to get out of his seat, aggressively.

'Hey, guys, calm down,' Wayne interjected. 'Let's just get on with it, shall we?' he said, reasonably.

Sam sat back down, still on edge. But he picks up his cards, and flashes a forced smile, and the game continues. Glancing at the bar, he sees the bounty hunter hand over a small piece of paper to the bartender. He had a cold feeling that on it his name was writ.

Cheech looked at the paper which had been offered him. It was neatly folded, with a single name in longhand. Beneath that was a drawing of a bird enclosed by a series of woven rings.

He lifted his gaze to meet that of the stranger. Cheech stood a couple of inches taller, but the man was menacing nonetheless.

Important to hedge one's bets though. He had to figure who he was gonna get the most from.

'Yeah, I think I could take a good guess as to who you're lookin' for,' Cheech said, testing the waters. 'Not that I've the best memory for names, you know,' he added. 'Faces yeah, names no.'

Cheech leaned across the small bar, close to the bounty hunter, saying confidentially, 'An incentive could jog my memory, of course...'

The man across from Cheech looked on with no emotion, other than perhaps boredom. He took a long pull on his cigar. Slowly, deliberately, he then stubbed it out on the bar, between himself and the bartender, spreading the final shards of skin with ashes. Then, with a sudden speed that one would not have expected from the tall calm man, had you observed his demeanour, the bounty hunter grabbed Cheech by the shirt with both hands, and lifted him from the ground, ever so slightly.

It was enough though.

Eyes wide, Cheech gagged. 'Yeah... um... Not quite the incentive I had in mind...'

The bounty hunter gave a sharp tug upwards, indicating quite clearly that this was the most agreeable incentive he intended to offer.

'But good...' Cheech commended, terrified. 'Very good incentive.'

The elevated bartender took a deep, ragged breath before continuing.

'There's this guy been comin' round,' he explained. 'I know he's the one you want!'

The bounty hunter slackened his grip, now that Cheech was being more co-operative.

'He's got the box you're after. And the gold. He showed me it last night when

Thirteen

I was tryin' to throw him out,' Cheech continued, filling in the details. His interrogator lower him so as his feet touched the floor again, but maintained his grip around his collar. 'He's got a lotta money, that's for sure. He musta got paid off too. Never works, I can tell ya...'

The man, face clad in the shadow of his hat brim, listened as Cheech told him more of what he needed to know.

Sam was sweating. He was nervous, both because the game was coming to a head, and what was transpiring at the bar in the black and white of the corner of his eye.

He pushed a wad of cash into the centre, hoping to scare Jim. Wayne had already folded, and was watching, leaning back in his chair, arms crossed and smiling.

'Call,' Sam hears this as if under water. His hands shake violently.

Jim leans over the table, catching Sam's attention. '*Call*,' he said, with emphasis.

Reluctantly, Sam turns over his hand, which is laughably poor.

Jim's face breaks into a huge smile, as he shows his straight flush.

'Thank you very much gentlemen...' he says, reaching into the table, scooping the various moneys and valuables.

Sam's face returns to that dark colour associated with anger. Rage, in fact. He had been hoping to out bet Jim. Hell, he ought to have without a problem. Those two must have been conspiring against him.

He is too engrossed in his surprised anger that he fails to notice the bartender pointing towards their table – to Sam himself in fact. All he sees is Jim, laughing with that cowpoke, Wayne.

While the two are celebrating having cleared out Sam's coffers, the small explosive man pulled his trusty Remington 1875 from the bundle of his long leather drover, and brought it level with Jim's face.

From across the saloon, the bounty hunter let go of Cheech, and, drawing his gun, made his way towards the poker game, knocking over tables and kicking aside a slouched man sleeping beneath his sombrero.

'Cheating crow roost...' Sam growled at Jim, pulling back the hammer, cocking his shooting-iron, while the other man breathed protests, unbelieving.

Outside, a horse began to bray, disturbed by the commotion.

With the bounty hunter closing, and Sam's finger depressing the trigger, Wayne lurched into the fray. He pushed Sam's arm just as he was about to fire.

The shot rang out loud through the saloon.

Sam looked nervously around the room, grabbed his bundle and ran from the Watering Hole, knocking his knee hard off a chair and almost slipping on the straw mat.

Ears ringing, the bar was silent for a moment as people recovered from the shock of the close call. Jim sat stunned, eyes wide and blank. His cigarette fell from his lips and struck the floor with no notice.

Attention elsewhere, or entirely absent, nobody noticed that there was a hole in the window by the horse rail, and that the loud nag had become oddly silent. Everyone except the bounty hunter, who had redirected his course to take him to the batwing doors. He had noticed the pinched whine that had preceded the total silence, and recognised it for his mount. Had to be, for there was not another single horse on the rickety street.

Just as he reached the straw mat before the doors, a large shadow blotted out the blaring sunlight from outside.

'Hey, Cheech, I heard me a shot,' came a new voice. 'Everythin' ok in...'

Not even slowing down, the bounty hunter slammed into the man who had

Thirteen

just entered the saloon. He felt his arm grasped. Looking up, he saw the glint of a sheriff's badge.

'Whoa, boy! Where's the cattle stampede...' began Sheriff Brown, breaking off when he notices the drawn gun, pointing just ever so slightly away from himself.

He scowled at the tall man he had restrained. Tall yes, but the sheriff was larger. 'Sonny, I think we better go for a little chat down the way,' he said, a hint of menace in his voice. 'Free accomodation for the night I reckon. Ain't ya lucky, boy?'

As the sheriff lead the bounty hunter from the saloon, Jim finally relaxed, slouching against his chair. Fluttering in the air, a card dropped from his sleeve.

Sam may have had the head start, with the bounty hunter spending the night in lock-up, but neither of them had a horse. On foot, the desert seemed an endless ocean of fire and sand.

He hadn't seen a campfire that first night – that was how he knew that Sheriff Brown had docked the guy. He had seen him lead the man, who was so clearly after his neck, out of the Watering Hole and towards the sorry excuse of a jailhouse, as he'd left his rented room for the final time.

He knew it had only been for a single night, as tonight – only two days down the road – a campfire haunted him, just beyond the horizon. How the man had caught up so quick, he had no idea, but he had no intention of letting up more ground.

Unfortunately for Sam, the man had little options here, and was not exactly the most skilled trail-man. The bounty hunter tracked his quarry easily, and knew he was getting closer as, day by day, the ruined campfires he came across became slightly warmer, the tracks a little clearer. Finally, after five days of living in the blaring hot desert hell, he lifted a still burning cigar from the wreckage of a smouldering fire, lifting it to his sun cracked lips.

The nights froze Sam to his bones, and he found it difficult to sleep. The coyotes seemed to be crying his name, listing his past deeds. He knew it was probably just dehydration, but that didn't help him sleep.

The bounty hunter had no such problems. He slept little to begin with, and having renounced his family and history, was nothing but a cold machine. He felt little – had to keep those emotions locked away, or else he may be forced to face his past. He had been doing this for so long that it seemed to take little effort, and he could almost believe he had always been this way. Almost.

Halfway through the following day, Sam broke into a final run. He had seen the dark figure of his pursuer when he had crested a sandbank, and was shocked to find him so close. But then, it was no surprise that he hadn't heard him. He'd waited until the rock had broken once again, and the soft sand dampened all sounds other than those of the soaring carrion birds.

Ducking down the far side of a dune, he hurriedly drew his gun, and sent a wild shot over the top in the vague direction of his hunter.

The bounty hunter, reflexes tuned by hundreds of gun battles, broke into a roll, drawing his gun fluidly as he came to a final crouch behind a rough thorn bush. It was scant protection, for sure, but his brain automatically picked out the best cover in any area. He didn't even need to glance around to confirm this – so sure of his abilities.

A moment of silence, with no follow up shots, and then Sam peered over the summit of his dune. The man who no longer thought of himself as a person noted that his game had removed his drover.

He saw Sam's mouth open, and a moment later came the sounds, buffeted by a headwind.

Thirteen

'Sorry 'bout that man! Just ya freaked me out a little is all!'

The grizzled bounty hunter sat in silence. He never dignified such people with a response. They'd wear themselves down asking to be spared, and then, later, mercy. That was good. He didn't care for anything this small time bandito had to say, but the effect that it would have on the man was psychological dynamite.

'Think we could have a little chat, man ta man?' asked Sam. Always the same, reflected his enemy. That was about as far the bounty hunter would ever allow himself to reflect. After aspects of his new life – or, what had now become the majority of his life – he didn't care to remember his past.

'See, there's been a misunderstanding,' Sam added, as they *always* did when they saw their end as inevitable.

The bounty hunter judges this as the best time to start laying some added pressure down. He let off a shot aimed just below the crest of Sam's dune.

Sam ducked back before the bullet hit home. Sand erupted in a plume, which showered down on the cowering man.

Gritting his teeth, Sam loaded the empty chamber of his 1875 model pistol.

'No, no!' he called out, whilst loading, not looking over the hill this time. 'I didn't mean misunderstanding as such...' he paused to think – what did he mean? 'More, I have a proposition for ya.' Yeah, that was good.

Thunder rolled out again, and sand fell over his head, scratching his skin.

What was wrong with this guy? He thought, frantic. *I just wanna talk!*

'Hear me out!' his voice had sped up to a good tempo. 'I could pay ya more than Jefferson. Much more!' That had to get his attention. 'C'mon, my philosophy's take double if it's there... I could give you that! What d'ya say?'

Sam rose slightly, showing his head for good measure, only to have to dive quickly as a bullet grazed the air where he had just been.

'Awww... c'mon...' he almost whined.

A fourth shot rang out in the apocalyptic wastelands.

'I just want you to know!' he called in response, his anger (and fear) reaching heights he'd never thought possible. 'I'm takin' that as a no!'

His loss... he thought, although not quite believing it.

The ensuing shoot-out was intense, and despite the entrenched cover, with his opponent effectively out in the open, Sam found it to be the most trying of his life. What's more, he didn't land a single shot even within one foot of that man! It was as if he were pitted against a demon sent from the fiery depths of Hell itself, to finally collect what Sam Hall owed the world.

In fact, Sam found it very difficult to resist this idea. It chilled him to his bones.

Whilst fumbling to reload his gun in a brief lull in the battle, Sam felt it important to try to reason with this *man* (for he had to be just a man, didn't he? There were no such things as demons and ghosts...). Moreover, he felt it in his *gut* – this was his last chance.

'Hey, ok. How 'bout a truce... ahh!' he swung his hand. The heat of the used chambers had burned through even his thick calluses. He leaned over the top of the dune, and continued. 'I'll even let ya take me in – alive, if ya don't wanna go for takin' my gold 'n' jacket or summthin' back ta Jeff...'

Sam saw as the bounty hunter finished reloading his gun, and with uncanny speed levelled it. The shot was through Sam's upper right arm before he could even think to dive. Blood ejected from the wound as a violent volcanic eruption, and the impact sent him flailing down the other side of the dune. At least that was a small mercy. He doubted he'd have lived another second had he fallen down the bounty hunter's side.

When the bounty hunter reached the top of the dune, he found no trace of

Thirteen

Sam Hall bar a splash of blood. There were no tracks even.

He must have covered them using his jacket to dust sand over them. The bounty hunter would have seen the marks left if it had just been dragged over.

Looking from left to right, all the way to the far horizon, and even the spine of the Rockies, he saw no sign of Sam .

The deep breath, bordering on a sigh, was the only indication of his mounting frustration.

Squatting on the top of the dune Sam had used for cover, head lowered, the bounty hunter tried to organise his thoughts.

Suddenly he reached out and picked up something he'd noticed in the sand next to him.

He lifted it to his face, and examined the small cigar stump.

Raising his head, he sniffed the air.

He could smell the acrid smoke.

The man may have covered his tracks well, but the fool had forgotten that nothin' but a strong opposing wind could hide the signature his habit. It was enough to make a man grin.

But the bounty hunter didn't. He didn't even twitch at the corners. He simply stood up, that fluid deliberate motion ebbing menace. He pulled down the brim of his hat, and headed in the direction of the pleasant smell of cigar smoke.

Sam walked along, wafting his long drover behind, kicking up clouds of dust that settled into his footprints. Suddenly a shot thundered out, kicking up a pelt of sand and shards of the underlying rock.

Sam dropped to the ground, landing on his injured arm.

'Damn sum-bitch!' he hissed under his breath, both at the flaring pain and the persistent hunter.

'Don't you ever give up!' he yelled at the man he thought he'd lost hours ago. It was mostly for his own benefit, he knew. That relentless hunter cared for nothing his potential (*yes, keep telling yourself that*, a voice whispered) had to say.

Sam lets out a couple of wild shots, trying to force the hunter to stay under cover, while he himself dove for the nearest bush.

The madness of desperation began to work its way into Sam's dark mind. 'He don't accept money, don't accept me alive, proof I'm dead where he'd still get paid,' came the constant, comically exaggerated panicked jabber, sanity frayed. 'He don't give up when I disappear, goddamn!'

He twisted up, and let out a volley in the direction of the bush the bounty hunter had taken refuge behind. In this section of flat, open desert, where the erg gave way to the relentless, desolate hamada, these struggling dry plants were the only cover available.

Sam fires until his gun clicks dry.

As he ducks back into cover his nemesis let out two final shots in his direction, before he also emptied his chambers.

Sam reached into his pocket in the silence, and drew only a couple of empty shell cases and a match. He had wasted almost all of his ammunition in the first gunfight, and now he had used his last bullet.

Fear gripped him by the balls, but a silence stretched longer than it took even a novice to reload – and this demon was *no* novice. Peering through a gap in the scant foliage of the thorn bush, he saw the bounty hunter walking towards him in the open.

Sam smiled – couldn't help himself. Hope poured into his worn soul.

'All outta bullets are we?' he asked, standing with his gun levelled on his

Thirteen

would-be (*and, oh yes, he* would *be*, came that voice, even now) assassin.

The man didn't respond, merely continuing his walk towards where Sam stood.

Somehow he knew that his quarry's gun was empty.

'Ain't that a pity,' Sam continued, trying to at least reach that cold heart – make it question its convictions just the once. 'Lucky for you...'

Sam pulled the trigger, hammer already cocked. The bounty hunter didn't even pause to listen for the 'click'.

'... so've I.'

The bounty hunter stops only a few feet from where Sam stands. He is expressionless, as always.

The cold blue of the man's shadowed eyes sends a shiver down Sam's spine.

They looked dead.

Sam replaced his pistol in its holster. His had snaked into the folds of his jacket, which he'd re-adorned during his pointless jabber behind the bush.

'So, it's gonna be a manly punch-up, is it?' Sam said, trying to keep the man's attention on his face. 'Well, I can't think of a more fittin' end than this.' His hand found what it was looking for, and grasped the hilt. 'A fair duel between two equally matched opponents.' He'd begun to circle the inhuman bounty hunter, trying once again to put him off balance – something he should now know to be impossible. 'Poetic really. Just one thing...'

He drew his katana quickly, fluidly, whipping it just inches from the unflinching hunter.

Sam laughed, although anyone would be able to see the concern through that petty disguise. 'I ain't that kinda guy.'

The bounty hunter just stood, watching Sam calmly, knowing that there would be another speech to hear. And it was better to let them get it out. Always was. That way their moral could be raised that final bit, using that last reserve of emotional energy, ready to be crushed by *him*, the relentless hunter.

'Oh yeah... I forgot to mention this, didn't I?' Sam said, indicating his sword, as he continued to circle the bounty hunter. 'Spent some time travelling, I did.' The bounty hunter could almost taste the salty fear in that frantic voice. 'Saw a fair bit of Asia. Fascinating place.' It was amazing that the man couldn't see this final speech for what it was, but they never could. 'Made a few friends. Was a good laugh.' Of course, he missed the reason's why he was so far from home. The inference said a lot about his character. 'And it taught me a few skills, which have been very useful since.'

The outlaw waved his sword, and laughed. He was on the brink of insanity. The bounty hunter could see it. Above all, the man was afraid of his hunter's calm.

'I tried to be reasonable with ya,' Sam entered into his final plea. He gestured with his arms outstretched, sword wavering. The bounty hunter knew he could have killed him there and then, in that short moment, but he preferred to wait. 'Hell, I even tried to bargain with ya! You can't say fairer than that.' He gave a sickly grin. 'But you wouldn't accept. And now,' he spun a quarter circle. 'Now, here we are. Bet you fuckin' wish you'd bargained now, yeah?'

The man laughed, but his smile was quickly snatched from his face as the bounty hunter, judging the time right, drew a machete from his left hip, from under his pommel slicker.

'Shit...' was all Sam could think to say. The dull blade had had a similar effect of the sheriff.

The final conflict was fast. Sam made the first move, as the bounty hunter intended. He, of course, parried with ease. Although no expression ever crossed

Thirteen

his leathery face, the bounty hunter did become concerned as the duel progressed. Sam was a better swordsman than he had expected. Better than any of the others had been. They were evenly matched, despite their differing weapons and styles.

For a moment – less than a second – the bounty hunter wondered if he had made a mistake in letting the man live so long, passing up open opportunities to end his life.

The sword clinked lightly against the heavy machete, but it was strong and didn't show any sign of breaking. The grit of the hamada flew around them, as if they were enclosed in their own personal sandstorm, cut off from the outside world by the dustdevil. Sam's long jacket, open down the front, swung around them. The two were too close for this to make any difference, but it gave the scene a greater feeling of intimacy.

Finally, Sam made his last swing, slashing upwards. The bounty hunter stumbled backwards, but continued nonetheless. Leaving himself exposed, the machete cut through Sam's belly easily, and into his ribs. The bone cracked under the brutal force of the crude weapon.

Eviscerated, Sam collapsed, a look of shock on his already dead face. The small wooden box, beautifully hand carved, tumbled from Sam's leather drover.

Looking onwards, unseeing, the bounty hunter's face showed a hint of something. It wasn't surprise. It seemed more like fear.

After a moment his head moved, and he looked down at his chest. There, cutting deep through his ribcage was the wound Sam had given him. It was mortal, there could be no doubt.

Falling to his knees, all the strength gone from him, his machete clattered to the rock. His dead eyes locked on the box. Hatred and greed flashed simultaneously across those blue, disquieting eyes.

He fell, his head landing beside that ancient gold, on the heat-baked rock.

It was not the first time he had fallen because of this dark treasure.

His fear was borne of the possibility that it would not be his last.

PLAYTIME
ALIYA WHITELEY

"You killed him."

"Didn't," Wendy said.

"He's dead, isn't he?"

"And it was an accident."

"You threw him against the wall!"

"It bit me," Wendy defended.

"That's because you were poking him." Sal crouched down next to the peeling skirting board and plucked the furry ginger body from the carpet. "He's gone all floppy."

"Is it like a rag doll?" Wendy asked, chewing her gum faster. "Give it here."

"No."

"Listen, I've got this brilliant idea of what we could play next. Let's play vets."

"No." Sal held the dead hamster in her hands, torn between her desire to cradle it and her revulsion at its emptiness. Something fundamental had disappeared from it. She felt the small bag of fur deserved a new respect. "I want to bury Fudgie properly. We should put him in a box with some flowers and say a prayer over him."

Wendy sat down on Sal's bed and gave a few experimental bounces in time to her audible chewing. "I want to play vets or doctors. You can choose which one."

She had played doctors with Wendy before, and if it was a choice between herself or Fudgie being subjected to the poking and prodding of her friend, then Fudgie was it. He was dead anyway. It was strange how quickly that had become a hard fact. The object she was holding so tentatively was already becoming a cold, light thing, like a discarded sweet wrapper. "Vets."

"Okay!" Wendy bounced upwards to land on her feet. She swept the bottles and brushes from Sal's white dressing table and threw them on to the bed. "You're the assistant. Put it there and we'll examine it."

Her commitment to every game was total. Whenever they played together Wendy seemed to immerse herself so far into the fantasy that Sal always felt a little afraid. It wouldn't have surprised her if, one day, Wendy produced a real scalpel or a syringe for her experiments instead of an imaginary one.

But with the fear came curiosity. She lay the hamster on the dressing table, on top of the hand crocheted doily, and stood back as Wendy bent over it in silent awe.

There was the tiniest of hesitations, and then Wendy's thumb and forefinger closed over a front paw, manipulating it with professionalism. "Mmm... it's broken. We'll have to set it. Get some tape and a hairgrip."

Sal retrieved the grip from her hairband tin on the bed and passed it over. Wendy positioned it parallel to Fudgie's leg, stretching out the muscles so that a small hairless patch appeared at the juncture of its thigh. "Tape."

"Haven't got any."

Wendy clicked her tongue between her teeth until she reached a decision. "Put your finger here." She pointed at the thickest part of the leg and Sal obeyed with a mixture of fascination and disgust. With her free hand Wendy took a plug of chewing gum from her mouth and stretched it from her teeth to her thumb. It elongated and eventually snapped, leaving her with a long pink string which she wrapped around the hairgrip and the hamster with quick movements, as if reeling in a fishing rod. "Right."

"Can I take out my finger now?" Sal asked. The warmth of the gum against the fur of the hamster was making her queasy.

Thirteen

"No. You have to wait for it to set in place," Wendy said knowledgeably. "Hold still until I complete the examination."

Sal dared not move in case the corpse twitched in response. She could feel the gum drying and hardening against her finger. Wendy was busy poking the stomach with tentative jabs, rubbing the fur the wrong way to expose the button-like nipples. Then she turned her attention to its head.

"We should check its teeth," she said, fingering the tight black line of its closed mouth.

Something about peering down into the darkness that now inhabited the hamster body was too much for Sal. She shook her head.

"How old are you?" Wendy asked scornfully, and then prised the mouth open. It came slowly apart, the curved yellow teeth and the blue-veined tongue becoming exposed to the sharp spring light from the open window. Sal deliberately looked at the wall instead; at her framed picture of the happy little girl swinging a basket of flowers as she skipped along in an alpine meadow.

"Uck," Wendy said. Sal had to look back at the corpse. Its mouth was still open even though Wendy had turned her attention elsewhere; she was pointing with her index finger at one of its eyes, which had come out of its socket and was lying on the furry pouch of its cheek. It looked like a tiny black conker that had been drilled and strung, ready for battle.

The object on the dressing table did not remind Sal of Fudgie any more. Hamsters did not have open mouths and eyes on stalks; only this thing had those characteristics. Part of her felt utterly detached from the matted ginger fur and rapidly blackening tongue, but another part still felt a stubborn desire to protect it from further examination, to try to put it back together again.

"What did you do that for?" she shouted, as loud as she dared.

"I didn't! Honest! It just popped out!" Wendy touched the eyeball once. It moved slightly on the cheek and she squealed. "Weird."

"Put it back in."

"No way! You put it back in."

"No!" Sal looked at the eyeball, trying to find the courage to act. Her finger was still caught between the chewing gum splint and the leg. The weirdness of that contact had passed; maybe she could feel the same about touching the eye. "We can't bury him like this."

"Well, you'll have to put it back in then, won't you?" Wendy said. She crossed her arms and raised her chin. "Go on."

Sal leaned over the remains. The eye was too much to ask. But maybe, if she could just close the mouth, she would be able to bury it in the back garden and picture it lying peacefully there; maybe just next to the apple tree. Or underneath one of the rose bushes. She reached out with her free hand and inched towards the open hole, trying not to look past the teeth and the tongue to the ridges on the back of the mouth that slipped away into the darkness.

She wasn't aware that Wendy had moved around her to stand by her shoulder until her friend grabbed the finger that was stuck to the chewing gum and the corpse, and forced it upwards towards her head as she bent over the dressing table.

Her own hand made contact with the side of her face, making a sharp, slapping noise that set off a momentary buzzing in her ears. Sal closed her eyes as a reflex. She could feel her finger, still matted with gum, sticking to her hair. It was causing a painful, dragging sensation that forced her to open her eyes and stare at Wendy, who had clapped one hand over her own mouth in a pretence of shock.

"Thanks a lot! Now I've got gum in my hair!" Sal said, trying to work out her finger. It brushed something soft. Something furry.

Thirteen

"Umm..." Wendy said. She looked as if she didn't know whether to run for the door or burst out laughing. "That's not all you've got in your hair."

Sal jerked her finger and the hamster corpse swung round into her peripheral vision, dangling close to her ear. She felt the brush of fur against her lobe and panicked, pulling her finger hard despite the pain until it came free, with a clump of hair attached to it.

"Is it still there? Is it there?" she asked. "Get it out!" She couldn't bring herself to touch it. Instead she leaned over and shook her head from side to side, hoping to dislodge it.

"You're just making it worse," Wendy said. "It's all tangled up now. Sit on the bed. Where are your scissors?"

Sal obeyed instructions, sitting with her head tilted far over to one side. She grabbed her nail scissors from where Wendy had thrown them on the bed earlier and proffered them. "Quick. Get it out."

"Okay okay." Wendy approached and took the scissors. The look of concentration told Sal that she was in the throes of a new game; hairdressers. "Hold still."

The snipping began.

The snick of the blades close to her ear sent shivers through Sal's back. She forced herself to sit as still as she could, but her back would not stop arching away from the noise. She tilted her head further and put one arm on the bed to steady herself, brushing Wendy's leg in the process.

Wendy started and the scissors clipped together as a reflex. There was a silence and Wendy stepped away, her hands behind her back, her mouth screwed into a tight purse. "Ummm..." she said.

"What?"

"You made me slip!" she accused.

"What?"

"I kind of stabbed it."

"What?"

"Just a little bit!"

"Get it out! Get it out!" Sal screamed, jumping up from the bed and clenching her hands into claws by her chin. Her voice was beyond her control now, becoming higher and louder as she imagined each squirt of blood. Wendy shook her head, her eyes wide.

"It's going in your hair!" she squeaked.

Sal lurched to the dressing table, grabbed the doily, reached into her hair and cupped the ruined corpse. Then, before she could lose her nerve, she jerked her hand away as hard as she could. There was a moment of hot, tearing pain before she felt a patch of her hair come free in her hand, along with the doily wrapped bundle.

Then she threw the entire package out of the window.

Wendy rushed to her and leaned over the sill, following the trajectory of the corpse as it sailed through the air, resembling a large shuttlecock, to land on the opposite pavement. "Look!" she said excitedly.

A short woman dressed in a red shirt and faded blue jeans was the only person on the street. She was pushing a large pram and looking into its depths rather than at any mysterious flying objects. Sal and Wendy watched as she unknowingly approached the bundle in slow, even steps, the wheels of the pram lined up in a collision course. It was too much for Sal to watch.

She pulled Wendy back and shut the window with an unintentional bang, sinking under the sill to hide herself from view. "What's happening?" she asked Wendy, who was staring avidly at the incident waiting to unravel.

"She's coming up to it... she's right on it... she ran over it!" Wendy told Sal.

Thirteen

"She hasn't noticed... she's gone now. You gotta look... you gotta see this."

Sal stood up cautiously and let her eyes work their way to the scene of the crime. The doily had rolled open and was flopping in the wind like a stranded jellyfish on the pavement. There was a tiny trail of red spots that led down into the gutter, and there, nestling against the kerb, was the little orange body that had once been her Fudgie.

Wendy was looking at her critically. "You need to wash your hair."

"Yeah." Guilt was threatening. Fudgie looked just as he always had at this distance. She could almost imagine him crawling around down there, wondering where she was, hoping she would come to take him home. She should have stood up to Wendy this time, his abandoned corpse told her sternly; she should have said no at the beginning and meant it.

"I've got to go home now," Wendy said. "But I'll see you tomorrow, yeah?"

"Okay," Sal said.

Wendy walked to the bedroom door, looking once at the empty hamster cage as she passed it. "Remember to wash your hair and get a new hamster before your kids get back from school."

"Okay."

"I think I'll meet Jack at the school gates today. Do you want me to pick your two up as well? Give you more time to get cleaned up."

"Okay," Sal said. "Thanks."

"See you tomorrow. Oh, and I've thought of a great game we can play!"

Wendy walked out of the room with a vague wave and a smile, and Sal turned to watch her leave the house from the window, noticing how her friend kept well away from the opposite pavement and the orange blob lying in the gutter.

Thirteen

KLAUS
MATTHEW KING

The doll in my son's room is trying to kill me. I won't let him; I know what he's up to. He's been watching me as I put Nic to bed every night, sitting in the corner chair with his diamond-shaped eyes staring at me, just waiting for the opportunity to strike. He'll bide his time until later when I do my last check before bed. There's a maddening intelligence in his grin. He knows that's the perfect time to attack, but I'll be ready for him.

The sweat is starting to build on my forehead now. It's coming up on one in the morning and I know the time is close. By one, Nic's completely asleep. He's like his father and can't hear a thing once he's a few hours in. I'm afraid that if he's awake, Klaus may try to kill him too. Nic's a good boy and I know he would fight with me, but I can't have him interfere. Klaus is too smart. He might even go for Nic first, like those hostage situations in the movies. Yes, I'm sure that's what he'd do.

Twelve-fifty. I can barely clasp my fingers around the hammer. I have to rub my palm on the couch before I try. I'll need a good grip. Klaus is strong and made of thick, Austrian plastic. I remember my wife bringing him home from Germany and remarking about that. "The man told me his name was Klaus. He's a hearty fella. Don't you think Nic will love it?"

The doll hadn't made it out of the bag before I knew what kind of dark malice he contained. His red hair stood on end, reflected in his black, pointed eyes. The green suit he wore reminded me of a Christmas elf, and as she took him away, I saw a hint of red just inside his blazer. I recognized it as a thin streak of blood, and he saw me staring at it. "Shoot, my pen must have dropped in there," my wife said. Klaus grinned.

The point of my tack hammer is sharp. If I catch him square with it, I might be able to end this quickly. Five minutes now. I should exercise before I go in. Doing pushups helps my arms to loosen up a little. Klaus knows about the stiffness in my shoulders. Nic asked me about it tonight after reading. I tried to laugh it off, but when I turned around Klaus was already looking at my right arm with a greedy smile.

One minute left and I can't stop pacing. The hammer is nearly cemented into my right hand. I practice my quickness by sparring with the fly Nic let in after playing. I finally catch him on the arm of the recliner and the blood makes a tiny stain on the end of the point. I can only pray that Klaus's blood will run as free. I wipe the end of it on my arm and check the clock: the numbers flip over to zeros. I take a deep breath and say a prayer. As I always tell Nic, if you aren't asking, God's not hearing. Lord protect me. Amen.

The hinges on the door don't squeak; that much I took care of before the bedtime routine. The red night light is glowing in the far corner just above Klaus's chair, but the seat is empty! My eyes dart over the room and then I see him in the shadows. His unflinching stare beams at me from the corner of Nic's bed. I feel like screaming but this is no time to lose my strength. Klaus will make me pay for showing my weakness. Instead, I show my hammer to him and close the door, locking it behind me. I see Klaus's arm move slightly, like he's tensing it. He's inching his fingers towards Nic's throat. Despite my rage, I can't seem to move. The smile on the doll's face grows larger.

The sweat rolling into my eyes is starting to burn. I let it, because I can't lose sight of Nic. My chest is heaving and I feel like I can't make it stop. Klaus knows the time is near. What is his plan? How can I beat him? Wild thoughts are pounding through my head until I feel as though my whole body is about to burst. I can't contain it anymore! A wild scream erupts from inside me and I charge the

Thirteen

bed with my hammer cocked in the air, ready to strike. I aim the first blow at Klaus's head and miss, sending the tack point smashing through the wall above Nic's shoulder.

"Daddy!"

Nic is awake. God! My worst fears are coming true. Nic turns around and Klaus falls onto him, sending his dagger-like teeth baring down onto my son's neck. In a rage, I swing at him again and this time I catch him flush against his unruly mop of hair. Klaus careens off the wall, landing at the foot of the mattress. Despite the blow, he's still wearing a grin. Austrian plastic, the finest in the world.

My weapon rises and falls like a jackhammer as I throw myself into the blows. They're landing, most of them, and I can feel Klaus's armour starting to break. My son is behind me, screaming. I picture this demon with his hands strangling my boy and the hammer begins to fall harder. I lift my knee to pin him against the bed and use both hands to drive my weapon down. With a final gasp of air, I strike at Klaus again. The hammer breaks through and lodges itself in the head of my enemy, shattering his armour into a spray of chalk and dust. What's left of him crushes easily beneath my weight.

The room begins to settle as I struggle to regain my thoughts. My Nicky is safe. I repeat those words to myself as I climb down off the bed. I let the hammer drop to the floor.

"Daddy?" He's crying now. A soft cry, just like his father.

"It's okay, son. Daddy wouldn't let him hurt you."

Nic looks to the end of the bed. He won't pull himself away from the corner to see Klaus's head laying in pieces on the floor.

"Where's mommy?"

"Locked in the wood shed," I say. "For protection."

Nic's eyes glance toward the window. He's still shaking. He looks so nervous. I curse the name of Klaus once more for making him feel this way.

"Does this mean you'll be going away again?" he asks me.

"No," I say. "They can't do that. Not this time. Not when I'm only trying to protect my son."

SWEPT AWAY
RICHARD HIPSON

The rolling waves playfully tug at her long hair while the sun beats down upon her back. The river, in all of its innocence, embraces her naked beauty like it would a lost child in the belly of danger.

Silently, no, lovingly she drifts through the ominous canyon until settling in upon a shallow bed of rocks. The passing current pulls at her limbs and taunts the young woman to come away with it but she refuses this gesture of grace and remains beached where she is. Gradually, the sun is consumed by an army of clouds as a light drizzle begins to fall.

The cold wind cries a sad song, becoming more aggressive, more urgent. The young woman, oblivious to all save for the enchantment of her peace, is nestled further onto the rock bed. And this is where she waits.

With the tenderness of a snake, the current lashes out to kiss her, shoving her again and again into the jagged edges of the canyon wall. Small pieces of flesh are torn from her swollen body. She does not bleed.

Seven days. Seven days since she was last seen playing, laughing, living. Seven days of fear and panic for those who had known her and for many who had not. Around here, everyone looked out for his or her neighbours; that's just the way it was done. For seven days a sweet young smile is splashed over the local papers and behind the screens of supper time televisions all over town. Yet, her name remains less than a whisper on the lips of those who dare to mention it. To lose one of their own couldn't possibly happen to them, surely not in this innocent little town. However, seven days ago, someone, a reckless stranger no doubt, had invaded their sanctuary, their home, and stole one of their own right out from her bed for reasons they would never understand.

And somewhere out there, in the dying light of the evening, a restless group of men, women and dogs search mournfully at the edge of a small town that cannot sleep for a body they cannot find.

Thirteen

THE COCKROACH COLLECTOR
BEN REPTON

The little slut was there again, the very fact that she came back meant that he almost had her now, there was no escaping him, no going back. A smile crept across his unshaven face.

His nicotine stained fingers danced across the keyboard to the tempo of his heart, bitten tips caressed the keyboard.

Alice : lo Nicky, how R U today?
Nicky : lo Alice, I'm good. I finished school for the summer now :)
Alice : Sweet :) Me too, no more slave work :P
Alice : R U doing anything this summer?
Nicky : I might be going to see the back street boys :) I'm very excited about that.

Alice smiled to himself once again, the name of that particular boy band never ceased to amuse him.

His gnarled fingers did a quick dance on the keyboard, the old alt-tab shuffle and the genie of google was there, ready for his command. Two seconds later the full details of the back street boys hung in front of his eyes, a quick hunt and he located the concert date that Nicky would probably be going to. He already knew that she lived near Chicago. That was far enough away from his home for it to be safe for him, no danger of people recognizing him.

Alice : OMG, so am I! I'm going to see them on July 18th.
Nicky : That's the same time I'm going to, we're going to the same concert! SCREAM :) LOL
Alice : What a coincidence, they're like so cool :)
Nicky : We have so much in common, it's so cool that we met.

That was almost the moment; the little fish was swimming around the bait, sweet mouth open and ready to swallow. But it wasn't quite time yet. Alice had developed instincts, he'd been playing this game for a long time now, he knew that if he appeared too eager now the little fish would swim away.

Alice : Yes, I think IRC is great. I wonder if we have anything else in common?
Nicky : I collect cockroaches. Do you like cockroaches?

"Cockroaches?" Alice's cracked voice betrayed his confusion, this was one strange little fishy, but who looks a gift horse in the mouth?

Tappy tappy went the fingers across the scum-encrusted keys. A couple of heavy breathes later and google had served up the details of the wonderful world of the cockroach.

Alice : OMG!!! I love cockroaches :) My favourite is the Madagascar hissing cockroach, I think they're SO cool :)
Nicky : OMG!!! We must be sisters or something like you know separated at birth :P

The smile returned and grew larger this time, down below Alice felt something stirring.

Alice : Get out of here, I was about to say that. Hey, I've had an idea, would you like to, you know, meet and we can show each other our collections?
Nicky : That would be so cool. But my mom and pop wouldn't let me come, they don't know you.

Time to appeal to that good old female contrariness, thought Alice.
Alice : Blow your mom and dad. I could show you my...

There was a pause as Alice flicked back to her web browser.
Alice : Death's Head cockroach.

Thirteen

Alice let a small laugh out at this little joke; he never let a little fishy swim away once it was landed. No throwing them back into the stream, a swift knife to the back of the head before disposing of them somewhere safe.

Nicky : You're right, parents are a drag, what do they know? Do you know where we could meet?

Alice : Do you know Grant park by the sea?

Nicky : That's near where I live :)

Alice allowed himself a little chuckle at this one, of course it was near where Nicky lived, that's why he'd picked it.

Alice : Meet me by the Clarence Buckingham Fountain in 1 hour :)

Nicky : I will :) And don't forget your Death's head :)

Alice : I won't. c u soon :)

Nicky : c u soon :)

The sun had set by the time Alice approached the fountain, his stale breathe began to come in little hurried pants as his anticipation built. Would he have netted himself a cute little fishy this time?

Through the gloom he spied her, it had to be her, a little fishy, a sweet little twelve year old fishy and all alone in a big dark park. Who else could she be waiting for but little Alice? And my, but she was a cute one, her blonde hair all neat and proper, her skirt was long, but that didn't matter, that could be changed soon enough.

He walked over to her and smiled his best smile for her.

"Are you Alice's little friend?" He asked, trying to keep his breathing under control, he'd let himself become too excited at this point once before and ruined the game.

"Who're you?" The little girl asked, her blue eyes framed by blonde hair briefly flickered with concern and a little bit of fear.

"Don't worry Nicky. I'm Alice's dad. She couldn't come here to meet you but asked me to come instead. I can take you to her if you like, she's just over there."

He indicated a copse of trees not far from where they stood.

"She's twisted her ankle and can't walk far, but she asked me to tell you that she's brought her Death's head with her. Would you like to see it?"

"Oh yes please." The anxious glint vanished from her eyes, replaced with a childish enthusiasm.

"Then come with me."

He lead the way, walking in front of her so that she couldn't hear how desperate his breathing had become, the tingle in his pants was now close to exploding, this was it! The moment he'd been waiting for for one month, ever since little Nicky had entered the chat room and started chatting to little Alice.

They made the safety of the trees. The smile on his face had spread to ludicrous proportions; a clown's smile would look sane in comparison. As he turned he undid his fly, his bold and sweaty deflowerer bouncing out like a flagpole.

The look on Nicky's face was one that Alice would remember for the rest of his life.

The pointed teeth and glowing red eyes particularly stood out.

"Hello little cockroach." Said little Nicky, her voice sounded more like the growl of a large cat than the gurgle of a little fishy.

Mr Smith sat in front of his computer, the pile of unmarked homework sat at his side, ignored for now; he had bigger fish to fry.

His fingers flew over the keyboard in a virtuoso display of typing skills as his creative mind brought into being yet another bright young thing.

Thirteen

Tonight he was called Mandy, she was a little over twelve years old and loved listening to the music of Justin Timberlake.

Lucy : I love him too, that's such a coincidence :)

Mandy : We have so much in common.

Lucy : Maybe more than you realize ;) Do you like cockroaches?

Thirteen

CATALYST
BRIAN DOWELL

After a tough day at work, Steve Price took two cold cans of beer from his refrigerator. He always took two; the news lasted for thirty minutes. There were commercials, but he was afraid to get up. He might miss something.

He sat on the recliner in his living room - the only decent piece of furniture in his whole apartment, and he knew it - and turned on the TV. Steve cracked open a beer, pulled the wooden handle on the side of the recliner, and leaned back.

The news started with the regular opening; there was an overhead shot of Louisville as music played. Then, there were shots of the reporters out on the streets, chasing bad politicians and suspected murderers. The shot then moved into the studios, where the anchors were studying their notes and discussing something with the producers. Then, they switched to the live-feed in the studio. Steve loved the opening, especially the music, and hoped they would never change it.

The camera moved through the studio and up to the anchors. The male anchor, a smug bastard named Jake Domino, concentrated on his notes as the camera approached. He reminded Steve of the guys in tuxedos who escort beauty pageant contestants at county fairs. Jake Domino had once hit on a girl Steve knew at a bar on Bardstown Road. She said he had a dirty mind.

After Jake Domino looked up and smiled his expensive smile at the camera, the shot moved to the other anchor, the reason Steve had watched the local news every night for the last three years. Veronica Hightower smiled and looked up into the camera. Her teeth were perfect, but Steve doubted that she had ever had any work done. Her long, dark hair was up in a clip and her soft blue eyes glimmered under the studio lights. She was perfect.

The music faded and the anchors introduced themselves. Steve loved Veronica's voice; she sounded so intelligent, he knew they could have great conversations together. The top story was about a fire at a shoe factory on the west end. Steve ignored the story and picked up the notebook on the end table beside the recliner.

He opened the notebook and in the next available space wrote the date and a description of Veronica's wardrobe. She was wearing a charcoal suit with a skirt—they kept a light on her legs—with a white blouse and a diamond necklace. Steve could never buy her a diamond necklace, but he knew the one she was wearing wasn't hers, anyway. In the credits at the end of the show, they always told which companies had provided the wardrobes.

Steve placed the notebook back on the table, took a sip of his beer, and continued to watch Veronica Hightower work. As he did most nights, Steve wondered about her life. He had tried to look up her number in the phonebook and on the Internet, but she wasn't listed. Steve had even once taken the day off and waited outside the TV studio downtown the whole day, hoping to see her. At the end of the day, he had left without seeing her or Jake Domino.

They went to one of the reporters on the street; he was covering the extortion trial of one of the mayor's former assistants. The reporter followed the accused down the courthouse steps, but a team of lawyers blocked him. Other reporters shouted questions; they were left unanswered. The reporter, who looked like Steve's high school Spanish teacher, turned to the camera and said: "Back to you, Jake and Veronica."

Back in the studio, Veronica had a strange look on her face before she smiled and announced another news story. Steve saw the look, but he was too focused on Veronica's legs to give it any thought. He wondered what kind of exercise routine she used to keep her legs looking so great.

378

Thirteen

That look came back to her face; it was something he'd never seen on Veronica. What he liked most about her was her composure. No matter what was happening or how irate her guest was, she could always smile and maintain. Now, it looked like she had seen someone murdered in front of her.

Veronica continued, "...I've said, we can't verify it at this time, but we want you at home to see it and make your own decisions. We now take you to a live feed from our network affiliate WXAY in Cincinnati."

The screen flashed and changed to a scene in the living room of an old house. A man was speaking rapidly as the camera moved around the room, following a floating red mist.

The man said, "We're getting word that some of our affiliate stations are putting up our feed, so let me catch you up with what's happening here. My name's Jeff Durbin. I'm a reporter for WXAY here in Cincinnati. We were doing a live piece about this house -the Buckner House on Carl Lane - for our local news here. The house was built in the 1840's and has recently been renovated and opened to the public. We were about halfway through the piece when we came into the living room, which has been redone to look like it would have back when the house was first built, and we saw this. Stay on him, Tim."

The mist shot around the room and stopped in the corner beside the fireplace. The camera moved closer.

"Nice work, Tim," Jeff Durbin said. "Well, folks, we were here in the living room when our cameraman Tim Puckett spotted what you see on your screens at home. Tim's followed it around the room several times, and I call tell you what you're looking at is real. The owner of the house, Alma Gibson, left the room as soon as she saw it."

Steve finished off his first can of beer and said, "Well, hell." He picked up the phone. As the phone rang, he cracked open his second beer and took a drink. His mother answered the phone.

"Mom, you watching this?" he asked.

"What's that? Tim, you all right?"

"Yeah, I'm fine, Mom. Turn on channel eight."

Seconds later, his mother said, "What is it we're looking at here?"

"That's a ghost, Mom. I don't want to say I told you so."

There was silence on the line and then his mother said, "I want to watch this. Let me call you back."

Back in the living room of the old house, the ghost hovered in the corner, two feet off the ground. It's shape constantly changed, but at times it looked almost human.

Jeff Durbin whispered, "I'm going to try to talk to it."

Durbin stepped in front of the camera and crossed the room. Even though he could only see his back, Steve thought Jeff Durbin looked younger than his voice sounded; he looked like he belonged in high school, not reporting for the Cincinnati affiliate.

Durbin moved around the sofa and kneeled in front of the fireplace. The ghost swirled, looking as if it wanted to run but couldn't. Tim moved the camera closer, just over Durbin's left shoulder.

Steve took another drink of beer, wondering why the ghost didn't just go through the wall. When he was six, he had seen a ghost in his parents' closet. A white glowing hand had reached out of the wall and tried to grab him. His parents hadn't believed him.

Durbin leaned closer to the red mist and said, "Hello."

The mist spun wildly, and it looked like it might fly away, but then it stopped and its shape started to change: it twisted and swirled until it had taken an almost human shape. Steve thought it looked like a baby, except it was too thin and the

Thirteen

facial features were too defined.

Durbin said, "Hello."

The ghost looked at him with swirling eyes, but didn't say anything.

Durbin looked back at the camera, showing his square jaw and white teeth, and said, "If you're just joining us, as far as we know this is the first time anything like this has been caught on live TV. We're not sure why the little guy can't just up and leave or disappear. I've been trying to make contact with it, but I haven't had any luck, yet."

Durbin leaned closer, until he was just inches from the figure's face, and said, "Hello. Can you hear me?"

The thing looked frightened. It looked around, as if it was trying to find a way to escape, and then looked back at Jeff Durbin.

"Can you hear me?" Durbin repeated.

The thing moved its mouth, but there was no sound.

Durbin turned back to the camera and said, "I think it's trying to talk to me."

As Durbin was talking into the camera, Steve saw that the ghost looked even more frightened than before, as if something was coming after it. When Durbin turned back around to try to talk to it again, another red mist started to roll out of the wall near the ghost.

"Something's happening here," Durbin said.

Steve finished off his second beer and said, "No shit. You better get out of there."

The second mist was larger than the first. Its shape changed, but it never came close to a human form. The first ghost squirmed, barely keeping its human form.

Durbin leaned forward and said, "Hello. Are you his friend?"

There was no reply.

Durbin turned back to the camera and said, "Well, as you can see, there are two of them. The first one looks scared of the second one. I'm going to try to talk to them again."

Durbin turned and said, "Can either of you talk to me?"

The second ghost moved closer to Durbin, until it was just in front of his face.

Steve didn't like the way the ghost was moving; it was spinning quickly and moving in quick jerks.

As the first ghost, which was still in human form, cowered in the corner, the second ghost moved across the room. The red mist rolled as it floated to a lamp on an end table beside the sofa. It then stopped and floated for several seconds before surrounding the lamp.

Steve shook his head and said, "They didn't have big electric lamps like that back in the eighteen hundreds, you dumbasses."

Durbin said, "As you can see, this new apparition has moved across the room and has now put itself around the lamp. Tim's followed this second ghost, and I want him to stay on it—but what you can't see at home is that the first ghost has disappeared."

The camera jerked, as if Tim was going to turn to look back in the corner, but he stayed on the mist around the lamp.

"Now, I'm certainly no expert on the subject, but maybe the camera's what kept that little guy from disappearing. Maybe once we've got them on camera, they can't disappear or do whatever they do to get away. Wait a minute, something's happening with the lamp."

The lamp started to rock and then it lifted off the table. The red mist rolled around it as it moved.

"It's moving the lamp," Durbin said. "I wonder if it's doing it just to show us it can. Maybe that's a sign it's trying to communicate."

Thirteen

The lamp floated in the same spot for several seconds before flying across the room and striking Jeff Durbin in the head. Durbin fell to the floor.

The camera stayed on Durbin, who didn't move, and Tim the cameraman said, "Jeff, you all right?"

The mist rolled around the lamp and started to pick it up again. The camera fell to the floor and Steve could hear Tim's footsteps. Then, there was a crashing sound followed by a thud.

The screen went black.

Steve picked up the phone and dialled his mother. As it rang, Veronica Hightower and Jake Domino appeared on the screen. The light was still on Veronica's legs.

Steve's mother answered the phone.

"Mom, hold on, I want to hear what they say."

"Me, too," his mother said.

Veronica Hightower smiled into the camera and said, "We're trying to contact WXAY to get a report on what happened there. We're sure what we saw couldn't have been real. We'll let you know as soon as we hear anything."

Jake Domino then went into the next news story, something about a bus bombing in the Middle East.

"Mom, you still there?" Steve asked.

"Yeah, what *was* that?" she asked.

"I don't know, Mom. You think it was real?"

"Well, it's hard to say, but it sure looked real. I can't imagine why they'd fake something like that on the news."

On the screen, Veronica Hightower was talking about a food drive downtown. As she spoke, a red mist rolled out of the wall behind her. She stopped speaking and turned around after apparently noticing the thing on one of the monitors.

Veronica Hightower screamed and jumped over the desk. For one glorious moment, Steve Price saw up Veronica's skirt. Jake Domino was crawling across the desk when a boom mic came down on his head. He lay flat on the desk; blood poured from the side of his head.

Steve assumed the camera operators had all run away, because the camera didn't move as more red mist continued to roll out of the studio's back wall. Soon, most of the screen was covered with red; people screamed from behind the camera. Steve was sure one of the screams had come from Veronica Hightower.

Then, a scream came from the telephone.

"Mom, you all right?" Steve asked.

"One of them's here," she said. "I love you, Stevie."

"I love you, too, Mom."

There was another scream from the phone and then silence.

Steve stood and looked around the living room. Red mist was coming out of the wall by the front door.

He ran to the bathroom, cleared the counter, emptied the medicine cabinet, and threw everything into the hallway.

Steve closed the bathroom door and locked it, sat down on the edge of his bathtub, and waited.

Thirteen

LESTER
STEVEN SOUTHWORTH

Lester is a normal man. You probably walked past him today. He's the type of man who reads newspapers and drinks espressos. He wears a dark suit and a navy tie and carries a brown leather briefcase with shiny bronze catches.

When he gets home from work, he kicks off his shoes and forgets about the strains of the day. He spends the evening lounging in his dead father's armchair, reading or watching television while he eats half a ready meal off a tray on his lap. He has a glass of wine or two as well, just to help him relax.

But after dinner he gets restless. His sits and stares at the clock on the wall, shifting awkwardly in his chair. He watches the little hands moving around, willing them to tick faster. Every inch of him wants to get up and give in to his urges, but he knows how much better it is when he waits. He knows how much fun torture can be.

When the hands eventually land in the right place his heart almost stops with excitement. He runs upstairs; one had sliding on the polished banister, the other swinging happily. He pauses at his bedroom door, treasuring the sound as he gently squeaks it open. He stands in the doorway, eyes fixed on the tight space under his bed and sighs a deep, uncontrollable sigh. He wants to go in and end his misery, but he knows that it's still too soon.

So he hides away in his bathroom, scrubbing and brushing and rinsing until his eyes burn with scent of aftershave and lavender soap. He looks at his naked body in the full-length mirror, long limbs trembling slightly, and feels the familiar fits of disgust and arousal bickering inside him, fighting for acknowledgement. But the quick thrill of adrenaline surges through him and he makes his way back to the bedroom.

He locks the door behind him and slips the key into a secret place behind the wardrobe. Then he sinks onto his knees and waits until his thighs start to quiver before he carefully slides the long, homemade wooden box from under his bed, barely feeling any of its substantial weight. His heart shudders against his ribs, a little flip of fear jumps in his rolled belly.

Slowly, he removes the lid, ignoring the repulsive odour that attacks him and a gasp of relief slips from his lips. Finally, he is once again gazing upon his boxed goddess, his princess, his angel.

A tear forms in the corner of his eye and trickles down his cheek. He looks longingly at her wide, bloodshot eyes, at her withered face and at the bones that jut out from her emaciated body. He examines her stretched grey skin, following the contours of her flesh and the trails of sweat that run over it.

He reaches out a hand to tentatively touch her perfectly pale face, but his fingers recoil as they discover her cold features and retreat to the safety of her damp matted hair. He strokes it with overwhelming tenderness, embracing every greasy stand with his fingertips.

As he strokes, his eyes fall onto her lips. He remembers a time when they were pink and pouting, like the day he'd watched her talking to a friend outside the butchers. He'd wanted to race over and kiss her and love her forever. That was the day he realised how much he needed her around, how far he was willing to go to have her.

Her lips had lost their colour since then, but he still wants to kiss them, to run his tongue over the cracks. He feels a nudge of guilt as she doesn't appear to be aware of him. But the temptation is too great and she is too wonderful.

He bends down, trying not to inhale the stench that rises from her, and presses his mouth against hers. He murmurs contently, then pushes his tongue forwards, forcing it into her mouth.

Thirteen

Suddenly, he hears a crunch inside his head. He withdraws his tongue, filled with stomach-twisting pain and the horrible realisation that his angel, his perfect angel, has bitten him. He glares at her, shock mounting into anger as her little voice hums below him.

"You'll rot in hell," she whispers.

He howls with animal rage, slamming the lid onto the box and shoving the whole thing back under his bed. He storms out of his room, tears welling up inside him, and locks himself in his bathroom.

As soon as he enters he catches his eye in the mirror and gags, revolted at the sight of himself. He looks at the blood drying on his bottom lip and sticks out his tongue to survey the damage.

The wound is small, only a row of three shallow puncture marks. Easily explained once the blood has gone, he decides.

He looks away from the mirror, picks up the lavender soap and starts to scrub at his body. His skin turns red and raw, but he doesn't stop until her smell is gone and he can hardly remember she exists. He scrubs until he doesn't feel dirty or bad, until he is clean and unsoiled and normal.

Because Lester is a normal man.

You probably walked past him today.

Thirteen

ME, MARC AND IT
MATTHEW BATHAM

Marc was filing his nails. They were already buffed and manicured to perfection, but he was letting me know he was bored. White flecks snowed down onto the car seat between his legs, some onto his lap, which he brushed off irritably.

Perhaps he just wants to look perfect because he knows the car is going to break down.

Marc had admitted this was his fantasy – to run out of petrol in a dark lane and be fucked on the back seat.

"How long till we get to your brother's place?" he asked.

"Hour, hour and a half," I replied.

"Mind if I smoke?" asked Marc, lighting a cigarette.

"As long as you open the window."

Marc tutted, but wound the passenger window down.

"It just gets in my eyes and I need to see the road," I explained.

"Yes, John," he replied.

"Are you sure you don't mind meeting my brother?" I asked. "I know we've only been seeing each other a couple of weeks. It's not like meeting my mother or anything; I just think the two of you will get on."

"I'm sure we will," said Marc, although his tone suggested otherwise.

"It's actually our two-week anniversary," I said. "Since I pulled you at The Oak."

Marc took an exaggerated drag on his cigarette and blew the smoke into the car. "It seems longer," he said.

It wasn't hard to see why he'd had success with men in the past. His features were boyishly pretty, hair light blond, fringe hanging across his high forehead. But his brittle personality was seeping through now, etching lines around his mouth and eyes, draining colour from his cheeks.

I knew what had attracted him to me – middle-aged, balding and fat round the middle – the £50 note I'd held under his nose when I'd asked if he'd like a drink. And all the subsequent notes I'd waved at him or thrust into his hand since.

We were passing through the middle of a dense wooded area. The trees formed a natural arch over the road. I squinted, straining my eyes to see ahead. A man stepped out from the trees to our left. He was dressed in a long dark coat and a neck scarf that covered half his face. He stared into the passenger window as we drove past.

Marc shivered. "Freak."

"Just someone taking a stroll," I said.

"In a wood at this time?"

"Don't tell me you've never taken a walk through a wood after dark," I said.

Isn't that part of the thrill, Marc? The risk of being caught by a casual passer-by? Isn't that the part that really turns you on?

Marc tutted and took an angry drag on his cigarette.

"John!"

I slammed on the brake. The man was in front of us, his dark-clad form like a shadow in the headlights.

"How did he get there?" asked Marc, voice higher than usual.

The man began walking towards the car, his right leg dragging behind the left. As he drew nearer his face, or the top part, became visible.

"What's he doing?" asked Marc, as the man leered into the car. "Look at his eyes. I told you he was a freak."

I had to admit, there was something feral about the eyes that peered above the black scarf.

Thirteen

"What's wrong with his head?" Asked Marc. "It looks all mashed up or is that just the light?"

"No, I think it is all mashed up," I said. "Looks like he's been dragged along a gravel path on his head. I think that may his brains we can see."

Marc looked uncomfortable. "Drive round him."

"Road's too narrow."

"Drive over him then."

"Now, now."

The man was unravelling his scarf as if it were a bandage. He tugged it free. Marc screamed. It was a manly sound, but definitely a scream.

"His face!"

It was hideous. Putrid looking. Like a fruit that will turn liquid the second it is touched. It may have been the headlights distorting things, but it looked as if things were squirming amongst the destruction.

"Drive!" screamed Marc.

He sounded serious, so I managed to squeeze past the damaged man. It meant driving on the narrow grass verge, so that branches clawed at the side of the car.

"Call the police from your mobile!" said Marc, staring at the man through the rear-view mirror – it was good to see him using it for something other than to admire himself.

"And tell them what? A man showed us his face and he was ugly?"

"He stood in the road, he was trying to stop us getting by."

"He was just a bit drunk."

"Don't be fucking stupid. He was after us."

Maybe it's already time for the 'oh dear I've run out of petrol' routine. Fancy that Marc? Fancy getting fucked senseless while that creature comes staggering through the dark, dragging its left leg like a piece of dead meat?

Instead I suggested we stop for a coffee at a small café at the next town we came to.

"Why do we have to stop here?" asked Marc, eyeing the dusty interior and sparse clientele with distaste.

"I thought you might like some coffee."

"Doesn't your brother have coffee?"

"Maybe not," I said.

Marc screwed his face into a sour pout. He really was too old for pouting.

We were served by an old woman with a neck like a brown paper bag.

"This place is a shit hole," said Marc, not bothering to keep his voice down.

"I thought you might want a break from the car after what happened," I said.

Marc didn't speak again. He drank his coffee in quick jerky motions, like an actor in a silent film, then walked back to the car.

"Great coffee," he said, when I joined him. He'd left me to pay.

Fuck you! I thought and drove on.

The car felt smaller. Marc's breathing was loud and irritating. I wanted to punch him. Hit that once peachy face until it looked like a pomegranate.

I chose another narrow unlit road.

"Can't we use the motorway?" asked Marc. "Why do we have to take the fucking scenic route?"

Can't do the "no petrol' routine on a motorway you stupid fucker. Can't shag your slack arse on the hard shoulder.

The man was there again, running towards the car, stooped like an ape, grotesque face exposed, carnivorous glare fixed on Marc.

Marc screamed loud and shrill. There was nothing masculine about this one.

I slammed on the brakes again stopping just feet from the man. He slapped

385

Thirteen

his hands on the bonnet and grinned at us. A gob of blood flopped from his mouth and hung from the remnants of his chin.

"Drive over him!" screamed Marc.

The man was walking around the car towards Marc's side, still grinning, the blood hanging like a red string of snot.

"Your window's open, Marc," I said.

"Shit!" Marc began winding his window back up, but the stranger's hand was already reaching in, grabbing at his hair, black nails raking at his face.

"Drive for fuck sake!" He kept winding until the man's spongy hand was trapped. The rotting face was pressed to the window, leering like a drunk – a drunk that has washed his face with a flannel full of razor blades and drenched in acid.

"Drive!"

"Okay," I said, and pulled away. The stranger yelped like a kicked dog and a ripping sound filled the car. Marc was screaming again. I really wanted to hit him now.

"I know him!" he finally spluttered. "I dated him!"

"Please tell me you don't always go for the same type," I said.

"He didn't look like that then! I met him in the Oak too. His name is Marshall."

"How do you know it's him?" I asked, genuinely intrigued.

"I gave him this ring," said Marc, and I saw that he was holding one of the man's fingers – the ring finger apparently – that had been torn off when I pulled away.

"How do you know it's the same ring?"

"Because it's inscribed," said Marc, peering at the silver band like a jeweller – a jeweller that's had a recent shock.

"Mine forever," he read. "Love Marc."

"That's very romantic," I said.

"I can be," said Marc. "I did really like him."

"What went wrong?"

"We had a row. I finished it and he drove off after drinking two bottles of wine at mine and wrapped his car round a lamppost. He was thrown through the windscreen and landed face-first on the road. I saw him in the hospital before he died. It was horrible. I couldn't even look at him let alone talk to him."

"Not very compassionate is it," I said. "Still, you were more romantic with him than with me. Perhaps we should try spicing our love-life up a bit. Live out a few fantasies."

Marc scowled.

It's time!

I pulled the car over to the side of the road.

"What are you doing?" Marc glared at me.

"Oh dear," I said. "I seem to have run out of petrol."

"You're joking."

"Shame to waste a perfect opportunity – dark road, car, no petrol."

"Dead ex-boyfriend!"

I undid my seatbelt and leaned across, kissing Marc's cheek. He flinched away and continued glaring at me. I kissed him on the lips, shifting across and twisting so that one of my knees was pushed against his crotch. I kissed more forcefully and his mouth opened, his hands gripped my hair and he returned the kiss. I felt him growing hard.

"Wait!"

He pushed me away.

"Not now for God's sake."

"But you're turned on," I said. "You like being watched."

Thirteen

"Who's watching us?" asked Marc, and at that point he would have felt hot breath on the back of his neck and smelt the death on it.

"Marc," I said, nodding to his dead ex-boyfriend in the back seat. "I'd like you to meet my brother."

Thirteen

IN HER PLACE
M.S. HART

They considered her insignificant if they considered her at all. Why she chose to walk that way, along the dark side of the buildings no longer matters to anyone else.

She checked over her shoulder often. She felt as though she was being followed. She was you know. A rush of thin stale air climbed her back scraping her nerves, sending wisps of hair into spiked jolts of dread.

It may have only been a feeling after all. The only time she would have known for certain was when it was too late.

It was pouring. The street noise was muffled, distant. Her gait would have sounded uneven as she sidestepped the puddles. She was a fast walker at the best of times. Your leg muscles twitch involuntarily imagining her pace, imagining you in her motion.

Her thoughts may have slipped back and forth between practical realities and intangible wanderings. She had been carrying dry cleaning, office attire; two merino sweaters and cream gabardine slacks. The wine stain never did come out - a Hungarian red, Szekszárd 2003 - your birthday or hers?

You suspend your breathing to consider her desolate moment. Obsessing over images, rhythms, creating textures, you can't stop building the incident with incomplete fragments. Your life stops locked in her whorl.

Her thoughts and ideas, plans and emotions lost. You agonize. Your mind tortures senses. What became her reality, you force down into your own essence. Her tangible terror is swallowed in supplant shards, skimming over your vital organs, screeching across your thoughts. You beg to be consumed, removed: to be in her place.

Replaying how it must have been, locking one mangled night in an endless eight-minute loop. You are desperate for one last element, something to finally connect you.

You want to believe there must be a reason for it – for everything – a comfort to be found. There isn't, not for any of it. Nothing will ever fit quite right; you'll simply have to find the reason that fools you into calm. Find the reason to make you let go.

Frenzied; the dissembled projection takes your mind again.

You watch her leave. She steps out into the downpour wincing at the first touch of slivered rain.

You sit numb: watching her tug at the collar of her navy coat then drape her cold right hand with the fringe of the pink scarf, the one you bought her for Christmas the year before last.

She shivers, visibly agitated. She speeds up veering down the alley; her short cut to meet you.

You slip out of your body; floating over the horrid scene allowing the details to sting your mind, burn your eyes.

You float just high enough for her to reach, close enough for her perfume and the night to be real.

Clearly now, this time you can see, always unable to prevent it.

This time you are there at the moment of her death.

Thirteen

WHITECAPS
THEA ATKINSON

My first memory. Mother lifts me from a soft cushion into the air and points at a womblike fluid similar to what I left so few days ago to say, "Ocean, Georgie. That's the ocean. Your daddy's out there today." Then she dips my lower part into the liquid and I find it's not womb-warm. It's different. Much different. I don't like it and use the only sound I have to tell her so. The white bonnets of fluid disappear beneath the liquid, only to come again like the cotton caps she forever ties onto my head.

She holds me and says, "Come now, Georgie. If you want to be a fisherman like Daddy when you grow up, you have to get used to the water. That's it, Baby. Jump for Mommy. Jump. Jump."

The fluid is all I see as she jumbles me up and down, up and down. The little bonnets aren't happy at my invasion; they tease my face until I open my mouth in protest. Before they dissolve this time, they tease my tongue. I think the white tastes like crying.

Then whitecaps froth around me and erode years into another memory.

She rocks quietly. Even in the dark I can see she has the quiet posture of a woman lost to sorrow, and I recognise my daughter immediately: Annie, sweet Annie, looking as she did days before we lost her. Gone... what... three days now? Despite the shadows I can see her clearly. The wide lips she got from her mother are mouthing silent words as she creaks forward and leans back. I make out one: ocean. Then another: damn. Damn ocean.

Darkness flashes to white and fades to a foam of bubbles in a cooking pot. Images of a small kitchen come to me like a television warming to picture. Standing over the pot, I watch seals of elbow pasta roll and play in the boiling water. I'm with Annie again, yet strangely the kitchen where we stand - hers - has no fragrance. A vacuum is all it is, with light and shade and shape but no texture, no... feel. I search my bank of images, casting about for a buoy to mark the timeframe. There's none, or it's lost. Pulled under perhaps by the storm of recollections rushing in: Annie at ten begging me for candy: black liquorice, our favourite, one I bring home for her every time I stop at the convenience store at the head of the wharf; Annie as a toddler sliding in a playground; or asking me for a story before bedtime. "Tell me about God, Daddy. Is he big or small? Does he have toes like mine, or is he just like an angel without hair?"

"He's light, I think," I tell her, thinking about it. "Bright light. So bright he's hard to look at."

Annie, again as a girl, grieving a pet hamster. "I want him back, Daddy. Please can't I have him back?"

"He'll always be with you, Annie. You just have to think about him, is all."

"That's not good enough." She pouts. "You can't love a memory."

The grown, now gone, Annie mumbles something into the boiling water, and for a second, I think she's heard my thoughts. I can't hear the words, but I know their formation. "I want him back," she says.

"Just think about him, Baby," I tell her, imagining she'll respond, but she turns away from the stove and lets the water boil over.

Again I see whitecaps; this time the memory shows the boat's deck during my first trip as a hired hand. It's storming, nasty, with the sea casting angry fingers into a dawning light of sky, but not nasty enough to cancel the trip. Dumping day - most important of the season. If the traps don't get out today, there'll be no lobsters to sell tomorrow - a whole day of pay lost in a season far too treacherous and short to lose an hour. I'm staring over the rail, praying my three a.m. breakfast of bacon and fried eggs won't litter the water only four hours

Thirteen

into the seventeen-hour day. The waves throw their white hats relentlessly at the stern wall, froths of ocean heave into the gunnels and freeze on the platform. I'm careful to avoid the coils of rope that can catch my ankle and pull me over as I skate across the deck to throw over a pot. It's going to be a hell of a long day.

My seasickness will go away; I know it will. The last person in our family to have suffered such affliction was a wife two generations back who climbed aboard the dory my grandfather loaded every morning with lobster traps. She only did because, with his hundred and two degree temperature, she didn't think he could possibly fish safely. She wanted to make sure he was okay out there. So, with such stalwart stomachs in the family, I know my sickness is only temporary. Still. The churning of the waves matches the churning of my stomach, and before long, I'm praying for another memory.

Something comes before I have a chance to finish my prayer, and it's pleasant. I'm sitting on a driftwood log staring out into the full expanse of Atlantic Ocean. Seals bask on a sandbar halfway to the horizon, a lone seagull worries a scrap of seaweed on sand wet from the retreating waves, and whitecaps break against a crop of boulders surrounded by eelgrass. Annie sits cross-legged on the other end of the log; I sense her presence long before I turn to look at her.

I have a sudden urge to change the memory, to ask her why, with all the wonderful things she had to live for, why she was taken from me. But memories can't be changed; they can only be revisited, and I sigh, wishing things could be different. I stare at her and she stares at me, and within moments I realize something's missing. As full as this memory is, it's not complete. Like the memory of her kitchen, the air holds no taste. Here, the gulls make no sound, and Annie, my lost Annie, has no fragrance when I know she should smell strongly of patchouli perfume and bubble gum.

These images of her are not memories after all.

She's come to me, I realize, fought against time and space and even death to comfort me in these days since she's been gone. She knows that I only have to think of her, to bring her to me. I can ask her things, if I dare.

"Why, Annie?" I whisper, but she only watches me. Her hair is still lustrous and black, her eyes wide and green. I'm grateful she's chosen this manner of appearance for me; I'm not sure I could stand seeing her as a pale froth of air, or a blinding spot of light.

" Annie?" I whisper again, thinking maybe she hasn't realized she's come fully through. "Annie, are you OK?"

I watch a look of shock spread across her face, surprised she's broken through the barrier, and I throw her a reassuring smile. "It's OK, Annie. You're here. You made it."

She tries to speak: her mouth opens, her lips move, but no sound emerges.

As she fades from view, I determine to work on strengthening another sense for the next time: sound. I need to hear her voice. I close my eyes and let brightness dissolve into the darkness behind my eyes. I'm content to let the memories take me again; there is little pleasure in a reality without my daughter.

I see her again as a girl. Her pigtails dip under slightly and I curl one around my index finger.

"I don't want you to die," she says when I explain that her hamster, like every living thing, can't live forever.

"Well, I won't for a long, long time."

"Promise."

"I can't promise that. But I can promise I'll always be with you."

"How will I know you're there?"

I shrug, wondering how I could possibly comfort her without lying. "You'll just know."

Thirteen

Hearing her becomes all I think about. Even when the various memories come: tying up the boat at the end of the day, seeing Annie with her mother on the wharf waiting for me, starting the day again with a thermos of hot chocolate to stave off the numbing cold of ice-heavy water that I repeatedly plunge my hands into day in and day out. Even when those memories fill my space as if they're truly happening again, I focus on hearing sound. I will hear sound when Annie comes to me again. If she comes again. I hope she comes again.

"Dad?"

The sweet sound of her voice dispels the latest vision of me hauling a trap over the rail. It's filled with lobsters and with a small treasure that glints at me from the parlour: a 52 calibre bullet housing from the second World War when the allies target practiced near a large rock face here in the Atlantic. Sometimes strange things show up in traps and they always break the rhythmic monotony of hauling pot after pot. I'll give this to Annie. Annie. Didn't I hear her voice?

Her image comes into focus. A dissipating light reaches from my space into the darkness to find her. She looks startled to see me, and as I realise this, I get a whole picture: bedroom, dim light, Annie in her bathrobe staring into the shadows. More senses come: I smell soap: Noxzema, her favourite night cream. Electric heat gives off a dry odour of burning dust, and there's another fragrance...

"Daddy? Daddy are you ok?" The grown Annie whispers and I see her creeping toward me. As blessed as it is to hear her voice, I notice that there's something queer in the way she moves. She doesn't float like I imagine a ghost would; she doesn't hover. Because I can hear her, I catch the distinctive sound of slippers scraping against wooden floor. I hear the creaking of boards trying to embrace each other.

I want to wipe the sudden tears that catch the light on her cheek that slants from my direction. She does it for me and nods quietly.

"I know it was you; I could tell by your scent. You made it," she whispers. "Tell me you're ok. I can let you go if you say you're ok."

A familiar fragrance swirls around me, intensifies until I sense it on my palate. Liquorice. Black, fragrant liquorice.

Black liquorice...

Black liquorice...

And I remember.

Whitecaps: last memory.

I struggle against ropes and the liquid that sustained me these forty years, now filling my boots, dragging me down, absorbing me. I know that above me these bubbles are caps breaking on the boat into foam beneath the surface. I think of Annie. My Annie. "It's okay, Baby," I mouth, hoping she can still hear me. "I'm all right. It's not so bad. Like being a whitecap sinking beneath the waves..."

It's cold here as a ship's rail in this winter storm. White brine invades me the way I did it so many years ago.

And it does taste like crying.

THE EULOGY PILLS
KEN GOLDMAN

"Harris? This is Dr. Lazarus. I'm afraid I have some bad news."
I didn't really need to hear more. I knew . . .

I loved my father. But then he died.
During the last few of his eighty-one years Lewis Goulding had beaten a broken hip and a cancerous prostate, and on the final birthday of his life he golfed nine holes before breakfast. But death, that he couldn't beat. Not really wanting to, I picture his last moments. He's watching Letterman's Top Ten and suddenly turns to Mom in bed, gulping for mouthfuls of air like a man trapped underwater. He manages to grunt "Cora..!" before his heart quits on him and is already dead by the time Dave is wrapping up his bit.

["And the number one phone call you don't want to receive in the middle of the night . . ."]

You spend years readying yourself for that call. It's the shittiest fact among the Top Ten shitty facts of mid-life. Beloved parents wither and grow frail; you watch their bones snap and their bodily functions shut down. Among the aged life is a fragile thing, yet when death finally comes it's a sneak attack. You're unable to absorb the simple fact that a parent's life is over, that nature is clearing space for the next generation to die, and that generation is yours.

At first the pain comes as a dull and indistinct ache that quickly finds its centre in the core of my belly. An entire belief system has gone balls up during the course of a phone conversation, and following Dr. Lazarus' call my guts feel nailed to my backbone. The great cosmic plan that necessitated my father's dying does not accommodate any concept of a caring and benevolent deity because God's message to me now has only one interpretation.

"Pssst! Hey, Harrison! Tonight I have taken your father. There is no one to care for your sick mother and not much money either. Death happens, Harris. And by the way, here is some acid reflux to make your day complete."

"So, will we be seeing you in church next Sunday?"

So much to do in such little time, I am telling myself. I must put aside my religious concerns for the more immediate practical ones. I will need to select a suitable casket among the dozens displayed like nursery bassinets inside the funeral home's parlour. There is also a eulogy to write, a clergyman to locate for the final service, relatives and family friends to notify. The arrangement of a cold cut soiree during these most traumatic moments of my life seems ludicrous and vaguely obscene, but I will follow the necessary formalities at the Staemans Funeral Home as Edgar Staemans presents them, even while my insides are on fire. During my divorce I had believed my acid stomach could not become more excruciating. But those pains were just warming up for this day's gastronomical fireworks, and now I almost wish Lewis Goulding had been loved considerably less.

So much to do . . .

We had used Edgar Staemans' services to bury Dad's older sister, so I felt comfortable calling upon him for his burial. While Staemans is gibbering something about which of Dad's suits I would like my father to wear during the ceremony, I am idiotically picturing Dad inside his shiny new coffin wearing the ratty pee-stained pyjamas he had on when he died. His favourite blue suit hangs inside his closet mummified in plastic wrap, and an image flashes of my father sealed inside zip-lock plastic like last week's garbage.

Christ, the way a stressed mind works.

Although his insurance policy will cover the immediate funeral expenses, I

Thirteen

know Dad's savings will not stretch far, especially since Mom has been enduring the effects of a stroke she had suffered the past summer. Ailing parents of modest means tend to spend frivolously on such things as prescription medications, food, and rent, while divorced accountants with vindictive ex-wives are not in the best of financial circumstances to assist.

My heartburn is inching towards agony. I am hoping I won't topple face forward from my chair upon Staemans' polished mahogany desk.

A properly sombre man who keeps his smiles in check, Edgar Staemans snaps into sympathy mode. I half expect some rehearsed inanity concerning death's mysteries and uncertainties, maybe "Death is like a box of chocolates." Instead he dutifully reaches into his pocket and offers a Rolaids, insisting I keep the pack. But after sucking on several lozenges I experience no relief. Watching me writhe in my chair Staemans asks, "Would you like something a little stronger?"

I attempt a smile, cannot manage it, and settle for excising my grimace. "Have you got a pill inside your drawer for an ailing soul? I think that's what I really need right now."

"For the moment a little stomach relief may have the same effect," he answers, rifling through another compartment. Locating a small packet he taps two chocolate coloured capsules into my palm, offering a cup from the water cooler. "These should be potent enough, Mr. Goulding."

"We're burying my father together, Edgar. I think you can call me Harris."

Staemans doesn't miss a beat. "All right, then . . . Harris. An upset stomach is understandable when death takes a loved one from us. Such pain doesn't go away without a little pharmaceutical help. These next few days will be difficult. Take two more pills before you deliver your father's eulogy."

Although I have always been the pragmatic sort, this seems good advice. What the man lacks in charm Staemans makes up for in mannered trustworthiness, and he has probably dealt with this situation before. I gulp the capsules down like an addict in need of a fix. I suppose during this moment that's exactly what I am.

The pills help a little, and the burning sensation subsides. Edgar Staemans permits himself a smile that evaporates before I feel certain I have seen it. He offers several small packets.

"In case you need more," he says.

Edgar, old pal, you can bet the ranch on that one.

Night time.

I take two more of Staemans' pills to see myself through the task before me. In longhand I plan to compose an eloquent eulogy befitting my father with words sincere and heartfelt.

"My father was not a perfect man . . ." the testimonial begins. My tribute will rebut this pronouncement with examples of how perfect a parent he was. I will have to exaggerate his virtues, of course, but is any man ever so unblemished in life as he becomes in death?

Sleep overtakes my efforts to write any further. Edgar Staemans' wonder pills work their magic all too well. The pain is almost gone, and I drift.

Floating. Nothing but a dull memory, unformed and unwelcome.

[Dad's funeral is tomorrow!]

Floating . . . floating . . . floating . . . the pain far far away . . .

[Dad is dead and his funeral is tomorrow!]

I see something. It's out of focus at first, but the image sharpens. My father appears before me alive and much younger. His hair is coal black, not white and thinning. His skin is smooth and unlined. He is maybe in his early thirties, many years younger than I am now. This is the man I remember when I was a child. He

Thirteen

is with my mother who is also much younger and even more impossibly beautiful than I have memorized her as being.

The two are in bed. But they are not sleeping.

Edgar Staemans stands alongside my parents' bed like a sentry, and he turns towards me.

"Would you like something a little stronger, Harris?"

I am too absorbed by the scene before me to answer him. These are my parents and they are both unthinkably young. They seem about to make love. But something is wrong, something is very wrong.

There is a bottle of Old Ironsides whiskey on the nightstand. It is almost empty. And there is something else I see.

My mother is not a willing partner! Dad seems to be shouting, although I hear nothing. He is angry and he is shaking her. He continues to shout while Mother struggles beneath him.

Their voices are muffled, but gradually I can hear them.

"Goddamn you, Lewis, you're drunk again - "

"Yes, Cora, drunk's what I am. Drunk as a skunk is just what I am!"

She slaps him across his face and he hits her back very hard, so hard his wedding band etches a red crescent moon into the flesh just above her eye. He keeps hitting her until she stops her struggling. Her sliver of torn skin bubbles blood and a thin streak snakes down her cheek like an opened vein.

Holding her down he is forcing himself inside her! He is laughing and turning towards me, speaking to me across the years from another time.

"Go back to bed, Harris. There's nothing to see here."

Staemans stands alongside me and whispers close to my ear. I feel his breath warm my flesh.

"Such pain doesn't go away without a little pharmaceutical help, Harris . . . just a little pharmaceutical relief."

I awake inside Edgar Staemans' parlour. I have never left.

"Did I dose off? Christ, what a dream I had! How could I just fall asleep like that in the middle of all this--?"

"The pills are strong, Mr. Goulding. They sometimes have that effect, and for that I do apologize. How does your stomach feel?"

"A little better," I tell him. "Still a bit queasy."

"That's to be expected."

"Christ, I'm really sorry. Give me a few seconds to collect my thoughts, okay? You know, I still feel groggy. I apologize, Edgar. Maybe if I could just rest for a moment longer . . .?"

"Certainly," Staemans says. "The couch is comfortable. Take all the time you need, Mr. Goulding, all the time you need . . ."

" . . . Mr. Goulding? Can you hear me, Mr. Goulding?" Edgar Staemans' voice calls from some faraway place.

"Where am I?"

The coffin is before me, the one I have selected for Dad's burial. His remains rest inside. The lid is closed as I have requested.

"You're at your father's funeral, Mr. Goulding."

"Call me Harris, will you? I'm dreaming again, aren't I, Edgar?"

"Of course you are, Harris. Take your pills. It's time. The mourners are waiting."

I remove two capsules from their foil bubbles. I swallow them dry.

"It's time? What are you talking about? I was inside your office not one minute ago! I'm probably sleeping on that big couch at this very moment. Besides, I haven't prepared anything to say."

"That doesn't matter. It's time."

Thirteen

I find myself standing on a pulpit. Many faces are before me. They must be friends and relatives although everyone is shrouded in the darkness and I can't tell one person from another.

"The mourners are waiting for you to deliver your father's eulogy, Harris . . ."

"All right, then, Edgar, since you insist. How badly can I screw this up if I'm only dreaming, right?" Like the obedient son I have always been I mutter the first words that come to my lips.

"My father was not a perfect man. In fact, there is the possibility that he used to beat the crud out of my mother, although my memory is not very clear on this. But let me tell you this now, here before all of you and God. I loved my father and I forgive him because he was drunk at the time and he just didn't know I'd be getting up here like this telling you about it.

"Then again, maybe I was dreaming the whole thing. Hell, maybe you should forget I even brought this up, okay?"

I turn towards Staemans. "How am I doing? Is there a dry eye in the house?" I feel certain my father's mourners have been shocked out of their wits to the point of complete indignity. But, no, they are grieving for real, as if I am delivering a testimonial that has moved everyone present to tears.

Mother's face comes into soft focus, and she is wiping her eyes with a shaking hand gnarled with arthritis. I notice the small crescent scar above her right eye that she has had for as long as I can remember. She never speaks about it, has kept its secret all these years, and maybe I have some suspicions concerning it. One look at her convinces me that I have done enough eulogizing for one day.

"In closing, let me say that I would like to enjoy the rest of my nightmare alone. Just fucking go away, all of you."

Like a magician's vanishing act the mourners fade into nothingness although the residue of a few ghostly sobs lingers. Staemans joins me wearing the black robes of a church minister. He places one hand on my shoulder.

"A wonderful eulogy, Harris, a heartfelt and touching tribute befitting the memory of a wonderful man."

I almost laugh myself sick. "What are you talking about? My eulogy was an insult to my father! It was pure shit! I hated it!"

He isn't listening. Instead, the mahogany casket catches Staemans' attention. He speaks close to my ear.

"Your father has something he would like to say to you, Harris."

I feel more amused than shocked by what follows. Organ music fills the chapel and the lid of my father's coffin creaks open with all the drama of a low budget horror film. There is no surprise when Dad rises from the small silk pillow. His newly embalmed flesh appears anything but corpse-like. He has not been dead for very long, and in a few days he will probably look and smell considerably riper. He is still wearing the ratty pee-stained pyjamas he had worn the night he died.

"Dad?"

I know that what I see can't possibly be there.

"My blue suit, son. Where did I leave my blue suit?"

My father has returned from the dead to ask about his damned suit! I am performing a vaudeville routine with a cadaver.

"I thought you had the suit on when we buried you, Dad."

"Do you see me wearing the fucking suit? Do you?"

I half expect a drummer's rim shot, ba-da-boom.

My stomach pains have returned. Dream or not, this shit is getting to me.

"Christ, Dad, that doesn't matter any - "

Mother steps forward using her walker, moving with difficulty toward the

Thirteen

casket.

"Damn you, Lewis. You're drunk again!"

"Shut up, you two-bit whore!" my father shouts.

Ba-da-boom!

"Now, Lewis, Cora . . ." Staemans interrupts, his voice as firm as a headmaster's.

"Show some restraint on this day of all days."

I have to ask.

"Tell me about Mom's scar, Dad!"

My father ignores me as he climbs out of his coffin. His movements are stiff but not altogether ungraceful. He turns towards his wife.

"May I have this dance?"

Mother cannot help smiling. "Oh, Lewis, you old fool."

"The scar, Dad! How did Mom get that scar above her eye? How many other scars are there, Dad? How many other scars don't I know about?"

He does not answer.

The chapel organ plays an old tune from the 40's. I remember the song from when I was very young.

"That's 'Beautiful Dreamer!'" my mother exclaims, tears filling her eyes. "Oh, Lewis, you remembered!"

"Our song, Cora," he whispers. He takes the walker from her, and she enters his open arms. They dance.

Edgar Staemans is wearing priest's robes that would rival the Pope's. He motions for my attention. "So, will we be seeing you in church next Sunday, Harris?"

Some idiot on the P.A. system who sounds like Ed McMahon announces, "And tonight, in the role of God, Mr. Edgar Staemans of the Staemans Funeral Home located midtown at 53rd and Third! Memorial services, wakes, cremations and burials. Business hours 9:00 to 5:30 weekdays . . ."

This is crazy. This is fucking insane! Enough already! I want to wake up now! My stomach is on fire and my heartburn is killing me.

All right, so my father was not a perfect man. But he never laid a hand on my mother! He never drank! That was not the man I knew! [. . . not the man I want to remember . . .]

[. . . not the man I would ever want to remember . . .] I loved my father.

But then he died. "Hey, son," Dad calls to me. "What is the number one phone call you don't want to receive in the middle of the night?" "Pills," I mutter to Staemans. "P-pills, please . . ."

"I'm sorry, Harris. There are no more pills."

"P-Please . . ."

"Sorry. I'm so sorry . . ."

A curtain slowly drops. The light fades.

I'll be waking up now. Any second I'll find myself on the long black vinyl couch, waking up inside Edgar Staemans' Funeral Home.

Business hours 9:00 to 5:30 weekdays . . .

"Harris? Harris? Are you there?"

"Yes, Dr. Lazarus, I'm still here. My mind drifted for a moment."

"Harris, I'm so sorry. It's about your father . . ."

"Yes, Doctor. I know. I was expecting your call . . ."

LAUGHTER IN THE DARK
JOSEPH WAKELING

Laughter. Laughter is the enemy of power. And power is everything - power is what we all dream of, whether it's the power to command, the power to act or even just the power to stop others having power. When people ask me what I write about, power always comes first, because what else is there to say?

If people laugh at you they take that away, because how can you be powerful if you're ridiculous? You should never let anyone laugh at you. They should never dare. Perhaps they still laugh behind my back when they think I can't see and hear, but I know they are afraid to, and that's what matters. They never know, too, when I might hear. Now that's power.

That's what being an Author is all about, in my opinion. Writing your own story, relegating all the others to minor parts - you can cut them out, maybe focus on the ones you like momentarily, giving them something nice to say, but they can never be bigger than your voice. They dance like puppets as it pleases you, for your entertainment. Maybe one of them does something you don't like, so you can have him break his leg or kill his firstborn son or end up being crucified. I especially like killing firstborn sons. The grief of bereaved parents, especially when it was an only child, has a scent and taste that nothing else really matches.

I wrote the first words in a flash of light and everything that has happened since is down to me; my name is on the title page and it's staying there, alone. When one fellow suggested to me a collaborative project I threw him out of my house, thrust him down to the ground and kicked him too. If I use ghost writers they do exactly what I tell them or not at all. The copyright stays mine.

Some of them try to find the reason behind what I make them do. Some say it must be for the best, that since I tell them what is moral and what is not, I must be telling them about something absolute, something beyond me, because if I was just telling them whatever I felt like, it wouldn't be moral. And I am telling them morals, so...

Sometimes they don't like what I tell them to do and they beg to be let out of the story. That nice young man with the beard pleaded on his knees and sweated blood to try to get me to change my mind, but of course I would not. And the best thing is that then, when it happened, he willingly went and let them flog him half to death and nail him up. Those last words of his when he realised I'd really left him on his own, those I treasure. The moment when they realise they are utterly in your hands, and you're closing them into a fist. Ashes to ashes, dust to dust... Like Playdough, when you're done with them you scrunch them up and start on something new.

Laughter in the dark is the only way some of them can deal with it. They suffer, but they convince themselves others are suffering more, or will end up that way in the end. I've given them subplots of lakes of fire and seventy-two virgins; they all laugh at the others, convinced that they are the only ones on the train to the Promised Land. I still haven't decided quite how the ending will go, but that idea of dividing the sheep and the goats is quite attractive, watching the half of them bleat with pleasure as the others are plunged into oblivion. But who'll be laughing when the tide turns and they too are swept away? Will they turn chill with horror or will they even have time to realise, will they die with the laughter still on their lips?

And then in the end, when I put the word-processor to sleep and turn out the study light for the last time, I'll sit there in the dark and I'll have the last laugh:
Ha
Ha
Ha

Thirteen

Ha
Ha
Ha
Ha.

THE TRUE MASTER OF THE DESERT
SEAN M. FOSTER

The town of Pul stood in the Ezinef Oasis,
Which lay among the vast desolate stretches of sand
To be found in the heart of the Great Southern Desert.
Pul was home to a proud tribe that felt it could command
The world around; it boasted of its ability
To persevere and claimed to have tamed the arid land.

Now in this town lived a simple man named Haš. Haš worked
Silver as a trade, but on his farm he also raised
Various animals to feed his small family.
When dawn arrived, he awoke and yawned; when the sun blazed,
He toiled; when night fell, he rested with his wife and sons.
The beauty and mystery in life left him amazed.

One morning Haš rose early, eager to face the day.
He climbed to his feet to find that the floor of the room
Which he shared with his family was littered with sand.
The night had been quite still, so he was forced to assume
That some swift rogue breeze had blown the grains through the windows.
In the growing light he swept the floor clean with a broom.

After giving food and water to his animals,
Haš slipped into his congested workshop to complete
A delicate silver torque begun the day before.
When he reached the table, though, and sat upon the seat
In front of it, he discovered that the torque was gone:
Only a ring of sand remained in the growing heat.

At first he supposed that the collar had been stolen;
Closely inspecting the sand, however, he discerned
That the tawny circle displayed features quite like those
Of his creation. Even more, a small citrine burned
Among the grains; no, not a citrine, but the citrine --
The very stone that the beauty of the piece had earned.

He plucked the stone from the sand and held it to the light.
For a moment it smouldered gold, just as it had done
When he had traded that mated pair of vids for it.
Yet then, all at once, it started to crumble; soon, none
Of its life remained, and the smith pinched just grains of sand.
Bewildered, he stepped outside and stood beneath the sun.

Haš peered to the end of the road beside which he lived;
Had not a trio of palm trees grown there yesterday?
He then noticed that some of his neighbour's vids were gone;
Maybe someone had quietly carried them away?
Turning an ear toward the centre of town, he perceived
Shouts and screams and other sounds of life in disarray.

Haš rushed back into his home and found his family.
"Something strange is happening," he told his sons and wife.

Thirteen

"Although I can't explain exactly what's going on,
I fear for us all: I fear for your lives, and my life,
And the lives of everybody in Pul. I believe
That we have to ride south to escape the coming strife."

"What did you see?" asked his wife, Seca. She set aside
The tunic that she had been mending. "Soldiers? A storm?"
"No, nothing like that," replied Haš. "But I swear to you
That the world around us is beginning to transform
Into sand; and I sense we no longer have the time
To search for supplications, spells, or rites to perform."

Briefly Seca stared; then she laughed. "You worry too much,"
She declared. "'Turning to sand'? Your imagination
Has gotten the better of you, I'm quite sad to say."
"It's true!" countered the smith, his voice full of frustration.
"I witnessed a citrine turn to sand as I held it.
We *must* go; if we stay, we risk annihilation."

"You worry too much," Seca said again. "Far too much,
In fact, you probably just dropped the stone on the floor,
And then, when you looked for it, found a small pile of sand.
There's nothing to worry about, and no need to roar
And howl about the impossible, that's for certain.
We are safe: the desert is ours to use or ignore."

Seca returned her attention to the torn tunic;
When she grasped it again, however, it proceeded
To dissolve into pale grains just as the gem had done.
She cried out, astonished, but her voice soon receded,
And her hands began to quiver. An instant later,
She grabbed her slender throat; with frightened eyes she pleaded.

And then, before her horrified husband and children,
Seca started to fall apart: her body crumbled;
Her skin split and from the tears cascades of sand poured forth;
Her bones dissolved. Snatching up his two sons, Haš stumbled
Out the door. Yet by the time he collapsed in the road,
His young children were gone; with sand alone he fumbled.

The desert had taken his cherished family from him,
And now began to take his home. Around him the town
Shuddered, collapsed, melted into sand; the oasis
Became a wasteland of yellow and orange and brown.
The arrogance and the pride of the people of Pul
Had ensured that the desert would devour its renown.

Haš kneeled among the dunes, defeated. The burning sun
Stared down: perhaps it mocked him, perhaps it pitied him.
The man had learned that the true master of the desert
Allowed people to survive there only on a whim -
And just as it could permit, so too could it forbid.
He sighed softly, renouncing his hope; his face grew grim.

Thirteen

And with that Haš felt a sharp, searing pain in his chest;
From there it coursed though his body. He started to scream,
Like his wife had done; his scream was swiftly silenced, though,
And soon Haš had begun to dream that peculiar dream
Which we know as death. And thus the land had been reclaimed:
Once again the spirit of the desert reigned supreme.

Thirteen

CHICKEN LIST
ZOE LEA

The names were on the board. Block capitals as always, and written with the same hard lines. Chalk was gathered in small mounds at the ends of the letters and the dust had blown back on the board. Mickey was overly excited. He was walking about the classroom with his arms bent and flapping like wings. His head jerking in and out and his clucking noises irritating everyone, especially the girls whose names were on the board. Shelly was particularly embarrassed, she hadn't done very long.

Some other girls whose names were up there were sniggering, recounting how Shelly had ran from the building claiming to have felt a hand on her shoulder. Everyone thought this was amusing, apart from Shelly, who didn't have an ounce of bravado in her skinny body and who was terrified at the sight of her name on the list again.

My name was also on that list; Tina Longly. I saw my name on the board, it was no great surprise. I didn't feel fear, or dread, but just a pang of regret at wanting to come to this school and having made my mum stop teaching me. I thought I was missing out, what did I know?

"I felt it." Shelly was staring at the board and talking to me. "I felt the hand. Ice cold, on my shoulder." She looked at me, patting her shoulder, and I believed she really did feel a hand on her shoulder.

"Whose do you think it was?" I asked. Her mouth opened slightly.

"That girl's. The dead one. Who else?" We both looked back at the board.

"Who else?" I wondered aloud. I had a few ideas.

When the time came, a group of fifth year girls gathered at the school gates, ready to catch the 'chickens' as they tried to leave school un-noticed. They stood together, their skirts rolled up above the knee, socks pushed down in there school shoes, shirts pulled out and just the barest hint of make-up. One grabbed my blazer as I tried to pass. I tasted hairspray.

"Tina, you gonna be chicken?" I turned slowly and looked at her, this girl only a few years older than me. "Oh," She looked at my stare and called to the others. "We have a live one here." The other girls looked up and grinned, a group of lads had gathered to watch.

"I'm not playing." I said quietly. It was enough for the blonde haired one to hear.

"Not playing!" She shouted. "Like you have a choice. This isn't a game, new girl, this is the way it's done around here. This is the way it's always been done. The first years go on the chicken list. That girl died in that burnt out building, and if she doesn't see all the new comers in there, she gets mad. And she'll burn down another building, and this time, no one will escape."

"Rubbish. There is no girl in C-Block. This is just an excuse to bully."

She lent in close to me, so I could see the jerky line of eye-liner under her lid.

"Excuse or not, you're going tonight Tina, or your name will be up on that board every day until you do, and the whole school will know you are the biggest chicken alive."

She released my blazer with a shove and I walked home slowly. A stupid game. A stupid game that had to be played. Looking at my options, it seemed I had very few, I was already considered 'weird' because this was my first school and I liked to play chess instead of an Xbox. I didn't really need to give people any more ammunition.

That night, at nine o'clock on the dot, I walked up the playing field to C-Block. I could make out a group stood together and as I approached they all turned quickly. Shelly let out a sigh.

"S'only Tina," she said. "Thought you weren't coming." I shrugged my shoulders.

"So what happens now?" I asked digging my hands deeper into my duffle coat. All of my thoughts were of my warm bed.

"Chickens!" The girls jumped in unison. I couldn't help sniggering, and the blaze of the flash light blinded me

"Tina Longly, how nice to see you. Glad you decided to play after all. Now then first years, let's see who else is here." A girl chewing gum loudly took down our names and wrote an equals sign beside each of them, it was the chicken list.

Another girl who was trying to light a cigarette held a stop watch. The blonde haired one who had stopped me at the gates was shouting the orders, whilst another girl swigged something from a can.

"Here's the deal." She shouted, her breath hanging in the air. "You run through that building, whilst we time you, so that the ghost of the dead girl can see you pay respect to her. You must pass through this broken window." The beam of light swung round to show a window with the boards removed. "And walk through to that one." The torch was swept along the length of the building and stopped at a broken window on the far side. I looked inside the building as the torch rested. The floor was littered with bricks and empty cans, wooden boards and glass.

"Shelly, this is your second run on the chicken list. You go first." Shelly was trembling as she stepped forward.

"Wait," I shouted. "I'll go first."

"No." The light blinded me as Shelly gasped at my suggestion. "You, Tina, you go last."

"You won't have to wait long," The one swigging from the can giggled.

"Shelly, go!" The girl pressed the stop watch and started counting aloud as Shelly made her thin legs climb through the window. We all heard her scream within seconds of being in there, and then saw her body re-appear as she climbed straight back out.

"Five seconds." The girl shouted. "Better than last time," Shelly was white, muttering about feeling icy breath on her neck, refusing to leave until someone could walk her home.

The three other girls didn't do much better, they all returned out of the same window, all talking of cold hands, hearing voices, and the feeling of a spirit being present. Not one of them made it across to the other window.

"Tina, you're up" I walked up to building with a smile. My hands deep in my pockets and I reassuringly felt the small torch. Climbing through the window, I walked far enough so I was out of sight and switched it on. I darted it around, the small beam of light barley cut through the dust that was hanging in the air. It caught in my throat, making me cough and gasp in more. I slowly started to walk across, my only fear was spiders. My boots echoed, crunching down on something as I walked. I saw crumpled bits of paper on the floor, no doubt other chicken lists, and small piles of cigarette butts. It looked like C-Block was in use after all; there were beer cans and crisp packets. Someone had been here recently.

"You alright in there?" It was Shelly's voice, I could hear the tremor. I could visualise them all huddled together, the stop watch ticking as they waited and I got a bit giggly.

I wondered how long they'd wait if I didn't come out, I thought who they would send in after me, who they'd force in. I thought about pretending to be the ghost and do some howling, and then I thought of my warm bed and my mum's reaction if she found me missing and I walked on. Reaching the far window I saw

Thirteen

it was higher up than I thought; it would be a struggle to climb out of. There was nothing I could use as a step-up. Obviously no one had come this far before, I grinned and imagined the reaction in class. It was worth it, so I decided to take a run at it. As I ran toward the open window I grabbed the frame with both hands and catapulted my body through. I felt the rotten wood give way and heard a crash around my head. The last image I saw was a sparkle from a blade in the moonlight.

Three months later and the names are up on the board again. The same hard lines, the same pressure. Mickey's the first to see them; he frowns and rubs his cheeks. The others are close behind him and they all stop as they see the list. They all stare, some one mutters about rubbing it off and what a sick joke it is; but they know if they rub it off, the names will only be written on again. That's the way the chicken list works; the names stay on the board until the girls run through the building to pay their 'respect' to the dead girl in C-Block.

Perhaps no one likes it any more because the names on the board are not first years, they are of fifth years. They are not a random selection of new-comers, they are carefully selected. And they are always the same. They are the names of the fifth year girls who arrive at school every day for counselling. Who no longer wear eyeliner or grab the blazers of first years. They are the names of the girls who invented the game, and now I'm waiting for them to play it.

Thirteen

THE ASYLUM & THE SUNDOWNER CAPTAIN
JAMES FIELD

Outside, the bone of the moon glows, but within, we lie, destroyed in the dark.

I say 'we' - that isn't technically true. In fact it's just plain untrue, dammit. Royal 'we'. Can I say 'dammit'? It doesn't matter - the children aren't listening anymore. Anyway, outside, the bone of the moon glows, but within, we lie, destroyed in the dark. I've said that already? Sorry if I bore you. Mr. Ribald would have said if I was being boring. Did I mention Mr. Ribald? He's my friend. Sort of. He comes and goes. To tell you the truth, I care not for him. He's a little irritating. Mostly he goes. The dullard.

Do you know what he said to me the other day?

'Man,' he said, 'what is it with this moon? It's so big!' Did you know that the moon is nearly as big as Pluto? I'm not sure if that's right. The moon is a small place. I digress, he continued: 'All the other planets in the system have much smaller moons - this one's huge.'

'Well,' I observed. (I'm quite good at that, observing. And interpretive dance. But Mr. Ribald made me stop. He said it was unbecoming. I don't know whom it unbecame.)

'The moon is quite big because it is the collected debris of the collision of two planets.'

This was fairly accurate, I was sure.

'The result of which was primarily the Earth. The dust formed what we stand on.'

'Then why isn't the Earth a sort-of peanut shape? Being as it is made up of two spheres?' I put forward that this was no way for planets to behave, and he concluded that this was true, and also that I was an idiot. Then he left.

It was always the same. He came, asked me about the moon, called me an idiot, and left. I don't know where he goes. There isn't a door. There's a window, but I was told not to open it.

When Mr. Ribald comes, he insists I sit on the carpet, so that he might sit on the chair by the fireplace. The only other chair is a wooden one beside my writing table, but I don't like it. I don't write, and it's uncomfortable. It's one of the old-fashioned contoured ones you find in farmhouses. I sit on the carpet because Mr. Ribald tells me to. If I go to stand he scowls at me. It's hard to scowl when you have no eyes, but that does make it more intimidating when the desired effect is achieved. It's to do with his hat too, his top hat- the brim furrows downwards at the centre, like eyebrows as he does it. And the bump where I suppose his mouth is moves unsettlingly- I imagine that it would be a pursing of lips.

Mr. Ribald is only a small fellow, his skin is quite unhealthily grey, and looks to me to be made of the material that dressmakers dummies are- that odd plush material. Anyway, I'd quite like to poke it. Stitches run down the left and right of his face. When he sees my eyes follow the neat rows down to the high collar of his starched shirt, he crosses his legs, ankle resting on knee, as if to say 'I dare you to mention the stitches running down the left and right of my face.' Then he taps out his pipe on the hearth. Which is obviously just to irk me because he doesn't smoke. Or it's to look stylish.

'What are you thinking about, man?' He looks impatient. I was thinking that it was pretty lonely. A dressmaker's dummy is no company, even if it is elegantly dressed, especially such an arrogant dressmaker's dummy. Personally, I don't see what he has to be arrogant about, what with the grey face and the stitches. He says he's impermeable. I looked that up in the dictionary. A geographical dictionary. For plot purposes. And it said that 'impermeable' was an adjective associated with rocks, water and the combining of the two- or the absorption of

Thirteen

one into the other, rather. I brought this up with him when he appeared the next day. The bumps of his approximate-eyes and his approximate-nose and mouth all scrunched up with what I suppose was scorn. He said simply: 'I do not permit passage.' When I reread the definition in the Geographical Dictionary, Second Edition, Revised, it did indeed have very similar words to those that Mr. Ribald had used, except without the pronoun and hence some subsequent and slight change of meaning, but I got the gist. I thought this was a little odd. Creepy even. Having said that, Mr. Ribald is creepy. Frightening. I don't know where he comes from, where he goes, when he's next going to appear or what he's thinking. I'm always here, and he knows exactly when I'm thinking about his stitches, or of poking his plush dressmaker's doll face. I'm not sure when he had the opportunity to look at my Geographical Dictionary.

He came again this morning. It's always the same. It's just after I've breakfasted, and I let my mind wander to the bright disc of the Earth, outside the oval lead-paned window of my room. It's more of a chamber actually. Or a shaft. I'm at the bottom, and the window stretches to the very top, out of sight. I can see far enough up to make a slight curve out in the glass. If I gaze up there while lying in bed at night, breathing as if asleep (I do that- breathing like I'm asleep - deep and rhythmic, I don't know why- it's relaxing I suppose). Anyway, I lie in my bed and breath as if I'm asleep, and I think that I can see up to the roof of my shaft. And if I squint, I can almost see, just for a second, always a second, the stars beyond, like a hatch has been opened, and then the stars are obscured like something has come in, and then they disappear altogether. It's rubbish of course - there's nobody here except for me and Mr. Ribald. And he's not even real. You do know that right? He's a figment of my imagination. He arrived in the restless period after the children stopped wishing and I was considering leaving. He must be imaginary - he'd tell me if he wasn't. He'd tell me why his face is made of the plush grey material of a dressmaker's dummy and why he knows the words of my Geographical dictionary and how he can just appear like that behind me and he'd tell me if he was using a hatch in the ceiling of my cell. As he doesn't, and as I am on the moon, he must be a figment of my imagination, and almost certainly my sub-conscious imagination, as I know the answers to none of those things. Consciously.

After I see the hatch close (which I don't - I imagine it), I hear a shuffling in my cell and I ignore it, for this too is my imagination at play, and I'd be scared if it was real and it can't be real and Mr. Ribald can't be real and I hate Mr. Ribald.

I

Hate

Mr. Ribald.

I'll tell him next time.

No I won't. I'll stare at his grey stitched-up face, and I'll know that I can't tell him and that even if I did he wouldn't leave, and I wouldn't leave and I'd still be stuck on this lonely satellite and he'd say 'Man On The Moon, you're an idiot and you'll stay here till the children dream again.'

Thirteen

THE URGE
BRYAN WOLFORD

The cart's wheel kept squeaking as it was pushed down the aisle of the grocery store. Numerous items littered the bottom of the cart: bread, eggs, orange juice, cheese, and cereal. Now Robert was searching for milk. The last gallon had gone sour, and if he was going to buy more cereal, he'd have to have milk. He pushed the cart into the dairy aisle and headed straight for the milk. It seemed odd to that he hadn't picked it up when he had gotten the cheese, but then again, he hadn't grabbed the Lucky Charms yet. He stopped and picked up a gallon of skim milk. His eyes wandered to the 2% milk. He shrugged as if to say, "Why the hell not?" and put the skim milk back down. The 2% milk quickly made its way into his cart and he wheeled off into another direction.

He stopped in the candle aisle and grabbed numerous sized scented candles. Some aerosol room deodorizers were a few shelves over. Robert picked out five different scents and threw them into the cart. As he wheeled the cart around to go to the check out counter the wheel let out a loud shriek as if protesting the direction he had just chosen.

When he reached the check out lanes he saw that the woman on lane five was actually quite attractive. She had a slim build with brown hair down to her shoulders. She smiled at the customer she was helping, and her whole face seemed to light up. He made his way over to her and patiently waited for the few customers in front of him to finish with their shopping. When he finally did reach her he saw that her nametag said her name was Andrea. He gave her a courteous hello and she responded, smiling the whole time. She moved his items across the scanner and it beeped as the prices jumped onto the screen. By his judgment, she was around twenty-five. He was only twenty-nine himself so she landed right in his age range. His looks weren't bad either. He may not pass for Brad Pitt but he had his assets. His jet-black hair was trimmed neatly and his face was blemish free. She passed his last item across the scanner and pushed a few buttons on the register.

"Twenty-seven thirty-five," she said. He dug through his wallet and handed her the appropriate bills. She turned to get him his change and he opened his mouth to say something but quickly shut it. The register spit out his receipt; she tore it off with ease and turned back to him to give him his change. He thanked her and picked up his items. She gave him a smile and he was about to say something, but the guy behind him began to ask her a question. Robert slumped his shoulders and headed out to the parking lot.

The keys jingled as he pulled them out of his pocket. He hit the unlock button on the car remote and a Mercedes chirped as the alarm shut off. The bags slid smoothly into the back seat. Robert looked at them resting on the leather upholstery and decided it might be better if he put them in the trunk just in case something happened in which the leather would be ruined. With a push of a button on the car remote the trunk was opened and the bags were placed neatly inside.

He began to open the driver's door when he felt a pang in his stomach. Guilt for not talking to the cashier was invading him. After standing there for what felt like an eternity he shut the door and began to walk back inside. When he entered he saw that she only had one customer in her lane. He quickly jumped into her lane and grabbed a pack of gum off the shelf. After she was done with her customer she looked up and gave him a sly look that made it seem like she knew what he was doing.

"Back again I see," she said.

"Yeah. I forgot my gum." He held it up and smiled. She took it and ran it

Thirteen

across the scanner. He knew it had to be now or never. "I don't usually do this but I was wondering if I could get your phone number. Maybe we could go out some time." She began to look at him as if she were analysing him.

"I tell you what," she said. The receipt for his gum popped up out of the register. She tore it off and flipped it over. "This is my cell phone number. If we have a decent conversation sometime then I'll think about that date." She scribbled a number on the receipt and handed it to him with his gum. He took it with a smile on his face.

"Alright. I'll be in touch," he said. She gave him a smile that almost melted his brain. He headed towards the doors. When he reached the parking lot he let his joy overtake him and he swung his right arm in delight. He dug the keys out of his pocket again and thumbed the unlock button. The Mercedes chirped again. He jumped into the front seat and turned the ignition. A song he liked came on the radio and he turned it up. He was having a good day.

The garage door opened as he angled the Mercedes into the driveway. He turned the wheel and lined up the car perfectly as it entered the garage. When the car had completely entered, he pressed the garage door remote located on the sun visor. The door slowly began its decent back down its track. Robert shut the car off and made his way back to the trunk. He grabbed the groceries and headed for the door that would take him inside. It opened into a spacious kitchen. The floors looked like a professional company had waxed them. All the appliances were top-notch quality. It seemed that you could roast a whole pig over the large stove.

He put the groceries on the island in the middle of the room. As he pulled the contents out of the bag he began to hum to himself. The groceries went into their respective places. On the wall by the door to the garage was a bulletin board. Robert pulled Andrea's number out of his pocket and pinned it to the board. He let out a sigh and smiled at the handwriting. It was very feminine and bubbly.

"Honey, I'm home," he called out. Nothing but his echo came back to him. He turned and headed into the living room. When he entered the living room his eyes directly darted to the couch where a man and woman sat. Their eyes looked off into space as they sat motionless. The woman looked to be around thirty-five. Her hair was a light blonde, more than likely dyed, and her skin had a nice tan. "Right where I left you this morning," he said with a chuckle. "You two need to be more productive." They both just sat unmoving. The man wore a black turtleneck. The front of it had a large, dark stain on it. The man appeared to be close to forty. His temples were starting to grey a little and deep wrinkles on his forehead showed that he had a stressful job. On the woman was a yellow scarf that was turning a red colour, and a green blouse. Robert walked up and began to adjust the scarf. He moved it to one side revealing a large cut across her throat that was leaking fluid.

"You're still leaking after three days?" He readjusted the scarf and turned to the man. When he pulled up the front of the man's shirt it made a squishy sound. "You're still leaking too? My God." Multiple knife wounds were apparent on the man's stomach. Robert pulled the shirt back down and took a step back from the bodies and smiled at them. "I've got some good news. I met someone today." Both of the bodies just sat there. "So it looks like I'll be inconveniencing you for a shorter time than I thought. If all goes well I'll be able to move onto my next place within the next couple of days." He looked at the bodies as if he expected a response. When they didn't seem to give him what he wanted he began to get angry. He stepped forward and backhanded the man. The man's head lolled to the side and stayed there.

Thirteen

"Listen to me when I talk to you!" As soon as he said it, he began to laugh at himself. He looked over at the woman and walked over to console her. "Oh, don't worry honey. I would never hit you." He grabbed her left breast as if to show her that he cared. Laughter escaped his mouth again as he got up to go to the kitchen. "Dead people are so much fun," he said. When he entered the kitchen he turned on the stove. Dinner had to be made.

As he began to prepare dinner, Robert thought back to how easy it was to enter the house. Rich people were usually more cautious. The woman had opened the door as if he were a long lost relative. He claimed to be collecting money for a children's relief fund. She had been all too eager to contribute. When she turned her back to get some money, he pushed his way in the door. His hand produced a blade that he had hidden behind his back. The tin can he had been holding cluttered against the porch as he reached up and grabbed the woman by her hair. He pulled hard and jerked her head back. She began to let out a scream. The blade flashed forward and drew a line across her throat. The screaming stopped, but her body began to squirm as she panicked from lack of oxygen. He stood in her entryway holding her hair until all of the fight had left her body and she finally went limp.

For three more minutes he stood silently listening for any sounds in the house to indicate that anyone else might be home. No sounds came. The husband must have been at work. Robert looked at his watch and smiled as he saw it was just a little past noon. Plenty of time before the hubby came home. He made his way out to the garage, by way of the kitchen, and found a tarp neatly folded on one of the shelves. Spread across the floor it had to be at least ten feet. The woman was placed in the middle of the tarp and the sides were folded around her. She wasn't too heavy and he carried her upstairs easily.

The bathroom tile was a sky blue colour. On the towel rack were two white towels adorned with blue flowers. He set the woman down on the floor and turned on the faucet on the bathtub. The wound on the woman's neck was still bleeding, but it had slowed down. Once the heart had stopped beating, blood wasn't rushed throughout the body as quickly. Gravity was the only other force that helped it get from one point to the other. Without the heart, the blood's movement was slacker yet it still seeped through. Robert unfastened the buttons on the front of her shirt. Underneath he found a white bra with a silky sheen to it. He felt himself getting excited and had to make himself calm down. As much as he liked looking at naked women, he had always felt that people who had sex with dead people were absolutely deranged. He had never had sex with a dead body before. Crazy he was, sick he was not. Very delicately he sat her up, reached behind, and began to undo the fastener on her bra. He could perform the most delicate of procedures such as pulling a knife out of his pocket, opening the blade, and slashing someone's throat with one hand in a matter of seconds. Yet he still had trouble getting a bra undone.

Finally the fastener unlocked and the silky fabric unleashed its hold on its owner. Without even looking at her he lay her back down and immediately unbuttoned her pants. With one pull he pulled down her pants and underwear, which matched her bra, and threw them off to the side. He stood up and looked at her. She was completely naked on the bathroom floor. He could see definite tan lines on her breasts and pelvis. Obviously from a tanning bed as it was early March and a slight chill still swam in the air. Her pubic area was well trimmed, telling him that she enjoyed sex. He bent forward and cupped her left breast in his hand. The weight of it felt good. When he gave it a gentle squeeze he began to shudder. He was getting excited again. A long breath escaped him as he closed his eyes trying to restrain himself. Someday he may just give in to his

Thirteen

urge. When he opened his eyes he was once again focused on his task.

With a quick turn, the bath faucet shut off. He lowered her body into the water. As she sank to the bottom of the bathtub small air bubbles escaped the wound in her throat as the air that was trapped in her chest escaped through the water. He looked at her through the shimmering water. To him she looked beautiful. He had thought she was beautiful to begin with. Now she seemed dreamlike. Her hair flowed around her head as it was given weightlessness by the water.

The husband had been a little harder. Robert heard the car pull into the garage so he had hidden in the kitchen, waiting for him to enter through the door from the garage. After five minutes, it dawned on him that the husband may come through the front door. Robert ran to the living room and peeked out the front window. Sure enough he had gone to the mailbox to check the mail. He was now coming up the front walk with his head down while he sifted through the mail. Robert pressed himself against the wall next to the door. When the door opened the husband walked in. His eyes immediately darted to Robert's position. The husband was a little more alert than he had anticipated. He put up more of a fight than his wife had. Robert took a few shots to the face, but in the end his blade found itself into his stomach.

He had performed the same ritual for him but was drastically less excited about stripping him down and putting him into the tub. While the man soaked, Robert went downstairs and cleaned up. Very little blood had splattered onto the carpet so cleaning up had been simple. No one would have known that two people were just murdered here. He dressed both of the bodies up with clothes he found in their room. Over the next two days he had taken them down stairs and sat them around the kitchen table while he ate dinner, sat them in the living room while he watched television, and put them in bed with him at night while he slept. He talked to them all the time as if they were still alive. Now Robert stood stirring the stew he had been making.

"Dinner's ready!" he exclaimed. The bodies were sitting around the kitchen table, slumped back in their chairs. Robert put the food on the table and dished out three platefuls. Steam rose up from the stew and danced through the air in the kitchen. His two dinner guests only looked off into the far away distance. Robert's spoon clicked as he ate heartily. A smile was on his face after every bite.

"I know I've been a burden, guys, but after a few more days I'll be out of your hair. That Andrea girl seemed to like me enough that she'll agree to a date. Then after I go pick her up I'll have a new place to live." He smiled. "At least for another week or so." A small laugh escaped him and he went back to eating. After three bites he turned his head sharply towards the woman. His face was angry.

"What?" No response sounded in the room but he seemed to get the answer anyway. "There's no need to get jealous. You knew this was only temporary." Still no response came. Robert stood up abruptly and slapped the woman across the face. She slowly slid off to one side and then fell off her chair in a heap. Robert looked upon her with a smile on his face. He sat back down and finished his stew. After his last bite he set the spoon down and knelt next to the woman.

"I'm sorry, love, but I don't like being questioned about my activities. You needed to be taught a lesson." When she was lifted up her head rolled to the right side. She was put back in her chair with such kindness it was almost a wonder why she was on the floor in the first place. Robert brushed off the side of her face to get rid of any dirt that may have gotten on her. Her flesh was ice cold but for him it was comforting. He stroked her other cheek and was immediately

Thirteen

feeling excited again. His heart began to hammer against the inside of his chest. To him the room sounded as if a large bass drum was being beaten. Blood was rushing through his veins. He was losing control. His urges were over taking him.

With a shout he let go of her. He walked into the living room and began to breath heavily. Sweat rolled off his forehead. His hands were trembling as he reached up to wipe the sweat from his face.

"Not now," he thought to himself. "I've come so far only to lose control now. I really will be sick if I follow through with it." He began to look around wildly as if someone was watching him. No one else was in the room. The drapes on the front window were wide open. He ran to them and looked out. No one was outside. Far off in the distance he heard a dog bark. "Of course if I do it no one will know. Not if I only do it this once. No one will know. Just this one time," he thought.

He rushed into the kitchen with his mind made up. With ease he lifted her and took her upstairs. Gently he put her on the bed and backed up to look at her. His body was trembling but he was still excited. He could feel it. Slowly he walked towards her. The green blouse clung to her breasts. She was not wearing a bra, as Robert couldn't figure out the complexity of putting one on her. The fabric of the blouse was so thin her nipples, though not hardened, still showed through. He reached towards her and unfastened the top three buttons of her blouse. His hand reached inside and cupped her breast. The breast was a little stiffer than it had been the other day but it wasn't yet repulsive. He caressed it softly. His excitement swelled. Sweat poured off of him. He leaned over her. His eyes found her lips and the rest of him began to follow. Their lips were only centimetres apart when a loud crash broke the silence of the house.

Robert turned his head towards the noise and away from the task he had been thinking about a second ago. His hand that was holding her breast relaxed. The noise had come from downstairs. Robert walked to the door and listened for further noise. Slowly he walked into the hallway. Nothing came from downstairs. He continued on until he was at the top of the stairs. Still nothing came from downstairs. From his pocket he pulled out the knife he had used only three days earlier to kill the people he now lived with. He descended the steps as quietly as he could, hoping to catch the intruder by surprise. A soft shuffle seemed to come from the kitchen. He peered around the corner into the kitchen but could not see anything. Walking further into the kitchen he saw the man sprawled across the floor. Somehow he had fallen over and managed to take a plate of beef stew with him.

"How did you do this?" Robert asked him. Beef stew was now all over the man's left arm. Robert set his chair up straight and began to pull him over to set him up again. As the man was being put back into place a small sound escaped him. It almost sounded like a grunt. Robert looked at him suspiciously. With his index finger he poked the man in the cheek. "Must have been gas." Robert said to himself. Out of nowhere a loud thud came from upstairs. Robert looked up at the ceiling. He hurried up the stairs and ran into the master bedroom. Now it was the woman that was on the floor. Slowly he walked towards her.

"What in the fuck is going on?" he asked. His hand trembled as he reached out to turn her over. Without warning her arm jumped up and fell back to the floor. Robert jumped back in surprise. He stood by the door and looked at her. No more movement came from her. Robert looked around cautiously and walked back towards her again. He pulled the knife out of his pocket and held it in front of him.

Carefully he bent over again and reached out to touch her. Before his hand could reach her, she began to flail around wildly. Her arms and legs flew this

Thirteen

way and that. Robert backed away again and held his knife in front of him. As he stood watching, the woman pulled herself up into a standing position. She turned to face him and he saw a blank expression on her face. Slowly she walked towards him. Robert struck out with his knife and caught her in the chest. She stumbled backwards and he ran for the door. He looked over his shoulder as he took the steps two at a time. When he reached the bottom he turned into the kitchen so he could go out into the garage. As he turned the corner he ran right into the chest of the man who had been dead three days now. Robert began to scream at the top of his lungs.

"You're dead! You're fucking dead! I killed you!" he said. The man had the same blank expression on his face that his wife had upstairs. Robert turned to run towards the front door but quickly realized that the man had a hold of his arm. He began to punch at the man to try and get him to release his grip. The man only pulled him closer. His other hand went up and grabbed Robert's neck. Despite the pressure on his windpipe and his dwindling air supply he let out a scream. As dots began to dance in front of his vision he saw the woman walk down the stairs. A large red patch had grown where he had stabbed her. She stumbled over towards them. Finally all of Robert's strength gave out and he fell to the floor with the man's hands still around his throat. His vision began to give out and everything faded to black. The last thing he ever saw was the two people he had killed only days earlier kneeling over him.

Thirteen

THOUGHTFORM
DEE WEAVER

It remained unseen in the morning mist, travelling at speed through the trees. It had been hunting all night but its quarry was elusive and the sun was rising. It was more than capable of hunting at anytime and in any condition. The dark of a lightless cave, the searing brightness of sun on snow, meant nothing. But it had been created to hunt only at night and it didn't have the thought processes to question or override that.

On the edge of a clearing it banked to the left and entered a narrow tunnel, making its way to the darkest deepest part of the cave. Humans, insensitive beings that they were, wouldn't see it if it flew into their eye, but animals would sense it. They would become restless, they would draw attention.

Only bats, the most intelligent of creatures, recognised it for what it was, and knew it would not threaten them. They acknowledged its presence as they settled down to sleep away the day.

At dusk it flew out of the cave with them and continued its mission. All through the night it hunted tirelessly, its energy supplied remotely from the Source.

As the sun breached the horizon once more it was among buildings. Densely packed, hard-edged and angular. A bat-ley led it to a gap under the eaves of an empty house. It slipped inside and spent the day in the papery depths of an abandoned wasp nest.

When the last starling fell silent, it emerged again into the dusk, its sensors buzzing. It cruised unseen among the buildings, probing through them, sensing ahead. It was close. Very close. And yet the night was well advanced by the time it passed a message back to the Source that it had made contact with the target.

The man stirred in his sleep. He rolled onto his back and a small sound, somewhere between a moan and a whimper, escaped his dry lips. His eyes moved rapidly under their lids. The woman beside him half-woke and slid an arm across his chest to soothe him.

Miles away in another town, sitting at the table in her new suburban kitchen, with an opened bottle of red wine in front of her, the Source smiled. She raised her hands in front of her face, as if rolling an invisible tennis ball between them. Her eyes were closed and her lips moved although she made no sound. Her silent instructions were heard only by the Thoughtform, the invisible mental projection she had created from her own malevolence and sent out on its mission to seek and destroy.

It felt her hunger for revenge as it waited indifferently for the signal to move on to the next stage. The quarry was a good man and the Thoughtform would have admired, possibly even loved him - as the Source once had, if it were capable of judgement and feeling.

In the morning he would tell his partner he'd had a nightmare that he couldn't recall. Only that something had been watching him in the dark. She would tell him to lighten up. It was just a dream. She couldn't know that this was different. A nightmare, certainly. But no dream.

The signal came through. The Thoughtform moved down to hover against the man's temple. Delicately, almost gently, it melded through into the tissues of his brain. Now it became him. Now the Source could experience his being, the blood swishing through his veins and arteries. She could watch his dreams, hear his thoughts, the internal dialogue running through his mind even in sleep. She could feel how much he loved the woman sleeping beside him. Sense that he wanted to live the rest of his life with her.

Thirteen

The Source smiled at the irony that she could grant her ex-husband his last wish. He had vowed to spend his life with her, yet now he slept peacefully beside his new lover.

She poured herself a glass of wine and drank it slowly, savouring its taste while she anticipated her coming victory.

He would wonder why the nightmare continued to elude him and yet remained lodged in his head. He would continue to feel the gnawing in his mind. He would be anxious but wouldn't know why. He would jump at shadows. Lie awake at night staring into the dark, uneasy about something he'd forgotten to do. He would fall into a restless sleep and wake with a headache.

He would lose his appetite and drink too much. Start smoking again. Struggle to concentrate on his work. He would worry about his future.

He would cling to his new woman. Tell her he wanted to spend the rest of his days with her. The Source almost wished she could add to his distress by letting him know how few he had left.

But she still hadn't decided when she would send her Thoughtform its final instruction.

Thirteen

APPETITE FOR DESTRUCTION
JOHN GLASS

Tuesday: 09.47 am.

"What!" Billy bawled down the phone. Its continual ringing had finally nagged him out of sleep, and falling out of bed, he'd crawled across the floor to answer it. There was a sharp intake of breath on the other end, then silence for a few seconds, before a female voice meekly piped up, "Is ... is Greg there, please?"

"No! Now fuck off!" Slamming the phone back down on its cradle, he hitched up his duvet and bunny-hopped back to bed. And as Greg wasn't there to fuss and cluck, he could afford to have a bit of a lie in. He really needed it: he'd made a right arse of himself last night. He vaguely remembered something about a strip bar in the Cowgate; a fumbled poke up a close with the gogo; and then throwing up over some stupid fucking cat in the stair; but after that, well, he hadn't a clue!

As he lay tossing and turning, trying to get back to sleep, Billy thought of the voice on the phone. Dumb bitch, what the fuck did it want with Greg anyway? They always wanted Greg, nobody ever phoned for him. Bastards! What was it with him and these bitches, could he lick his eyebrows or something? So, another new woman, eh? Well, he couldn't allow that! If Greg moved out, or worse, the bitch moved in, what would he do? Who'd look after him? Who'd replace Greg? No, it was probably some daft bint from the library, telling him his books on Leyland fucking buses, or AEC trucks were in! Still, he should check it out, and maybe even have some fun in the process.

He dressed before going back to the phone. Dialling 1471, he noted the number before punching out the keys.

"Good morning, Central Library, Sarah speaking." Ah, the meek little voice again. Good!

"Aye, hello. You phoned earlier, lookin' for Greg?"

"Oh! Ye-es?" She seemed apprehensive, even better!

"Em, look ... I'm, eh, I'm sorry about what I said. I'd a heavy night, an' you woke me up," Billy paused to stifle a belch before carrying on. "Anyway, Greg's not here, and I'm not sure when he'll be back."

"Could I leave a message then?" Christ, what was he, his fucking secretary?

"Okay, fire away then."

"Tell him I will be able to make tomorrow night after all, I've managed to get out of working late."

"Okay, no probs." Billy slammed the phone down. Now he was worried. And when he was worried, he paced. He kept going over the conversation again and again.

Billy sat down by the window, his mind racing, doing cartwheels and somersaults to Olympic standard. Tomorrow! What was Greg up to tomorrow? Giving this new whore a good seeing to no doubt! He had to stop this shit before it went any further. After all, hadn't he moved in to look after Greg, protect him after he'd been beaten up?

He began pacing the room again, wondering, and thinking. Always thinking. Invariably about Greg: and now he's got a new friend. Bastard! He'd never even said anything. And another thing, when was the last time the two of them were out on the piss together? Time he was taught a lesson: he was turning into a right ponce these days; Christ, just look at the way he dressed; and what about all that veggie crap! Subconsciously, he began biting nonexistent nails. He eventually sat back down by the window and waited for Greg, though the view was lost on his glazed eyes.

Thirteen

Tuesday: 20.19 pm.

"Billy, look at the mess in here! I suppose I'll have to clean up, again?" Greg had his back to the window, and was surveying a good hour of cleaning. He was increasingly concerned that this was happening more and more frequently: Billy could at least tidy up after himself.

"Stop your fucking moaning! Christ, you're getting more like a woman every day!"

"That's just typical, Billy. Never anything positive to say, always have to slag me off."

"Well, no wonder! Fuck me, a man can't drop a crumb but the hoover appears before it hits the bloody carpet!" Billy began to pace the floor.

Greg knew that another argument was looming. But things simply couldn't go on as they were, not now that he'd met Sarah. Should he move out, and find a better place? But what would he do with Billy, who'd look after him, where would he go? Greg knew Billy wouldn't, probably couldn't manage without him. Granted, he was becoming an embarrassment, he'd got himself into a right state last night, again: was it any wonder that they never went out together? But Billy needed him, relied on him. They relied on each other; it was very much a symbiotic relationship.

When Greg had apologised earlier to old Mrs. Perry about her poor cat, she had suggested that Billy was mad. But to Greg, the question was still open to debate: whether madness is or is not a higher intelligence; whether all great things of genius, great thinkers and better understanding, do not in some way have their roots somewhere in madness. Hadn't he read something recently that likened madness to 'dreaming by day'; and that those who were 'afflicted', or 'blessed' with this, were far more cognisant of a great many things than those who merely dreamt during sleep.

"Billy, please sit down. I need to talk to you." He kept on pacing, fingers continually going to his mouth, trying to excise the last fragments of nail. "Come on Billy, we should talk."

"Fuck off! If it's about that bitch, I don't want to know!"

"Well, yes, it is actually." Pausing, Greg was uncertain whether to continue.

"Her name is Sarah, and she's coming here tomorrow. I've ... I've asked her to move in," Greg sat down by the window, and waited for the explosion.

"Greg, you're a total bastard! After all I've done for you! Well, you can go and take a running fuck to yourself! Why the fuck should I move out? So you and your bitch can rut like bastards all the time!"

Greg let Billy rave on for several more minutes. He knew the score. After ranting, he'd probably storm off, and be gone for ages. And true to form, that's exactly what he did, though his parting comments struck a note of alarm with Greg.

"She'll never move in here, fucking whore!"

"Billy! Billy! C-c-come back ... w-w-what do you m-m-mean ... B-b-b-i-l-l-y!" Greg slumped down onto the sofa, sobs raking his body. He didn't deserve all this aggravation. Why couldn't Billy just accept his new friend?

It took Greg more than the hour he had originally thought to tidy up Billy's mess. Why did he have to be such a slob? There was no need for it. But it did fit the pattern of his behaviour lately. Maybe he should suggest seeing somebody, get some kind of professional help. Greg could well imagine the reaction that this would produce. He decided on a nice long bath, then he could have an early night to think things through.

Thirteen

Wednesday: 18.36 pm.

She was early. Billy had jumped at the doorbell. He'd only just managed to finish the preparations in his room: he'd moved all his furniture to one end, and covered everything in heavy-duty plastic sheeting. A swivel chair, which normally lived by the computer, dominated the centre of the remaining floor space.

It had been so simple to fling open the door, grab her hair and pull her in, trip her and give her one good rap with a hammer to the back of the head.

After the row the previous evening, Billy had decided to teach Greg a lesson. A serious fucking lesson! Why didn't he ever come out with him anymore? More interested in his whores! He'd teach him to mess up their relationship with bitches! How could he even think of bringing one home? Well, now Greg was out of the picture, he had him locked up safe and sound. Shaking his head, he turned his attentions back to the girl.

She was sitting in the swivel chair. Brown parcel tape secured her feet and legs to the central spindle. Once he'd taped her torso to the backrest, he'd done the same with her arms along the rests. There was even a length over her mouth to shut her up, but he'd remove this later, as he didn't care who heard her screams. He certainly wouldn't. Anyway, round here, there was always folk screaming and bawling at each other! He pushed play on his Walkman.

He noticed how her mascara had run, giving the impression of two huge black tears running down an ashen face, like a female Pierrot. He never did like clowns, but Greg did. Well, she wouldn't look like that for long! After circling her several times, he grabbed up her ponytail and used it to spin the chair round and round, mimicking a lasso. Yee ha! He was oblivious now to her frantic, high-pitched screaming: Axl Rose and Slash were giving it large into his earpieces. Welcome to the jungle, baby!

The sudden flash from reflected metal as she whirled round and round brought fresh panic to the girl's eyes. Laughing, Billy thought this hilarious: it reminded him of Tom and Jerry cartoons, where one of them, after seeing something terrible about to happen, popped their eyes miles out of their sockets to the sound of a claxon. Billy's laughing seemed to petrify the girl even more: her nostrils began to flare in and out, her chest heaving as she constantly tried to draw in more air.

As the chair's revolutions began to slow, Billy circled in the opposite direction, shadow fencing each time she came into view. The first stroke took her high on the forehead, leaving a six-inch slice above her right eye. As her brow creased in pain, a thin trickle of blood ran down her face: capillary action sent little red rivers running to fill up the wrinkles.

On the next turn, he managed a penetrating downward jab to her right cheek: her momentum drawing her off the blade before completely severing the tongue. Billy marvelled at the resistance put up by her flesh before yielding the blade. As she came round again, he fancied himself one of those Matadors in Spain, and ducked in to deliver an over arm strike to the other cheek. Ole!

He let her spin for a few turns, watching pretty patterns of red appear on her white blouse. They looked like those Rorschach inkblots he'd seen: and what do you see in this picture, Billy? Fuck off!

Blood was falling in steady drops from her nose, and the desperate shaking movements of her head sent them flying in all directions. He saw one particular globule describe a perfect arc through he air, before splashing onto the toe of his left trainer. He couldn't help whistling as it fell, mimicking a bomb.

Giving her another few turns to build up speed, Billy stepped in close; this next part required some skill and strength. He jabbed the knife into the middle of her forehead, and keeping pressure on, let her momentum carve out a spiral

Thirteen

around her head. This continuous cut lacerated her right eye; sheared hair; took off the top of her right ear and the lobe of her left; opened up her left cheek and sliced through her bottom lip. It finally ended under her right jaw line. Her screams had died down to a whimper. Blood soaked them both, and was pooling with her urine under the chair, running along troughs in the plastic.

Stepping back to admire his work, Billy wondered what Greg would say to all this? No! Fuck him, and his bitch! He didn't need them anymore. See what he could do on his own! The heady mixture of adrenaline, the thrash in his ears, and blood lust sent him into a slashing frenzy: jabbing, slicing, and hacking at the face, head and neck of the girl, yelling with each attack. "Bitch! Bitch! Bitch! Fucking bitch!"

After several minutes of this frenetic butchery, Billy staggered back exhausted. He could only stare at the carnage in front of him: the chair had stopped revolving, and the girl now wore sodden red clothes. Gravity had pulled her head down onto her chest, giving her the appearance of dozing. Flesh hung in long, ragged and dripping strips from her massacred face: some pieces had flown up and become lodged in her hair, on the walls. Billy could even see bone at several places.

He knelt down to gaze up at a puréed face. Her right eye was missing, but miraculously the left was relatively intact: it was wide open, and staring coldly back at him. Images of all those dead fish that so captivated him in the supermarket swam before his eyes. He poked a finger into the useless socket, all the way in to the second knuckle, before twirling it around the bloody hole and pulling it out again, dripping with gore.

"Sarah, wakey wakey! No? Guess you'll not be seeing him tonight after all, eh bitch?"

Billy began looking for her missing eye, planning to shove it back in. Fits of uncontrolled laughter soon brought Billy to his knees: the eye, with black glutinous liquid oozing from of it, was still impaled on his blade. Christ, what a fucking rush! He would definitely have to do this again, now that he'd an appetite for it!

Wednesday: 17.03 pm.

Looking down at the bloody knife in his hand, Greg screamed, "Billy, what've we done!"

Thirteen

SIDEWALKS
JOSHUA SCRIBNER

"Can I help you, sir?" the old man in the red vest asked.

Mark Waller could tell the man was nervous. And he thought he could understand why. He knew he probably looked like a thug, his shirt drenched in sweat, his messy hair coming out of his hat.

"Yeah, I noticed that these bikes were on clearance, but there's no price on them."

The old man squinted as he looked over the rack of chained bikes that sat outside of Oliver's Marketplace. Mark had never seen an Oliver's Marketplace before today, but he suspected he'd soon see a lot of new things in this town, half a country away from where he'd spent the first twenty-two years of his life.

"Which one in particular are you interested in?" the old man asked, his tone reflecting his wariness.

"The blue fifteen speed," Mark said, then pointed at the only bike on the rack that was big enough for an average sized adult male.

"That one's on sale for sixty dollars."

Mark smiled. Sixty was cheap. He was hoping he would get a break. His car had broken down a few days after he got here. And he wouldn't have the kind of money he needed to get it fixed until next month, when school started and his scholarship kicked in.

"I'll take it," Mark said.

As Mark pushed his new bike through the parking lot, he entertained thoughts of not getting his car fixed at all. This was South Carolina, after all, and the climate would be generally warm. The college, where he would spend most of his time, was only a couple of miles from his apartment. He could use the money he would have to spend to repair his car elsewhere, and he could probably make a couple hundred extra selling the old thing for scrap.

But when he got to the road, he had second thoughts about his new idea. The road that ran in front of Oliver's was the business route off the interstate, and it was the main road in town. As he looked around, he remembered more about walking up here. He'd had to walk through the lots of several businesses. The business route was packed with traffic, and there was no sidewalk. And now he could see a little blue sign with a picture of a bike crossed out. The business route was the most direct route home. But if he wanted to take the bike, he'd have to find another way.

Mark thought he might have taken longer getting home on the bike than he had taken walking to Oliver's. The roads behind the store curved around in all directions. He thought he'd have to use the town map in the phonebook to find a better route.

While parking the bike behind his apartment, Mark realized that he'd forgotten something. He would have to go back to Oliver's and buy a chain to lock his bike to the rack. Tired from the long trip home, Mark figured he could do that tomorrow.

Inside his living room, Mark saw the answering machine light blinking. He hit the button and heard his cousin's voice.

"Hey, Mark, buddy. How ya liken South Carolina? Have you reconsidered yet? I think you should, because I think you'll find this place ain't so bad."

Mark laughed to himself as the message came to an end. His cousin, Dave, had bought a club in California. He'd called Mark on the day he graduated from Kansas State.

Thirteen

"Don't go off to graduate school. Come work with me. I'll cut you in. We'll get rich."

Mark had declined. Even though Dave's plan sounded fun, and it did tempt Mark, there was no way he was going to give up what he'd already earned. His high GPA and entrance exam scores had earned him a hefty cash scholarship here.

Dave was persistent. He even sent Mark bus tickets, knowing Mark hated to fly. Mark had torn them up and left for South Carolina the next day.

That night, Mark woke up in a sweat. He had been dreaming again. It was the same dream he had a lot lately. He had taken up his cousin's offer and was on his way to California. Mark hated this dream. He hated it because of the feeling it left him with. He felt like he was missing out on something.

Mark went early the next morning, while it was still relatively cool. He took the back roads to Oliver's, a little disgusted, having checked the map, finding nothing even near a direct route. He went inside and bought a cheap little chain.

He was dreading the ride back. His legs were still tired from yesterday. And now, having forced them to peddle all the way up here again, they felt like jelly.

Mark was just getting on his bike, when he thought he saw something. But what he saw couldn't be right. It was quite a distance away, so Mark thought his eyes might be deceiving him. He got on his bike and rode up the lot, toward the business route. He got clear up on the road.

There it was, though he didn't remember it being there yesterday. But then again, maybe he hadn't looked across the busy four-lane road, or maybe the thick traffic had blocked his vision. But, anyway, across the street from Oliver's, running on the business route, toward the apartment complex he lived in, was a sidewalk.

The sidewalk ended on Miracle Drive, which was fine, since that was where the apartment complex was. It had only taken him about five minutes to get home. And now Mark felt good, like he'd gotten a break. He parked his bike in back and locked it.

Inside, once again, the answering machine was blinking. Mark hit the button.

"Come on, buddy," Dave's relentless voice said. "I know you can find your way to me. I'll be waiting right here."

Mark laughed, even though he was kind of annoyed. This was the life he had chosen. Who was Dave to second-guess it?

The next day, Mark decided to take a ride around town. He thought it would be a nice little tour. He'd be able to get to know the place better. He took the business route up to the college, which was about a mile on the other side of Oliver's. He rode around looking at the buildings. He looked inside the building where most his classes would be. It was very modern looking inside. He liked it very much. But somehow, it made him sad. He didn't know why.

Mark rode around aimlessly for a while after that, then got hungry. Back the other way, about half a mile from the street his apartment was on, was what he craved. It was a Taco Bell, right off the entrance ramp back onto the interstate. Mark wanted to go there. But he'd have to walk from his apartment, and, with the morning ending, it was starting to get pretty hot.

A little dejected, Mark thought of what he had in the fridge, as he made his way home. He had just crossed the business route onto Miracle Drive, when he hit his brakes so fast that he skidded a couple of feet. He couldn't believe it. It

Thirteen

was yet another sidewalk he hadn't noticed. He followed it all the way to Taco Bell, where it ended, just before the interstate began.

It was like clockwork. As soon as he walked in, he saw the answering machine blinking away. He hit the button and heard Dave.
"That's it, buddy. You'll find your way to me."
What an odd way to put it, Mark thought. And he was sick of this. He picked up the phone and dialled Dave's place in California.
"Hello," Dave said after picking up on the first ring.
"Hey, asshole, give it up already."
"I can't give it up, buddy. I feel personally responsible for you being where you're at."
"Well, you're not. So stop trying to talk me into something I have no interest in doing, because to tell you the truth, you're starting to bug me."
There was a pause. Then Dave's voice was serious. "You locked yourself away, man. Now you're the one who has to decide if he wants to be in the real world or - "
"Yeah, Dave. You're right," Mark said, cutting his cousin off. "And I don't want to be in the real world yet. I have to finish up my education first."
"Alright," Dave responded in a sad voice. "I guess you'll come here when you're ready."
Mark started to lay into him again. He hated the way Dave was presuming that he'd come there. But before Mark could say anymore, Dave hung up.

That night, Mark awoke from the dream again. He had been on the bus, and he had been happy. Actually, he had been happier than he was right now. The prospect of the club was more exciting than the prospect of graduate school. And Mark had already learned enough that he could probably make the business go.
Maybe he had made a mistake, Mark thought. Maybe on a subconscious level, he knew that. Maybe he was going a little bit crazy because of that.

Mark shocked himself the next day. He got on his bike and rode up to the Taco Bell again. But this time, it wasn't to eat. In fact, it was way before lunchtime, and they hadn't even opened yet.
And Mark saw what he came to see. Sure as can be, on the other side of Taco Bell, running past the entrance onto the interstate, running out of town, was another sidewalk.

By the time Mark got home, he had run the different explanations through his head. Maybe, in his excitement, he was just missing things lately. Or maybe he just wasn't looking carefully the first time, causing it to seem like these sidewalks were magically appearing later.
But, of course, when he got inside, the answering machine was blinking.
"What the heck? Does he know when I leave?"
Mark hit the button and listened.
"Come to me, buddy. This place ain't so bad."

That night, Mark stayed up late thinking about it all. He considered the thought he'd had earlier, that he'd gone crazy. He didn't think he was completely out of his mind. He wasn't hearing voices, and his thoughts generally didn't seem strange, yet. But it was a little bit loopy for him to not notice the sidewalks the first time he came across them, especially when the sidewalks were of use to him.

Thirteen

What was his mind trying to tell him? He did the math. For years, he had planned on going to graduate school after college. Then he had been rigid in his old decision when a different path arose.

"That's it!" Mark shouted with the excitement of insight hitting. His mind was trying to teach him a lesson. "I'm supposed to be more watchful in the paths I choose. I'm supposed to make sure I find the right path."

That night, Mark awoke from the dream again. He had been so thrilled to be on that bus. The future had seemed so wide open. It was almost as if the dream were beseeching him. He suddenly knew that he had to do it.

The next day, Mark rode his bike around with a new invigoration. He felt free now. He felt free from an old plan that was tying him down. He rode around looking the town over, and at the same time, saying goodbye to it. He rode up to the college and did the same. He knew he should probably go to the registrar and maybe to the academic advisor he hadn't met yet and tell them he was going. But he could do that later. Today, he was celebrating.

Mark was at the corner, getting ready to go back to his apartment, when he got the idea that he wanted to go down the sidewalk that went out of town. Or maybe he just wanted to see if it was really there. He wasn't sure.

Unable to resist, he took off that way. He made it to the other side of Taco Bell and confirmed the sidewalk was real. He kept going, riding it out of town.

The sidewalk ran adjacent to the interstate for a couple of miles, then continued into a forest.

"Cool," Mark said, feeling like a kid exploring for the first time. The sidewalk curved through the thick trees, which actually ran above in places, blocking out most of the sunlight. Mark was surprised not to see anyone else back here. It was a pretty cool place. A place he would think would attract lots of bikers and joggers. But Mark was glad to be alone. It felt more like his that way. He rode for miles.

Then he hit his brakes when he saw the light up ahead.

Now Mark was sure he was hallucinating. Because the light had just come out of nowhere, right after he came around the curve. It was a perfect circle, two-dimensional, its diameter about six feet. Mark thought he could hear something coming from inside. He laid the bike down and moved closer. A few feet away, he could make out a steady beeping sound. Then, when he was right up to it, he heard a voice come from inside.

"Come to me, buddy. This place ain't so bad."

Mark turned and ran. He got on his bike and sped out of there, without looking back.

That night, Mark tossed and turned. He couldn't sleep, because he feared the dream. For the first time, there was an ominous feeling associated with it. He didn't want to be on the bus. He wanted to be where he was. He wanted to be in South Carolina. He wanted to be here, and he didn't want to sleep anymore.

But there was another reason he couldn't sleep. He couldn't sleep, because he could still hear his cousin's voice beckoning.

"Come to me, buddy. This place ain't so bad."

Over and over, it repeated in his head. But he couldn't go to Dave, not now.

But the voice kept going, well into the night. Finally, around 3 am, Mark got out of bed. He went outside and got his bike. He rode into the night.

He had expected it would be quiet at this time. But he had expected he would see at least one or two cars. He didn't even see lights on the interstate as he rode beside it toward the dark woods ahead.

Thirteen

Mark peddled as hard as he could, taking the curves at a dangerous rate. He had to get there, and he had to get there fast. He didn't know why. He wasn't even sure if the light would still be there. But sure enough, he came around a corner and found it sitting in the same place.

Mark rode the bike right up close to it. He was close enough to hear the beeping. Then he heard Dave again.

"Come on, buddy."

Mark got off the bike and walked into the light.

"Death is a hard thing to accept," Dave said to him.

They were in the sky, looking down through the ceiling and one of the hospital floors. There were people in blue scrubs trying to revive Mark's body. The machine, which Mark now knew and been the source of the beeping, showed a flat line.

"For me, it was your impending death that was hard to accept. I felt responsible. That's why I killed myself, while you were still in that stupid coma."

Mark looked at his cousin. Dave had the same ratty look here that he'd had on Earth.

Dave said, "For you, it was also your impending death that was impossible to accept. In the real world, your body clung futilely to life, as you created a world in your mind where you had never gotten on that bus. In this false world, you weren't there when that bus crashed. You'd stuck to your original plan."

"Why then?" Mark asked. "Why didn't you just let me stay in my head?"

Dave nodded as if acknowledging that it was a good question. "You would have eventually figured it out. False realities have holes in them. They never last."

Mark nodded. "Alright. So what do we do now?"

Dave looked around. "You'll see. There's a lot to do here." He smiled. "This place ain't so bad."

DARKNESS
BILL WEST

The moon lit a path towards the shore, as though pointing the finger of guilt at me. I walked across shingle, and into the sea, stopping only when the waves washed round my ankles, soaking my shoes.

I felt bone weary.

The doctor had said, "There is nothing organically wrong, you need rest, take a holiday." And so I came, here, to Whitby.

Attacks are more frequent now, always at dusk. Shadows detach themselves, slithering about me. Sometimes I lose track.

Everyone has been so kind here.

I fight the memory. Buttoning my coat I retrace my steps.

A dog snarls and whines. Approaching the Crescent I notice the hotel is in darkness. Nausea seizes me and I tremble.

Shadows are shooting towards me again like iron filings flying to a magnet. I am seized by nameless dread.

I stumble up the steps, fumble the key from my pocket, and open the front door.

The smell hits me first, the metallic tang of blood, lots of it. I flick the light switch. Overhead a fluorescent tube flashes. The jumping light catches severed heads in neat lines up the stairs, their eyes reproachful.

I drop the knife. And finally, darkness comes.

Thirteen

TWO FACED
PAUL MCAVOY

We all thought that Colleen Fletcher was just moody, prone to sulks and generally paranoid at the worst. We blamed it on her youth; she was nineteen. We thought she had a lot of growing up to do. We never thought anything sinister was at work. But you never do, do you? Demons don't exist in our world. Not this world of normal and generally sane people. Demons were alcoholism, were actors in masks, were graphics and cartoons. Beelzebub and Co did not really exist, did they? None of these demons were living normal lives as students, house sharing with other pimple-faced young adults. Getting by on Pot Noodle and chocolate. They were of myth and legend; stories to tell children so that they behaved.

Some might suggest and believe there is a God, but can these same people really think there is a devil? I have seen lots of things to support *and* counteract these beliefs - but I don't know if there is a God or Devil. What I do know is that evil does exist in a form, and it has many tentacles...

Colleen started working at the office in the summer of '02. She was a student, studying business at a nearby university. One of the female members of staff was on maternity leave, and we were short staffed at a busy time, so we took on Colleen to help out with photocopying and answering the telephone. At first we all found her pleasant, and hard working. She learned all her new tasks quickly, so we gave her more demanding and interesting things to do. We liked her and she seemed to like us - well, at least everyone else but me. I had the feeling, right from the start, that she despised me. Why, is anyone's guess. I was married with two children. I was in my early thirties. I got on with everyone and had no enemies, so it puzzled me why Colleen did not like me. I cannot go into great detail here, but it was just a feeling I had. The odd look here and there, the ignorance and one syllable answers she gave me when I tried to make conversation.

I found myself looking forward to summer's end when she would return to her student life and we would be free of her. But I did not realise that she was as off-hand with everyone else in the office as she was with me. It would appear that she treated everyone with the equal amount of contempt. We all carried on as normal, but her sulks and mood swings grew stronger. It was really no surprise when she was 'laid off' a week or so before her short-term appointment should have ended.

Colleen had a leaving do, of sorts, and it was on that night out that I found out what she was.

Why I even went to her leaving do is anyone's guess. We met up at an eating out place – one couldn't really call it a restaurant, nor was it a café. It was called 'Cartoons' and on the walls were paintings of various cartoon characters, such as Roadrunner and Tom and Jerry. The menu was pretty cheesy and boasted dishes such as 'Steam Boat Chilli,' and 'Hong Kong Suey.'

The office where I worked was small and had eight staff. I was the only male, save for our manager, Mr Watson, but he could not make it that evening. So I was the only male that night, standing at the bar, waiting for my colleagues to arrive. I felt uncomfortable and thought of excuses I could use to make to make an early getaway.

As I waited, Jill and Shelly came in and we found our table. Soon Jane and Susan arrived, informing us that Lisa could not make it. Colleen entered the place half an hour later and we ordered food. We all pretended to like Colleen and told her how much we were going to miss her. It was all lies and I wonder if she knew this deep down, if she expected it.

At one point I got up to use the toilet and when I was returning to the table,

Thirteen

Colleen was going to the toilet. She passed me, totally blanking me, as though I did not exist. I felt anger rise in me, but did not say anything.

I finished my meal and we all moved onto a pub nearby, where I had a few lagers in quick suggestion. The place seemed smokier than usual and I felt my eyes sting. I was not used to going out much, having a young family, and the drink was going quickly to my head. Though I worked with an office full of females, I got on well with them all (save for Colleen) and I had a fairly good evening. Even so, at nine o'clock I made my excuses and left.

I caught the bus home and I sat at the back of the bus, checking my mobile for messages and deleting items from my In Box. It was a cold evening, and the bus seemed to take an age to leave.

Suddenly, I felt someone sit down next to me and I was aware of the smell of perfume, as it was familiar to me. I turned and saw that Colleen was next to me.

'Hi,' I said. 'You left early too?'

She did not say anything at first, and I thought she was ignoring me again. Nothing new here then. It annoyed me though; why did she even bother to sit next to me? Then Colleen did speak. And it was the weirdest thing. I think there and then I knew there was something genuinely not right about that girl.

'I don't ignore you on purpose, Robert, it is just my nature,' she told me.

I think I stuttered some sort of reply.

'You are a very nice man,' she told me, and I was aware how close she was to me. Perhaps she had drunk too much, as she seemed to be coming on to me. Colleen was flirting with me, the man she had despised the last few months. I found the whole thing strangely funny, even though I really ought to have been angry.

'I am married,' I said.

She frowned. 'I know, to a very pretty wife. I have seen you, and your children. You make the perfect family. To be part of something like that... it must be so harmonious. Like music..?'

You're crackers, I thought, but said, 'It... is... erm...'

'Sorry I have not been nice to you this summer. But you will understand why... later...' she told me. There was a pause, then the bus jerked into gear and set off.

'Do you live my way?'

She paused, as though to think about the answer. 'You might say that.'

Suddenly I felt the need to get off the bus, there and then. I did not owe this girl anything, and she certainly did not deserve my company, not after the way she had treated me that summer, like some kind of leper. But it was not only I; everyone in the office had had to bear her sulks and paranoia. I turned to the window. I intended to stare out into the night until my stop arrived and go home and forget about this strange girl. I did wish she would not sit too close. I felt suffocated.

'I would like to live there,' she continued. 'And I would like to kiss your children.'

I turned to face her, not sure if I had heard to right. She turned to me and smiled. I felt myself staring into her cold blue eyes for just a moment. I felt chilled and began to shake. This girl was dangerously strange.

'I have waited for a long time. But a change is a good as anything, isn't it? You can be someone for a long time and just end up becoming so very bored and that is when you become ignorant and rude and that is when you sulk when you feel you are being treated badly by people. It is good to change, but it also takes a long time, and lots of scrutiny to be able to make the right choice. I have always made the right choices and I have no regrets.'

I nodded blankly, not too sure what she was talking about now. I just wanted

Thirteen

to get off the bus and go home. To my wife, to my children. I pictured them in my mind's eye. I thought of Alice and Michael both in bed now, and Jenna sitting up watching TV. I would kiss my children good night and hug my wife. I suddenly realised how much I missed them all, and how I would be the one who normally read the children a story, but Jenna would have took on that role this evening.

'People come and go, don't they, Robert? Like the ebbing and flowing of the sea pulling down sand castles or clawing at wet sea weed.'

I craned my neck and looked out of the window to see if we were any nearer to my stop. 'I guess they do,' I said.

'Like the sun burning up dry leaves and sparking a fire that can destroy miles and miles of trees. And take life too.' She paused. 'What to you think about the taking of lives... Is it necessary or what?'

'I don't know what you mean.' Before today I had thought she was slightly disturbed, now I thought she needed certifying. I looked at her for a moment, wondering what to do. She could well have been taking the Mickey out of me; or perhaps she was just being over friendly and nervously talking gibberish, as some people do after a few drinks...

I decided to remain calm, whatever, and wait patiently until my stop arrived.

Colleen continued: 'I am talking about useless people here, should they be destroyed so that other, more useful people can fill their boots?'

I thought about that, realising now that she wanted some kind of answer from me. I decided that I would walk the rest of my way home. 'Oh, look it is my stop... Well, it was very nice working with you and good luck with your career.' I got up and made my way to the front of the bus. I did not wait for any response from her, just got off the bus as soon as I could. I could feel her eyes boring into my back. It was a cold evening, but I was sweating quite a lot.

A premature wintry wind blew at my face; the dark night was star-less. I zipped up my jacket. I was on Chain Lane; I worked out that I probably had a ten-minute walk before I got to my house. Little payment, I decided, for a trip home with sanity.

The sound of footsteps hurrying behind me broke me from my thoughts and I turned around, expecting to see Colleen heading towards me, having got off the bus and decided to continue her strange conversation. I braced myself for more weirdness, but sighed a breath of a relief when I saw a middle aged woman hurrying along Chain Lane behind me looking anxious. She had a mobile phone in her hand and was muttering something. She glanced through me and hurried passed.

I watched her briefly and headed home along the quiet, but breezy road. I felt quite sober now, which I supposed could be the result of my odd conversation with Colleen and the cold night air. I was, however, quite relieved to be away from the strange young lady.

But that night's strangeness was only just beginning. I arrived at my house feeling cold and tired. I reached into my pocket and pulled out my keys, looking over at the front window. The lights were not on, and I found this quite strange, but decided that perhaps Jenna was somewhere else in the house, reading the children a story..? Perhaps they had not been able to settle with me not being home.

I slotted the key into the door and turned it for a moment. I removed it from the slot, frowning and checking to see if it was the right key, as the lock did not turn. Finding it was the right one, I tried again, and again the lock would not turn. I frowned, listening out for Jenna inside, wondering if she had heard my struggles. After a third fruitless attempt I rang the doorbell.

After a moment the door opened and I waited to be greeted by Jenna's curious look. But the door was answered by a man in his seventies. He had a thin

Thirteen

face and white hair that was balding. He stood at the fresh-hold unsteady on his feet.

'Who are you?' I found myself asking.

'I...' he began, then he frowned. 'What do you want?'

'What are you doing in my house?'

He stared at me for a moment. 'I beg your pardon?' he asked, to which I replied with the same question. 'It is my house,' he told me. 'I have been living here for seven years.'

'You have not – I have been living here for seven years. Where's Jenna and my children?' I tried to look behind him and into the house. But everything appeared to be in darkness. I started to walk into the hall, but he stood in my way. I don't know want stopped me from barging past him... a feeling I suppose... or his look of genuine honesty.

'You must have the wrong house,' he told me. 'I live here.'

I looked around. 'This is number six, Doncaster Road, isn't it?'

He nodded. 'Yes, young man, it is. And it is my house.'

'It bloody well is not!' I said. 'What are you up to? What have you done with them?'

'You're mad!' he said and he turned around.

'I'm calling the police,' I said, reaching for my mobile.

He shut the door. 'Do what you want!' he said, as it slammed shut in my face. 'Bloody nutcase. My house, indeed!'

I stabbed 999 on my phone, then paused. I disconnected the call and thought for a moment. The man seemed very sincere; could I be wrong? I stepped away from the house and looked up. I remembered the first time Jenna and I came to view the house. It was just over seven years ago. We fell in love with it from that first moment and after three months we moved in, vowing never to change house again as the move had been so stressful.

I remembered choosing wallpaper with Jenna for the living room. I remembered bringing Michael home from the hospital for the first time. There were many memories in that house. So what was going on? There was only one thing for it, I thought as I phoned the police again. This was my house and this old man was there unlawfully – what he had done with my family was anyone's guess. I just hoped there were all right.

Many unsettling thoughts came flooding in my mind, but I tried to steer away from them. I felt a great urge to smash the door down but I managed to refrain myself. This was a job for the law.

The police seemed a bit sceptic, but luckily there was someone in the area and a police car pulled up outside the house five minutes later. Two PC's got out and I walked over, quickly explaining what had happened.

'You say he is in your house, sir?' the older of the two asked. 'Have you tried your keys?'

'Well, yes, but they don't seem to work.'

The policemen exchanged glances.

'I know it sounds crazy, but I am worried about my wife and children.'

The policemen walked up to the door and rang the doorbell. The man appeared moments later. 'Hello,' he said. He was still as angry as before and shot me a frustrated look. 'Has this nutter got you believing his story? I think he is on something.'

'Can we have a look inside, sir?'

'I tell you what,' he said. 'You can *all* come in, Mr Crackpot as well. He can look around and see that it is my house, with my belongings. Things the wife and I bought before she died.'

The policeman looked over at me. 'Want to have a look inside, sir?'

Thirteen

I nodded, hoping that this whole business would be over soon. But when I entered I knew that what the old man said was true. It was baffling; as though I was in some kind of dream. The place was filled with things I did not recognise. It was not my home. I recognised the place, its shell anyway, but it was not my house at all. What was happening? I mumbled some kind of apology towards the old man, not knowing if he heard, too numb to even care.

I left, surprised the police did not arrest me for wasting their time. In fact they were all right about the whole thing and I think they felt sorry for me really.

I stumbled down Doncaster Road and stepped back onto Chain Lane. I pulled my mobile out and rang my home number. It was quite possible that I was going mad, or that I was suffering from some form of temporary amnesia and that I had only *thought* number six was my house. My wife would know the answer, she would tell me. But my home number just rang and rang without answer. It was possible she was busy with the kids. I tried my sister's, but her number seemed to be faulty. As did my mother's number.

I stood still on that cold dark night, looking around me. I felt suddenly alone. What was happening? Should I go to the hospital? I tried to think. I might well be ill. Perhaps I had some kind of virus or even a genuine mental illness. These seemed the only plausible explanations.

'*You really should* not *go off like that when someone is talking to you, you know!*'

I turned around towards the sound of the voice and saw Colleen approaching me. 'Colleen,' I began. 'Something really weird has happened…'

'I know,' she said. She stopped walking and stood less than a metre away from me, arms folded.

'You *know*?'

'I did it to you, out of punishment. It was the final straw, you see. All I have had from you is distain… all summer… I have read your thoughts. Sometimes lustful, at other times just evil. I have waited and I have been patient, but then you start being rude and getting away from me when I know that your bus stop was seven stops away!' her voice rose as she spoke, her eyes burned.

'You did this, how?'

'The easy way, believe me; nothing too complicated, so don't go thinking you're special or anything.

'But how did you manage to talk that man into… how did the furniture…?'

'I did not talk anyone into anything… I simply removed you from existence. It was quite simple really. Because you did not exist anymore, you never bought that house with your pretty wife, and never had your children.' She shook her head. 'All this because I was being *nice*.'

I stood there, looking at her. 'Sorry,' I mumbled. My mind was a maelstrom and there was too much to have to take in. Much of which was stretching the boundaries of reality. I felt faint, as though I might fall over at any moment. I also felt a surging anger inside of me.

'I realised I had been rude to you also, during the summer and I tried to make amends. When you are like I am, you tend not to worry about pleasantries and niceties. These things do not seem important. But I saw that it bothered you, tried to make you feel better and you shunned me.'

'What are you?' I found myself asking.

'Something far more old and powerful than you could ever imagine. Something much more evil too. Life goes on, Robert: even to immortals. Even the eternals need to have something to do: lazing on beaches, living in villas, having all the money you need – all these things can become tiresome. Normality can be quite inviting sometimes. The fun of chatting with mortals. Daily interaction with mere normals. But that is all I am going to say, for if I reveal my true name to you, and reveal who I really am, then I will die. And I do not wish to die... not yet.

'But...' she looked thoughtful. 'Do I, though? Perhaps that is why you have intrigued me so, why I have done what I did to you, so that I can say who I am... Perhaps not. Not yet, anyway.' Suddenly a dog barked, breaking the silence and cutting into the moment. A bus rattled past. 'I supposed I was wrong, was wicked. But I am evil. I was once good, but we all are good... to begin with. Eternity can change you, and so can waiting, waiting for things to happen. Things that might not come to pass...'

She looked in the distance as though searching for something. Then her eyes cleared again and she turned back to me. She smiled.

'Goodbye Robert.'

Another bus hurried past and I turned to watch the double decker as it journeyed along the road. When I turned back to Colleen she was gone.

She was gone, and all I could hear was the sound of my mobile. I answered it, seeing that it was home calling me.

'Hello,' I asked, my voice shaking. I knew I would not be able tell Jenna about this evening for a long time. One day, yes. I did not fully understand what had happened, anyway...

'Hi Robert? Where are you?'

I looked into the dark night. I remembered her words. Words of an immortal.

Normality can be quite inviting sometimes. But that is all I am going to say, for if I reveal my true name to you, and reveal who I really am, then I will die. And I do not wish to die... not yet.

'I'm on my way home,' I told my wife.

What Colleen Fletcher actually was I do not know. It is something I can only surmise at. She was some kind of demon, of that I am certain. I did a bit of checking. The university she supposedly went to had no records for her. A friend of mine worked at the bank her wage had been paid into. He told me none of it had been withdrawn.

I told no one in the office about what happened that night. I have yet to tell my wife. This evening something happened which prompted me to write all this down, something I had been meaning to do for over a year.

I finished work at the usual time and decided to get off the bus at the same stop I had done that night. As I walked home I felt a presence and a smell of perfume. I am pretty sure if was the same perfume Colleen used. I heard a whispered name. It might have been the wind, but I think it was a whisper.

'Arizell.'

I stopped walking and looked around the dark night. It was quiet, there was no traffic. Cold, I could see my breath chase across my face. Silence filled the night, a silence so thick I could almost touch it.

'Arizell...'

My temples began to pound. The air grew thicker and I felt it almost impossible to breathe for a moment. An eerie chill filled my body, a coldness that invaded every part of me, crawling through my veins so much I felt I might explode from within. Dark shadows crept over my vision and I felt so very tired. I leaned forward and retched. The vomit splashed on the floor. I retched again, but this time nothing came. I stood up and wiped my face with my handkerchief. I inhaled a deep breath and struggled home.

Later I recalled the feeling I had had before I had vomited. I can remember it now, and I know I will not forget it. It had felt so palpable and frightening.

It had felt like dying itself...

thirteen

the editorials

Thirteen

JANUARY EDITORIAL

I must have been eight or nine years old the night I was allowed to stay up late to watch a horror film all by myself. It was the first time my parents had granted me such a privilege and, despite being attired in my Action Man pyjamas, I felt as though I had finally started to cross the divide between boyhood and manhood.

Until that night, my movie experience consisted mainly of ITV's 'Friday Film Specials'. In fact, the scariest film I had ever seen was without doubt 'Willy Wonka and the Chocolate Factory', which my brother, sister and I would watch again and again on video, giggling with nerves every time Mr. Wonka sang his strange song on his magical boat. Perhaps if my brother and sister had stayed up with me that night, my experience would have been different.

But they were safely tucked up in bed and I was all alone.

To this day, I don't know the name of the film I saw. I can remember the basic plot - a woman moves into a large house in the middle of nowhere and before long strange things start to happen. At first they are small; a cup falls to the floor and breaks, even though there is nobody near it; a musical jewellery box starts to play by itself.

Then things get worse.

A hearse appears out of the darkness one night as the woman is driving home, the deathly pale face of the driver clearly visible when she looks in her rear-view mirror. There is no doubt it is out to get her and just as it finally looks as though it's going to catch up with her... it vanishes.

One evening, the woman runs a bath for herself. In my naiveté, the calmness of the scene didn't suggest to me that something scary was about to happen. After all, I'd just witnessed a car chase featuring a hearse. How much scarier could things get?

The bath fills.

The woman turns off the tap.

Silence.

And then came thirty seconds which would stick with me for a very, very long time.

An almighty noise from downstairs freezes the woman (and a nine year old boy in Action Man pyjamas) as she is about to get into the bath. It isn't the sound of breaking glass or splintering wood or anything as easily definable as that. It's more of a single, distorted bass note, out of tune and unpleasant but with a very clear message. Something extremely evil has just entered the house.

The sound comes again. And again. And again.

It's getting closer!

Closer to the landing, closer to the bathroom, closer to the woman, closer to poor little me! Thud, thud, thud, like giant footsteps, thud, thud, thud, like the beating of an excited heart. The woman slams the bathroom door shut and locks it.

Thud, thud, thud, so close now. How I wished to be somewhere else - in my bedroom, whispering to my brother, or even on Mr. Wonka's boat. Anywhere but alone in the living room.

The bathroom door shakes violently as something slams against it   Once, twice, three times. "Leave me alone!" screams the woman.

The door continues to shake in its frame.

"Leave me alone!"

The door seems ready to come off its hinges.

"In the name of God, leave me alone!"

The door stops moving and after a few moments the thudding resumes, but this time it's in the other direction, the right direction, still scary but mercifully

Thirteen

moving away from the bathroom and back down the landing. The camera cuts to the stairs, where we should see whatever was responsible for the noise, but there is nothing, only the retreating sound.

I had just 'not seen' my first ghost.

I can't remember much more of the film. I seem to recall the woman being driven away in the hearse which followed her earlier, screaming and banging on the back window, but whether or not she escaped, I'm not sure. I certainly didn't care at the time - I had my own problem to deal with, namely the walk from my living room to my bedroom.

I was convinced I would hear that thud.

Years passed. I saw hundreds more horror films, read hundreds of horror stories, and even managed to shed my Action Man pyjamas. Despite the genuine fear I had felt that night, I was hooked on horror. Part of me was always (and will always be, I'm sure) listening out for the sound of that thud.

And I've heard it.

Several times.

Whilst reading 'Dracula', confined to my bed with the flu.

When Carrie White's hand shoots up from her grave.

While sat in the front row of 'The Woman In Black' in Covent Garden.

And now, for you, thirteen thuds of your very own.

Sit back, make yourself uncomfortable, and enjoy Thirteen.

Andrew Hannon
Editor

FEBRUARY EDITORIAL

I was recently invited to attend an acquaintance's leaving party. She was about to embark on a year long travel and wanted, so it seemed, to gather everyone she'd ever known in the same place.

I showed up a little late at the venue and followed the sign 'PRIVATE FUNCTION' to the first floor. The party was in full swing and I scanned the faces of the crowd until I finally located the party girl.

"Hi!" I shouted to her over the sound of the live band after I'd forced my way to her through the crowd.

"Hi!" she returned. She looked delighted to see me. "I'm so glad you could make it! Have a nice night!"

And off she went. Oh dear.

I desperately looked around for someone else I might know but, despite half of North London congregating in the same place, I didn't see any familiar faces.

It made for an interesting night. For a while, I propped up the bar. Then, after the alcohol had oiled my social hinges, I got chatting to a group of girls for about half an hour. They introduced me to a newly engaged couple, who I spoke to about property prices and mortgages. I then got talking with a couple of Australian lads who, it turned out, had sneaked in to see what the private function was all about.

By the end of the evening I'd covered pretty much every topic I could imagine with people from all walks of life. It got me to thinking about how similar meeting a stranger and reading a short story are.

Some may interest you, others may bore you. Some might make you laugh, others might make you think, or make you change your opinions.

You might forget you ever met them.

Or you might wish you could get to know them better.

Nothing more remains to be said, other than I'm glad you could make it and have a nice night. You are about to meet thirteen strangers. I do hope you get along.

Sit back, make yourself uncomfortable, and enjoy Thirteen.

Andrew Hannon
Editor

MARCH EDITORIAL

For self-conscious people like myself, contact lenses are an invention inspired by genius. It's not that I have anything against glasses; it's just that I don't feel comfortable wearing them.

Anyone else who wears contacts will, I'm sure, have gone through the experience of losing one while out and about. If you can manage to locate it and find a mirror, you are usually okay.

But if you can't find it... if you lose it in the long grass, or in a dark cinema, or in a public toilet (in which case finding it wouldn't necessarily mean putting it back in your eye)... it can be quite unsettling.

To close the naked eye and to look with just your other eye, the world maintains a sharp, well-defined focus. To change eyes, all becomes blurred, hazy, and indecipherable. Open both eyes and peer into a combination of the two, a peek into two separate yet simultaneous realities, where the real and unreal meet, mingle and mesmerise.

What follows in this issue is an eye test for you. I want you to read the lines from top to bottom. Don't worry if reality starts to distort or blur – it is to be expected. At the end of the test you might prove to have twenty/twenty vision.

Or better yet, thirteen/thirteen.

Sit back, make yourself uncomfortable, and enjoy Thirteen.

Andrew Hannon
Editor

Thirteen

APRIL EDITORIAL

Suffering from an overactive imagination, I used to harbour many peculiar interpretations of the world around me. It would often be embarrassing each time I discovered the truth behind one of them – indeed, most of my moments of awakening occurred when family members or school friends would stare at me blankly after I had uttered some innocent yet bizarre comment.

Most of them, I suppose, were common enough misapprehensions. I was convinced that my grandparents had lived in a black and white world because old television footage was in black and white. Only after asking my mother if colours had been invented when she was little did the truth emerge.

One of my favourites was my notion that an earthquake was a large animal that lived underground. Hearing on the news one day that over one hundred people had been killed by one, I bravely announced to my dad that I wanted to become an earthquake hunter. Five minutes later, after a gentle explanation from my amused father, I found myself strangely upset that an entire species which never existed had been wiped out, at least in my mind.

But I want you to imagine that some of your childhood fears are back, and that they're very, very real. There's an earthquake beneath you, waiting to attack, and I'm guessing he'll hit a thirteen on the Richter Scale.

Sit back, make yourself uncomfortable, and enjoy *Thirteen*.

Andrew Hannon
Editor

MAY EDITORIAL

I stopped walking and stood completely still.

I had to, because I could not see a thing.

The moon had, moments earlier, gone behind the clouds, plunging me into darkness. I had to force a smile – I thought that kind of thing only happened in horror stories.

By day, the woods in which I stood offered a pleasant short-cut between my new house and the shops. But by night, as I was now finding out, they were an arena where your senses are heightened and your imagination replaces the voice of reason. Especially when you're a little bit drunk.

I knew from my day-time walks through it that the path through the woods was no more than a hundred meters long, but with absolutely no light to guide me it may as well have been a hundred miles. I considered using the light from my mobile phone to try and illuminate the path for me, but after a few seconds I realised it wasn't strong enough and a very annoying part of my brain whispered that it would give my position away. Sitting here now, in front of my computer, I can laugh at myself, but at the time I knew that the advice was sound.

Step by tentative step, I finally made it through the woods, welcoming the sight of the streetlights at the other end.

Now it's time for you to take a walk through the dark. Thirteen steps, all by yourself, with no promise of a light at the end.

Sit back, make yourself uncomfortable, and enjoy Thirteen.

Andrew Hannon
Editor

Thirteen

JUNE EDITORIAL

Unfortunately for me, regular rush-hour journeys on the London Underground are not something I can avoid. It amazes me that with all the recent technological advancements made by our species, there is no real alternative to being crammed in a carriage with two hundred or so other commuters.

I don't know which is worse – the person blaring music out of their headphones who invariably chooses to sit or stand next to me; the large woman eating crisps who coughs in my direction without covering her mouth; the strange person who I catch staring at me, as though he would like to cause me some injury; or the baking heat, and its subsequent effect on the odour of the carriage.

Perhaps I'm being a snob – it's not as though anyone else is enjoying the conditions, and we're all in it together anyway. Between us, we don't really have much of a choice.

But you have chosen to ride this train... the ghost train which will take you through dark tunnels and into strange lands. I shall leave you here on the platform and wish you a pleasant journey.

Wait, I nearly forgot. Here are your tickets – they're thirteenth class.

Sit back, make yourself uncomfortable, and enjoy *Thirteen*.

Andrew Hannon
Editor

JULY EDITORIAL

We've all done things we're not proud of. One of mine was a mis-spent summer with a 'bad crowd', terrorising people in our community with late night pizza deliveries.

In my defence, I was only twelve.

We'd gather in one of our houses and my friend Tom (who had the deepest voice) would phone up the pizza place and order whatever we told him to say, asking for it to be delivered to any house within easy running distance. After the hoax order was placed, we'd rush down to a safe position with a decent view of the unsuspecting house and watch the ensuing confusion unfold as some poor chap was confronted with half a dozen family pizzas.

As you may suspect, we eventually got caught. After several lectures on how irresponsible our pranks were, affecting innocent people and the hard working pizza staff, many of us spent the rest of the summer under careful watch.

But old habits die hard.

And I've just ordered a pizza for you.

It's thirteen slices of pure horror, topped with screams, shivers and suspense and guaranteed to leave a bad taste in your mouth.

Sit back, make yourself uncomfortable, and enjoy Hirteen.

Andrew Hannon
Editor

Thirteen

AUGUST EDITORIAL

A couple of months after having moved house, I am still in the process of unpacking. Most people use moving house as an opportunity to get rid of a load of stuff they don't need - I seem to have picked up more!

I'll be honest - I'm useless at the unpacking process. If I come across a book I read years ago, I'll abandon the sorting and spend an hour flicking through it. If I find a collection of photos, I'll sit there and look over them.

So when I unpacked my guitar, it wasn't surprising that I spent several hours going through every song I'd ever learned (or half-learned) to play. The music probably wasn't pretty to hear - at least, not for anyone else who was listening. To me, however, the songs I strummed were heard through rose-tinted ear-plugs.

Now it's your turn to get musical - there are thirteen strings for you to pluck, one by one, and they're all going to resonate. One string will sound like a scream, another, a whisper, another, an unexplained sound of someone else's footsteps when you know you should be alone...

And the sound of all thirteen strings will be a chord like no other.

Sit back, make yourself uncomfortable, and enjoy *Thirteen*.

Andrew Hannon
Editor

SEPTEMBER EDITORIAL

Handing in your notice at a job you don't like is often a bittersweet experience. Depending on the boss, plucking up the courage to take them aside and announcing you're off can take some doing. However, countering this is the immense feeling of relief that comes with the words "I'm tendering my resignation."

I've worked my fair share of undesirable jobs and have made the professional acquaintance of more than my fair share of undesirable bosses. I've noticed that having the gall to hand in your notice causes a bit of a sadistic change in some of them.

It's as though they see your notice period as a time limit in which they have to try to break you.

Suddenly, you are 'volunteered' for the big pile of filing which has become an urgent project, despite having been hidden away under your boss's desk for goodness knows how long. Your aggrieved employer leaves mountains of work on your desk for you to sort, photocopy and file – and it all has to be finished by yesterday.

You even have to make the teas.

Now, it's time for you to work your notice – thirteen days, to be precise. I've put aside some special jobs for you, far more unpleasant than photocopying and filing. I know you're leaving us soon, but I think you might need to work a few extra hours… maybe even a few midnight shifts.

Your reference depends on it.

Sit back, make yourself uncomfortable, and enjoy Thirteen.

Andrew Hannon
Editor

Thirteen

OCTOBER EDITORIAL

I have imposed upon myself a ban which prevents me from listening to music stations for the next month or so.

The reason?

A girl.

Possibly even *the* girl.

For four happy months I have had the pleasure of her company, but now she has gone on a year long travel around the world. I always knew she was going – I tried to prepare myself for it, but you know...

The other night, I stood at the sink, washing up, listening to the radio, as is my habit. Every song played seemed to be about us and it was too much for me to take. I switched over to Medium Wave and tuned into a twenty-four hour news station.

The result?

My heart is slowly mending and I have acquired an uncanny knowledge of shipping forecasts.

But don't let me keep you with this tale of sadness. It's almost midnight and my favourite radio show is about to start. They don't play love songs. Why don't you tune in too? Turn that dial all the way to the left until you find Thirteen MW.

You need to be very precise... there... in between the static and the screaming...

Sit back, make yourself uncomfortable, and enjoy Thirteen.

Andrew Hannon
Editor

HALLOWE'EN EDITORIAL

Stood at the airport bookshop with a few spare Euro left in my wallet, I decided to try and vary my reading habits slightly. I spent a while in the 'True Crime' section, reading blurbs about gangsters and bank robbers. Nothing was really grabbing me.

But then I happened to pull out a book with a red spine and based purely on the front cover I knew I had to have it.

The book was about one man's experiences as an illegal fighter. The front cover was a close up of his head and shoulders, blood and mud covering the expression of unsuppressed animal rage on his face.

I read the book in two days. The most powerful scene for me came at the end, in which the fighter describes various fights, each with their own bizarre and sickening permutations – glue-and-glass covered fist-fights; fighting with maces; upside down, closed quarters combat.

It's your turn to step into the ring tonight. The crowd are baying for blood and there are no holds barred as thirteen Hallowe'en heavyweights attempt to put you out for the count.

Sit back, make yourself uncomfortable, and enjoy Thirteen.

Andrew Hannon
Editor

Thirteen

NOVEMBER EDITORIAL

I was kept awake last night by rain lashing against my window and the sound of gale force winds rubbing shoulders with trees. Usually, I'm out like a light, but I enjoyed the opportunity to just lie there and think.

That might sound odd, but with hectic days taking up my calendar, it's hard to find time to meditate on life. I don't mean legs crossed "Ooooomm ooooomm" meditation – just the chance to take a step back and look at where things are headed; if certain things need changing; or even if certain friends are due a phone call.

So I was thankful for the wind and the rain, and after my hour or so of deep thought, I think I would have been thankful for any insomnia-inducing effects – a hot and humid night; a party near-by; someone snoring.

It's your turn to lie there in the darkness and think. You're about to have thirteen not-so-sweet sugars and, if you finally manage to get to sleep, I'm predicting thirteen nightmares.

Sit back, make yourself uncomfortable, and enjoy Thirteen.

Andrew Hannon
Editor

DECEMBER EDITORIAL

I write this editorial with senses of pride, relief and sadness.

I am proud of the achievements of Thirteen – it has far surpassed my early expectations of it. In the early days, I thought the idea was possibly too ambitious to succeed, but it has, and here we are. For this, I am forever indebted to my friend and colleague, Andrew Levy, whose creativity and hard-work have been an inspiration and without whom there would be no Thirteen.

My debt of gratitude extends to the writers of the stories – over 140 of you, I believe, have been published. I have been corresponding with many of you for quite a while now and it has been my absolute pleasure to work with you and read your stories. Many of you have made quite an impression on me and it is an honour for me to have published your work. Special mention has to be reserved for the following – Matthew Batham, Lee Betteridge and Leisa Parker. You have all been published in several issues with consistently excellent stories and I thank you for thinking of Thirteen.

Another word for the writers – I have no doubt that many of you will go on to be very successful writers and am sure you need no urging on from me, but with the amount of talent that many of you have demonstrated, I feel it is my duty to say "Keep it up!"

And for the other writers, those who have yet to hear from me regarding their submissions – my apologies. The bad part of having so many writers sending their work into the magazine means that response times have been far too long, particularly in recent months. Most of you have been extremely patient and understanding, and thanks for that. There just aren't enough hours in the day to get everything done and I hope you can continue to be patient while we work on the future of Thirteen... but more on that in a moment.

I am relieved that we made it to this issue. Regular readers might have noticed a few tenuous links between the theme of the editorial and the number 'thirteen'! Contact lenses, drunken walks through dark forests, girlfriends going travelling for a year, bare-knuckle fighters... how did I get away with it?

I am sad that this might be the last edition of Thirteen, but equally hopeful that it could be just the beginning. At the time of writing, we are putting together a presentation for a national magazine distributor with the aim of becoming a 'proper' magazine, available to buy nation-wide, out on time, that kind of thing. If this isn't successful, the only way for the magazine to survive will be with some fundamental changes. Andrew and I have discussed this at great length and an announcement will be made on the website once we know where we stand.

Other plans include an anthology of our hundred best stories and even a possible radio show. These plans are still struggling to squirm their way out of the pipelines, but I'm doing my best to help them out.

So keep your fingers crossed. It's meant to be lucky. And so is Thirteen... lucky for some, anyway.

Sit back, make yourself uncomfortable, and enjoy Thirteen.

Andrew Hannon
Editor

thirteen

thirteen

thirteen – volume two

coming to get you soon...